I0741114

Shatter

shat·ter (shăt'ər)

To break or cause to separate into pieces, as with a rapid and violent blow.

To injure gravely; disable: *His health was shattered by his addiction.*

To cause the demolition or decline of; annihilate: *The war shattered our hope of peace and prosperity.*

FOR MY FAMILY

SHATTER

O n e

Friday, April Seventh, 2:30 pm.
Spokane

"Carl! Hand me that two-by-six," I said as I steadied my right knee on the slippery roof, left foot planted on the bucket-truck platform. My safety harness dug into my shoulders as I reached out for the lumber. My knee was throbbing from a near-fatal slip earlier in the day. I'd really pay for that tomorrow, I knew.

"Here you go," my son said as he passed me the last roof rafter. He was working inside the house, and passed up materials to me as we finished up the gable. I secured the pre-cut rafter in place in with a metal strap anchor, and nailed it in with my big Senco framing nailer. April seventh, three p.m., my watch said. By tonight, we'd have the roof sheathed and papered, and re-roof the damaged part tomorrow. Eighty-four days after the Domino tore up the house and wrecked the Pacific Northwest.

"All right, that's the last of the framing. Here, take the nailer—unplug the hose first," I cautioned as I began to pass him the nail gun. "I'll finish up the fascia up here by hand, then we'll get the plywood up here and we'll have a roof again. Go down and get that roll of thirty-pound tarpaper from the garage, please."

"Already got it. Uncle Alan said you'd need it today."

"And he was right," I said as I passed down the air hose. I looked around the newly completed chimney enclosure across the field to Alan's house, where he had just finished spreading compost in their new kitchen garden. I gave him a wave signaling the framing was done. He waved back and gave me a 'thumbs-up'. "Pass that on up," I told Carl as he rolled the tar paper across the stair landing, seven feet below me.

Carl struggled for a minute, climbing the step-ladder inside the house while weaving the two bulky rolls of thirty-pound paper up to me through the ceiling joists and roof rafters. I struggled a bit to get them in place, and finally stacked them up behind the chimney. The misty rain had continued all day, and was now dripping from the bill of my Spokane Indians baseball team cap.

"Ready for that three-quarter?" Ron called up. He was working on the ground, cutting and running lumber for the roof.

"Yep. Here's my pad with the dimensions for the panels, and a sketch of how they need to be oriented for strength," I tossed down the paper for him to cut. "Two uncut panels are good to get me started though. I'll tie-off to the roof and use the pulley on the ladder for the panels. Carl, go give Ron a hand."

"K," he said.

John, Marie and Libby were over at their 'new' house, along with Karen and Kelly, working on cleanup. We'd been working on perfecting the art of multi-tasking for the past three months on everything from structural engineering and home rebuilding to gardening and equipment maintenance—in short, the skills of any normal honest-to-goodness farmer, which I was not in former days. The Martins new home would be habitable by next week, we hoped. The plan for today was to get the roof framed up, sheathed and roofed, and tomorrow we'd attack the needed repairs at their place en masse. As usual, today had not gone as planned, and things were taking longer than I thought. Slipping off of the ash-slickened roof in the soft drizzle wasn't on my plan, nor was the safety harness catching me and abruptly smacking me into the access ladder welded to the front end of the big Ford. I hadn't broken the skin, but did give my wife a good scare as I came flying down. My leg felt like I'd been hit with a baseball bat. Ribs were a little sore, too, where the harness had caught me. Without the harness of course, I'd have been toast.

I took a few minutes to look around from my rooftop perch, as Ron cut the panels to my measurements.

From up here on a clearer day, I could see many miles around us, off to the southeast, where Mica Peak dominated the view, to Browne's Mountain off to the south, the downtown area ten miles off to the west, and the nearer hills to the north. Mica used to house an Air Force long-distance radar station, it's white dome a long-familiar sight, now a misshapen form, obviously wrecked, on the days that we could see that far, which weren't many anymore. Browne's Mountain still held a few of the broadcast towers for radio and television, most of them wrecked, and snapped off in the quake. The low clouds today obscured most of those, and only allowed shadowy outlines of the formerly trendy hillside neighborhoods on both sides of the Valley, now abandoned to nature or scavengers. The Valley, first settled in the late eighteen hundreds as an agricultural area, then suburbanized, had plummeted in population in the past few months. I wasn't sure of the current population, but I knew that it had to have regressed back to a nineteen-twenties or –thirties level. There were only four families on our block, and I was related to or a part of three of them. Pre-quake, there were dozens of families and a couple hundred people, at least. The block to the east, split up more than ours with sixties-era ranch houses that didn't function in the extended power outage from the quake, had only one family in residence that we knew of, and they spent the cold months in their big RV. The roofs of many of the homes around us, built at a slope of three-in-twelve or four-in-twelve, were still covered with the heavy ash from January, and two more bursts in February. If the ash were thicker, it might've collapsed some of the homes. Coupled with the Domino of course, was the flu. The outbreak had caused everyone to look toward a self-imposed quarantine long before the government made it official, so social contact had been very limited since the first of February. Only in the past few days had the quarantine been lifted, and then with uneven interpretation, we were finding. I hadn't been out of my zip code in two months. Longer than that, for Karen and the kids.

"Pull…" Ron called out to me from below. We'd rigged up a very simple (Rons' term, 'stupidly crude but effective') pulley system to winch the heavier or bulkier members and sheeting up to the roof. We'd already packed up six squares of roofing shingles, or eighteen eighty-pound bundles. They were perched on the peak of the roof, waiting for me to finish sheathing. I pulled the half-inch hemp rope up tight, while Ron and Carl pulled the lifting rope through the pulley system, and up came the first two sheets of plywood. My rope was used to pull the lower edge up, and stabilize the load. After a precarious dance of unloading the sheets, and another half-hour of nailing, I was ready for the tarpaper, then we (meaning 'I') could roof over the gable. By five p.m., the tarpaper was on, and I'd moved the roofing bundles onto the peak of the rebuilt gable.

Our roof was now weather-tight for the first time since January.

During February, after things had settled down to a point after our last real firefight, we were all antsy to get out of the barn and do some physical exercise that had the added benefit of not thinking about how bad things were. We'd been cooped up in the houses and the barn for weeks, and we needed to get out.

We continued to clear out the wreckage of the house, and established a game plan to get the place habitable by sometime in the summer. This was prefaced of course on the hope that the foundation was repairable, that the structure of the home wasn't as beat up as I thought it might be, and that we didn't get ourselves overrun while we were just having coffee on the porch.

I still had 'gas station' duty, on an infrequent basis, usually with only an hour's notice or so, due to breakdowns in line power that were all too frequent. This wasn't a major problem, but the influenza outbreak certainly curtailed interactions with the 'outside'. Other than waves, and hollered instructions across parking lots, we didn't talk too much to either the deputies or the firemen or the emergency service workers gassing up at the station. I dutifully kept log of how much gas of each type was used, and my 'share' of fuel for the use of my tractor. By the time power was restored in early February, the little Ford had 'earned' nearly two hundred-fifty gallons of gasoline in service of pumping a little less than ten thousand gallons of gas and diesel for evacuation buses, police and military vehicles, fire trucks, and ambulances. By our estimates, there was still about nineteen thousand gallons of fuel in the underground tanks I wondered what the 'shelf life' of underground fuel was.

This 'payment' presented a unique short-term problem: Fuel storage. The majority of my storage cans were full before the quake hit, as were all the cars and most of the equipment. Other than the gas we used to run the small generator or fill up the Martins and Alans vehicles, and topping of the Expedition, those cans were still full. I topped off the cans as much as I could, and kept log of what was owed me, leaving my share in the underground tanks at the convenience store. Finally, as power restoration was looming, and therefore ending my obligation to help the County provide gas, I was faced with finding a place for one hundred ninety four gallons of fuel.

Mike Amberson 'loaned' me two fifty-gallon fuel transport tanks, usually found in the back of farm trucks. That took care of a large part of the requirement, but Mike would want those back soon. Alan, Ron and I looked for answers.

"What about your friend, the Italian guy. Pauliano. Does he have any cans?" Ron asked.

"I don't know. We'll have to look. He said he had a tank that had about three hundred gallons in it, hidden in his barn."

"Three hundred! What's he use that for?"

"Used to be a contractor. I'm sure he buys gas when it's cheap, and fills it up for his use during the year."

"Did he say the tank was full?" Ron asked.

"No," I remembered. "He said something like 'there was pretty close to three hundred' in it.

"Better check there first then," Alan said.

We did just that. The tank, hidden within a false floor and wall, appeared to be a five hundred gallon tank. Problem solved, with the addition of the appropriate mixture of fuel stabilizer.

"Even with the stabilizer," I said, "That fuel may go bad before we use it all."

"Now that power's back on the way, shouldn't we be getting shipments back in?" Alan asked.

"Should be, sure, in a normal world. Who knows what shape the pipelines are in coming into town? Or for that matter, how much foreign fuel is still coming in to the country? I'm betting, not very dang much. If that's the case, the price spikes that we're hearing about and the shortages will only get worse."

By late February, it was apparent to all of us that this would in fact be the case. I was out in the shop when I heard a sound bite of an interview to be broadcast the following day. Our newly minted Secretary of Energy, in his post for all of six weeks.

".....gas rationing in effect throughout the United States today, formalizing the already-obvious, that gasoline and petroleum products in general, in short supply since the start of the Second Depression, now are limited to those users designated as crucial to the National Recovery. The wholesale rebuilding and reorganization of the Nation's energy policy, use and priorities has concern on the Left that the government, with the minority leadership stating that the reorganization has deprived the poor and city dwellers of the right to transportation. The Administration response was that transportation for anything other than non-crucial activities wastes limited fuel resources, largely assigned to defense, the war effort, and food production."

The news commentator continued on. I thought that the rest of the interview ought to merit my full attention, and I made a note to watch it tomorrow morning. Carl was listening in as well.

"So what does that mean, Dad?" The gas part."

"That means that unless you're using gas or diesel for food production, or the war effort or in recovery, you're not going to get much, or any, gas."

"Well that really sucks," he said, beginning to realize the depth of the problem.

"Yeah. In more ways than we can imagine. That sixty-six Mustang of ours might get finished, but it may never be driven."

"Seriously?"

"Yeah. Seriously. Gas will be hard to come by, and expensive. It may even be restricted in use. That means, even if we have gas, we may not be able to use it for pleasure driving."

"So how are we supposed to get around?"

"For us, we've had a taste of what the rest of the country…and a large chunk of the world…might be experiencing real soon now. We haven't really gone anywhere for more than a month. The tank for the rest of the country's been running low and lower since the Domino. It will get worse."

"So what then?"

"They'll ration it first. That means farms, factories, essential transportation. Then, if there's adequate supply, the 'rest of us' will get some, too. I think that's the way it worked in World War Two. They had coupons that allowed different people to get different amounts of gas, based on their occupations."

"And that's fair?" he said sarcastically.

"No, not always." The news broadcast continued as I hushed him with my hand. He put his gloves back on and went back up to the wreck of our house.

"New rail lines, the first put down in decades, were started today on parts of former rail rights-of-way in the Midwest, and in some cases, in the center of the eastbound freeway lanes in Iowa, Kansas, Nebraska, and Colorado, in anticipation of the need to transport the grain harvest to population centers throughout the country. Rebuilding and salvage repair of worn rail equipment, including boxcars, grain transporters, and diesel-electric engines adapted to run on multiple fuel grades, was stated to be behind schedule at numerous rail centers throughout the US. Critics are demanding that the effort be nationalized, and put under the authority of the Federal Government to force the railroad companies to meet the critical deadlines of the fall harvest. The Government has

responded by stating that a free market, and as a result a larger share of shipping, is the only way to meet the projected demand."

"This is ABC World News from New York. It is four p.m., Eastern Standard Time."

The sharp--and bitter--parts of the interview with the energy secretary were broadcast the next morning on ABC. The hostess, seated in her phony living room set piece, was drinking her Starbucks, logo placed prominently for product marketing reasons.

"Can you provide an estimate of full recovery, Mr. Secretary? Meaning, when will we be back to our pre-Depression levels?" the blonde hostess asked, mock concern on her face.

"Levels of what? Consumption? Never, in my best estimation."

"You mean that we will NEVER enjoy the lifestyle that we enjoyed before the Crash?"

"You ask the question—but in this case, you asked it in a manner that can have only an unpleasant answer."

"How would you phrase it, then?" I could cut the sarcasm with a dull knife.

"I would state that the United States will recover. That our lifestyles will be different, but not worse than they were before the Crash. Our energy use must be more efficient, as should the use of all of our resources. The President's new policy—adopted by the Acting Congress—of the combination of exploring new energy options and conservation of existing resources, is painful in adaptation and implementation. Every sector, every man, woman and child in this country is being affected, and will continue to be affected, for years to come. We will recover, however."

'Well, at least he was optimistic,' I thought to myself.

2

After our first letters from my brothers scattered far and yon, we wrote back and received uneven responses in return.

From my next oldest brother, Alex and his wife Amber, now living with their kids at her parents place near Colliersville, Tennessee, we received four letters, and a large package. Amber's mother was recuperating at home after her knee surgery, and her father had been re-enlisted by FEDEX to assist with shipping and relief operations. Another letter followed that cryptically told me that we'd be receiving a couriered package, which turned out to be our 'junk' silver and some gold coins. Nearly two hundred pounds in all, most of my retirement fund, cashed in, literally. Alex in subsequent letters told us about their 'place', about seven acres of old farm land, and that he and Amber, taught by her father, were both learning to shoot. Food at that point wasn't much of a problem--that was back in early February. The stores were still open and the selection good. Within two weeks though, Amber's mother started canning whatever she could, including meats, vegetables, soups and sauces, as the stores began to run low on produce and staples. They were starting to have issues with power, phone, and of course the Internet had long gone. Alex was teaching his young ones, Lucas and Jaime, the fine art of planting a garden (a task that Alex despised in youth.)

The last letter we received was written on February 27th, with the sad news that both of Ambers' parents had passed on in the flu. We've written several letters each month since then, and received no response.

Jeff and Barb, in Utah, wrote us several times as well in February, with news of his businesses' collapse in the Depression, and news of the flu. Graveyards now dotted the landscape at the LDS Stake buildings, where baseball and sports fields used to be. Jeff also reported some thefts at LDS canneries and storage warehouses, as well as armed robberies in some cases. Barb's classes of course were cancelled as the University closed. The last we heard, in a letter dated February 18th, was that their daughter Lynnie was ill, but "not with the flu, thank God." It's been months now, and we've never heard from them either.

Jack, my oldest brother, and his lovely wife Emily (my favorite sister in law, but don't share that), have written faithfully through the weeks and months, although we've missed getting some of their letters.

Two seminary students from Jack's college ended up moving in with Jack right after the flu outbreak happened, because they couldn't stay in the unheated school (it was heated from oil-fired boilers), and couldn't get back to their homes in Nebraska and eastern Colorado. Jane, Jack and Em's daughter, widowed last Christmas Day due to a mortar shell in Fallujah, moved back into her old room as well after her former neighborhood on the north side of the Twin Cities, got too dicey with rampant gang activity that the police cannot hope to contain. Jack's house, a three-bedroom rancher in Little Canada, was heated with gas, but fortunately had a wood stove for backup heat. We've missed letters from the middle of February through the middle of March, but the letter on March 15 brought some news of Patrick (their son) and his girlfriend Deborah. Deborah had gone missing from their twenty acres near Cloverdale, while on the way back from a shopping trip. The store, Pat later found, was looted and burned. No one's seen any trace of her since then.

We're hoping to hear more, but their letter this week is late, and we missed last week's letter as well. We hope and pray for all of them, and hundreds more.

I still wonder if the 'net is going somewhere, if some of my Internet 'friends' are faring well in all of this. Still up on that mountain, 'muleskinner?' Is "C" still hunkered down in DC, waiting for things to get better? Is R. doing well in Oklahoma, with the varied contacts to local farmers, just trying to make a difference? And Linda, up on her farm. How's she doing?

Will I ever know?

During the late winter, one thing that kept coming up in our conversations around dinner was the status of the other homes on the street. Nearly all of the residents of our neighborhood—and a large percentage of the urban population-- had evacuated to warmer climates during the last two weeks of January, right after the quake as the train started to go off the rails. I knew, as well as everyone else, that there were still food products in those homes that might still be good while they were still cold. Once spring got here and things thawed out though, it'd be a different story. It seemed a waste to me to let it rot.

I posed the question to Mike Amberson on Lincoln's Birthday, February twelfth, after requesting a meeting with him to discuss several areas of interest. Since the flu outbreak, when we left the house, we talked with folks at the gas station, from a good distance. Handshakes were rapidly seen as an anachronism, and a way to help spread the virus. Of course now, we were also openly armed as well, and 'miked up' with our radios.

We'd developed a sort of a routine in our conversations, with neither party being upwind of the other, in case the virus spread by airborne means. One party usually stayed in his vehicle, the other within ten to fifteen feet. Not exactly private.

"So what's your next topic?" Mike asked. We'd just reviewed the amount of gas left in the unleaded tanks. The diesel tank was pumped dry the day before. I'd returned the empty fuel transfer tanks to Mike already, lashed to the tractor, which now had its back blade for snow plowing, since power to the store was back on, however infrequently.

"Winter's going to be over soon, and there are some things we might do to help save some food in the abandoned homes."

"You don't think it's already spoiled?"

"Some, sure. But if it was frozen in January, it probably still is. The other stuff—canned goods, should still be fine. Boxed stuff, you know, cereal, sugar, flour, is probably fine, too. But once spring gets here, it'll be mouse season, and that frozen food will rot for sure."

"So you want to salvage it?"

"Yeah. But more importantly, I think that YOU need to salvage it."

"Meaning the County?"

"Well, if they're the authority, yeah. It would be stupid to let it go to waste, and that will happen when things warm up. Which could be any week now."

"I'll talk to my logistics folks. How do you figure this would work?"

"You supervise, observe, make sure that what's taken out of the houses is food or perishable or in short supply, no looting. Inventory it as it's removed. Take it to the food bank or a store with refrigeration cases still intact. Make it available for sale or trade. Heck, give it away, whatever. If food shipments aren't coming in, and I doubt they are…"

"They are, but not enough," Mike interrupted, "and we don't know if they'll ever increase, or if they'll stop altogether."

"OK, all the more reason. What's being shipped here is or was, already in the pipeline. It was made pre-Crash and in a warehouse somewhere. There are, or were, what, three big food distribution centers before the Domino?"

"Yeah, how do you know that?"

"Clients, a couple of them."

"And are any of them still standing?"

"I'm not at liberty to say…"

"C'mon, Mike. What do I have to do, walk up the hill to the freeway fence and look over the interstate to see if the Supervalu warehouse is still there? Can't do that with the others, they're on the north side. But I'd wager that in ten minutes I could find out on the radio." I had him, and he knew it. I didn't know why he was being so secretive.

"The Safeway distribution center was looted. The Army and some of my guys hold what's left of it. The URM center collapsed and then part of it burned."

"OK, so there was our cities' three-day supply of food, gone. Right?"

"Yeah."

"So we're standing in the middle of a ghost city, where a couple hundred thousand people lived until January fourteenth. Then some died. And a whole lot more left. Then a whole lot more died. There's gotta be food and medicines and other stuff that people will need, either now or soon, and it will go to waste unless you do something about it."

"Like I said, I'll talk to my logistics officer."

"Do it soon. Time's a-wastin'."

February fourteenth, Valentines' Day, started out with a bright sunrise that quickly turned to heavy snow as a frontal system came in from the west. We worked on 'normal' chores in the morning hours, or moving snow about with the tractor. In the afternoon, we all worked on a nice dinner, prepared for our loved ones. The menu, partly planned, partly what was on hand, included a beef burgundy stew favored by my late father (and only made on rare occasions), fresh dinner rolls, butternut squash with brown sugar, chocolate cake, and pink sugar cookies for the kids. Carl and John put the kids to task in making Valentine's Day cards for everyone, from craft supplies from Karen and Kelly's craft stash. Alan and I had retrieved a couple bottles of old cabernet for dinner, in addition to the jug of burgundy for cooking the stew in its clay pot. I think in the end, we enjoyed the preparation of the meal as much as the meal itself.

As I set the table at Alan's, the kids were watching the latest news on ABC, our only operating station at the moment. The TV stations locally had their transmitters well--removed from the 'core' areas up on high foothills and surrounding mountains--and as such far from main transmission lines. All three continued to operate on standby generator power until permanent power was restored...if power was restored. Today, we had ABC. We'd had to dig up an old set of 'rabbit ears' for reception; because of course the cable was now useless.

The permanent state of emergency that we seemed to be living in since the Domino and the start of the Second Depression also dramatically affected what was being broadcast for 'entertainment' and 'information.'

Other than the 'top of the hour' broadcasts on the radio that we picked up usually once a day during those first weeks after the quake, and monitoring the CB and scanner, we didn't listen to the radio all that much. After the first two weeks, we settled into work and chore routines that kept us pretty well entertained. With the damage caused to our local area by the quake, and lack of fuel, and slow repairs, commercial television was spotty as well. We did tune in once in awhile to watch the national news in the evening, before the television stations shut down at seven p.m. The hour-long national news, once filled with the predictable patterns of "national news, international news that affects the US, scandal of the day/week, emerging medical crisis of the day, human interest story of the day," etc., now was three hours long, starting at three p.m. our time. There were no 'human interest' stories anymore; it was all 'hard news.' There was plenty of that to go around.

"Dad, where's Riyadh?" Kelly asked.

"Saudi Arabia. Capital city of the kingdom. Why?" I turned and looked at the grainy picture on the TV.

"Look," She said.

ABC was picking up a Sky News feed (apparently no American coverage there anymore?) showing many columns of smoke around the city. The news crew, filming from their room at the Radisson, showed dozens of buildings in flames, including mosques, Western hotels and companies, and explosions within areas identified as compounds of the royal family.

"Whoa," I said.

"What's going on?" Karen said as she came into the room with a handful of mismatched wine glasses. "Where's this?"

"Saudi. Looks as if the royal family's got a problem," I said.

"Yeah. Big one by the look of it."

The news in January that the strange bedfellows of Iran, Saudi Arabia and other middle-eastern nations would be supplying China with substantial amounts of their oil production to meet China's burgeoning growth had unsettled things in unpredictable ways. Once the US had defeated the Chinese, and now that world economies were in collapse, no country was willing to step up and defend the royal family from their own people, now revolting against the loss of their many social programs and Western 'guest workers'. First, the Chinese had offered far more than the US thought reasonable (or in fact, could pay), and then with the Chinese loss to the US in the short war, the neither the US nor China could afford the oil. The US was instantly, dramatically and permanently affected by the immediate cessation of oil shipments...not just the Saudis, but any country who worked with the US on 'credit' ceased shipping as soon as the US declared itself unable—and unwilling—to repay its debts. The Chinese now of course were struggling with a new government and an imploding economy and an influenza epidemic of their own making. The fuse that the Saudi royal family had crafted through decades of control and abuse of power, had been lit for some time. Within hours it would be over for them, it seemed.

"Dad, they said the 'wahabis' had taken over? Who're they?" Marie asked Ron.

"Nine-Eleven ring a bell? Them," he said as he put down a stack of plates on the table. "Radical Muslims."

"Oh."

For most countries in the world, the collapse of the economy in the US, and the default of US obligations resulted in the collapse of their own economies. The collapse of the economy, the too-coincidental seizures of US owned or operated businesses around the world within a day or so, all fuel for the fire. By the end of January, tens of thousands of companies had shuttered their doors and turned their poorly paid employees out, with the loss of income from their Number One customer, the US. Hundreds of millions of workers were instantly unemployed. Millions of them would not survive to see another job.

We watched as the palaces burned with thousands of people attacking and killing. After a few minutes of that, I picked up the remote, and shut off the TV. It was only a month after our discussion about the US as we knew it not being able to exist without cheap and abundant fuels, to see one of the largest supplies of petroleum go permanently off-line. Rumors flew about the status of Ghawar and Safaniya oil fields, and their reserves. Saudi refugees—former members of the Royal Family—stated unequivocally that the fields had proven reserves for more than fifty years of production at current levels. The fundamentalist "government" that had taken Riyadh and most of the rest of the country within days put bounties on those responsible for the looting and desecration of the wealth of the country, decrying the former leadership as 'wicked and evil for the depletion of the treasures provided by the merciful Allah.'

On the sixteenth, one of the Deputies showed up out front, while I spelled the boys on watch. He let me know that the next day, I was to meet at the convenience store to participate in a pilot program of the salvage of perishables from our neighborhood. I was to come unarmed.

"Sorry, my forty-five is part of me now," I said.

"Orders, sir," was the reply.

"Understood, deputy. But, I'm not a Department employee, and I don't take orders. I would be happy to assist the department, but if someone thinks that I go anywhere unarmed these days, they've got rocks for brains."

"These orders come from Commissioners Williams and Markweather."

"OK, so there's two out of three, what about Sam Jackson?"

"Commissioner Jackson dissented on the vote."

"Can't imagine why. Listen, Deputy, with all due respect, and there is plenty for what you and your fellow officers are going through, would you go anywhere unarmed?"

"No, sir."

"Then you can understand my hesitation."

"I can. Meeting's at ten."

"Understood."

The next morning, Alan and I, both armed and not subtle about it, as well as equipped with our radios, took Ron's Jeep down the road. The wind was bitter, from the east again. The wind chill was below zero. Again.

At the convenience store, we were met by two Sheriff's patrol cars; four patched and abused Humvees, and a number of green-clad men, armed with gloves, hats, and some with clipboards. Two had a video and digital still cameras. All had surgical style masks on. An Army corporal handed Alan and I masks as well. Rather, he placed them on the hood of the Jeep and we picked them up.

"Good morning. I'm Lieutenant Pete Wolfson, logistics officer for the Spokane County Department of Emergency Services. You have been requested to participate in a program of inventory and salvage in this neighborhood as a pilot program for the Inland Northwest region, Washington section."

"Serving here today are members of the Community Emergency Response Team, the Washington Army National Guard, the Sheriff's office, FEMA, and resident civilians. Our civilian representatives live in this neighborhood and will serve as guides to the two teams in this pilot program. They are Rick Drummond and Alan Bauer. Mr. Drummond has been a resident of the neighborhood for some years now; Mr. Bauer has relocated recently to this neighborhood. The civilian representatives in this and other neighborhoods may know in advance of potential risks, threats, and resources in each home. Do not hesitate to ask them."

Alan and I glanced at each other, thinking the same thing: 'They think we've already been into the other houses.'

"Pete, if I may interrupt," I asked.

"Certainly, Mr. Drummond."

"We have some specific knowledge in some cases. We have not set foot in any home that, pre-quake, we were not looking after or homes that were owned by friends. This may not be the case in other neighborhoods, but it is the case here."

"Thank you, Mr. Drummond. All right. Our procedure will be to quickly inventory with a first team, with a second team tasked with removal of perishables. For this exercise, perishables consist of foodstuffs only. These perishables get a blue tag. Any other personal possessions or contents of homes, garages and outbuildings are to be left in place. Other materials, specifically fuel, will be inventoried and removed later—those get a green tag. Each houses owner has been identified. Any dead from the quake have been removed. No residents in these homes were present prior to the flu outbreak. Each side of the street will be served by a separate inventory and removal team. Mr. Drummond will serve on one side of the street, Mr. Bauer the other. Both will lead the inventory teams, assisted by a CERT official. FEMA reps are on each team as observers, security will be provided by the Sheriff's department. The

Guardsmen, as usual, do the heavy lifting on sorting, transport to these two step-vans, loading and off-loading at the community center when we're done. Questions?"

None came.

"Good. Let's get moving before we freeze. Team A, east side of the street, with Mr. Bauer and Mr. Lewis of CERT. Team B, west side of the street with Mr. Drummond and Mr. Chase. Team leaders have flashlights, salvage teams have spotlights. Use them. If something doesn't look right, don't go in. Feral dogs are all over the place, and rabies meds are impossible to get. Work accordingly."

Alan and I both nodded to our CERT representatives and introduced ourselves as we moved across the street toward the first two houses. The deputies, charged with protecting the squads, were armed with flashlight-equipped M-16's and were attired in riot gear. I didn't know what they were expecting, perhaps an attack from squatters. 'Not in this neighborhood, guys,' I thought to myself.

The first house that our team arrived at was twisted and seemingly frozen in mid-collapse with the eastern half of the house pancaked, and the west half pulled toward it. The Sheriff's deputy, another guy I didn't know, opened the door, declared the house 'clear,' and we went inside.

The CERT guy—Sam Chase--both flipped on our mag-lights and went inside, wary of what we might find. The back half of this house appeared to be a bedroom wing, with maybe a family room on the main floor, bedrooms above, no basement. The kitchen was off to the left, and a dining room to the right. We were in a one-story wing, which still stood. The later addition had twisted and collapsed in on itself.

"OK, now what?" Sam asked.

"We look in the kitchen cabinets, refrigerator freezer, and closets for food. Then off to the garage and look for fuel or whatever. First though, we need the video guy so that if anyone ever comes back here, we can prove what was here and what we took."

"OK. Video! Front please," Sam barked.

"Yes, sir," a Spec 4—a young lady at that-with no rank showing--replied.

"All right. As we enter, we need you to film us, and film the contents of the house. Inventory crew will list what's being removed; salvage crew will box it up. You need to film our portion of the work. Clear?"

"Yes, sir. I assume that I will use both motion and still pictures?"

"Correct."

"Very good, sir."

Sam and I made quick work of the kitchen. There couldn't have been more than two people living here before the quake. Two cupboards and the freezer unit—still closed—were tagged.

"OK, on to the garage." Our photographer, Specialist Ross, trailed behind us after shooting digital video of the interior and stills of the blue-tagged cupboards and the freezer.

The garage, a single-stall structure dating from perhaps the nineteen thirties, was intact and nearly undamaged. We gained access by reaching through a broken windowpane in the door, and simply unlocked the deadbolt, after the deputy looked things over.

"All right, no freezer, no food," Sam said. "Two gas cans, empty. Lawnmower," he said as he checked the fuel, "Empty."

"At least they winterized it right," I said. "Would've been easy to fire up in the spring, if we were still in 'normal' times."

"Yeah. 'Normal.'

"OK, let's look for tools," I said as I played my flashlight over the dark brown wood framing of the walls and rafters. Nothing.

"Well that's a bust," Sam said.

"Yeah. Next house. OK, inventory and salvage team, you're good to go. We're moving up to the next house."

"Affirmative," the corporal replied. He motioned to his men as they quickly moved into the house with empty boxes and plastic grocery bags. One of the deputies stood guard over them as they went in. The three of us moved to the next house. Across the street, Alan was already on the next house, since the first place appeared to have been looted already.

I learned from Sam that the CERT teams currently serving in our area were all locals. All of the teams from out of the region had been sent home, wherever 'home' might be. Sam was about thirty, and worked in his former life as an accountant and one-time volunteer firefighter for our District Nine fire department. District Nine covered a large chunk of northern Spokane County, now without water due to the quake, and home now to a small percentage of its former population. He'd relocated to the far eastern portion of the Spokane Valley to be with his wife's family right after the quake. They lived within a few hundred feet of the Spokane River, which was currently their backup source of water. The home they lived in had a well house, attached to the main house. They were actually living in tents, inside of their damaged house, rooms sealed up as best they could with plastic and duct tape. His in-laws were living in their RV, parked in a large metal building. I gave him precious little information in return, to the point of being cryptic. I could tell that he understood.

The second house, minus every scrap of glass, had drifted snow in most of the rooms. One quake victim had been removed from here, according to the deputy reading the checklist of homes, this one likely a victim of a heart attack.

Sam and I moved into the house after the 'all clear' was given. We entered into what would've been the living room, in this case, it was filled with exercise gear, well used by the looks of it. In the kitchen some animal had scratched the cabinets to the point of taking off the outer layer of maple veneer, but had not succeeded in getting fed.

"Start left?" I asked Sam.

"Sure. I'll start right." The Nineteen Fifties kitchen was well laid out, at least, before the quake. One cabinet had popped open, and the contents of it, and the stuff on each countertop, was all over the floor. Each cabinet door had decorative hook and eye latch, built in Colonial fashion of wrought iron and solid knotty pine.

"Holy smokes," Sam said.

"What's up?" I said, looking over my shoulder.

"Look at these cabinets!"

Specialist Ross let out a descending whistle as she took digital stills.

Sam had opened up four cabinets so far, each one full, front to back and top to bottom, with canned goods, packaged foods, spices, salt and sugar, labeled with expiration dates on the front of each shelf, each item done similarly. One cabinet had liquids, which had frozen and burst, leaking onto the floor in a multi-colored goo.

"This guy had it together," I said. My two cabinets so far were cleaning supplies, labeled with only a little less detail than the food cabinets.

Seven other cabinets, two floor-to-ceiling, the rest 'above' the food preparation area, where also loaded up. The freezer was a separate unit from the fridge. Both were big Sub Zero stainless steel models, very much out of character with the modest home.

"Deputy, got a sec?" I called outside.

"Yes, sir?"

"How many people lived here?" I asked.

"One by our records, male, age thirty-eight, deceased of a probable heart attack in the quake," the deputy, Gary Simmons, replied. "Found him in the bedroom, next to the bed, face down, say the notes. Why do you ask?"

"Got enough food to last a long time," Sam said.

"OK, that's it for the kitchen. Let's look at the rest of the place. Deputy, have you checked the basement?"

"Briefly, yes. It's clear."

"OK, Sam, You wanna lead or follow?"

"I'm perfectly happy following, thanks," he said with a grin. More than half of the kitchen was tagged with blue tags. "Inventory team, you're good to go in the kitchen,' he called out.

"And here we go," I said as I headed downstairs, turning the beam from the flashlight from a tightly focused beam to a wider play.

"Whoa," I said as I looked around the basement.

"Whatchya got?" Sam said.

"Too much to tell. C'mon and have a look," I said.

"Ross, better get this photographed before we do anything," I said. And what's your first name? I'm not much on rank."

"Annie."

"Well Annie, it's all yours. Shoot it all. Are you from around here? You look familiar." I couldn't place her, not quite. She seemed all of twenty-two.

"I was born here. I live out in Greenacres with my parents, or did."

I looked at her nametag again. "Ross. Any relation to Brian Ross?"

"He's my dad. Do you know him?"

I chuckled a little. "Since the first grade at Progress Elementary, yeah. And your Mom is the former Tammy Jones." Annie looked like her mom, as I recalled her at about that age. I could tell by the eyes, even with half her face hidden by the surgical-style mask.

"Yes, sir." She said as she lowered her mask.

"Nice to meet you. They doing OK?"

"Yes, sir, the last I heard. They were on a ski vacation in Colorado when the quake hit. I was at WSU helping in the ROTC program, and got a phone call before the lines went down. They were planning on staying at Estes Park until they could come back home. I was mobilized the next day, and have been on active ever since."

"Brave new world."

"Yes, sir."

"Are you barracked with the troops over at Felts?"

"When on duty, yes. On days off I've been out to the house with my squad to try to clean it up a bit and put it back together."

"Much damage?"

"Yeah, not as bad as some. We've got it boarded up now, and the roof is in good shape. Lots of water damage, but it's drained now at least. One of the big water towers was across the street, and when the quake hit the tank came down and sent most of the water through the main floor. Quarter-million gallons, the guy from the utility said. The damage looked like Katrina when I was down there, without the smell."

"You were down there for that, too?"

"Yeah, mostly evac. We didn't stick around for Rita."

"Wonder if they'll ever get it put back together," I said almost to myself. "Hurricane Gay probably put an end to that."

"I expect you're right," she said.

The windowless basement walls were sheet rocked, and there were no interior walls to break up the fifteen hundred or so square feet. The room was basically one big storehouse, with more than a dozen racks of shelves, enclosed by wooden-framed wire, from wall to wall. Behind the stairs to my right, was a reloading press, metal lathe, and other gunsmithing tools. Very little had been disturbed by the quake, other than a couple of sheets of ceiling sheetrock that littered the floor.

"This will fill the truck," Sam said.

"Yeah. Maybe twice," I replied.

"Remember, we're just salvaging food," Sam said.

"Yeah, but still…"

"I know. This stuff's unreal."

We followed Annie down the aisle, looking at the various foodstuffs, dry goods, and gear. Two full pallets of freeze-dried food were in the corner, barrels of rice, wheat, corn, flour (noted that it was preserved with DE, on such-and-such a date, at such-and-such a cost).

"What's 'DE'," Sam asked to no one in particular.

"Diatomaceous earth. You mix it in with grain for storage. Bugs don't like it if you blend it in with your grains," I said before I could check my words.

"Oh." Sam said.

There were literally, thousands of pounds of grain alone, in addition to non-hybrid seeds, severe weather gear, lanterns, camouflage clothing in four different patterns, medical supplies, and four cabinets with locks. I assumed, the weapons locker.

"C'mon. We're done here," I said to Sam. "Annie, we'll wait before we go into the garage."

"Thank you," she replied through her mask as she continued to take pictures.

Sam and I stepped outside into the cold, around the salvage team. "Quite a stash," Sam said. "Makes my preps look like sick by comparison."

"Makes EVERYBODY'S look that way," I said. "Just goes to show you though."

"What's that?"

"You can prep to your heart's content, or your wallet's limit, and you can still die or get killed by something you didn't even see coming."

"Yeah. But so much stuff," Sam said as we looked over at Alan's crew, now on the fourth house.

"Planned for the end of the world. He reached it before it reached him," I said. "C'mon. Let's go look over the garage."

The garage was an unremarkable structure, no windows, a single man-door on the side, two doors on the front. The garage was set back from the street, and hidden behind a gate.   The white siding was stained with liberal amounts of blood on the side with the man-door. That question would remain unanswered.

"Deputy? Ready for the garage," I said as Annie joined us.

"Got the keys from the house," the deputy replied.

"Beats kicking it in," Sam said.

"Look again. You're not kicking that door in," I said.

"What? Looks like a door to me," Sam said.

"Solid steel frame, pardner. I'm betting that's a solid steel plate with a decorative skin on it. Look at the lock. That didn't come from Home Depot," I pointed out. The lock was a very heavy duty Schlage stainless-steel lockset. I'd only seen one like it, on a Federal building that will remain nameless.

The deputy unlocked the door, with a single key on a tagged key ring, and swung the door open. Lighting immediately snapped on in the garage, startling us all. From what I could see, this was a very well equipped shop, including a hydraulic press, large air compressor, and a fairly good sized multi-axis milling machine. Other tools adorned the walls. Late-sixties Dodge Powerwagon, in grey camouflage, resided on the far side, with a canvas-covered load in the bed. The near side, held a 'stock' late-sixties Powerwagon, chromed wheels, roll bar, off road lights. Pretty much a standard Spokane toy, pre-Domino.

"Whoa," I said again. "This place is full of surprises. Emergency backup lighting that's lasted this long off of line-power must've cost some bucks."

"Gimme a minute, the deputy said as he prepared to enter.

"Deputy, you might want to back out of here, real slow," I said as I took a step back.

"Why?" Sam said.

"Security system. A non-conventional security system, I'm thinking. Look over at the bench," I nodded toward the bench on the wall to the right of us. "Looks like a infrared motion detector focused on the door." A lighted LED display was just above the bench, on the wall. Something was blinking near the doorframe, reflected on the paint of the 'stock' Dodge truck inside.

"Discretion," deputy Simmons said.

"…is the better part of valor," I finished the saying as we backed up and closed the door.

"Now what?" Sam asked.

"We let the Army deal with it, and we move on to the next house when the inventory crew is done with the basement."

3

Thursday
February Sixteenth

Opening, inventorying, and removing the perishable foods from the vacant homes on our street took five hours, including a fifteen-minute lunch break. We knocked off, dead tired and cold, a little after three p.m., and headed back to the convenience store for a debriefing in the parking lot.

"All right," Pete Wolfson said. "You had a good day. We're done with the test exercise. By your records, you've retrieved four truckloads of foodstuffs from this single street, excluding the stored bulk foods and at seventeen-oh-one, which is being guarded, occupied homes, and homes being kept or watched over by Mr. Drummond and Mr. Bauer. Fuel products of various grades and types total eighty-six gallons in containers and additional fuel in parked vehicles. Comments?"

"What will be the implementation of this program on a larger basis?" I asked.

"It will start tomorrow morning, with assistance of residents in the area. Are you available tomorrow?"

"Let me check my Palm Pilot," I responded with a smile. The guardsmen chuckled as well.

"Where's the stuff going, and who gets it?"

"All food products from each neighborhood will be kept at each neighborhoods community center, food bank, local school or where possible grocery store. The distribution of these salvaged materials remains in question."

Alan and I looked skeptical. "Hokay," I exhaled. "Are you telling me that they're going to be sold, given away, traded, shipped out, or what?"

"The plan at present is undefined," Lt. Wolfson said.

"Then it is no plan at all," I said. "If this is going to be successful, meaning the salvage of food, you need a fair method of distributing it. Not everyone can pay for it."

"I understand," Pete said. I could sense some discontent in the Guardsmen ranks. They obviously had families to feed as well. "This is a matter that the Commissioners are dealing with at present."

"They best figure it out damn fast. Once word gets out that this 'pilot program' is going house to house, you'll have unbridled looting to lock up whatever's still out there by whoever's still left. Then, you're hosed. You'll lose a big percentage due to waste."

"Understood." Pete was silent.

"Then," I pushed him "when can we expect an answer?"

"The Board…"

"Pete, don't give me 'the Board.' We're talking about accountability here, not power. If they want to hold on to whatever little civilized society they've got, this is where it starts, or ends. But you understand that, don't you?"

"I do."

"Good. What time tomorrow?"

"Nine."

"Sounds fine. We'll see you then," I said as Alan and I headed back to the Jeep. "Alan, hang on a sec. I'll be right back."

I walked towards the nearest Humvee that Annie Ross was headed for. "Specialist Ross? Got a minute?"

"Yes, sir," She replied as she left her group.

"I just wanted to let you know that if you need anything, you let me know, OK?" I told her quietly. "Your folks and I go way back, and it's the least I could do."

"Thank you. I'm doing OK for now."

"All right, but like I said, you need anything you get in touch with us."

"Thank you. I'll remember that."

"We'll see you tomorrow."

"See you then," she said with her Mom's smile.

I walked back to the Jeep, where Alan was waiting.

"Extending the hospitality of the house?"

"Yep. She's the daughter of two classmates of mine from grade-school on up."

"Seems like a good egg."

"Yeah, like her folks as I remember. Of course, I haven't seen them for more than ten years, the last reunion. So how'd you do on your side?"

"Probably about as expected, except for the cats."

"Cats?"

"Third house from the end of the street. It looked like three house cats, trapped in the house after the owners bailed. Looked like the big one ate the other two, then died from dehydration or cold. They darn near clawed through a three-quarter inch thick hunk of maple to get at their food. Didn't quite make it."

"Bet that smelled good," I said as I closed the duct-taped Jeep door.

"Would've if it'd been warmer. Still, managed twenty-five gallons of gas and a fair amount of food. Looked like a lot of folks just bailed right after the quake. Lots of stuff still in the fridge, all of it long gone. Freezer stuff was still good, if you like mystery food. How about you? Do OK?"

"Yeah," I said, filling him in on the deceased bachelor's most-impressive preparations, and his untimely demise.

"Guess you can't plan for everything," Alan said.

"No, but you can plan for some things," I said as we pulled into the driveway.

Once our neighborhood—our street and two others east and west of us, as well as north and south of the large block—had been 'collected' we were released from the pilot program. During the three days of inventory and salvage, Alan and I noted the foodstuffs with some interest, but hid another key goal—reviewing and inventory of available tools, equipment, land area, fruit trees, building materials, and useable buildings that we hadn't been able to fully inventory previously from a distance or due to access. We also subtly kept an eye on security provisions for the block, with the goal of limiting vehicle access to the interior (dang near impossible) and ground attack by another gang. The latter was all but impossible. We could though, make it more difficult, and create some concealment of our position, and our walk arounds during 'collection' gave us some good ideas of better tactical positions for our observation posts.

On our last day of 'collection,' I was becoming a bit overcome by the surreal nature of it all. Here we were, our extended families and friends, in the midst of a medium sized city in America, figuring out how to defend ourselves against attackers. 'This is just wrong,' I thought to myself. I was starting to sound like Carl.

We closed up the last house and headed back to the community center, and it's now-overflowing food-bank. Refrigerated goods had ended up getting shipped to two grocery stores in the area, those that could be defended and had operating coolers from line power.

"So, Mike," I asked the Sheriff, "what's been decided on distribution of this food?"

"We have a plan, finally. Although there are several folks up a few pay grades from me that fought it tooth and nail."

"Do tell," I asked. A number of the Guardsmen were listening closely as well as we stood in the parking lot in the cold afternoon haze. No one had left after the last box was unloaded, and no one spent a lot of time 'close' to each other. The Flu was still a threat.

"We now have as complete a population count and distribution of population as we can get. In short, we know who is where and how many, down to the block. The County does not know how much food the population has, and we will not inventory the assets of each family unit."

"Why's that?" a Guardsman asked.

"Frankly, if someone's still here, they've got food, or at least enough to get to this point. I believe it's an intrusion into areas that we don't need to go if we have County or military personnel ask you how much food you've got. I'm not going there."

"And besides that," I said, "You all might get fired on for asking questions like that."

"That was a concern," Mike said with a steely look in his eyes. "Primarily of my department, not so of those who aren't actually making the decisions."

"Gee. Go figure," I said with no small amount of sarcasm.

"Distribution of food will be made on a equal basis without charge. Each family will receive an equal amount of food—weekly--based on the number of people in the family or group. If there are special dietary needs, these needs must be proven to the distribution office prior to food being distributed. That proof needs to be in the form of doctor's or nutritionists orders, medical history, something of that nature. Regarding quantities, each neighborhood will receive food based on what was salvaged from that neighborhood, and food amounts equal within that neighborhood area. Meaning, the five major inhabited neighborhoods in the Valley, stretching from Liberty Lake on the east to Park Road on the west, will share food equally within each neighborhood. These neighborhoods happen to be as well off, or slightly better off, than some areas of the City, South Hill and North Side. Food will not be transported out of one part of the city to feed another. From what we're hearing from on-high, food shipments into the city will be resuming within two weeks. The shipments will very likely not be enough to keep the residents fed in the style to which we have become accustomed. There are no imports coming into the country, and as you can imagine, distribution and manufacturing of processed foods is becoming a mess."

"No shock there," another voice responded.

"Mike, how are you going to get the word out about this?"

"Each resident will get a flyer, stating the days that they are to pick up food, locations, etc."

"How about medicines?" a voice from my left asked. "My wife has diabetes, and my son is on medication, too."

"Local clinics—in each neighborhood—will distribute prescriptions as proven needs arise. If you have medical conditions, you need to show up personally, with proof of the condition, at the clinic and make arrangements for receipt of the medical supplies.

"And what's that gonna cost?" the same voice asked. I looked over to my left. A young Guardsman, maybe late twenties, in dirty desert-camouflage utilities and a forest camo parka. The name tag read 'Morris.' He was part of Annie Ross's squad.

"Prices for foodstuffs and other products in retail stores are fixed at pre-quake levels in stores still operating. Cash. Salvaged medicines are not to be used in any regard, and may not be sold. Medicines distributed through clinics are available free with suitable proof of need."

"And if we don't have cash for store purchases?" A voice behind me.

"You can ask for credit, with suitable proof of identity. Men, we are not going to operate this for our convenience or profit. This is a service. If you can't afford something, that doesn't mean you're not going to get it. Clear?"

"Yes, sir," Morris answered with several others.

I quickly thought over our stocks of medicines, vitamins and first-aid stuff, and came up short. I made a mental note to have Karen update our inventory and make it a priority to get our stocks back up…if we could.

"If that is all, you are dismissed. A distribution list will be available here at the community center at oh-eight-hundred tomorrow."

I motioned Annie to follow me, and she met us at the Ford while the rest of her squad headed for their ride.

"Here's a couple of packages of cornbread. My wife thought your squad might enjoy it."

"Thank you very much," she said with a smile in her eyes. "We will."

"You remember what I said. You need something, you come look us up."

"I'll remember. Thanks again," she said as she gave us both a quick hug.

The rest of the guardsmen and deputies were now loaded up in their various cars and trucks, and Annie piled in the back of a Humvee equipped with a canvas top and bench seats, a configuration I'd never seen before. Alan and I went back to the Ford for the ride home.

"Nice kid."

"Yeah, and remember, she can probably out-shoot both of us."

"I have no doubt about that. Still got a couple hours of daylight left," Alan said.

"Yeah, and the weather service said we've got more cold on the way. Let's spend a little time on the tool inventory from today's walkabout. Tonight I can get it all compiled and we can figure out where we really are," I said.

On that first day, we mentally noted hand tools, any three-point implements, harness gear, outbuilding types, motorized and non-motorized equipment, bicycles, trailers, a dozen other items. By the second day, we just decided to openly note and list the equipment, telling the Guardsmen and the CERT teams that the tools might come in handy later in the spring. Unlike the food and fuel, the tools remained uncollected on each property. By the end of the 'collection', Alan and I had visited three hundred fifty-seven homes. Eleven had legal residents. At least ten more had squatters, who quickly left when our 'collection team' appeared. No food remained—of any kind—in any home within hundreds of feet of the squatter or 'legal' residents. They'd obviously been forced to look to the vacant homes for food already. Once the 'collection' was done, the squatters moved on to other neighborhoods with better pickings. They usually took any sleeping bags or bedding with them, as well as anything they perceived as 'valuable' from the homes they broke into. We found one shopping cart filled with electronics, another with ladies shoes. It seemed that not everyone had a common definition of 'valuable.'

"Firewood?" I asked Alan.

"Maybe three cords in my section today, cut and stacked, but none of it dry."

"Downed wood?"

"Another five, easy, on the ground."

"Building materials?"

"Eleven sheets of OSB, I think five of three-quarter plywood, two of those furniture grade. Thirty seven two-by-fours, eight foot; thirteen two by eights, eight foot; four two by twelves, ten foot. Six bags off mortar mix. Four bags ready-mix concrete; four buckets of chain, mixed sizes. Four rolls roofing paper, fifteen pound. Four sheets fiberglass sheet…"

I had a hard time reading Alan's notes. It was easier just to have him dictate to me as I put things into Excel.

"OK, that's about it then for now. We can finish up the small tools after dinner."

"Pretty easy in my part. Here's my list," Alan handed me one of our checklists. Only a dozen or so tick marks were on the sheet.

"Wow. Not much there."

"Duplexes and rentals. And what's there isn't worth much."

"You two want some coffee?" Libby asked.

"That would be great. How's Ron doing? Feeling better?"

"He'll be OK, if he just takes it easy."

"He's had three days away from us, so his back ought to recover just from the lack of exercise!" I said. Ron had twisted his lower back a few days before, and it hadn't fully recovered yet. While I kidded Libby, I also suffer from back problems (as in, doing-things-that-I'm-really-too-old-for), so I was certainly sympathetic.

"Chiropractors are hard to come by these days," she said as she finished pouring Alan's coffee.

"A lot of skills are. And will continue to be, I'm afraid."

4

Monday
February Twenty-Seventh

The occasional bursts of gunfire continued off in the distance, even though we knew that there weren't that many residents in the area, and police and military patrols were noticeably less frequent. We were unable for the most part, to determine from the scanner, CB, FRS or AM radio what the shooting was all about. In late February, a few weeks after our lopsided firefight with the teenaged attackers, my friendly contact with the Sheriff's office came to an abrupt end, I assumed at the direction of the Commissioners. Mike Amberson stopped by one day to pick up some eggs for Ashley for her birthday. He let me know that although patrols would continue in our area, that all informal 'fraternization' between the department or the military, and civilians was as of that day, not allowed. Apparently one of the commissioners had done a ride-along with a deputy when I'd called Mike on the FRS the day before, and told him that his eggs were ready, and that I wanted to talk to Mike regarding the fuel and food situation. Mike got a royal butt chewing for it. Most importantly, and more disturbing to us than anything we'd experienced recently, was that we were to allow only the Sheriff's department and the military units still in the area to deal with looters and raiders.

"You do realize that that is a complete pile of horses**t, Mike," I said.

"I do. You also realize that I have my orders from my employers, and I've been warned that my position is not as firm as I might like it to be. None of ours are."

"They'd can you for us calling the department on a radio—because we have no phones--saying that we need help because we're being shot up?"

"That was the implication."

"What are we supposed to do without phones? String a damned can with strings? Lie back and think of England while we've got bullets tearing up the barn? Get real, Mike."

"I understand your position Rick. You understand mine. Don't think that they're picking on you alone—it's this way county-wide."

"County-wide my ass. They've got a phone at the community center that's not available for public use. They have no phone service to the neighborhoods, and none for the foreseeable future. Cell-phone towers are down all over, there's no fixing them anyway. Your staff can't patrol the whole county and you know it and so do I. So does the Board. Who are they protecting, or where?"

"Rick, don't go there," Mike said sternly.

"Fine, I won't. I hear you. We're literally on our own, unless a deputy or a military patrol happens to be parked right in front of our house when we're attacked. And we will deal with raiders accordingly. The Commissioners, in their protected enclaves wherever they are, will have all the protection they can muster, while the rest of the citizenry fends for themselves."

"Rick, that's..."

"No, you listen, Mike. You know reasonable and you know unreasonable. You know right and wrong. You know what the score is with the flu, and the chances of this city ever getting back to anything approaching what it was before the quake and before the economy went in the flusher. Maybe five percent, and that's being generous. I'm telling you that someone better get some balls down there and stand up and tell the Board the what-for or there will be very little left to put back together. What you just said, assuming there are any sheep still stupid enough to listen to such crap, is that they are supposed to die rather than defend themselves, unless some officer or military unit comes by."

"Now wait just one damned minute...."

"No, you wait. Defend your employer's position. Go ahead. You can't and you know it."

"I do. I cannot change that position, you realize."

"Really. Then you better find yourself a surviving judge for the interpretation of those directives, because I will guarantee you this, if this rule is implemented, people like me are going to find us a judge, and when he rules on it and finds it to be an unconstitutional order, you can damn sure bet that should one innocent person die as a result of this, we will come hunting. And you will be part of a housecleaning the likes of which you have never seen. You don't want to be on the wrong side of that, Mike."

"Is that a threat?"

"To you? Mike, you know me better than that. I've known you a long time, and I think Ashley was lucky to marry such a good man. But imagine some other father out there who's daughter was raped and killed by someone that your staff should've stopped, but didn't, because the orders to stop them didn't come through your pre-quake 'normal' channels, or because your resources were……. misallocated."

I knew where the 'missing' patrols had gone. They were defending a couple of the commissioners' homes and businesses. I knew this with a very, very high degree of confidence.

"You think that he's not going to get out his thirty ought-six and pick you off at his leisure? Think again. You think your wife will be safe in this kind of culture? She won't be. None of us will. This isn't a dictatorship run by those three elected representatives, even though they seem to be leaning that way. The resources are available to protect this community. You cave, we all lose. You cave, and we're back on our nightly patrols. We see an unmounted individual after curfew, there will be a shot. We see a darkened vehicle driving up our street, there will be a shot. The next day, there will be a body. 'Looters will be shot. Survivors will be shot again.' There is no question about that."

Mike was silent as I wound up my diatribe. "You need to decide if you will follow an illegal order, or…..not. 'Not' could be more of a problem for you if you and your staff aren't prepared to deal with it legally, quickly, and with overwhelming support."

"You're talking about a coup."

"I'm talking about a coup. Do you see an alternative?"

A long silence passed. "No," Mike responded.

"Then you need to get your ducks in a row. Your orders are probably in writing, knowing the board, right?"

"Yes."

"Who's providing counsel?"

"No one. Staff counsel hasn't been seen since the quake. Two prosecutors are still around, and a couple of public defenders, but they're not being consulted."

"Imagine. Maybe you ought to have a nice, friendly chat with them, and get their legal opinion on what you just told me. Then you might want to poll your department on what I just told you, and remember the hypothetical father coming after you."

"This is going to take some time."

"It might. Good morning. You've just woken up in a minefield with no map. Here's your eggs. Give Ash our best," I said as I shook his hand. I was still ticked off.

"Thanks. Rick, this will take time," Mike said as he got back into his cruiser.

"Understood. Night watch will start up this evening, armed appropriately."

That night we put a rotation back in place, with two armed observers outside at all times after dark in the observation posts, all adults armed whenever outside of a building, and one person manning the radios. This would put another crimp in our plans, by designating man-power and energy towards security, instead of towards rebuilding.

Over the next couple of days, we analyzed the larger block again, to determine threats to us from hidden shooters, aiming to pick us off. In the end, there was very little we could do to still maintain a good field of vision 'out', while protecting the barn from observers. Our impressions gained during 'collection', were seemingly correct.

We did, however, come up with four specific areas that we could address, and during daylight hours we thinned out shrubs and trees four properties to the north of us, and moved and built some fencing to at least provide some sense of enclosure. The fences ended up being a 'zig-zag', so that we could pull out the center portion when it came time to plant, so that the tractor could maneuver through the block. Two additional observation posts were also built, that when manned, provided a clear view to the north and west, toward Alan's. This new post was perhaps the biggest security improvement we could make, as it protected the north side of the barn, which was windowless. The new post was built partly of large tree branches, scrap and found lumber, and, well, two scrap metal hoods from my collection of Fords for a roof. The entire contraption was screened with cut branches, downed tree limbs and brush. This 'pile' was built about thirty feet north of the barn, nine feet high. It covered most of the barn wall from the view down the slight hill to the north, and if the shooters were stupid, (we were counting on this) they'd have to be almost on top of us before they saw the barn. Access to the post was from the south, directly on the west side of the barn. With little effort, we could leave the barn in a crouch, and make it to the post without being seen. None of our posts was what we'd consider bullet-proof, or even bullet-resistant. The ground was like concrete as well, although if we felt the need, we could've probably gone after it with picks and shovels. (We didn't, although we probably would've been wise to.)

Both north- and south of the barn, we created several man-traps using found spools and rolls of rusty barbed wire. At least someone approaching in the dark couldn't walk right in without some difficulty.

In the end, we were counting on people to be reasonable and civilized and not shoot first. It was as simple as that.

The national news, and the international elements during February and March gave us the news of virtually complete withdrawals of US forces back to US soil. The lone bases remaining in US control included Diego Garcia, a base in Turkey, and one in Guam. All other bases, no matter what branch, were systematically abandoned, apparently after useable components were either removed or in some cases, demolished in place. After our forces were 'sequestered'—as the media now called it, and the President showed what he was really made of---the host countries allowed the full withdrawal. When certain countries complained about the loss of the bases and the mess that the US was leaving, sixty-eight percent of Congress decided that those European countries should be sent a bill for the US involvement in two world wars and defending them for the better part of six decades. No further comments were made regarding US operations. One evening, during a dinner of chili and cornbread, we watched with no small alarm the tape of massive runways at one of the German bases systematically blown up by our own forces, the last plane out using a remote control detonator, apparently.

The world-wide protests against the US, after the 'war' was all but over (except for Mexico, of course) focused on the 'arrogant greed' of the US's new foreign policy. On February 1, the President announced that all foreign aid provided for decades for 'development' of second- and third-world countries was permanently terminated. The US would now use its revenues within the borders of the United States and its territories, and for defense of the country. By this point, any Americans planning on coming back home were either here already or...probably never would be again. The window had closed. This included virtually all American correspondents abroad. If they were discovered to be American in a hostile country, there was virtually no getting them out. What little we did learn about what was going on in the rest of the world came from the BBC for a while, and later from other European shortwave receptions. It seemed that after the Americans were dispatched, the English seemed a good second. Five correspondents were killed in Africa, three in the middle east. One, on the air during a live broadcast.

Sit-coms, variety shows, and anything less than 'serious' matter on television faded immediately after the words 'Second Great Depression' were spoken by the President's Treasury Secretary. They were replaced with hours and hours of mindless talk about the Economy, How to Save Your Retirement Fund, and other pointless topics. If, at that point, you still had investments in dollars, or in real estate, you'd lost it all, except for the numbers on the statements that you were mailed each quarter. There were of course the Pollyanna pundits continuing to state that this was a 're-set' of the excesses run up over the past few years, and the Market Would Soon Be The Place To Be. Damned fools.

Within a month of the stock market 'bottom' call, though, the Big Brains in Hollywood brought a series of the sit-coms and dramas back, dealing with imagined scenarios set after the Depression had started—trying to get advertising revenue flowing, trying to fill time. Problem was, in the end, no one really wanted to see the famous starlets learn how to cook dinner using what the food lines handed out, and scrounging for a latte. It just wasn't funny. The soap operas, Kelly told me, were even more stupid.

"'Survivor' for real now, hon," I told her.

"Yeah. With no 'immunity challenge' or 'reward challenge," she replied.

"Kinda. Our real-world 'immunity challenge' is to build a safe community. Our 'reward challenge' isn't really found here."

"I don't get it."

"We're tasked with storing up treasures in Heaven. Not here."

"Yeah, but how does that apply here?"

"Do what's right, even when no one's looking. Give until it hurts. Then, give some more. I start with those. Go through Proverbs. You'll find lots of good advice. But you already know that."

"OK, so what about all that silver and gold that Uncle Alex sent?"

"They're tools, that's all. If we didn't have them, we probably wouldn't miss them. Should the day come when we CAN use them, we will. But I'm not working to gain material goods…..in spite of the fact that I do seem to have a lot of stuff."

(The courier shipment—through FEDEX—had arrived as Alex had promised in February, nearly two hundred pounds of silver coins and some gold Eagles as well. The funds that bought these coins had comprised a large percentage of my retirement fund back when mutual funds still existed. Alex had adeptly moved my money from mutual funds to gold and silver stocks and then to physical metal before things came completely apart. I figured--figuratively speaking--I'd never see a dime of it. Now, literally, I had tens of thousands of silver dimes, and nearly twenty thousand silver quarters. I have no idea how he did it, and I probably never will.)

Sports broadcasts were similarly affected, and as dramatically. The Super Bowl was still held, with the Patriots losing to the Forty-Niners. The game was moved from Ford Field in Detroit to Vikings stadium, due to a car-bomb attack at the Detroit Airport a few days before the game, with continuing rioting reaching out from the empty core of Detroit into what passed for suburbs. Major League Baseball was still planning on spring training, but obviously facilities in the southern states were affected by the war, including a couple of the fields in Arizona that I'd visited before. One of them was looted and burned in the initial Mexican attack, another seemed to be turned into a holding area for possible prisoners of war, tents pitched on the now brown grass of the Seattle Mariners' spring field. A great percentage of foreign players were…missing from the rosters, either in their home-countries when the war started and unable to come to the States or perhaps lost to the flu.   The Mariners of course, were missing completely, their surviving players filling out the rosters on a dozen other teams. The NBA season was still running a full schedule, although with dramatic fall-offs in game attendance, until the third wave of attacks targeted sports venues. After that, games were played sporadically, through February. By March, with the melt-down approaching full steam, they halted play.   My favorite TV sport, NASCAR, continued on with the Daytona 500 on February 19, and other races limited to the Southeast only. Spectators, almost to a man, were openly armed. Travel was 'iffy' beyond the Southeast for the Cup drivers and their teams, or so someone thought. Oddly enough, after the initial wave of attacks by the Mexicans, there was no second or third wave in the Deep South. The retaliation in the Old South was swift, effective, and relentless. One TV news broadcast showed a scene in Northern Georgia, where one small town—Summerville?-- near the border with Tennessee and Alabama, had all adults wearing sidearms or carrying long-guns. The commentator stated the obvious, 'an armed society is a polite society.' Four hundred sixty illegal aliens—not all Mexicans, and certainly not all guilty of an attack on the US—had been rounded up and summarily executed in six neighboring counties within eleven days after the attacks. They did not comment on whether Summerville had seen such activity. It was also stated that the attacks were conducted by both black and white members of the population. The commentator stated that travel to Atlanta, however, was difficult due to rioting and looting.

Go figure.

When we weren't watching or listening to "the wheels come off the wagon" so to speak (which was a continuing source of concern, anxiety, worry, and downright fear), we worked and deliberately shut off the news. There were still lives to live here, and being paralyzed by the rumors of shortages, of riots, and battles was no way to live ours. I think that what surprised me most, was how long things were taking to grind down.

To take my mind off of the outside for awhile, I put a rough calendar together on when certain things 'needed' to happen, regardless of whether we wanted them to or not. Seedlings for the garden, for example, had to be planted and 'up' by a certain day to ensure early harvest, given our 'normal' growing season of late April through mid-September. Fruit trees needed to be pruned and sprayed for pests….assuming we had enough spray or could make an organic spray from stuff on hand. Two big greenhouses up on the north end of the block would need to be reskinned, cleaned, and prepared well in advance of planting. We'd have to plow up the ground with the Ford's two-bottom plow, or maybe a scrounged rototiller for the three-point, for field crops. Whether we wanted to do the work, or not, it was still there for us. Hunger, and starvation, might be the alternative.

5

The flu outbreak, by the second week of February called Guangdong Flu, tore through Asia, Australia, major cities in Africa, and the whole of Europe, as it progressed only with a little less fervor in the US. Mexico, Canada, and major importers of Chinese products in South America were similarly hit. By the first of March, the peak seemed to have passed in the States, with death tolls hitting fifteen percent in rural areas, thirty-five percent in urban regions. Europe's 'peak' hit a little sooner for some reason--I thought that the virus had been introduced a little sooner. Their losses are estimated at forty percent, nearly as bad as those in China and throughout Asia.

When I heard those statistics, I thought to myself of how the Native American societies and cultures changed, specifically the Inland Northwest tribes, when faced with such catastrophic reductions in population. European diseases, spread through the first explorers in the fifteen- and sixteen-hundreds, introduced diseases that wiped out whole tribes and left decimated survivors in their wake, far beyond the physical contact of the Europeans. Traditions died. Ways of life disappeared. Trading opportunities and routes disappeared with the dead.

It seemed, we were now re-visiting history, first-hand. They say that those who do not learn from history are doomed to repeat it. I think it's more complicated than that. We just seem to find new ways to kill ourselves, rather than repeat verbatim the old ways.

We gained far more news of what was going on in the rest of the world through shortwave than through our own news networks—American reporters and their crews had mostly come back home with the military withdrawal. Those that didn't....often died. We'd listen in the evenings to the macabre reports, of the progression of the virus, the climbing death tolls, the futile attempts to corral the urban population within the cities to control the spread. Invariably, the initial reports discounted the outbreak, stating that the health departments had things under control. Within days, reality kicked in, and the extent of the losses became apparent.

41

The CDC thought that the lower US death toll was mostly due to another unrelated strain of influenza that preceded the Chinese-engineered bioweapon. The 'natural' virus apparently had built up some immunity to the 'engineered' strain, which either left the victim ill, but not dead, or killed them quickly with a progression of aggressive symptoms that ended up drowning them in their own fluids, Ebola fever-style. Of course it remains to be seen if the virus will mutate is it did in the nineteen-eighteen and nineteen-nineteen outbreak. Many who made it through the 'fall' outbreak, died in the spring of the next year, when the mutated virus came back, batting cleanup.

It also seemed that here, at least, the virtual inability to travel has helped slow the spread of the virus. Commercial air travel into Spokane had ceased on January fourteenth, and only relief flights and military flights had gone in or out since then. No rail traffic. Very little commercial trucking. No inbound bus traffic.   We heard on Fox News radio that virtually all major US cities had been closed off from the rest of the country as the virus spread. Many small towns, like Grangeville, Idaho, seeking self-preservation, closed themselves off from the rest of the world, occasionally going as far as tearing up the roads and building trenches across them. Those attempting to get in around the roadblocks were fired on. Even today, little traffic is allowed in, or so we hear.

For us, the 'other' strain probably saved our lives, or in Grace's case, exposure to the nineteen-eighteen variety or some later version, which built up immunity. For others, like Andrea, and Ashley Amberson's family, Mike's wife, they had no such immunity and died quickly once they'd contracted it. Mike had gone up to check on them, up in the hills outside the town of Chewelah, the third week of February. Ashley's parents, her brother and his wife and their four children, her sister and her husband, newlyweds at Christmas. All dead, in the locked house.

Rebuilding

Once the house had been cleared of the mountains of plaster that had fallen from the walls and ceilings, we were able to determine the extent of structural damage that had been caused by the quake.

By the second week of February, we all knew that the limited amount of assistance that had already arrived from other parts of the country would probably be all we would get. There were simply too many problems to deal with at one time for the United States, and limited resources to go around. In that view, we were both better- and worse-off: better in that we were forced to do for ourselves; worse that we had to do so while the rest of the country enjoyed a few more weeks of stability....and civility. It was sometimes too much to listen or watch on TV, the morning anchors, interviewing some poor hapless soul, and talk about another in a string of major disasters hitting the country in a years' time. The public was even weary of fundraisers for the disaster victims. Not that

I could blame them, I was weary of the whole thing myself. So, we went to work trying to put our lives together. We started with the house.

The plaster and lath walls and ceilings in most of the rooms were now lath only, covering the balloon frame built atop the stone foundation. The west-to-east shaking had shattered about half of the windows, all those facing north and south, as the building racked in the direction of the quake. The windows on the east- and west-facing walls were more-or-less intact, although some (such as our bedroom window upstairs) had blown out for unknown reasons. The clearing operation took weeks to get through, but I didn't want to even start repairs until we had a good assessment of the size of the project. Twenty plus years of remodeling work had at least taught me that much. 'Know What You're Getting Yourself Into.' (Had I learned this in my early twenties, I'd have never bought this house).

Starting at the foundation, we'd stripped off the paneling and insulation that covered about half of the walls up in the basement. Other than one major breach in the wall over the bar area, the foundation was very much intact, although about half of the mortar holding the stones in place had cracked, and about ten percent had separated completely. The major posts holding up the floor beams and joists—big ten-by-tens—were in perfect shape, along with their toenailed connections to the beams. That surprised me. During part of February and into March, we re-installed the big hand-cut stones that had collapsed into the basement, and re-mortared where we could, until we ran low on mortar. I then had Carl and John salvage the mortar that had collapsed, and experimented on crushing it back to dust and re-wetting it. It worked, although I wasn't sure of how well. For surface work though, I thought it would suffice for now. Most of the time in the basement was actually spent moving stuff around, rather than rebuilding. There wasn't room to store our 'stuff' outside, so we did the move, move, and move-again routine.

The final basement reconstruction element in this phase of work was to replace the broken windows that the Domino had taken out. Both windows, one on the south, the other on the west, were gone. The west lost completely when the wall collapsed, the south shattered in its frame. Years before, I was visiting a development that our firm had designed, and scored new windows for an entire house. A builder had ordered the right ones; the factory had built them incorrectly with the wrong mullions installed between the panes. The factory didn't want them back, and the builder was going to dump them. I got them for free, double-glazed argon-filled glass panels, minus their wood frames, which were re-used when the correct glazing panels arrived. The glass had been stored in the barn ever since, waiting for a use. I certainly had one now.

On a very wet day in late February, we cleared out the 'woodshop' out a bit so that I could use some of the power tools to build the wooden window frames for the stair case window, and the two simple windows for the basement. The original at the top of the stairs, a small thirty-inch tall, twenty-inch wide window, was lost in the debris from the quake; I'm sure pulverized into very small bits. The replacement would be wider, and instead of opening 'in' to the house on hinges at the top, would instead have two double-insulated panes that would swing 'in' towards the walls, rather than 'up' towards the ceiling. This was more due to the sizes of the windows than anything else. One benefit though, would be the ability to better vent that part of the house, once the windows were in and screens built. Right now, of course, the house was about as well ventilated as you could get, with the large hole where the gable roof was supposed to be. Andy Welt's man had delivered a double insulated window, but it was 'fixed' and there was no way to convert it to an 'opening' window. I'd find another use for it, I was sure.

It took me a day and a half to build the window frames and the sashes, and scrounge the shop for four hinges to make the stair windows operable. For simplicities' sake, I used the same overall design for all of the windows, and built everything from cut-down dimensional lumber. Not the greatest stuff to use, but it's what I had. Two leftover window locks were ready to go to secure the windows to the frame. Carl, John, Ron and Alan joined me for the cutting, routing, assembly, and final fitting. Let no one tell you that building a window is an easy thing. More complicated than cabinetry, and that's saying something. I'm sure that I'd be better at it if I did it more often, but that's a skill I'd prefer to let someone else perfect. The finished stair window assembly was a monster thing, and weighed almost a hundred and thirty pounds.

We fit the basement windows first, which were installed in the cut stone foundation, and then mortared and 'foamed' with expanding foam to fill any gaps. The frames were built of pressure-treated two-by-sixes. The rooms warmed noticeably when we'd installed them and closed out the winter.

The houses' waste stack was in surprisingly good shape, and we tested it with rainwater fed into the drains on the upper floors, after I'd cobbled up a new connection from the waste lines to our 'old' septic tank over the space of about three days. This was accomplished using PVC drain line parts from the James' house, my Sawzall, and a couple of flexible sewer line connectors, also from the James'. Two supply lines were split, feeding the hot water tank (also split) and a line to the kitchen sink. With much effort, we salvaged some galvanized pipe from Tim's house, and also liberated his nearly new eighty-gallon hot water tank. I scrounged up enough pipe to do the job, and re-threaded the three-quarter inch pipe with my threading tool (one of the coolest tools ever, if you need a pipe that's not standard length). Once we'd tested the lines and drained them all again after working on them (no heat in the house still, and it was still 'winter' outside), we could progress to the next phase of work, structural repairs on the damaged framing.

The main floor structure was virtually undamaged, with the exception of the damage around where the chimney had collapsed from above the second floor roof down onto the main floor, and the complete loss of the enclosed back porch. The motion of the quake had popped almost all of the plaster off of the walls, and about half of the ceilings. The kitchen, remodeled a number of times since about nineteen-fifty was all sheetrock (I dated one remodel from a newspaper stuffed in a wall for insulation), all still in place but damaged. The back porch, added onto the house after it was built, had suffered the greatest damage of any single part of the house. Its foundation had failed right off, dropping the floor framing into a crawl space, and the rest of it had settled about a foot from its previous elevation onto the rubble of the foundation. We'd end up tearing the whole thing down and adding a new door from the kitchen to the porch, just to keep the weather out. We planned to rebuild it during better weather.

The second floor was a different story. The chimney collapse had torn through the landing and half of the stairs, opening up a hole through the middle of the house from the first floor through the roof. Carl and John had salvaged the brick, and stacked it up in neat squares on the front porch and in the front yard. Destroyed woodwork and balusters had been similarly salvaged, just in case we could somehow repair or reuse them. A roll of the dark green carpeting that once covered the stairs now resided in the living room, complete with two pieces of framing and some of the varnished fir trim that had been rammed through the carpet and the stairs, and resisted all efforts to pull them out. We now traversed the hole where the stairs were supposed to be with two stepladders, placed on temporary supports on the old stair stringers or on new temporary framing. The hole was lit only with the eerie blue glow of daylight coming through the tarp that Carl and I had covered the roof with. It leaked a little, but not enough to really worry about.

When we stripped off parts of the lath in suspect parts of the second floor, we discovered that the collapse of the north gable had shattered the framing members eight feet either side of the gable location. Before we could rebuild the gable, we'd have to complete more demolition on the outside of the house and replace the damaged framing just to get to something solid. Two ceiling rafters in our master bedroom had also split, but could be left in place and patched with new lumber, sistering the old parts together with some new framing. By the last week of February, with the basement work wrapping up, we were able to get this little piece of work done as well, pulling the cracked and separated ceiling joist ends back together with twin come-alongs attached to the north and south walls. Once the parts were approximately at their former lengths, we put new two-by-fours on either side of the broken joists, and fastened them to the originals with a combination of epoxy wood adhesive and sixteen-penny nails from my framing nailer. That little task took four of us all day long. We left the come-alongs in place for two days, until we were sure that the glue had set up.

During a break in the action, I had Carl collect all of the pieces of broken or nearly destroyed wood trim from the house, and arrange them so that they could be reassembled if possible. Most of the small stuff was no big deal to piece back together again, some of the larger parts—Kelly's five-panel bedroom door for example—would be a bit more interesting. I didn't know if I'd take this on right now or not, but part of the reason we fell in love with the house in the first place was all of the original woodwork. It would be a shame to put the place back together without it.

On March thirteenth, after finishing up the hole for Alan's new septic tank, I dug out the keys to my big F500 utility truck.   A couple years before, after putting off the repaint of the house for almost as long as possible, and dreading the prospect of setting up scaffolding, working, tearing it down, and re-setting it, I'd scoured the ads for options. I found a nineteen seventy-one F500, with a thirty-four foot hydraulic ladder and bucket, for less money than I'd spend on either renting or buying scaffolding. I went right over to Coeur d'Alene and bought it on the spot. It had saved me countless hours in the two-year repaint of the house, which included removing almost all of the decades of paint, re-nailing all of the siding, dozens of tube of caulk, and forty-five gallons of paint. Now, we'd use it to remove some of that freshly painted siding and trim, and help us hoist new lumber up for the new gable and repair the damaged walls.

"Think she'll start?" Alan asked through the drizzle.

"Heck yeah. It's only been sitting four months. No, five," I said as I turned the key and the big six-cylinder turned over and coughed.   A little less choke, and the big Ford fired up.   "See? Told ya."

"How much fuel in the tanks?"

"Should be pretty close to full. I filled it up before I parked it. The cab tank holds around twenty gallons, the saddle tanks about thirty each, I think. The gauges are shot, so I can't tell you exactly."

"Dipstick measure," Ron said.

"Yep, that or thunk 'em."

"Helluva lotta fuel for a six banger."

"Top speed's maybe forty five miles per hour. Just 'cause it's a six doesn't make it economical. It weighs almost five tons. Besides that, I didn't buy it for a commuter."

"Good thing. Gas OK this old?"

"Should be, I put stabilizer in it. Still, it won't last forever."

After a few minutes of warming up the monster, and making sure that Buck and Ada were out of the way, I pulled the truck up into the yard, about fifteen feet from the house, so that we could use the hydraulic boom to lift materials up to the second floor, either hanging from the boom or carried up the ladder. The boom had a three hundred pound limit, so we couldn't do too much, too fast, or carry much.

By the twenty-sixth of March, we had the demolition work done, framed in a new chase for the double-insulated metal chimney for the wood stove, re-framed damaged rafters on either side of the 'hole', and were ready to start framing the new side walls for the gable. The end wall had already been framed, with a new window opening sized to fit the new stair window. We were on track to finish up the sidewall and roof framing by the end of March when the weather shut us down, starting with a thunderstorm like I'd never seen in this part of the country. It poured for six straight days. We received six inches of rain in that time. A record, certainly, if the weather service was still keeping track.

Our rain delay on our house was offset however, by the fact that Alan now had a flush toilet, septic tank, drain field, running water, and the chance that 'line power' might be back within a few days. The tank and drain rock were placed by a private contractor hired by the County. We installed the piping and finished the backfill. We gave Grace the honors of the first flush.

6

Friday
April Seventh, 5:15 p.m.

"Hon, dinner's in an hour. Or do you plan to work all night?" Karen asked on the FRS.

"On my way. Just taking in the satisfaction that my dear, we have a roof again."

"Rain tight?"

"Yes ma'am."

"Good for us. Now get down here and help with dinner. Paulianos will be here any minute."

"On my way."

I climbed back onto the bucket truck, hooked my safety harness to the metal loop on the end of the ladder, flipped the remote master 'on' switch with my foot, and retracted the ladder as I lowered the boom, coming to a rest just ahead of the hood on the big Ford. I shed my safety gear to the dry cab, and shut off the master switch to the truck's electrical system.

Dinner, tonight at Alan's house, would be the first chance we'd really had to talk with the Paulianos since they got back. For the past three days, they'd been either putting their own place back together with help from Alan, Karen, Kelly and the older boys when we could spare them, or out at Don and Lorene's place out near Newman Lake. The Martins house was also one of our 'projects', so we never lacked for something to do.

Even though we'd covered over the windows and the obvious damage, they still had the quake damage to really address. Joe's age didn't help matters, as he wanted to do more than he was now physically able to.   The first night at least,

49

we were able to get their bedrooms habitable, and the second night, their bathrooms functioned again, even with flush toilets and showers.

The menu tonight included a large ham from Joe's friend 'Peretti', who I'm sure had a first name, although I've never heard it. We also had mashed potatoes on the menu, the last of the winter squash, bread, and a number of pies that the girls had worked on for two days. We would, if nothing else, be well fed.

I stomped off the volcanic mud from my boots, and wiped off as much as I could before I shed the boots and slipped into a thrashed pair of Reeboks that were on a rack inside the outer barn door. The 'inner' door was a conventional three-foot wide insulated steel door, opening 'in'. The outer door with the shoe rack was just a barn-wood rattletrap that was more for aesthetics than security and opened 'out'. It was nice and warm inside, and I wasted no time in getting over to the woodstove to warm up.

"Any news?" I asked Libby, who was working on the potatoes.

"Yeah. Some. Another quake in California. Six point seven."

"No way."

"NBC reported it ten minutes ago. Shasta again. I-Five is closed again.

"Eruption?"

"Haven't said."

"Dang. What's Ron up to? After he finished up cutting my panels, he vanished."

"Double checking his to-do list for tomorrow over at the house," she said looking out at a now-driving rain.

"Tomorrow will be good. We'll toss a lot of bodies at the place and have a lot of the work knocked out quick. Better than the piece-meal fashion we've had to do here."

"We had an advantage. We didn't have a staircase that led to the sky," she said with a smile.

"Gotta love a challenge. Any other news, other than California sliding into the sea?"

"Yeah. That Mexican oil complex, what's it called…"

"Cantarell?"

"Yep. Said that it had been fired on. Marines took out whoever did it. Also, the Army has stopped the advance, and is pulling back. Set up a hundred-mile wide clear zone."

"Huh." I thought about that for a minute. "Wonder what that means?"

"The newsy from CNN did, too. I could hear him sneer through the radio."

"I'll bet."

I excused myself to my blanket walled bedroom and changed out of my work clothes into something a little cleaner and drier. I wondered if my flannel-lined Carhartt's would ever come clean.

I helped Libby carry our prepared foods over to Alan's house (bundling everything up in blankets to keep them warm and dry, and using my grandfather's contractor wheelbarrow in ways he never intended.)

The house was a hive of activity already, with everyone from our family but Ron, already at Alan's. The dining tables included the 'formal' table, a card table, and the kitchen table with two sheets of plywood over both to create a sixteen-foot long banquet table, covered with deep red linens that my late Mom used for Christmas dinners that seated twenty or more. We also had two sets of our 'fine silver' out, our wedding crystal, and crystal that belonged to my parents and grandparents. None of it had broken in the quake, stacked up in its cabinet, and protected by layers of felt. Seemed like a good idea to actually use the stuff, instead of polishing it once a year and putting it back in the dark.

Kelly lit the four candelabra on the table, more for decoration than light, as Joe, Joan, Don and Lorene arrived at the back door. They'd driven across the fields, and around a couple of our barricades, opened up since they'd come back home.

"Welcome home!" Karen said as she passed each a glass of wine. "Come on in and make yourselves comfortable."

"Oh, that smells wonderful. It's been years—well it seems like it—since we've had a ham like that," Joan said.

"Come in and sit down. Dinner will be a few minutes yet," Mary said. "Rolls aren't quite done."

"That's fine dear. Joe, come sit down now."

"Oh, you never mind now, you. I'm fine here," he said with mock anger. We'd enjoyed his play-acting for years.

"Codger," she replied.

Don and Lorene seated themselves in the living room, heavily. They'd obviously been working too hard. This was the first time I'd gotten a good look at them both; they were both drawn and thin. Don looked twenty years older than the last time I'd seen him, five months before. His hair had thinned noticeably.

"You guys must have quite a story to tell," I said to Don quietly as the younger kids were teased by Joe in the kitchen.

"Yeah, you could say that," Don said as he took a sip of wine. "Like waking from a nightmare."

"Only to find that it's real."

"Yep."

"Save it for after dinner. We can for a little while, just enjoy the company. I didn't think you were going to be able to leave the farm until Memorial Day – That's what your Dad said anyway," I said.

"Rick, Dad's getting a little confused with all of this," Don said quietly to me.

"I understand." I replied. It's a sad thing to see one once so sharp start to falter. "Still he looks pretty good."

"This has worn on him and Mom far more than their appearance will tell."

I nodded at him as I sipped my wine. Karen and Mary soon called us to dinner.

April Seventh, 7:40 pm

"The farms and ranches up in the hills are holding their own, but we'd had enough. There were just too many attacks coming and our place really wasn't defensible," Don said, finishing another bite of pie. The dinner course, now finished and cleared, had given way to dessert and the story of their stay in California and their trip north.

The girls, assisted by Alan's young ones, were listening intently to the story that Don and Joe were telling. Lorene and Joan were in a side conversation with Mary, Karen, and Libby. I felt that Joan and Lorene were filling in details.

"Here. Have some more coffee. It's the real thing," Alan said, pouring one of his perfectly strong black concoctions. Karen always had to thin it down with cream or milk.

"Thanks. Haven't had coffee in a....while."

"Alan did some bartering. Got lucky," I said.

"Anyway, even after the Farm Association—that's what they called themselves—tore up the bridge up the valley, they kept coming. At first, it was just 'normal' people. Families, trying to get out of the crime, get food, whatever. We sold or traded with them as long as they were peaceful. Then they thinned out. Eventually, it was just predators. Took until March for that to happen. Since then, it's been bigger and better armed groups coming up the valley to steal cattle or sack a farm. None of the ranchers have been killed yet, but five hands were shot up in the first two weeks of March. Picked off, one by one."

"How are they getting in to the valley?"

"On foot, ATV's with silenced mufflers over the ridge on the west side. Some motorcycles. No one on horseback. Nothing from the north or east," Don replied. I glanced over at Joe. He had the Thousand Yard Stare in his eyes. I'd seen that look in my fathers' eyes when he'd had too much bourbon, and the ghosts of nineteen forty-four returned. I'm sure Joe'd have something to add before long. I'd known Joe twenty plus years, and never seen that look before on his face.

"Defenses?"

"Fixed bunkers on either side of the ravine, above the old bridge location. Smaller bunkers within thirty-ought range of game trails and hiking paths. Twin bunkers at the fire road, which is now the only way in, or out. Everything manned, all the time, twenty-four seven. Made getting meaningful work done difficult."

"Bastards," Joe said almost to himself.

"What was the last straw?" Ron asked.

"It was everything. The last night I was on patrol at the forward position—above the bridge—I saw them massing below us, maybe a mile out. More than a hundred. We called it in--Denny Jenkins and I were on duty, Arkwright and McCandless on the other side. That night it was different. Pre-emptive strike. Fifty-seven riders went out. Fifty-five came back alive four hours later. None of the raiders was left. They brought back six kids. I won't go into what was done to them by the raiders. You can imagine. Two died the next day," Don said in a low voice. "We'd had five battles like that. In defending that valley, the Association has killed more than three hundred attackers."

"They never shoulda done that to them kids. Burn in Hell, you bastards," Joe said, again, almost to himself.

Don said quietly, "Mom and Dad took care of the kids when the mounted patrol brought them back in." Don was quiet for a moment before continuing. "I think in the end, we just realized there were too many people coming up into the hills to keep fighting week after week. The last batch, the captain of the riders said, was from San Francisco. Before that, some of the smaller towns were hit. Mill Valley. Corte Madera. San Rafael were all burning. We talked it over with the Association, and Jenkins bought me out on the spot. Paid me in gold and silver coins. We loaded up Dad's Suburban and our Silverado and left the next day."

"How could you know you'd get through?"

"The Association mapped us a route all the way to Susanville through their mutual-aid network."

"Their what?!" I asked.

"Farmers and ranchers network from the word go. It's basically families and friends and business associates looking out for each other. Did it all on ham radio, all the way across the state. We had a situation report for the whole route by the time we left town. Saved our butts for sure. Told us lots of detours, missed most of the checkpoints, kept checking in with us on progress all the way."

"Unreal," I said. "I never would've thought. What about gas? How did you get enough to make it?"

"Big tanks on the trucks, and two transport sleds in the back of the Silverado. Gassed up at Susanville and again at Burns in Oregon. That was the last time."

"How long did it take? I mean, did you do it all in one shot?" Ron asked.

"No. Took a day to get to Susanville. Two more to Burns, three more to get here. A lot of it on dirt roads and forest trails down south, some paved roads up here. Got shot at a few times too, but more in warning I think to stay on the road than to hurt us. There's not much left of a lot of towns. The crash…well, more correctly, what people did after the crash wiped them out. No gas. Nothing in the stores. Some burned out. I mean the whole town."

"Flu?"

"Yeah. It's really bad in the big cities we hear. L.A., really the whole urban area from San Francisco south to the border. Radio and TV don't tell the story the way it is. Shortwave and first person accounts paint the real story. Pandemic. They say on the national news that the peak has passed. It sure hasn't down there."

I knew that in 'normal' times, we could've made that drive in two long driving days. Now, six to do it, while in fear for your life.

"No trouble with highwaymen or anything though?" Alan asked.

"No, not much. Stayed alert and ready for ambushes on the back roads. Other than the quake damage and the shortages, which are nothing compared to what we've got here. Did have to bribe our way through twice though, which damned near got us killed anyway. Once on a bridge in California, cost us two hundred rounds of twenty-two long-rifle. Then a State cop right south of the Oregon border decided that we needed to pay him all of our money and half our gas. Fortunately, we had three guns on him to his one."

"How much did you have to pay?"

"Six hundred dollars, cash."

"Federal Reserve Dollars?"

"Yep."

"Which aren't worth anything. Literally."

"He seemed to think otherwise. We gave it to him, but not the gas obviously. I told him that if he came after us or tried to shoot us as we left we'd hunt him to the ends of the earth. About that time, Dad took out the radiator and battery of his Impala patrol car with my Wingmaster. I thought the guy was going to wet himself. We left him there, twenty miles from anything."

"You said 'checkpoints'?" Alan asked.

"Yeah. Closer to the urban areas and you have them all over the place. The farther out, they thin out to one at each county line crossing, big ones on the interstates. If you're not from that county, or zip code or area code, you're not getting in. Or out. Some of the cops can get rough. Only reason we made it into Washington is because of Mom and Dad's ID showing Spokane as their residence. That wouldn't work most places."

"Well you're lucky. Up here, we don't have the cops to worry about as much as the throw-aways," Alan added.

"Throw-aways?"

"Most of the attacks around here, according to the cops and the military have come from people that before the Domino, depended on public assistance, illegal drug sales, out-and-out theft, prostitution or other below-the-board enterprises to survive.....or a combination of all of the above. Not many of them had the means or inclination to evacuate after the quake, and just decided to loot and pillage instead. From what we've heard, there are seven major gangs within the urban area. We've had a few experiences with them, personally."

"Attacks?"

"Yeah." I replied. "Not for a while here, but we've heard some chatter on the radio about closer to town. Marines and Guardsmen are very welcome around here."

"How about out in the rural areas?" Don asked.

"Out there, it's shoot, shovel and shut up," Alan said. "So say the folks we have on the barter network."

"Barter network?" Don asked. "Let's hear about that."

"Alan, it's your project...."

7

Wednesday
March First

Within a few weeks after the quake, it became apparent to us and to other folks that we talked to on the CB and some of the longer-range FRS talks that people wanted or needed to buy things that weren't available through the neighborhood stores (our group included).

Desired items included twenty-two long-rifle, shotgun shells and other low-powered shells. Hunting rounds or anything that might realistically be used in a 'combat' weapon were not offered, and when asked for, potential traders were politely told that such rounds were in very scarce supply and not available. Really, those that had them didn't want to provide the very bullets used against the seller! The barter list of common items was long, and getting longer and more creative as the spring wore on. Examples of oft-asked for items included gloves, boots, seeds, food plants, vines, and canes, fertilizer, manure, pesticides, rabbits, goats and other livestock, rain-gear, harnesses and custom leather, finished meats, eggs, chickens, geese and ducks; canning supplies, soap, and most often, toilet paper.

Alan, being the natural salesman, was the first to suggest creating the barter network. One evening we mapped out how a network might work, security and privacy for all parties being the most notable issue that I was concerned about. We were sitting around the table saw/food prep area, with the light of one of the Aladdin lanterns around us. It wasn't our 'night' for power, with the rotation that the power company had set up. Kelly and Marie were playing cards—'Animal'—while John and Carl listened to the radios and kept the younger two entertained with an ancient game of 'Tip-It.'

"So what happens when you've got it set up, the transaction I mean, and someone jumps the buyer? Or the seller for that matter?"

"We'll have to have security," Alan responded, thinking it through as he stared through the piece of pie on the table, wheels turning. Kelly and Marie had made the pie, using dehydrated peaches. We were saving the last piece for Carl, who missed dessert due to 'watch' duty.

"Not good enough. We're undermanned, and not in the sales business. Not yet at least. We need to make sure this is as secure a transaction process as possible, or any sort of barter store or whatever will just be a target for the picking," I said.

"Encrypt it," Libby said. "Put it in a code."

"What? Encrypt what?"

"You're talking about broadcasting items that are available or desired on the CB or Ham, right?"

"Yeah," I said, starting to see where she was going.

"You do that and you're advertising for trouble. You need to provide both buyer and seller security in the advertisement and purchase or trade of the item."

"And we do that how?" Ron said.

"Code of some kind. Can't you come up with that? Like those spy novels that Rick likes—Tom Clancy, isn't it? They use codes."

"Sure," I said, "that would work…."

"Enlighten us. We don't all read about made-up top-secret stuff you know," Ron said.

"I know, but we need to treat it that way. It is important that all parties—including us—feel safe in doing business. Here's a thought, Libby chime in. First, we need to create a unique series of list items for each trader. Times, dates, specific items that might be commonly needed or available for trade. The point of that is that we can broadcast in the clear, and that each traders words—times, dates, and items—will be different than every other on the network. That means that only we will know who will arrive when, for or with what items. Anyone hanging around hoping to pick someone off would have to be around all the time, therefore, probably up to no good. They could be encouraged to move along. Second, we'd need the parties on the barter network need to come to a central location to pick up their sheets and we'd give them instructions on how the network would work. Third, or maybe first, we'd need to find a location that works."

"Way more complicated than I would've come up with, but makes sense," Libby said.

"Why not the convenience store?" Karen said as she filled my coffee cup.

"Don't own it, for one. But I certainly don't want the barter operations taking place here, either."

"Well, the store's close, but not too close, and you could talk with Mike and see if you could open it up," Karen said. "It's not like there's anything left after they collected what was left and moved it to the Community Center."

"I could ask, I guess."

"Hey, Dad," Carl interrupted, "You're going to want to listen to this I think."

"'K, be right there," I replied before turning my attention back to the barter conversation. "You all figure it out from here, now that I've done all the work..." I said in a distinctly upper-crust accent, acting as Upper Management used to do when we were Blessed with their Presence. That resulted in of course the predictable barrage of thrown items in my direction.

"So what do we get out of this operation," Ron said. "Sounds like a lot of work to me, and Rick, you've already said we're going to be working pretty danged hard just growing food."

"Well, it puts us first in the line for selling and trading, for one. That might be worth it all by itself," Alan added. With the egg production we've got, we've got built-in customers."

"What about dealing with the flu? Who's going to want to go shopping?" Libby asked.

"We can set up pick up and drop-off times to avoid most contact. I think at this point, for us anyway, the first scare is over. We've all had a bug or something go through, and we're all still here. I'm praying that what we got was the 'flu-light' version."

"OK. What's up, bud?" I asked as I tuned out the conversation in the next room.

"They announced that the Re-Valuation has been cancelled."

"No surprise there," I thought. "Can't fix something that's totaled."

Carl was talking about the Federal Government's last gasp at maintaining the 'old' FRN 'Dollar' as the standard for financial transactions in the country. We adults were skeptical of the whole deal, the others less so than myself at first.

"Yeah, but the news guy said it in a way that implied there was no other way to save the economy," Carl said. He had a worried look that a fifteen-year-old just plain shouldn't have.

"There isn't, not by their standards. It's just taking longer for them to figure it out."

"So what's going to happen?" John asked, half-listening to the BBC reports coming in on the shortwave band.

"They need to re-establish money as something that has physical backup. Gold. Silver. Something tangible."

"But what about our Dollars?"

"They're now for all intents and purposes, toilet paper. They've defaulted on bonds and debts owed, and gone as far as admitting that they flat-out will not pay back the debt. That's pissed off every creditor to the US. We win, they lose, we're now their enemies. We robbed the bank, thumbed our nose, and got away with it. There is no going back now. They have to start fresh, be honest, be open, and learn from their mistakes. The problem with those ideas though, is that they are all completely foreign to anyone in power, anywhere."

"So now what?" Carl asked.

"Son, no one living in this barn has gone through this before. But let me ramble. The government lives off of taxes. Taxes need to be collected in a transportable form. Used to be metal, then paper, then electronic transactions. Problem is that the denomination is now meaningless. Without a currency system of some kind, government dies. And it is not in governments' nature to die. They will come up with something, and very, very quickly."

"What about the Reorganization?" John asked, referring to the dramatic ongoing downsizing of the Federal government.

"Can't do it without money. There are basic things that need to happen in any country that's worth anything. Defense. Protection of the common good. Protection of private property and individual rights. Commerce. Basics that were spelled on once on a single document that were perverted over two hundred odd years of bureaucracy. From what the President and his staff have said over the past couple weeks, they intend to push the 'reset' button. I gotta believe that they've known this was coming, and that the death of the paper dollar will quickly be followed by the birth of something…" I searched for the right word, "better."

"Rioting's getting bad, too," John said.

"What'd you pick up this time?" I asked. Six nights running, riots had been spreading.

"Shortwave skip I think. They said that they were 'holding the line at the river, and that most of the population had made it to Covington.' Problem is, I don't know where 'Covington' is. It faded out before I heard much more. Two-meter broadcast. Totally a civilian. Something about a 'skirmish line,' too."

"Did they say any of the route or highway names?"

"Yeah. Seventy-one and four-seventy-one. Why?"

I thought for a moment. "Covington, Kentucky. Across the river from Cincinnati. Friend of mine used to live there, until the race riots in two thousand one. Burned his business out, right downtown. I visited there a couple of times, before you kids were born. Lotta troubles there. Anything else?"

"Not from there. Picked up someone in Kansas earlier. They were trying to pass on a message to someone in Colorado. Didn't sound like they had phones."

"Huh. That doesn't sound encouraging either. Keep listening and writing down the stuff you think is noteworthy. Watch starts soon."

"We're ready, whenever," Carl said.

"Fifteen minutes, and we'll man A, D, and E tonight."

"K," they both responded.

"Remember your rain gear. Supposed to pick up after midnight."

"Stellar. I've done post in the rain since, oh, night before last," John said with perfect sarcasm. "I think I'm starting to mold."

"Remember to keep your feet dry."

"Yes, Sergeant Major, sir."

Over the next day or two, we wrote up the common list of items, and then randomly generated an associated code word for each item, different for each trader but not unique across the board. We then created code names for days of the week and times of the day, again, unique for each trader on the barter network. The code sheet looked something like this:

Item	*Trader A*	*Trader B*	*Trader C*
Eggs	Daisies	Concrete	Brick
.22 LR	Rainfall	Pizza	Oak
Gloves	Pine Tree	Speaker	Lincoln
Boots	Carpet	Frame	Trashcan
Jeans	Post It	Microwave	Phone
Sugar	Nail	Poster	Granite
Salt	Desk	Pencil	Cable
Rice	House	Underline	Basket
Beans	Handle	Cut Out	Opportunity
Batteries	Teacher	Light Bulb	Outlet
Laundry Soap	Zip Tie	Laminate	Logo
Hand Soap	Spring Clip	Pen	Flip Top
Bandages	Binder	Merchant	Business Card
Aspirin	Mask	Pebble	Metal Box

I contacted Mike Amberson—literally, by flagging him down one day as he drove by the convenience store—and told him of our idea. He dropped off the keys to the store (now of course stripped clean of inventory), and told me to 'go for it,' but 'keep it low-profile'.

'Now what is that supposed to mean?' I asked myself.

Two hundred items per list were put together this way, starting with an estimate of twenty members, and a companion list of unique words and numbers designating times of day. If we had elected to have the two-hundred-item list use unique words for each seller and each item, this might have driven us all a little closer to the edge of sanity, coming up with that many unique words and cross-checking them. As it worked out though, we managed to add a few more buyers to the network, and change the code words for each member each month. A number of members of course, wanted to discuss future transactions or items not on the list or quantities or whatever in more detail, and we did that in person....as much as we can with the flu of course....and set something up for later transactions.

April Seventh, 8:20 pm

"That's quite a system for buying a tube of toothpaste," Don said, quite seriously.

"It is that. I hope that within a few more weeks or a month or so, we can drop the cloak-and-dagger. I'm—we'll more correctly, 'we're'—more concerned that we might drop our guard too early and someone will get hurt."

"Tough to build trust in your fellow man," Don said.

"Yeah. Thin skin of civilization these days."

"Yeah," Don said as we finished our coffee in the back yard, under the somewhat-mangled patio cover. The rain was picking up again, with thunder rumbling off to the west of us. I hoped that the main storm would head south.

"So how's the farm? Your Dad said that your cousin hasn't been seen since the quake?"

"Nope. Place was locked up tight. The neighbor between my property and the road kept an eye on it."

"Get much damage?"

"Nothing I can't handle. No water damage from the winter, thank God. A broken pipe in the basement drained the cistern, and without power a few things broke. That, and broken windows. Sergei—the guy on the lower farm—boarded them up, and cleaned up the barn so he could shelter his draft horses. The fields are a mess. Evan, my cousin, just let them go. He bought it for the space, not the pasture and garden and fruit trees. Wanted to 'be one with nature.' The pastures and the garden both have three to five-foot-tall Ponderosa Pines in them now. Got our work cut out for us there."

"Still have a tractor and implements?"

"Yeah, although it hasn't run in nearly twenty years. I'll be working on that soon too."

"Let me know if you need anything, and I'll see what I can do."

"Will do. I appreciate it. I saw that old 'N' of yours. Looks great."

"Thanks. I changed the fuel filter a year back or so, and ended up repainting the whole thing by the time I was done, one thing leading to another. What do you have?"

"I've got a fifty-one."

"Eight N? Small world. Great little tractor."

"Yeah, but could really use power steering with that front bucket loaded."

"Yeah. I bet. I wish I had a loader sometimes. When you get a chance to look it over, let me know what you need. I've got a bunch of spares and normal maintenance stuff for mine. Oil filters, seals, belts and a couple sets of hoses."

"Thanks. I'm sure that we'll be needing some parts."

"What do you plan on raising?"

"I've got a built in market for hay, with Sergei and his horses, he's got Belgians and a couple of quarter-horses and not enough fenced land for them. We'll need to get the garden cleaned out and planted soon, too. It's almost an acre. The fruit trees need to be thinned and pruned too, those have almost gone wild. Dad's friend Peretti has beef cattle, pigs and goats. We'll try those too this year. Fences and cross-fences are still intact though. Used black locust for the posts, which are just this side of concrete for durability. Still, it's not going to be easy."

"Nope. Nothing is this year. Or next year. Or the year after that. How're you fixed for firewood?"

"Need some?"

"We will, I'm sure."

"I have nine acres of bottom land and thirty one of upland pasture and forest. I think we can set you up there. Evan never cut a tree up there, except the ones that came down in the Ice Storm in ninety-six. And then, just the ones in the road or next to the house. The rest of it looks like it did the last time that I saw it in ninety-eight. Doug fir, red fir, pine, spruce. Needs to be thinned bad."

"How about tools? You fixed up OK?"

"Yep. All of my stuff...well, the stuff that I sold to Evan is still there. I ended up leaving most of the newer stuff that I used in contracting down there. No way to move it."

"What'd he do? Evan, I mean," Alan asked.

"Not a thing," Lorene added. "Trust fund kid. 'Kid', wrong word. What was he, forty?" She said to us.

"Really. Hmmm. I wonder what happened to him?"

"The neighbor have anything to say about him?" Alan asked.

"Saw him once right after the quake, didn't think too much about it. Thought he was OK then. Went up to check on him a few days later and he was gone. His Escalade is still in the garage. Sergei thought that he lost it and walked off. He said he'd seen that sort of thing before. Sergei made it through Sarajevo."

"Oh." I said.

April Seventh
Late evening

Karen and I compared notes later that night, after we went to bed. It was well after eleven by the time we hit the sheets, far later than we'd become accustomed to. It was a very enjoyable evening, even if Alan, Carl and Ron had to leave early to man the observation posts. The wine had also gone to my head. It'd been a while since I'd had three glasses in an evening. Not long before, I'd have a bottle to myself, and maybe another half. Certainly, no longer. Fortunately for me, tonight was a night off of post duty.

"Joe's been hit hard by this," Karen said.

"Yeah, that's what Don said. He's, how do you say it, starting to lose it."

"Lorene said that his faculties started to slip right after the last fight they had. She thought taking care of the kids sent him over the edge."

"That I'm sure, and age. He's no kid. Joan seems to be holding up OK though," I said.

"Yeah, but I can tell she's more worried than she lets on."

"Being married for more than fifty years to someone, and then seeing them go downhill is plenty reason for her to be shook."

We didn't say anything for a while, as Karen snuggled into my shoulder, tucking her head under my chin.

"It'll be OK," I said before we drifted off to sleep. "They're both steering by the same star."

"I'm worried about Mom, too."

"I know, babe. I know."

Before the flu, we'd planned on restarting school at the local elementary, with some assistance from the school district in supplying books and materials. There seemed to be enough students and parents within the local area—meaning walking distance—to make it work. Once the flu hit, and with it the fear of contracting it, that plan hit the wall. Karen and Libby had both taught, with Karen teaching kindergarten through sixth grade, and Libby teaching middle and high school. Karen had 'retired' when Carl was born, but Libby was still an active teacher in one of the tougher neighborhoods in the City. We needed to keep up with the kids school-wise, assuming that 'real' school would someday come back about.

After things had settled down to the new routine caused by the quake, the kids found themselves 'bored' because there was 'nothing to do.' The odd schedules caused by our increased security needs, working on the house and barn, and cooking and cleaning, didn't leave a whole lot of time left over, though.

We (parents) decided after three weeks 'off' of school, that with the flu pandemic, normal schooling wasn't going to resume any time soon. The 'original' plan had been to start up a small multi-grade school at the damaged elementary school, using some of Central Valley's normal elementary through high-school texts, and teachers as we could. Once the flu shut things down though, that idea was shelved. So home-schooling was now the only option, with an unrivaled teacher-to-student ratio of two trained teachers and one teacher's assistant (Karen, Libby and Mary, respectively) to six students. "Classes" split up fairly evenly, with John and Carl both in high school; Marie and Kelly in middle school; and Mark and Rachel in elementary school. Alan, Ron and I also helped when we could, and as we finally got into spring, we 'taught' while we worked around the properties. We had a running series of 'classes' that taught the kids how to plant each type of seed, how and why to prune, how to identify various trees, shrubs and weeds, how and why to weed and when not to, how to use tools correctly, and covered dozens of other topics. We knew (and still know) when we are successful when they use their knowledge long after we've finished teaching, or at times well outside of 'normal' classes.

We didn't forget the 'play' side of things, and cleared off our driveway for basketball, foursquare and hopscotch. We had a bunch of other field toys for them too, including swings, a couple of slides, and a tetherball. The slides and swings came from one of my private-school clients, whose insurance company would no longer cover them if they kept the equipment in place. The insurance company obviously figured that having no toys with anything resembling a moving part or something that you could fall from was infinitely better than something that you could actually have fun with. For now, until the ash settled, most play on the swings and slides was restricted to damp days or days when the rains had just stopped. Dry days kicked up winds from the southwest and quickly brought up dust storms so thick that our visibility went down to a mile or two within minutes. We didn't want the kids out in that, and when we were needed out side (frequently, with the gardening) we donned dust masks or one of the paint respirators that I used to wear for spraying the trees or painting. We only had two of those at first, though the County did come through with six more, none of which would fit the youngest kids. We made do with keeping them out of the severe dust, and wearing tight-fitting dust masks when ever it was just a 'light' storm.

Someday we'd be able to play croquet, volleyball, and set up the inflatable swimming pool again. Someday.

Our kids and the Martins had brought most of their textbooks home the day before the quake, for the three-day Martin Luther King holiday. On three-day weekends, we usually made the kids spend at least an hour with us reviewing their current assignments and upcoming tasks, which gave us a good litmus test on where they were at and how thoroughly they'd learned the material. I placed little faith in the letter grades given out, when valedictorians in the local high school went from single digits to more than thirty per graduating class. Getting an 'A' is more than showing up. I expected my kids to know the material and understand…and strangely enough, reason and know how to think. Karen and I were in a distinct minority of parents who thought like this. Karen got to see this first-hand as a school volunteer, who knowing the system, was able to affect things in positive ways that the teachers couldn't, working within the political boundaries of the school district. We also challenged our kids on what they were being taught, and directed them to think for themselves rather than accept the material presented, which was often at odds with history. Once, I perused Kelly's 'history' book, only to find four sentences devoted to the founding of the United States of America, and a page and a half to the ACLU. Seemed a bit out of balance to me. We made it a point to have the kids read several history books on the country, the world, and key historical figures, which gave them a depth of understanding and an ability to discern what most other students only achieved much later, if then. They then became interested in historical fiction, which only deepened their understanding.

History books--certainly not all of them would've been 'sanctioned' by the school district--were drawn from the ample supply of my own books, and those I'd inherited from my parents, grandparents, and great grandparents. They included the seventy volumes of The Harvard Classics that belonged to my maternal grandfather; Decline and Fall of the Roman Empire; The Defeat of the Spanish Armada; United States History to 1960, a textbook that belonged to my oldest brother; The Second World War, by Churchill; Sandburg's Lincoln; Jefferson's writings, including his Autobiography and Notes on the State of Virginia; Recollections and Letters of Robert E. Lee, leading to Stonewall

Jackson's Book of Maxims; and Shirer's Rise and Fall of the Third Reich. Not light reading for an adult, let alone high school and middle school students.

Our 'class' schedule was by necessity flexible due to work and weather. In addition to the 'history' topics, math, science, literature, spelling and current events were taught both 'in the field' and in the classroom we'd set up at Alan's, in a basement room with a big daylight window. The goal was to provide three hours of instruction per day, six days a week, with three hours of independent study as well. We've found, over the spring, that this usually works out to three hours of class time spread over the day, with 'study' happening when it can. The kids are, though, keeping up with their studies, and that is the point, isn't it?

Today, even though it was a Saturday, was a school day. Twice a week at least, we made it a point to have all the kids in the same class at the same time. The older kids set the pattern of behavior for the younger ones, a situation sadly lacking in public schools.

Saturday was typically Grace's turn to teach, more story-telling than teaching, about 'the way things used to be,' which might be 'the way things will be done.' Saturday's classes usually were pretty casual, and ranged from 'history' to practical things like cooking, cleaning, and working together. Today, Grace, Mary, Alan and Karen would be outside with the kids, and would be planting raspberries and layering some grape vines for propagation. Grace's raspberry patch, at her now abandoned home, was the most prolific I'd ever seen. What she also brought of course, was the chance for her grandchildren (and the Martins' kids) to interact with her in ways that they'd never done before. Grace always looked forward to her 'teaching days.' Eighty-five, going on sixty.

While the school kids and teachers learned their lessons, Ron and I started collecting tools for the repair work of their new home. The rains had picked up again, so I had no desire to apply three-tab roofing in the rain. Our house for now was again rain-tight, with all the windows back in place, after a fashion. Today, after lunch, we'd hit Ron and Libby's new house with all available hands. The youngest, Rachel and Mark, would stay with Grace while the rest of us worked. No one was on watch duty during daylight, and the barter store was closed for the day. I double-checked the list on the clipboard, along with the tools that we needed for each.

To Do:
Replace broken glazing, bedrooms and basement.
Repair broken pipe to water meter in basement.
Sheetrock repair, throughout and paint.
Electrical check, all circuits.
Repair rear porch. Torn off of back of house.
Patch crack in basement wall.
Repair waste line from kitchen to main drain

Check chimney liner for damage.
Repair front yard fence.
Build woodbin in basement for basement wood furnace. Forced air wood furnace as backup, gas as primary.
Add: Computer, printer, inventory list, FRS radios and charger, hand-held CB radio and charger.
Tools: sheet glass, glazing compound and points, glasscutter. Pipe wrenches, threading tools, female coupling, Teflon tape. Multi-tester. 12/2, 12/3, 14/3 wiring, stripper, wire nuts, junction boxes, clamps. Skil-saw, framing tools, nails, dimensional lumber. Hydraulic concrete and quick-patch concrete. Fence pliers and wire.

"Curfew's at seven, right?" Ron asked.

"Yeah. Changes on the fifteenth to seven-thirty."

"Can't keep track of it."

"Yeah, used to be 'sundown'. Now they want a 'time' to have everyone off the streets. Got the plumbing stuff?"

"Everything but the pipe wrenches."

"On the wall, above the breadbox," I said, pointing to my pegboard tool rack above our temporary kitchen counter.

"OK, I think that's it."

"Good. The van's about full."

While I gathered up the last of the tools, I listened with one ear to the eleven a.m. news. The word 'assassination' piqued my interest and I turned up the radio.

"……Jameson on March twentieth. Jameson, the new Treasury Secretary, was traveling in a motorcade in suburban Maryland when the attack occurred. Four members of the security detail, apparently in the lead car, were killed outright by a car bomb, and Jameson was wounded in the blast and ensuing gun battle. Seventeen suspects were captured or killed in the attack and the ensuing investigation, which has ties to five major international financial institutions, according to sources inside the investigation. Our Washington bureau chief will have a special report tonight at six p.m., Eastern time."

"Well. I wonder what they're NOT telling us," I said to myself as I sat on the edge of the table saw, listening for more.

"In news from the Republic of China today, cleanup and restoration of services was interrupted by the arrival of the USS Antietam at the naval base at

I shut off the radio, filled up a thermos with some tea, and headed out the door, and wondered who was writing the copy for the news guy. Not really well put-together.

"What's with the long face?" Ron asked.

"Complications," I said. I then recapped the news for him.

"Just gets better and better, huh?"

"Yep."

Saturday
April Eighth, 2 p.m.

"OK, scratch windows off the list," Alan said as I worked on the house electrical system.

"Already? You had four windows upstairs and two in the basement?"

"Yep. Done. What's next?"

"List is over there," I motioned toward the clipboard as I tested another apparently bad circuit with my multi-tester. "How're Ron and the boys doing with the sheetrock?"

"Good. Ceiling cracks are all patched, after they used those drywall screws to make sure everything was nice and tight. Ron's putting on the base coat over the tape now. Might even get the skim coat done today," he said as he looked over the list. "I see that no one seems to want to go after the drain line."

"That was next for me, after I get the circuit problems figured out. We've only got nine of twenty circuits working right, and only one of them in the basement. Pretty dark down there. No lights in the bedrooms either, and half the kitchen is dead."

"What've you found so far?"

"Seven of the circuits are easy. Wires pulled loose from their junction boxes or switches or whatever. Three had broken receptacles or switches. The two-twenty circuit to the range is totally fried. Fabric and paper insulated wires tore open. Lucky the whole place didn't go up. We'll have to see what we can scrounge up from Tim's place for a replacement wire. I know I don't have anything that heavy laying around."

"How are you checking it? I mean you're not running line power."

"Yeah, we are. Dan's guys checked out the service panel, and we're good in there. They just turned the breakers on and I'm checking out anything that flipped when they tested them. They also repaired the water meter service. You must've been working on the fence while they were doing that."

"Glad you're doing it. Scary."

"Just gotta be careful. Treat all the wires like they're live, all the time. Haven't been bit in years."

"I'll go take on the back porch project until you get done. Then we can do the plumbing."

"Not sure I have the right pants for that."

"What?"

"Mine don't ride down far enough to be a plumber."

Alan laughed like he hadn't in a long time. "I needed that."

"Don't ever miss the opportunity to poke fun at yourself, I always say, unless you can poke someone else and get away with it."

"I'll be outside."

"Coffee break at three, Libby said."

"Good. I'm about due."

For the better part of the next hour, I replaced damaged receptacles and switches, or in one case, ran a new twelve/two wire to the basement stair lamp circuit, and a salvaged ceramic lamp base to light things up. The old wire had a spiral burn from one end to the other, and cooked the ballast of the florescent lamp at the top of the stairs. Must've been a power surge. By the time I was done, we had eighteen of the twenty circuits working again. The garage feed, only a twenty-amp circuit to the receptacles and lights, had a bad breaker. The stove circuit was also not yet repaired.

I gathered up my tools in my two five-gallon buckets and headed upstairs, where things were still pretty dark. We'd all become used to working in dim light, and it was more than a month after the quake before I quit turning on light switches instinctively upon entering a room. This time, I did it on purpose as I went into the small dining room, which adjoined the living room where everyone was taking a break. I flipped the switch.

"Wow!" Libby said. "Light!"

"Yep, you're about good to go. Got a problem with the garage circuit breaker, and the stove feed line needs to be replaced. Other than that, you should have power everywhere. Heat too—the blower circuit for the wood furnace checks out OK."

"Thank you so much, for this, everyone. I can't tell you how nice this will be."

"It will be a distinct improvement over our barn."

"That was nice, too," Lib said backpedaling a little. "It's OK Libby." I said with a smile. "Where's Ron gone to?"

"Roof. He's looking at the chimney."

"Yeah, that was on the list," I said as he appeared in the doorway.

"How's she look?" I asked.

"I could actually tell if someone would've opened the damper," He said, mildly irritated, glaring at Marie.

"Oops! Sorry Dad. Here. Have a cookie and some coffee."

"Forgiven," he said as he warmed his hands around the mug. "Man it's cold out there."

We went over the progress of the day and the remaining items to address before we thought it 'smart' to move the Martins into the house. Alan thought he'd have the small porch deck put back together by the end of the day, minus its shed roof (smashed hopelessly), and John and Carl would be assembling a wood storage bin in the basement to feed the wood furnace. The gas furnace, still in place, would likely wait a long time before natural gas would be available again…if ever, I thought. Earlier, Ron shut off the gas meter, the valve inside the house, and would cover the chimney flue for the gas side of the chimney as well to keep moisture and birds out. The rooms were humid with the unique smell of drying sheetrock compound and fresh paint. The former occupants of the home—a very sparsely furnished rental—had not been seen since the quake, and the place left a lot to be desired in the way of cleanliness. Mary, Karen, Libby and the little kids had spent quite a bit of time cleaning walls and floors over the past few days, and Kelly and Marie had sorted and stored belongings of the former occupants. Two small stacks of boxes were now stored in the north half of the garage.

"Anyone heard the weather forecast?" Alan said as he finished his coffee. "I swear it's only about thirty out there."

"No," I responded. "Is there a radio over here?"

"Not one we brought, but there's a clock radio in the bedroom," Kelly said

"Bring it in if you would, babe."

"K."

"Something wrong with the TV?" Ron said.

"Duh. No. I never thought about turning it on." I reached over and pushed the power button, and got static at first as it auto-programmed itself. Finally, it settled on channel two, our local CBS affiliate. The rental folks did not have cable, just a small rabbit-ear antenna in the back of the set.

Since the quake, we'd become accustomed to having almost full-time news on the AM band on only one or two stations with power, and we usually had one or two TV stations broadcasting as well, on low power. When two stations were up at the same time, one usually had news full-time, both local and national. The second station either ran new programming, sports, or movies. We'd not had all five local stations operating since January.

About the time Kelly made it back in with the radio, we were able to tune in the local CBS broadcast. They were showing us some of the salvage and retrieval work in the Puget Sound area, devastated by Rainier's eruption and the earthquakes that still rattled the area. We'd just missed the weather forecast, but the 'crawler' at the bottom of the screen told us the current conditions, as if we couldn't open a door and look outside. Everyone watched as the helicopter on TV hovered, somewhere above what used to be south Seattle. I hushed the kids and turned up the volume.

"These are rows of new BMW's, Jack, buried in the ash fall from January," the reporter said to his anchor, who was in L.A. *"The ashfall varies from three to seven feet throughout the southern Sound area, here it's about four feet."* I could see the nose of one of the BMW sport-ute's poking out of a drift of ash.

"You can tell from our satellite location," the image changed to pinpoint the helicopter superimposed on a recent satellite image that shocked us all, *"that we are over the heart of the Southcenter area. There is very little here that is recognizable as far as landmarks go. We literally have to look around to find the Space Needle and the remains of the downtown area for reference points on*

cloudy days. The rescue efforts that ended in February managed to save more than thirty thousand people through the use of helicopters alone. Tens of thousands more walked out of the zone, and even today, we've seen signs of people still living in the area. In the Tacoma region however, we were met with the gruesome images of human skeletons exposed on the ashfall and mudflows, literally miles away from anything green or alive."

"Danny, can you tell us the status of the salvage teams? Are they mobilized yet?"

"No, Jack, they're not mobilized, certainly not fully equipped yet either. The ash, followed by the unprecedented rains, have turned the ash and mudflows into virtual quicksand or concrete, depending on where you are. You cannot walk across most of what we're looking at right now, and on more than one occasion in the past week, we've seen where people and animals have died, trapped in the mud and unable to free themselves."

"Terrible news. Danny, now that overflights of the area have resumed, and the eruptions seem to have ended, can you give us some insight into the Navy's recovery efforts?"

"Sure. Bremerton is a write off, and it's likely that Bangor is as well. The shift of the Earth's crust in the quake has raised parts of the Sound, especially near Bremerton, by as much as forty feet. Parts of the Olympic Peninsula, especially along the central Washington coast, dropped by a corresponding amount, submerging the coastal highway and several small towns. The deep-water berths that once housed aircraft carriers and battleships now are clogged with silt and you can literally see the bottom of the Sound, just a few feet below the surface. Ships that were stored in Inactive Status are literally aground, probably permanently. The Naval Shipyard is similarly unusable. Of course, you already know about McChord Air Force Base and Fort Lewis, both lost in the eruption and quakes. Even without the ashfall, the earthquake has destroyed the usefulness of much of Puget Sound as a military or commercial shipping port. One other thing to consider is that under all that ash, in addition to several hundred thousand missing people, is a toxic waste nightmare. Those leachates are starting to be detected in surface waters and within the Sound itself."

"Danny has any effort been made to....recover ordnance from these bases?"

"DOD....Sorry, Department of Defense spokesmen in Bellingham—that's near the Canadian Border and now a temporary homeport--decline to comment."

"I would assume that DOD has been working on that for the past couple of months while civilian air traffic was banned?"

"Probably a safe assumption." The picture changed to a tape of the downtown core, zooming in on the Columbia Tower, devoid of its glass skin, thick grey ash covering each of the seventy-six wrecked floors. The 'copter flew close enough to see where the rains had eroded the ashfall near the missing windows, small channels eroded through the ash, a computer monitor on a desk further inside the wreck.

"Jack, we're about ready to wrap up here, DOD is telling us that broadcast power from the ground repeater will go off-line in a few minutes. This happens about every day at this time so no big deal."

"One last question Danny, if you would. Where are the deceased being buried?"

"We've seen two mass grave sites, one in Monroe, a second in Arlington, both north of the Seattle area. I understand that there are also several more south of the blast and mudflow area, near Centralia along Interstate Five."

"Thank you, Danny."

"You're welcome. More when we can get..." The broadcast went to black, and then cut back to the CBS studio in L.A. *"We'll be back at the top of the hour with the latest. Now over to our local affiliates."* A commercial for a 'fully-ready emergency kit' came on the screen as we sat in silence for a few moments. None of us had seen the devastation in Seattle since those first broadcasts, two months before.

"I knew it was bad over there, but..." Alan started before trailing off.

"Yeah," I said. Libby got up and left the room for one of the back bedrooms. Her sister Marie hadn't been heard from since the quake. The commercial ended, and a weather guy, not one I knew, came on with a special report.

"A severe weather warning has been issued for the Spokane Coeur d'Alene region, with cold temperatures this evening reaching into the low twenties or high teens. A chance of snow—that's right, you heard me correctly—snow—is possible in the overnight hours. A very cold low-pressure system, more familiar in late February than April, is on it's way south out of Canada at this time. This puts any outdoor crops in severe danger of freeze damage, including fruit trees, row crops, and in colder microclimates, even crops in greenhouses or under cover. Obviously those people living out of doors or in rough shelters are also in danger of hypothermia if exposed to these cold temperatures without adequate protection. This severe weather alert will continue to be broadcast hourly, and is in affect until Monday morning at the earliest."

"Great. Just what we need," I said with no small measure of frustration.

"What can we do?" Carl asked.

"The cold-weather crops are in and up, and about the only thing we can do is put out some smudge pots or small fires, which we'll have to tend. That MIGHT keep them warm enough not to freeze. We'll also have to light up the woodstoves in the greenhouses and keep them tended. All of the really tender stuff hasn't been planted yet. Except for the fruit trees, which are just starting to bloom. And those are pretty well scattered, too. Ours are pretty close together and maybe we can put some heat under them. The rest of them, they're all over the block. Not much we can do. The bad thing is is that this is a cold spot…rather, the garden spaces are. The cold air settles in these areas and freezes before other higher areas do. Not good. If it snows more than a little, or doesn't warm up soon, we're screwed."

"Hon, did you hear that?" Karen said on the FRS. She was over at Alan's busy making some bread, but really keeping an eye on Grace so that she wouldn't overdo.

"Yeah, we did."

"Do we need to cover stuff up?"

"Yep, at least. We'll figure out something and let you know."

"K. Dinner's at six—split pea soup and fresh bread."

"Don't tell me that. I'm already hungry."

"You know how I like to tease."

"All too well, baby."

"Now quit you two," Mary chimed in on the other radio.

"Yes'm," I replied as I signed off.

"Rick, we got about six of those old fifty-five gallon drums over by the trees there. Can't we burn in those?" Mary asked.

"Yeah, that's a good start. Alan, did you see anymore when we did the inventory?"

"Never noted them, but I'm sure there were some north of here. I'll take John and Carl in my truck and go round 'em up. I know there were at least three."

"K. Bring them back to the plot northeast of the barn. That's going to be the toughest to heat, and it has the most stuff up right now. We can take a couple and put them in the aisle between the fruit trees too, and maybe that outdoor fireplace I've got, the one on wheels, and keep the fruit from freezing. When you're up that way, Carl, you check the wood in the greenhouses for the boxwood stoves. We didn't put that much in them, and I'll bet we need more."

"OK. Do we go...armed?" Carl asked.

"Yes, just like watch, and you need to wear all dark clothes just like watch, too."

"'K. So who's going to run watch?"

"We'll figure that out. Anything else?"

"No."

"All right, let's go. The rest of this can wait until after dark or tomorrow, can't it?" Alan asked.

"Probably. I didn't leave anything that can't wait. Still gotta do that drain line."

"I did that yesterday," Ron said.

"When? It wasn't crossed off the list."

"Couldn't find the list. I did it when I came off of watch. No big deal, just a new hunk of PVC."

"Cool. Then your new home is just about ready for move-in. We can do some painting tomorrow, and you'll be good to go."

"Works for me. How's watch going to work tonight since we're lighting nice bright bonfires all over the place?" Ron asked.

I hadn't thought about that.

"Really good question. I'll let you know when I figure that out, unless you'd care to answer it for me."

"Standard watch rotation plus a fire-tender or two," Ron suggested. "Dressed in all black, and keeping a very low profile."

"Agreed. Let's go," I said. "Not like I can come up with anything better."

"'Git 'er done." Carl said, imitating Larry the Cable Guy.

10

Saturday evening
April Eighth

We'd rounded up what we could in the form of old fifty-five gallon and smaller (thirty gallon?) drums that we'd scavenged from around the neighborhood. Open burning of yard waste and garbage had been banned in the County (and much of the State) for more than thirty years, so finding any surviving barrels was a chore. Finally, around six, we had the barrels and other improvised containers set and wood supplies were stashed close by, covered with whatever we could find to keep the wood a little drier. The rain had tapered off to a sprinkle and then a mist, before the sky cleared and the temperature really started to drop. By seven-thirty, sundown, the sky had cleared and the temperatures were already dipping into the high thirties.

Karen had watched the 'late' weather as we hauled kindling and wood to the barrels and burner locations. The snow wasn't likely until after midnight, after whatever heat trapped beneath the low clouds had radiated away. The snow might keep things insulated, if there was enough of it. Or, the cold could just be too much for our burn barrels, and we'd lose everything that was 'up' in the gardens, and the blossoms on all of the trees.

"What time do we start lighting things up?" Ron asked.

"Probably by nine. I figured that Carl and John could run the barrels during the night in the center of the block, one of us could take the north end with the greenhouses, and someone else pulling watch duty and watching the burners around the garden plot."

"Good thing not much is up yet," he said.

"Yeah. These late frosts can be a pain. We've never had snow this time of year before, at least not in my memory."

"But you've lost blossoms and stuff, right?"

"Oh yeah, every eight or ten years or so, and even up into mid-May. That's why we don't really plant anything tender outside until the first weekend of May."

"That's the 'snow is off the mountain' week, right?"

"Usually. Probably not this year."

"You guys about done?" Mary called from the house. "We have an idea."

"Yeah. We'll be right in." I keyed the mic on my radio and called the boys home.

"Right there," John replied.

We met around the kitchen table at Alan's, an ancient early Fifties chrome table and chair set from my parents' place. I hadn't had the heart to get rid of it when we closed out the estate, so I'd stashed it in the barn. Amazingly, that style had come back with a vengeance. Karen filled my coffee cup with strong coffee as the boys came in the back door.

"What's up?" John asked.

"Couple ideas," Mary said. "Back when I was growing up, the growers would use fans to move the air around, and not let it settle in any one place. With the burners running too, they were able to ward off frost pretty well. They also used surface water at night, which was quite a bit warmer than the air. Saved a lot of oranges that way. Can't we do something like that, too?"

"We've got some small fans, nothing like the big ones that they use in California," I said. "Except for one," I thought. "I've got an old furnace blower that I use to collect paint fumes when I paint in the garage. That moves a fair amount of air."

"Can't you hook up some of the fans around the barrels, and move some air that way?" Karen asked.

"Sure. We'll dig up what we've got. Good ideas, ladies," I said. "Remind me to ask you first next time."

"Fault of all men," Mary said with a grin.

"Funny." I said. That water idea though got me thinking. "Have the kids already showered tonight?"

"The little ones, yeah. Why?"

"I was thinking we could hook up a bunch of hoses to the hot water line in the basement, and run the heated water out to the garden. That would help ward off the cold, too."

"It'll cool off awfully fast though," Libby said.

"Yeah, that's OK. It doesn't have to be hot, just warm things up a little. We'll have to have someone run more water through it once in awhile to keep things warm. If we do that, we can move a couple of the burn barrels somewhere else. And hopefully, save more of the trees."

"Let's get John and the girls on that," Ron said. "Carl's gotta get to bed for late watch. You do, too," he said to me.

"I suppose so," I said looking at my beat up Timex Indiglo. I was 'on' in a little more than four hours. "The hoses are stacked up...."

"We'll take care of it," Karen said. "Get some rest. I don't want you getting yourself all worn out again."

"Yes ma'am!" I said. "Walk me home?"

"Sure! It's a date!" she said as she took my hand, pulling on her coat awkwardly. "I'll be right back," she said to Mary.

"Take your time."

We walked across the field toward the barn, which was unusually darkened with everyone busy at the Martins or at Alan's place. Buck led the way, roused from his nap under a big spruce tree at Alan's. Ada trailed behind, pausing for a long stretch along the way.

"You think this will really work?" Karen asked. "If we lose the fruit on those trees...." She trailed off.

"Yeah. I know. Not good. I think we've got a fair chance. If it drops to the low twenties, we've got a problem. There's no way we can keep up with that."

"Will the greenhouses be OK?"

"I think so, even without the heat they'd probably be OK for one night. The batteries on the fan units up there are charged up too, so we'll be able to move some air around in there are keep things warm."

"I thought you only used those in the daytime."

"Usually, yeah, to keep things cool enough. We can use the same fans at night to keep them warm."

"Will the batteries last all night?"

"We don't need to run them all the time, maybe a couple times an hour just to spread the heat."

"Oh," she said as we got to the barn. Buck wanted dinner, and Ada wanted her nap—the eight-hour kind. She took my hand as she led me into the darkened barn, and….locked the door.

The greenhouses, which were several properties north of our land, were re-skinned in March, and we traded for a couple of small woodstoves to heat them. Our small greenhouse hadn't been re-skinned or planted yet, although that was on the agenda two weeks out. We'd taken a couple of small oscillating fans from our house, and wired a number of salvaged car batteries together with an inverter to generate enough power to run the fans for a good long while, on hot days (of which, we'd had almost one) when we needed to move air through the greenhouses. The intention was that the batteries would be recharged with our small homemade generator. Tonight, we'd use the fans to move warm air. I hoped it would work. For now though, other much more interesting activities occupied my attention.

I woke for watch duty at twelve-thirty, even though my shift wasn't supposed to start until one. Karen had mid-shift radio duty, and relieved Mary. Kelly was sitting in a chair playing cards with Karen.

"What's the temp?"

"About twenty-eight, that's what Carl said about midnight."

"Any sign of snow?"

"No, but the clouds are back."

"That's good and bad. Clouds mean it won't get really cold, but it could snow on us."

"Yep."

"And how come you're up, young lady?"

"Couldn't sleep. Everyone else is up, at least it seems like it."

"Yeah? Any problems keeping the fires going?"

"Not so far. The boys have been keeping a pretty low profile, although that's not as easy as it sounds."

"Alan and Ron in the watch posts?"

"Yep. They're due for relief at one. The boys said they'd stay up and work the fires for the next shift. Carl was supposed to be on watch later, wasn't he?"

"Traded with Libby."

"Libby's then on watch in the south post and I'll be in the north?"

"Yep. Alan's taking east. The dogs are out with him. He's going to pull a double…assuming someone brings him some coffee."

"Dogs're better watchmen than we are."

"Six to Helena," the radio crackled. That was Alan. 'Helena' was the codename of the base station tonight for our second watch shift.

"Helena, go," Karen said.

"Corvette passed one ago, lights out, loaded for bear," Alan said quietly. 'Corvette' was our name for a loaded troop carrier.

"Get everyone outside under cover," I said. Karen gave the command 'Houston' on the radio, our code for 'hide'. ('Houston, we have a problem').

"Destination?" Karen asked.

"Cabo," Alan responded, which meant 'north'.

I took the radio from Karen. "Everyone down and away from the fires. Respond."

Four radios clicked. They already knew something was up and didn't respond with voice traffic..yet. I looked at the small white-board, with the names of the manned watch post locations on them and the 'incoming' and 'outgoing' names.

"Bad Moon Rising," I said into the transmitter, echoing one of my favorite Creedence Clearwater songs. The signal meant that no one was to move for sixty minutes, be absolutely silent, and defend themselves if needed. Four radios clicked.

"Anything on the other radios?"

"Not on the frequencies we've got in memory," Karen said.

"Turn it to open scanning," I said.

She reached over and pushed a button to scan the frequencies available within the bands on the radio. Not all-encompassing, but we'd noticed that since a couple weeks after the quake, the police and other emergency services abandoned the remains of their trunk-broadcast system as the emergency generators went off-line, and went back to broadcasting over 'old' frequencies. In order for the military and the police to be coordinated, they sometimes broadcast in the clear for limited amounts of time. The normally 'stored' frequencies covered what these days amounted to our 'beat' cops, State Patrol frequencies, fire and emergency service channels.

"Any other news? I mean, AM band?"

"No. No local stations are up. A whole lot of static every once in awhile."

"Huh," I thought. What was going on?

"The FRS channels quieted down just like normal after dark, nothing odd there," Karen told me.

We usually talked in the 'clear' during daylight hours, which in retrospect wasn't all that smart. But considering how much other traffic was on the FRS bands, we didn't think that it was all that dangerous. After dark, we went to code names for locations and people. Anyone listening long enough though, could easily have determined the size and composition of our 'force' by listening to the voices. Like I said, we were not all that smart. Some lessons need to be learned the hard way.

"Stage down the hill," a strange male voice said on one-fifty-four four hundred, the scanner locking in on the transmission.

"We're nominal," came another voice.

"Fifteen seconds," a third voice said. Silence from the other end.

"Hon, dim the light. I'm going out for a sec."

"Are you nuts?"

"No. Trust me." She turned down the small kerosene lamp. We'd become accustomed to the soft light, and didn't use the 'line' power, even though it was working some of the time.

I moved to the door that led from the craft room to the 'outside,' and opened it. Other than the soft glow of the warming fires in their barrels, it was utterly dark outside. I was dressed in dark blue insulated Carhartt coveralls, my winter boots, and gloves. I opened the outer door, a beat-up weathered barn wood door just as a helicopter passed over the barn, low, fast, and un-lit. I quickly ran around the west end of the barn to follow the sound, just as a large explosion lit up the sky to the northwest of us, a half-mile or more away. The sound arrived a moment later, accompanied by the sounds of automatic weapons and….grenades or other small explosions. In less than a minute, it was over and I went back inside.

"What happened?" Karen asked.

"Not sure. Hang on a sec."

"Emerald City, Emerald City," I called into the radio after checking the post-name. That was Alan's post location. The radio clicked once. If he could talk, he'd call in with his 'incoming' call sign, 'Six'.

"Notify if clear," I said. He didn't click back.

"We've got company," I said to Karen.

"Good guys or bad?"

"Good question. If they're good guys, I'm hoping we're safe. If they're bad guys, I'm hoping they're stupid and on the run."

"Chicago," I called. That was Carl's call sign.

He was whispering into the VOX microphone. "I'm here. North house flat on my stomach." That meant the north greenhouse, a hundred yards or so north of us.

"You inside?"

"Yeah."

"Stay put. Where's Lumpy?" 'Lumpy' was one of my many nicknames for John.

"Cherry orchard." That put him two hundred yards south of the barn.

"Keep your head, buddy."

"Right," he replied back.

"Newport," I called to John's location.

"Here. Noise to the north and east, people on foot headed south. Not real quiet about it either."

"Where are you?"

"Fifteen feet up a Picea pungens 'glauca'," he replied. I was teaching him botanical names of trees earlier in the week. He was in a Blue Spruce, south of the cherry trees.

"Hold there," I said.

"Oahu," I called. The radio clicked back.

"Click once if hostiles on the road," I asked. The radio clicked once. Ron's position was northeast of the barn, beneath a brush-pile between two houses on the road on the west of our block. Alan's position was east, and south of the barn. We were bracketed by people on foot, moving down the east and west roads. If they cut through between homes, they'd be right in the middle of us. To do that though, they'd have to climb fences and get through other obstacles that we'd pre-positioned. Either Ron could already identify them as 'hostile', or he was being careful. Either way, we'd keep our low profile.

Long minutes passed.

Karen and I, and now joined by Libby in her 'watch' gear, listened for any news. The commotion had also roused Marie, who was huddled with Kelly around the radios with us. We could hear outside that there were vehicles passing to both the east and west of us, and shots fired to the south of us as two helicopters came in…as if to herd cattle. No further radio traffic came through the scanner, and finally Ron came back to us.

"Seven," Ron said quietly.

"Go," Karen said in reply.

"Large armed force, with hostages, disorganized and fleeing south."

"You OK?"

"Yep. It was a near thing, though. Passed three feet from the end of my rifle."

"Status?"

"Guard units and Regular Army moving them south. Sounds like they've crossed toward Sprague in a running battle. Out."

"Out."

"That won't be a good thing for them, then," I thought out loud. Karen and Libby both looked at me. I answered before they could ask. "Open ground. No cover."

"Oh."

"Emerald City," Karen asked.

"Ditto Seven's report. Looked like a gang with hostages. Way too many to confront. Running with their tails between their legs. Some wounded. Hold on…."

The radio clicked. "Got company. Regular Army, looking for me," Alan whispered.

"Same here," said Ron. "Holy crap. They're headed right for me."

"Surrender. Now." I told them. Silence was the response, and then heavy static…on all the radios, I noticed, one after another.

"What's happening?" Libby asked, scared.

"I don't know. But they obviously know we're on watch, if they're moving right to Ron and Alan's positions. Or they think that they're hostile."

"What about the boys?" Karen asked.

"Hopefully they'll stay low."

Fifteen minutes later, radios still filled with static, both Ron and Alan checked back in, in person.

"What happened?" I asked both as they came in, followed by two Army soldiers, one with an M-16, the other cradling what I thought was an M249, or Squad Automatic Weapon, and a backpack, obviously with spare box magazines.

"FLIR spotted us. These young men were sent to make sure we weren't hostiles."

"And to make sure that we stayed off the streets, just in case." 'FLIR' was an acronym for 'Forward Looking Infrared'—meaning, they spotted people by their body heat signatures. The helicopters were probably first to spot our watch.

"Come on in," Karen said. "What about the boys?" Ron and Alan came in, rifles slung, followed by the two young soldiers, who looked a little unsure as they entered our makeshift residence and looked around. Kelly peeked around the doorway from the woodshop, and Marie was behind her with an old wool blanket wrapped around her shoulders, both looking scared.

"They're feeding the fires and they'll be in."

"Why didn't they check in?"

"Radios are jammed, ma'am," the taller of the men said. "Will be for a while yet. Everyone needs to be inside for the rest of the night. Got hostiles on the run."

"Who are they?"

"AP's. Sorry, Aztlan Posse, or so they say. Hispanic gang. Slavers, thieves, murderers," said the taller of the two.

"And executioners," added the second.

"I'm Rick Drummond, this is my wife Karen and our friends Ron and Libby Martin, and Alan Bauer, my brother in law."

"Corporal Danielson," the taller of the two said. "This is PFC Akers."

"Nice to meet you both. Coffee?" Akers, obviously brand-new and wet behind the ears, glanced, eyes-only, sideways at his corporal.

"That would be most welcome, sir," the older man said. 'This guy's too old for a corporal', a little voice in my head said. 'No, not only that, too....something...for a corporal.'

Carl and John came in behind the two soldiers, who both turned a weather eye toward the door as they heard the outer door open.

"Hon, got any fresh?"

"Yes, hang on a sec." Karen was trying, and doing a good job at, acting like she hadn't had the wits scared out of her. I thought I was doing a pretty fair acting job myself. I could've used a shot of Johnny Walker Black Label about that time.

"Infra-red in the helos picked our watchmen up?" I asked as I unwrapped a bag of oatmeal raisin cookies that Kelly had baked the previous afternoon.

"Yes, sir. That and the fires. Lit things up pretty good. Not too many people around, so you weren't too hard to spot. Had to sort out the friendlies from the chaff."

"I appreciate your discretion," Alan said, passing a cup of coffee to each.

"Yeah, thanks for not lighting us up!" Ron added as he stowed his rifle.

"Well, to be honest, if either of you had made the least threatening move, we wouldn't be talking right now," Danielson said. Libby and Karen both were taken aback by that comment.

"This isn't a war zone," Libby said.

"Well, ma'am, not to offend, but yes, this is a war zone, as long as gangs like these are around."

"Where are they from? I mean, obviously you're saying they're Hispanic...."

"Only partly. They've managed to collect the worst elements and banded together. The AP's are only one bunch. We've been fighting them for a month now, this way and that. This unit's done for; the helo took out their leader at their camp over on Montgomery. The ones we caught here got out before we hit 'em. We haven't got them all yet."

"You said 'slavers'?" Ron asked.

"Yeah. You can imagine what kind of slave I was talking about," Danielson said, glancing at the girls in the other room.

"I can. How bad is this problem? The gangs I mean."

"Bad enough," added Akers, now munching a cookie. "Nothing I'd care to discuss in present company, sir."

"Understood. Let's warm up a bit and maybe we can talk in private, outside," Alan stated, before I could suggest the same thing.

"Where you guys from?"

"Used to be from Fort Lewis. We were over at the Yakima Firing Range for training when the quake hit. We're assigned to First Squadron, Fourteenth Cavalry. The rest of the brigade's deployed in Mexico Territory. You might know us as Stryker Brigade."

"Fourteenth served with Pershing in Mexico, if I recall." I said, remembering my grandfather's background in the Cavalry, before and during World War Two.

Danielson was surprised. "You know your history."

"A little. My grandfather served in the Cav, way way back. There's his sword," I said, pointing to the dress sword hung on two sixteen-penny nails on my tool rack.

"May I?" Danielson asked.

"Sure," I said, taking the old sword down. He carefully pulled it from the plated scabbard, and examined the fine engraving and my grandfather's name, and the old leather tassels soft and still pliable after decades of display.

"Thanks. I've never seen one that old. First war, right?"

"Yeah. He got in too late to go to Europe, and was too old to see much action in the Second. Still got to go fight the Japs in the Pacific as a light-colonel...Sorry. 'Japanese'." That drew a chuckle from both.

"No need to be 'P-C' with us, sir," Akers said. "Check-in time, sir," he reminded his commander.

"Affirm. Let's step outside for a few minutes."

11

Sunday
April Ninth, 1:20 am

Alan, Ron and I went outside with Corporal Danielson and his PFC, still cradling the SAW.   Danielson stepped away from us for a few minutes, as we talked with the young private.

"How long you been in, Akers?" I asked as I watched the Corporal, talking into an extremely small walkie-talkie.

"Finished basic in December."

"Choose Infantry?" Alan asked.

"No, sir. I was supposed to be going to Combat Engineers School after basic. Didn't quite work out that way."

"Yeah, we know what you mean. This isn't exactly the life we had planned, either. Where you from, originally?" I asked.

"Little town in Kansas. Cottonwood Falls."

"Tallgrass prairie. Home of the Kaw and the Osage," Alan said. He was born in Oklahoma, so he was familiar with the region.

Akers was surprised. So was I. "You know the area?"

"Yep. I was born down in Enid. We used to hunt off of Thirty-One over near Lawrence, and then on down to Independence."

"Dang," Akers said. "It's a little different terrain, here." Danielson was wrapping up his conversation and headed back to us.

"OK, Corporal, fill us in on these gangs. We've heard scuttlebutt on the shortwave, but damn little else," Alan said.

"The gangs have carved up pretty significant parts of the city that are under-policed. Murder, robbery, looting, knocking off supply trucks, raiding clinics and hospitals for drugs. Taking hostages. Killing them after they're done 'using' them. By our count, about half of the gang members are convicts, a high percentage of illegals, most are drug users, most are barely literate. Most can shoot, though, and are heavily armed, including stolen or captured military weapons."

"Holy crap," Ron said.

"This gang, who called themselves the Aztlan Posse, was only about twenty-percent Hispanic. Their leader ran things from a little house over on Montgomery, amongst the industrial buildings over there. Used a lot of runners to set up scouting missions throughout the north side and the Valley. You weren't long in being hit. They had digital pictures of this whole neighborhood, especially your barter store."

"How did they do that?"

"Easy. They were customers. One of our men was an infiltrator. He was on the mission that came to the store for a pick up."

I was flabbergasted. So were Alan and Ron. "We had no idea."

"I'm sure you didn't. This gang…and the gangs in general, pick over an area, doing what they can do with minimal interference from the cops, and move on."

"Why has this just come out? I mean, why didn't we know about this already? We could've prepared."

"Might have something to do with your County leadership being a bunch of horses' asses."

"Can't disagree with that," I said, remembering my earlier meeting with them.

"Well, your Sheriff seems to be doing the best he can, which isn't near enough. He's pretty well hogtied. Got all the right ideas and absolutely no tools for implementation."

"How so?"

"Eleven percent of his force requirement, pre-quake."

"I had no idea it was that bad. What about the State Patrol? Or the City?"

"State is about thirty percent of pre-quake. City is about fifteen percent, with more than half of the county population. That's where most of the problems are…for now."

"How long have you been fighting the gangs?"

"First of March. Wiped out five major groups. Fragmented a dozen more. This was the last of the big groups," Danielson said, nodding off to the south. "The small ones are harder to find and take out."

"What do you consider 'small'?" Ron asked.

"Less than six shooters, plus support. Lotta small ones over in Idaho, we hear."

"Support?" I asked.

"Snitches. Whores. Spies. Sycophants. Pick a label."

"How are they getting around? The small groups I mean."

"They're not. Which works in our favor. Without gas, which they'd have to steal, they're stuck in a walking distance radius. If they steal gas, they drive. If they drive and get stopped, they have to prove that they have ID and they can't just be tooling around. No one wastes gas just driving. Gas is for approved users. Farms. Shipping. Critical needs."

"So these are 'minor league' predators, huh?"

"Only in size, not viciousness."

"So what happened to this bunch?" Ron asked.

"They were trapped in the parking lot on Sprague, which was fenced at dusk."

"Then what?" I asked.

"They were told to surrender or die. Some chose the latter. The survivors will be sorted to determine their status either as combatants or as hostages. The latter will be treated and likely released. The former, well, we don't go into that much."

"Executions."

"Like I said, we don't go into that much. Most are so cooked on meth that, even if they're cleaned up, there isn't much brain power left."

"Good God," I said. Here we were, minding our own business, never knowing that we could be next on the list to be attacked and…worse.

"Can you shed any light on the rest of the country? The news is pretty well sanitized."

"Yes it is, which no uniformed soldier agrees with, by the way," an emphasis on 'uniformed' soldier. Interesting, I thought. "Any urban area with rioting is, or has been, contained. Which means, if you're in there, you're not getting out."

"We'd heard some of that. What about the flu?"

"If hospitals can be supplied from the air, they are. If they can't, they aren't. That Chinook that was shot down in St. Louis taught us that."

"We hadn't heard that," I said.

"Not many have. It was hovering, waiting for its slot on the helipad. Small arms fire took out the cockpit crew. It ended up in the trauma center. Six hundred dead. CNN had it on their feed, which was squashed before it was broadcast."

"When did this happen?" Alan asked.

"Two weeks ago, now. Swiss-cheesed a Blackhawk down in Reno, too from what I heard. I think only the crew died in that one."

We were silent after that.

"You gotta understand," Danielson said, almost apologetically, "There isn't any way that we can go into those cities and not get our asses shredded or not spread the flu. You don't have the population density up here, or the shooters that the cities do. You got it good."

"Well, Hell," Ron said. "I thought we were turning a corner there. The CDC said that they thought the peak was a month ago."

"Not from what I'm hearing," Danielson said. "USAMRIID says this will run 'til it's done, whatever the Hell that means." His radio beeped twice. "We gotta go. Remember, inside tonight. We'll have a Guard patrol or Army unit on station tonight and tomorrow. Keep that store of yours closed until Monday. We'll have a unit there on Monday morning."

"Understood. Thanks, Corporal, Private," I said as we all shook hands. They walked off over toward Alan's cut through the yard to the north, and disappeared. We stood watching, not quite knowing what to say.

"So, how much of that was bullsh•t?" I asked.

"That is a very good question," Alan replied.

"Let's get inside," Ron said.

"Yeah," I said as I felt snowflakes on my neck.

The boys had already shucked their outerwear and were getting ready for bed, and the girls were huddled under their covers. No one was ready for sleep yet though.

We recapped our conversation with Danielson for everyone, sanitized a bit for the girls. We were still pretty well shook up by the whole evening.

"So that's it, in a nutshell," I said as Alan finished the recap.

"So things really are as bad as the shortwave says."

"If not worse." I said.

"So now what?" Libby asked.

"Now, we all hit the hay. Snow's started, so there's probably nothing we could do outside now even if we were allowed. Tomorrow we'll go to church, and it's a stand-down day anyway, other than some work on your place."

"That's not what I meant. I meant, what about what they're doing in the cities? What about these gangs?"

"Can you think of anything that we're not doing now that we can do to make us safer and not be walled inside some castle somewhere?" That got her, I could tell. Not that I meant to…

"No," she said. "It's just that we were…targeted."

"Yes, we were. And could be again." Ron said.

"We just need to be vigilant," I said, "And live our lives."

I elected to stay up until four and listen to any radio broadcasts that I might pick up…once the Army got done jamming in our area. I watched from the barn as Alan headed home, making sure he got there in one piece. I could still hear in the distance the transport trucks moving the gang members out, and once, a helicopter passing to the south of us. The snow turned out, mercifully, to only be a passing flurry. By the time I went back inside, Karen was in bed, as were the Martins and all of the kids. Knowing earlier that I'd be on watch over part of the night, I'd mentally geared myself to be 'up'. On past occasions that I'd done this, and had plans change, I had a tough time getting to sleep. Finally, I just resigned myself to being up, and found things to do in the middle of the night.

Around two-thirty, the jamming finally stopped abruptly; I suppose that someone must've turned a switch. The rain began in earnest not long after, so hopefully the cold temperatures hadn't done too much damage to our early crops. The first plantings of potatoes (which comprised the last of our seed potatoes from last falls' harvest), onions, cabbage, Swiss chard, and a few other things were just out of the ground.

I kept turning the conversation with the corporal over and over in my head. We'd been infiltrated. The gang had one of our code sheets, and may have 'shopped' with us for some time. They knew the store location, and probably knew where we all lived. They knew our staffing. They knew what local traders 'had' and 'could get', if they'd been part of the network long. They could figure out our weapons complement by just being observant. I never thought to ask, 'who' it was that was the infiltrator. Which meant that now that they had dropped off-line—or more correctly, been moved to another assignment, that we'd have to treat everyone with suspicion. I continued to mull this over when the three a.m. news came on, six Eastern Time.

"….cities remain in lock down mode this Sunday morning, after an unprecedented day of protests and rioting took hold. The Administration's new 'containment' strategy, marked by some as racist and elitist, effectively isolates urban areas that have been wracked by unrest and devastated by Guangdong Flu since the start of the Second Depression and the war with Communist China. These areas, isolated by regular units of the military, have effectively been abandoned by the rule of law. An Administration official, speaking on the conditions of anonymity, said that 'these areas are far too dangerous to enter due to the high infection rate and rampant violence.' Humanitarian air drops in

*parts of Detroit, Cleveland and Pittsburg were halted after supply helicopters
came under fire from multiple locations, joining St. Louis in a full quarantine of
the area. A breakdown in order in downtown Chicago late Saturday led to a
series of arson fires on Michigan Avenue's famous retail row, which joined the
Board of Trade on Jackson Avenue in flames. The Board of Trade, a major
player in commodities and futures markets, continues to burn at this hour."*

I pondered both of those stories as a commercial for some commercial
'security service' came on, with a threatening voice and music. I'd been to
Chicago a couple of times on business, and was very familiar with the landmarks
they mentioned. I'd even bought my first Power Book at the Apple store there, a
lifetime ago. My first visit there left me with the impression of 'this is what real
cities are supposed to be like.' That seemed to no longer be the case I thought, as
the raindrops slapped the skylight over my head.

*"The nation's last solvent mortgage broker declared bankruptcy late
Saturday evening, stating unrecoverable losses in excess of nine-hundred
thirteen billion dollars in residential and commercial paper. Royal American
International joined the last of the top-ten mortgage brokers in collapse, this less
than forty days after the collapse of Freddie Mac, Fannie Mae and Ginnie Mae,
driving yet another nail in the coffin of the New Economy. On a related topic,
the massive foreclosure rate has created a new 'bounty hunter' mentality on the
part of creditors, who are searching worldwide for debtors bound by new
bankruptcy laws to pay their debts. Thousands of these debtors have simply
dropped out of society or assumed new identities in an effort to hide from their
past."*

The radio 'beeped', apparently signaling the local station to 'wake up' and
add the next segment of programming. More than a minute went by before
someone pushed a button and gave us the weather report…for the previous day.
Finally, 'live' programming from somewhere filled the void.

*"This is Financial Outlook, I'm guest-host Peter Wilkenson, and thank you
for joining us for this special outlook for the coming week. This really seems to
be the bottom, with the mortgage meltdown and the utter collapse of the
residential and commercial real estate markets. I'm joined by Abe Bowman, a
private investment banker from northwest Arkansas. Abe, thank you for joining
us."*

"Thanks, Pete. Rough week ahead."

"So it would seem, another in a long string of them."

*"Yes, and overdue, although no one wants to admit that," 'Abe' said with a
gravelly, no, a seasoned voice.*

"Abe, given what we know right now, this really is an unprecedented crisis, isn't it?"

"Suitably understated for this time of the day, yes."

"Can you offer any advice for our listeners?"

"Advice? I offered advice for thirty-six years, and damned few people listened. There will be a new economy, a new currency, and eventually, some sense of order will be restored. Whether that resembles anything that we're accustomed to still remains in doubt."

"What form of currency to you forsee?"

"Me? I'm just a worn out broker and full-time grandfather. It will not though, be paper-based."

"That brings up another question. Millions of people with money in banks..."

"That's not money. Pardon the interruption."

"But..."

"Pete, I know you are...most of the time-....a morning talk show host in Denver. Right?"

"Yes."

"Money in the bank is paper. It isn't money. Heck, most of the time it's not even that—just numbers on a computer screen. It might have its uses for satisfying obligations for companies that still believe in it, but on the street, it is worthless. I'm frankly a bit surprised that you still think it has value."

This was getting good. You could almost see the guy blubber. *"Well sure it does. I just paid my rent."*

"Pete, money has to be tangible to have the trust of those using it. Paper money that can be redeemed for precious metals, silver and gold, for example, has that trust. Paper that is not redeemable in metal...isn't trustworthy. In addition to all of the troubles facing this country, the financial crisis is just now being recognized as perhaps the key to the survival of this nation."

"Abe, I'm...I do not know what to say."

"Welcome to Sunday morning. The Federal Government, as it exists right now, is aware of this crisis and has been working to figure out a way to get through it and simultaneously trying to make nice and keep the population calm. Which it cannot do for much longer and without destroying the old way. And the old way is the power that nations strive for. Economic rule of the world. And that day, for the United States, has passed. Why in the heck did we pull out of our foreign bases?"

"Because we were..."

"Because we are bankrupt and it was obvious to the whole world that we are."

"The Acting Congress has stated that they intend to issue new currency based on a much smaller Federal budget and..."

"And that currency still isn't money. It's paper."

"Well what do you suggest?"

"Gold. Silver. Re-establish the standard and do it now. There isn't time to screw around with another option. There simply isn't time."

"Is that possible? How...."

"Sure it's possible. Sorry, I keep cutting you off."

"No problem. Go on."

"The government has to establish the value of the currency based on the weight of actual metal. Silver should be something like a buck forty an ounce. Not sixty-eight bucks an ounce that it is. Gold should be twenty bucks an ounce, not thirty-eight hundred. Why do you think we used to have twenty-dollar gold pieces, anyway?"

"Abe that was before my time."

"And you've had the wool pulled over your eyes your whole life. Most of America has."

I decided that I'd like to meet this guy. He was good.

"The problem is, Peter, that there isn't enough gold or silver coinage to go around, and probably not enough mined bullion to satisfy the demand."

101

"What happens then?"

"You have products, and no money. You have no means of exchange other than trading or bartering them. If you operate that way, you have no way of generating taxation revenue. Without revenue, governments collapse from the top down, and rot from the inside out. The Administration has already taken a battle-axe to the Federal Government, which is all but chopping off one's own rotting limbs to save the torso."

"So how do we get through this? I mean we've been hammered with the war, the virtual loss of all imported goods.…"

"That's due to a currency collapse, remember."

"OK, fine. But our manufacturing capacity…How can we meet the demands for our nation without foreign manufacturers and suppliers?"

"Listen to what you just asked. You asked, 'how can we take care of ourselves.'"

"That's not really what I meant."

"But it is in fact the question. How can the United States, which allowed so much critical manufacturing and supply structure to go off shore, ever hope to meet its needs."

"Yes, I suppose that's right. That's what I mean."

Years..no, decades to get back our manufacturing capacity."

The host was quiet. "That can't be right."

"Sure it is. How long does it take to build a steel plant? How many machine-tool plants are left in the nation to supply tool-and-die equipment for those plants? How many large-scale steel plants are left in the States, anyway? How about textiles? How many are left in the Carolinas? How about shoe factories. Any left in the Northeast? Anywhere? Do you know the answers to those questions?"

"No."

"Well, let me tell you. There are damned few machine tool plants left in the states. There are damned few steel mills left. They're in Brazil and China. Textiles. Same. Shoe plants. Indonesia. For all intents and purposes, there has

been a war all right, and we lost it. We've completely lost our industrial base. And we did it to ourselves."

"So where do we start? How do we do this?"

"We're not done with hitting the bottom yet. We might be getting close though."

"Can....can you explain that?"

"The bottom is found when everyone admits it is. And they haven't. Some people still think that things will get better. Until everyone essentially loses faith in the current system, the bottom isn't in. Besides that, with the flu quarantines going, and the riots, there is no hope of meaningful recovery on a national scale. The best the Government can do at this point is station keeping, unless they intend to write off large urban areas of the country permanently, which I doubt. In any regard, this is nowhere near what is needed."

I was glad that I wasn't the only uber-pessimist up at this time of day.

"The question is this, Peter. Can the American people ride things out where they are with what they have for the foreseeable future?"

"I don't see how that is possible," the host replied.

"Then may God have mercy on those who believe that, because your fellow man will have none."

The host went off. "What're you talking about? 'Mad Max' for Christ's sake?"

"Mad Max? No. They had gasoline."

"I've gotta take a break," the host said. *"This is Financial Outlook."*

I poured a glass of water from an old stonewear pitcher, and pondered this fellow's outlook. He'd been around a lot longer than I, had probably seen the tidal wave coming even when I was a kid in the sixties. And neither of us had a chance of changing the outcome. The radio went to dead air where an advertisement at quarter past the hour was supposed to be. By three-twenty, I figured the broadcast was not coming back. It didn't.

The silence left me wondering if someone didn't like Mr. Bowman's outspoken comments. Certainly it wasn't a local station decision, if they couldn't bother to push a button for an ad.

I wondered what northwest Arkansas was like for a few minutes, looked over our 'to do list' for the upcoming week, and finally went to bed.

12

Sunday
April Ninth

The pastor closed the service in prayer a few minutes after ten, and for some reason, I was thinking 'it was about time.' I'm not usually like that in church or when I'm listening to something that is important. This was both. Still, I was anxious. For the past two weeks, we'd made a concerted effort to have us all up and clean for church, leaving a rotating 'watchman' or two back at the property, just to keep an eye on things. They could listen in on the church service with one of the FRS's tuned to a different channel than our 'normal' voice channel, which we'd changed to four, side channel seven…for today.

Our 'normal' church, not quite destroyed in the earthquake and the aftershocks, was not quite salvageable, either. Our neighborhood, within a mile or so of the community center and the elementary school across the street, had a wealth of churches of several different faiths. Just before the flu quarantines were put in place, we'd helped a couple dozen remaining residents move hymnals, bibles, and other materials from several churches into the schools' multi-purpose room, where we hoped to have Sunday services on a regular basis. Or Saturday services, depending on faith. Those materials sat, unused for most of February and March, until inquiries came through the barter network on when services might resume. We put the word out for a pastor, hopefully still in the area, and received six replies. Only two could come, due to distance. Still, that was plenty for what would be a tiny congregation. Both, it turned out, were within a mile, so travel on foot wasn't really that big of an issue.

Music this week was actually 'live', with two guitarists, a base, and two volunteers leading the hymns, which last week were from hymnals, this week on Power Point slides. We'd learned this was preferred by several folks who'd lost their glasses in the quake, and couldn't read the fine print in the hymnals without them. We had thirty-one people in attendance and leading the service. I was tapped to read the New Testament verse, which I picked on my own. I chose Romans 12.2, 'And do not be conformed to this world, but be transformed by the renewing of your mind, that you may prove what is that good and acceptable and perfect will of God.'

The pastor, originally from an evangelical church, this week spoke on Zechariah 8.14, a verse that I wasn't all that familiar with: "This is what the LORD Almighty says: "Just as I had determined to bring disaster upon you and showed no pity when your fathers angered me," says the LORD Almighty, "so now I have determined to do good again to Jerusalem and Judah. Do not be afraid. These are the things you are to do: Speak the truth to each other, and render true and sound judgment in your courts; do not plot evil against your neighbor, and do not love to swear falsely. I hate all this," declares the LORD."

Last week, he'd preached on Genesis 19.19, which seemed at the time appropriate, "Your servant has found favor in your eyes, and you have shown great kindness to me in sparing my life. But I can't flee to the mountains; this disaster will overtake me, and I'll die."

Had a theme going there.

Finally, (and why did I think 'finally?') the service was over and we filtered into the hallway, where two men, formerly who might've been ushers, watched over the plastic barrel that held a variety of long guns carried by the worshipers, one of our captured AK's included. I didn't want to ding up the Garand, nor did I want one of the scoped rifles mishandled. I pointed out the proper gun to the bulk of Randy Thompson. Randy, one of our barter store clients carefully retrieved it. In former days, he was sales manager at an outdoor/sporting goods shop, that specialized in 'non-hunting' sports, especially aggressively competitive mountain biking, rock climbing and whitewater sports. Good sports for someone in his mid-twenties, but not for me. These days, we were in discussion about carving out a corner of the corner store for Randy to sell re-fitted bikes of all kinds. These were becoming high-value items as we'd expected they would, when gas prices and later availability became an issue. We'd salvaged a number ourselves, around the neighborhood, abandoned in backfields and downed homes and garages. Alan had stashed a number of them in his garage, waiting for time to refurb them. I nodded to Randy, not letting on to anyone else that our 'store' might be expanding its offerings. Alan had a meeting set up for sometime this week with Randy.

"Mr. Drummond. Remember me?" An older man asked. "I'm Aaron Watters. I delivered a message to you from your brother-in-law?"

"Yes, I'm sorry, I didn't recognize you there."

"Quite all right. I'm not wearing my Elmer Fudd hat," he said with a smile. "Did you meet up with your brother in law OK?" he asked, referring back to a ham radio message that he'd passed on to me, right after the quake.

"Yes, he's right over there. That's Alan Bauer. He runs the barter store most of the time." I pointed over to my gregarious brother in law, who was enjoying some conversation with folks who were obvious clients of the 'store.'

"Right! I've met him. Never made the connection."

"How've you been doing?"

"Fair to middlin'. Alan's been a big help. Question for you though, if you don't mind."

"No problem." 'Wonder what this is about,' I thought to myself.

"There's an abandoned home on your block, used to be owned by a ham like me. Sold it to some other folks after he moved into a retirement home. Light green, white trim, a rancher. North of you."

"The Jacobson's place." I was familiar with it from our 'collection' of food and later, tools and other items that we could use in the garden. We'd never really been into the house though, other than to salvage the food inside. We'd done what we could to cover the broken windows, to keep animals and the weather out. We'd learned that the Jacobson's' had abandoned the home to the elements not long after the quake. Financially, we'd learned they had negative equity, so just walked away from it, after taking what little they could pack in their mini-van.

"I was wondering if there's a chance I could salvage something over there," he asked cautiously.

"Don't know why not. What is it?"

"An extendable mast for my antenna. Mine was damaged in the quake and there's no way to salvage it. Tore loose from the base and collapsed on top of the neighbors' garage. I was using it when the quake hit."

"At two am?" I asked with some surprise, remembering that night a little too clearly.

"I'm a bit of a night owl, since I lost my wife a couple years ago."

"Oh, I'm sorry. There's a mast over there? I've never seen it."

"It's in a retracted position, and the hinge pin was pulled, and then the mast laid down. It's only about twenty feet long, retracted on the ground. It's out behind the garage, where Ray used to have his shack. Probably covered with a tarp or hard shell, too. I bought the antenna from Ray when he sold the place, but I already had my own mast. Till the quake anyway. Can't really listen like I used to nor broadcast with any real range."

"Sure. Come on by this afternoon. We'll go see what it takes to get it moved."

"How much?" he asked with a wary eye.

"For what?"

"The mast."

"Mr. Watters…"he interrupted me.

"Call me Aaron."

"OK, Aaron, no charge. It's not mine, it's more useful to you and hopefully all of us, if you get your 'rig' set up and would be kind enough to keep us apprised as to what's really going on out there. God knows the media coverage isn't worth anything."

"I can do that," he said, obviously relieved that I wasn't going to try to extort some obscene amount of …..money? for something that didn't belong to me in the first place. "Come by around two. I'll meet you down at the Jacobson's' place."

"Thank you so much," the old man said as he turned determinedly, heading for his little beat up pickup truck, which had no less than six antenna masts visible. I thought that there couldn't be any room in the cab for anything but radios, if they were all hooked up.

"What was that all about?" Karen asked, carrying a large backpack full of books.

"That guy…Aaron Watters, lives over on University, I think. He's the ham operator who put us in touch with Alan."

"Oh. Did he need something?"

"Yeah, and we'll get him set up. I'll fill you in later. Looks like you got what you were looking for."

"Yep. Raided the library, too."

Karen, Libby and Mary had asked the new Center manager, who also ran the school building, if we could 'borrow' some school books and materials for the kids. They had to share on occasion, and having the 'teachers edition' of some of the books would be very helpful.

"Get anything for Carl and John?"

"Some, not much. They did have some middle school and high-school books here for the home-schooled kids in the neighborhood, but not the heavy-duty stuff. Not that it matters much. We have what we need. I put a note on the secretary's desk that we'd 'checked out' some books."

"Good. Now are we ready to go?"

"Why so antsy?" Karen asked, obviously noticing my anxiety.

"I don't know. Just am." I said seriously.

"K. We can go. Let's round up the kids. And I got a nice surprise for you and the kids," she said with a grin.

"What's that?"

"Traded some eggs for…two gallons of milk."

"No way," I said. It'd been a long time since I'd had anything but re-hydrated milk.

"Yep. Elaine Gustafson, that nice lady in the flowered blouse."

"I know her through the store. I never knew she had a cow."

"Umm, she doesn't. It's goats' milk."

I was a bit taken aback by that.

"Never tried that before. Not too late to learn I guess."

"It's not bad. I've had it before."

"OK, I'm game. Let's get it home."

We collected everyone and loaded up the big Ford, which didn't really appreciate sitting around for weeks on end. Ron and John had stayed home on watch, and Grace had listened in on the radio. Her arthritis was flaring up, and she didn't feel like sitting on hard chairs or bleachers.

After an early lunch of home made tomato soup and muffins, Mary, Libby and Karen poured over the school materials that they'd retrieved from the elementary school, which included a wide variety of materials for local home-schooled kids of all ages. Most of the gaps in our made-do curriculum were taken care of quickly.

Our afternoon watch was cancelled after a run-in (well, that's not the right word, but it seemed like it) with an Army patrol. This particular unit had just been shipped in from Portland, and they didn't really care for civilians with long-guns in their area. The Lieutenant in charge, when summoned by his sergeant, let us know that for at least the next twenty-four hours, they would be providing security in our area, meaning line-of-sight coverage to each other patrol. It would seem that not all the gang members anticipated had been rounded up. That was fine with me; it had turned into a nice day, with temperatures going above sixty for the first time this year. A fine spring day. Had I been able to find one of the hammocks, I might've napped outside.

Ron, John and Alan put the finishing touches on the painting at the Martins' new home, and most everyone else, myself included, 'stood down' for the rest of the day. The schedules that we'd been trying to keep since January really began to wear on us, resulting on more than one occasion in verbal outbursts that were more of frustration than anger. During a 'family meeting' one night, we agreed (I think most of it was directed at me, being a 'Type A' personality in a 'Type B' persona) that we'd knock off as much as possible on Sunday, with no major work, projects or anything other than 'normal' chores. We also thought it a good idea to not take on more than one major project at a time (This was a big thing for me. I think I liked the variety of working on multiple big things at once. Problem being of course, is that it's hard to get any one of them done within a reasonable time frame). It was a good day for a nap, so Karen and I snuggled up in our blanket-walled 'room' and snoozed for a while.

At one forty-five, my watches' alarm sounded, reminding me of my meeting with Aaron up the street. I gently moved off of the bed, leaving Karen to snooze a bit more. Ada quickly took my place while Buck decided that he'd like to tag along with me. I went into the next room, where Carl was reading Michener's 'Centennial', and listening to something playing on the radio, through his headphones. The girls were nowhere to be found.

"Join me?" I asked as I clipped on a chain leash to Buck's collar.

"Where to?"

"Up the street. Jacobson's place. We're going to meet that guy I was talking to after worship this morning. He's the guy that put us in touch with Alan after the quake."

"Oh. Do I need to bring anything?"

"No, probably not. I'll bring my radio. Who's monitoring, anyone?"

"Mary is. Libby was supposed to but with watch cancelled, she and the rest of them are working on the house."

"Gotcha. Put your boots on. Probably muddy up there."

"I assume we're walking."

"You assume correctly," I said as I moved to the door. I noticed the small pile of stuff we'd agreed to position—and share with—the Martins. Among the supplies, one of the FRS radios and it's charger; one of the twelve-volt CB's with a hopped-up antenna (engineering courtesy of Alan); one of the AK-47's and one of the beat-up Taurus .45's Colt we'd captured; a couple of the kerosene camp lanterns and fuel, one of the several Macintosh computers and my treasured, older copy of Carla Emery's Encyclopedia of Country Living. (May God rest her soul.)

It would be odd not having the Martins' in the next room as they had been for the past three months. Odd, but not all in a bad way…

Libby had pulled watch duty four times so far, and with some practice with one of the Ruger 10/22's and one of the AK's, had become a fair shot. She was less skilled with the Garand, and absolutely despised the twelve-gauge. Still, for coming from 'never fired a gun' two months ago to today, there was a marked change in her personality. More assertive, confident, and…..questioning of authority.

"C'mon," I called to Carl. "What's the hold up?"

"Sorry, wanted to listen to that last play."

"Baseball?" I asked.

"Yeah. Opening day was last Monday, Dad." Carl was a rabid fan, and back before the Domino, was glued to SportsCenter.

"Sorry. Who's playing?"

"Sox and Yankees." Carl's favorite team, the Red Sox, like his great-grandmother, and his least favorite team, the Yankees.

"We winning?"

"Five zip in the third. Manny Ramirez just lit them up. Three-run homer."

"Who's pitching?"

"Big Unit." We'd watched Randy Johnson pitch for the Mariners in Seattle once, in the now-ruined Safeco Stadium. Not the friendliest guy, but man could he throw the heat.

"Bummer for him. Grab that little Sony AM radio. You can listen to that while we meet with Aaron."

"Cool." He quickly took my ancient Sony, a little chrome-silver plastic radio that I'd had since I was twelve, and it's companion earpiece, and found his game. "This would've been handy on watch," he said as we headed out the gate, Buck trying to sniff his way there.

"Sure, if you're not serious about your work."

"Yeah, I guess."

"C'mon. We'll be late. Here, take the leash," I said as I handed the six-foot leash to him.

"They said on the radio that there's only about ten thousand people there at the game."

"Not surprising. I'm surprised that anyone's there at all."

"Why?"

"Money, or the lack of it."

"But if they bought their tickets before the Depression, wouldn't they still be good?"

"Sure, I suppose. But the cost of the ticket isn't all of it. You gotta get there, which means gas, which is in short supply and expensive and people are getting killed for it. In Boston, getting around isn't easy. Can't imagine what the traffic or neighborhoods would be like. Probably not real friendly. Then you gotta park. Maybe it's dangerous. Gotta eat. Some gotta stay overnight. All of that costs money. Meanwhile, people around them are going hungry. You go to a baseball game these days; I'd expect you'd be a rich man. And a target. How're the teams making out, with so many players gone?" Many of the players had died in the flu outbreak. Many others couldn't or wouldn't come back to the States.

"It's weird. I don't think that Johnson did that bad a job pitching, but half of his team is new."

"Stands to reason with the flu and the attacks on anyone that sounds like they're from Mexico. I'm kind surprised that Ramirez is even there."

"He's from the D.R., Dad," referring to the Dominican Republic.

"I know. That doesn't mean that somebody else is going to give a rip about that though."

"The color commentator said they'd been marketing their foreign players as 'not from Mexico,' and they had a big fund-raiser for the victims in Virginia," Carl said, referring to the car-bomb attack on a day-care in the D.C. suburbs.

We'd been pretty well 'bound' to the property since the quake, with most of our outdoor work focused on breaking ground, pruning and thinning fruit and nut trees, the greenhouses, and salvage of tools and goods that we thought would be better out of the weather, or could be better put to use. To date, we'd documented 'what' came from 'where', in case the property owners or residents came back. Other than the Paulianos though, no one had moved back in. I really wasn't expecting anyone to, either.

The dozens of yards in the neighborhood were all looking well-overgrown, first, with no one living in most of the homes, and second, with lawn-mowing a distinctly bottom-of-the-bucket item on our to-do list, both in time and resources. The grasses were green and lush, and most of the pavement still had a fair layer of ash, which facilitated the growth of grasses and weeds over the pavement. Coupled with the numerous downed trees, the neighborhood bore little resemblance to that of the previous spring.

One heavily damaged home, which appeared nearly abandoned before the quake (the homeowner refused to mow, trim, prune or weed-spray, and not because they were on some organic gardening kick) exhibited what the rest of the neighborhood yards would soon resemble: Grass mixes of Kentucky bluegrass, fescue, and rye, eighteen inches tall, liberally decorated with dandelions, Canadian thistle, yarrow, and dozens of other 'weeds', as well as saplings from Norway Maple, Elm, Mountain Ash, Smoketree, Pine, and a few other tree varieties. I'd been tracking how long it had been since a mower had been used on that property—a little more than three years. The land was being reclaimed by nature, surely as the sun rose.

"There's Aaron," I pointed to Carl.

"Why're we here again?"

"He's a Ham radio operator. His antenna mast was snapped off in the quake. He says there's one at the Jacobson's, and he wants our permission, and probably our help, to get it moved and set up."

"K."

"Afternoon, Aaron. This is my son, Carl."

"Nice to meet you, son." Buck sniffed Aaron's coveralls and wagged his tail madly.

"You too, sir."

"Got the game on?"

"Yes, sir, Boston."

"You mean the Yankees, don't you?" he said with a smile. "I was born in the Bronx."

"Oh, boy. Don't get started on that," I said to both of them.

"Well, nobody's perfect," Carl said with a smile. "Just kidding."

"That's OK. It's good to see there are other things to think about these days that don't involve the end of things as we know them."

"Amen," I said. "Let's go take a look at that mast."

We walked toward the garage; a small detached two-car frame building, set to the northwest of the house. As we rounded the corner of the house, Buck stopped short, lowered his head, and I watched the fur on his back go straight up, and a very un-Buck-like growl came from deep in his throat. I quickly took out my nineteen-eleven and motioned for Carl and Aaron to step back.

"If anyone's there, you got about ten seconds before I loose the dog. When he flushes you, I open fire. You choose."

No reply.

"Let'im go," I told Carl.

"No! Wait!" a voice came from deep inside a blackberry thicket called.

"Cover, you two," I said to Carl and Aaron, quietly. They moved behind the corner of the house, Buck standing ready for me to set him loose. Carl had released him from the leash, the growl still rumbling. "Carl, try to get the Army of the FRS," I said quietly.

"Give me a second. It's sticky getting out."

"That's your problem," I said. "Not mine." I heard Carl get through to someone down by the store, and the sound of an engine starting up in the distance. Within a minute or so, a stocking-capped face appeared from the brush, watching me in my combat stance. Behind me, I could hear a number of soldiers running fast, leapfrogging ahead to maintain cover.

"Stand down, sir," a voice came from behind me.

"You got it. He's all yours," I said as I safed the old forty-five and put it back in my holster.

Two troops pulled the very dirty and heavily tattooed man out, long beard filled with nettles, his bare skin scratched and bleeding. His torn jeans and filthy white tank top were not what one would call adequate clothing.

"You match the description of one Jozefo Vankin Mihhaelo," one of the soldiers stated flatly.

"Yeah, what of it?" Tattoo said as a wire-tie was fastened around his wrists, another around his ankles, a boot to his neck.

"What of it? Well lessee," the sergeant next to me said. "You killed three of my men the other night, and rumor has it, you got a thing for young boys."

"**** off."

"You are headed to a firing squad, asshole. I'm personally going to put a bullet in you."

Tattoo then went off on a yelling and cursing fit until one of the soldiers calmly and efficiently gagged him with a bandanna. Four more soldiers joined the first two and quickly picked him up, none-too-gently placed him face down in the back of the truck-style Humvee, with four additional aiming their M-16's at the prisoner.

"You two, put the muzzle on his neck. If he so much as twitches, blow his head off," the sergeant said. Carl and Aaron looked on in a little bit of shock. I suppose I had that look on my face, too.

"Peterson and Macklin, fan out west. Douglas, light up that pile."

"Yes, sir," the soldiers replied. 'Douglas' retrieved a small shotgun-style weapon with a large bore, adjusted something on it, and fired a single, fat round into the blackberry mass, which immediately ignited the green, lush thicket. Within moments, we had to stand back from the heat.

"What the Hell is that?" I asked.

"You might think of it as portable napalm," the Sergeant said. "Anything?" he called out to the other soldiers.

"No, sir."

"Saddle up. He was the last of the leaders."

"Anything else we should know?" I asked the sergeant, whose uniform bore no name.

"No, sir. Thanks for calling that in," he said as he climbed into the back of the Humvee.

"No problem."

As quickly as they'd come, they were gone again.

"Now that was damned odd," I said.

"What isn't these days?" Aaron said, all three of us looking down the road as the truck disappeared. "This Army ain't the one I'm used to."

"You served?"

"Nam. Sixty-six to Sixty-eight. I was what the front line guys called, a supply puke. Still didn't keep me from getting both eardrums blown, though. Goddamned VC."

"Well, thanks for your service in any regard. A couple of my friends served there, and a bunch of my older brothers' friends, too."

"Thanks. Lets get a look at that tower."

We walked around the back of the garage, keeping a wary eye, even though the Army had theoretically 'cleared' the area. The heat from the burning blackberry bushes was still formidable, and let off a fair plume of smoke. Alan noticed and checked in with us, and Carl told him everything was OK, and that we'd fill them in when we got back, with another close call.

"There she is," Aaron said, pointing to a non-descript pile of wood siding, covering a triangular-shaped form under a blue tarp.

"Big thing," I said.

"Twenty-three feet plus retracted, weighs about twenty-four hundred pounds."

I let out a long descending whistle. "That'll be fun to move."

"Indeed. And it's not like I've got a crane handy these days, either."

"I can put out some feelers on the barter net. All you really need is a wrecker. Those'll hoist this easy. Just gotta find one, and get some justification for using the fuel. I can do that I think," I said hopefully.

"You sure?"

"Even if that falls down, we can round up a couple of engine hoists, get it off the ground onto a low trailer, then tow it over to your place. Setting it up'll be interesting."

"That's no big deal. I have a winch setup on mine."

"OK, then we'll see what we can do. Where'd you get a thing like this one, or yours?"

"Bought mine at the same time as Ray did, over the internet. US Towers. They were about ten grand apiece then."

"Wow. Expensive hobby."

"Well, maybe. But I can't golf, don't really care for collecting crap, and don't really like to do anything else."

"How far up does this thing go?" Carl asked.

"The mast will go up about ninety feet. The antenna another twenty or so."

"What's your range?" I asked.

"Depends on the weather. Can cover a lot of the West if things are good, a lot farther than that sometimes. We can find out a lot of stuff going on with the right setup, a lot of which isn't seeing the light of day on TV or on network news."

"That's what we've figured, too. Between the rioting, the flu, the economy…"

"And all the rumors."

"We haven't heard much of that."

"Got a shortwave?"

"Well, sort of, a couple. The better of them is an ancient monster of a console from the forties. Tubes and all. That does a great job at pulling things in. The smaller one, a Sangean, does OK. Digital tuning is nice, but we get more with the big one. We just moved it out of the basement a couple of weeks ago. Had to replace the plug and the wire. Works like a champ."

"Good for you. Listen to it every chance you get. From what little I've picked up on, things are getting damned interesting in Europe and the Middle East."

"How so?"

"Israel and Syria've been duking it out for a week or so. Nothing serious yet, but it sure could be pretty soon."

"Hadn't heard boo about that," Carl said, surprising me. Current events and world affairs were not his favorite subjects. I guess things change.

"And you probably won't. Not on the networks."

"Anything else?"

"Yeah, the E.U. is getting hammered on by their guest workers. Demanding equal representation based on race and religion."

"Well. The E.U.'s about to go Muslim."

"Yep. Sure as the sun rising, if they cave."

"When they cave," I suggested.

"I was preferring to be optimistic."

"I'm afraid in this case I'm being a realist."

"One in every crowd." Aaron replied.

We agreed to meet Tuesday afternoon at the store, after we'd had a chance to put the word out for some heavy-lifting assistance on Monday, through the barter network. I'd also try to get 'permission' to use a wrecker or tow truck or whatever to accomplish the task, which wasn't strictly 'related to food-production or essential functions.' That latter statement was debatable, I hoped.

13

Monday morning
April Tenth

Morning curfew had been pushed back to six-thirty a.m., which meant we could 'officially' be on the streets. We had two pre-arranged deliveries and one pick-up from the store scheduled for eight a.m., and we wanted to get our broadcast out to our network done before that. I knew I needed to get going, but still couldn't resist seconds of the oatmeal/honey cereal that Karen and Libby had made, even with just a small portion of goats' milk.

Ron and the rest of the Martins were making their final cleaning pass through the new house, and would spend their first night in the house this evening. Karen and Mary would be working on some housewarming gifts, covertly.

With an obvious Army force still present, that meant that we could stand down off watch duty again today, which put a few more hands in the fields, although not much remained to do…at least that we could be motivated to work on. We'd lost none of the blossoms on the trees near the warming fires on Saturday night, and all of them where no heat was available. This cut our expectations of fruit and nut production by a whopping seventy five percent. None of the cold-weather crops in the heated areas were lost however, so perhaps there was a trade-off.

Alan and I biked down to the store, Alan on my beat-to-heck Specialized mountain bike and some ill-fitting pannier baskets, while I was on Karen's forty-plus year old Schwinn Typhoon, my favorite bike of the several that we owned. We passed the Pauliano's house, and waved at Joe though the window, and he returned the wave with a stiffened arm. As we came into view of the store, we were greeted by the view of two Humvees and their crews, positioned as if under attack. A new wall of sandbags was present at the northeast corner of the lot, with a crew of three manning a machine gun. I was immediately reminded of similar images from Baghdad.

"Well, now. Ain't this friendly," Alan said under his breath.

121

"Why do I feel we've been occupied?" I replied.

"Because we have been. Now if this isn't going to stifle commerce, I don't know what will. Every trade made under the watchful eye of big brother? I don't think so." We waited on our side of the intersection for a large transport to pass-- Army again.

"And I've damn little in the way of warning the network."

"Broadcast in the clear. Who gives a rip at this point?"

"Probably right," I said, as we pedaled across the street. "Morning," I called out.

"Good morning, sir." An unfamiliar face in an unlabeled and unranked uniform replied.

"We OK to open up?" I asked.

"Yes, sir." The reply came from one of the trucks. "We're pulling out around oh-seven-thirty."

"Sounds good."

"Sir, one of the higher-ups will be visiting you by oh-nine-hundred."

"And who will bless us with their presence?" Alan said. That drew a chuckle.

"Not sure sir, I just got the message a few minutes ago. Said he met you the other night."

"Danielson."

"Could be, sir. Like I said, no names were given."

"Thanks, soldier."

"Quite welcome, sir."

'Nice kid,' I thought. 'Kid.' He was probably only three years older than Carl.

Alan and I moved our bikes up onto the sidewalk, and unlocked the heavy chain holding the plywood-covered storefront doors open as we brought our bikes inside. "This just gets better and better," I said in a hushed tone.

"Don't it though?" Alan replied.

I went into the back of the store to turn the lights on, past the rows of bent and twisted shelves we'd set back up and tried to straighten, most now stocked with items 'for sale' or 'trade'. A cooler in the back of the store held twelve-dozen eggs, courtesy of our hens and those of the Paulianos. Only about two-thirds of the lights worked, the rest damaged or broken in the quake. We'd managed to re-work some of them so that the back half of the store was artificially lit, with the front, near the door and the improvised windows being lit with daylight.

While I checked the back room and the temperature in the cooler, and did a brief inventory walk, Alan broadcast in the clear to all of our trading partners that 'security was good this morning, with an Army patrol in place on site,' and that 'we would notify trading partners when security levels changed.' Only the most dense of our partners would not have realized the double meaning of the broadcast. And yet, I knew there were at least two who fit that category. Nice enough, kind, but not very bright.

The store, if it continued and could continue to be supplied, would eventually end up being a general store, as it had been until the convenience store craze in the sixties. Our 'inventory', some of it belonging to us, some salvaged from destroyed homes, some on 'consignment', included what you might expect, and some things you wouldn't.

Our current stock included used clothing, shoes and boots but no gloves; cookware and utensils; four gallons of Coleman fuel and two cases of Sterno (I don't think many people knew what it was or how to use it); several hundred rounds of twenty-two long-rifle; new and used rope, tarps, wire, nails and screws; window glass, almost all salvaged; caulking and glazing compound; dust masks (down to one box now from a case); sewing machines, thread, needles and yarn; two big jars of hard candy from Costco; a declining number of high-priced batteries and battery chargers; a number of small portable radios; and more electronic stuff than you could shake a stick at. These sat almost untouched near the front doors on two low shelves. A big seller when available were crock-pots, we'd sold or traded five so far. A thirty-two gallon galvanized garbage can held excess garden tools, which also were a pretty popular trade item. We also had some 'freeware' for our traders, including printed plans (printed double sided to save paper) on making a slow sand filter for water treatment; building a small generator similar to our little home made unit; and some guides for gardening, felling and cutting trees for firewood, and tips for keeping warm.

Other than the occasional loaves of bread or muffins (almost always made by our group); there was virtually no prepared food for sale. Nor were there seeds in stock, or fruit trees or any food crop, unless by special arrangement. We'd heard that some other traders had cow's milk, and we were eager to be able to buy some if and when it became available. How odd it was to think that.

Items in constant demand included toilet paper (none, ever available, and I wasn't about to sell from my stash); bleach, detergent and soap; larger caliber ammunition; charcoal; firewood (we were about to start working on our own supply, hopefully with Don Paulianos help); feminine hygiene products and baby supplies; juice mixes of any kind; window screening material; vitamins and painkillers; livestock; sugar, flour and spices; chain-saws, axes and hand-saws; matches and lighters, cigarettes, beer and other non-medicinal alcohol; first-aid supplies and antiseptics; cast-iron cookware; canning supplies (virtually none ever available in stock, and only a few times available for trade or outright sale); bicycle tubes and tires, bike trailers and bikes; razor blades; wagons; and any other pre-Depression pharmaceutical. Those that had these items did not often trade them, if they did, they had spares or Very Good Reasons for letting them go.

By the time I'd finished my walk through, and unloaded my old REI backpack of the twenty-two long-rifle (we didn't leave that in the store) and a couple loaves of cornbread, Alan had already found someone with a big tow-truck and trailer to move Aaron's antenna-mast, and given the nature of tow-truck operations, using fuel for the operation of the truck could be constituted as an authorized operation, under the military rules that we were sort-of operating under. The truck operator, living in Greenacres, offered to stop by the store later in the morning, and negotiate payment. Aaron was listening in, and concurred. I was sure that Alan would have fun negotiating that transaction. I'd heard the Army vehicles start up and leave, and decided to wait a while before going outside to see if they'd left anyone behind. No sense in being too nosy.

Alan had the local news on, KDA was back up and operating finally, although not at its former fifty thousand watts.

"Anything new going on?"

"Only listening with one ear. Said something about income taxes though from what I heard. Annick will be coming in by ten with his trade." Annick, no last name given or asked for, was Alaskan by birth, but had lived in the Valley for most of his sixty-plus years.

'Sure. I've had a banner year for income,' I thought. Well, last year I did. And how in Hell was I supposed to file my last year's taxes, when I'd never received my 1040 form, W-2's or anything else? I also realized, that I never filed my corporate tax return, or finished my fourth-quarter State tax statements for the company, or filed them. 'This could be bad,' I thought at first. 'There's a whopping understatement.' All of that information was probably still in the wreckage of my office, near downtown. Assuming of course that it hadn't burned or been bulldozed since my only visit back since the Domino.

I turned up the radio, and hoped to figure out the discussion.

".....tax amnesty? Is that what they're talking about?" the show host asked.

Another newsy, I assumed, replied. *"More- and less-complicated than that. The Reorganization advocates have successfully pushed for the elimination of the Internal Revenue Service as we've known it for decades, by Executive Order. Revenue will now be collected by the Federal Government from the States only, as a flat consumption tax across the board."*

"If you spend, you pay. If you save, you don't pay."

"Precisely. And this is only subject to sales of new items, not used, not traded, not wholesale. And ITEMS only, not SERVICES."

"Excuse me while I get some duct tape, wrap my head with it, and you repeat that. I think my head might explode," the host said. I was chuckling at that. 'This will be interesting,' I thought.

"You heard me right."

"So no more 1040's? No W-fours?"

"Correct. And of equal or greater importance, no double or triple or quadruple taxation. No taxation on corporate profit."

"OK, I think I'm getting this," the host said. *"But how can the government cut their own throats like this?"*

"Sure as Hell beats open revolt, doesn't it?"

"Well, I can't say that it's actually avoiding it given what we're seeing in Philadelphia, Atlanta, D.C. and Chicago today."

"The Federal Government is downsizing like there is no tomorrow, because if they do not, there IS no tomorrow! We've already this morning heard of the complete elimination of massive portions of the Federal bureaucracy, following up on the 'interim suspension' of those departments in February. Today they're

gone. Department of Education. Gone. Most of Health and Human Services. Gone. Foreign aid we've already seen go away. We've already gotten out of the UN and sent them packing. We're paying for that, and will continue to do so with all the animosity out there. Social Security cut back to damn near nothing, and I predict it will be gone by the start of the new fiscal year in July. FEMA: completely redesigned. Bilingual Language Office: Gone. I could go on for hours with the list...it was eleven pages long, listing all the departments, offices, bureaus. It's now three pages long. Three."

The host stopped for just the barest moment. *"How....OK. What is left?"*

"The military. Some parts of the State Department, now essentially the Trades and Treaties Department. A dozen others. Basically a gutted Federal Government that appears to be geared toward protecting the Nation from other countries, and enable us to trade freely within a framework not seen since the early eighteen-hundreds. Protection of national assets, resources, and open space, which are not mutually exclusive. Encouragement to companies founded and wholly based in the United States. That does not mean 'protection'."

"I'm not hearing anything about the protection of the individual and things that the Government has provided for us."

"That's because the Government doesn't PROVIDE anything for us. They take it from us as we've allowed them to. This is a vast shift of power from the Federal government to the states. Responsibilities and activities taken on by the Federal government through such actions as interpreted by the Supreme Court, and I'm speaking about 'interstate commerce' here in particular, are going to be restored to their proper place, and that means the States. Any cotton-picking politician out there who wanted to put his greasy thumbprint on the rights of the individual just had to make the thinnest of cases for it, wrap it in some half-wit 'protection of interstate commerce' legislation, and Poof! Your rights were gone and you now had more government mouths to feed. No more. If the states want to duplicate the Federal bureaucracy, its now completely up to them. If they want to run lean and mean and be accountable, then there you go. The failure of the Federal government was because of the lack of this accountability and the constant grabs for power and control. Those came at our expense."

"OK, so what's the Acting Congress have to say about this? This has got to mean that their power is being diminished."

"Reduced, yes. To a level that will be appropriate. Congressmen and Senators accumulated too much power that was completely out of proportion to their contributions to leadership, and that is attributable almost exclusively to the influences of lobbyists."

"And that's going to change? 'The best government money can buy?'" the host said with only the barest camouflage on his sarcasm.

"It will, assuming that what I'm hearing is correct. Two-term term limits on all Federal elected offices. Retirement mandatory for elected officials at age seventy. Retirement paid for by the individuals elected, with no contribution by the government or any other contributor. A virtual ban on retaining former elected officials to lobby the Federal government. They gotta work for their paycheck like the rest of us."

"And how will this be put in place? Fairy dust?"

"Bear with me, Mr. Perry. Elections to seat the new Congress will be held July first. The interim Congress, including almost forty-percent non-elected Representatives and Senators, are calling for this internally. That forty-percent, composed almost entirely of men and women appointed by their respective Governors after the deaths of so many in the flu outbreak, are leading the way in this call for change."

"What about the respective parties?"

"This is a bipartisan effort, as far as this item goes. The domination of one party over another really isn't all that relevant anymore. Both parties, except the radical fringes on both the Democrat and Republican sides are for this. It is literally, down to a choice between success and failure. And failure isn't an option."

"What about those 'fringes' you mentioned?"

"Both have their visions of what the Federal government is supposed to be. Both are obsolete as of the start of the Second Depression. The far right wing wants more representation of business within the administration. Damned near to fascism. The far left wing is demanding outright Marxism with some half-assed environmental bent to it. But the American people are demanding change, and this is what they're demanding. They're done with central government."

"You listening to this?" I asked Alan.

"Yeah. Pretty good stuff. Fantasy is good this time of day. Never listened to story-time in the morning before."

"Ever the cynic."

"Well, it's my turn. You've been slacking lately."

"Only in public. Trying to be the figurehead and all. Don't think it's going to work?"

"Not a snowball's chance in Hell. Too many people with too much power that don't want to let it go."

"Where do you think it will go?"

"South, and in a hurry."

A few minutes later, another Army Humvee rolled up to the doors, and shut off the engine. A single occupant, hidden in the dark of the interior, apparently talking on a radio.

"And why did the hair on the back of my neck just stand up?" Alan said quietly.

"Ditto," I said as 'Danielson' climbed out the drivers' side.

"Good morning," I said in my best-faked 'I'm in a good mood' voice.

"Mr. Drummond," he nodded. "Mr. Bauer."

"All quiet on the front this morning, Corporal?"

"Yes, sir. And I assume you realize I'm not a corporal," he asked.

"I was figuring on 'Captain,' actually, unless you're one of the oldest corporals in the Army, which makes you a dolt, which we have observed, you are not."

"Thank you. Captain is close enough."

"Regular Army or what?" Alan asked with no inflection to his voice.

"Intel."

"Figures. So is 'Danielson' your real name, or have you changed that too?" Alan asked, again flatly.

"Doesn't really matter now, does it?"

"Probably not," I replied. "What brings you out today?"

"Wanted to give you a heads up. You are firmly on the radar screens of your county leadership. More accurately, within the cross-hairs."

"And that is no surprise."

"Yes, but what they're planning may well be a surprise for the population."

"Which is what exactly?" Alan asked, finally settling down a little.

"It appears from my sources that they plan on foreclosing on any and all property that is behind on taxes or vacant, and seize it for the County's use. Which means, 'their' use."

"That certainly sounds constitutional," I said.

"Hardly."

"And don't tell me, we're on the top of the heap."

"Yep," 'Danielson' said, sipping a travel mug of coffee. The mug had a label that read 'Fort Belvoir' on it. I'd have to see where that was, if I could. "You really must've pissed them off in a former life."

"No, in this one actually. OK, taxes are normally due on April thirtieth and October thirty-first. Notices are mailed at least a month ahead of time. We haven't gotten mail in three weeks of any kind…."

"Their doing."

"You're kidding me," I said.

"Nope. All mail is being held at a warehouse on Freya, after it's left the Terminal Annex by the airport."

"And that's not a Federal issue?" Alan said with some irritation.

"Sure it is. If we had time and manpower to do something about it. Which we don't."

"Suggestions?" I asked.

"Proactivity would be advisable," he replied.

"Pay them now," I said.

"At least make the effort. I'm trying to get military command to take charge of this, but so far the Brigadier in charge seems to be preoccupied with polishing his desk with his secretary's behind. That will be rectified shortly, but not until it's too late for you."

"When do they plan on this?"

"End of the month, latest. If taxes are due the thirtieth, plan on May first as the day they seize your property."

"How do they plan on doing that?"

"They've retained a number of individuals that they rely on for certain services. These men have already been used in the aggressive harassment of other problem citizens in Spokane County, Stevens County and Lincoln County."

"Mercenaries?"

"All but in name, yes. That's your heads up. I suggest you spread the word, quietly, and be prepared for it," 'Danielson' said as he got up from a wooden bar stool.

"Thanks. Where you off to?"

"Coeur d'Alene. Seems we have some issues over there to deal with."

"Issues. Interesting way to put it."

"Beats 'armed gangs who burn down occupied nursing homes,'" he said as he walked out the door.

"Thanks," I said to his back. He raised his hand and waved in a single pass without looking back, got in the Humvee, and drove off to the east.

"Holy smokes," I said, standing there for a minute.

"'Remember, Government is Your Friend,'" Alan said as he took out a pad of paper.

"Notice for the barter group?"

"Yep."

14

Monday Afternoon,
April Tenth

Around ten I left Alan to man the store, with our friend Ellen McDonald there for company. Ellen's husband died from the flu, and her son and daughter-in-law were lost southeast of Tacoma when Rainier went off. Predictably, she had not recovered, but was making a life day by day. I frankly wondered how she did it. Stronger than me, for sure.

Alan's note to specific barter operation members was brief and to the point, and was almost put out on the radio, before we thought better of it. 'Specific' barter members because we trusted them as much as our own blood and wanted to avoid entanglements like the gang member who infiltrated our operation. Both Alan and I suspected that our County Commissioners had a mole inside too, or some other lackey that was making a concerted effort to provide as much info about us as possible. We decided to have a meeting on the matter and to get the word spread as quickly as possible. The memo was entitled 'Wildfire.'

"In the first Great Depression, many homes, farms and businesses were lost and foreclosed on because of the inability to pay property taxes or house payments. Now that we're in the Second Depression, we are concerned that this may happen again, with facilitation by the County government to seize properties and displace those that are or have been opposed to their leadership in the past. We ask you to meet at the community center at high noon, April 11th, to discuss this possibility and actions that may be taken to prevent this."

That said a lot, especially between the lines.

We printed twenty-eight copies of the memo on my Epson printer, for hand delivery to the recipients. That was my afternoon job, as many as I could hit on the Specialized, hopefully twenty-one. Seven we'd call in for 'special trading, immediate action required' and they would come to us. Hopefully. They were beyond comfortable (or timely) biking range.

My delivery run was pre-planned and highly scripted, having a map of each trader's location hidden inside my boot, and working with a homemade scabbard for one of the Ruger twenty-twos, mounted on the back rack. I started off after lunch, in a circuitous route that was actually far longer than it needed to be, just to throw off anyone who might be watching me. At stop number seven, I noticed for the second time, a very dirty green and white Spokane County Sheriff's patrol car more than four hundred yards off, and seemingly a lone figure behind the wheel. Almost as planned. It was too bad. I was starting to enjoy my time on the bike and the nice sunny spring day.

Again this time, he appeared to be speaking into a microphone. 'Great', I thought. I didn't stop at trader number nineteen, whose home was right across the street from where the car was parked. Instead, I just rode by the cruiser, waved at the non-deputy behind the wheel (the driver was dressed in a dirty plaid flannel shirt, thick moustache and dark glasses. 'No way was that guy a cop,' I thought. Had to be one of the hired thugs. Sure looked like one. Even thought things had hit the fan, the cop cars were at least clean enough to be seen as police cars. I also noticed that instead of the dashboard-mounted shotgun, the muzzle of an AR-type weapon was visible. Hardly standard equipment.

I biked another half mile down the two-lane arterial, and noticed in the little rear-view mirror that I'd poached from my old Schwinn Varsity, that the patrol car was lazily following me, although trying to be subtle about it. All through my deliveries, I'd maintained a fairly constant slow speed, to set my observers at ease.

I made a quick right, shifted gears and dramatically sped up. I cut between two homes, deep mid-block in a virtually abandoned neighborhood similar to ours, but much more heavily in filled with apartments and single-family homes with no useable garden or farming space. I made a quick run across unfenced yards, still on my bike, doubling back towards the deputy. I stopped behind a rancher, and peeked around a big arborvitae hedge as the police interceptor screamed past, continuing south toward Sprague Avenue. I snuck around the north side of the house and peeked around the corner. The cruiser had stopped a few hundred feet south of me, and the driver had slammed the big Ford into reverse, hoping to back up and catch me. I decided to play possum rather than run anymore. He sat there for a moment, trying to see if I was coming back out to play. I heard my little FRS earbud beep at me.

"Fireman," I replied. "Ready for transmission." Our radio play was about to begin.

"What are you doing? One of the CB channels is all over following someone on a bike with a gun," Ron said, on cue and on script.

"Who's doing the talking?"

"Don't know. They're using proper names, not military, not police. You OK?"

"Yep. Here's the skinny. I'm on Locust," (not correct, I was actually on Farr Road) "at about eight-oh-five north." (Also wrong, I was at about fourteen hundred north). "There is someone posing as a Spokane Sheriff's deputy in a Spokane County patrol car. He's been following me since I left our street." That part at least was true.

"You gonna make it home OK?" Karen asked, with real concern in her voice.

"I don't know. He's been talking on a radio to someone. This looks like an ambush."

"There's at least two parties tracking you, maybe more," Ron added. That wasn't scripted.

"Then I've got a big problem."

"What are you going to do?"

"Head toward Sprague, hopefully I'll be able to get to one of the Army patrols down there or stay under cover, and make my way back home." With that last comment, the police car spun around and headed south. I thought I heard another one on the street to the east. 'Check,' I said to myself. 'Now, if the Army or the real deputies are listening in....'

I went on with the act. "Hold on. I think they're coming. I hear engines." I was no more than a half-mile away from where the phony cops were trying to corner me. "I'm moving," which in reality would've been the last thing I would have done had I been there. I needed to move over to the next street though, to continue my acting job. It took me about two minutes to cover the ground, hoist my bike over a small fence, and take up cover again. I could just see the patrol car with a small pair of binoculars I had in my courier bag, next to four spare magazines for my nineteen-eleven. Two more dirty Crown Victorias pulled up behind the first, and at least seven heavily armed men, none appearing to be actual deputies, got out and quickly fanned out towards my reported position.

"Jesus!" I said. "There's a dozen of them! I gotta go!" I heard random firing down the street as our act concluded. "They're shooting me!" With that, our play was done, and appropriately timed, as a pair of Bradley's and an up-armored Humvee turned south on Farr from Broadway and rapidly accelerated towards the positions of the phony police. The first arriving at the cluster of Crown Victorias stopped and held ground, while the second passed the parked cars and continued south. The Humvee followed the first Bradley to a stop, where the infantrymen had disembarked and were under cover behind the cars and the Bradley. "Checkmate," I said aloud after shutting the VOX feature off on the radio. "Pawn takes king."

Automatic weapons fire continued off and on for nearly two minutes, before silence returned. 'Time to head home,' I thought, as I got back on the bike and moseyed along home. If all had gone as planned, one of our pending problems might've just been eliminated.

I biked the four blocks home, and was greeted by Mike Amberson's own Crown Vic, and a very odd-looking truck wearing Army livery. I'd never seen anything like it. I dismounted and walked my bike the hundred yards or so to the truck, and convinced the gunners that I was not a threat.

Mike was obviously there to tell Karen and the family the bad news. I wish I had a picture of the look on his face when I walked my bike into the yard, safe and sound.

"Hiya, Mike. How's it going?" I said with a smile. The whole family, including Grace, was standing on the front porch or in the front yard. A fair number of Army uniforms stood watch in a fan pattern around the group.

"Better now. I better call Danielson's patrol and tell them to quit looking for your body."

"Thanks," I said, shaking his hand. "Can I talk you into a shot of single malt?"

"You may," he said as he picked up his mic. I thought I heard him say 'bastard' after that. I did see him shaking his head.

"Alan, can you set us up please?"

"Way ahead of you," he said as he opened a small wooden crate that camouflaged a Styrofoam box, pulled a bottle of Laphroaig (Gaelic for 'The beautiful hollow by the broad bay") and four crystal shot glasses out of a little velvet bag that belonged to my Dad.

Mike rejoined us as Alan set up some shots on the front porch rail. A dozen infantrymen came back to their truck after orders, and stood informally, waiting for something else to do. A Lieutenant—this time, appearing to actually BE a lieutenant—joined us briefly and said that they were returning to their post positions. Mike nodded, and they began to load up.

"How long have you been planning this?" Mike said as Alan passed him the Scotch.

I looked at my watch. "'Bout three hours."

"And how did you know it would work?" Mike asked.

"Didn't. How'd we do?"

"The Valley Protectors seem to be no more," he said.

"Protectors? That's what they called themselves?"

"Yep. 'Informal militia' authorized by Commissioner Markweather."

I'd had a run-in with Markweather once, a couple months ago when I proposed that the County take the lead on resettling the area along more resource-sustainable methods. He was not amused. "Really. And what about Earl Williams or Sam Jackson? They approve of these guys?"

"Jackson's' dead. Flu got him. Commissioner Williams has the North Side Protectors operating in his district."

"And you can't stop them?"

"With the force I've got? Not even remotely. I'm outnumbered by a significant percentage. And the Army? Don't even ask. Stretched too thin too."

"So how much trouble am I in?"

"With me, none. I have no proof that you did anything wrong or against the law. With the Commissioners, that's another story."

"What about the Army?"

"Army got the radio call same as me. They were moving to assist a civilian apparently being chased when they were fired on by persons impersonating Sheriff's personnel."

"So what now?"

"Not sure. Danielson's on his way up here. He might have the answer on that."

"So who's really running things in this County, Mike?" I said as I downed the straight shot.

"The Commissioners have run rough-shod over every legal check in sight. They're literally carving up the county for their own uses and replacing people who were elected or hired with their own hand-picked staffs."

"So what about the legal department of the County? We talked about someone in Counsel reviewing their orders to you."

"Chief Prosecutor and a couple of the remaining D.A.s woke up dead over the period of four days. Two were supposed to have died from the flu. One in a house fire. One dead in a robbery."

"Sure they were."

"I know. I lost a deputy as well who spoke up one time. Turned out one time too many."

"Mike we gotta get this cleaned up."

"Army will help us soon. Danielson's got the 41st Infantry Brigade from Oregon coming up as soon as they get detached from Mexico."

"How long?"

"Too long, probably," he said as an open Humvee showed up outside the fence. 'Danielson' was driving. He spoke to a pair of the soldiers—two in unmarked camouflage—and they took his ride back down the street, double time.

"Sheriff. Mr. Drummond, Mr. Bauer."

"Nice to see you," I said. "Scotch?"

"Absolutely," he replied. I was starting to like this guy.

"Busy afternoon," I said as I poured a shot.

"So it would seem. You haven't heard anything about a civilian being in distress around here, have you?" he asked with a glint in his eye.

"Hmm, no, I don't think so. I was actually out making some deliveries until a few minutes ago."

"Good thing. Hate to see an innocent man get himself on the wrong end of a gun," he said as I handed him one of the crystal shot glasses.

"Indeed," I replied as I saluted him with a shot and downed it. 'That better be my limit,' I thought to myself.

"So, I understand you had a little business down near Sprague?"

"Yep. Bunch of fellas deciding to pretend to be some of Sheriff Ambersons' deputies. Managed to liberate some of his patrol cars, and a few mismatched uniforms. When challenged, they decided shooting was better than responding like outgunned folks ought to. There's twenty-seven men who will not be around for dinner tonight."

I was shocked. I only saw maybe a dozen. "That many? Well," I trailed off.

"Yep. Seemed to have the idea that there was a person of interest down the road a piece. Tried to flank him when we came up on them from all sides."

"Any of the good guys get hurt?"

"Nope. Turkey shoot."

"Any chance of this happening again? I mean, are there others out there pretending to be cops?"

"Might be. Better not happen again like this though," 'Danielson' said, almost an order.

"I'm fairly certain it won't. Not around here, anyway."

"So, what were you out delivering?" Mike asked.

"Meeting notices. Calling a special traders meeting tomorrow. You're invited if you'd like to come."

"Got an agenda?"

"Still working on that."

"What time?"

"Noon. We'll have some soup or stew in big ol' pot, and some of that cornbread with the jalapenos."

"Count me in," Mike said.

"I'm afraid I will not be able to attend," 'Danielson' said. "Other obligations."

"Stop by around two if you're in the neighborhood. I'll save you some lunch."

"I'll see what I can do," 'Danielson' said as he turned to go. "Thanks for the shot. Been awhile."

"Hey, before you go, can you tell me about that truck? Never seen the like."

"Not likely. Most of 'em were in Iraq. It's called a 'Cougar'. Weighs about sixteen tons. This is the only one in the state so far."

"What makes it so special?" Alan asked, intrigued.

"It keeps its crew alive after getting shot at or bombed. Layered hull. Ceramic, steel, composites. All the stuff a good soldier needs so tomorrow he can kill the guy to tried to kill him today."

"You need trucks like this here?"

"Not yet. We hope. Lost four Humvees in L.A. this week so far, with full crews. Roadside bombs."

"Haven't heard that on the news."

"And you won't, either. Gentlemen, good afternoon. Oh, Sheriff, your cruisers will be moved to the community center."

"Thanks," he said to 'Danielson's' back. We watched him mount up in the monster truck and our eyes followed it down the road.

"How 'bout you kids get that kindling picked up like you're supposed to?" I said to the collection of kids. I received a grumbling reply. Karen and the ladies filtered back inside, working on sorting out some of our belongings that we were donating to the Martins, who'd move into their home tonight. That left Ron, Alan and I out with Mike.

"OK, what's this meeting about?"

"Our kindly Board of County Commissioners."

"Figured as much. What's your game plan?"

"We've heard rumors that the Board is planning actions that will result in the seizure of private property for non-payment of current year taxes. Taxes are due April thirtieth. Notices have been mailed and are being held up from delivery. We should've received them by now. We haven't."

"I've heard such rumors, but don't have any confirmation. Where did you get it?"

"Can't say," Ron said. That didn't set well with Mike. "Trust me. We think it's a reliable source."

"Fair enough. Again, what's your game plan?"

"Pre-emptive strike."

"And this afternoon wasn't?" He was getting angry.

"Partly. I wanted to see how reliable the information was. They proved that it was highly reliable."

"And your next step is what?"

"We're going to pay our taxes based on last years amounts, since taxes haven't gone up. We didn't pass anything new for the schools or you or the fire department. Things cannot have changed…legally, that is."

"Pay with what?"

"Checks, drawn on our banks, same as last year. It's not like we've heard officially from the County that Federal Reserve Notes aren't being accepted. And we'll have them there ahead of the April thirtieth deadline. Well ahead. Who's running the Treasurer's office, or the Assessors?"

"Clark is in Treasurer's and Assessors. Was deputy, and promoted to head both after the quake. Neither of the department heads made it through the flu."

"Good guy? Trustworthy?"

Mike corrected me. "Yes, SHE is. Daphne Clark. Caught between a rock and a hard place. She's almost the last of the old staff still left. Playing her cards close though. I've known her for a couple years. But if you think this will play out in your favor, you're wrong. If she works with you on your behalf, she's dead."

"I don't plan on delivering payments to her. I plan on delivering them in person to the Board. And I plan on doing it with you standing next to me, and a few other folks as well."

"You got big brass ones, don't you? Trying to get yourself killed?"

"Not on purpose. But neither will I stand for this kind of crap," I said, pointing towards the location where I was supposed to be ambushed. "You think they'll shoot me down in broad daylight?"

"Probably not. But if this isn't done right, you are done for."

"Then we best be careful," Alan said.

15

Tuesday,
April Eleventh

Monday night we outlined our 'plan' for the inevitable confrontation with the Commissioners. We knew that we couldn't do it alone, and we knew that the legal system that we'd thought would protect our rights was virtually no more. We were hoping that with the participants of the barter store joining us, with some assistance from the small Army presence, we thought we might have a chance of defusing things until some real legal authority could be put in place from outside the area.

With the Army patrols running, we were all able to turn in early. For me, that meant a nice long stretch of uninterrupted sleep. Most days I felt that I was a walking zombie, working too hard during the daylight hours, functioning on too little sleep, waking for watch, and being forced to stay awake to keep us 'safe.' Whatever that meant. Tuesday night, we turned in at the unheard of hour of eight o'clock, with light still coming in from the skylight in the barn, and I slept until Buck woke me licking my face at six a.m. I was a new man.

After a quick breakfast of a couple slices of Spam, eggs, and a new muffin mix that Libby had perfected specifically to imitate McDonalds' egg McMuffin (no cheese though), and some too-strong coffee, we were ready to go. The day was turning out to be clear and sunny, and relatively warm. If the winds stayed down, we might actually have had a day without dust. They never seemed to stay calm for long, though.

Alan, Mary, Karen and I worked most of the morning on making an overly large stockpot of stew for lunch, with Kelly and Marie working on batches of jalapeno cornbread over at Alan's place, keeping his kids busy as well. Some of the last of our previous-years' carrots went into the stew, along with some stew-meat that the Paulianos contributed. The older boys were working on getting both of my chainsaws ready for a long days work, cutting firewood from downed trees that we'd already limbed for kindling for the winter ahead.

Ron and Libby, after spending their first night in their 'new' house, enjoyed sleeping in for a change. The Army was kind enough to have full patrols running through the neighborhood all night on irregular schedules, so we cancelled our own watch. Karen had made a housewarming gift of brownie pudding for the Martins, and I'd contributed a bottle of cabernet that I knew went particularly well with Libby's favorite dessert. Hence, the need to sleep in.

Around nine I turned the radio up, figuring that someone had turned the volume down—it was almost always on during the days. Nothing on KLXY. I punched the next button that we'd programmed, KDA. Nothing. I manually scanned the AM band. Nothing but static.

"What's up with the radio?" Kelly asked as she came in to borrow another pair of nine by thirteen baking pans.

"I don't know. Nothing's up. None of the local stations."

"Anything on shortwave?" Karen asked with some concern.

"Don't know. Might not get much during the daylight," I said. I searched the 'usual suspects', and other than heavy static, managed to pull in a few broadcasts, a couple seemingly from the Midwest. Probably not unusual, I thought.

"How about CB?" Alan asked.

"Let's try." I put the radio on 'scan', to pick up any active channels. A little chatter, same as always. Nothing sinister there.

"I dunno. We've never lost all local AM stations since the quake hit. Something's up."

"You think it has anything to do with us?" Mary asked.

"I'm paranoid, but not quite that paranoid. Yet." I replied. "We know the media's being controlled by higher ups. What we don't know is is it the Federal government that's doing it, and if so, shutting things off, or the networks working for the government, or something else."

"Or maybe the Commissioners just decided to shut things down," Alan said. "Make everyone come to them for information."

I was skeptical. "Think so?" I asked.

"Whom do you run to when you want to find out what's going on? The authorities. And they are appearing to be the highest civilian authorities around."

I thought about that for a minute. "Could be, I suppose." I paused again. "If that is the case, then we ought to move faster. Like a lot faster."

"Yep."

At eleven-thirty, we packed up my Expedition with the stew, cornbread and paper plates and spoons, raiding our summer party stash for the occasion. Drinks would have to be limited to water from the community center. We weren't really planning on feeding an army, just a little meal between neighbors.

Buck and Ada both thought it was a good day for a drive, and on this rare occasion, I relented and brought them both, on their leashes. We waved at the soldiers down at the corner (the store was closed today, although that had nothing to do with the meeting); and passed no one on the way to the community center. It was a beautiful day. We were unprepared for what we found at the center, though.

Thirty-five cars filled the parking lot, with a larger number of bikes, and two horses tied up to the chain-link fence inside the schoolyard next door. "Well, now," I said. "Word does spread."

"Like wildfire," Karen replied.

"Hope we have enough stew," Mary said with a smile.

"Not worried about that. That cornbread's going to get gone quick though."

Mike Amberson's freshly washed cruiser, and two others, were parked flanking the front door. One deputy watched the parking lot and street from the door, joined by an Army Humvee at the far end of the lot. We parked temporarily right in front of the door, and popped the tailgate open to unload lunch.

"Need a hand sir?" One of the deputies asked, as Alan and our wives unloaded our semi-precious payload.

"No thanks, we can get it. I'm Rick Drummond."

"John Stewart."

"Good to meet you. Worked for Mike long?"

"Three years next Monday."

"Wow, then condolences are necessary," I joked.

"Best boss I ever had."

"Yep. Good man. He inside?"

"Yes, sir."

"Thanks."

We made our way into the multi-purpose room, which now held more than sixty adults and an untold number of smaller kids. Flu or no flu, we had a turnout far larger than we'd planned.

"There is no way that this is enough lunch," Karen said with wide eyes.

"Loaves and fishes, babe," I said.

"Don't be sacrilegious."

"Sorry. We're not the only ones who brought lunch. Look over at the table on the far wall. Smells like chili."

"Good for them. Don't want anyone leaving disappointed," said Mary.

"Can you get set up, while I talk to Mike?"

"Yep. Go on and get started," Alan said.

I made my way through the crowd over to Mike, who was near a portable podium at the front of the room. "Nice little gathering you've got here," he said.

"Yeah. A little larger than I thought. Like five times bigger."

"You ready?"

"Yep. Let's go." I moved to behind the podium, and asked for everyone's attention.

"Thank you all for coming today! This is a better-attended meeting than I thought; so let me apologize in advance if we run low on stew and cornbread. I see that there are some other dishes here, and I'd like to thank those of you that brought those. Your generosity will be remembered." A number of folks found their seats, while some of the smaller kids were herded into a smaller room, I assumed to be entertained and not distract the adults.

"If I could, I would like to ask for God's blessings on this meal and our work today. I see Pastor Allen in the audience. Pastor, would you provide the blessing?" He looked a little surprised for an instant, and then was 'on'. I found it difficult to ever really surprise a pastor.

"Certainly, Mr. Drummond," the room grew quiet. "Dear Heavenly Father, we have come here today for fellowship and for guidance for these difficult times that we've lived through and those ahead. We have lost loved ones, but gained friends; we have lost possessions but gained and renewed faith; we have seen the mighty fall and are challenged by a future that we are unfamiliar with. We ask for your blessing, your guidance, your strength in these things and in the decisions that we make today. We ask you to protect your children and help them to hide your Word in their hearts. We ask these things in the name of your Son, Jesus Christ. Amen."

"Amen," we responded.

"Thank you, Pastor," I said as he settled back in.

"Most of you know why we're here today. We are faced with a potential crisis brought upon us by our elected leadership, the two remaining County Commissioners. For those of you that hadn't heard, Commissioner Sam Jackson passed away, apparently from the flu." A minor buzz went through the room after I said that.

"The crisis is upon us. There is reason to believe that the Commissioners intend to foreclose on properties that are delinquent on their property taxes, which in years past have been due by April thirtieth. No notices have been received, but we have reason to believe that they were indeed mailed out, and are being held along with all other U.S. Mail that has come into the County recently."

"Rick, is that why we haven't gotten mail in two weeks?" Aaron Watters asked. The room came alive after that question.

"That's what we think, Aaron."

"Well that's gonna stop, right-damned-now....apologies, Pastor," Aaron said.

"None necessary, sir."

"So what's our plan?" Ellen MacDonald asked. 'Our' plan, she said.

"Ellen, what I'm thinking is this: They intend to hold our mail until it's too late for us to respond. Even though they've tossed the legalities in every other case, they're either waiting for the thirtieth or they're waiting to consolidate their power. They no longer have a legal department apparently, and even if they did, they'd probably ignore laws that weren't convenient to them. They're using hired thugs to intimidate people that are rabble-rousers. We had a little of that in this neighborhood yesterday, or so I hear," I said. No one in the room questioned that, or who the intended target of the ambush was. They'd heard on their CB radios just as we hoped they would.

"So, I propose that we pay our taxes. En masse, tomorrow morning. Pay with checks drawn on your bank accounts, even if the banks are closed. No one's told us the FRN's aren't being accepted by the County, we haven't had an increase in taxes since last year, either. So pay what you paid last year. Dig out your checkbooks and figure out what that was. Put it in an envelope addressed to the County Assessors' office, put a stamp on it. We deliver them tomorrow. It might not do a damned thing, but they cannot legally tell us that we didn't pay our taxes and swoop in like a bunch of Civil War carpetbaggers and steal our homes."

"Appropriate date, then, isn't it?" A tall man in the back asked.

"I'm sorry? I don't get the connection." I said to the unfamiliar man. "And would you mind introducing yourself?"

"Victor Beard. History teacher at Gonzaga University. On April 12, 1861, the Confederacy shelled Fort Sumter in South Carolina. First shots of the Civil War."

"Well, I'm fresh out of sixty-nine caliber musket balls, which I think were used by the Confederates, but I can tell you this. I'm going armed. I suggest that everyone do likewise. I'm not planning on a confrontation. I don't want provocation. But I'm also not stupid."

After an hour of sometimes-lively discussion and the creation of a tentative schedule, we broke for lunch. I was famished. Mike took me aside for a moment.

"Nice job. Hope it doesn't get you killed."

"That'd be nice. I'd like to see my kids grow up."

"See any problem with the caravan idea?" We planned on 'commuting' using our own private vehicles, to make the trip into downtown, ten or twelve miles to the west.

"Not from my side. But don't be surprised if you raise the hackles of the Commissioners' private army."

"I won't be. How bout the route?"

"No problem," he replied. "Might be nice to have more Army units around or that detachment of Marines back here."

"Yeah, I really miss Gunny McGlocklin. We could use him about now." Gunnery Sergeant Scott McGlocklin saved my butt right after the quake. He'd been shipped from Iraq directly to the Spokane region after the quake, and then down to Mexico after the war started. We hadn't heard from him since, although we'd written a couple of times.

"Talk to Danielson. He might be of assistance."

"I hope so, I'm counting on him," I said.

The afternoon was spent cutting firewood. Carl and John had successfully cut seven trees to length for our woodstoves, and now were working loading up one of the trailers to move the rounds home before it was split. We had more than forty trees to fell or cut up in place where they were already downed. More than a little work.

Knowing that we were unlikely to get natural gas back, and that being our former primary source of heat, made it all the more important to get our firewood cut, split and seasoned as soon as we could, and continue to do so throughout the year. In 'normal' times, I had maybe five or so cords of wood around the place, and used a couple of cords per winter for supplemental heat when we didn't feel like paying Avista for natural gas. Our house being, even before the quake, as airtight as a screen door, we went through a fair amount of heating dollars. Even after all the remodeling and weatherizing and such, there is only so much you can do with a house that is nearly a hundred years old.

With our home, Alan's place and the Martins, as well as 'spare' wood for the 'just-in-case' kind of winter, we were going to have to lay in a lot of wood to keep us warm in the coming winter. My late father, raised in cold, wet Northeast winters in the nineteen-twenties, said that in his day, five cords per house of seasoned wood was the absolute minimum. Our disadvantage at the moment was that in order to have the wood ready for the fall, now only four months off, we'd have to work our tails off to generate enough wood, salvaged, dead and standing, or felled, to be ready. We'd also have to find a place to store that much wood relatively close to each home.

We estimated that roughly twenty cords could be readily cut within our block, with probably another ten that could stand to be cut. With a wood supply from Don Pauliano out at Newman Lake (all softwood Tamarack, Red Fir and Pine), we'd do OK for wood. Splitting it would be no one's favorite job, even with the small hydraulic splitter that I owned, a hand-operated beast that basically used a hand-pumped hydraulic ram with a wedge on the end to split the wood. Same principle as on a motorized unit, but much slower.

By dusk, we'd loaded all of the cut rounds to the trailers, moved them to a spot north of the barn where we'd split them, and sharpened our saws for the next time we'd use them. The volcanic ash was having a serious effect on the saws, with much more frequent changes of air filters and much more wear showing up on the chains and bars. Most of this was due to the downed trees being cut with ash still layered on the trunk, hardened into a crust. Not much we could do about that.

Our late supper was some leftover chili and the last of the cornbread from lunch. Turned out there was plenty to go 'round, even after some of the young Army soldiers joined us.

Before turning in for the night, I tried the radios again. Managed to pick up Coast to Coast from a Salt Lake City station, but that was it. Nothing local.

I lay sleepless, next to Karen, who was also troubled by what was coming. It would be a long time before we slept.

16

Wednesday morning dawned overcast, and by the time we were ready to load up the Expedition and head over to the community center at eight-thirty, the southwest winds were beginning to howl, stirring up dust and ash in a cloud as thick as fog. Our commute would probably take longer than an hour, at this rate. I had a paint respirator/dust filter with me, hanging around my neck and ready for when I was due to be outside for long. With the change in the weather, no one would be working outside today.

After a long discussion, we decided that I would go alone to pay the tax bills, in the event that something happened. This left me driving seven other passengers downtown, including Aaron Watters, Ellen MacDonald, Joe and Don Pauliano, Sandy Grant (who lived northwest of us, husband Dan was pulling a double, working on power restoration), and Deputies Paul Schmitt and John Stewart, in civilian clothes, at Mike's suggestion. Besides that, they were property owners too. I carried checks for our property; both the Martins' current home and their former (burned down) place;

I was surprised at the number of vehicles already at the community center when I arrived to lead our group downtown. More than a hundred cars, from what I could estimate, most of them full it seemed, although through the dust, it was tough to see. I'd turned the Ford's air conditioning on to 'recycle', rather than suck in a bunch of ash.

I'd already picked up Joe and Don, who were seated in the middle row of seats. Ellen, Aaron and the rest of them were waiting in the vestibule, trying to stay out of the blowing dust.

"You all ready?" I asked after getting out of the car.

"Yep. That Danielson fella said he'd lead the way," Aaron said as he climbed into the third row of seats beside Ellen.

"Well that does beat all."

"Said the dust made traveling a hazard, and he was going to ensure that we were safe while driving."

"Danged considerate," I said as the two Deputies arrived. "Morning, gentlemen. Ready for a little adventure?"

"We're happy enough with peace and quiet, thanks," Deputy Stewart replied.

"I am, too. Funny how that doesn't always seem to be the best course of action though," I said.

"Paul, good to see you. Been a long time."

"Yes, sir. I've been working the north end of the County." Paul Schmitt was one of the first of the Deputies that we'd met after the Domino. Darned near ventilated me one day when I was coming out of the wreck of the house.

"How's the farm?"

"Well enough. Shorthanded like we haven't been in thirty years, so my Dad says."

"Lose anyone to the flu?"

"No, sir….not yet at least."

"Well, we'll hope for the best." 'Danielson's' unique truck showed up in front of my Ford. His masked figure, for all the world looking like Rommel in North Africa might've, waved us to fall in and follow. No orders, conversation, nothing. Just 'let's go.' The rear-seat passengers were discussing local conditions, farming, the weather. Just like normal. Not a normal day, though.

"Let the adventure begin," I said quietly as we drove west. I'd forgotten to check in with the house. I pushed the little VOX switch on my radio and called in. Karen answered.

"You OK? Leaving already?" She said, concern thick in her voice.

"Yep, got a few folks ready to go. Looks like times four 'x' ," I said. We'd estimated twenty-five cars or so in our caravan. 'Four X' made it a hundred. We didn't want to alert anyone that we were…numerous though.

"Good. Remember the toast."

“Will do.”

“Toast?” Paul asked.

“Code from my wife. Remember to check in. Toast has nothing to do with it.”

We drove west, then turned north on Argonne to cross Interstate Ninety, up towards Millwood, and then left on Trent Avenue, which was also an old state highway. Trent led directly into downtown, and according to Mike, was our best option as far as decent road conditions (no blockages from the Domino remaining) and little chance of being shot at. That was certainly comforting.

The weather continued to deteriorate on our drive, or perhaps we were just going through a dustier than average patch. Over the interstate, we were just able to see the southbound bridge, cracked in the middle of the northern span, and sagging towards the freeway below. We could barely make out much beyond that distance, scarcely a hundred feet. I hadn’t been this far from home since my one trip downtown to salvage materials and equipment from my office, back in January. All of my passengers were quiet, looking out into the grey dust and looking for familiar landmarks. Not many of them had been out of their neighborhood either, since the quake.

The roads had uneven cracks from the quake, and in more than a few of them, grasses and in a couple cases, trees were starting to grow through the pavement. It wouldn’t be long and we’d have few roads left, I thought.

Passing through a commercial area north of the freeway, I noticed that the grocery store that the Martins’ had tried to shop at—and been shot at instead—now appeared to be completely looted and abandoned, along with the rest of the strip mall. The main railroad line bridge, passing over Argonne was still intact and apparently undamaged. We hadn’t heard a train since January though. Too much damage on other parts of the line, and derailments in other parts of the region where the trains were then stripped and looted. On the west side of the street, a collapsed pile was all that remained of one of our local institutions, the Longhorn. No one made barbeque like that place. Well, now maybe no one did. I used to ship the sauce to my brothers, along with some of our Cougar Gold cheese, for Christmas each year. (And the one year we didn’t, and elected to send something else, we heard about it.)

Turning west onto Trent, we passed the partly lit Albertsons store, which although closed, now had lights inside and folks apparently working. We wouldn’t see many more businesses with similar activity for the rest of the trip. Much further west, we passed a City of Spokane police checkpoint, at the intersection of Trent and the entry road to the Police Academy, near Felts Field, a small public airport, where some of the military units were housed. Just after the quake, we'd had attack helicopters operating out of there. We hadn't seen them since early February though, when they were transferred to the Mexican Territory. We could've used them now. I guessed that our military forces in the County were probably less than five hundred men and women, a fraction of what we'd had right after the quake.

The big Burlington Northern train yard had some activity in it, with at least a few railroad men working in the big shop, and a number of trains back on their tracks. A train with a crane on it, used for righting derailed cars, was on the track nearest Trent, on a line that led east to Idaho and the Continental Divide. I hoped that it was on the way out to help clear and repair the lines.

East of the train yard, the road came to a 'Y', where Mission Avenue headed straight west, and Trent veered slightly to the south. A series of concrete jersey barriers now blocked Mission, and I knew that beyond the blockage lay a derailed train, once laden with chemicals. That train, when it derailed in the quake, killed hundreds of people downwind, briefly exposed to the cold and wind of the cold winter, then blanketed with toxic fumes from a dozen different cars. The joint City/County Emergency Operations Center was also a victim, as was the National Guard's Readiness Center, both located within yards of the train tracks. Not the best of planning.

"EOC open yet?" I asked Paul.

"Nope, not completely anyway. Hazmat teams still working it. Retrieved all the bodies and got the building secured back in January, but the chemical contamination covered everything, inside and out. So in addition to the quake damage, and all the windows getting blown out in when the train went up, the toxins are on, and in, everything downwind for about a half-mile."

"I thought the windows were supposed to be blast-resistant," I'd done some work on similar facilities, so I knew the criteria.

"Sure. But you take a train car full of ammonium nitrate, mix it with gasoline, diesel, and a few other nasties, let it soak a while because you can't fight the fires, it's gonna blow. There's a sizeable crater over there, about a quarter mile up the line. Wiped the rendering plant clean off the map, along with about three hundred feet of track. Just gone."

The Purina and Centennial Mills grain elevators and mills were still intact, and had power. The Centennial Mills plant on Trent, and the bigger mixing plant on Sprague, were both now owned by ADM. I wondered if the industrial farming giant was still in business. Someone was still there, a few light trucks were in the parking lot, near the grain cars, sitting derailed on their tracks in the off-load

152

area. I used to drive to work this day five days a week. I could just make out the other big mixing plant over on Sprague, although no lights were visible on that building. Drifts of ash and dirt had covered the curbs on both sides of the four-lane road, looking like grey snow.

Passing near Gonzaga University, we entered the downtown area. We stopped at Division and Trent (which in this part of town was called Spokane Falls Boulevard), where 'Danielson' turned north over the Spokane River bridge, following the path we'd taken last time downtown. The quake-damaged downtown looked almost untouched since January, piles of brick, belonging to the building that once held one of my favorite lunch bars, Fast Eddies, spread across both Division and Spokane Falls. Across the street from that, the wrecked but brand-new Convention Center and the Opera House, built for our World's Fair, thirty plus years ago. Karen and the kids and I had seen The Lion King there, just last fall.

Up and over the bridge to the north, I saw the wrecked and partially collapsed Pier One building, and the burned out shells of two hotels and one office building. None of those had burned because of the Domino, it had to have been looters or squatters. I knew the owner of two of them, and helped design one of the sites. It was odd to see blooming trees near the burned out six story office building.

Coming up towards the Spokane Arena, a couple blocks from my office and from our destination, the County Public Works building, we met another stream of cars coming down Washington Street.

"Well, now. What do we have here?" I asked no one in particular.

"Friends from the north side. I made sure of that," Paul said.

"This is big." I said, suddenly surprised at how our small actions had resulted in such large effects.

"It is that."

"So where are we supposed to park?"

"Follow Danielson. You'll park right behind him at Mallon and Monroe. Everyone else should follow behind you and park as they can."

We followed 'Danielson' up to the intersection, which was blocked on the opposite side with concrete jersey barriers that weren't there in January. As I looked in my rear-view mirror, the cars behind us were now three wide, stretching to the east and back up to the north. There had to be hundreds of cars.

There was already a crowd of people on the north sidewalk, apparently waiting….for us. Mike Amberson was at the intersection, ahead of the line, which seemed about six people wide and God knows how deep.

"Paul, this is way bigger than I thought it would be."

"Should make a statement."

'I just hope we come out with our skin,' I thought. "Everyone ready?"

Joe answered for everyone. "God-damned right we are."

We climbed out of the Ford, and walked up to 'Danielson's' odd-looking truck. I looked to the east, and hundreds of men and women were getting out of their cars and filtering toward us.

"Good morning, Mr. Drummond."

"Corporal," I winked at him. "Anything I need to know?"

"Other than my troops have been in position since oh-five-hundred, no."

"Insurance?"

"Or something like that. Do me a favor though."

"Sure, what?"

"Walk around the north side of the Cougar. That's the signal for my troops to move."

"Done," I said as we headed to the passenger side of the truck. My heart was pounding, and we hadn't even 'engaged the enemy' yet.

By the time I rounded the front of the truck, his soldiers were crossing the street and heading toward the Public Works building, set back from the street and fronted by a row of small businesses, now boarded up. I made an effort not to look their way so as not to draw attention to them. There weren't many of them. No patrols or security were moving against us. Then again, I hoped they wouldn't either. They didn't even have a post on the roof watching. Good for us.

The Public Works building was fully lit, which for Spokane County meant 'dim', energy conservation measures and all, put in place the previous fall. The four-story building held the County's planning and building departments, engineering and public works offices, the Commissioners' conference rooms and the main public Chamber room where meetings were typically held. The ornate Courthouse, modeled after a French chateau when built in 1893, looked in good condition, but also appeared to be abandoned. The Commissioners offices were formerly in that building. Behind the Courthouse was the Public Safety Building, which translated into normal language, meant Sheriff's and City Police offices and the jail. The black glass south wall, facing the Courthouse in its concave shape, was completely void of glass. The majority of the building was obviously abandoned. I wondered for a moment what had happened to the six hundred prisoners inside?

Don, Joe and I were at point, followed by the Deputies, Ellen and Aaron. More of our Valley neighbors were behind them, and hundreds of others, walking slowly towards the building, most with long-guns slung over their shoulders. We passed the empty storefronts, turned towards the building, and saw exactly two armed men, on either side of the door. Both were smoking and trying to protect themselves from the wind in the small vestibule on the north face of the building. Both were in mismatched camouflage, with M-16's carelessly stacked up in a corner by the door. No sidearms visible. 'Danielson' was to our right. I glimpsed to my left, twenty or so of his men, moving to flank the entry. A second group, further to the south, was rounding the south end of the building, to cover the south end. The parking lot held a Ford Excursion Limited, an Escalade pickup, and a dozen more cars. All had the dealers' original placards where license plates should've been. Obviously liberated from the dealers.

We were twenty-five feet away before the 'security men' noticed and immediately challenged us, obviously startled that anyone was here. They scrambled for their weapons. We didn't challenge them, but 'Danielson' did. His gun was up and ready before they could put their fingers to the triggers.

"Hold it right there, gentlemen," 'Danielson' said.

"And just who the Hell do you think you are?" the larger, and less intelligent of them said.

"United States Army, asshole. On your knees, now." 'Danielson' nodded his head, and his men rapidly advanced from both sides towards the door. Both dropped, although the larger of them needed some persuasion from one of the troops. Both were then dragged to the east, out of direct view of the doorway, where soldiers were now flanking the door, trying to avoid being seen by anyone inside. I immediately recognized one of them as Annie Ross, the daughter of two of my school classmates. I hadn't seen her since the food collection, back in February. She was all business now.

"Mr. Drummond, come with me if you would. Ross, Anderson, Mitchell, Wilson. On me."

"Sir," they replied.

"All right, dirtbags," 'Danielson' said to the prone figures, both with rifle barrels in their necks and boots on their backs, and by now efficiently wire-tied, "let's hear about who's inside."

"Commissioners are on the main floor or second floor. They got heat and clean air. Four security each. All on the main floor," the larger of them said. He had wet himself in the excitement, and had the unfortunate positioning to have his head lower than his groin, pressed into the now wet pavement.

"Who else?"

"I dunno. Maybe a dozen others. No other security."

"Where's the rest of your 'security?'" 'Danielson' asked sarcastically.

"South hill. Mop up down at Manito Country Club."

"Mop up? We'll talk about that later."

"Able Team, ready," 'Danielson' told his troops. "Drummond, hold here," he said, not looking at me as his troops were in position to enter the building.

By this time there were more than a hundred people in the parking lot, with many more behind them, patiently waiting, but all of us were in a field of fire. 'Danielson' strode towards the door either bravely or foolishly, and was almost in lethal range when the shotgun blast tore into the inner vestibule doors. The doors and windows in this building, as in the EOC, were blast and bullet resistant. 'Danielson' quickly moved to cover.

I'm sure I jumped back a bit. The crowd might've as well, but we were all still standing there.

Danielson yelled to the door, "We can do this the hard way, or we can do this the easy way. You've got five seconds before we do it the hard way."

Eleven seconds passed. I heard a distinct 'ka-whump' from the south side of the building, obviously we were a distraction and the main force was entering the building from the south. The flash-bang I'm sure, inside that building, was going to result in a lot of headaches. Hopefully the innocent among the population were far enough away from the entries to avoid much injury. Automatic weapons fire, and shotgun blasts, echoed from inside the building.

"Team, Go!" 'Danielson's' troops quickly moved into the north entry, to be met by the troops from the other side.

"Report," I heard 'Danielson' say.

"Six down on the main floor, all shooters. At least two holed up in the upper floors. They were shooting at us from the stair tower," one of the 'south' troops called out.

"Clear the main floor out this door. Hold the occupants in that bike cage over there," 'Danielson' ordered. The 'bike cage' was an eight-foot tall chain link box that the building employees used to secure their (expensive) bikes. "Search 'em after that. You find Markweather or Williams, you hold them for me."

"Yes, sir," the soldier replied, entering the building again with weapon ready, eyes scanning. Shots were still ringing out from the inside.

"Mr. Drummond, if you would be so kind as to step over here, please," Annie said.

"Nice to see you Annie. Nice work there."

"Thanks. We've been waiting for a chance like this."

Our conversation was stilled as another flash-bang went off on what I thought was the third floor. Another round of automatic weapons fire, and the shooting stopped.

A sergeant (nice to see someone wearing rank, I thought) hustled fifteen people out in a group, followed by a second smaller group. Most looked as if they hadn't slept in a week. I recognized two, Walt Ackerman, the County's chief financial officer, looked as if he'd been roughed up. Jake something-or-other, I couldn't remember, was in the Engineering department. The remaining 'staff', although wearing their County I.D. badges, I didn't know.

I was, as I suspect many others behind me, bewildered. We wanted to push the issue, be proactive, and ensure that at least within legal means, we would keep our property. Those on the other side of the table didn't care about the legal side though, ignoring their sworn oaths, and took advantage rather than offering needed leadership. The question now remained, What Was Next?

Several hundred folks had filtered in behind our group, now filling the vacated street north of the building, and stretching west to fill the lawn area between the Courthouse and Public Works. Most stood quietly and watched, waiting for whatever was next. Nearly all had masks or scarves of some kind over their noses and mouths, to help filter out the dust and ash. One guy had a full-face respirator. I was a little envious.

A single shot was heard within the building, and a few minutes later, 'Danielson' re-appeared.

"Mr. Ackerman," 'Danielson' said. "With me please. Mr. Drummond as well, please."

"What's going on, Rick?" Joe asked.

"I don't know, Joe. I'm thinking we're down to one commissioner, though. That last shot…"

"Yeah. You go find out now," Joe said in his hurried Italian accent.

I walked up to the door, where the grey pallor of Walt Ackerman met me at the door of the bike cage, guarded by four of 'Danielson's' men, their weapons ready for any moves by the captives inside the cage. None moved, most were cowering in the far corner. They all looked awful.

"Walt, you look like Hell," I said.

"And I feel like Hell too, Rick," he said, averting his eyes from both the crowd and me.

"Ross, make the announcement when we get inside please," 'Danielson' said to Annie.

"What announcement?" I asked.

"The commissioners are out of power. We're putting a new civilian authority in charge today. You two get to help put it in place."

"Why me?" Walt asked.

"Because according to my sources, who've been on the inside during all of this sh•t, you are one of two people on the inside in a leadership role that actually tried to do the right thing. Drummond, because he seems to have a clue as to what's coming our way. A couple more folks are being brought in from the crowd to help out too."

"This beats all," I said as we walked inside. I heard Annie begin her announcement over a bullhorn that showed up from nowhere. Within a moment, loud cheers resounded outside the building.

"Strength in numbers. I figured that even the Commissioners wouldn't be so stupid as to shoot on a crowd this big, especially armed. Turned out to be serendipitous when you conveniently had us eliminate a sizeable portion of their thugs."

We paused for a minute inside the main building and hand a chance to look around. Gun smoke was still thick in the air, and acrid in our lungs. Two soldiers were bagging up four bodies in the main entry hall, which soared the four stories to the roof. Several of the large windows, facing west, had been broken and replaced with non-tinted glass. Nice to see that the seat of power in the County was so important to the former leaders. Or maybe they just wanted to keep warm.

"With me," 'Danielson' said.

We headed up the open, circular staircase, past the first-floor 'planning and building' offices, up to the second floor. Through the open doors, and to the left, we went into a large conference room that I'd presented projects to the Planning Commission in former days. It had been converted to a private office, and I noticed that dark mahogany furnishings and a side bar had been added. I assumed that one of the surviving commissioners had taken over the space, which held a commanding view of the downtown area. Today, the view was grey and fog-like, with the blowing dust and ash.

On the floor, behind the desk lay the body of Commissioner Markweather, his hand still holding a plated revolver. Blood from his head wound was staining the tan carpet, and a window was ruined by the bullet he'd shot through his mouth, apparently exiting at the back of his head.

"There's one," 'Danielson' said. "Williams is in here," he said as we entered and adjoining office, once an employee break-room. It also had the best view in the entire building, and was now furnished with the best furnishings in the City. Looted, I was sure, from the residences of the wealthiest. Williams was face down on the ground, a boot to his neck and a rifle muzzle to his temple. His hands and feet were bound with plastic ties, shackle-style.

"Good morning, Commissioner," said 'Danielson'.

"You sonofabitch. I'll get you for this!" he spat.

"You sir, are relieved of your office. Mr. Ackerman will be assuming the position of County Executive until proper elections can be held. Mr. Rick Drummond, Mr. Andrew Simons, Mr. Cletus McKinnon, Mrs. Stacey Womack and Mrs. Tonya Lincoln will be serving as advisors to Mr. Ackerman on the reconstruction of this County's governmental operations and resettlement. You will be assisting them I'm sure, after your trial and your sentence to life at hard labor."

"I've done nothing....."

"You have directly ordered the murders of law enforcement officers and military personnel. You released prisoners to serve as your personal henchmen and armed them with County-owned weapons. You stole and looted for your personal gain and disregarded the public at large who remain in great need. You ordered the contamination of water sources in areas that were unfriendly towards your domination. You have deliberately hindered the recovery effort in this county and the surrounding counties. You have tried and succeeded to loot recovery food shipments again for your personal gain. Save your excuses for your trial, which will be short and sweet. Your military tribunal will be the first thing that I attend to when the Forty-First Division arrives."

"You and your little piss-ant Army? What do you have, fifty men? I have more than that at my house."

"You might...if it were indeed your house, which it is not. When word spreads that you're out of power, I think your influence over those men will drop significantly. Cooper, get this sack of sh•t out of my sight. Seems to me there's a jail nearby with his name on a cell door."

"Sir!" 'Cooper' replied, hauling Williams to his feet.

"You ready to get to work?" 'Danielson' said to Walt and I.

"And where are we supposed to start?" I asked. Walt was still in shock.

"Come meet your fellow Recovery Board members. They should be downstairs about now."

"Mind if I head up to the roof? I need to check in with my wife. Radio reception should work from there, I hope."

"Sure. Gun crew said it's clear all the way up. I'll tag along. Mr. Ackerman, you can head downstairs. Ross will introduce you around." Walt walked off silently. I thought it would be a miracle if he survived long, looking the way he did.

“Fifty men?” I asked.

“Fifty-six,” ‘Danielson’ replied. “The airborne guys don’t count.”

“And how many of them are there?”

“Twelve, including maintenance crew.”

“And that’s your entire force?”

“That is the entire military force under my command in the County. That is, the entire force that we’re able to field. We have twenty-four wounded at the hospital at Fairchild. The Air Force has a small guard contingent out there keeping an eye on things, but since there are no active operations going on out there anymore, there isn’t much left to guard. There are however, a sizeable number of former servicemen who have been of great resource to us throughout the region. One of them was ‘inside’ here. He wasn’t here today. ‘Out sick.’”

“No small wonder you needed a crowd. Where the heck did everyone else go? There were thousands of Guardsmen and Marines….”

“Pulled out quietly and sent south. Mexico wasn’t as easy or as quick a walkover as they say it was.”

“Neither was Iraq.”

“Yep.”

17

Wednesday morning,
April Twelfth

"I'm fine. It's over," I told Karen on the FRS, barely able to make her voice out.

"What happened?"

"Unexpected events. Don't worry about me."

"Easy for you to say," she said.

"I know. I love you most though."

"Come home soon."

"As soon as I can. There's some business we need to attend to."

"Check in later then. We'll be listening."

"K. Talk to you soon. Bye."

"Bye."

We'd used a frequency we'd never used for this type of transmission, and didn't use any names, code or otherwise. If someone was listening, there wasn't a whole lot of information gained from it. The chatter on the FRS was usually pretty thick. Today was no different.

The dust storm up on the roof was every bit as bad as it was down on the ground. Visibility was less than a hundred yards in any direction. The ash burned my eyes, the same as St. Helen's did back in May of Nineteen-Eighty.

'Danielson' and I headed back downstairs. We were to meet briefly with the rest of the newly appointed 'Recovery Board', and then head over to the

Spokane Arena, where we used to watch our mostly-Canadian Spokane Chiefs hockey team play. The rest of the small army that came with us in our property-tax protest were already heading over there, to get inside and out of the blowing ash.

"Sir, you're gonna wanna see this," Cooper said to 'Danielson.'

"Whatcha got, Coop?"

"Williams has blood on his hand and his sleeve. And he's not bleeding. Looks like gunshot residue on his shirt, too."

"Well, in addition to everything else, he probably shot Markweather," 'Danielson said.

"And you sound surprised?" I said.

"I shouldn't be. I've seen too much already. Go on to the first-floor conference room and get introduced. I'm going to visit Williams for a minute before he heads over to his cell. Amberson's down shuttling the rest of your crowd over to the Arena. We'll be over there in fifteen minutes and get to business."

"You sound like you've got an agenda for today."

"I did. My part's about done in this part of town. It's up to you and Mr. Ackerman and the rest of your fellow Recovery Board members to figure out what's next."

"Thanks. I guess."

"Don't thank me yet. Your work is just beginning."

I hurried downstairs to the Planning Department conference room (appropriate enough), passing two young soldiers who were finishing up bagging the commissioner's 'security' team.

Walt Ackerman was starting introductions as I walked in.

"Good morning, everyone. There is honest to God coffee over there, and some orange rolls from the Spokane Club. I'm Walt Ackerman. In a former life I served the County as the chief financial officer. For the past several months, I've been charged with looting the resources of the county at the behest of the Commissioners," Walt said emotionally.

Before anyone could say anything, I responded. "Walt, welcome back to the land of the living."

"Thanks, Mr. Drummond."

"I'm Rick Drummond, everyone," I said for the benefit of those I didn't know, which was pretty much everybody.

A stately black woman responded, "We know who you are, Mr. Drummond. You are one reason that we're here today."

"Me?" I asked, sounding a little stupid.

"Yes, sir. You seem to have inspired us to stand up for our rights," she said. "I'm Tonya Lincoln."

"Nice to meet you."

"These are the rest of our Board Members," Tonya motioned, "Mrs. Stacey Womack from Colbert; Mr. Andrew Simons from Cheney; Mr. Cletus McKinnon from Liberty Lake; I live up on the South Hill, on Glenrose." I nodded to each and smiled. Shaking hands still wasn't 'back' as a custom.

"Anyone here from the City?"

"No, the City of Spokane has...or will have their own Recovery Board," Tonya replied.

"You seem to be well-versed in what we're doing here. I'm thinking that you ought to be Chair," Mr. Simons stated to Ms. Lincoln.

"Walt, are you parliamentarian here?" I asked.

"I sure can be. Let's have a seat. We've got to get over to the Arena in a few minutes."

I could not believe the change in Walt within the past half-hour. His pallor was not quite so grey, and his attitude had improved markedly. His late-fifties physique, which could only be called 'rotund', now seemed to have more stature and, well, less width.

We went through some additional introductory conversation, to learn a bit more about each other. Tonya Lincoln, originally from South Carolina, was until the Domino the owner and chef at a trendy South Hill restaurant, after working for twenty years around the world as a civilian employee of the Air Force. After three ulcers, she decided to do what she loved, rather than what she was merely good at. I knew the restaurant, and although I hadn't met her, I'd certainly enjoyed her cooking.

Cletus McKinnon, 'Clete', appeared to be in his early fifties, and worked as a floor manager for Kaiser Aluminum, formerly a major employer in the Valley. He lived in the hills above Liberty Lake, east of Spokane near the Idaho border, and by all appearances, was as a hard-core a survivalist as you could imagine. I was amazed that he was in as good a physical condition as he was.

Andrew Simons, 'Drew' to his friends, was a retired professor living outside of Cheney, home of Eastern Washington University. Now working the family farm that his great-grandparents homesteaded, his career in ecology, biology and earth sciences was being put to practical use. He was also more than a casual hobbyist in old-world farming, with Belgian draft-horses who annually put on a show at the Cheney Rodeo on plowing, harvesting, and hauling with the massive horses.

Stacey Womack was a very pleasant, and very pregnant thirty-something; this child would be her second. About five-foot five, her flaming red hair reminded me of my ancestral Irish forebears. She and her parents owned two farms in the Colbert and Chattaroy areas, in the north end of the County. Her husband Dane was lost due to a ruptured appendix the first week of February. No medical facilities were available to treat him. He was only thirty-four. Together, they ran a small tourist-farm shop. Now, it was back to straight farming and working the small family dairy.

"OK. So now that you know a little about each other, we need to get moving," 'Danielson' said.

"We haven't elected anyone chair," I said.

"Time for that later. Besides that, Recognize that being 'chair' will not necessarily make you a popular person. Let's go, if you would."

"OK, meeting adjourned." Walt said.

"So what's happened with Commissioner Williams?" Walt asked 'Danielson.'

"He murdered Commissioner Markweather, and set it up to look like a suicide. One of the folks in the cage outside heard the whole thing."

"Good God," Walt said. "I've known him for fifteen years."

"We'll talk later. We have an audience waiting. Get your coffee and let's go."

We quickly refilled our coffee cups with what seemed to be a Starbucks blend, and hurried over to the Arena, two blocks north and east. We covered our coffee cups to try to keep the dust out. Futile, but we did it anyway.

Entering the Arena through the service connection between the former sales offices and the building (both now void of glass), we passed from the darkened hallways near the team rooms to a barely-lit hockey floor, ice long-gone, although the painted markings were still in place. A pile of wreckage, probably the center-hung speaker cluster, lay at center-ice. Only part of one bank of utility lighting seemed to be working, giving us almost as much light as the filtered daylight streaming in through the broken windows. Like everything else these days, dust covered everything.

Specialist Ross and several other troops had seated our guests in two sections of the lower seats, centered on the south side in the lighted section of the spacious Arena. Some folding chairs were set up for us on the 'ice.' We took our seats as 'Danielson' asked for quiet.

"Good morning to all of you gathered today," he began. "Many of you know me as 'Corporal Danielson' of the United States Army. The Army part is correct. I am James McCalister from Fort Belvoir, Virginia, on temporary duty to Eastern Washington. I work in Army Intel, and until today, have been working to unseat the Commissioners and oversee the military action against gangs and rampant criminal activity. I apologize for first trying to impersonate a Corporal, and second for any deception that you may have suffered."

A number of people stood, and slowly at first, applause began. Soon, all present were standing and applauding McCalister and his troops. More than a couple of the soldiers were wiping tears away. Captain McCalister hushed the crowd, and called our meeting to order.

"Please stand for the Pledge of Allegiance," he asked.

All eyes found the huge flag on the west end of the building, and renewed our allegiance to our Nation. I realized that it was the first time since the Domino that I'd heard the pledge, or said it. It seemed never more appropriate than then.

Captain McCalister introduced each of us to the thousand or so present, and told the assembly that commencing immediately, our Recovery Board would be tasked with putting a new civilian government in place from the ground up. Progress and notifications of the work of our committee, which seemed huge, would be broadcast on local news stations, as often as practical.

"Why haven't we had any news for the last couple of days, Captain?" 'Clete' asked.

"We arranged to have all broadcast personnel take a few days off. It helped freak out the powers that be, or so we heard. Broadcasts, both local and national when available, will begin today at noon, or as soon as the staffs can be notified."

"When are your reinforcements coming?" the question came from the audience.

"End of the month is our best projection. Forty-First Division is scheduled to be detached to Eastern Washington about then. Last I heard, which was Friday, they were still pretty busy in the Mexican Territory. Busier, I might add, than the media is letting you know about."

"What about the rest of 'em? The Protectors, I mean."

"They're not all dead or captured, yet. From what we heard a little while ago, a significant number of them were on the South Hill near or at Manito Country Club, probably looting or attacking someone who opposed Commissioner Williams. Commissioner Markweather's thugs were eliminated or captured not far from Mr. Drummond's home, while trying to eliminate Mr. Drummond. Let me make a point here. The Protectors are composed of former prisoners of the County Jail, as well as some of the meanest, most psychotic humans on earth. They are ruthless, violent and literally no remorse for anything they do. And as you know or suspect, the United States Army is probably outnumbered at the moment. Not that that bothers us a bit, mind you, we like target-rich environments." That drew a few chuckles from the audience.

"There were, at last report, one hundred and fifty Protectors working for the Commissioners in Spokane, Lincoln, and Stevens County, with additional forces in Kootenai County, mostly in Coeur d'Alene. These people are now leaderless, and will very likely attack any target as they see fit. Nearly all of them are using official police vehicles, and in some cases, they have literally driven right up to their targets and killed them outright. Several City Police and Sheriffs' Deputies were attacked in this manner, as well as three of my own men."

"Great. So how are we supposed to tell the difference?" A voice from far up in the crowd asked.

"Gasoline will tell the tale. Most, if not all of the gasoline in the County and City is under the control of either the 'real' police, the military, or you in this room or people that you know. Gas supplies that were under the control of the

Commissioners will no longer be available to the Protectors. When they're out of gas, they're afoot. And less mobile and less of a threat to the general population. More of a threat to the isolated individual."

"So what's next?" a woman in the front row asked. She could only be described as 'severe' in appearance.

"I'd like to let all you folks get going back home. The Recovery Board's work will begin soon, they'll meet as soon as we're done here and set up a meeting schedule and start to work on an agenda."

"We will?" I asked jokingly. "Good. About time someone did some work around here that doesn't involve manure," I said as I stood up and rubbed my hands together. "No offense, Walt."

"None taken," Walt said as he sat up, straightened his tie, smoothed a single wrinkle in a much-wrinkled suit-coat, and got out a pencil. "Can I trouble you for a legal pad?" he asked a very young soldier standing at ease to his left. The perfect straight man. The room erupted in laughter.

"On that note, we are adjourned," Captain McCalister said. "I would recommend that you return to your homes via the routes you took here today and quickly. The weather is deteriorating as we speak. No sightseeing. Not that you'd see much in the ash, anyway. An address will be made later today to the general population on all available AM stations in the area with the announcement about the change in leadership here in the County. Good day."

A smaller round of applause this time, and then our fellow attendees filtered out, back to their cars. I could imagine the traffic jam that they'd be dealing with. And, I had passengers to bring back home. Joe and Don Pauliano, Aaron and Ellen were about three rows up, watching the proceedings. My other two passengers, the deputies, were having a word with their boss.

"OK," I said taking charge for a minute. "Who else has passengers that we need to get back home, other than me?" Everyone but Walt raised their hands. "All right, then a short meeting that we can ruminate on, and how bout we get together tomorrow morning, down at the Planning Offices?"

Tonya asked for the vote, "All say aye?"

"Aye," everyone said.

"The floor is yours, Mr. Drummond."

"All right, thank you. First thing, name's 'Rick'. Second thing, I move that we postpone 'elections' until tomorrow. I don't know if anyone here knows this, other than Walt, but right after the quake, I met with the Commissioners and proposed what they thought of as a radical tack on recovery. Since that time, I've been on the 'B' list."

"What were your ideas?" Tonya asked, her interest piqued.

"That the settlement patterns fostered by the automobile are unsustainable without gasoline. Basically, anything post nineteen-twenties or so as far as the original development goes. That the expenditure of precious resources to reconstruct infrastructure outside of those areas that remain habitable post-quake would be incredibly wasteful. That everything depends on cheap and abundant gasoline, which now is neither abundant, nor cheap, assuming that we actually had money to work with. That food needs to be produced locally, as does most everything that we're going to need from now on, or at least until we as a country settle into the new reality. And that we have a very limited time to respond to our obvious needs with what limited resources we have at hand, because there is no contingency plan. I personally believe that the rest of the country is about three months behind where we are right now. They will catch up in a hurry though, come winter. These are the things I think we should be thinking about."

I didn't catch them completely flat-footed, but it took awhile for anyone to respond. When they did, Drew Simons' voice carried above the others.

"Walt, is that right? That this information was given to the Commissioners in January for Christ's sake, and they didn't listen? Pretty damned obvious to me," he said, looking to the others. "I can barely get enough fuel to run our tractor to haul the seed drill. And fertilizer isn't to be had for love or money."

"Yes, Mr. Simons, Mr. Drummond's statement is a fair representation of that conversation."

"Four months wasted," Drew said, almost spitting.

"OK. I didn't mean to hijack the meeting, or push my own agenda here, but I wanted everyone to know where I'm coming from. And we do not have time to waste. What is going for us is that because of the quake, we're becoming used to adapting, and that we have the remains of a city that was much larger, population-wise, than it is at present. What is against us is the damage, the increasing shortages of medical supplies, and soon enough, food and fuel. We're also chronically short on labor. I don't know about you folks, but I never planned on raising my kids to be subsistence farmers."

"Let's talk more tomorrow," Clete said.

"Agreed," Said Tonya. "The drive home will almost be by Braille."

"Nine a.m., Unless we can't see to get here," I said.

"Done. See you all tomorrow," Drew said. Besides my passengers, there were a good dozen more folks, clustered together, waiting for us to break up.

"Rick, a minute please," Walt said.

"Sure, Walt," I said as the others met with their friends and filtered out of the gloomy Arena, into an equally gloomy day. "What's up?"

"I wanted to thank you for being the spark that lit the fire. You literally saved my life and the lives of everyone in that building. Their henchmen were to the point of torture to get people to work. Two women who worked there for more than ten years were found raped and murdered down by the Public Health building. Of course, no one had any knowledge of that," he said sarcastically. "Denise just happened to be there. Sheryl rebuffed Commissioner Williams' advances. I'm sure she was killed for it, after those thugs had their way with them."

"Hopefully that is over now."

"Let's pray to God for that to be so. Is there anything that you need before your meeting? I know you've got ideas about putting things back together."

"I don't know about 'back together', I think it's going to end up being 'put right.' And yes, there is," I thought quickly. "GIS department—sorry, Geographic Information Systems department had a pre-packaged set of CD's that had the entire county's database on them, saved in .pdf format as well as the proprietary program. Can you get me a set of those?"

"Sure, I guess. I don't think anyone's set foot in that department since the quake."

"They were in Wally Dretke's office." Wally was the GIS coordinator. "I'll send someone over and check. "I'll be right back," he said as he headed toward a group of former County staff, now freed from the bicycle storage cage. The group was smaller than it had been when we were there earlier. I wondered if some were being treated, fed, or…jailed.

I'd known Walt for the better part of fifteen years off and on, working on various tasks for the County departments that we consulted with or on the 'other' side of the table working with developers on new projects. I knew that he was married, and lived not far from Downtown, in the very old Corbin Park neighborhood. If I remembered, he was married and had a couple of kids.

"Rick, how're you doing?" Mike Amberson asked.

"Better, I guess, although I seem to have stepped into an alternate reality where people think more of me than is actually due."

"Don't underestimate your impact on the community. I've heard that you were the focus of more than a few tirades in the Commissioners meetings. That you were targeted by them, and nearly attacked, was no coincidence."

"I know. Good thing Danielson—er, McCalister was listening," I said, referring to the ambush that we'd help turn against our attackers.

"That? Sure. I'm talking about the other one. Aztlan Posse. That was a Protector operation."

I was silent for a minute. "What did you just say?"

"You heard me right. McCalister just found out about it as well. He thought it was just criminals. He was right on that count, he didn't think that they had sponsorship and logistical information provided by the County. They tapped into our secure channels and heard every move we made. Williams was taking a cut from their operation. Markweather found out about it this morning as you and the general public was moving in toward the Public Works building. They had an argument and Williams popped Markweather. Then of course tried to make it look like a suicide."

I didn't have anything to say.

"You are damned lucky, Rick," he said. "Or more properly, well blessed."

"I am at that," I said quietly. "How're you doing? It's been a while since we could talk much."

"Doing OK. Getting these bastards out of office will allow us to sleep better. We need more officers though. Too much ground to cover and not enough men."

"Beat cops."

"Huh?"

"Beat cops. You'll need to re-think your patrol strategy. In the old days you had precincts that were responsible for certain areas, and the cops in those precincts lived there. That's going to come back, whether we want it to or not."

"Still leaves the issue of the larger county. We have a lot of roads to cover."

"We'll get to work on that," I said. "Are you going to be at the Recovery Board meeting tomorrow?"

"Probably not tomorrow. We need to get the rest of the Protectors taken care of. The Captain and I have some work to do in that area. We're not out of the woods yet."

"Drop by or let me know when you can come to a meeting. Essential services are pretty high on the list of things that we need to address. If not the highest."

"That's nice to hear. Sure as Hell haven't heard that in *this* neighborhood lately. Take care."

"You, too."

"Don't worry about the deputies getting back out to the Valley. They'll take a couple of our cars out there. Two of the cars will be parked at the barter store. Permanent-like."

"Thanks," I said as a very thin twenty-something young man stood patiently waiting for us to wrap up our conversation.

"Mr. Drummond?" he asked quietly.

"Yes?"

"Mr. Ackerman asked me to deliver these to you. He was called away and could not return."

"Thank you. You are?"

"Brandon Yake. I was interning in the Planning Department before the quake."

"Good to have you around. We'll keep you busy, fairly soon," I said. He perked up at that.

"Thank you. It's been....difficult the past couple of months."

"That may be the understatement of the day. Will you be in the office tomorrow?"

"Yes, sir," he paused for a moment. "Actually, I've been living there."

"On purpose?" I asked jokingly.

"No. More like 'prisoner'."

"I'm sure that will change effective immediately. Where did you live before?"

"Apartment, over in West Central. Burned three days in. I've been at the office in the emergency shelter ever since."

"One more thing we'll talk about tomorrow. For today, pass this on to Walt if you would: Close up shop, get out of the office, sleep and rest up. We will need all of the staff we can muster, and we need them sharp."

"Yes, sir, Mr. Drummond. I'll see you in the morning."

"Will do. Thanks again for the discs."

"Oh! I almost forgot your pass," he said as he reached in his rumpled sports coat. "You'll need this. This is the Sheriff's new Universal Access Pass for your car. It'll let you go through roadblocks without searches. Assuming roadblocks and checkpoints might come back that is. It'll at least let you find a place to park," he said with a slight grin. "Like there are a lot of cars on the roads these days."

"Thanks. See ya."

Brandon turned and headed out the service door that we'd entered through as Joe hollered over to me.

"You done yet? Good Christ you can talk!" Joe said loudly, with pretended frustration.

"On my way!"

We headed back outside after covering our mouths and noses with scarves and masks. Joe and Don both pulled out industrial-type dust masks, and Aaron and Ellen held a couple of lighter-duty dust masks against their faces. I noticed that Aaron also had on some clear goggles. Ellen was using some clear safety glasses. I was stuck with my sunglasses, which were more than useless. My safety-goggles were in the car.

"Thick as fog out there," Don said. "Good thing Lorene and I planned on staying over."

"We ready?" I asked as I tucked the laminated parking tag in my pocket, along with the CD case.

"Yeah," Aaron said. "This'll be interesting."

The ash and dust was far heavier than it had been just an hour before, and there were even some operating street lights that had come on, at nearly mid-day. A thinning stream of cars threaded their ways back to their destinations, at no more than five to ten miles per hour. We were thirty feet from the Expedition before we were able to see it. The buffeting winds were blowing at perhaps thirty miles-per hour, with gusts much higher. I wondered again about our light-duty greenhouse, and how it would perform. Thank God we had the windows in the house sealed up with either salvaged glass or oriented strand-board and duct tape. Several of our Valley-bound neighbors were in their cars, waiting for us to lead the way. 'Thanks for that,' I thought. I was hoping to follow someone else!

I unlocked the car with the remote, and let the rear-seat passengers get in before I opened up the front. Don sat up with me, and Joe, Aaron and Ellen in the middle seats. Finally, we were out of the dust.

"Jesus. I've never seen anything like it before," Don said.

"Me either," I said as I started up the SUV. I was definitely going to have to clean out the air filter after this trip. I hoped that all those behind me were traveling with clean filters—when St. Helen's went up in nineteen-eighty, more than a few cars stalled due to clogged air filters. Those that ran without filters soon found out that their engines were ruined from the gritty ash sucked into the combustion chambers. I remember that I used both the 'stock' Fram filter on my old Falcon, as well as a series of feminine sanitary pads used as filters over the intake. Worked like a charm. (I did get a number of odd looks from the cashier in Pullman, when I walked out with a case of Budweiser and four boxes of pads....)

"We need to make sure we don't lose anyone behind us. Gimme a minute and I'll be right back," I said as I put on my goggles.

I went back to the line of cars behind me, on the downwind side so that the ash wouldn't be quite so thick while we talked, and told each car of the ten behind us, that we needed to make sure the car behind us was still there. If anyone stalled, it might be a long night before anyone came along. Anyone friendly, that is.

Back in the Ford, I took a long drink from one of the water bottles stashed in the console. "There's more here and under your seats, and Karen made some sandwiches. Don't be shy," I told everyone. I was pleased to see that no one was. Ellen dabbed her face with water and a well-worn, but clean handkerchief, which after a moment was a dirty grey.

"OK, here we go," I said as I started the Ford up and turned on the emergency flashers. Each car behind us did the same. I could see the second car, not the third. With luck, we might not lose anyone. If anyone disappeared from our rear view mirrors, the driver ahead was to flash his high beams and slow down. I hoped that the signal would work. I know that I wouldn't want to be stranded miles from home in that kind of dust.

We moved down to the end of the block and made a wide u-turn, and headed back home.

I tried to raise Karen on the FRS, but got no response. No small wonder with the terrain and the buildings around us. I knew she'd be worried about us. Next I tried the hand-held CB radio, which was plumbed into a magnetic-mount antenna on the roof.

"Broadwater, you there?" I asked into the radio, before repeating it.

"Here," Libby's voice responded. "Didn't expect you on this band."

"Other one's not cutting it. We're on our way back. This storm is way-ugly. It is going to take some time."

"Understood. Any ETA?"

"Not even a guess. I have a full tank, that's about all I can say."

"I'll pass it on to interested parties."

"We'll be checking in on the hour or so. Radio's on, we'll move to Zulu at the prescribed time."

"Agreed. Watch yourself there, sir."

"I'm all over that. Out."

"Out."

"What's 'Zulu'?" Don asked.

"Today, Zulu is channel thirty. If anyone wants to track us, we move frequencies around per a schedule. The casual listener it can frustrate. Someone with a CB scanner will pick right up on it. We haven't had a problem…other than the people with access to official police scanners monitoring us."

"How did they get those?!" Aaron asked.

"The Commissioners gave them to them," I told them as I related the information that I'd been provided, checking my mirrors every few seconds as we threaded our way out of the downtown area.

Turning east on Trent again, we met a roadblock and were asked to stop. Thankfully we weren't rear-ended. A City of Spokane police officer came up to my window. I fished out my pass, to see if it really worked.

I rolled my window down and the officer, who I at first thought was a guy, spoke. "You're not headed east, are you?" she asked.

"Yes. Is that a problem?"

"Got any room for a passenger?"

"Sure. Room for two. Cars behind us might have more."

"Just one. Me. My partner's staying in the unit. I was hoping to get to the Community College."

"That, or the EOC?"

"EOC actually."

"Climb in. We're going right by there."

"Great. Thanks."

She waved to her partner in the car, who was all but invisible, and came running back to the passenger side, front. Don had moved to the back seat, behind Aaron, Ellen and his father. The wind gust helped close the door for her. I noticed she was wearing twin nine-millimeter side arms, as well as a too-short-to-be-legal sawed-off twelve gauge in a custom holster. With the body armor, boots and helmet, accessorized by the dust mask and goggles, it was easy to see why at first I mistook her as a man.

177

"Thanks a lot for this. We've been having problems keeping our posts and getting shift-changes taken care of without leaving holes all over the place."

"I know exactly what you mean. I'm Rick Drummond," I said, and introduced everyone else in the car.

"Penny Jacobson. Nice to meet you all."

"What's your job at the EOC? I thought it was contaminated by the train wreck."

"Dispatch. I used to work in the nine-one-one center downtown, and then transferred over to patrol duty when I graduated from the Academy. Back to my old job. The contamination in Dispatch has been cleaned up. The offices aren't though."

"Good thing you weren't there for the Domino. Lotta folks killed that night," I recalled.

"Good folks too. My old boss and half of my old shift."

"That's quite the shotgun you've got there," I commented.

"Certainly not ATF approved, but we're all using them pretty regularly. Dog packs don't give you much warning. Some of the people left don't either."

"Yeah. Welcome to the bright, new future."

She smiled. "You sound just like my partner. You a cop? I see you've got the purple pass."

"Nope. Just an ordinary guy."

"Not if you've got one of those, you're not."

"County Recovery Board. Just appointed."

"You're him."

"'Him, who?"

"The guy that got the County leadership to cave. We've been talking about it all morning. You set up the Protectors for an ambush."

"I think they did that all by themselves. I was just there for the assist."

"Well if you want to volunteer to take care of the second unit, you let me know."

"Those are the ones up at Manito?"

"Yeah," she said warily. "How did you know that?"

"I was there when McCalister found out."

"Who's McCalister?"

"You might know him as 'Danielson.' Poses as Corporal. Actually a Captain with Army Intelligence."

"We knew he wasn't who he said he was."

"Now you know for sure."

"He and his unit are moving up the hill right now. They've got half of our force with them."

"Showtime, then. If fortune favors the foolish, then the Protectors won't know what's coming."

"Keep thinking that," Penny said. "May I have one of those waters?"

"You may. Cold ones are in the bottom."

"Awesome," she said as she dug one out.

18

1:30 pm,
Wednesday, April Twelfth

Top speed was just over five miles per hour. We were averaging much less than that, most of the time rolling at idle. That need was generated by both the safe following distance and as fast as I felt I could go, seeing just feet in front of the bumper.

Aaron and Penny hit it right off, with his ham radio background and her job as dispatcher. At eighteen, she'd gained her Novice Class license, and then rapidly progressed to the Advanced Class. Aaron seemed impressed, as they talked about Aaron's 'rig'. Penny's equipment was lost in the quake. They were surprised that they hadn't met during the ham-fest swap meets around town. Ellen's late husband was also involved in broadcasting, but on the commercial side. I was glad they all had something to talk about. Joe and Don were discussing their plans and needs for Don's farm and more work at Joe and Joan's home. I was merely gripping the steering wheel with white knuckles, and hoping that I wouldn't hit anything on the way home. So far, I'd only (almost) missed a turn once. This, on roads that I'd driven every day for twenty years.

Coming up to one of the smaller cross-streets near Greene Street, the western edge of the Spokane Community College campus, we met another 'checkpoint', this time set up by the State Patrol. The Trooper was in the 'police' version of my Expedition, strobes and flashing lights going. I was amazed that anyone would be out in this kind of storm, other than us idiots. I pulled up slowly as he motioned us to stop, and rolled my drivers' window down—fortunately on the lee side. The trooper had a full-face mask on, similar to a chemical mask, with a belt-mounted filter. It was a little tough hearing him through the mask.

"Good afternoon," I said. My 'pass' was visible, barely, on the dash. I noticed the Trooper looked over at my front-seat passenger.

"Afternoon. Nothing good about it. Where you headed?"

"East of Argonne. Got a row of folks behind us. I'm dropping this young lady off at the EOC on the way."

"OK, just a warning. The train wreck up ahead's being cleared, one lane road, twenty-minute delay probably. This storm came up about halfway done, and we're diverting you down to Mission, then back to Trent. You can get right to the EOC though on this side of the wreck."

"Any other problems out east?"

"Nope, not that I know of. There's no one out today, small wonder," he said.

"Need any water? Got a spare bottle," I asked.

"You bet. That'd be great."

Penny fished one out from the console and I handed it to the Trooper, and we slowly turned left to head north up to Mission and then right. Within a few hundred yards, we were stopped by cones in the road. I could almost make out a crane mounted on a railcar, and a dozen or so workers struggling to work in the dust. I shut off the car, and decided to go back and tell the others behind me what was going on. If we were held up, there was no good reason to run the engines with this dust and ash. That took about ten minutes. Once I was done with that chore, I started the Ford back up, turned left and headed the hundred or so yards to the Emergency Operations Center, past the remains of Fire Station 8 and the City's Fire Training Center. The 'retired' or 'surplus' fire engines were stored here as well, all burned to the pavement, I assumed because of the train wreck.

"Not too fast. There's a jersey barrier up ahead, with a machine gun behind it."

"Pity the poor bastard who's running that today," Joe said.

"No kidding."

We soon came up to the barrier, as Officer Jacobson put her mask back on. "Thanks again for the lift."

"Anytime. Stay safe."

"That's one of two things I do really well," she said. I could tell she was smiling under the mask. The big door slammed closed as a gust of wind caught it. She was invisible after four seconds of walking.

"That young lady is a world-class flirt," Ellen said.

"Good for her," Aaron said. "Probably helps to keep her sane. I can't imagine what it's like to be a cop these days."

"OK, Don, if you can look out the back for me, make sure I don't do something stupid like plow into a rock, I'll try to turn this thing around," I said. I had literally no reference points behind me, and I knew there was a series of big boulders, of course grey in color, off to my left. After much maneuvering, I was able to get turned around. The crane was still working when we got back to our caravan, and took our place as lead again. I decided to check in again with 'home.'

"Broadwater," I spoke into the radio. The 'Broadwater' was the name of a resort outside of Helena, Montana in the late years of the eighteen-hundreds. It's famous natatorium, fed by natural hot springs, was closed after an earthquake in nineteen thirty-five irreparably damaged the magnificent building. It fell into decline and was eventually torn down in the forties. I had a lithograph of the original resort at home.

"Broadwater here," Karen said. "Where are you?"

"Not far from Cathy's office." Cathy was a friend of ours who worked at the college. We hadn't seen or heard from her since the quake though. She used to live in one of the newly converted residential lofts downtown.

"Then you've got a long way to go."

"Yep."

"Everyone OK?"

"Fine, I think everyone could use a nice walk after sitting here so long though."

"Not in this stuff you don't."

"I know. I'll check in later. Remember, radio's on."

"K. Out."

"Out."

I shut off the engine again and sat there, relaxing for a minute. The AM radio, tuned to 920 AM, KLXY, but receiving nothing but static, suddenly came back to life.

"This is KLXY 920 AM Spokane, resuming broadcasting. It is now two-twenty p.m. A severe weather system over the area has forced the closure of all public facilities including shelters, utilities and all open businesses and gathering places. A mandatory road closure has been in effect since twelve-noon today, and will continue until this storm passes, currently estimated to be tomorrow evening. Wind-blown dust from the Columbia Basin and points west have affected the entire Spokane region, as well as areas as far north as Bonners Ferry, Idaho, and reaching as far south as Clarkston Washington. The dust has also closed public facilities throughout North Idaho, and is affecting western Montana as well."

"In other news, we have reports of military activity west of Manito Country Club along High Drive apparently taking place at this time, between law-enforcement and military units against heavily-armed escaped prisoners from Pine Lodge Correctional Facility and the Spokane County Jail, apparently in a running battle through the Manito Ridge neighborhood and the adjacent Quail Hollow area. If you are in this area, please take shelter in a basement or wherever you can. Reports of heavy machine-gun fire in the area have come in on various civilian radio frequencies."

"In news from the Southeastern U.S., telephone service in the Southeastern states was disrupted today and remains inoperative, due to a reported shortage of switching devices in one of the main telephone centers in Atlanta. Replacement parts for the system, originally manufactured in Communist China, have been unavailable since the war in February. Bell South, the major telecom provider in the area, lost one of its major facilities in rioting in past days, along with significant damage to Georgia Power. Also from Georgia, the default of both the Southern Company and Georgia Natural Gas has left energy supplies throughout that region in a shambles, with massive ripple effects throughout the struggling economy in a dozen states."

"In other news, clamp-downs on 'civil unrest'--as local government spokesmen call it-- in major Northeastern and Rust-Belt cities has reportedly been heightened, but local reports of major urban battles and extensive civilian casualties cannot be confirmed due to communications problems in the area. Much of the recent unrest is being attributed to intermittent disruptions in electrical power in the areas, apparently by vandals. The riots of course began following the complete cessation of Federally funded public-assistance programs throughout the nation, and have continued in one form or another since early in the year. The situation continues to fester and with increasing summer-like temperatures and aggravated by sporadic utility failures, authorities believe that the future holds more violence rather than less. The continuing decline in the ability of local authorities to respond to the situation seems to have stopped, however in some cities, as those authorities finally quit asking for Federal

*assistance and taking matters into their own hands. Federal officials have been
stating this very thing for a number of weeks now."*

*"From near Memphis, Tennessee, a reporter in Crittenden County,
Arkansas reports that massive riots in Shelby County have been stopped only by
sealing off those areas from adjacent Desoto and Fayette Counties, with some of
the rioters escaping into predominantly white areas. Many of these areas are
exhibiting all of the worst examples of race riots from the nineteen-sixties. The
Federal Government has dispatched a very limited amount of military assets to
the affected cities, more to contain than to quell the violence. The President
today again asked for prayers for the country, and urged the states again to act
'as needed' to restore order."*

*"In manufacturing news this morning, representatives from major tool-and-
die firms announced that expansions in tooling for domestic manufacturing had
increased by twelve-hundred percent, after the loss of similar facilities in Asia
due to the war. Industry insiders state however, that this number is much
inflated, with only a half-dozen new plants planned or under construction at this
time. Part of the problem, insiders say, is that the equipment to build the plants,
including the steel and the steel mills themselves, simply no longer exist and
must be rebuilt from scratch to provide the raw materials for the tooling plants."*

*"Agricultural producers, including the super giant Agnew Middleton
conglomerate, have stated that the reorganization of their domestic operations
will take at least twenty-four months, assuming that natural gas and petroleum
supplies return to pre-Depression levels this year. The loss of the majority of the
firms' fertilizer supplies, all imported, and the extreme shortages of
petrochemicals in general have cut the nations' commercially –grown grain
supplies to a fraction of their previous yields. This news has sparked runs on
grain supplies across North America, with two major grain facilities in the
Midwest posting large armed forces to keep last years' harvest safe."*

"This is KLXY, Spokane. You know Jim," the newsreader said to his partner,
"You have to wonder if there's enough food to feed the nation."

His partner replied, *"Might be a lean winter."*

"Amen to that, I said under my breath, as the wrecked train was finally
cleared. A trainman waved us through the wreck site. Back to the crawl.

Two more hours of crawling along, and one missed turn, and we were back
at the community center, which was actually open. The dust had lessened a bit
by then, providing almost a hundred yards of visibility now. We were able to
drop off Aaron and Ellen at their homes, and then the Pauliano's at Joe's place.

Finally just before five p.m., I was home. Six hours for what used to take me twenty minutes.

I was greeted by Karen in the tool-room of the barn with a bathrobe. My clothing was covered with ash and dust after being out in it several times during the day, and she didn't want me to have to traipse over to anyone else's house to get cleaned up. The tool room itself was an example of why: everything was covered with a thin layer of the grey dust.

"Just leave your clothes here," she said. "Here's a washbasin too."

"Will do. How're the dogs with this?"

"Not well. Buck wants out every hour. Ada could care less. They're in the shop and I'm keeping them there, and off of the beds. I've used the shop-vac on them each time they come in. She hates it, he thinks it's a game."

"Nice to see you," I said as I gave her a kiss, almost from a distance.

"You, too. Now get changed and I can do that properly."

"Where're the kids?"

"Over at Alan's for the night. They're playing a marathon of our board games. Last I heard, the little ones had Carl and John down four to one playing Chutes and Ladders."

"What's for dinner?"

"Tomato soup."

"Yum. I'll be right in."

I quickly changed out of my (much dustier than I thought) clothes, and washed what I could in the washbasin Karen brought me. I began to actually feel normal again.

"Hiya, babe," I said as gave Karen a big hug.

"Hi back atcha, love. You look better."

"Feel better too. I didn't think we'd ever get home."

"I was worried. Lots."

"I know, sorry. What'd the kids do all day?"

"Studies for a while after you left, then they watched 'The Day After Tomorrow,' then games. They were worried, too."

"I know," I said. I then spent the next two hours going over my day with Karen and the adults, helping her fold clothes and putting in some 'dog time' with our gritty Golden Retrievers. The Martins and Bauers headed home about eight after my recap. After a cup of mint tea, Karen seemed to settle down.

"Do you think you're going to be able to keep that meeting tomorrow?"

"Entirely up to the weather. If this dust storm keeps up, nope. And I'm OK with that. I'm sure the air filter in the Ford's gotta be plugged pretty bad. We need some rain."

"Not likely. Weather service says next week at the earliest."

"Great. I've still got more ground to plow up, too. Not to mention planting in two weeks or so."

"Yeah. And firewood to get in, and the roof to finish, et cetera."

"Ad infinitum."

"More tea?"

"Sure. I want to upload the CD's from the County onto my Mac. I've got a lot of work to do. I'd like to have some done before our meeting, whenever that is."

"What does that involve? I mean, what work do you need to do?"

"The CD's have the entire county GIS database in them. Maps, raw data, demographics, infrastructure, everything. The information will help guide us on how to remake things. It won't be popular. We'll end up essentially abandoning big chunks of the developed parts of the Valley."

"Why?"

"In economic terms, they're now unaffordable. We have to figure out first what works and what doesn't. Water, power, phones, sewer, major public service functions. What roads are passable. What schools are useable. What commercial areas are viable…meaning close to people to work in them. Ag lands. Where we can grow food. Water wells. Firewood supplies. Establish a transportation network that may or may not include cars. Then it'll be on to salvaging what we can before the weather hurts it anymore than it has already."

"I'm glad you've got it all figured out," she smirked.

"If only."

By 'bedtime', around ten, I'd managed to get all of the information that I thought I'd need loaded up on the computer. I didn't have the raw storage capacity in my workstation that I did on my office server, but I didn't have the server set up yet, either. 'This would work for now,' I thought. 'Dang there's a lot of information here. I wonder how much if it is chaff?'

The ten o'clock news would be the last broadcast tonight, on KLXY and other local stations. More news, mostly bad, from around the country, news of unrest in Quebec, with the fifth night of rioting in a row. A brief and cryptic report about the Syrians threats against Tel Aviv which left me wondering, and the National Anthem before they signed off. I hadn't heard that on a radio station in years.

I dozed off not long after, still hearing the wind.

19

Thursday,
April Thirteenth

Buck woke me up at five, way earlier than he normally did when I wasn't on watch, whining and wanting out, NOW. There was something out there that he wanted after. We still had a good hour or more before sunrise. It was gloomy outside, and the brief glance that I had across the field looked like fog. It turned out to be dust, still.

Buck was at the door to the tool room, which led to the garden to the east, and the chicken shed (and home to our lone dwarf rabbit) to the south. I grabbed my Remington shotgun, now equipped with a small maglight attached to the barrel, after I pulled on some jeans and stepped into my moccasins. Ada was now wanting out too, and Karen was of course roused by the commotion.

"What is up with him? Do I need to get on the radio?"

"Dunno. Let me send 'em out and we'll know," I said as I unlocked the door. "Here we go," I said as I opened the door and the dogs tore out, pushing open the door to the chicken shed, creating quite a commotion along the way.

"Racoon!" Karen said as I followed the dogs. "It just went off across the field!! There's another!"

I looked around the chicken shed and saw at least three hens dead as I called the dogs back. I opened the door to the field and the two raccoons were about fifty feet away. I fired twice, hitting the nearest one. The first one out of the shed, now farther away, was also hit by the pattern. I ran out and finished it off from ten feet away. Both of the 'coons were very thin. I'd never seen one, let alone two, work in the near daylight or just stop running like these two did. The dogs were now at my side, and I had to call them off so they wouldn't pick up the carcasses. The first one I shot...still with it's head intact, its eyes were glassy and almost white, like cataracts. 'They must be all but blind,' I thought.

Alan and Ron both came running, long-guns in hand. Both were hastily dressed. "What the Hell's going on?" Alan yelled as he came through the fence.

"Raccoons in the hen-house," I said. "Look at this one," I pointed to the remains.

"Blind," Ron said, kneeling next to the raccoon. "Not an old one either. Too small to be much more than a year old. Awful thin."

"Other one blind too?"

"Can't tell anymore," I said. "Took its head off. But they both ran out, then kinda stopped. That's how I got them. They're usually a lot faster than these two. Not that I've had any raccoon experience in the last fifteen years. I better get these buried."

"Don't want the pelts?" Alan asked.

"No, absolutely not. You?"

"Just kidding," he said. "Storms not over yet. No travel today. Heard it on the radio at five."

"What were you doing up that early?"

"Morning constitutional," he replied. In former days for Alan, that would've been a trip to the outhouse. No longer for the Bauer family. For us, it still was a trip outside for the necessaries.

"Hope you had reading material," Ron said. "I hope this is enough excitement for one day."

"Yeah. How 'bout you come over about nine. Kids'll be in studies by then I expect."

What's up?" Ron asked.

"I want to pick your collective brains about the recovery."

"Then you better have coffee ready," Ron said. "And maybe some fresh biscuits too…"

"I'll see what I can do. See you in awhile. Go grab a few more winks."

"Indeed," Alan said as he safed his AK and walked off.

After getting the dogs back in the tool room, I took care of the dead hens and raccoons, burying them deeply and piling some of our field rocks on the site. Karen had cleaned up the dogs again for the umpteenth time in two days before I was able to get cleaned up myself.

"So much for sleep," she said as I came back into the shop and stowed the Remington.

"It's overrated anyway," I said with a smile as I kissed her good morning.

"What'd Alan and Ron have to say?" she said as she covered up with a quilt made from blue-jean scraps.

"Not much. I've invited them over later today to pick their brains. They requested coffee and biscuits."

"Well they're out of luck. They'll have to make do with English muffins."

"Been holding out on me?" I said.

"Made them yesterday. Took my mind off my troubles."

"You're a peach," I said as I kissed her.

"That's a well known fact."

Karen snoozed under the quilt, listening to her 'Casting Crowns' CD, a Christian pop band, as I had my first cup of coffee, today a Thomas Hammer blend, and began to study the maps of the County. Only a pound of that coffee left, before we opened up a big can of Folgers or whatever. I'd miss that high-octane stuff, I knew.

I managed for the next couple of hours to get some work done before the business of the day really got going. Working over the various maps, beginning with rail lines and land uses, then the infrastructure of water wells and lines, power distribution and roads, layered-up each one of the maps in my computer program to examine the 'bones' of the urban areas of the county.

I was half-listening to a CNN news broadcast on my headphones. Syria had occupied most of Lebanon overnight, and was supporting the Palestinians in reinforcing Palestinian enclaves in Israel. As if we didn't have enough to worry about. The diplomats seemed to be flailing about, rather like the French leadership when the first wave of attacks came to France. The Israelis' silence was deafening on the matter, which worried the news folk all the more. They viewed, probably correctly, that the Syrian action could only lead to a major war. Our president had had no comment on the situation as of yet. I could imagine what he'd have to say though, something to the effect of 'They'll kick ass and take names, and I suspect they're fresh out of paper.' CNN's coverage was pretty poor, having to piece together the story from other news sources in the region. They no longer had a major presence in the Middle East, they said. I suspected that that was true for a large portion of the world, these days.

As the endless commentary went on, I worked on the premise that rail should be the primary people mover and transport method for goods into and out of the area, first and foremost. Second, that business areas must be located close enough if not adjacent to the transportation backbone. Third, that residential areas and business areas must be integrated. Fourth, that healthy business areas must contain enough of the essential services required by the residents that rail travel, walking travel, or in a worst-case scenario, travel by private car was minimized. Networked into all of this of course were schools, hospitals, fire stations, police stations and post offices.

What I found of course when I began to apply these ideas to the existing conditions were in all cases the opposite of my 'ideal' configuration, which wasn't 'mine' by any means, but merely the reflection of what worked, pre-automobile, throughout most of North America. Residential areas were now strictly defined and limited to specific zones, far away from businesses and manufacturing. Business and manufacturing were almost universally located these days away from rail lines, and along major five to seven-lane streets. Medical offices and hospitals were clustered together in a single area or two. Police stations in the Spokane Valley, consisted of a single 'substation', a branch of the main office downtown. Nearly all small businesses were located along medium and large roads, many as parasites to larger 'anchor' stores. The retail 'blend' or mix of types of retail stores in existence prior to the January Domino quake were heavily weighted with 'non-essential' types of stores, viewed from my present-day. Bird feed stores. Stores specializing in painting fingernails. Hot tub stores. Car-stereo and cell-phone stores. 'Dollar' stores, which even pre-quake, held little that interested me, but at least had variety in their contents. Video stores. Coffee huts.

There was not one single area in the Spokane Valley, the area I was most heavily focused on due to the high level of post-quake residents that resembled the original settlement pattern that formed the majority of my premise for recovery.

For starters, two major, and one minor rail line remained of the original five or six, and the 'minor' line was actually in serious decline due to lack of maintenance and lack of traffic. That line used to serve the southeast corner of Spokane County and northern Whitman County, both to supply those areas with passenger and cargo traffic, and to feed the large grain mills in Spokane with wheat and other crops of the day, from the rich Palouse dryland fields.   The Milwaukee Road line had been pulled up in the seventies, with the right of way at least remaining, if crossed with some public development. The two electric rail lines, designed for efficient passenger traffic in the late eighteen hundreds and in operation until the thirties or forties, when passenger car and municipal bus service ended the operations. I knew that at least some of the original transformer buildings for the electric line were still in place, crumbling red brick structures from Spokane to Colfax, southern Coeur d'Alene Lake, and a few others. A third abandoned line, that used to run just a mile south of our house was pulled up in the fifties, and the right-of-way abandoned and sold off for development.   The Spokane River, meandering generally in the middle to north side of the Valley, was only recently recognized as an amenity, more for rafting and recreation. No commercial use of the river was possible due to the shallow depth and fluctuating water levels, driven by the use of the river as a power-generating resource.

Any of the 'original' settled areas had been so redeveloped since the rail lines were lost or their uses changed, that there were literally no 'mixed use' developments--meaning that you could live within walking distance or 'upstairs' from your office—anywhere in the Valley. There were buildings that could be remodeled, assuming they survived the quake, and there were residential areas near businesses, within walking distance, but the densities required for the businesses to survive were a question. I recognized that any business has to have a certain number of people around it or other businesses, to draw customers, vendors, drive sales, make a profit, expand. The 'linearity' of strip development countered the 'cluster' development of the pre-automobile age. Karen rose, and found me staring at the flat panel display, and had to poke me to get my attention. CNN was still babbling in my ears.

"You sleeping with your eyes open?"

"No, just thinking," I said. Actually, I think I was beginning to realize how depressing my work was, and how depressing things were looking.

"You have that look. The one you get right before you figure out that you can't fix something," she said as she handed me another cup of coffee.

"You're right. I can't fix this. More correctly, there is so much to change that I wonder if it can succeed."

"You know for a fact that it can't though, if you don't do anything, right?"

"Yes, I certainly know that much," still staring at the screen as I pulled down the headphones to rest on my neck.

"Then quit trying to solve all the worlds problems in a day. You can't do it."

"I know, I'm just of the belief that my first shot at something is usually the best."

"It might be. From what you described last night though, this isn't something you can do quickly."

"It's not. But we have to move quickly to make up for lost time. The longer things continue to deteriorate, the harder it is to rebuild."

"Are you talking about buildings, or what? How much more damage can the weather cause that hasn't already happened?"

"I'm talking about buildings only as an accessory. Really I'm talking about re-establishing neighborhoods. Community."

"Then you're out of your depth and you know it. You just are starting to realize that."

"Yep. You're probably right."

"So put that stuff away for awhile and get some breakfast. Here's a muffin for you."

"Thanks."

"Strawberry jam is in the fridge. I'm going to collect eggs."

"Get your mask on. It's nasty outside," I said as I looked out the window. I could now at least see Nate Woolsley's shop to the south of us. A hundred fifty feet of visibility at ten after eight in the morning.

"What's on your list today?"

"Alan and Ron will be over 'round nine, you knew that. I figured I'd spend an hour or two going over my ideas with them on the recovery. We need to get some water on the stuff that's in the ground, and the crops in the greenhouses. I thought the kids could be inside again today. I don't want them out in this stuff. Bad for the lungs at least. No idea what other effects might be. You?"

"I'm going over to help Mary and Libby with the kids today for class, then I think we'll be at Libby's working on the house. They're almost done getting it fixed up. If you have time after that, I'd like to have you do some work on our place."

"Tired of barn life?"

"Yes."

"Ditto."

"You have the sheetrock inside, and can start that, right? I mean the walls. I know the ceilings are done."

"Well, not done. The joints need to be taped and mudded, sanded. Then painted."

"Seems like a good day to do that," she said hopefully.

"I'll talk to the guys. We can probably have our bedroom and Kelly's room rocked today, and maybe taped, too. I just have some patchwork on the upstairs bathroom, and all of the taping and mud work on the main floor. The half-bath of the first floor you know I have to rebuild. Again."

"I know. I'm just anxious."

"Spring fever. That and three months living in a barn."

"Yeah. Exactly."

I munched through breakfast, a muffin and some homemade granola, and another cup of coffee. Karen was right, I needed to work the problem with a little less expectation of instant results. Getting my mind off of it for a while was probably smart, too. And if we made some progress at getting our own house habitable again, so much the better.

Carl drew the short straw between he and John, to suit up in my only Tyvek painters' suit and slog about in the dust to get the water going, and rotate it through the day, on the early crops. It beat cleaning out the chicken coop, but just barely. The suit kept ones' clothes much cleaner, although that was a relative thing. John got to do his work indoors, watering the greenhouse crops...by hand. I hadn't had time to rig up anything automatic, and probably didn't have the right stuff to do so even if I had the time.

Kelly and Marie, Rachel and Mark were getting ahead on their class work, with a six-hour school day, and the promise that they'd be out of school all day

Friday and Saturday, too. Friday was after all, Good Friday, and we were planning on having a relatively big dinner on Sunday. I searched through a number of boxes of stuff we'd moved out of the house, and found my DVD copy of The Ten Commandments. We'd watch that over the weekend, and remember that sacrifice. John and Carl had worked ahead of where our teaching staff, mostly Libby and Karen, were at in the teaching materials. Let no one say that teaching high school material is easy.

I spent about an hour going over the material that my Mac now held, maps, lists of utility purveyors, and land-uses, with Ron and Alan.

"You're talking about the problems you have with the existing conditions. Where the buildings are, all that, right?" Alan asked after I'd told them how I didn't know if we as a 'government' could pull it off.

"Yeah, pretty much. Buildings….and the condition they're in, don't for the largest part match the types of architecture probably needed for the uses."

"Who cares?" Ron said. "Adapt to what's there and get that through your head. Just because you have a forty thousand square foot building and you only need ten thousand, shouldn't make you give up. So what if you carve up an existing building for housing and retail in one shell?"

"I hadn't even thought of that."

"Take a big box like a Fred Meyer. That one over on Sullivan and Sprague. Not near a rail line, so probably not a great location. Or one of the stores at the Mall," Ron said.

"Rail lines are on the wrong side of the river," I said.

"Fine. Pick a big box near a rail line. Not all the rail lines are all that close to the big box stores, but they're in walking distance, some of them, right?"

"Yes," I said, looking at the flat panel, using the rail lines as my guideline, and worked from memory. I had in my mind, the two-story mom-and-pop type architecture, small stores, streets with angled parking…..and all of that was getting in the way of what I really had to work with.

"So one big box gets working again, air handlers, convert the heating from natural gas to a boiler or something, electrical is fixed, and you carve up the interior space into a bunch of smaller businesses. Like department stores used to be, but more like a co-op. That is probably not the right word either, no matter. If there's a strip mall that's part of the development, maybe that's carved up into businesses up front and housing in the back. You could do the same thing with the big box buildings, but most of them don't have enough windows for someone to want to live there," Alan said.

"Yeah. That could be fixed though. They could retrofit them." This was good stuff.

"Sure, just get the right architect and structural guy. Assuming that the buildings haven't been too compromised by the quake, or the weather," Ron said.

"What's your next step?" Alan asked.

"I'll outline your ideas and get them ready to present to the Recovery Board. I'll have to look at the map overlays and figure out where, based on rail access and working utilities, we have building inventory that can work like you're thinking."

"That's one thing only. What about farms? Small farms I mean. Those have to get up and going this year…and you know that," Alan said pointedly.

"I do. That's actually the first thing I want to talk to the Board about. We have a very limited amount of time."

"Right. Businesses and getting an economy going and whatnot is all well and good, but without food, nothing else matters," Ron said.

"Yep," I said. I was beginning to feel a little better about the situation. Not a lot better, a little better.

"OK, enough of this stuff. Ready to do some sheetrock?"

"You owe me five bucks," Alan said to Ron.

"Damn. And I thought it was going to be roofing."

"You two slay me," Karen said as she topped off our coffee and brought us the last of the muffins, and raspberry jam this time. "I will gladly trade you both in at the drop of a pin."

"Trust me boys, don't mess with ulterior motives, especially when there are women involved, and those women have been patiently living in a barn for three months."

"I believe you," Ron said. "Common background and all."

"Let's finish these up and get a move on. If we're lucky we can finish hanging most of the rock today, or rather you two can, and I can set a tape-and-mud record."

"Not gonna happen," Ron said. "I've seen you work. It's almost painful to watch."

"Trade you in a heartbeat then, old friend. I've seen the way your wife looks with what can only be lust, at the five-gallon can of ceiling white paint yonder, and dreams of the olive tan paint at your house suddenly transforming to something a little less mortuary-like."

"You sure got her pegged," Ron said with a laugh.

"Yeah, it's the look on her face when she walks in, stealing glances at the paint can, I can see the wheels spinning…"

Ron was laughing hard by now, and nearly choked on a bite of the English muffin.

"If the Evening at the Improv is over now, you have work to do," Karen said, shaking a wooden spoon at us.

"Yes'm," Alan said. "Right away, Ma'am! C'mon boys, the natives are hostile."

"You have no idea," she said.

20

Good Friday,
April Fourteenth

I woke slowly to the sound of KLXY's morning news, just at six. As I learned each time I worked with sheetrock and mud, I had discovered a whole new set of muscles, as evidenced by the stiffness and soreness in every part of me. Eight hours of putting on drywall mud will do that to you. And I still had two more rooms to do, and no more mud to finish them with.

".......for business and official work today, with police substations, community centers, hospitals and clinics resuming normal operations at curfews' end this morning. A meeting of the City Recovery Board has been scheduled for nine a.m. this morning, first floor City Hall, with the County Recovery Board also scheduled at nine at the Public Works Building."

"Chief of Police McKinnon and Sheriff Amberson confirmed at a predawn news conference this morning that the County Commissioners are no longer in power, and that the so-called civilian militia formed at the direction of the Commissioners has either been wiped out by legally-authorized civilian or military units yesterday on Spokane's South Hill. The battle took place at the Manito Country Club clubhouse, which was destroyed in the battle and a subsequent wind-spread fire that destroyed more than six dozen homes in the neighborhood east of the golf course. An estimated eighty-one dead of the Protectors have been recovered, with two soldiers wounded in the battle. Both are recovering at Sacred Heart Hospitals' trauma center. Approximately seventy members of the Protectors remain unaccounted for in various parts of the County."

"Weather today is a marked improvement over the past two days, with the dust storm finally over for now, and calm conditions expected to continue for the next forty-eight hours. Temperatures today will be in the sixties by noon, and will dip down tonight into the low forties."

"No news since late yesterday has been received through any channels regarding the Middle East situation, but ABC News has learned that the

European Union has voted to enact economic sanctions against Israel due to their ongoing battles with the Syrian Army. Israel late yesterday responded by telling the E.U. that their sanctions, and the E.U. themselves, were irrelevant in the world situation. The E.U.'s executive committee, as of last week composed of a majority of European-born Muslim representatives, demanded immediate termination of diplomatic relations, with thirty percent of the representatives, Germany, Belgium and France in particular, demanding military action against Israel should they not cease military action within twenty-four hours. That deadline will pass at two p.m., Pacific Daylight Time. The President stated forty-five minutes ago that any action against Israel, or against any remaining US forces anywhere in the world, would have only the gravest repercussions against any aggressor, and that action would be taken immediately. Sources in the Department of Defense and Department of State confirm that this action can only mean retaliation with a nuclear response. Subsequent contacts with sources in the White House confirmed that this is in fact, the case. The President is scheduled to address the nation at seven a.m. our time."

"Did I hear that right?" Karen said, now sitting bolt upright.

"Yes you did."

"They wouldn't do that would they? Attack Israel?"

"Yes, they would, I think. I don't think they believe that we'd retaliate with nukes."

"Would we?"

"Absolutely," I said. "The time that we will tolerate bullies is over."

"And you don't think we're being a bully?"

"By threatening to open up a can of whoop-ass on someone who attacks somebody else for defending themselves? No. But then again, my glasses these days are colored by the memory of bullies trying to come after me, and I will not tolerate that."

Both dogs greeted me with thumping tails, Buck also choosing to grab hold of my hand with his soft mouth and 'growl' as he tried to parade me around the barn. Karen tried to snooze, but I noticed she was staring up at the cracked ceiling as I dressed, and moved some of the files from my G5 Mac to my Powerbook, and grabbed some papers I'd printed up for the meeting. The horsepower of the bigger computer would've been nice to take with me, but the smaller laptop would do for now.

"I'll make you some coffee. I've got some stuff I've got to get gathered up for the meeting," not to give away the surprise due her.

"How long do you think the meeting will take?"

"It's Good Friday. I'd like to be out of the meeting by noon and on my way back home. This will be more of an organizational meeting today, and assigning folks to gather information. That's my game plan anyway."

"Are you chairing this?"

"I hope not. I'd rather just be the worker behind the scenes, and not the guy catching the flak."

"Weather looks good," Karen said as she looked up at the unfamiliar blue sky.

"Yeah, if you like shades of grey. Everything is dusted. I'll check the greenhouses before I go, and I'll have to vacuum out the air filter for the Expedition."

"What do you want us do get done today?"

"How're the kids doing on their schoolwork?"

"A day off would be good."

"Then do it. Have them write some letters to their uncles and friends. I'm going to check on the mail status today too, among a hundred other tasks. If you feel so motivated, you can finish-sand the wallboard joints in the bedrooms. And then paint them."

"You've got to be kidding. You got that far?"

"Yeah, me and my Extreme Makeover crew. We can be in the house by the end of the month. We need to try to find or trade for some sheetrock mud, so we can get the stairwell and the dining room finished. I did our bedroom, Kelly's room, the upstairs bath, and the living room yesterday. Main floor bath is still a shell though. Need new fixtures in there." The collapsed brick chimney had destroyed all the cabinetry, smashed the sink, toilet, and an antique beveled mirror that had been in Karen's family for most of a hundred years. The brickwork also left some new character on a marble floor and backsplash that I'd put in during the remodel, four years before.

"Can Alan trade for that?"

"I asked him last night. He was planning on opening the store today and putting the word out. Open 'til noon, afternoon off. Probably open for the morning tomorrow and closed on Easter of course."

The news was still going on as we talked, and I heard a commentator talk about a topic near and dear to us: Food gardening. The Federal Government was strongly encouraging everyone to plant food crops to minimize (and I noted they didn't say 'prevent') food shortages in the coming months. Information regarding food gardening would be available nationwide through local extension agents and local authorities. If they were 'strongly encouraging' such measures, I was extremely pessimistic that things were going to be recovering with the assistance of the rest of the country. The rest of the country had its problems to, and we weren't really one of them.

"Hey, got any eggs to spare?" I asked. "Thought I might gift some to my fellow board members."

"Dozen apiece work?"

"Sure."

"Shouldn't be a problem. We haven't sold or traded any most of the week."

"K. I'll take ten dozen if we have them to spare. Oh, almost forgot. The 'facilities' in the house are working."

"You mean I can shower? And use my own toilet?!"

"Yes you can. Right after me."

"Maybe I'll join you."

"Gotta love water conservation," I said with a grin. "Grab your clothes. The water heater was programmed to start warming up at four-thirty. Should be good by now. And the coffee should be ready too. I used the old one with the timer on it."

"You sir, are a man among men."

"Don't go giving me a swolled up head, now. Someone will just come along to prove that I'm just me, warts and all."

"Maybe. But you are just right for me."

After the first shower that we'd taken in our own house for three months and a day, Karen and I had two squares of cornbread and honey, and apple juice and coffee, made in the house and not the barn. We used a small microwave and a spare coffee maker from the basement, saved and moved upstairs for this mornings' breakfast. The house was almost a cave, with nearly no furniture in any of the rooms. The kitchen, still partly a wreck, was at least useable. More so even after the quake, than it had been in six months of remodeling it. We lived in it nonetheless, breakfast, lunch and dinner.

As with most Presidential news conferences, it was late. Nothing at seven, although the newsies were waiting with baited breath.

Before I headed downtown, I went over the sheetrock with a sharp eye, to make sure that it'd all dried to the point where it could be finished, and showed Karen where all the paint stuff was. Alan and Ron and their families came over, led by Carl and Kelly, all enjoying Karen's broad smile and sparkling eyes at the prospect of moving back in. It was a good day. Alan and I talked for a bit about the store, and some more needs that we had, and Ron spoke to the boys about the days' watering schedule on the early crops, and told me he'd check on the greenhouses for damage from the wind. My initial look, from a couple hundred feet away, showed no obvious damage. Thank God for that.

By eight, it was time to go. I was hoping for a quicker drive today. Carl retrieved the big shop vac from the barn and plugged it into the garage's lone working circuit, while I retrieved my trusty Powerbook. The K&N filter, once a kind of red color, was not quite completely plugged, but close. The last half-mile, facing into the wind, had probably done most of the clogging. Within a few minutes, we had that cleaned out and back in place. I knew that an oil change would be in order and soon.

"Check in on the CB when you're on your way. Marie will be listening this morning," Karen said as I hugged Kelly and Carl, who this morning didn't seem too old for such public displays.

"Will do. Love you babe."

"You, too. Thanks for the house," Karen said with a sparkle in her eye.

"Just like moving day, huh?" I said.

"Yeah. You going off to work and leaving all the work to me and my folks."

"Gotta know how to delegate," I said.

"Get going. You can't afford to be late."

"Nope. See you for lunch."

"Bye--and thanks again for our house!" Karen said as I closed the dusty door. The interior of the big Ford, that I'd once tried to keep clean, was now an evenly dusted grey. Someday, perhaps, it would come clean. No time soon though.

The weather, what could've been a brilliant sunny spring day, was blue sky above and dusty haze below. Little wind blew, and the only birds I saw flying were crows, in murders larger than I'd seen.....ever, I thought.

My purple 'pass', which theoretically identified me as someone 'important' (or 'im-poe-tant' as a friend used to say) hung from the rear view mirror. I hesitated to use the wipers and washer fluid, knowing that it would scratch the glass and not really result in a better result. KDA, todays AM station of choice apparently, fired up a little past eight as KLXY shut down. A talk show on the national situation was welcome relief to endless, mindless nattering of the news people. I missed the familiar voices of a few months before, most of those voices silenced permanently because of the Flu. I turned on my emergency flashers for the trip, just to draw more attention to me. No sense in getting shot up by the good guys....

"...shortages are far more serious than the Administration is letting on. The minority leader is putting the blame squarely on the President for these problems, unfairly I might add, and I'm an unabashed Liberal."

This would be interesting, I thought to myself. *"Sure. Blame the poor sucker in office for the short-sightedness of two generations past......"*

"Pete, it's more complicated than that...." The first commentator said, before being interrupted.

"I know that for Heaven's sake. The fact remains though, is that first there is no capital to build new factories, there is little ability to manufacture, fabricate or mine materials critical to the Nation, there aren't enough machine-tool manufacturers left in the States to build what we need! There aren't enough steel mills! Surgical steel used to come from offshore. Where are we supposed to get spare parts? Short answer is, we can't!"

"The Administration....."

"Is over their heads. This is beyond what the Government can do, even given broad emergency powers which they fully realize. You cannot invent these things out of thin air. You cannot magically impart knowledge in manufacturing,

*mining and specialty engineering out of thin air. You cannot deprogram a
generation of wards of the government—who do not know how to work, because
they've never had to—and expect results. They want to be fed the same as
always, by their food stamps and their welfare. They're not workers, they're
eaters."*

"As the nation recovers...."

*"Don't use that word. Sorry, I don't mean to interrupt here, but it's not
about recovery anymore, in my opinion. I would suggest that you phrase things
like this: 'As we progress into the Depression....'"*

"Pretty pessimistic view."

"Cascade failure is indeed that."

"Please define that term, Pete. It's not one I'm familiar with," the show host
asked. I was all-too-familiar with the concept though.

*"'For want of a nail, the shoe was lost.
For want of a shoe, the horse was lost.
For want of a horse, the rider was lost.
For want of a rider, the battle was lost.
For want of a battle, the kingdom was lost.
And all for want of a nail.'*

*"That, David, is cascade failure. The problem we face now of course is that
the financial system we've become used to is now wreckage. That's a nail. The
second problem is that we have little in the way of manufacturing ability in this
nation. That's another nail." "Another problem is that we have little in the way
of a skilled and motivated and educated workforce to put things together. I know
that the Administration realizes this. I just don't know if the American People
realize this yet."*

The show host responded. *"It has been nearly a full quarter since the Second
Depression began, and the Government seems to have done little in the way of
fostering recovery."*

*"For good reason. It is not their job to do so, and I think they've said as
much."*

"So how do we truly recover?"

"We don't. We adapt. If we're lucky, we'll adapt quickly."

I wondered if this was a reasoned discussion or a scripted effort. But then again, I do have a cynical streak in me a mile wide and nearly as deep.

By this time, I was well on my way back into town, passing the Burlington Northern yards again, where more trains were being righted and tracks apparently repaired. Today I could see that a good portion of the main railroad shop, an ancient brick building with Palladian windows looked to be partly rebuilt with a pole-building type structure over the sidewalls, and a new metal roof spanning the old shell. Lights inside meant that folks were working in there. 'Good for them,' I thought.

This trip though, also included seeing a train-mounted crane at the ADM Centennial Mills plant, righting two grain cars that had rolled over. A small crew was also rebuilding the covered off-loading and loading dock, which was in a heap on top of the rails, blocking the operation of the mill.

"Maybe it's a new day after all," I said to myself. The talk show ended as the White House commentators started back up, speculating again on what the President would say and when he would say it. I'm sure phone lines were burning up around the world today….

I passed two military checkpoints along the way, one manned, and saw four police or Sheriff's cruisers. As the Courthouse came into sight a mile away, I noticed that Old Glory was flying from the huge flagpole, a couple hundred feet up the main tower of the building. Someone had a long climb of those stairs.

By eight forty-five, I pulled into the parking lot, dodged the concrete jersey barriers, and parked the Ford next to two other cars; a small Subaru wagon and a Toyota so thrashed that I wondered if it still moved under it's own power. A pair of pickups and a minivan were parked on the other end of the lot.

I balanced my coffee and my computer backpack as I headed toward the building, leaving the eggs in their plastic bags for later. A new large sandbagged emplacement was now taking up the handicapped-parking space, with a single soldier. The tall, tired soldier, sans nametag or rank, was at his post near the door, well-worn vest, waist-packs, a patched helmet, manning 'Ma Deuce', the M2 fifty-caliber machine gun. 'That' certainly wasn't here a couple of days ago.

"Good morning. Nice 'fifty," I said to the young man.

"Yes, sir, and Ma can sing."

"I don't doubt it for a minute," I said as I entered the vestibule, the shotgun-blasted inner glass still in place, but taped over with plastic and blue tape.

Inside the lights on the upper floors were shut off, with only the lights in Planning and the lobby space turned on. I noticed two more cars come into the parking lot as I went into the conference room.

"Good morning, Mr. Drummond," a voice from behind me said. 'Yake, what's his first name? That's it. Brandon.'

"Brandon, right?"

"Yes, sir."

"Thanks again for those CD's. Very helpful."

"Glad to help sir."

"You still camped out here?"

"Yep."

"We'll see if we can arrange something a little more agreeable."

"Thanks, but I think Mr. Ackerman is seeing to it already."

"Good for Walt. You joining us for the meeting?"

"No, sir, I've got a crew tasked with getting the upper floors straightened up."

"Well, we might be calling on you anyway. I have a number of things we need to run down."

"Just let me know," he said.

"Will do. Thanks."

I knew that as a former intern of the planning department, he could lay his hands on information, and contacts, that I'd have to figure out the hard way. Hopefully we could get what we needed over the next few days and get a better sense of what we had to work with.

The conference room, this one on the far end of the department and not appropriated by the former Commissioners, held Walt Ackerman, Tonya Lincoln and Stacey Womack, sipping coffee and reclining back with her feet up. I remembered the discomfort that Karen had with the last few weeks of her pregnancy, and Stacey looked like she was more than ready to be done with being pregnant.

"Morning, all. Weather the storm OK?" I asked.

"Living the dream, Mr. Drummond," Tonya said with a smile. That got us all laughing.

"I understand completely! Stacey, how you holding up?"

"It could be worse. It could be August."

"Yeah, so my friends with September babies said. And their wives too," I added. That drew a smile.

"Any word on the rest of the Board?"

"Not yet. Hopefully everyone will make it. I planned on today being a meeting about goals and big-picture items, and wrap up in a couple hours. I have Mass today at noon that I'd like to attend," Walt said.

"Thanks for that. I was planning on attending our service later today as well. Where is your service to be held?"

"St. Al's. Latin service, too."

"Good for them." St. Aloysius was the twin spired Catholic Church on the Gonzaga campus, just east of downtown. While I wasn't Catholic, the architecture certainly provided me inspiration for my faith. "Much damage from the quake?"

"Plenty. Most of the stained glass was lost. One of our projects will be its restoration."

The rest of our board members showed up, including a County staffer, Drew Simons, Clete McKinnon and Clete's grandson Rusty, a young man perhaps in high school. Clete introduced him and then sent him off with his truck to round up some stuff for his farm.

"OK, looks like we're all here," Walt began. "Thank you for attending. I plan on a fairly short meeting, mostly to get us moved along toward determining how to get our civilian government re-established, but obviously dealing with the overall recovery effort. Also, I have one of the staff listening for the Presidents' address, and we'll stop the meeting when the address starts."

"Thanks for that. Walt, do you have a formal agenda?" Tonya asked. "I planned on one, but was down with a cold."

"No. I'm open to suggestions."

"I've got one…agenda that is for your approval. Here are some copies that I printed up," I said.

"That's fine, Rick."

"Well, wait until you see the agenda before you say that," I said with a smile.

"I'd like to introduce Kamela Gardner, my administrative assistant. Kamela was working in the Human Resources division before the quake, but has worked for the County for most of her career, which if I recall is about fifteen years. Is that right, Kamela?"

Ms. Gardner, a very well put together professional seemingly too young to have fifteen years professional experience behind her, confirmed Walt's statement. "We also have some fresh coffee on the way, and some bottled water, too. Our normal drinking water was tested yesterday and we have a boil order in place for this area."

"Thank you, Kamela. She'll be assisting me in working with our staff, which at this time includes about thirty folks on this campus, and perhaps sixty more that are non law-enforcement throughout the county. Pre-quake, Spokane County employed more than nineteen-hundred people, although that included law enforcement and corrections officers."

Clete let out a long descending whistle at that.

"You could say that again," Walt said. "Not only are we hugely understaffed, even with massive reductions in programs, but we can't even locate most of our former employees. They're gone. I've had our current staff try to locate many of our former County staff for the past two days without much luck. Enough of that. Rick, let's get on your agenda."

"Before I forget, this is Paul Howard of KLXY, and Jeff Johnson of CBS," Walt said, waving two more into the room." I invited them to report on the meeting. Come on in, both of you and help yourself to some coffee. Rick, go."

"Thanks, Walt. First up, I recognize that you're the County Executive and that we report, or more properly, advise you. In that effort, I think we need to have a formal board structure. I'd like to nominate Tonya as chair."

"Second," Drew Simons responded.

"I appreciate that, Rick, but I was thinking that YOU might be a better chair," Tonya replied.

"You know, I'm just happy to be a worker bee behind the scenes. I'd rather not be chair."

"Vice chair then," she said.

"Second," Clete said.

"You two are awfully good at that rapid fire 'second' thing, aren't you?" I asked with a grin.

"Yep. I figure if you're Vice Chair, that'll leave the rest of us to really run things," Drew responded with a smile, nudging Stacey at the same time and nodding to Clete.

"And that's just fine. I've had enough heavy lifting with my own recovery plan….not that the rest of you haven't," I said, catching myself before I really put my foot in it.

"We're all full of stories of adventure, I'm sure." Drew said. "Let's get on to business."

"You need to vote on the election of officers," Kamela said.

"Sorry, we forgot. Not really good at Roberts' Rules of Order," Clete said.

In short order, Tonya and I were elected to office, term of one year or at the discretion of the County Executive.

We next moved on to the agenda that I'd cobbled together. Mike Amberson conveniently showed up at quarter past nine, and had a report prepared for us on the public safety side of things, which happened to be my first agenda item. Mike was wearing more 'official' attire, a traditional uniform and not the Sheriff's department camos that he seemed to live in for the past few months.

"First, thank you for your cooperation and patience with the Sheriff's Department and the past three months. I think we can now really get some work done on putting us back in shape. Second, Captain McCalister asked me to convey his regards as well, unfortunately he was wounded in the action at Manito and is at Fairchild's base hospital. He received some wounds from shrapnel, and should recover. His executive officer will be taking over for him until the Forty-First Division arrives, which is estimated at one May. An advance force will be deployed to the region by the end of next week."

"Mike, can you give us a general overview of your present force, equipment complement, communications, et cetera?" I asked.

"Sure, Rick. We're at eighteen percent of force pre-quake, including all divisions and staff types, corrections, patrol, investigative, etc. That means that we have about sixty staff under my command for the County. The City's level is not much different, percentage-wise. The EOC—Emergency Operations Center—is about ninety percent operational. All pre-quake dispatch functions have been restored, but the trunking system for communications is dead and isn't coming back. We're back to using the pre-EOC system, which was still in place, but not in great shape either. Communications for the past three months, well since the military arrived, have almost been fully integrated with military units in the area. Some areas are only accessible by ham radio. We hope to have full, countywide communications back under County operation restored by the end of May. Parts are a problem. Vehicles and armament supplies are not at this time a problem, but I'll have a better handle on that next week. We've recovered a fair number of Sheriff and Police vehicles that were used by the Protectors, and their stolen weapons as well."

"Are they on the run?" Clete asked.

"More or less, yes. We know of two isolated areas where they seem to have holed up, one on the southwest side of one-ninety-five in the Eagle Ridge subdivision, the second headed northwest and are out in the Indian Trail/Rutter Parkway area. We also know that they're damned near out of gas, and won't be driving much longer. That will either precipitate into an effort by them to steal fuel or overthrow us. We're ready for both, as long as the weather cooperates. McCalister's air operation will see to that."

"Anything else?" Walt said.

"Probably, but not that I can lay a hand on right now," he said.

"Are you going to be in the building for the next couple hours? Might have need of you," Walt said.

"I'll be over at the jail. You can hail me on channel five."

"Thanks, Mike," Walt said. "Next item, communications."

My turn. "First I want to say that there are a number of the upcoming agenda items that we can't address today, but the reason they're here is to get some information coming our way on what kind of shape we're in. This is one of them. Walt, what I was thinking here is that we need to hear from Cingular or Qwest or whoever ran the phone systems, both land-line and cellular, what it will take to get service re-established. I know that at least parts of the land-line system are working, but we obviously need to know what's going on with that and when and if we can expect phones to work again. We also need, as a board, to have better communications between the County and the board members."

"Taken care of that. You're each getting radio units we pulled from some of our wrecked vehicles. You'll have to hook them up to twelve-volt power, and each has been checked and is good to go. Think of them as a radio in a back pack," Kamela said. "Each of you will be calling in using the number printed on the radio face. That way we can get you all in touch for meetings and let you know if things change."

"Better than finding out on AM," Drew said.

"Yep. That's what we figured, too. Forty-mile range, too. Got three of the repeaters working out of five, so that's about as good as we'll do unless we can get some more parts somewhere," Walt said.

"OK, that's all I had there. Anybody got anything else to add?" I asked.

"TV and radio. There is no formal schedule of broadcasting. Not that big a deal for me, but a lot of people see that as a sign of instability, disorganization. Can we do something about that?"

"Walt?"

"We can do that," the local reporters for CBS and ABC replied. "We'll get ahold of NBC and put a schedule together. It's been a rotating schedule due to staffing and fuel."

"I'll put the word out to the radio side as well," Walt said.

"All I'm thinking is that if the general public knows that Channel Four will be on in the morning, Two in the afternoon, etc., we might be able to inspire a higher sense of confidence in things," I said. 'If not real confidence,' I was thinking to myself.

"If you can get back to us next week on that, or better yet, get it implemented by next week, I think we'll make some progress there," Walt said.

"Engineering-wise,the biggest issue is power," the CBS guy responded. I can say that for both us and NBC. Our power is generator-fed, and without fuel, we're off the air. We need power restored to Brown's Mountain to be able to ensure that we can meet a set schedule."

"Ditto, Mount Spokane," his ABC counterpart responded. "We've already worn out two Cummins generators, and we're danged near out of fuel."

"We'll see what we can do," Walt said.

21

Good Friday,
April Fourteenth
9:40 a.m.

"How long will she be?" Walt asked one of his assistants down the hall. He sounded displeased. "Tell her to get here as soon as she can. Yes I understand. Now go."

"What's up?" Tonya asked.

"Doctor Sorenson will likely miss this meeting. For you who don't know her, she is the head of County Health. Good doc, not much on procedure. Rather, not much tolerance for politicians."

"I think I like her already," Clete said.

"I saw your agenda item, Rick, and wanted to have Rene here to give you the up-front."

"That can wait 'til next week. Where's she at?"

"If you can believe it, she's making house calls. Concern about some extinct diseases."

"Outbreak?" Stacey asked.

"Potentially, yes. Measles."

"Then given my current condition, I'm just as happy not to see her," she said.

"Of course," I said. "The baby."

"Yeah."

"Well, we can do it on a speakerphone. Assuming that we have some working phones next week. Internal phones work. We just can't get anything outside of the building," Walt said.

"Can you pass on my ideas for info from her?"

"Yep. Anything to add?"

"I don't see the overall death toll from the Domino here. The other stuff about the hospitals, medicines and such are fine. How many did we lose in the quake, where'd the survivors evac to. Are they coming back? Can we handle them if they do?" Drew asked, perhaps more pointedly than he intended.

"I'll pass that on to Rene and other staff. We should have answers next week."

"On to Utilities," Tonya stated. "Can we get all of these purveyors to reply by next week?" I'd made a list of each water and energy purveyor in the county, with the intention that we'd get a report on each of the respective systems.

"Most of them, yes. There were draft reports prepared right after the quake, before my employers got a god complex."

"Tuesday? Wednesday?" Drew asked. "Sooner we get the info the sooner we can figure things out."

"Probably."

"Travel and transportation," Tonya continued on. I'm glad she was making good use of my agenda. Didn't bother me one bit, either.

"We have exactly two of our engineering staff left. Of thirty. We do have a complete inventory of all county roads, bridges and overpasses, whether State highways or county roads. We can present a summary next week."

"Great. Food supply."

"We've got a handle on that too, and it's less than good news. After the food collection efforts in the county, and the wise decision to keep it in each neighborhood, there is less than a months' worth of food within the county, ready to eat."

"How 'bout the grain supplies," I asked. "I noticed work going on at the Centennial Mill. I thought over at the Purina plant too.'

"I'll check," Walt said. "Short answer, I have no idea."

"Have we heard anything from the Federal Government about food shipments?"

"No."

"Then we better press them on it," Stacey said. "We cannot feed the county based on what we're growing right now, unless there is a huge farming operation out there that I don't know about."

"There isn't. There are, as many of you have figured out or done yourselves, a lot of what we used to call truck gardens out there though. Probably not enough."

"OK, unless I'm wrong and I doubt that I am, we haven't seen a food truck come into the County since February. And no trains since the Domino. Right?"

"Right."

"So we've been eating on borrowed time," I said.

"Yes."

"Enough said for now. I heard the ad—I won't say news story—on the radio 'encouraging' all Americans to plant food gardens to 'minimize', not 'prevent' food shortages. I seriously doubt that we're going to see anything meaningful come into Spokane from out of the region. Am I wrong here?"

No one disagreed. "Then that's likely going to be our biggest issue. Walt, we need an updated inventory and we need to hear through channels that we're going to get food shipments, or we're not."

"I'll see what I can do."

"Allied recovery boards," Tonya moved on. "Do we know who is representing the City? And their meeting schedule?"

"They're adding new people today. I'll get you what I can next week. They're meeting right now as well, and will be meeting Monday, Wednesday and Friday next week. Tentatively, I'd like you all here on those days as well next week, with potentially weekly meetings thereafter."

"Sounds OK. Half a day or a whole day?"

"Your preference. It's not like we don't have a lot of ground to cover."

"Half a day if you please," Drew responded. "I have a farm to run."

"Ditto," said Stacey.

"Fuel supplies," Tonya continued.

"Good news there at least. The pipeline to Billings is intact and functioning to the East Spokane storage facility. The bad news is that not much is coming through it. Most is going elsewhere."

"But we're not dry."

"No. And won't be. We will have chronic shortages, gas will be very very expensive and we'll have strict rationing, and absolutely no tolerance for wasting fuel, as in punitive measures taken for wasting it. But we're not dry."

"Hoo-rah," Clete said. "Now you need to define what you just said for Joe Schmuck who needs to use his chainsaw and might be afraid to."

"I'll work up a draft."

"Please. I don't want to get tossed in the clink because I'm letting my tractor idle too long," I said.

"CERT Report," Tonya went on. "Rick, what are you looking for there?" CERT stood for Community Emergency Response Teams. Dozens of volunteer teams worked in the initial recovery efforts in January and February. I knew that they had begun a comprehensive inventory and census. I just never knew what became of it.

"Inventory of damaged/destroyed houses, businesses, percents inhabitable, salvageable, distribution by zip code, distribution by arterial, distribution by proximity to specific public facilities, transportation and..."

"I get it. That was a mouthful."

"I see that as one of the critical building blocks for recovery, actually. Walt, did you get a final copy from the CERT teams after the quake?"

"I never saw it. It went straight to FEMA."

"Can you look into that?" Tonya asked.

"Yep. Gotta track down FEMA anyway."

"OK, Rick, the last item you have here is titled 'Resettlement Concepts.' Can you explain that for us?"

"I spent the dust storm looking at the County's Geographic Information Systems documents on the county's development patterns, with an eye towards how things will need to change based on new transportation needs. Basically, the loss of the private automobile to take us everywhere, which also fostered sprawl and miles traveled to get to ones' business, the grocery store, whatever."

"How do you think this can be implemented?" Clete asked. "You aren't forcing people to move, are you?"

"No. But on the other hand, if your house is six miles from the nearest rail link where mass transit is, coincidental where food and goods and services are, are you going to want to walk or bike that far if your car is out of gas or too expensive to run or you can't get parts for it?"

"No, I don't suppose so."

"Me either. There are places that will naturally grow. There are places that will not. These will be determined by how easy it is to live and work there."

"Sounds too simple."

"It is. There are a dozen-dozen things that factor into this idea. Rail lines. The ability to have rails work for passenger and freight traffic. The ability to have businesses and residential areas in the same building or within a close proximity. Public services being nearby. Food grown nearby. Schools nearby. Medical care, et cetera. I'd like to, if you agree this is an idea worth pursuing, to present this in more detail after we get the CERT report and other information from the utility purveyors."

"Assuming gasoline does not come back to the degree that we had pre-Domino, is there any other substitute?"

"Not that I know of, no."

We wrapped up the meeting shortly thereafter, and before I left, told my fellow board members to meet me at the Expedition for a dozen eggs each. Stacey and Drew passed, as they each had laying hens. The rest of the board took a dozen each, which left me with six-dozen unclaimed. I gave McCalisters' men a couple dozen, and then the rest to Mike Amberson for his family and the deputies working the Jail. I think I made some new friends because of that.

Back in the car, I checked in with Karen on the CB, again, not identifying myself or where I was, just that I was 'on my way.' I then hooked up the County radio to the power point, which we used to call a 'cigarette lighter,' and 'checked in' with the County radio dispatcher, with the big clunky push-to-talk microphone. I was now known as 'one thirty seven,' and would have to call in as 'one thirty seven to Spokane,' whenever I needed to talk to someone. Some of the Board members, including Drew and Tonya, would have to figure out how to rig a twelve-volt supply in their houses. I had a couple of car batteries to work with, and somewhere a twelve-volt step down box that used line power to supply twelve volts to portable radios and other gear for testing, outside of a car. Of course, I had no idea where that was....

"Spokane to one thirty seven," the radio crackled as I turned onto Division, headed south.

"One thirty seven," I responded.

"For your information, from the Sheriff, you are authorized to proceed to your destination along a route of your choosing. Way is clear, over."

That was certainly a surprise. "Understood, thank you. One thirty seven out."

"One thirty seven," the pleasant voice replied.

"Well, now. I get to take a tour if I so desire," I said to myself. I decided to take advantage of the opportunity and do a little exploring. My blood pressure went up at the thought. Silly. I was excited about not driving the same old road home, and looking around at other parts of town along the way home. Stuff that used to be background noise was now interesting to me. I turned the emergency flashers on as I took off.

"Broadwater," I said into the CB.

"Here," Libby replied.

"Hiya. Going to be a little longer coming home than I thought. No problems though."

"I'll pass that along."

"Thanks. See you in a while."

I headed further south, passing the Trent intersection, and wound my way past the wrecked Chili's restaurant, down to Sprague. I hadn't been on Sprague but for one trip into town, for my first and fateful visit to the Commissioners, months ago now. My impression then was of the surprising amount of damage. Today, it seemed changed as to the surprising amount of buildings that still stood. I don't know why my view changed.

Many of the older--oldest in fact—buildings in the downtown area lost their brick facades in the quake, which were then bulldozed up onto the sidewalks to create winding paths of the once-wide streets. Most of the Seventies-era aluminum light poles were down or tilted at odd angles, and I noticed that many of the overhead power lines out of the core area were draped low over roads (in the core, most lines were underground), or in the case of the silver Cable TV lines, downed altogether. Most of the individual service phone lines were road spaghetti now, too. In retrospect, not much had changed from January 'til now, other than the obvious looting. Had the Commissioners acted as they should have, much of what I was seeing would've been taken care of, in some manner or other.

Farther into East Central, a notoriously rough part of town well known for drug problems, low income homes, more than a few rough folks, and prostitutes plying their wares on Sprague Avenue at all hours, the merely collapsed buildings gave way to collapsed and burned buildings and cars, block on block. At Sprague and Helena, four blocks of clear ground, sporting nothing but foundations, separated Interstate Ninety from Sprague. Hundreds of homes once stood there.   I stopped in the middle of the street, not far from where my first employer's office once stood...a skeleton was being picked on by two dogs. They paid me no heed.

North of Sprague, one of the trains that used to pass through town all too frequently lay partly on its side, blocking the underpass beneath the trestle. Several of the cars were car-carriers, at least one of which had spilled its contents of new cars in the derailment. Someone I suppose then decided that burning them, and the train, seemed like a good idea. Both the train and the wrecked cars were now bright red with rust after months in the weather. I moved farther east.

By the time I reached Fancher, nearly to the point where Ninety passed over Sprague, I observed that virtually all of the commercial buildings between the tracks to the north and the freeway to the south were all but gone. Lowe's, Home Depot (both recipients of lots of my money for a good number of years), Costco (burned now, and not from the quake), many manufacturing and warehouse buildings, custom fabricators, small retail shops. What hadn't been destroyed in the quake and burned then, was looted and burned later.

I suppose that I was surprised on how little was left.   Was there something to actually rebuild anymore?

"Broadwater," I called.

"Here, what's up?" Karen said. "You OK?"

"Yep. Should be home soon. Have I missed anything on the radio? Thought the President was supposed to speak."

"You haven't missed it. Nothing so far. VP was spotted getting on a helicopter though. Where are you?"

"Three miles, west-southwest."

"Hmm. See you soon."

"K. Out."

"Out."

She'd have to figure it out on the scaled map I'd cobbled together on the wall, a bunch of eight-and-a-half by eleven sheets taped together, covering most of the county. I'd printed it off the GIS database the day before. I'd put a 'dot' on our house with a thumbtack, and a string marked in miles that ran to the far end of the county. Three was pretty close.

I passed under the interstate and made a left on Thierman Road, heading north and then east again. Residential areas, north of Sprague and within a stones throw of rail lines heading into town. Most of the housing fabric looked predictably run-down, this was a lower income area, pre-quake. There wasn't much evidence that anyone was living around here, but I wasn't about to go sticking my nose into a neighborhood that I didn't know like my own just to prove that.   Further east, one of the cities' 7-11's, burned and gutted. I thought of Paul Milne when I saw that. ('If you live within five miles of a 7-11,' Paul wrote on the misc.survivalism website pre-Y2K, 'you're toast.)

'West Valley School District' the bus said, what I could read of it, stuffed into the side of Centennial Middle School. Someone went joyriding, and then lit it off. The seventh-grade wing was a gutted shell. Most of the rest of the school looked OK, though, worse than Broadway Elementary, not far from our place. I turned north again, up toward Mission Avenue, along the western edge of the subdivision. I slowed in front of the school, and I made sure my nineteen-eleven was handy, just in case.

Turning west onto Mission, I saw an older man in a front yard a couple blocks up, working in his yard. He took note of me too, and was wary as I pulled closer. At least he didn't go for a gun. I stopped in front of his small house, and noticed that the entire front yard, and those on either side of him, was planted in cabbages, on about sixteen-inch spacing. Wall to wall cabbages. I rolled my passenger window down and introduced myself.

"Morning. I'm Rick Drummond of the Recovery Board."

"Manny."

"Nice to meet you. That'll be quite a crop of cabbages."

"This is nothing. You should see the back yard."

"May I?"

"Sure, I guess."

"Let me check in with my wife first," I said as I radioed home.

"Short leash, huh?"

"Naw, I've just had more than a few opportunities to be a target. More than my wife cares for."

After I checked in, I shut off the car and climbed out, and let myself in the gate. The house, built perhaps in the forties, was well kept and well repaired after the quake.

"Nice job with the house. Much damage?"

"More than should be my due."

"Yeah, I know what you mean. You here alone?"

"No, my wife and I. Lost our youngest son in the flu."

"I'm very sorry. We didn't lose any family, thank God. Friends though. Most of our neighbors are gone though, either evac'd or were out of town when the Domino hit. We're putting things back together, sort of. We'll be meeting and trying to get things organized over the next few weeks. You'll hear about it on the news, I hope."

"Don't listen or watch much anymore," Manny said as we went around the back of the house. "Not since the Army crossed the border, and all they have on is bad news anyway. My parents were from Juarez. I still have family down there. Or did."

"I'm sorry. I know that's not worth much though."

"More than most would say. We can't even leave the street without someone throwing crap our way. Calling us 'wetbacks' or 'spics'. Juanny—that's my wife, is third-generation American. I spent too many damned winters in the Army in the sixties in Korea. And we get treated like this. Bunch of squatters down the road a piece threatened us once, after Juanny gave them some food too! Damned strung-out teenagers. Ran them out in January."

A cold chill ran through me. "What did they look like?" I paused. "How many?"

"Six or seven of 'em. White kids. Two or three of 'em were girls. One pregnant. Why?"

"They came after us on February first."

"Bad?"

"Yeah. I still have nightmares about it," I said. The blond girl with the violet eyes and perfect teeth that someone spent a lot of money on. The hole above her right eye from my Garand.

"Damned waste."

"Yeah. At the very least."

"Anyway, here's our garden. Six hours a day. Rest of the time is on the livestock."

I was impressed. More than an acre, cultivated by hand, Asian style, with rows perfectly aligned and spaced only wide enough for careful walking. An adjoining yard held dairy goats, ducks and geese, in pens, and a small barn probably held more.

"No chickens?" I asked.

"Haven't found any yet to buy. Haven't gone too far a field."

"Well, then, let's go back to my car and let me get you set up."

"You're kidding me."

"No, sir. I'm sure we can work something out that's mutually beneficial. Dozen laying hens and a rooster work?"

He looked at me warily. "Yeah, in exchange for what?"

"We'll work something out."

"You got a deal."

"Let me make a call to my family. I'll have her pick some out. Rhode Island Reds."

"Need any rabbits?" Manny asked.

"Meat rabbits?"

"Yeah. Got…plenty."

"That sounds like trading material," I said.

"Yeah."

"Tell you what. I'll be back tomorrow about ten or so with the hens…do you happen to have a CB radio?"

"No, why?"

"We have a little barter network that we run, mostly over the radio for security reasons. I think you'd benefit by being part of it."

"Know where I can get a radio?"

"Yep. I'll bring one by. Little hand-held thing with a power adapter. See you then, Manny…" I said, looking for a last name.

"Alvarez." I stopped in my tracks. Probably a common name, I thought. 'What the heck. I'll ask anyway.'

"Any relation to a Jeremy Alvarez?" Manny looked at me warily. "In the Army?"

"I have a nephew in the Army…he was anyway. Got shipped to Iraq last year. My sisters' boy. His name is Jeremy."

"'Bout twenty? Tall?"

"Yeah."

"Back in January. Week or so after the quake, we had an Army unit down the street from us. Just shipped back in from Karbala or someplace. Spec-four by the name of Jeremy Alvarez. West Texas, if I remember. You didn't know he was here?"

"No. We only moved here from Redding in December. I'm sure he hadn't heard."

"Well, if he's the same kid, your sister should be proud."

"Do you know…is he still here?"

"I don't think so. I think his Division shipped out to Mexico."

"Damned war."

"I'll check though. I've got some connections with the Army."

"I would appreciate that. My oldest is in the Navy. She's a surgical nurse on a carrier. We haven't heard anything from her in weeks."

"That could be because of the commissioners. They stopped the mail. We should be seeing the mail deliveries start up soon. Like, Monday. I know I've got his address at the house. I'll make sure I get it to you."

"Thank you," Manny replied quietly. "We figured we'd never see him again. I thought he was still over there."

"You take care. I'll see you tomorrow. Are you attending any Good Friday or Easter Services?" I asked as I got back into the Ford.

"No, the St. Anne's is gone. There's nearly no one left in the parish. God knows where the priests are."

"The community center east of University has a Good Friday service at noon today, and a sunrise service on Easter. Services just started back up a couple weeks ago; most of them have been Protestant. Easter though will be a full Mass."

"Thank you. We've missed that," Manny said.

"I'll see you tomorrow, if not sooner."

"Thanks. See you then."

Sometimes, it just pays to go off the beaten path.

22

Good Friday,
April Fourteenth
1:40 p.m.

"Thank you again for stopping this morning. We appreciate it," Juanita, 'Juanny' Alvarez said with a smile." Manny and I have only been out of our neighborhood twice. Got shot at for the favor the first time. The second, we went over to Inland Seed for dried peas. Very romantic." Juanny's eyes had that sparkle that only people married for more than a couple of decades have, as she stood arm-in-arm with her slightly rotund and graying husband.

"It was nice to be with others at worship. It has been a long time since confession."

"The priest on Sunday is from St. Mary's. Do you know him?"

"No, I think he was new. Installed after the scandal with the bishop," Manny said.

"Well, you'll have your chance Sunday. You mentioned Inland Seed? Is there someone running it?"

"Guy named Rockins. Can't remember his name."

"What do they sell?" Not wanting to ask if he'd 'liberated' some seed, or if he was dealing with a looter.

"Peas, beans, lentils. Used to be mostly wholesale by the looks of it."

"Not livestock feed," I said.

"Nope. You wouldn't want to live on the stuff, but it's been good to fill things out," Manny said.

227

"I think Karen and Kelly are done now," I said. "Let's get you properly introduced to the rest of the bunch. Let me go track her down."

I'd introduced Manny and Juanita Alvarez to the Bauers and the Martins, before they left for home. Carl and John were keeping an eye on the place for us. Grace didn't come to the service, because her hip was bothering her. Karen was finishing up cleaning after coffee. She'd just had time to say hello to Manny and Juanita before running off for more coffee. Most Good Friday services that I'd attended were somber events meant for reflection of the Sacrifice made for us. This was more like a 'normal' church service. I think that people were hungry for human contact. The news that the commissioners were no longer in power, and that I'd had a hand in it, made me something of a minor celebrity, which I brushed off immediately and assigned credit where it was more properly due.

When I came back out of the kitchen, off of the multipurpose room/sanctuary, I noticed that Randy Thompson was speaking with the Alvarez's. There was plenty of help in the kitchen (for a change) to finish up.

"Hiya, Randy. How's things going?"

"Thankful every day," he said. Alan and I still needed to meet with Randy to talk about his bike shop idea, I remembered.

"Attaboy," I said. "Manny, Juanita, this is my wife, Karen and my daughter, Kelly. My son is home keeping an eye on things."

"Very pleased to meet you both," Karen said. Kelly was respectful as she said hello. "Rick told me that we may be trading for some rabbits! That will be a nice change."

"As will some eggs and fried chicken," Juanny said. Both Karen and Juanny enjoyed a small laugh. "Manny told me that you have a store?"

"Well, of sorts. We connect people who want to trade or sell something. Problem being, there isn't much money. Anyway, if people have things to trade or things they need, we can put out the word, without exposing folks too much to robbery or worse. It's worked OK so far," I said, not mentioning that we were not long before on the list to be exterminated.

"What kind of stuff do you have?"

"It's a long list. It's only a couple blocks down if you want to stop by. We're 'closed' today for Good Friday, so no one's there trading, but we can let you have a peek and if there's something you have to trade, I'll have Alan put out the word."

"That would be exceptional." Manny said. "Maybe there is some hope for civilization after all."

After retrieving my beat-up AK from Randy, Karen, Kelly and I went the short distance to the corner store. Kelly had plugged in some headphones into the rear-seat CD player and was listening to The Beach Boys. Manny and Juanita followed behind us in a very well worn Mitsubishi mini-truck, surprisingly enough a diesel. I didn't know they even made one.

"What year is that?" I asked Manny when we stopped and the abundant dust settled.

"Eighty-six."

"And it's a diesel?"

"Yep. Got a Trooper that's a diesel too."

"I had no idea they made diesels."

"Great rig. This one's got three hundred thousand on it. The Trooper's got over four hundred thousand."

"You gotta realize that Manny is…well, was an over-the-road driver. Cut him and he bleeds diesel. Won't even consider a gas car."

"Too many problems with them."

"Come on in. You can at least look around and get some trading ideas."

I unlocked the door and made my way to the back of the store, and flipped on the lights that still worked. I could hear Juanita draw her breath in sharply when the lights came on. I guess she was surprised.

"My Lord," she said. "Sorry. I didn't mean to say that."

"Are you all right?" Karen asked.

"Yes. I am now. These are things to sell? And to trade?"

"Yeah," I answered. "Alan, Karen's older brother, pretty much runs the store. Please, look around."

"Thank you," Juanny said. She and Manny walked down each aisle, talking quietly to each other.

"Are they OK?" Karen asked.

"Yeah, I think so. I would suspect that there are a number of things in here that they haven't seen for a few months, is all."

"Do you think it's like this in other parts of town?" Karen asked as she held my hand.

"I honestly hope it's a lot better than this. I'm afraid it's not though, based on what I saw this morning."

"Can we buy some of this today?" Manny asked.

"Well, we're really just set up for trading, and no one's using paper money any more."

"Pre-sixty-four silver work?" He asked. I was more than surprised.

"I'm sure that it will. I don't think we've priced any of it in silver though. I think Alan's worked up a price list, but I haven't seen it yet. What did you need?"

"A few things. Toothpaste. Soap. A pair of leather gloves. A pair of sunglasses that'll fit under my goggles…"

"I think we can work that out. Let me get Alan on the radio."

I moved to the door, next to Karen. "Hon, go help them out. I'll see if Alan has a copy of the list here."

"K," she said with a smile. "Nice to be married to a knight in shining armor."

"Stop that. It's the right thing to do."

"I know, I was just saying."

Out in the parking lot, I turned on the FRS radio and plugged in the earbud, and was immediately yelled at.

"Dad! Where have you been?" Carl said.

"We stopped at the store with the new folks. The Alvarezs. What's going on?"

"The President is supposed to be on at two. I was about ready to come and get you."

"What's the rumor of the hour?"

"Iran's taken Iraq. The Israelis have taken most of Lebanon, and are moving into Syria. The King of Jordan was hurt in an assassination attempt. That enough?"

"Is that rumor, or fact?"

"Like you can tell," Carl said, fading back into teenage sarcasm. I had to remind myself, that he was yet to turn sixteen.

"We'll turn it on here. Is Alan around?"

"Let me buzz him. I think he's on yesterdays frequency," Carl replied. A few moments passed.

"Hey—Carl tell you the latest?" Alan asked.

"Yeah. I'll turn it on down here. Hey I've got the new folks here, wanting to buy stuff with pre-sixty-four silver. I need to know what to charge them."

"There's a list under the inventory pad, right against the clipboard. All I did was convert pre-Depression prices to silver, and rounded up a little. If something costs twenty FRN's, pre-Depression it's a fraction of that now. I basically used a twenty-dollar per ounce value on gold, and something like a buck-forty in FRN's per ounce of silver. That's how I came up with the prices. I wanted to talk it over with you though, in case we're not charging enough."

"And? I don't get it. How does that relate to price?"

"Sorry, it's tough without seeing it. If something was twenty bucks pre-Depression, it's five bucks silver, now."

I was quiet for a minute. "Is that right?"

"Yeah, as I figure it. I took the values from the Pre-First Depression money standard. I figured that's as good a place to start as any. And with silver and gold pieces up to sixty-four still being around, sort of, that gives us a basis for exchange.”

“What about post-sixty-four money?” I knew that at least up to sixty-nine, there was still some silver in some of the change, forty percent or some.

“Pennies are still useable up to something like seventy-eight or so, they were still copper. Some of the silver dollars and quarters and dimes were too, up to sixty-nine, with forty percent silver content. Anything later than those dates of course is play money. They have no silver in them. Unless we run across a Gold Eagle or one of the commemorative silver pieces.”

“Right. OK. I’ll find your list. Did you price the entire inventory in coins?”

“Yeah, as a first run. I put the pre-Depression prices in, then converted the prices in your Excel program. Resulted in the original price divided by a factor of five.”

“K. Thanks. That’ll work.” I noted that our protocol on using names other than our own needed to be brought up tonight. I didn’t think we were back to the point where we could go by proper name. I went back into the store, where Karen had provided one of the little plastic baskets to Manny and Juanita, who had promptly filled it up. I hoped to avoid an awkward situation if they didn’t have enough money.

“OK, I think we’ve got that figured out. Let me get the price list,” I said as I walked behind the counter and turned on KDA, waiting for the President to speak. I could tell that Juanny was still eyeing some items, and kept looking into the basket, perhaps to figure if one item was more important than another. “Ready?” I asked.

“I think so. I hope we have enough,” Juanita asked with a little worry.

“How are you pricing things now?” Manny asked, with some backbone.

“We went back to a pre-Depression standard,” I said. Manny looked uncomfortable, knowing that ‘silver’ was worth far more than ‘paper’ dollars. “Sorry. Pre First-Depression standard. Silver comes out to about a buck forty an ounce, gold at twenty an ounce. Basically, the prices are twenty percent of what they were pre-Second Depression.”

“That’s more like it. So this ten dollar pair of gloves,” he pointed, “Is now two dollars.”

“Yes.”

"Then we have a deal."

The gloves, a tube of toothpaste, two bars of soap, two toothbrushes, a knock-off pair of polarized sunglasses, a bottle of aspirin, a bottle of elderberry extract (home made by one of the Traders), a box of band-aids, some heavy thread and a sleeve of sewing needles, a box of razor blades—the old-fashioned kind that my Dad used to use when I was a kid.   I added up the total on a solar calculator. "Eight dollars, eighty cents."

Manny reached in one of the deep pockets of his vest, and pulled out a cloth bag, I could hear the coins inside. He counted out eight dollars and eighty cents in Peace and Morgan Dollars, Franklin Halves, and Liberty Dimes. I was impressed.

"Nice coins," I said.

"Never believed much in banks, bein' on the road all the time. Bought these when I could. I got these in Oklahoma, I think."

"Then if you bought enough of them you may be a very wealthy man. There aren't too many folks around that have money."

"Mebbe," he said. "Mebbe so."

"Here's a bag for your things," I said as the radio switched to Washington for the broadcast. We all went silent as the anchor began to speak.

"Ladies and gentlemen, the President will be speaking to the nation from an undisclosed location. The President of the United States," he announced.

"Well, this sounds bad already," I said. Little did I know.

"Good afternoon to the citizens of the United States and those around the world who are listening as well. I know that both friends and enemies of this country, those that believe in freedom and those that would deny it are listening, and I will speak to both the Nation and the world about events today."

"Through our national strategic assets, this broadcast is being made on all spectrums of radio and television, world wide. This is possible through the temporary interruption in the normal traffic of communications satellites belonging to, and being used by, any and all nations. This unprecedented broadcast is also being translated in near real-time by our communications specialists and broadcast in native languages world wide, to inform all people, and all governments, of the seriousness of events today."

"They hijacked everyone's satellites?" I said, and was hushed for it.

"Approximately six hours ago," I checked my watch, seven a.m. our time, *"the United Nations, dominated by French, German and a mixture of Islamic nations and interests, attempted an attack on the sovereign nation of Israel. This attack was repelled primarily by Israel herself, but with some assistance and forewarning by the United States of America. United States forces were also attacked at Diego Garcia by conventional submarine-launched weapons; at Incirlik, Turkey by conventional weapons; and an aborted attempt at our base at Guam. This last attack was a nuclear-equipped ballistic missile launched from China. The United States Navy responded upon my orders and has destroyed any remaining space-launch capability of the Chinese. It is understood at this hour that elements of the former Communist regime attempted a coup today, the second in as many months, and gained control of that nation's nuclear arsenal. That arsenal at this hour no longer exists, nor does the offensive capability of that nation. China is by all appearances now in a state of civil war."*

"Since this morning, our naval forces have been assisting the Israeli military in the defense of that nation. A number of attacking warships and ships that ignored repeated warnings have been destroyed. These include four submarines carrying intercontinental ballistic missiles belonging to France, recently re-named as vessels in the service of Allah. These ships were sunk off the east coast of the United States by fast-attack submarine forces of the U.S. Six German-built submarines, also similarly named, were destroyed by U.S. forces after they threatened U.S. ships and in two cases, shadowed a U.S. carrier fleet in the Mediterranean, providing assistance in the defense of Israel."

"These ships were lost with all crew." I could almost see the President's expression. *"No losses have been incurred by forces of the United States at this time."*

Manny, Juanita and Karen all had the same expression.

"The nation of Israel at this time is engaged in significant battle with forces from Iran, moving through and overflying Iraq, the Syrian Army, and elements of the Egyptian military. Israel has responded with forces appropriate to that used against her as well. European forces that participated in the attack have been repelled from their initial surprise attack, although intelligence suggests that these forces and the nations behind them are bent on continuing to fight."

"I direct this next message to nations that are engaged against Israel and the U.S. Should offensive operations, anywhere in the world or in space, continue past midnight Universal Time, the United States will conduct offensive

operations using conventional and nuclear devices against all military targets in enemy combatant nations and all capital cities of those nations."

A pause in the broadcast. *"Yes, you heard me correctly. That was an ultimatum, there is no negotiation. Cease your attacks or we will destroy you. For the forces of our military, the United States, the nation of Israel and the people of the world, I ask that all Americans offer their prayers for His protection and guidance. I pray for all of them. Good day."*

"Here we go again," Juanita said.

"I was thinking something like that too, but with a couple of expletives," I said.

Karen and Manny both remained silent. "C'mon, hon, let's go home," I said.

"Let's."

"Manny, Juanita, we'll pray for you tonight," I said. We were all feeling the threat.

"And we for you. Thank you for these things."

"You are most welcome. I hope we can continue."

"Us, too," Manny said as we walked out the front door. He nearly crushed my hand with his gnarled grip. Juanita gave Karen a kiss on the cheek. I could see tears streak both of their faces. I could tell that the joy of being able to buy such simple things as a new toothbrush and some toothpaste and some other things, was now lost in the dread of, again, war.

"I'll stop by in the morning," I told them as I locked up the store.

"We'll look forward to it," Juanita said, knowing that our 'tomorrow' might be much, much more different than our 'today.'

Karen and I got back in the Ford, where Kelly was singing harmony to 'Sloop John B.'

"Do we tell her?" I asked.

"She'll know soon enough," Karen said.

A few minutes later, we were back in the barn. Grace, Alan and Mary were at their house, Carl was listening to the radio for more news, while John put on a

DVD, our collectors edition of "The Ten Commandments." I didn't think ABC would be airing it this year...Kelly plopped down on one of the kid's beds, to watch the show. Mark and Rachel had studied Exodus just a few days ago, in preparation for Easter.

"Any more news?" I asked Carl.

"Nothing. A lot of blabber. What time is midnight Universal Time here?" he asked.

"Four," I said quietly as Karen lit the stove for a little heat. It was a bit chilly, in spite of the filtered sun. "Eight hours difference to here."

"I'm going to run over to Alan's for a minute," I said. "Ron, would you join me?"

"Sure," he said. "I know how this ends," he said with a smile.

"What's up?" Karen asked. "Other than the obvious."

"It's the obvious. I want to go check the temperature with the boys on getting the fallout shelter equipped...or contingency plans."

"What contingency plans?"

"That root cellar is nowhere big enough for everyone we have now."

"Oh," Karen said. "How long before the fallout from China gets here?"

"Couple days," I said, remembering how the U.S. tracked one of China's early weapons detonations, and our ability to determine what kind of weapon it was by its fallout.

"Do you think we should...get it ready?"

"I don't know. That's why I want to talk with the guys. If we've taken the Chinese factor out, that leaves either small players or former allies or the Russians. Who've been awful quiet since the Depression started."

"It's not like we have a lot left to destroy," Karen said. "The quake pretty much took care of that."

"Tell that to a warhead programmer on the other side of the world," I said. "Fairchild was...the biggest refueling base on this side of the country. It may still be a target. I'll be back in a bit."

"K," she said. "Kiss." I obeyed orders.

"Right back," I said as I went outside.

2:42 pm

"There it is, then," I said. "My assessment of the situation."

"Agreed," Alan said. Ron nodded as well.

"OK, so we have little time," I said. "And a lot to do."

"Let's get at it. Do we want the boys to help?" Alan said.

"Moving stuff into the shelter with more than just the three of us will likely have us tripping over each other," I said. "We'll be working them soon enough. Besides that, it's not that much stuff. Couple hours, maybe three for the cellar to get a good start. A lot more time in getting stuff moved around over here. With the old coal room you've got, we only need to worry about getting mass overhead. Three concrete walls and one of block will help a lot. We'll see what it takes to get enough mass overhead to provide the same protection factor. I've got a book on it."

"Why am I not surprised," Ron said. "What's it called, 'Do it Yourself Bomb Shelters?'"

"Not quite. 'No Such Thing as Doomsday.' And that other one I was telling you about when we cleaned out the basement, remember? 'Nuclear War Survival Skills.'"

"You're kidding," Alan said.

"Dead serious."

We'd decided that we would equip the fallout shelter, which doubled as our root cellar, and was in fact probably capable of keeping some of us alive in case of a blast within the city. It was built long before we owned the home, and I'd modernized it somewhat, and built a few items that would be needed in case of actual nuclear war. Two blast doors, being among them, and a new escape ladder.

In addition to equipping the root cellar, we looked over both Ron's and Alan's houses with the supposition that one or the other would also need to be equipped for fallout protection. Alan's quickly became the best choice, with an enclosed coal room, used once for storing coal for the now-gone coal furnace. It was built into a corner of the basement, and constructed with concrete block walls, reinforced, with a large metal door. Two vent windows in the eight-inch thick concrete foundation walls could provide ventilation with proper encouragement. Should power fail, a manual air exchange system, similar perhaps to our big Kearny Air Pump in the cellar, would need to be built. Soon.

The house was built with two by twelve floor joists on sixteen-inch centers, on top of which we'd have to figure out which form of 'mass' would be most thorough in providing a good degree of protection from fallout. Concrete would be best, if I recalled, a whole lot of dirt would be a second.

"OK. I'll go get started getting the stuff ready for the shelter. You guys know what you need here, right?"

"Yeah. I'll come get that water barrel," Ron said.

"I'll go raid the upstairs," Alan added. "You think the wives will think we're off our nut?"

"You mean any more than normal?" I said.

23

Good Friday
April Fourteenth
4:07 pm

Before the 'deadline' set by the President, we tasked ourselves to move a lot of material into both shelters. All the kids knew what was going on, Mark and Rachel included, but I'm sure they didn't fully grasp the situation. Mary stayed with them for the rest of the movie, now deep into the third hour, and kept them focused on Moses and Pharaoh.

I'd made a quick trip down the street to Joe's, and found a note that he and Joan had left for Don's place, ten or twelve miles further away from Fairchild than we were. Aaron passed me by on the way back home, and stopped to let me know that he and Ellen MacDonald would be sheltering at his house. I reminded him that he should remain a gentleman for the duration. That comment got me a startled look, and then a quick, deep laugh. It was good to know that even in times like these, I could still zing someone.

I went back to work with Carl, getting the food and gear moved in, and keeping an eye on the water barrels as they filled. Sleeping bags, clothing, a Coleman stove and fuel, lanterns, basically all the stuff that we camped with....a long list. We'd set it up and put it 'away' when we were 'in' the shelter. I had checked the air pump that I'd built years-ago first-thing, wishing that I'd done so weeks ago. The 'air shaft' that it would be installed in was filled with sand, with a trap door on the bottom, locked in place with a steel brace. A heavy concrete pad covered the vent stack on the 'top' of the shaft. The theory was, after the 'bomb' went off, and before the fallout hit, someone (me) would remove this cap, dump the sand out of the shaft, put a 'fallout' cap on the shaft, and we'd be able to breath 'filtered' air from the air intake. The filters weren't much, just several series of common furnace filters. I put Karen on task with raiding the tent-trailer for it's utensils and kitchen stuff—it was already pre-packed in bags and easier to load up, lock, stock, and barrel, than raiding the barn. Besides that, if things 'simmered' rather than 'flared', I didn't want to be living in the shelter or running back and forth looking for whatever we needed to make dinner. I continued to kick myself for not double-checking the theoretical operation of this shelter, and its shortcomings, long before.

Ron and Alan, assisted by John, moved a ton of stuff into Alan's basement while we were working on the root cellar. Their first task was to upgrade the mass-shielding overhead. For this room, I handed them my hard-copy file of shielding against radioactivity info, in addition to the two reference books I had and a couple of FEMA brochures on home-made shelters. One of the ancient-- nineteen-sixties era--brochures had plans and sketches of constructing infill-mass that fit between floor joists, constructed of brick, block, and earth. This was the task at hand for both of them. Alan was building as they went--Ron and John were scrounging materials. The collapsed brick house opposite of Alan's provided ample brick, a carport to the north of that house provided three-quarter-inch plywood and a fair amount of the framing needed. My supplies of screws, nails and metal brackets helped put things together.

The plan allowed for sixteen inches of bricks stacked as tightly as possible and as deeply as possible on top of a wood frame, which was assembled just below the floor joists. On the floor above this room, a nearly empty bedroom (more so now, with the bunk bed scheduled to be moved to the shelter room), boxes and bags of dirt would be piled to a depth of at least a foot, preferably sixteen to eighteen inches. This wouldn't provide as much shielding as we had in the shelter, with its concrete and earth cover, but probably adequate. Far better than a simple basement.

As soon as a section of 'ceiling' was paneled, framed and filled, contents of the shelter magically appeared....Libby and Marie worked on moving a substantial pile of stuff into the room. When they weren't hauling 'stuff', they were hauling bricks.

We knew when we started that there would be no way to complete the work by four p.m., though. If we were lucky we'd have another day. Of course, if we were really lucky, we wouldn't have to finish it at all...

By a few minutes before four, the root cellar shelter was about as well equipped as we could make it in an hour. I sent Carl over to Alan's, and checked in with Kelly, who was now finishing the movie with Mark and Rachel, and listening to the radios. Mary had headed home to help 'stock' the shelter, taking along a well-padded wheelbarrow load of our home-canned goods.

"Kel, heard any news?"

"Sounds like the entire east coast is evacuating. There's not enough gas though so people are going out on foot." I knew that if this was the case and attack came, they'd never have a chance.

"Anything from the President?"

"No, the CBS broadcast said he'd left D.C. this morning. No one has any idea where he or the Vice President are."

'Airborne, I hope,' I thought to myself. "How about shortwave? Anything there?"

"They said that no radio broadcasts have been heard from Europe for the last half-hour. Some guy in Tennessee said he was listening to the BBC and it went off in mid-sentence. What's that mean?"

"It might mean that we've hit them with a pulse weapon. That would fry their electrical systems. It would be the first step to an attack," I said, anticipating her question. To myself, I said, 'Pretty hard to let the other side know that you're going to back off if you can't talk. That makes no sense though....'

"So with China out of the picture, then who is it who wants to attack us?"

"Might still be some of the Europeans, since they're now pretty much ruled by the Muslims. Might be Russia, too."

"Do you think that we'll ......be attacked, Dad?"

"I don't know. I do know that before the quake, we were high on the list with Fairchild and all. Now, I don't know. I wouldn't be surprised if we were though. Turn up the radio so I can hear it. It's almost four." A local and not national broadcast came on. Should that have surprised me as much as it did?

"Local and regional authorities advise all in the Spokane metropolitan area to take shelter or evacuate out of the urban area in case of attack. Communications with national authorities have been interrupted due to an attack on telephone relay systems in Denver, Colorado. Most commercial satellite communications have been disrupted by an unknown cause. The response to the ultimatum put forth by the President, now just passing, is unknown. The U.S. has stated that the communications blackout over Europe was not caused by a pre-emptive attack by the U.S., however. A limited amount of commercial radio traffic is still being broadcast in the local area and will cover events as they arise. Again, repeating, local and regional authorities..."

"What does all that mean?"

"That means that it's probably a good idea to get to the shelters," I said. "The movie's almost over. Let's get the little ones packed up and home."

'So Europe can't talk to us, and some of our domestic phone systems, especially those used for official communications, are out. European? Russian?' Who did this?' I asked myself as I tried to keep calm.

By four-twenty, Karen, Libby and the Martin and Drummond kids were in the root cellar shelter, getting things squared away. I continued to both feel silly about the precaution and worried that we'd be hit anyway. Grace and the kids were already in their cellar shelter as well, still not finished, with Mary, Ron, Alan and I working on finishing the installation of the brick mass in voids between the joists above the room. We still had to fill whatever boxes or bags or whatever with soil, and put them in and around the room above the basement shelter. I knew that that task would take hours all by itself. We would at least today, get the brick and blocks installed, and get things situated for the night. Tomorrow we'd hit it again, unless we heard otherwise. 'Otherwise' of course, meaning that sense had prevailed and that nuclear war was not in our future. Or perhaps not in our 'immediate' future.

Each shelter included bedding for most of the occupants either in bunks or regular beds (Alan's house) or improvised bunks (our cellar—shelving that served in normal times as storage, but was also sized similar to Navy sleeping berths. Not generous). The list of things that each shelter required was sizeable. Much more so than we would think of in non-war times. Until we were actually attacked, we could use 'line' power for whatever we had in the shelters, which in our case included lighting, radios, and fans. The shelters, with limited ventilation, were both quickly becoming warm and 'stale'. The weather outside wasn't particularly cooperative, either, with dust again, kicking up, but at least there was some cloud cover coming in, so perhaps rain was in our future.

Power for the 'cellar' shelter was run across the field underground, in a PVC conduit that I'd put in, running two GFCI outlets and two shielded incandescent lamps along the center of the aisle. In the event of an electromagnetic pulse, this line would probably send an electrical surge into whatever was connected to it, possibly—probably—killing it. I had no provisions for building a Faraday cage---which would insulate whatever was inside it from such a surge—it was one of a zillion things that I never got around to. The underground power, and a small air connection and air pump that was run by hand, provided us 'fresh' air. These connections to the outside air would render our shelter useless as a blast shelter, since the overpressure would overwhelm the shelter through the air inlets. In the case of an imminent attack, these could be capped with a steel threaded cap, and we'd take our chances on the carbon-dioxide buildup until the blast passed. In theory. Theory depended on a single attack though. Spokane was likely targeted, at least in the good old days by the Soviets, by multiple warheads, and was definitely a first-strike target. These days it was anyone's guess. Would they de-target us because we got whacked by an earthquake, causing the vast majority of our military aircraft to move to other bases? Probably not.

A few minutes before five p.m., we decided to knock off for the day, and take up residence in our temporary shelters. We had our FRS radios charged up, and both shelters had AM radios listening to KDA, the last local station still broadcasting. The others, with their studios in the downtown area or not being scheduled to run at all were off the air, after shutting down fairly quickly after two p.m. My portable Sangean radio with the shortwave band, picked up little more. My scanner was all but useless, picking up massive traffic on the CB channels. Alan and I shook hands and gave each other a hug, and we headed off to our caves. We both felt the apprehension that we might have only minutes….and both felt that we were worrying too much about it. Karen and her Mom had already hugged and said some things quietly to each other, before heading off to their shelters. I looked away, a lump in my throat.

Karen was hunting up dinner, tonight that would be some of the 'collected' food in cans, some home made wheat bread, and some juice from powdered drink mix. We were using more of the 'collected' foods these days, but we knew that the supply of them was running low, soon there would be no 'pre-Depression' pre-made foods left anywhere. Most of what we were using were early-date packages, and would not last more than a few months in any regard. We had enough canned food—meaning in metal cans—and home canned goods to survive in the shelter for three weeks of spare meals. A large portion of the shelter walls were lined with cans. The jars, including quarts, pints and the odd sized half-gallon, were padded with rags and paper, to keep them from breaking in the event of another quake or…ground shock from a nuclear blast. Each shelter had about a hundred-fifty gallons of water as well, in cleaned food-grade barrels treated with a touch of bleach. The drinking water portion would be filtered through one of the two Berkey filters that we had.

Uncertainty.

One of my least favorite things to endure. Not knowing if we were at war, would be at war, or were already 'victorious'…whatever that might mean, was arguably the most stress-inducing event that we'd experienced since late January. We agreed en masse that until we heard otherwise, it was probably advisable to remain in the shelters until we 'heard otherwise'. The thought of a flash of a nearby explosion left little time for considering other courses of action of course, so we 'hid' from whatever might be coming.

How could it come to this?

I shut the door at ten minutes after five, both dogs already settled in on their dusty dog-beds. Provisions for their bodily functions were already a topic of interest, we'd not thought of it before. 'That'll be fun to clean up,' I thought.

Ron and Libby were at the far end of the shelter, around a card table, John and Carl were both listening to, or trying to listen, to different frequencies on two portable radios. 'This will get tight,' I said to myself. Both Kelly and Marie had retreated to their respective bunk areas, head to head, and were talking. For middle-school sized girls, the bunks were probably adequate. For John on the other hand, I'm sure it was much like a seaman on some submarine, stuffed into a too-small berth. The thin foam pads over the wooden shelf provided nothing in the way of comfort, either.

"Spokane to one thirty-seven," the County radio barked, startling us all. It was sitting in it's backpack, with a couple of alligator clips snaking over to the twelve-volt battery I'd pulled out of the Mustang, and then charged up.

"One thirty-seven," I responded.

"Spokane EOC requests your location," a flat voice asked.

"My home root cellar," I answered back.

"Thank you, our EOC staff is verifying locations of all County personnel. EOC operations have been relocated out of the urban area until further notice."

"Understood. Good luck and God bless. One thirty-seven out." I said.

"Thank you. Spokane out."

I wondered for a moment about others in the neighborhood and the city, and how they were preparing, or were they fleeing? Dan and Sandy, just north of Alan's place, hadn't been seen all day. Dan's Modern Electric four-wheel-drive was gone, as was his travel trailer, which sheltered him in the days following the quake. Maybe they'd bugged out after all.

"Kinda eerie, huh, Dad?" Carl asked.

"What's that?" I said.

"Like in the movie. 'And evil shall pass over....'"

I thought for a minute. "Yes, but we are dealing with a whole different kind of bondage," I said.

24

Friday Evening,
April Fourteenth

I took Buck and Ada out for a short walk after dinner, tasked with a trip over to the barn to pick up a few things that we'd forgotten, toothpaste being one thing, some books (entertainment, not technical) being another. I had one of the FRS's in my pocket and earbud plugged in as well, and my forty-five on my hip—tonight it felt odd to be wearing it, like a pea-shooter. Karen and Libby had done a good job getting things put together for the cellar in short order, but our supplies in the root cellar were in disorganized heaps and piles. We'd have to do some sorting so that we could find things. The box containing the potassium iodide tablets were at least where I could find them. I knew that I'd also printed the balance of the web-site information regarding their use as well, and put a copy with the pills and with one of my binders. The one labeled 'Radiation.'

The weather was pleasant, the last traces of daylight fading, the dusty ash still blowing about. Each step the dogs took in the native grass pasture, now a foot or more tall, stirred up more clouds of grey, almost a wake behind them in the play of the flashlight. Dark clouds obscured what might have been the last bits of sunset to my left, moving in from the southwest. I hoped they held rain. The Falcon van, one of my many ancient vehicles, was parked up by the gate, gassed up and ready to go if we needed to leave. Behind the van, my equally old Falcon station wagon. Both were pre-transistor, so if an electromagnetic pulse hit, they'd still run. Hopefully. The van could hold normally six, as could the wagon. Add in supplies, and we'd need the trailer. I was praying that we wouldn't need either. Besides that, where could we go?

As I stood there in the field not really watching the dogs, I thought to myself that I could not ever remember being this….depressed. Buck startled me back to reality and out of my thousand-yard stare, grabbing my hand with his soft mouth and urging me to play, growling with that deep growl while his tail went crazy. I snapped out of my bad humor and went over to the barn and collected our things.

Back in the shelter it seemed everyone was in the same mood that I'd been in. Carl had his back turned to the rest of the room, John on his back. The girls were playing at cards, not really playing the game. Libby and Karen were sorting, stacking and trying to organize. The static of the radio crackled in the background next to Ron. He was reading Nuclear War Survival Skills, propped up on his lap.

"Nothing on the radio?" I said.

"No, KDA signed off until tomorrow morning. We tried to find some other station, but nothing's coming in strong enough to be clear," Karen said. "Get everything?"

"Yeah, for now. Might have some rain tonight."

I put the bag of books on the shelf with my binders, rescued from the basement after the quake, and holstered the FRS in its charger just as the ceiling lights flared and then died.

"Whoa!" Ron said.

"Well, now. This complicates things," I said as I found a flashlight. I'd picked up a couple of the power-failure lights from the barn, and flipped them on. Karen dug out one of the kerosene camp lanterns and was about to light it. "Hon, don't light that. Let's use the battery lanterns. That'll just use more air."

"OK," she said quietly. I could tell she was either crying or about to.

"Listen up. We know this: The power is out. We don't know that we've been nuked, all right? How many times has the power dropped out since it came back on two weeks ago?" I asked, knowing the answer.

"Dozens of times," Karen said.

"Right. This may be no different. Don't make it a big deal," I said to Karen but really directed at everyone. "Besides that, we may only spend one night in here. We're here as a precaution, remember."

"OK," she said.

"Let's check with Alan," I said.

"Y'all got your ears on?" I said into the FRS.

"Yep. You just lose power too?"

"Yeah. Checking to see if you did or if it was just us."

"We're all in this together, my friend."

"Indeed. Talk to you later."

"Yep. Take care," Alan replied. I'm sure Mary and the kids were scared too. I decided not to look it, even though I was worried too. I checked my watch, eight fifty-seven p.m. Deadline plus four hours.

"OK, not just us. Don't worry about it because there's nothing we can do about it anyway, and we're plenty used to living without it. Right?" I asked everyone, knowing in the back of my mind that without power, coming by drinkable water could be a problem once our stored water was gone. We had no well of our own, and hauling water from the Paulianos well would not be…convenient.

A number of mumbled affirmatives came my way.

"All right. I'll stay up 'til eleven and try to find something on the radio. Ron, you want to go after that?"

"Sure," he answered, still reading.

"Carl, John, you two after Ron?"

"OK," they answered.

"All right then. You should try to get some sleep. I'll screen off the door area with a blanket, and we'll keep a light on here. While you're up, you'll need to open the door for five minutes every half hour enough to get some air in here. The air-pump we use only after we're sealed in. It's capped now. Right?"

"Yep," Ron answered. The boys nodded.

"OK. Libby, Karen, you all get ready for bed, and that might want to start with a trip to the outhouse, unless you prefer to do your business in here."

"No, thanks," Kelly answered. "Is it OK to go out?" Kelly asked.

"I was just out there," I said for example. "We haven't been hit by anything or we'd've heard or seen it. So yes, sort of. The shelter is more for fallout than blast," (this was not true) "although it would work for blast when we know that we're in imminent danger. If a bomb goes off, the flash is the first warning we might get, which is why we're in here. We're protected from the heat, which might flash-burn your skin or set wood buildings on fire. We can quickly close the door until the heat and the blast wave passes, then get the air-pump set up so that we can stay inside until the fallout decays to a point where it's not as dangerous as it would be right after the blast. That's a short-course on how the shelter works."

"Oh," Kelly said. "I didn't know that. I thought we had to stay here for good."

"No. Just for a while. So why don't you and your Mom go across the field to the 'facilities' and hurry back. Then Libby and Marie, then the boys. No sense in having everyone in a line. OK?"

"K."

"Then you get settled in and get some rest. I'll see if I can find anything on shortwave."

"All right," she said.

"Hon, don't worry. We'll be fine," I said softly to Karen.

"Says you."

"Yes. Says me. Now help me string up a blanket here."

"K."

By nine-twenty, everyone had 'done their business' and was settling in. Karen had helped me string a rope across the entry to the shelter, and I'd tossed a blanket over the line. I turned off the 'bright' setting on the battery powered lamp, and then shut it off altogether after I turned on a very small LED headlamp, which provided barely enough light to see the radio dial, but which would save battery power. I spent the next two hours fine-tuning the radio on AM, FM and SW bands and never did get a coherent signal. The last time I opened the door for a bit of fresh air, the dust was settled by a light rain. I thought I heard thunder off in the distance.

A little after eleven, I roused Ron, and he took over, bringing the copy of 'NWSS" with him. I noticed by his bookmark, he was well over a third of the way through it.

"Nothing on the radio," I said. "And I mean nothing."

"K. Thanks."

I climbed into 'bed' across from Karen and lay atop my sleeping bag. It took a long time to get to sleep.

Saturday, April 15

Karen stirred; I could tell that I'd been sleeping for a long time by the kink in my neck. I got up with her, and checked the time. Five minutes after five a.m. I had slept a while.

John was up, reading the book that Ron had left out.

"Morning," I said as we went to the barely-lit side of the blanket.

"Hi. No news."

"Go on and head to bed," Karen said. "I'll stay up."

"K. Thanks." John ducked behind the blanket and I heard the shelf/berth creak as he climbed back in.

"You OK?" I asked Karen.

"Couldn't sleep, that's all."

"I'm going out for a sec," I said.

"You all right?"

"Yeah, just going to get some air. I'll take the dogs out." I slipped into a jacket and stepped into my boots.

"K. Don't stay too long."

"C'mon you two," I said to Buck, who was ready to go, and Ada, who'd prefer to sleep."

I opened the steel door as quietly as I could and took the dogs out into the pre-dawn. Sunrise wasn't due until a little after six, an hour from now, and the stars were fading from a crystal-clear sky. I had a difficult time believing that somewhere right now World War Three might be raging. Was likely raging?

I took the dogs up around the house, past the cars. Buck as usual was nosing after something, then flitting after something else. A few minutes later, I was back at the cellar door with wet boots and wet dogs. I enjoyed the very fresh air, wondering how long it would be before we really had to worry about fallout here from the China bombs—not very long. And probably others we hadn't heard about. Now we had to decide what to do next.

I went back inside, holding the door briefly open for fresh air, and found the lights on in the shelter—line power was back. We'd left the switch on last night I guess, and the lights coming back on managed to wake up everyone.

"Well, that's a good sign," I said.

"A little rude way to wake up, but yes," Libby said.

"Morning, beautiful," I said to Karen.

"The bright lights reveal the true me. Unwashed, uncombed, unkempt."

"Yep, and I'm all over it. I don't suppose the radio is back as well," I said.

"Too early. They said six."

"Yeah, but let me hope."

"That you can do," she said.

"Rick there's some notes that I made in your book. Hope you don't mind," Ron said.

"Me, too," said John.

"Whatchya got?"

"If this is a fallout shelter like the one in the book, don't we need a place to put our contaminated clothes and to wash down?" Ron said.

'Well, duh,' I said to myself before saying the exact words out loud. "I never said this was a perfect plan. Especially since we put it together in an hour."

"That's OK," Ron said. "We're only counting on you with our lives."

"Funny. What else."

"Shouldn't the stairs have a cover over them? For dust and…fallout?"

"Yeah. Next?"

"Couple other things. I don't mean to beat up on you."

"You're not."

"Alan's shelter. Sidewall shielding on the outside wall, exposed to the atmosphere. Shouldn't we pile up some dirt on that side?"

"Yes. I think you are our new expert in surviving fallout. I haven't read that book in awhile," 'since the first round with China,' I remembered.

"Rick, what do you think we should do today?" Libby asked.

"By and large stay inside. Not for fallout, but in case we actually get attacked. That should be the rule for the majority of us. There are some things we still need to do obviously to get the shelters finished for fallout; you've identified most of them. I want Karen to read up on the potassium iodide tablets too, and we should think about taking them soon, today or tomorrow."

"What are those for?" Libby asked.

"They will help prevent radioactive iodide...or iodine, I can't remember...from settling in the thyroid gland and causing cancer."

"Where did you buy those?"

"Guy on the internet. Shane Connor. KI4U.com, I think the address was. Dosage is one pill per day for adults...probably the same for the older kids. Younger kids will need less. We'll need to check to see if anyone is allergic to iodine before we take this stuff though."

"Do you have enough?" Karen asked.

"Yes."

"For everyone? There's thirteen of us," Karen said.

"Yes. I have enough for twenty people."

"Why twenty?"

"Why not? Really, it was in case of a protracted nuclear war. Longer than thirty minutes, perhaps weeks or months of war, at random."

"What if this is that kind of war?"

"Then we'll not have enough."

"We have regular iodine," Karen said.

"Not the same stuff. Iodine is poisonous taken internally."

"Oh."

"On to more current matters. Do we want to make breakfast now, or later? I'm starving."

"Us, too," the kids answered.

"Then there you go. Did you have something planned already?" I asked Karen.

"Yes. We made some breakfast bars yesterday. Dried peaches, raisins, oatmeal, and popped wheat, among other tasty items, one being chocolate chips."

"Count me in," I said. Anyone else want to go use the latrine?"

"Yep," Ron said.

"Tallest to shortest, one at a time," I said. Take a new roll. The last one was getting a little thin.

Each of our cellar residents made a trip over to the outhouse, a much shorter trip than up to the house, which never even crossed my mind at the time.

By six, when the radio broadcast was supposed to start, we had each had a square of the breakfast bar, which was more filling than it might've appeared. The girls settled back into their berths, while the boys tried to come up with a more comfortable place to sit or relax. They were currently working on a plan for snagging my two summer hammocks from the storage shed and putting them to a new use in the root cellar. I was skeptical that it would work, but it kept them occupied for a while.

I had the radios tuned to KDA and KLXY, the most reliable of the local stations these days. I was surprised when my County radio was the one that spoke first, although not to me.

"Spokane to one oh-one," the dispatcher began. One oh-one never responded. The count, up to my 'one thirty-seven' and beyond. No communication beyond determining who was listening or in range was allowed at this time. 'One oh-five' was barked at for asking questions.

"Good morning, this is KDA Spokane. It is six a.m. local time."

"About danged time," Ron said.

"It is just six," I said.

"Hush, you men." Libby said.

"KDA overnight has received information that the United States has been attacked overnight in a number of locations within the lower Forty-Eight states with nuclear weapons. At least one of these attacks was not successful, with one warhead failing to explode above it's intended target."

"Oh my God," Karen said.

"Information is still coming in on these attacks, and it is our understanding that U.S. military forces are in direct conflict with military units of the European Union and Russia, after Russian missiles were launched at Israel. The attack, as described by the Undersecretary of Defense as 'disorganized' and 'haphazard', does not appear to be an all-out attack on the U.S., but has destroyed a number of military assets in the U.S. and, as we understand it, at least one Navy Carrier Group in the Mediterranean and a second in the western Pacific Ocean. Telephone service and communications throughout the U.S., continue to be widely disrupted, and most of the information that we are reporting is being forwarded to us by amateur radio broadcasts relayed across the continent. We can report however with confidence, that a number of U.S. cities lie in ruins this morning, and it is likely that millions of Americans have died in this attack. These cities and their military bases include Vandenberg Air Force Base in California; Kennedy Space Center in Florida; Huntsville, Alabama, which historically has had a significant role in the development of the U.S. space program; Norfolk and Newport News, Virginia; Groton, Connecticut and Quonset Point, Rhode Island, both known for their fabrication of nuclear submarines. According to an un-named NASA source, the United States has no non-military space launch facilities left after the attack. In addition to the cities listed above, an explosion was seen at least a hundred miles west of San Diego, perhaps a warhead that was short of the target. A warhead impacted in rural Houston, Texas, after failing to explodåe above the city."

"We cannot confirm that either the President, the Vice President or the majority of the civilian and military leadership of the United States are safe at this time."

We all looked at each other when the anchor said that, wondering if the country we knew still existed, even though battered and burned.

25

I quickly moved to write down what the newscaster said. 'Norfolk, Newport News, San Diego, Cape Canaveral, Connecticut and Delaware.' No West Coast impacts. Yet.   If the winds were from the south almost due north-northwest, we might get some fallout from the explosion off of San Diego. The rest of the fallout, other than whatever we'd launched at China already, would have to cross the Pacific, or circle the globe, before it reached us.

"It should be stressed that although we do not know of the status of the Federal leadership, sources in the government that are available, primarily in St. Louis, Minneapolis, and Denver, expect the President to address the nation later today," the news anchor said.

"Local officials continue to urge residents to remain in shelters for the majority of the time until further notice. It is not known at this time if military actions are still taking place between the United States and Russia or the E.U. As such, it is not known if Spokane or other potential targets in the Pacific Northwest might yet be targeted. These potential targets include Fairchild Air Force Base, Grand Coulee Dam, the Hanford Nuclear Reservation, the Puget Sound region, Portland, Oregon, and major population centers in the region."

"We are going to be speaking with Spokane County's interim director of emergency operations, Lieutenant Pete Wolfson, who's with the County Sheriff's office. Pete should be joining us within fifteen minutes or so. I would like to inform you at home throughout the region, that KDA will be on the air until noon today, after which KLXY will be on the air until eight p.m. or later this evening. No television stations are operating at this time within the Spokane area. Additionally, as we stated at the top of the hour, our primary sources of information—hard news—are news outlets nation wide that pre-war, would communicate heavily through the use of satellite networks. These satellite networks are now not operating, and we're frankly trying to find a way to work without them. News right now is being gathered and broadcast on ham radio networks across the country, as well as on a limited number of commercial telephone lines, but not of course here in the Northwest. Our land-line telephone systems, and the great majority of cell phone service was of course lost in January."

"Wolfson was Mike Amberson's logistics guy. I met him right after the quake. Must've got a field transfer," I said. 'Doesn't sound like a promotion….'

"Our news-reporting capabilities are, well, rather informal. We're trying to ascertain what is 'real' and what is rumor, and report that to you as soon as we can confirm the accuracy of the reports coming in. There are very few reports coming in from outside the country, but reports have been coming in that state that Israel's Air Force has destroyed Damascus, Syria—I repeat Israel's Air Force has destroyed the capital city of Syria, through the use of a nuclear weapon. It can be assumed that nuclear weapons may have also been used by Israel against Iran, whose forces have been attacking Israel with conventional forces and gas attacks since hostilities began. We are attempting to confirm these reports first-hand, but due to the failure of the satellite systems, this has not yet been possible."

"Isaiah, Chapter Seventeen," Karen said. I realized immediately she was right. Carl and Kelly got the reference, too.

"What?" Ron said.

"The burden of Damascus, 'Behold, Damascus is taken away from being a city, and it shall be a ruinous heap. …… At evening, behold, terror; and before the morning they are no more. ….'" That's not complete, though. The first verse and part of the last," I said. Ron looked pretty pale.

The news broadcast was now repeating the previous statements about the attacks.

"What did they say about our space stuff?" Carl asked.

"That we can't launch anymore," Karen said. "Or not for a long while."

"Sucks to be up in the space station right now, then," Carl said.

"Maybe. They have a 'Soyuz' capsule to get back home. Their 'lifeboat', I guess," I said. For two months we'd been trying to get a shuttle up to them for re-supply, finally the Russians sent one of theirs. Pretty tough to grow food and spare parts in space.

"That's gonna be an interesting trip. Who was up there?" Ron asked.

"I think only one American. The rest were Russians. I imagine they're having an interesting day," 'assuming they're still alive at all,' I didn't add. 'What do nuclear detonations in space do to people in space?' I wondered.

The broadcast finally had Pete Wolfson to talk to…. *"Pete, can you tell me what the County's preparations are for the war?"*

I could almost see his pained expression. *"The County government, what is left of it, as well as many key personnel, technical and physical resources, have been relocated out of an immediate projected blast area or are in shelters in the region. We are recommending that until further notice, the majority of time of each persons' day is spent in these shelters, either underground or in basements or best of course, out of the urban area. We do not know if Spokane or the base will be targeted, or how long the war will last."*

"How much warning will we have if we are attacked?"

"None."

Silence on the other end of the microphone. Pete continued. *"There is no longer an early warning system, and as you well know, communications throughout the country are a shambles. That's why we're recommending that everyone stay under cover. Literally, the flash of a nuclear weapon may be the only advance warning we get."*

"That's what you said, Dad!" Kelly said.

"Hush, now."

"What about if we're not attacked? What can we do to protect ourselves? The fallout from the attacks in Russia and China, as well as those in this country, will reach us eventually."

"He mentioned Russia?" Libby said.

"Yeah. Russia and the E.U. attacked Israel. We got involved. They said that earlier."

"Missed it."

Pete Wolfson replied to the anchors question. *"The County has a limited amount of medicines available—to be used before the radiation gets here and until further notice—to help prevent thyroid cancer. This will not prevent you from getting radiation sickness, and I need to emphasize that. This medicine will be provided to residents registered in Spokane County as of last Monday's food distribution cycle. Other precautions regarding protection against radiation sickness will be available at three community centers only: Spokane Valley, the South Hill center at Ferris High School, and the North Side shelter at Mead*

Junior High school. Other community centers are closed and again we urge that people within the downtown area make alternate arrangements for shelter, outside of the downtown area. These three community centers will open at eight a.m.—for one hour only-- for distribution of brochures on radiation protection as well as to distribute potassium iodide and allergic symptoms sheets."

"Allergies? I don't understand," the anchor said.

"A percentage of the population is allergic to iodine. The symptom sheet lists possible reactions to iodine. If they are allergic and still take it, it may make them sick. It may kill them in extreme cases."

That gave the anchor a pause. *"Will the medicine be administered by staff or medical personnel?"*

"There are no medical personnel available. Instructions are printed with each kit."

"Can you tell me where the medical staffs are, and the status of our local hospitals?"

"Most staff that have worked at each neighborhood clinic have been evacuated out of the area. Sacred Heart Medical Center remains operational for patients that cannot leave the hospital, I understand that less than twenty patients remain there," Pete said.

Sacred Heart once had over six hundred beds, pre-quake, and was the premier medical complex in the region, I remembered. I was born there.

"Deaconess Hospital's pediatrics and maternity unit remains in place at the moment, but will be closed by nine a.m. and relocated out of the region. Valley Medical Center has its full complement of departments, meaning the emergency department, pediatrics, internal medicine and radiology will remain open. Valley has a severe overcrowding problem as you can expect, with only fifty of the one hundred-thirty beds open since the earthquake. Holy Family hospital of course was lost in the quake."

"How about Fairchild? Has the Air Force evacuated the base?"

"I cannot comment on the base because I simply don't know. We did recommend that Airway Heights and Cheney residents evacuate." Airway Heights was a strip-city that lived off of the airmen at the base. Cheney, home to...or former home to...Eastern Washington University, was about ten miles south of Fairchild, or about the same distance to downtown Spokane. The

disadvantage of Cheney was that it was more exposed due to terrain than Spokane, which was sheltered a bit more in the river valley.

"Can you provide us any more information on sheltering or protecting ourselves?"

"Not beyond what is in the printed matter, no, other than the fact that we are monitoring background radiation with our own equipment, and will advise the public when we believe fallout is in the area. We have more than enough copies of the shelter brochures for the remaining population. We have adequate potassium iodide for our population. I'm sorry, Mike, but I really need to attend to business," Pete said.

"I understand, Lieutenant. Thank you for coming out here today. To our listeners, our KDA studios have been closed and we are broadcasting from our transmitter location south of Spokane. OK, we're going to dig up a weather broadcast for the day, as soon as I can find it...."

"Let's hope it's not 'a high of eleven million degrees and winds of eight-hundred miles per hour,'" I said, inappropriately. It was funny once. Not today.

Pete's discussion about monitoring radiation and fallout brought of course to my mind the fact that I did not have a Geiger counter of any kind, but I did have my Kearny Fallout Meter and made a note to re-read how the thing was supposed to work, and that we should probably build a couple more as well.

Karen made breakfast of scrambled eggs while Libby fought with a couple cans of Spam. Once only I would eat the stuff, but still had Karen lay in a stock of the stuff. Now the kids had acquired the ability to eat it, browned, seasoned, or otherwise fashioned into some form that might- or might-not have been recognizable. Libby was slicing up the second can into cubes, and would fry them up on the Coleman stove. I was nursing a cup of coffee, with a shot of bourbon tossed in for non-medicinal reasons. I was again fighting a mental wear-down, trying to figure out for the umpteenth time, what we needed to do 'first', and often finding that in conflict with both what I really wanted to do, and what was 'prudent.' Baaah!

Alan radioed over a little before seven, having slept longer than he'd planned. I told him to go somewhere a little more private before I gave him the update that we'd heard. His kids had had a good night though, sleeping in real beds, as had Grace and Mary. Alan had slept in a recliner that we hauled downstairs into their coal room shelter. For an improvised room, theirs 'seemed' bigger than ours, but we had more 'stuff' than they did. We agreed to meet at seven-thirty and put together the days' plan. Mary was cooking breakfast, in the kitchen upstairs, although they'd eat in the shelter.

The news was still continuing on in the shelter, Marie and Kelly were now taking notes, summarizing the important stuff. One day, those notes might tell a very interesting story, I thought.

At seven forty-five, I left the house for the community center in my ancient van, and listened to the recap of the previous announcement and what little local news was gathered. It mostly focused on gas thefts and reports of supplies being stolen…sometimes at gunpoint or worse. In short order, I arrived at the corner convenience store, shuttered tight. No traffic was visible on any of the streets. By ten 'til eight, I was sitting in the parking lot. Alone.

At five 'til eight, a very dirty Crown Victoria showed up, and a camouflage-clad figure climbed out and quickly went to the locked doors. I followed him inside.

"Good morning," I said to his back as he continued into the darkened building.

"That's a matter of opinion," he said.

"I'm Rick Drummond. You are…?" I was a little irritated with his attitude at first, but checked myself before I went off on the guy. We had, I kept reminding myself, been attacked today. I suppose this was going to be remembered for decades like Pearl Harbor, or Nine Eleven, which now paled in comparison.

"Morrison. John Morrison," he said, never looking at me, unpacking a cabinet of cardboard boxes. Each was stamped with 'KI' on the sides. A stack of Xeroxed instructions was rapidly tossed on the desk in front of the cabinet.

"Nice to meet you."

"Yeah. You too," he said sarcastically. 'Don't go there, Rick,' I said to myself.

"How many are you?" he said, finding my name on the census sheet.

"Four Drummonds, five Bauers, four Martins," I said as I gave him our street addresses. "And two dogs."

"Dog's and pets don't get anything," Morrison said. I decided to remain silent on the matter, for fear I might take his head off. This guy was really pissing me off. I suppose that everyone's fuses were just a little too short. I heard someone come into the parking lot outside, and I turned to look, having a tough time seeing through the broken glass, patched with translucent fiberglass and plastic sheeting. Aaron Watters was coming in, or at least that was his Toyota. Another figure, I thought maybe Randy Thompson, passed the window on a mountain bike.

"Here's your allotment. The instruction sheets tell you the dosage per the size of the individual. This is a month allotment."

'Weight', not 'size', I thought but didn't say. "Thanks," I said as Aaron came in behind me.

"Nice to see you, Rick."

"You too, Aaron. How's Ellen doing?"

"Very well. She's been a joy. Even through these troubled times."

"Name," Morrison said.

"Watters, Aaron C. I'm also getting medicine for McDonald, Ellen Louise."

"Addresses," Morrison again stated, almost spitting it.

Aaron and I looked at each other with the same thought, as he gave his street address, and that of Ellen.

Morrison then repeated his instructions and handed Aaron two bottles of potassium iodide and two sheets of paper. "You two can leave now," he said.

"We know, thanks," I said. Randy, Aaron and I exchanged 'hello's' and then Morrison went through his spiel again. No one else showed up by eight fifteen. Morrison then proceeded to take the still-full boxes of KI—there seemed like a dozen of them—down into the basement and locked them up. The partially used box, remained in the office.

Randy and his girlfriend were 'holed up' as Randy said in the basement portion of a converted barn that belonged to his girlfriend's parents. His wrecked apartment, even though he was still living there, was entirely unsuitable for fallout. He would've driven, but the battery in his ancient Landcruiser wagon had been stolen three nights before.

"Rick, can I ask you a favor?" he asked as we went back outside.

"Sure. Within limits," I said only half-humorously.

"I'd like to get some stuff from the store. I can pay for it."

"OK, let's make it quick then. Aaron, how about you?"

"I'm good to go. I'll let you know Rick, if I hear anything on my radios."

"Aren't you afraid of them getting hammered by EMP?"

"Tube radios. Ancient. And very resilient to electromagnetic pulses. And, I have spare parts just in case. And, one full setup in a cage," he said. 'Faraday cage,' I thought to myself.

"All right then. We'll have one of the CB's running on your barter network schedule. If you have anything to report, catch us then, OK?"

"Done. You watch yourself, you two. And Rick, tell Karen and Libby thanks for they'll know what," he said.

That caught me by surprise. "Uh, OK. I'll do that. Thanks Aaron."

"Toss your bike in the trailer. I'm going to get some stuff myself."

"Thanks."

We made the quick drive to the store and parked right next to the door. The radio was again, repeating the news we'd heard earlier. The same anchor was doing the talking. I suppose he drew the short straw.

"Whatchya need?"

"Coleman fuel. I think we have a pint left. I'd like to get another couple radios too, and some plastic sheeting. Maybe some other stuff."

"That's fine with me, if we've got it. What did you plan on trading?"

"This," he said as he flipped me a dull yellow coin.

I almost dropped it as I fished out my keys. It was an 1889 twenty-dollar gold piece.

"You sure?"

"Yeah."

"Well that'll buy you more than just fuel."

"I'm OK with that, if you're OK with me using future purchases against whatever's left."

"Absolutely," I said.

"I...I'd also like to get some ammunition if you have it."

I stopped in my tracks for a minute. "We don't usually sell that through the store, except the twenty-two long rifle, and that only on a limited basis. What are you looking for?"

"Two twenty-three and nine millimeter, and twenty-two long rifle if I can get it."

"I didn't think you were into guns," I said.

"Not until recently, no."

"I have the twenty-two long. I don't have, and can't get, the others. I can let you buy a brick though, or two."

"That'll work I guess. How much does it come to, with the fuel?"

"Let me add it up. The ammo is match grade Sellier & Bellot, so it's a little more spendy than standard ammunition, even for the lowly twenty-two. Probably will be a lot more spendy soon, if we can get it at all," I said as I checked our price sheet.

"What's that mean? Match grade?"

"Competition quality. Higher quality. Consistency. Accuracy. If you have a decent rifle and want something hit, this is it. Of course it doesn't matter if you're on auto, you're just throwing lead downrange. In the larger calibers, match grade is used for sniping."

"Oh."

"It'll be ten dollars eighty cents for the fuel and ammunition. We used pre-crash prices in Federal Reserve Dollars, and then used pre-First Depression values of silver and gold. Pretty much cut prices to twenty percent of what they were before the crash."

"OK, I guess."

"Gotta bag for the stuff?"

"Yeah. A pannier. It's folded up."

"OK. You better get going then. We don't know when or if it's going to hit the fan around here."

"Agreed. See you on the other side," Randy said as he got the pannier unbuckled. I headed back into the store to gather up anything that might be handy while we were 'underground.' I started with the masks, and within ten minutes, was ready to go. The other goods that I bought --although I didn't pay for it at the time and who was I to pay, myself? Little of what was there was on consignment--the remaining Coleman fuel and Sterno, all of the remaining batteries, regardless of condition; three pairs of heavy, and heavily-used coveralls; two beat up sets of rain gear; all of the sewing goods; and all of the edibles, which weren't many. I quickly put most of the stuff in the van. An unfamiliar car passed me, heading east very quickly. I don't think they even saw me as I got back into the van. About time too, with Karen wondering in my ear, where I was.

"Store. Picking up a frozen pizza and a nice Chianti for you, and some ice cold Heineken."

"I was worried."

"I know. I'll be there in a minute."

"K. Out."

"Out."

Within a few more minutes I was back home, and unloading the stuff from the van into the shelter.

"What's all of this stuff?" Ron asked.

"Stuff I thought might be handy. I owe the store."

"How much of this was consigned?"

"The raingear for sure, some of the batteries—the discharged ones. The rest was the stores' outright. I figured that if—no, when—the fallout gets here and we need to go outside, we should be wearing something easy to clean."

"Raingear," Ron said.

"Yeah. In addition to these, I have two sets of my own, and three or four ponchos. Hopefully we won't have to use them often."

"Dad, what about the ground? Won't it be radioactive too? How do we plant in that?" Marie asked Ron.

"We cover what we can with plastic. And tarps. And anything else we can get. The radioactivity will be in dust form, which will land on the tarps and maybe wash off."

"We can't cover all of our acres," Ron said.

"No we can't. We can cover at most a few thousand square feet."

"Dad, we got national news!" Kelly yelled to me.

"Here it comes," I said as I went back inside with an armload of stuff.

26

9:00 a.m.

"We're about to join ABC News ....here they come," the anchor said. The broadcast quality was awful, but the voice did seem familiar.

"This is ABC News Washington Bureau, reporting from Durham, North Carolina. A press conference, with no live radio or television available just wrapped up at an undisclosed location in North Carolina. The President will be addressing the nation later this morning regarding losses in the lower forty-eight states, but a Department of Defense official has provided the major news outlets a printed update on the current military actions around the world, which include nuclear attacks on the continental United States and on naval vessels around the world, and the American response. An Assistant to the Secretary of Defense has provided the following information:

"A nuclear first strike against U.S. and Israeli forces was made with a focused electro-magnetic pulse weapon centered over southern Europe and the Mediterranean, which most likely disabled the electronic warfare systems aboard the USS Nimitz and her associated Battle Group. This EMP blast was set off by a Russian satellite that was already in orbit, originally thought to be a communications satellite that never achieved proper orbit. Sources in Russia have informed us that the Russian President and a majority of the Russian government were in emergency session at that time, and were killed when a tactical nuclear device was detonated near their headquarters."

"Regarding the Nimitz, our protective technology was overwhelmed by the magnitude of the weapon. Four minutes after the initial weapon was detonated, seven other EMP weapons around the Earth destroyed virtually all communications satellites in space, and dramatically affected power systems in North and Central America, albeit temporarily. A side effect of these detonations was the loss of the International Space Station and crew, composed of two Russians, one American, Commander Matthew Cooper, and one Japanese citizen, Mission Specialist Hiroku Watanabe. The Nimitz Battle Group was then attacked with a combination of ultra-high speed nuclear-armed torpedos and surface-to-surface missiles by both Russian and E.U. forces. D-oh-D officials at

the press conference have stated that due to the nature of the attack, there will be no survivors."

"Upon learning in near real time of the nature of the attack against USS Nimitz, Israel launched short, medium- and long-range nuclear-equipped missiles at several targets, including targets in Syria, Islamic Arabia, Iran, Russia, and several locations in France and Germany. These weapons were launched after units of the Israeli Defense Force shot down an undetermined number of inbound missiles launched from Iran and Islamic Arabia. Targeting of nations in Europe focused on centers of military activity noted to have provided ongoing support to the conventional attacks on Israel over the past several days, including submarine-port facilities and launch-points for strike aircraft. The United States, meanwhile, launched both long-range nuclear missiles from ballistic missile submarines in the Atlantic, the Indian Ocean, and the North Pacific against targets in Russia. The D-oh-D states that no land-based missiles have been fired at this time."

"Approximately four minutes after the secondary EMP weapons were detonated, missiles were launched from Russian ballistic missile submarines in the Atlantic. These missiles targeted design, construction and maintenance facilities of the United States Navy; space-launch facilities of the United States, and the Federal leadership. The majority of these warheads were successful in their missions. One series of warheads was destroyed in flight as it approached the East Coast, its trajectory suggested that it was aimed at either Washington, D.C. or Camp David. This weapon package consisted of ten independent nuclear warheads launched from a single ship in the Atlantic. A second warhead failed to detonate over Houston, Texas and broke up on impact, creating a radiological event in that city. The nuclear detonations in Huntsville, Alabama and near Vandenberg Air Force Base were not missiles, but appear to have been fairly large tactical nuclear weapons enhanced with significant amounts of radiological material. Earlier reports regarding in-bound warheads falling short of the San Diego-San Francisco metropolitan areas are in error, the explosions seen were in fact American nuclear weapons used against inbound Russian warheads."

"In the Western Pacific, the Department of Defense confirms the loss of the majority of the USS John C. Stennis Battle Group, in a surprise nuclear attack by a Russian submarine, which was then destroyed by an American attack submarine. United States submarines are now pursuing several other Russian submarines and have destroyed at least six as of six a.m., Eastern Time. An undetermined number of American naval assets are engaged in hunting down the Russian submarines around the world. The U.S. has learned that each Russian submarine has been released to launch its weapons at the discretion of the captains in command."

"Nuclear detonations within the continental United States included both large- and small yield weapons. The submarine construction and maintenance facilities operated by General Dynamics, known as Electric Boat, in Groton, Connecticut and Quonset Point, Rhode Island, were both hit by high-yield weapons with significant blast radii. Shipbuilding facilities at Newport News and the naval shipyard at Norfolk, Virginia were hit by relatively low-yield weapons, although this is small comfort."

"Kennedy Space Center at Cape Canaveral was destroyed by at least one high-yield weapon, which virtually erased the space center from the Florida landscape. The three remaining space shuttles were lost, as well as all major space facilities located at the center. In the second leg of the attack on the United States' space launch capabilities, an attack on launch facilities at Vandenberg Air Force Base was carried out with what appears to have been a truck-carried tactical nuclear device that also contained significant amounts of radioactive waste products, which has spread radiological materials through both the explosion of the low-yield weapon and surface winds. The Department of Defense believes that the actions of USS Virginia, SSN-74, and her on-board weapons systems saved military assets and millions of citizens in San Diego, as well as other military ports and facilities in California, Arizona, and New Mexico."

"Department of Defense contacts on conditions of anonymity, and outside of this news release and the news conference, have confirmed that at least thirty nuclear weapons from the United States, and an unknown number from Israel, have been used in this battle. These sources confirm that a significant amount of the Iranian military was destroyed by Israel, and that Israeli high-yield weapons destroyed the Russian Missile Space Center at Tyuratam and the space-launch facility at Baikonur, Kazakhstan. Until this war, Israel was not known to have high-yield weapons or the means to deliver them."

The radio broadcast continued, but I got up and walked out of the shelter for some air. I just couldn't listen anymore. Karen came after me.

"Are you OK?"

"I'll be all right. I just…had to get out of there. Away from that."

She'd seen this happen to me before, upon the deaths of my parents, years apart. She knew that I just needed some time. I remembered a passage from MacKinley Kantor, upon reflecting on the deaths of so many at Andersonville prison during the Civil War. The losses now hit me like a loss in my own family. I went to the barn, retrieved the book that Carl had finished not long ago, and found the passage mid-way through.

'How many futures have we lost today?' I thought as I sat on the old elm stump south of the barn, the book in hand, my eyes on the closed binding yet reading the words inside. Did we lose the doctors and researchers who could stop the next plague, or the current one? Did we lose the astronaut destined to set foot on Mars? We certainly lost the men that would have designed the ship…The 'pop' stars and movie stars of tomorrow? The religious leaders that would convert millions? The future husband of my daughter, the wife of my son? What was the scope of our present loss? We could never know.

We knew that over the past months, that for example, we would never see a reunion of 'Friends', that wasn't possible with a third of the cast dead. U2 had played their last concert, as had the Rolling Stones, and a dozen more. The future King of England, struck down. Political and entertainment icons fell as quickly as the rest of us, but their impact seemed greater…at first anyway. We'd lost better than a third of Congress. In Washington, we'd lost nearly all of our state leaders in the quake, and more in the Guangdong flu. Disease would take more. So would famine, so would famine.

I wondered, as I sat on that damp stump in the April sun, a day before we were to celebrate the rising of our Savior; looking across the field to the mounded ground that held my root cellar, what would take us? Would our grave resemble that mound? Would there be a headstone for what was the present, and now passing, iteration of civilization?

Who would mourn? Were we to be mourned?

27

Saturday,
April Fifteenth, 9.30 a.m.

Buck dropped a tennis ball on my lap, and whined in that deep 'play with me' voice of his, as Ada waited patiently for me. 'Snap out of it you moron,' I said to myself.   Easier said than done, as I took the dirty grey tennis ball and heaved it as hard as I could towards' Alan's place.

'One day, maybe two,' I thought, 'before it gets here. Assuming that it's actually over. Worst case two, maybe three weeks in the shelter,' I pondered. 'Three weeks in a hole.' Buck dropped the now very-slobbery ball again, this time at my feet, as Ada now barked in a cry for me to throw it. What she really wanted was me to fake a throw to distract Buck, so that I would then hand her the ball so that she could play 'chase.' I complied.

"April fifteenth," I said aloud. "The day World War Three was fought. C'mon, dogs. I've stuff to do."

I got up and headed back to the root cellar, starting again to think about what we had still to do before the fallout arrived. Thank God we had still a little time.

"You all right?" Libby asked as she handed me a cup of tea, and Karen gave me a hug, immediately set upon by two jealous dogs.

"Yeah. I'll be OK."

"Good. You're supposed to be the foundation here," she said softly. "Don't go all wobbly on us."

"I'll try not to, Ms. Prime Minister," I said, referring to Margaret Thatcher and her 'wobbly' comment.

The kids were all up and dressed now, listening to the radio at the far end of the shelter. A makeshift changing-room blanket was now strung up, but pushed to the side of the shelter. My eyes struggled to adjust to the darkness. The air seemed close, too.

"The President's speech just wrapped up. They wouldn't say were he was," Ron said.

"Can't say I blame them. He have anything meaningful to say?"

"It was a nice speech, about what you would expect. What can you say after a couple million of your constituents are killed or wounded?" Karen said as she unpacked yet another cardboard box.

"My point exactly. Anything on the retaliation?"

"He said something like 'our attackers have paid a far greater price than they anticipated.'"

"Like they anticipated paying at all. Or gave a good God Damn anyway. I don't expect to know, ever, who started the war, why, or what their goals were. I'm sure the historians will chew on it for a long time though."

"That's probably a safe bet, since whoever started it is probably nothing but smoking atoms."

"Perhaps. Don't fail to look at the other side of the coin. We could've just as easily started it and haven't heard squat….and never will."

That caught Ron by surprise for a moment. "Attack our own ships? You're nuts."

"No, I don't think we'd go that far, but there may have been something that caused THEM to attack US, or maybe the Russians were infiltrated, and deeply, by the Islamics. Maybe all of this was supposed to be the end of the Great Satan. Maybe we poked them into doing what they did and waxed them when they DID act. We will never know, even if the evidence is out there."

"Why do you think that?" Libby asked.

"Because it is always better to fight on your terms, not somebody else's. Even if you pay for it with blood."

"Nice to see the cynic in you is still around," Ron said.

"Ever so. Anybody talk with Alan about getting to work?"

"Yeah. They're gathering up some boxes and bags to put dirt in, and then get to work. What do we still need to do?" Karen said.

"Tons. Assuming that we nuked Russia, we have probably two days before fallout gets here, maybe three. We nuked China first though, so that cuts us down to a day, probably."

"How bad will the fallout be?" Libby asked.

"Anybody's guess. Big bombs that are air-bursts put a lot of radioactivity into the air, but a lot of it is very far up in the atmosphere, and takes years to come to earth as dust or rain. By then, a lot of the decay has taken place. Smaller bombs—closer to the ground, spread more at lower elevations, that then comes out in rain or dust, while still very hot. The good news for us is that it's a long ways off. The bad news is, we don't know what we used on them, or where the winds are blowing. Or where the fallout will land and when."

"And we don't know how long we need to be in the shelter," Karen said.

"No we don't. If the war is in fact over, that's one thing. If it's not, we may be in there for a lot longer. If we even know what's going on out there, really."

"You made a fallout meter from the book, right?" Ron asked.

"Yeah. We need a couple more though, I think."

"Agreed. I don't suppose you have a Geiger counter..."

"Nope. The County probably has some. Strictly speaking, not all things marketed as Geiger counters ARE Geiger counters. Some are dosiometers—they measure an individuals' exposure to gamma radiation—bad stuff. Some are survey meters. Some are high and low-range. They don't all measure the same thing...No,that's not right either. Not all of them are applicable to our current needs."

"Right tool for the job," Ron said.

"Right tool for the job. The KFM will work for what we need it for. If we can build a few of them, we'll know how much fallout danger we're in. It'd be nice to have them in several different locations too. Alan's. Our place. Maybe a couple more. We could check them to see if they're behaving identically that way."

"What can we do here?" Karen asked.

"I want the kids to read a flyer. It's in the blue binder....what to do in a nuclear emergency. They need to know what we're facing."

"That'll be pleasant," Karen said.

"You also need to have them help you plan two to three weeks in here. As in, most of the time. If fallout is bad, we aren't going out much, if at all. And, plan on no power."

"What about the air? It's pretty stale in here."

"Once we have a reasonably good idea that we're not going to get nuked, and that may be now or in the next couple of days, we can open up the air vent at the other end of the shelter, that'll help a lot. The air pump will keep things pretty fresh then."

"What about the radiation? Won't it get in?" Libby asked.

"Probably not. I'd explain why but you should read it yourself. Grab that green paperback. Read it..." I said before Ron cut me off.

"Chapter six," Ron said. "Read it last night."

"Meanwhile, Ron and I'll go help Alan, and we have some work to do here as well. I also need you to read up on the potassium iodide, and we need to get everyone started on it. It blocks radiation from settling in the thyroid."

"Should we be taking it now?"

"Probably now or damned soon."

"Before it gets here."

"Yes."

"What then? For you? How long will you be at Alan's?"

"Probably a good chunk of time. We ought to be able to cover some of our plowed ground. Tarps, plastic, whatever, weighted down with dirt or something to keep it from blowing off. If we get radioactive dust or mud, it won't completely contaminate everything."

"What about the chickens?"

I hadn't thought about them, much, and I should've. "We should see if we can figure out a way to get some KI in their water, and keep them inside when we figure we have fallout," I said, still working things out.

"What about the eggs? The meat?"

"I don't know. And I don't know if I have anything that will tell me."

"Where can we look?"

"If it's anywhere, it's either in the green book, Nuclear War Survival Skills, or the blue binder, or in a computer drive."

"I'll get Kelly and Marie on it."

"And we need to cobble up an outer shelter. A place we can make sure we're clean of any radioactive dust before we come inside...."

"Plenty to do," Libby said.

"Yeah. And we better get at it. C'mon," Ron said.

Keep the radio on and someone listening to it. I'll let you assign marching orders," I said.

"Gee, thanks." Karen said. "And welcome back," she said as she kissed me.

"I didn't go too far," I said.

"This time. I know this is bad. Don't make it worse, on you I mean."

"I know what you mean."

"Tonight after quitting time I'll pour you a nice tall single malt. That is for medicinal reasons."

"Might be a good thing. Might also be a really long time before I'm able to buy a MacCallan's eighteen year-old again."

"Having it, and not using it, is the same as not having it."

"True enough. Gotta go."

"I'll be over in a while. I'll have Libby get started on provisions."

"Remember. Two weeks, minimum."

"K. Love you."

"You too."

Five hours of shoveling, filling, hefting, dropping and packing dirt later, we had a foot and a half of dirt, boxed and bagged, sitting on his first floor, above Alan's coal cellar. Alan had Mary working at getting 'stuff', primarily food, stowed away. It became apparent after not too much time that food would be an issue. We'd been depending on bulk foods by and large, but the eggs and meat from our chicken operation would be questionable, if not downright unavailable…which meant that even more of our bulk foods—rice, wheat, corn, rolled oats and such—would be a larger part of our diet. Less fresher stuff, more of our stores, a problem in planting and growing more due to the fallout.

Little in the way of reserves.

By two, when Libby handed me a sandwich (fried egg) and a cup of cold tea, both of the shelters had been provisioned with literally all of our food, more water, filling not only the barrels we'd had, but every empty container we could put our hands on. The water was stowed where it could be used for shielding, near the entry door to the basement shelter, stacked up on two plastic shelves that were completely underdesigned for the job.   Libby headed back over to Mary's place to keep the little kids occupied with picking out games to bring into the shelter.

I was leaning against the door jamb, sitting with my back near the outside door, wondering if I would be able to get up again after my tea. Kelly, then Marie, had read through the pamphlet I gave them ('What To Do If A Nuclear Disaster Is Imminent!) which promptly scared the cr*p out of them. Carl and John had read it as well, but weren't quite as dramatically affected by it. Marie literally, got sick to her stomach, so she was drafted for 'radio' duty, which meant listening to any 'news' and taking notes. There wasn't much 'new' information coming through, and hadn't been all morning. Nothing new locally, although the local guy was attempting to shine some light on how weather might affect fallout patterns, I read from her notes. I wondered where he was getting his information, since we probably had no working weather satellites, little in the way of 'national' knowledge (at least that we knew about) of the attacks, what the weather effects locally were (where the attacks took place), how big the bombs were…which made most of the anchors' comments just conjecture….

"Spokane to one-twenty-two. Respond please," the radio crackled.

"Marie, has the county radio been broadcasting long?"

"No, that was the first time."

"Thanks." I wondered who 'one-twenty-two' was. Whoever it was, they didn't respond. It would've been good to have a cheat sheet with all of the folks with radios….not enough time to put that together, before the War.

"Spokane to one-thirty," the radio crackled again. The voice was Mike Amberson's.

"One thirty," the radio responded. That was Walt Ackerman.

"One-thirty, and all the ships at sea," Mike began for all of us listeners, "Expect fallout by midnight, tomorrow. Concentrations unknown."

"Confidence?" Walt asked.

"High," Mike replied.

"What are plans for civilian information?"

"Broadcast at two-thirty p.m."

"Good."

"You all set?"

"Hell, no. But I'm as ready as I can be."

"Affirmative. Spokane out."

"Out."

I sat there for a moment. "Rick, what was that about?" Marie asked.

"That was Mike Amberson talking to Walt Ackerman. Walt is the county executive, and you've met Mike, the Sheriff. They're going to warn us about incoming fallout. Midnight tomorrow. Easter Sunday."

"Oh."

"Don't worry too much about it. We kinda expected it you know."

"I know, it's still scary."

"Yeah it is. Remember that we're still way better off than if Fairchild had been hit. The fallout will not be as heavy, so we'll be safer, OK?" 'In theory,' I said to myself.

"K."

"Do you have the FRS?"

"Yep, here you go."

"Thanks, kiddo."

I radioed Alan's and told them to get the radio on, with a few minutes to spare. "Midnight tomorrow is what I heard," I said to Alan.

"They sound sure?"

"Yeah. Mike did. No idea where he's getting his info though," I said.

"All right. We'll get there."

"You got enough bodies over there?"

"Yeah, probably and then some. Need somebody?"

"I wanted to get some help on covering some of the plowed ground on our garden, and the space beyond the barn up north, around the observation post. As much as we can. And I want to see what we can do about Joe's chicken shed and the hens."

"Cover?"

"That and covering the chicken yard if we can. I was thinking of yanking some of the sheetmetal off of the Woolsley's place, and Brad's house too. There's plenty there."

"OK. I can probably cut the guys loose in a little while. We're finishing up on the berm on the south side."

"Make sure that those two downspouts are directed away from the house too. You don't want hot fallout concentrating around the house."

"Waay ahead of you. I'll send the guys over in a bit."

"Thanks. Out."

"Out."

I put the FRS back in its charger, knowing now that the risk of fallout was suddenly now more real to me, now that I'd heard it was coming from someone else, and not something that I just 'knew' myself. I'm funny that way I guess, looking for confirmation….

"Marie, are you OK in here by yourself?" I asked her as I grabbed my little Sony AM radio and it's earbud, both of which were three times older than Marie.

"Yeah. Mom's got a pile of stuff for me to sort through and load up on the shelves."

"OK. Try to get out and get some air while you can, OK? We're likely going to be stuck in this box for a while. Like, two weeks."

"OK. I'll go out when I get done."

"Don't push yourself too much. You're still pretty green."

"Thanks," she said with a little sarcasm.

"You must be feeling better. Sarcasm is the first sign of recovery."

"Then I'm always recovered," she said.

"Well, I was going to say something…." I said as I walked out the door, catching a small bag of hard red winter wheat in the back of the head.

"See you in a while," I said as I tossed it back to her.

"See ya."

I went up to the garage, listening to the non-stop 'national' coverage of the War and the guesstimated death tolls (millions), and retrieved as many tarps as I owned, which when I piled them together, was pretty impressive if you're into blue and silver tarps. With the big (well worn) tarp that had covered the gaping hole in the house, I now had almost six thousand square feet of tarps, ranging in size from eight-by –ten to twenty four by forty. Those would make a fair dent in covering our plowed ground, but by no means would it cover all of it. I debated on using some of the rolled plastic, which was diminishing fairly quickly, and decided against it. I'd put the boys loose on the tarp job, and Ron and I could handle covering part of the hen yard for the chickens. We'd basically have to build a fenced-in carport, that shed its rainfall well away from the hens.

The local newscast began late, I noticed, and seemed a little odd in its presentation.

"Spokane County Emergency Services has learned through military sources that radioactive fallout will arrive by late Sunday evening, potentially earlier depending on weather conditions. Military officials do not know at this time of the potential levels of radiation in the Pacific Northwest or in the Spokane region. Emergency Services recommends that fallout shelters be prepared for a minimum of seven days stay and a maximum of twenty-one days. Spokane County officials will test radiation levels hourly at a number of locations and broadcast this information as conditions warrant. Repeating, Spokane County...."

"Dad! Where are you?" I heard Carl yell.

"Here," I said from the front of the garage.

Carl and John showed up, their dust masks hanging from around their necks.

"Don't need the masks yet, boys."

"We did over there. We were digging up dirt from across the street. It was dry. And almost all ash on top."

"OK, that makes sense. I need you two to start up at the north end of the garden, and cover up the tilled ground. The tarps need to overlap like shingles, and you need to weight them down all along the edges and in the middle to keep the wind from lifting them. Shovels are in the tool room."

"What about the stuff that's already planted?"

"Can't do anything about that. If we cover it and can't get out to uncover it, the sun'll cook it, or it won't get any rain."

"What about the greenhouses?"

"We'll set up an automatic waterer for them, that may have to do. The two big houses have automatic ceiling vents that open if it gets too hot. That's about our only option."

"You don't have the potato seed yet, do you?"

"No. That was supposed to show up next week. Joe's friend Peretti's got it."

"OK. What'll we do then?"

"Check with your Mom first. We'll need to build a small decontamination area outside of the door to the root cellar. We'll use some sheetmetal from Woolsley's shop—the stuff I used to cover the broken windows, and some two-bys. If she doesn't have anything for you, talk to Ron and he'll get you started on that."

"What'll you be doing?"

"I'm going to Joe's. I need to rig up a cover for part of the hen-yard to keep the dust out."

"We need to do that here too?" John said.

"No, we'll keep them inside. Dirt floor here. Concrete at Joe's."

"Why can't you keep them in over there too?"

"They need dirt and rocks for their digestion. Gizzards, specifically."

"Oh."

"When we're all locked up in the root cellar, I'll have you read up on poultry."

"Gee. I can't wait."

"Life of a modern farmer, boys."

"Thanks," Carl said. "Just what I wanted to be."

"I'll be back by four," I said as I got my mountain bike out of the garage. We'd put a scabbard on the front end, made to fit either one of the Ruger twenty-two's or a shotgun. Today it held the hugely illegal sawed off Spartan single-shot twelve-gauge. We'd cleaned up the butcher job on the nearly-new gun, working over the rough cut job on the stock, and dressing up the uneven cut of the barrel. The scabbard had a side-pocket with five additional shells, including both slug and shot shells. My forty-five was on my belt, along with two spare magazines.

"Do you have a radio?"

"No. I'll be fine. Grab the gate for me, OK?"

"K," Carl said. "Watch yourself."

"I will. No problem there."

The mountain bike was also equipped with three silly-looking milk crates for egg-retrieval mounted on the rear pannier, making it a little unwieldly when loaded. We used it for getting to the store during the day with deliveries, or when we picked up eggs from Joe and Joan's, before they returned. Now that they were gone again, off to Don's farm, we'd use it again. Which meant of course, that someone would need to make a series of trips outside, in the fallout I thought as I rode down the street. Or, we'd let the eggs stack up…and hatch? About half were fertilized. Water was automatic, as long as the power stayed up, and Joe had rigged a timer for feeding them too. I needed to figure out if we could add KI to the water to protect the hens' thyroids too. Assuming that the radiation was light enough not to kill them off anyway.

'Should I shield some of the hens?' I thought. 'How would I do that?'

I pulled into Joe's driveway and round to the 'back forty' as Joe called it, past the brilliant yellow daffodil and tulip display that Joan took so much pride in, fronted by grape hyacinth. The cherry and pear trees were in bloom, just, and the grapes were budding impressively. The hens heard me coming and greeted me with an appropriate level of noise. I'd never paid much attention to Joe's setup for his hens, but he had almost all the necessaries for sheltering the open hen-yard already, with an old RV awning that was folded up on its frame. I'm sure he used this to create some shade for the hens. All I needed to do was to fold out the awning, and make sure that any rainfall didn't find its way back under the awning. Easy.

I helped myself to a shovel from Joe's shed when the odor hit me. There was something dead upwind of me, southwest. Once you've smelled that, you never forget it. It wasn't close, but was still distinctive. I'd check that out, within reason, after digging a drainage channel away from the hen yard fence.

By ten to four, I'd managed to get the eggs collected, the trench dug, and fastened some pretty-well rotted plywood to the fence, inboard of the overhang. When rain fell, if rain fell, the splash would not come into the hen yard. Small protection, I was sure.

I left the mountain bike by the hen house, and walked off to the west edge of Joe's property, and then climbed a fence to the south, in the direction of the foul odor. It seemed to be coming from either the west edge of our block, a dozen or more houses south of Ron and Libby's, or somewhere farther southwest. I decided to spend ten more minutes investigating it, and then head home. There was still work to do.

I moved out of the area we'd cleared for planting, formerly the back half of someone's back yard, past a huge cherry tree in bloom, into a grove of eighty year-old Doug Fir, easily the tallest trees on the block, planted I was sure not long after the light blue farmhouse was built. The odor had grown much stronger as I neared the house, not too much younger than our own home. This house, in late 'teens or early twenties architecture, had once had a wide front porch across the length of the house, with fairly steeply sloping roofs to front and rear. A large dormer had been built on much later, and didn't quite match. Like many other houses on the block, this one was heavily damaged in the Domino, and no one had looked back since that day in January, other than our brief trip inside during the food collection. I unsnapped my holstered forty-five and slowly drew it out, and quickly readied it to the 'cocked and locked' position. I was beginning to regret that I didn't have either the shotgun or one of the radios. This was probably not the smartest thing I'd ever done. If I'd've listened to the little voice in my head, I would've turned around right then.

Most of the windows on the first floor were partially intact, oddly enough the upper panes broken, and the doors were both closed. None of the basement windows was accessible, with metal bars covering them from the outside. The smell of death was almost overpowering. I circled the house, about fifteen feet away from the walls, trying to determine if anyone or anything had gotten inside and died there. A chunk of this home's foundation, concrete unlike ours of stone, had collapsed under the front steps, creating a giant hole in the front yard.

The dogs came at me from the darkened hole without so much as a growl.

The first, a monster of a German Shepherd, tore up out of the basement at me as I backpedaled, my grandfathers' forty-five speaking as I did so. The first shot wounded it, dropping it at first but it still came on. The second dog was a clean kill, a Chow mix that crumpled on itself after the bullet tore through its chest. I was all the way across the street to the west, before the third and fourth dogs came out of the hole, dirt and dead grass flying as they clawed their way toward me. My left hand suddenly held a spare magazine as the Colt emptied. I was running for the front porch of a house opposite of the blue farmhouse as the third dog came at me from the left and the fourth from the right. A metal stair rail protected my left, backed by a hunk of corrugated fiberglass, and allowed me to back myself into a corner. The first shot from the next magazine went wide, nicking the dog in the shoulder as he leapt at me; the next was point blank into his chest, the remains of a studded collar scratching my arm as he fell. Dog Four was now barking and charging the metal rail at my side as his companion crumpled in a heap on the steps. My back was against the wall again as he rounded the end of the stair rail, and placed two rounds in his head. I was wishing that I had bigger magazines than the stock seven-rounders that I had inherited.

The wounded German Shepherd, still was trying to cross the street, growling at me even though the bullet had severed its spine. I placed another round in it, and it was still.   Alan, Mary, Karen and Ron spotted me, standing in the road, and ran towards me, Alan and Mary (!) both carrying long-guns. I waved my hand in the 'OK' fashion that we used when we were 'radio-less' and they slowed down to a fast trot.

It was only then that I noticed the smell from the dogs…like the odor that drew me here. They had to be eating something, or someone, that had died in that basement. The Shepherd I noticed, and the Chow, both had a bloody mess on their forelegs and snouts. Not their blood.

"You OK?" Karen asked. "Or do I just shoot you now?"

"I'm all right. Just a flesh wound," I said, holding up my arm, now with blood streaming down to my fingers.

"Good Lord. What happened?" Mary asked, holding one of Alan's shotguns.

"I smelled something when I was over at Joe's. I went to investigate."

"Without backup," Karen said, very coldly.

"Yeah. Stupid of me."

"Yes," she was really pissed. I couldn't blame her.

28

Saturday afternoon,
April Fifteenth

"Where's the sawed-off?" Alan asked.

"On the bike.'

"Didn't do you much good there then, did it?" Karen said.

"No. I didn't expect…"

"You have to expect. This isn't last year! It's *DIFFERENT* now!"

"I know. I'm sorry."

"Let's look over that arm," Karen said, shouldering 'her' AK-47.

I recapped my troubles, Alan kept his rifle aimed generally at the house as Mary and Karen looked over my arm. It was just a deep scratch. It would need a helluva lot of disinfectant, and soon, though. Mary radioed back to the house, to let the kids and Grace know what was going on. A medical kit was sent for.

"You didn't go in?" Karen asked.

"Nope. I'm dumb, but not stupid. Not entirely stupid, that is."

"No more dogs?" Alan asked.

"No idea. I am down to one full magazine, though, and I'm not about to go in there without more."

"We need to take a look. We can't have that…whatever it is…draw varmints or spread disease. Even if we're gonna be in a hole for two weeks. Mary, give Rick that shotgun. Let's go have a look."

285

"You have light?" Karen asked.

"Yep. A little maglight with my Leatherman."

"Be careful, you two," Mary said.

"Yes'm."

Alan and I moved to either side of the hole in the foundation. The smell was overpowering. No sound emanated from the basement.

"You searched this house during 'collection', right?" Alan asked me.

"No, Arnie Travers did this part of the block. I did the opposite side. You were further north, doing both sides. Remember?"

"I just remember that I didn't do it."

"There wasn't anything special that I remember about this place. It was abandoned right after the quake by the looks of it then," I said. "

"Ready?"

"No, but let's go anyway," I said as I climbed down the gravelly slope into the damaged basement. "My God."

"What?" Alan said as his eyes adjusted to the darkness, and the poor light from the double A maglight. He then ran to the broken wall and the afternoon sun, and vomited.

I discovered three bodies, partially consumed by the dogs. They had been dead long enough to decompose badly, in a back room of the basement, and were crawling with maggots and I thought, some other kind of worm. The dogs had clawed through a hollow-core door to get at them. I couldn't tell if they were male or female, by either the bodies or the shredded clothing that the dogs tore through to get to…them. I thought one might have been a woman, judging by what appeared to have been long, red hair. There wasn't enough left of them to prove that, without forensics, which of course was out of the question.

"Had to be part of that Aztlan bunch that the Army missed. Either wounded or drugged up or something," I said to Alan, who was on his third bout with dry heaves. "Look at the weapons stash," I said, pointing to more than a dozen long-guns in the corner, all but two wrapped up in a burlap gunnysack. The two that were 'unwrapped' were well used to the point of being filthy. M-16's, full-military configuration. A similarly dirty sports bag had probably been pawed at by the dogs for the food that was inside, a couple of candy bars judging by the foil-plastic that was on the floor. In addition to the candy bars, spare magazines for the M-16's were scattered on the floor, with more still in the bag. A small daypack was nearby, untouched.

"How can you stand that smell?" Alan asked as I looked around the room. Two bodies were on the remains of a mattress. The third had been dragged off into the middle of the room.   A dead dog—overdosed or poisoned—was crumpled near a bright yellow backpack in the corner. The backpack was torn up, exposing the contents. Something that could've been drugs was on the dog's muzzle.

"You don't want to know. This is not the first time I've been this close to a decomposed body. Enough said," I replied. It had been more than twenty years, but I still remembered that day, finding the remains of a man who had been in the Spokane River for more than a month. A summer month, at that. "Three more bags of weapons. Handguns and loose ammo. This one looks like drugs," I said as I slid the bags over to Alan. I made a quick pass through the rest of the basement, as a last check. "Let's get this stuff and get out of here."

"Amen."

I handed the bags up to Alan, who passed them up to the level grade that used to be the front lawn. I 'safed' the two M-16's and handed them to him, and gave him my long-gun as well. I then went back and retrieved the bag of rifles. They appeared to all be M-16's by the feel of them. Too dark to tell for sure until I was outside, though. Alan was talking with Karen and Mary when I came out of the hole, in a quick sprint up the loose soil, the big bag cradled unevenly in my arms.

"You all right?" Karen asked.

"I've been better."

"Alan told us. Three?"

"From what I could tell. I'm going to check the rest of the house though. Then, we're going to burn it."

"Take my gun," Mary said. "But let's get that arm cleaned up first," she said.

"Will do. Alan, you look absolutely green."

"Yeah. Feel it too."

"Can you round up some of that old gasoline? We're gonna need it to light this place off."

"Yeah. I'll have the boys run it down. Five gallons?"

"Should do."

I went back into the 'hole', and found the door to the main floor stairs. The door was jammed, probably from the quake. Two kicks of the cheap door, and I was 'in'.

The door led to the entry hall, centered between the kitchen to the right and the living room to the left. The house was a shambles, the quake, and later, looters. Nothing really useable was left. The looters had even taken out some aggression on an antique piano, a Kimball, its mahogany case smashed with boot prints on the top, and bits of real ivory scattered on the cracked maple floor.

I let myself out of the front door, a once-nice carved door with brass knob, now damaged from the quake and the weather. Carl and John had brought a five-gallon can of gasoline, now all but useless for motor fuel, on a hand truck. Alan was nowhere in sight.

"Thanks, guys."

"You're really gonna burn it?" Carl asked.

"Yeah. Let's get it done. I'll spread this around the house. You two take a look around outside and see if there's anything that the fire will spread to. We don't have a fire department to speak of anymore, so it's up to us."

"Do we need to run some garden hoses?"

"That's up to you to decide."

"We'll get hoses."

"Hustle then. I'm lighting this in about five minutes."

"K," John said.

Alan appeared from the south side of the house. "Should be OK to go. Plenty of distance between this place and the others," he said.

"You look a little better now."

"I've seen some things. Nothing like that."

"I'll be right back," I said as I took the metal can inside the front door.

The first trip was to the basement, where I used a liberal amount of the five gallons on and around the bodies, and around the wood framed interior walls. The remainder of the stale gas was used on the main floor. I left the stair doorway open, and the doorway to the second floor as well. The missing glass in the house, and the ample hole in the basement wall would serve as a perfect chimney.

The boys were ready with a hose, when I came out of the door.

"Who wants the honors?" I asked.

"To light it?" John asked.

"Yeah. I found a flare in the basement. Light it and toss it in."

"Flip you for it," John said to Carl.

"Deal. Dad, you gotta quarter?"

"The question for the centuries. Kids asking their parents for coinage," Alan said.

"Here you go. I want it back. It's a silver dollar from eighteen eighty-six," I said as I tossed it to John.

"Cool," he said as he took the heavy coin.

Carl won the toss. He had John light the road flare as he held it in his hand.

"Fire in the hole!"

'Literally,' I thought. Two whole seconds elapsed before the house went up with a 'whoosh'. In five minutes, the whole house was fully ablaze, a sizeable pillar of smoke climbing into the late afternoon sky.

"Carl, check the south side. Let's make sure we're not setting something important on fire," Alan said.

I stared at the fire for a minute. 'May God have mercy on them,' I thought.

By five p.m., the house had collapsed into the basement and was left a smoldering heap. The boys had watered down the perimeter around the home, and were having one of the last of the Vanilla Cokes that we had after retrieving my mountain bike, laden with fresh eggs, and taking that back home. We left John to tend the fire, with a rifle, until the fire was no longer a threat. I asked Carl to attend to cleaning the sand out of the ceiling vent in the shelter. The vent would allow more fresh air into the shelter, with the assistance of a small vent pump on the other end of the room.

Alan and I loaded up the hand truck with the burlapped wrapped bundle of M-16's, the two sports bags of loose ammunition, magazines and handguns. I carried the gas can and the two 'used' battle rifles, slung over my shoulder. The smell of death was on everything I'd taken out of the basement.

"Got anything in those books about getting rid of the smell?" Alan asked as we walked up the broken street.

"Not that I know of. Maybe we'll just let this stuff air out while we're in the shelters."

"Any guesses on how bad it will be?"

"No. I've been thinking about it plenty, though. We might really get hammered. Two weeks or longer in the shelters. Weather holds all the cards right now. You ready?"

"About as ready as we can be. You?"

"Yeah. The same," I said as we passed the Martins' locked up house.

"Dad! Your radio's calling!' Kelly yelled at me from the back yard.

"I'll be right there," I said. "See you in a bit."

"Yep. I'll stash this stuff out in the woodshed."

"Works for me," I said as I went into the field.

Back in the root cellar, the County radio was going through a call to everyone again, I'd missed mine. I decided to be rude and break in on the roll call when there seemed to be a break in things.

"One thirty-seven to Spokane," I called.

"One thirty-seven, hold please," the cool female voice replied. I either interrupted at the end of roll call, or I'd drawn attention to me.

"Spokane to all stations, stand by for a statement by Sheriff Amberson. No reply necessary or requested, please."

Alan and Ron had joined me now, listening in.

"Any idea what's going on?" Ron asked.

"Not even an inkling," I replied.

"This is Sheriff Mike Amberson. I am broadcasting on County radio frequencies and on the lone AM broadcast, KLXY, to inform all listeners that previous estimates of fallout reaching the inland northwest were in error. Fallout has been detected in Portland, Oregon, Vancouver, Washington, and in Bellingham, Washington within the past hour. Radioactive fallout will reach the Spokane area by midnight tonight. If there is good news, it is that the fallout is being measured in very, very low levels, known as picocuries, or a millionth of a curie."

"How does that compare to a RAD? Or a REM?" Alan asked.

"In a sec," I said. "And he's wrong. It's a **trillionth** of a curie..."

"...at this time if significant radiation will reach us. The County Emergency Services staff are still recommending that all residents of the region stay in shelters until further notice. Staff and liaison personnel from the military will provide updates hourly on radiation levels in the region and in other parts of the United States, which we can provide as we are able. Broadcasts will be provided on an hourly basis on KLXY until further notice. That is all. Spokane out."

"Well. I wonder if for a change we've dodged a bullet?" I said. "A picocurie is an extremely small unit of measurement of decay of radiation over time, if I remember. A Rad is the amount of energy absorbed in a gram of matter from radiation. A Rem is the absorbed dose—that's a Rad—multiplied by the ability of the radiation to cause damage. Damage in a biological sense....The problem is, I don't think that a picocurie relates to either a Rad or a Rem. I don't get it."

"Remember back when Chernobyl went off? They reported it here in picocuries."

"Yeah, that's true."

"Sounds less scary than 'Rads or 'Rems' anyway," Alan added.

"We'll need those fallout meters to be sure," I said.

"They're done. Kelly and Marie put them together from the instructions in the book," Alan said.

"You're kidding me," I said.

"Nope. Do not underestimate a fourteen year-old. Or a pair of them," Ron said.

"I guess I better not. What're the dinner plans? Do we know?"

"Mom's been working on that. Chicken pot pies, I believe," Alan said.

"That'll be awesome. It's been years since I've had one of those."

"Meet us at six. We'll be cleaning up by then."

"I'll be there."

I went back to the barn and grabbed some clean clothes, and took off for the house for a shower. I knew it would help a little with getting the smell off of me.

Even a cold shower, in this case, an ice-cold shower, was welcome. Nothing would clean those images from my memory, though.

After dinner, which was less a somber affair and much more filled with humor than I would've expected given today's news we again said our 'goodbye's' for a while, not knowing the duration of the stay in our respective shelters.

We'd worked out a schedule—Ron, Alan and I that is—for feeding and watering our hens, assuming that the radiation wasn't flat-out lethal. A trip or two per week to the Pauliano's was probably in order as well, but again, that was based on radiation levels. The fact that we still had both power and water was a massive bonus to our situation, even if we still had to boil the water for drinking. The tests on bacteria in the water, according to the local news, still showed potentially dangerous levels of e.coli.   We filtered and boiled all of our water anyway; so we were probably better off than most.

By sundown, about twenty to eight p.m., clouds had rolled in again from the west, and threatened rain. The non-stop news reports, scratchy, static filled, and utterly unlike the prepackaged and too-slick 'news' in the normal times, talked of radiation clouds that now were blanketing the Eastern Seaboard, spreading high levels of contamination in areas unaffected by the original detonations. The radiation seemed far heavier than anticipated, and the projected death tolls from the detonations in the East, coupled with projections of deaths due to radioactive contamination in the short- and mid-term (two months), ranged from just under a million dead in the blasts, to four million projected total deaths, in the continental United States alone. Late word had come in regarding a detonation in Alaska, although it was not known what target was hit. I suspected one of the Air Force bases or early warning facilities, or something more 'secret.'

News of the scope of our retaliation was even more sketchy, with 'breaking news' of late-hour engagements at sea between submarines and surface ships, another attempted attack on Tel Aviv, and confirmation that 'dozens' of American warheads had rained down on military facilities in Russia and her former republics. A dirty bomb had been found on the docks at the Port of London, aboard an Irish-flagged ship. I'd missed the Presidential Address in the morning, and was wondering how he was dealing with the world crumbling around him.

The 'local' news, broadcast at nine p.m., reiterated that radiation in the local area was expected by midnight, and added that radiation information had been provided by Air Force sources monitoring the fallout. They did this time state that all listeners should be now taking the provided potassium iodide, and should refrain from drinking fresh milk products.

"Why is that?" Kelly asked, listening with me.

"Cows could be grazing on contaminated grass. The radioactive iodine concentrates in milk."

"Oh."

At seven minutes after nine, the power flickered twice, and then failed.

"I guess that means it's time for bed," Karen said, who was just finishing up squirreling things away in small places in the shelter.

"Yeah. I guess so. Let me get the air filter set up for the night before we turn in though," I said to Karen.

I went back outside and set up the cap for the ceiling vent, basically a wood box over the top of the vent hole shaft. The box, basically plywood sides with two-by-two framing, had cheap furnace-filters that slip-fit into slots to keep out bugs. The airshaft, at the south end of the shelter, was basically an 'exit' shaft for the air coming in through the pump on the north end. We'd need to run a 'shift' of staffing for keeping fresh air in the shelter during our stay. Alan would need to do the same.

A few stars shown through a high overcast, the heavy clouds from the west looming larger, and I was sure by now, they'd crossed into our county. Did they contain radiation?

We'd know soon enough.

29

**Sunday,
April Thirtieth**

Fallout Arrival plus 16 days

For two weeks and two days, we lived almost completely in the shelters, only venturing out to take care of the hens, collect eggs, and run the dogs. Three times, we were warned (falsely) that significant radiation was coming our way, only to be confirmed later by local sources that the warnings were in fact in error.

Our Kearny Fallout Meters, once charged up and operational, never indicated any radiation whatsoever—the fallout was just too insignificant in our area. The County emergency management folks warned us all repeatedly that all residents should remain in shelters for two weeks after the Warm, to ensure that radioactive fallout, no matter where it was, had a chance to decay to a point where it was 'safer'. People who did not have a fallout meter of any kind, had no way of determining if it was 'safe' outside, or for how long it was 'safe' to be out there.

The two weeks we spent in that shelter wore on us all, on our spirits, our senses, and our relationships. It was an effort not to be snippy with everyone, or anyone, and in spite of the air pumps, the place stunk, I was reminded that it probably smelled a lot like a Navy sub after weeks on patrol. We gradually got used to it, but visiting 'the World' outside, and having to go back into that hole just reminded us of how bad it was.

We lost power several times during our stay, the first time the longest; three solid days. 'News' was almost impossible to come by. Either the radio— meaning the AM and SW bands, while not quite silent, had virtually nothing new to tell us. We heard on the second or third day in the 'hole' that the radiation levels on the East Coast, especially in eastern Virginia, New York, Philadelphia and along the seacoast around the detonation areas, had radiation exposures that ranged on the low end from fifty roentgens—the exposure to gamma and x-rays, both harmful or murderous in high levels—to over five hundred roentgens.   The radiation levels in the Huntsville blast were well over six hundred fifty roentgens, with lower levels radiating east from the blast site with the winds immediately after the blast.

If anyone was not sheltered in those environments, their death was not a question of years, but of weeks. Maybe, days.

On the late nights of our stay in the 'hole', I often listened, mostly in futility, to try to hear news from the rest of the country or the world. Our local broadcasts consisted of little more than repeated warnings, the occasional report on the radiation levels, and once a day, a 'roll call' of county personnel. Once in a while, a weather report. As if anyone were outside to enjoy it. I never did hear during our stay, which I began to liken to imprisonment, on whether the Navy and Air Force had finished hunting down the Russian submarines, or of any other battles.

We kept normal 'day' and 'night' schedules, with a couple people tasked with 'hen duty', which was a welcome respite from the boredom in the shelter. An adult, armed, always accompanied one of the younger residents, any time we went out of the shelter. Once it became apparent to us that high levels of radiation were apparently not in our immediate future, we treated ourselves to using the outhouse, rather than the porta-potti in the shelter. Alan's crew had it better; they just had to step outside of their coal-room to the basement bathroom. They even used the shower twice during their stay! Lucky.

Games, cards, books, the Bible, mending, figuring out what we'd eat when, trying not to say what you really wanted to but knew you shouldn't, sleeping in poor accommodations, wondering if we'd get through this; all were occupying our minds. I was very appreciative that the kids didn't, at least at first, behave like teenagers in too small a space for too long a time.

At eight a.m. the County radio crackled to life, plugged into the car batter, which in turn was plugged into an inverter to recharge the failing battery.

"Spokane County to All Personnel: The All-Clear is hereby given. Radiation levels are normal and projected to remain at normal background levels from this point on. Continue to take potassium iodide until prescribed dosage is exhausted. Announcements of the All Clear will be made on the hour for the remainder of the day. Official County personnel, board members and volunteers are expected to resume normal working schedules on Wednesday, May 3, at nine a.m."

"Well, Hoo-Rah!' I said to the mostly-sleeping residents of the shelter.

"What was that, Dad?" Kelly asked. Everyone was awake and paying attention now.

"They're lifting the shelter order. The All Clear. We can move out of here."

"Good. Not to offend anyone, but I would appreciate the change," Ron said.

"No offense taken. And, ditto." I made the last statement a little dramatically, throwing open the shelter door, and opening up the outer plywood door to the 'decontamination' area, that we never used, fortunately. The morning sun reflected into the shelter from the white plywood, and everyone squinted at the bright sun, the last day of April. "Come on. Let's get out of here."

"I'll call Alan and let him know," Karen said.

"'K. Kids, get some air with the dogs. After breakfast, we'll get our gear out of here and run some laundry. Then we'll move out what we need to. I think we'll still keep it the shelter stocked, just in case."

"OK," Carl replied. "Dibs on the shower."

"Twerp," Kelly said.

"He needs it more than you do, Kel," Karen said.

"I can't argue with that," she smiled. "Oh, the air is nice."

The kids took off across the field towards the barn chased by Ron, following the dogs, who were barking at each other and the play stick that they often played 'tug of war' with.

"It's good to hear them laugh," Libby said as she stood next to Karen and I.

"It is that," I said. "On to the strange, new world for us all, though."

"Soon enough. You can stand here for five minutes and enjoy it, you know," Karen said.

"Long as I'm with you, yep," I said as I squeezed her hand. "Get hold of Alan?"

"Yeah. They're making breakfast for everyone. Hope you like eggs."

"As long has he has coffee to go with them, yes."

"I'm sure he will. Your Mom hold up OK?"

"Yep. I'm going over to see her."

"K. I'm going up to the house to turn on the hot water heater. We'll shower after it's warmed up."

"That'll be like a dream," Libby said.

"Simple pleasures. None of us would've thought that a year ago, would we?"

"No. Not even remotely."

While we were sequestered, we'd talked about what we'd need to do once the fallout had lessened to the point where it was 'safe', namely, growing and trading for food to keep us alive for the foreseeable future. Our 'stored' foods were being depleted faster than I thought they would be, and I didn't think we'd see much in the way of 'processed' food coming down the pike anytime soon. If ever.

We'd been lucky with the hens, and our building relationships with local folks who could help supply us, and we, them. But we continued to also depend on our pre-Domino and pre-War supplies, and our 'thinking'. That had to end, and now.

'Things Are Different Now,' I kept repeating to myself as I went up to the house and fished out my little flashlight. Inside, I turned on the power to the majority of the empty building. Before we headed to the shelter, I left only one breaker in the 'on' position, the one that fed the barn, and by extension, the lights and utility outlet in the shelter. I flipped the basement light on, and checked the hot water heater 'active' light, and headed back up stairs. Maybe now, I could get the damned roof finished and we could move back inside. A month later than I'd hoped for. It was, though, a busy month.

I headed back to the barn, through our original garden, now to be converted to a kitchen garden. Through the tool room, I noticed that the mice had been busy, chewing up a burlap tree wrap into a new nest. I'd have to get out some D-Con or something. Or, better yet, get a mouser. The Golden Retrievers had been tasked with that in former days, which might've allowed the mice to get to places where we didn't want them to be....

"Power is on," I said to Karen. She was restocking our 'pantry', formerly the shelves where I stored my wood planes, with canned goods from the shelter.

"Thanks. How long 'til the hot water is ready?"

"Probably a half-hour."

"We've got time before breakfast then. Mary is baking biscuits in a camp oven. We can shower and run a load of dishes in the dishwasher. More like 'brunch' than 'breakfast.'

"No dishwasher. I haven't checked the drain lines yet for that."

"You shouldn't have been playing polo for the past two weeks, should you?"

"Nor you, eating bon-bons. Where are the kids?"

"I sent them up to check on the greenhouses. Armed, and with the dogs."

"K. The irrigation system was pretty hard to get programmed. I hope we still have a crop. Rube Goldberg would've been proud of me."

"The vent panels were open yesterday, they should be OK, right?"

"I hope so. We have a lot invested in there."

The 'houses' were planted on flats on tables and under the tables, with tomatoes, peppers, broccoli, cauliflower, head and leaf lettuce, with some sample plots of carrots, beans and small stuff here and there. The 'south' greenhouse was actually the 'warmer' of the two, with 'cool weather' crops in the north house. The automatic doors opened in the 'north' house when the temperature reached fifty-five degrees inside, which translated in measured soil temperatures to the sixties. The 'warm' house released hot air from one door at seventy-five degrees and from a second at eighty degrees. Our tomatoes and peppers were growing in that house, in large quantities. We also had some melons and squash starts, including some summer squash that was nearly ready to bloom...two weeks before.

I headed back over to the root cellar, and gathered up another load of 'stuff', including most of the radio gear. I left a small Radio Shack AM radio in its box, just inside the steel door. That could stay there, as part of 'permanent' shelter equipment.

By eight forty-five, Karen and I had moved the essentials back to the barn, and gathered up some clean clothes for a hot shower. We tasked the kids with getting their 'stuff' collected up and sorted. Ron and Libby were working on hauling their own things back to their house, and getting cleaned up as well.

"What will today's plan be?" Karen asked me as we headed up to the house, Buck trailing me and trying to play, grabbing my free hand and growling, as if I were a tug-rope.

"Not a thing for the kids. I want them outside to enjoy things. I was even thinking about a softball game. Kids versus adults."

"What about all the work we have to do?"

"One day will not make an iota of difference. We need some play-time. I do want to get the roof finished, but I can handle that myself. Couple hours, tops."

"How long until we can move back in?"

"The roof's the last thing that we absolutely need to fix outside. Inside, I can insulate and sheetrock the stairwell ceiling anytime after that. Until we get some more drywall mud, I'm done with joints. That'll mean the dining room and stairwell won't get done beyond the raw sheetrock. We can probably get final cleaning in the bedrooms done in a day or so, and get the primer coat done then. We don't have enough paint left…or anything we'd want to use anyway…to finish-paint much of anything. We can do the living room, and patch the kitchen up, and we're good. We still need more sheetrock in the basement, under the stairs, but that's no big deal."

"OK, let me ask again, perhaps more slowly so you actually answer the question. How long?" she smiled as we climbed up the ladder to the back door.

"Probably next weekend."

"That's better. I'd like to start cooking in the house again. Today."

"Should be OK. I can rig up some dust sheets to keep drywall dust down, and then we'll vacuum up the crud."

"How much time will you need to spend working with the County?"

"I don't know. We're going to be picking up the pieces from the War first I guess, and trying to figure out exactly what that means. After that, maybe we can get back to doing what we're supposed to be doing, 'recovery.'"

Getting to the second floor of the house wasn't exactly 'normal' yet either, with three smashed stair risers and treads to climb over, using an ancient stepladder laid over the hole. We had to balance ourselves against a wall, and carefully walk up the inclined ladder, to the bedrooms and bath.

The bath was remarkably undamaged, including the vast majority of Karen's makeup and stuff, left right where it landed in January after the quake, and most of the 'guest' towels, heaped in a plastic-covered pile on the floor.

"You first," I said to Karen. "I'll sand some sheetrock."

"Nope. Join me. We're conserving," she said with a come-hither look.

"Best not turn that down then," I said.

"Not if you know what's good for you."

After our long shower, and clean clothes (!), Carl and last Kelly showered and changed into clean clothes. The pile of dirty laundry was significant, and I didn't waste time on getting a load in the washer. I'd had to cobble up a 'grey water' drain for the laundry, because I didn't have a tie-in fitting to the waste drain. And probably never would.

Breakfast was fresh biscuits, scrambled eggs and some rehydrated hash-brown potatoes that we'd received from the food 'collection'...not half-bad with a little salt and some Tabasco sauce. Grace looked worn. I suppose we all did. Still, it showed on her more than the others. At eighty-five, I was amazed she was doing as well as she was. Alan and Mary's kids, Mark and Rachel, were similarly washed and dressed in clean clothes, and were relegated to the 'kids table', accompanied by Carl, John, Kelly and Marie, who were in an animated conversation with nine year-old Mark about his upcoming birthday. Kelly's was only a little over two weeks away, I thought to myself as I half-listened to the adults and the kids.

So, what do you get your fourteen-year-old girl for her birthday in a post apocalyptic world?

"Rick! Pay attention!" Karen scolded me. "Where were you? We've been talking to you for five minutes!"

"Sorry. Pre-occupied," I said softly. "Kel's birthday's coming. I was wondering what we should get her. And the other kids too. We have a slew of birthdays coming up in the next couple months."

"We'll figure something out, don't worry," Mary said.

"So what did I miss?"

"Teams. We were talking about your softball game idea," Libby said.

"So you all think I'm off my rocker for wanting to play a kids game?"

"No, a little worried I might get a heart attack due to the shock to my system," Alan replied.

"I figured that it was time that we do something completely illogical for a change. Besides that, I figured that the kids needed to do something kid-like."

"Good idea," Grace said.

"You've been pretty quiet during brunch, Mom. You OK?"

"Tired, that's all. Sitting and doing nothing does that to me."

"There'll be plenty to do starting tomorrow. We don't want you pushing yourself though. You're not...."

She cut me off. "Quit. I know. I'm not sixty anymore."

"I was going to say fifty."

"Flattery, my dear son in law, will win you favor," she said, disarmed.

"So what will tomorrow's plans be?" Ron asked.

"First of May and the snow is off of Mica Peak, and almost off of Mount Spokane. We get ready for planting our major summer stuff. Potatoes. Corn. We need to look at spraying some of the trees or all of them with pesticides, either 'natural' or some of our old chemical-type. We have a lot of work to do. We also need to see if we can get the store opened back up, get the barter network going again, and trade for some more seed potatoes and onion sets. I'd also like to find a source of wheat and rolled oats. Neither of those are coming from within the Valley. We'll need to see if we can stretch our trading area and get some new partners."

"How long to finish plowing and tilling?" Karen asked.

"I'm going to turn over those operations to the boys. Carl's run the Ford doing both, but he needs more time on the tractor to get better at it. John will need to pick it up too. Any of us can run the Troy-bilt tillers. At least three solid days of plowing, all day, to get everything ready. And we don't have enough seed to fill up that much plowed ground, unless we plant our own wheat. Which, I really don't want to do."

"Why's that?" Libby asked.

"No combine. We'd have to harvest it with a scythe or sickles, bunch it, dry it, thresh it. All by hand. Do-able, but not something I'd prefer to do."

"What if you can't find a source for wheat?"

"Then we plant our own. I'll need to secure a source this week or else we'll plant our own. Time's getting short. Harvest isn't that many weeks away."

"It's only May,' Libby said.

"Yes. And harvest is in July or August in normal years for winter and spring wheat, which is already in the ground normally, on the big Palouse farms. This year, I don't know how much of that is planted or harvestable. If there's not fuel enough to run the tractors and combines, we may see that last falls planting of winter wheat is all that got planted."

"How are we going to manage?" Mary asked almost absently.

"If we are lucky, we will do OK. We have to make our own luck though."

"What's that mean?" she asked.

"That means that ninety percent of luck is working your tail off," Grace finished for me. "Then, you are 'lucky' when you succeed where others fail."

"Couldn't have said it better," I said.

30

Sunday,
April Thirtieth, 1 p.m.

After a simple breakfast that never tasted so good, and a Bible lesson from Alan *(We are troubled on every side, yet not distressed; we are perplexed, but not in despair; persecuted, but not forsaken; cast down, but not destroyed…. 2 Corinthians 4:8-9KJV)*, we set our baseball game for two p.m. Karen and Carl were up at the greenhouses, tending to thinning and repotting some of the tender plants. Kelly was running another batch of laundry, as were the Martins and Bauers. We all started to feel a little more human, addressing the routines of the pre-War, post-Domino.

I snuck away, ostensibly to look over the dishwasher drain, which took a sum total of five minutes to check and repair. A clamp had popped loose in the quake, causing a minor leak. I then retrieved my big shop-vac from the garage, and cleaned up the drywall dust in our bedroom. The rest of my time I spent up on the roof, where my arrival was announced by my roofing hammer, with it's waffle-face, nailing up the composite shingles over the now-aged tarpaper. In an hour, I'd repaired all of the 'flat' work on the north face of the house, shingled the gable, and woven the shingles into the valleys on both sides. Once the ridge was done, I was out of the roofing business. Access this time on the roof was done the traditional way, an ancient wooden ladder that was new when my grandfather was alive, fifty years or more ago. The hydraulic ladder on the bucket truck wasn't working, the battery was discharged. No surprise there, it was dying before the Domino, but I didn't really want to spring for a new one, it was a monster, sized large enough to start and operate a semi. And besides that, they were very, very expensive. Today, they might either be unobtainable, or free, depending on the mood of a seller or the quantity available.

I sat up on the ridge for a few minutes before the scary trip back down the steep roof, like I'd done almost a month before, when I'd placed the tar-paper layer. I looked around at the clear air, so different than early April with that dust storm. So many changes in that time…we'd been through so much. What challenges awaited me THIS week?

"Daddy?" I heard my daughter call from below.

"Up here."

A moment later she appeared from under the eaves, squinting up at me. "Mom asked me to hang out the laundry if there's no dust. Where are the clothespins?"

"They should be in a pocket in that fabric laundry basket, next to the dryer. That's what Mom uses to move the laundry up, you know," I said.

"Forgot. How's the view?"

"Good. Nice and clear."

"How far can you see?"

"You mean, how many miles?"

"Yeah, I guess," Kelly said.

"Rimrock on the other side of downtown, that's probably fifteen miles. Mica Peak is probably ten miles. The mountains on the other side of Rathdrum and Hayden, fifty miles. Mount Spokane, twenty or so I guess. Clearer than I've seen in a long, long time."

"So I'm OK putting out the laundry?"

"Should be, yeah."

"K."

"Long winded way to ask about the weather," I said with a smile.

"I know. I just wish I could see that far. I'm afraid to climb the roof."

"I'll get you up in the bucket some time. K?"

"Cool. Thanks!"

I gingerly crab-walked down the valley to my ladder, and was soon back on solid ground.

"Sun-dried sheets tonight, huh?"

"Mom's orders."

"And we best follow them. Don't tell her, but we're sleeping back in the house tonight. She thinks it's next week or so, OK?"

"COOL!" My own bed again!"

"Yes, but keep it quiet. We'll move our beds in after the game. Some of our stuff is still out in the garage. We still need to paint the rooms, so it'll just be mattresses."

"'K, it's a secret."

"C'mon out to the barn when you're done. We'll pick teams for the game."

"K. Who're Captains?"

"I don't know, we'll decide later."

"K."

I stowed the ladder back on the big Ford's flatbed, and gathered up my tools in their buckets. The welcoming sun was I was sure, giving me a light sunburn after our stay in the darkened cellar. I never realized how much sensory deprivation we underwent in there...I noted the different bird songs, the occasional mosquito whine, several bees and the different 'pitch' of their flight. I'd never noticed them before. The lawn needed to be mowed, and would continue to need being mowed. Maybe for good. Could I stand that? We did have an ancient push-mower out in the shed, unused for decades just due to the sheer labor of using it.

Next on my short 'to do list' for the day was to change the oil in the Ford tractor, and top off the hydraulic fluid. A slow leak from one of the seals on the hydraulic lift arms leaked a little, just enough to be annoying. We'd need the tractor to run a full day to get our plowing and tilling done. The small tillers would need an oil-change too, especially with the volcanic dust they were plowing through. We had to clean the air filters daily, wash them down frequently, and grease all the fittings daily too, to deal with the abrasive action of the ash. The once-sparkling finish on my Expedition was now permanently dulled, just from the ash blowing across it and the rainfall. It hadn't really been washed since the first week of January.

I kept running through the things, the many things, we needed to do and soon. The planting, pruning, the fruit and nut trees, the grains. The store. The County recovery efforts. Of course my mind kept coming back to one thing.

The War.

Other than the occasional short-wave broadcast that we could pick up, we'd heard almost no 'outside' radio broadcasts. The 'local' broadcasts weren't much better; repetition of the All Clear, no 'network feeds' of any kind. I wondered if it was 'technical' in nature, or because 'someone' didn't want us to know what was going on. Or, that there could be no communications with D.C. and New York, because they didn't exist anymore. How long would it be before we'd hear? Ever?

We lost, thirty-one to twelve, we adults. The kids gloated mercilessly as we old, slow forty-plus parents attempted to play like we had in our teens and twenties. The biggest hit I had netted me a double. Ron managed a triple--but was thrown out at home on a rather foolish steal--by daughter Marie, who had the most wicked fastpitch I'd ever seen. I will not let him live that one down. Mary and Karen did better than they thought they'd do, at least getting on base. Libby never got a hit out of the infield. We were going to be sore tomorrow, but it was a good feeling at the end of the afternoon.

We called it quits at four-thirty, so that we could get cleaned up and get dinner going. Tonight, we'd be building a bunch of lasagna, and cooking it at Alan's, and eating it at the Martins, a progressive dinner of sorts. After dinner, we'd clean up and head to bed. Our brief time out of the shelter had afforded us only a little time to check on the Paulianos, whose home remained unmolested, as was the convenience store down the street. Knowing many, but not all of the remaining residents, we hadn't really expected any looting, but these days, we just never knew.

While the lasagnas (five!) were baking, I snuck out with the 'boys'— allegedly to round up some wine and to double-check that leak under the sink— but really to haul our mattresses, bedding, and some clothes back into the house. In twenty minutes, we'd done that, as well as retrieved four bottles of Ste. Michelle cabernet, nicely aged at ten years old. Our oldest reds were almost twenty. Before the Domino, I was saving them for something special. I vowed that we'd drink them all by the end of the year.

"We better get back, Dad," Carl said.

"And double-time. Don't let on now," I said, as I gathered up a couple bottles in my arms, and gave Alan a couple more.

"She doesn't know?" Alan asked.

"Nope. She hasn't the vaguest glimmer of a clue."

"Could be because you told her otherwise," Ron said.

"Well, could be. You know how 'contractor time is," I replied.

"Yeah. 'Ready in two weeks,'' Ron said.

"Sure, unless the Third World War intervenes," I said.

"Well, at least you had a good excuse. Unlike some contractors I've known…" Alan said laughing.

"It's been a good day," I said, watching the sun setting low over Alan's house. The 'girls' were in the dining room, it seemed playing cards.

"It has at that," Alan said, stopping next to me to look at the sunset. "But are we ever going to pay for it tomorrow."

"C'mon, Uncle Alan, you didn't play that hard," Carl said.

"The intensity of play and the injuries caused thereby is a direct invert of the age of the player, young man," Alan said. "And I am directly inverted."

"You can have an easy day tomorrow," I said. "I'll get the boys going on tillage, we can have the girls work on transplanting and planting with Libby, Karen and I. Mary and Grace can school Mark and Rachel until we're ready to plant. I'll do some more work on the house, you and Ron can get the store up and going. If the weather's good, I'll spray some of the fruit trees. How's that sound?"

"Good, unless it's raining," John said as we reached the back door.

"Man. Smell that. French bread!" Carl said.

"I guess the girls were figuring surprises, too," I replied.

"'Bout bedtime there, Sparky," I told my nephew Mark. I'd been sent out to round him up and get him ready for bed. It was a little after nine p.m., and the game of Sequence was winding down. I'd volunteered for 'dish duty', which left me free to watch the competition and provide color commentary, which was almost as much fun as playing the game.

"I know Uncle Rick. I was just watching the stars," he said, continuing to look east at the rising Dipper. We enjoyed a waxing moon and a clear night.

"Look!" he said pointing to the southeast.

Over Mica Peak, one of the two highest points in the county at about five thousand feet, a number of aircraft appeared, the first we'd seen in quite awhile. Relief flights had ceased before the war went nuclear, and we hadn't seen any planes since then, and none in our very brief trips outside of our shelters. I suppose that since the majority of our 'relief' military troops had been sent to fight in Mexico, we were now a 'non-priority' mission. The aircraft grew closer and increased in number, in a triangular formation, and then a second formation, vectoring toward the center of the Valley, and then banking due west. I was sure they were on approach to Fairchild, our all but abandoned Air Force base. There were over two-dozen planes, although I couldn't really be sure. They did at least, have all of their anti-collision lighting on and strobes, and the lead craft had its approach and landing lights on. The planes 'outboard' of the lead fell away to the north and south, circling I thought for their turn in the landing pattern.

"Keep count, Marky. Hey, everyone, get out here. We've quite a show to see," I called through the kitchen window. Mark and I were joined by everyone else, now clustered in the back yard, looking up at the Air Force, finally coming home. Most of the planes were C-17's or KC-135R models, although there were a fair number of planes that I didn't recognize. At least one was a twin-engine Boeing, with the signature AWACS gear. Had to be a 767. A third, and final group of planes appeared over Mica, this time a couple of 747's with fighters.

"I wonder what we've got here," I said.

"Very good question," Alan said. "I know the Air Force doesn't run too many seven-four-sevens."

"True. Air Force One and Two, the E-4B's—the Kneecaps--and the airborne laser platform. I think that's a cargo plane that they used. I think they've got some C-19's too. Those are basically passenger 747's belonging to the airlines that the Air Force has options on."

"What's a 'Kneecap?'" Libby asked. "Other than the obvious."

"That's the phonetic pronunciation of an acronym. They're the military's National Emergency Airborne Command Post. They're based I think, in Nebraska," I said.

"Offutt Air Force Base," Ron said. "My cousin worked there on them. Or their predecessors."

"There's at least three of them up there, whatever they are," Karen said. "See? There's another one trailing to the left. No lights though."

"Yep. This bodes well," I said.

"Why's that?" Mary asked.

"They wouldn't be bringing important assets to a target zone, would they?"

"No, I guess not."

"Sixty-one!" Mark said.

"How's that, son?" Alan asked Mark.

"Uncle Rick said I should count. Sixty-one."

"That's a lot of crews. I don't know how many one thirty-five's we used to have out there but I gotta believe that it's pretty close to our old complement. Where are they gonna put 'em all?"

"Why?" Karen asked.

"Look around. What's the percentage of broken buildings here?"

"Lots."

"Fairchild's gotta be at least that bad. Maybe worse. Government construction."

"Can't be much worse than living in a barn," Karen said. "C'mon everyone. Let's head to bed. Big work day tomorrow."

"Killjoy," Alan said.

"Hey, you'll be working harder than I will, big brother. Remember that. And you're substantially old-er," she said. I could hear her smile in the dark.

"Ow. Remind me never to get on the bad side of her, Lib," Ron said.

"She's kidding. She knows she'll work at least twice as hard as I will. I've perfected the art of relaxation, while working," Alan said. Not a great comeback....

"True, but I get twice the work done, too. 'Night, all!"

"Not 'til we see the surprise," Libby said.

"What surprise?" Karen said.

"We're sleeping in the house tonight," I said.

"You're kidding me. You said…"

"Not kidding, the beds are all in the house. Just have to make them, grab our pillows, and we're good to go."

"Thank you, Lord," she said. I think she was close to tears.

"And the late Andy Welt. Couldn't have done it without him, even with his shady background."

"And a shower in the morning!"

"And coffee ready when we get up. And an alarm clock set for six. Let's go."

"Thank you all. This is incredible."

"It's long past time, hon. You've done so much for us, it's payback time. Now off to your own house," Libby said. "And God bless you."

Karen was crying now into my shoulder.

"Jeez, babe. It's a bedroom," I said, knowing that it was much more to her. She'd been carrying too much for too long, like all of us. "Kidding," I said softly. "C'mon. Let's go."

"Goodnight. And thank you all."

A big round of hugs, and we were all off to our respective homes. I was trying to remember what a real bed—our bed—felt like. I flat out could not remember.

As we passed the darkened garden, awaiting its mission, I saw a lone fighter circling wide around the urban area, far off to the south. I never thought of fighter planes as something comforting to see. 'It's Different Now,' I told myself as we climbed up the makeshift back steps and passed into our home.

Our home. Again.

31

April Thirtieth,
11 p.m.

We all arranged our sleeping accommodations, placing our mattresses roughly where the beds used to sit, pre-quake. All of us thought the rooms seemed both 'enormous' and 'close', an odd feeling. Most of the furniture was either piled up in corners or out in the garage.

Karen dug out the flannel bed sheets for all of us, and we made up the beds. The house would not be as warm as the barn, due to the unfinished stairwell framing and lack of insulation. And, the lack of a furnace and no one tending the woodstove. We were becoming used to living in sixty-degree interiors, and if the temps were above that, we were shedding layers.

While Karen readied the kids' rooms for the night, Carl and I hauled some more stuff from the barn back to the house. Our communications equipment was unceremoniously stacked up in the dining room bay window, and battery chargers plugged in for the night. I took one AM clock radio from the garage and moved it back to the bedroom for the night, and kept our FRS radio 'on' for the night, sitting in it's little stand. By eleven-thirty, we were all in bed, and dog tired. Even the dogs beat us to sleep. I finally drifted off, after laying awake in the unfamiliar bedroom, with the occasional rumble of a far-off fighter or patrol plane.

May First,
5.30 a.m.

I woke with a start, from that common dream that I was late for work, and on a big meeting day at that. I hate those kinds of dreams, especially knowing that I'll never work in that company, with those people again. The firm died in the earthquake; likely with some of my co-workers. I'd never heard of any of them since the quake, and I'd tried to get in touch, more than a few times.

I was though, oddly rested, and remembered that I was sleeping on our 'old' mattress, a big latex foam slab that did wonders for my back. I hadn't slept like that in months. I quietly put my glasses on, punched the light on the clock to tell me what time it was—five thirty--and got up, trying not to disturb Karen. She was sleeping at least as well as I had been.

I quietly gathered up my clothes for the day as Karen and Ada continued to sleep in the dark bedroom. The roll-down shade on the east window let in enough light for me to see by, barely. Buck was up and stretching, not entirely sure he wanted to be up yet. Odd, for a two year-old retriever.

Downstairs, I slipped into my big farmer overalls, grabbed a clean flannel shirt, and headed to the kitchen. I knew most of my clean clothes were still in the barn.   The main floor windows of course were still void of curtains (how strange!), and construction materials still piled up in the corners. I made my way to the kitchen to start some coffee. There was virtually no food in the house…or at least the kitchen. I found a pan of honey-oatmeal-raisin granola bars in the kitchen, left over from 'dessert' last night, and munched one while I found the little 'backup' coffee maker. Outside, the day was clear and cool at forty-five degrees, the sun now peeking over the Idaho mountains. I absent-mindedly flipped on the AM radio in the kitchen, and was surprised by the broadcast. They were actually on the air.

"Good morning, this is Bill Owens reporting, it is five forty-five a.m., Pacific Daylight Time, this is KLXY Spokane broadcasting on nine-twenty AM. Nighttime curfew is now officially over."

In spite of my care to let Karen sleep in, I could hear her upstairs, starting the shower. Pre-Domino, she'd sleep until the last possible minute. 'Not anymore,' I thought to myself.

"Heavy military traffic began streaming into Fairchild Air Force Base and Spokane International Airport late last evening, heralding the arrival of elements of the Forty-First Division and other unknown military units. Heavy-lift C-17's and military 747's were seen landing and were accompanied by a large percentage of Fairchild's own KC-135's, F-16 and several F-22 fighters. No official report or statement has been made on the arrival of these units as of yet, although we are trying at this time to get an interview or a statement from the base. Heavy security at the main gate and along the entire base perimeter is visible this morning, and our reporting team was asked to leave the base area and make no further attempt to enter the base. Since the quake, early in the morning of January fourteenth, the base has largely been occupied by security and maintenance personnel, repairing the fourteen thousand-foot-long runway, as well as the nine-thousand foot main runway at Spokane International.   Air

traffic since the Domino has been limited to alternate runways at both installations."

"*We are anticipating a network news broadcast at six a.m., with news from the rest of the country. Since the attacks on April fourteenth, communications with regional and national networks has been all but impossible with the loss of nearly all commercial communications satellites. We literally have not heard any news directly from the East Coast since that time, and what news we have received has been relayed from station-to-station across the country. Communications with the southeast, and large portions of the Eastern Seaboard has been further limited by persistent high radioactive fallout in that region of the country and massive damage to the telephone system infrastructure. The nuclear attacks on military facilities in Alaska have only been reported in sketchy civilian shortwave broadcasts from that state, and appear to have destroyed both Fairbanks and Anchorage, and the installations at Eielson Air Force Base and Fort Wainright in Fairbanks; and Elmendorf Air Force Base and Fort Richardson near Anchorage, as well as substantial portions of the civilian areas around those bases."*

"*Radiological levels in the Inland Northwest remain at near-normal levels overnight, according to military medical sources charged with monitoring local, regional, and national levels. Through broadcasts received by KLXY staff over the past twenty-four hours, we have learned that radiological levels in the California Central Valley and Los Angeles-San Diego area have declined, but are still at dangerous levels. The high radiation has resulted in the dumping of dairy milk from herds throughout the region, and all but futile efforts on the part of the local authorities to keep the local population in shelters. Shelters in the affected areas are often without adequate power for ventilation, and the area is currently hitting highs of eighty-five to ninety degrees each day. The source for the radioactivity appears to be American and Israeli weapons, used against Russian and European targets two weeks ago, although investigations in the California area are also looking into a locally detonated radiological weapon. This has not been confirmed or denied by authorities, according to KFI radio in Los Angeles."*

"*Medical facilities in operation prior to the Shelter Order will be in operation after noon today, although services may not be fully restored for several more days. Residents within the listening area are reminded to continue to take the potassium iodide tablets provided at the specified dosage until the thirty-day supply is exhausted."*

"*Boil water orders remain in effect for all domestic water systems within the listening area, and will remain in place for the foreseeable future. Restoration of central portions of the Whitworth domestic water system in north Spokane is expected to begin again this morning."*

I made coffee, the last of the Irish Crème blend that I'd received for Christmas; a full pot for Karen and I, as the news continued. I knew that Karen had set her alarm for six, as had I. I would normally hop in the shower as soon as it went off, but I was really wanting to hear anything in the way of news from 'Back East.' I had some second and third cousins back there, in Massachusetts and upstate New York.

At six, I heard the characteristic 'ding' of the network news feed, sounding as if it were underwater.

"This is ABC news New York bureau, broadcasting from Pittsburgh, Pennsylvania, where tens of thousands of evacuees from the contaminated areas along the East Coast are crowded into public shelters and private homes throughout the western half of the state. This scene is repeated throughout the eastern States, with fallout and nuclear contamination from the initial days of the War continuing to plague the most populous region in the country," the broadcaster said.

"Used to be the most populous, anyway," I said to the coffeemaker.

"Official death estimates continue to rise as more victims are found from the radioactivity around the blast sites. It is estimated that more than a third of those residents downwind of the targets and who did not take shelter, will die before years' end, regardless of treatment."

"In Washington, D.C., now virtually an abandoned city, Federal troops continue to guard most vacant Federal buildings since the dispersal of governmental agencies and officials to dozens of locations around the country, mostly in areas free of fallout or benefiting from favorable weather conditions relative to world-wide radiological contamination. No plans have been announced on the potential return of the Federal government to the city, which has a relatively high radiation level even this day."

"Burn units throughout the country continue to report shortages of critical medicines and in some cases, skilled doctors to treat the more than forty thousand flash-burn victims. Euthanasia has been used widely in many cases, some estimate at more than five thousand, whose burns and injuries were so severe as to be a matter of time before they were relieved by death. Total death estimates from the nuclear attack in the United States are estimated at five hundred and six thousand killed outright, with an additional three hundred and four thousand projected additional deaths due to radiation, burns, and crushing injuries. Additional deaths can be expected due to disease outbreaks and other causes, according to the CDC."

The broadcaster paused, as if gathering strength, and began again, more respectfully than I'd heard in a very long time.

"An updated list provided by the United States Navy this morning lists known and projected losses from the attacks on USS John C. Stennis and USS Nimitz battle groups at nearly twenty thousand sailors lost. The following listing has been provided by the Navy, listing ships and crews known to be lost or not heard from since the initial attack and presumed dead. These ships include the following:

From the Stennis Group: USS John C. Stennis, USS Lake Champlain, USS Cheyenne, USS Tucson, USS San Jacinto, USS Howard, USS Ford, USS Carr and USS Laboon. Losses from the Stennis Battle Group are estimated at nine thousand fifty-nine."

He read the names of the dead ships as you would read a eulogy of a family member.

"From the USS Nimitz Group: USS Nimitz, the first carrier of her class, USS Princeton, USS Stethem, USS John Paul Jones, USS Lassen, USS Chaffee, USS Higgins, USS Louisville, USS Mustin, and USS Bridge. Losses from the Nimitz Battle Group are estimated at nine thousand four hundred forty-six."

Karen snuck in behind me and embraced me from behind. "What's up?" she asked.

"Hush. The list of ships lost."

"Oh." We listened as the broadcast continued.

"Lost in other action, and confirmed by the Navy, include the Ohio-class submarines USS Henry M. Jackson and USS Louisiana, and fast-attack submarines USS Augusta, USS Chicago, and USS Memphis. Losses from the submarine service are estimated at seven hundred sailors."

"On a personal note, my daughter, Amy Louise Paulson, aged twenty-three, died aboard USS John C. Stennis, where she served as a 'green shirt', responsible for assisting in launch and recovery of the Stennis' aircraft. Amy Lou was particularly proud of her work, running the aircraft catapult and arresting gear. To all of the Navy, Army and Air Force families out there, our prayers go out to you."

"This is Jonathan Paulson, with ABC News." The local broadcast returned, with an announcement of shelters and medical facilities scheduled to be open.

"Those poor families," Karen said.

"Yeah. We're lucky…and blessed, beyond our due."

"Any local news?"

"Some, I'm sure they'll repeat it. Good news on the radioactivity, and they said the Forty-First is here, or parts of it."

"What about those other planes? They were white, not green. It didn't have to be daylight to see that."

"No one's saying. Sounds like we might have someone important in town though. I don't know why we'd have fighter cover flying around without it, and they were up all night."

"The President?"

"Don't know. Maybe. Probably not though."

"Why not?"

"I don't know, just a feeling."

"Remember when he was in town a couple years ago? We were at Carl's baseball game? They flew then," she said, sipping her coffee.

"Yeah, that's true," I said, remembering the F-15's flying lazy circles across the sky during the campaign trip. We almost never had fighters around here, unless there was an air show. Other planes at the base, other than the tankers, were the little T-37 'Tweets', the twin-engine jet trainer, unlike anything else in the Air Force inventory.
"Probably just some administration or military people."

"Your turn for the shower. I'll make breakfast," Karen said, wrapped in her thick blue robe.

"In a bit. I want to get some stuff out of the barn, and I'd just get all dirtied up." Ada and Buck joined us, wanting 'out' and wanting it 'now.'

"Bring back some eggs from the fridge out there. This one's bare."

"As you wish," I said as I climbed out the back door and across the wrecked hole that used to be the back porch. The dogs tore past me, excited but not alarmed, and immediately headed around to the front of the house. This piqued my interest. Someone here? At this hour?

One of the County patrol cars was in the driveway, just outside the stock gate.

I called back to Karen inside. "Hon, get another cup out. We have company. Mike Amberson's here!"

Mike was on the radio as I approached the car, pulling my beat up Cenex cap on. The cap was actually part of a fortieth birthday gag gift, given by one of my employees to the 'farmer' in the company. He figured I needed an honest-to-God farmer hat, so he went to a co-op down in Rockford, ten or twelve miles out of town. He also brought me a bag of lentils. I never did tell him that I love stuff made with lentils....

Mike was finally off the radio. He looked thrashed, I thought, as he got out of the car.

"Good mornin' Sheriff."

"That remains to be seen. Everyone make it through OK?"

"Yeah. And you?"

"Yeah. This pregnancy thing is wearing on us though," he said.

"Pard, you still have two months to go."

"I know. Believe me. Counting the days."

"Is Ashley having problems?"

"Discomfort. Lack of sleep. Irritability mutating to occasional bitchiness."

"Welcome to the land of the Father To Be. You forgot wild mood swings."

"You're right."

"What brings you by so early?"

"You know we have visitors."

"The Air Force? And I assume the Army?"

"Among others, yes."

"Can you enlighten me?"

"Nope. Not sure myself. But I was un-invited to the bases' ops center yesterday. That was my first clue."

"That's pretty ballsy," I said.

"Yeah. I thought so. But since the guy was a two-star, and had four rather large young men with -16's in their hands, I decided that my presence was not needed."

"Well, at least they let you go."

"Yeah."

"C'mon in. Coffee's on."

"Thanks," Mike said as we walked around the back of the house. "Where'd you spend your two week vacation?"

"We were in the root cellar out back, with the Martins. Alan's family was in their coal cellar."

"We were damned lucky," Mike said. "It's bad down south. California's in bad shape."

"Fallout?"

"Yeah. We're going to lose a lot of people."

"Didn't the Forty-First come from down there?"

"Farther south. Other side of the fallout plume. Mexican Territory."

"Well, nice to have company," Karen said. "Please climb on up and on in," she said, referring to the traverse across the destroyed back entry.

"Nice to see you, Karen. Still putting up with this knucklehead, I see."

"Better offers are hard to come by these days. Who else would put up with me for two weeks underground?"

"And, vice versa," I added.

"C'mon in. Here's some coffee. I'll retrieve some eggs from the barn, and we'll cook up some biscuits. I'll get Carl to run out to the barn and get some provisions. This is our first day back in the house, so we're a little disorganized."

"Your hospitality is most welcome, Karen. It's…strange to say that."

"It's nice to see other people," she said. "We are starting to wear on each other, I'm afraid."

"Conditional hazard. Ash and I have the same problem."

"If there's anything we can do, or if we can get together, you let me know. We have a baby gift around here somewhere or other. Had it since just after you let us know you were expecting. And, a ton of the kids' baby clothes are up in the garage attic. I don't think Baby Gap will be available by July."

"Or ever," he said.

"You two go out and enjoy the morning," Karen said, knowing that Mike and I needed to be 'outside' for awhile. "I'll let you know when breakfast is ready."

"Thanks, babe."

Mike and I took our coffee out to the front porch, sitting on the wide railing at the early morning sun.

"So how did the County fare the last two weeks? I assume that you were not incommunicado," I asked.

"I wasn't. Ash and I spent most of the time at the EOC," Mike said, looking off to a fighter, completing its southwest-to-northeast transit, perhaps twenty miles out east of our home.

"I thought the emergency personnel were relocated out of the area."

"Backups were. Primaries—me, Walt Ackerman, a handful of others— stayed."

"Sounds backwards."

"Was, but our backups didn't, and don't know the systems down there like we do. Most of our skilled staff…died in the quake or the flu. We're training people on the fly."

"So does our recovery plan still hold water?"

"Yeah, probably now more than ever. I think the last of the holdouts that thought the Feds were coming to the rescue have now been awakened to the reality that we really are on our own."

"Good. We're maybe, if we're lucky, a hundred and forty days from first frost. End of the growing season. And we have to feed ourselves."

"Yeah."

"I know we're supposed to meet on Wednesday, with the Recovery Board. Is everyone on the Board going to make it?"

"Yeah. And we'll have the Health Department director, a half-dozen utility reps, a rep from Burlington Northern, and Rocky Mountain Petroleum. We should have your CERT census copied by then, and the overall death toll from the quake and subsequent causes."

"How about our grain supplies? The stuff in the elevators? Did anyone have time to get in contact with them?"

"Yeah, but I don't have the report.'

"What about outside sources? Are there any?"

"I doubt it. I would suspect actually, that what we have here is being eyed by the powers that be."

"You have got to be kidding."

"I'm not. I've seen a few too many olive drab vehicles around the grain elevators, the processing plants, and the remains of the warehouses."

"So what do they plan to do, sack the remnants of the ruined city?" I asked mockingly. "Sh*t. Have we not gone through enough?"

"Just telling you what I'm seeing. And that I don't like it."

"You're force is still less than twenty percent of pre-quake, right?"

"Yeah."

"And what's the resident population compared to the forces we've seen come in last night and over the past two weeks?"

"Maybe five thousand troops. Probably thirty thousand residents remaining, viable.

"Viable?"

"Fighting ability. Armed. Another thirty thousand or so in the urban and suburban region, non-viable."

"You think it will come to that? Armed rebellion?"

"Depends on the Feds next move. Which we'll probably know today."

"And I had such high hopes for the day," I said, entirely seriously.

"Listen, this is my speculation on what I'm seeing. Not the Gospel."

"Understood. But you also do not like what you see."

"True."

"And, you are also worried that the armed forces may operate against a peaceful civilian population. And deprive them of all things, food."

"I am."

"Then consider what may happen should the armed forces decide to tell those that give them illegal orders to shove it. Then what? The Forty-First, like its preceding Division, is largely composed of residents of Washington, Oregon, Idaho, and Montana. A slug of them are, or were, Reservists or Guardsmen. I don't know about you, but if I were a twenty-something kid, no matter what, I'd be thinking twice about taking food from my mom and dad."

"I'm all ears."

"If you see something that looks like it's leaning towards confiscation, you better be ready to get the word out, and pronto. You'll need people on the inside—meaning the media—that can broadcast it quickly before they're shut down cold by the government. Because once they decide to make their move, communication is very likely the first thing to go. If things succeed their way, it'll be over and we'll still be wondering what happened. Agreed?"

"I have contacts."

"Then make use of them. Have a pre-written statement or statements ready. If you need to broadcast something, label them differently, like 'envelope three' or whatever. Make it short and to the point. And scary as Hell. Even the military has to look at urban warfare on American soil differently once they're facing a few thousand deer rifles."

"Having been on the wrong end of them, I agree."

"Mike, consider that if we're just being overly paranoid, which is hard these days, you could be in serious sh*t if word gets out that you're organizing an armed rebellion."

"Should it come to that, we're all in the same boat."

"Well, here's to healthy paranoia, then," I said, toasting him with my coffee.

After a very pleasant breakfast, consumed while balanced on the front porch rail, Kelly and Carl came out to say hello to Mike, and brought him several dozen eggs for he, Ashley, and as he saw fit to his deputies and staff. I was sure that we had them to spare; thank God they keep well. We had many dozens of them loaded up in a cool spot in the cellar shelter, fortunately Joe had a huge pile of purple commercial-type egg flats. Our stockpile of egg cartons was dwindling before the War went nuclear—we'd have to encourage people to return them or find good ones so we could keep our enterprise rolling....

During breakfast, Mike let me know that all commercial ventures, especially those dealing with food to be sold or traded, would be protected by either Police, Sheriff or Army troops with now-standard shoot-to-kill orders for looters or thieves. Our little store, he noted, should be under protection by now, and would be, twenty-four seven. What little information he was able to get from the military overnight was that the Air Force personnel escorted virtually all of the Army's incoming Forty-First Division troops, which were ultimately supposed to number about ten thousand, off of Fairchild Air Force Base. They pretty much had to fend for themselves for housing upon arrival. They initially were staging at the Airport, close enough to Fairchild to be convenient, and probably irritating, to the Air Force. Mike had a meeting scheduled for eleven hundred hours this morning with the Division commanders, to review billeting options in their Area of Operations.

"AO. I never thought I'd hear that term used in my own city."

"Yeah. Me either."

"What are your recommendations?"

"Their mission is as far as I know, peacekeeping and law enforcement under Martial Law. I'm hearing from some of the underlings, mostly a senior master sergeant, that an engineering battalion is supposed to be coming too, overland. One Sixty-Eighth Engineers."

"That's a Fort Lewis unit, if I remember. Regular Army."

"How in heck do you know that?"

"I worked on a logistics center expansion over there. Site planning, consensus building, environmental mitigation."

"Warm and fuzzy stuff."

"Yeah. I don't imagine I'll use those skill-sets again for profit. One thing you said though—the Forty First should have fifteen thousand men, not ten."

"Well, now they have ten. I assume the war in Mexico took some, and the flu."

"Pretty hard to maintain force readiness of line units with that kind of attrition."

"Pretty hard when you're down to less than twenty-percent, too. You figure out what is possible, and what isn't. And you figure it out fast. Been there. Am there now. I think the best option for them is to disperse them in several areas around town. Valley, South edge of the south hill, down around Glenrose; up north around the Three Ninety-Five intersection with the Newport Highway. And of course, a decent sized element in or towards the downtown area. Probably staging at the Fairgrounds or the Community College."

"So we have a rivalry or schism between the boys in blue and the boys in green, huh?"

"Yep. More than 'normal.' Much more."

"This makes things interesting. You probably have no idea what the Air Force is up to, or how long they'll stay. Or if they're here for good."

"Nope."

"And you have good relations with the boys in green."

"Yep."

"Well, maybe their signals folks or command could lend you a little info on what's going on with their counterparts. All one big happy family here, and all. Maybe we finagle a little fresh food for some of their line units or middle management. For sure, their commanders are well fed, and usually ironed with a little too much starch. Mid-staff is usually a little more appreciative of the local population. Besides that, you know the ground and the hot spots, far better than they do, and the Recovery Board will need quite a bit of their help, especially the construction units, in getting transport put back together. And if we are getting an engineering battalion, then you could be ready for them before they get here. Pre-stage all the heavy construction gear and fuel you can justify. They never have enough of their own equipment, assuming that they're bringing any of there own. They may just show up."

"Word is, they're coming by rail."

"Well, that is good. Since they'll have to fix the rails to get here. Meaning that we can have outside rail traffic for the first time since January."

"That may or may not be a good thing."

"How do you figure?"

"Imagine a lot of folks might want to come to an uncontaminated and relatively uncrowded part of the country, don't you?"

"I hadn't thought of that."

"I'm sure a lot of people haven't thought of that. It might get real crowded."

"More than our capacity to feed them."

"Exactly," Mike said as he looked at his watch. "I gotta go. Running out to Liberty Lake before the meeting with the Army. And to meet with the Postal Service. Mail will be delivered to the community centers starting with the backlog, tomorrow."

"Use the eggs wisely."

"Indeed."

"The store should be open later this morning. We're probably going to have some traffic down there. Thanks for the news about the mail. Been a long time between letters," I said.

"Watch out for unfamiliars. We're not all sure that all the bad guys are gone, you know."

"Yeah," I said as he backed out of the driveway, remembering the funeral pyre we'd set, just before we went underground. I didn't tell Mike about the M-

16's, and I was debating on not telling him, for his own good. Plausible deniability.

Once everyone was up and fed and marching orders provided, I reviewed 'tractor operations' with John and Carl, making sure they could handle the plowing and tilling without getting themselves killed or damaging the tractor or anything around them. I watched with clenched fists more than a couple of times until they got the hang of things, and then decided that it was best just to let them go. I was not much better at it than they were, something you only gain by experience and feel of the soil and the machine.

Karen and the older girls headed over to the greenhouses to transplant, leaving me free to get the Honda lawn tractor out, and the spray trailer for the fruit trees. I'd decided after we'd inventoried the fruit trees on the block, and discovered that nearly all of them were left to go 'wild', that the commercial fruit-tree spray that I had would go toward the 'wild' trees, to get the bug infestations under control. The other trees and vines that were better tended (ours included), would get the homemade organic sprays. I had already sprayed once this year, a dormant spray that was sulfur based, with spray oil. Everything got hit with that—except peaches and apricots. They were sprayed with a fixed-copper spray, and spray oil. I had to be careful of the spray in order not to stir the Irish temper of Libby, who was hanging out clean sheets to dry.

By late morning, I'd sprayed all two hundred and seven trees, with eleven tank loads at fifteen gallons apiece. I could make enough organic spray based on what I had on hand and had salvaged around the block to last the rest of the year and through the year, but would run short of crucial components of the spray mix, and would have no spray oil at all, by this time next year. I guessed there were probably at least another couple hundred trees on the blocks surrounding ours, and without those trees being tended to, ours would be more susceptible to problems. Nothing I could do about that, though.

The boys had made quick work of breaking new ground with the two-bottom plow, over about an acre and a half of former 'back yards' and pastures of homes to the north of us. They'd then disked the fields, and finally raked most of the area, to leave a very well prepared seed bed. Both Carl and John now understood why I was so sore after being on the tractor for several hours, especially my calves and thighs and triceps. Both Buck and Ada were quite pleased with themselves, stretching and rolling around in the freshly tilled earth.

"So how much more do we need to plow up?" Carl asked, plainly ready to quit.

"We have about fourteen acres of area to work with out there. Almost all of it will be plowed up and planted."

"Why so much?" John asked.

"Beats starvation," I said as they rolled their eyes. "I'm serious. We need at least three acres and a good growing season just for summer and canning vegetables. Then we've got grains to grow and other crops to grow for drying. And we need an excess to trade with and sell."

"This is going to take forever," Carl said.

"Not. Probably a couple days to get all fourteen plowed, then more to disk, and not all of it needs to be raked. And you should be able to run literally all day on ten gallons in the tank."

"Great."

"There's lots of other things to do…like planting. You'll be all over that, too."

"We have to hand-plant all of this?" Carl asked, obviously remembering how much work it was to plant the dozen or so rows of corn we used to plant in our five thousand square foot garden. Must've taken all of a half-hour, this time last year.

"Not all of it. Corn, beans, any grains that we plant will be done with the seed drill on the tractor. That leaves squash, potatoes, tomatoes…."

"Auugh."

"Son, it beats starving. Look around. You see any bread trucks lately? You think Safeway and Rosauer's and Super One are coming back? They're not. We feed ourselves and friends and those that can help feed us. And by the way? I don't think we can grow enough food on this acreage to ensure we're not going to lose more weight, not without a good year weather-wise, anyway and a fairly boring selection of food to choose from, and still have the ability to grow in the future. We still need to develop some relationships with people that can supply us more. We're short on seed. Might be nice to have a friend who can get us milk for example. Or can provide us beef to eat, or a hog or three or six. There are thirteen of us here. That is more than fourteen thousand meals in a year. I can show you the math on how much food that means, if you really want. And it doesn't pencil out yet on what we have on-hand. And, I'm getting a little tired of eggs and chicken as my primary source of meat."

That was a sobering statement to them both, probably more brittle than it needed to be. I knew that they had no 'fat' to lose, well, Carl didn't anyway, and John was just built 'big' to start with, unlike his parents. I hadn't tracked my actual weight since the Domino, but I knew that I had to have lost at least twenty pounds since January, just by the new holes required in my leather belt. Karen, too, had slimmed down. Excess work, no 'junk food' or 'fast food' or meals out, had seen to that.   The twenty pounds however that I had lost, I could've stood to lose anyway…

"Let's get back at it. You now know the stakes of what we're dealing with. Correct?"

"Yes. Steaks. Good one, Dad," Carl said, getting the double-entendre. "I'll save you some A-1."

"Funny. I'm glad you understand the seriousness of this. Because if you do not, let me assure you that there is little in the way of a contingency plan for starvation. There are people in this country right now, four months after the earthquake hit us, and little more than two weeks after the War started, that have no food. In America. No food."

"Understood."

"Good, then, let's get back at it. And try not to be too concerned, now that I scared the crap out of you. We are still, and have been since the start, in God's hands."

"K."

"Remember to grease up those fittings I told you about. Every day."

"Got it."

"Knock off about noon and run the tractor back up to the house. I want to change the oil in the air filter. The ash is murder on engines. And keep those gloves on, unless you want blisters the size of your palms."

I hopped back on the little Honda and drove back to the house, looking up at two C-17's coming in, and the glint of the canopy of an F-16 to the south, circling.

'On to my next to-do-list item,' I thought, as I saw Mary wave me down. 'Or not.'

"What's up?"

"Alan and Ron need help at the store. They can't close for lunch. Can you run some food down to them?"

"Sure. Why can't they close?"

"They're swamped-busy, they said. Everyone's showing up looking for everything. You'll need to take the truck too—they're sold out of eggs. They said the place has a life of it's own."

I loaded up twelve dozen eggs into the Expedition (all I thought I could spare at the moment without getting into trouble), along with a couple of what looked like pita-bread sandwiches and tea, and some other stuff that I'd 'liberated' from the store prior to the Shelter Order. In a few minutes, I was at the store, and surprised by a crowd--of Army uniforms. Shopping. Thankfully, one of the faces at least was a familiar one, Annie Ross, daughter of two of my school classmates. She waved at me as I parked along the curb. The six Humvees in the parking lot, one with a rear-mounted machine-gun, left little room for civilian vehicles. A number of our regular customers though, had parked along the street, or ridden bikes with trailers.

"Annie! What'd you do, bring the whole Division?"

"No, sir, just my unit. Word spreads though. Sorry."

"That's fine, I'm kidding. How have you been?" She looked much younger than the last time I'd seen her. I had a difficult time thinking of her as a combat soldier.

"Pretty well all things considered. I heard from my parents finally, they're still in Colorado and will probably end up staying for the foreseeable future."

"That's good. I hope you pass on my regards," I said, noting that she was wearing a brand-new uniform, much unlike the worn, patched, and dirty one I'd seen her in last.

"I did already. They said they appreciate your 'looking out for me.'"

"More likely, the opposite is true. Your Captain still around? McCalister?"

"Yes, sir. Liaison to…..Sorry. I'm not supposed to say."

"Lucky him," I said. "And that's OK about not telling. We're not slow around here. We know we have important guests in town."

"Yes, sir."

"Ross, would you care to introduce me?" A voice came from behind my shoulder.

"Yes, sir. Sorry, sir. Mr. Rick Drummond, this is Chief Warrant Officer Woody Clifton."

"Nice to meet you," I said as I shook his hand. I'd seen that look before. In the Marine Gunny's eyes.

"You, too, sir. I understand that you're on the Recovery Board?"

"Yes, among other things. Farmer, store stock-boy, poultry-wrangler. I didn't know that infantry units had Warrant Officers," I said as I sized him up.

"They don't actually. I'm with Special Forces," he said. 'Well, that explains 'The Look,' I thought. "Northwest Command thought that I might be useful around here."

"Could be. We had a Marine Gunny here a while back that.... took care of business. I'm not sure, frankly, how many bad guys are left out there. Haven't been out of the hole that long." 'Northwest Command?' I thought to myself.

"The Sheriff said you might be agreeable to my stopping at your residence to discuss matters."

"Absolutely. This afternoon work? I've got some business to attend to here, but should be able to break away from all of my important meetings. With my chicken flock, for example."

I got a laugh out of him with that. "Sixteen hundred hours OK?"

"That'll be fine. Bring Annie, too. I wanted to get her introduced to the family. Her parents and I go back to grade school."

"Will do. Thank you, sir," Clifton said as he shook my hand again and went back to the Humvee, this one with a little darker paint job, covering up the 'up-armored' body.

"That guy is a mountain," I said to Annie.

"Yeah. A little intimidating," she said.

"I better get this stuff inside. Sounds like we have an old-fashioned market in there."

I unloaded two boxes from the Ford as the 'din' of the market rose and fell in waves. I approached the door, and the numerous soldiers and civilians made way for me as I carried my precious cargo inside.

"About time," Alan said. "We have customers."

"I can see that."

The store was crowded with both sellers and buyers, and I was reminded of a public market that I'd seen in Africa, a few years ago. Buyers were bartering for lower prices, sellers were aiming for higher. Almost all of our regular trading partners were there, with products that ranged from clothing (homemade and 'manufactured') to seeds; tools; flame-cut half-inch steel, sized in panels that conveniently fit un-armored Humvee doors and floors; loose rifle scopes and binoculars; soaps and toiletries; sunglasses; dust masks; grain alcohol and 'applejack' from Aaron Watters; knitted sweaters and hats from Ellen McDonald; a young blonde woman, completely unfamiliar to me was selling four-inch pots containing various herbs..legal herbs, it appeared. Someone in back, with a fairly large crowd of green uniforms around them, was selling fresh bread and muffins...for silver coins.

"Holy smokes, boys. You got anything left?" I asked Ron and Alan.

"More than when we started, actually, pending your egg delivery," Alan said.

"Here's the first load. There's more in the car."

"Don't even bother bringing them in. They're spoken for."

"For what in exchange?"

"Seed potatoes."

"No way," I said in a hushed but excited tone. "How many pounds?"

"Well, it's a complicated transaction, the eggs were the kicker, and they would like some fertilized to start their own flock too, by the way. On our part, two thousand rounds of twenty-two long rifle, a number of garden hand tools, and two copies of your CD's on primitive skills stuff. They're also looking for a computer that will run them. For fifteen hundred pounds of certified seed potatoes."

"You have got to be kidding."

"Nope. Best part is, you know the guy. And he says he owes you, big-time."

"Where is he?"

"Back with his wife in the back. They're selling the baked goods in the back. Says his name is Eric Moore."

"Dang. Good for him. They made it."

"Who are they?"

"Your neighbors. Their house is the one between you and Ron's. They evac'd the day of the quake, down to his parents farm, I think. Or her parents. Can't remember. Have two little girls. We got them warmed up, fed, and on their way. They were extremely ill-prepared for the quake."

"They said they were looking for a long-term market for their farm goods."

"They've found one. Right here. I'll go say hello. And damned good job you two."

33

Monday
May First
12.10 pm.

I waded back through the store, receiving access only when the soldiers realized that I wasn't 'a uniform.' When I finally got to the old sandwich counter, now the Moore's impromptu baked-goods store, Amy came out and gave me a big hug, and Eric nearly crushed my hand with his handshake.

"Where are the girls? Did you leave them home?" I asked Eric. Amy was back selling muffins of some kind—the size we used to get from Costco. They seemed to be an apple or fruit blend.

"They're with my Mom and my brother. We lost my Dad in the flu," Eric said.

"I'm very sorry. We've been blessed so far. How's the farm? Looks like you're doing OK."

"Yeah, shorthanded though. Dad was pretty well setup for mechanized farming, but without enough fuel, we've really had to scale back."

"Stop by the house later—it looks like you'll be sold out pretty soon in any regard."

"We have more in the truck. We were hoping to find a market—we didn't expect this though!"

"Good for you."

"We're pulling out though—moving our stuff back to the farm."

"You've got a better chance down there to succeed. Valleyford, right?"

"Yeah."

"Well, we'll keep the place secured in any event, just in case. Let us know when you're coming. Just tell Alan and Ron, and they'll radio ahead."

"For security reasons?"

"Not with the Army around. So we can have a little hospitality."

"Oh! OK. Thanks. See you soon."

I excused myself (not without another hug from Amy), and headed back to the front counter to talk business with the guys.

"Nice kids, those two," Alan said.

"Yeah. I invited them up to the house when they're sold out. How are we doing, trade wise?"

"Typical demand-shortages. Everyone wants toilet paper, bar soap, food, spices, beer, medical supplies, the routine stuff."

"Are we in the black or the red?"

"The store, or us?"

"The store. I'd say with Eric's trade, we're solidly in the black."

"Store's doing OK. We're up twenty-five dollars in silver, and six cases of home-made beer, traded for tools and a couple of radios, and two pounds of sixteen-penny nails. It looks to me like our other trading partners are coming away happy, too. We could use more of everything," Alan said.

"As always. Make sure you let us know when Eric and Amy are coming up. I have a meeting with a Special Forces warrant officer at four."

"What'd you do to deserve that?"

"Apparently, someone thinks I know about stuff."

"Well, we'd be happy to set them straight," Ron said.

"Thanks. Love ya, man. What time you closing?"

"When we're sold out or people don't want to buy anything."

"Make it five o'clock then. And make sure you know whom you're working with. Mike Amberson's idea."

"You think we're going to be robbed, with these guys around?" Ron said, waving to the small sea of camouflage."

"They won't be here forever. And someone might want to pick you or some of our traders at the end of the day. Easy targets."

"Fair enough. See you later."

"K."

Outside, the Humvee belonging to Clifton and Specialist Ross was gone, replaced by a large—no, more correctly, out of scale—military vehicle that looked like it could ford small streams. Or large ones. I'd only seen photographs of them before, the HEMTT, an eight-wheel monster that could crush normal vehicles flat, it seemed. This one was configured to be a fuel-carrier, and was UNLOADING fuel into the stores underground tanks!

The truck was surrounded by soldiers with 'that look' in their eyes, and automatic weapons were held by each. I decided to forego questions or conversation, and got in the SUV.

"Coming home," I called on the FRS.

"Good. Lunch is ready," Carl replied. "Better get home soon if you want any," he said.

"Thanks. I'll remember that when you have post duty."

"Awwww."

I pulled into the driveway, where Carl had the gate opened for me. I thought that I saw a stray dog up the road, just past the black locust that had blocked the road to the north since January.

"See any dogs up north when you were plowing?" I asked Carl when I got out of the car.

"No, why?"

"Thought I saw one. You be sure to be armed when you're on that tractor. And keep a wary eye."

I filled Carl in on the events down at the store on our way to the house, and then repeated it all for Karen and Libby and the girls.

"Is there any chance we can have something…." I began

"…for the guests that you have coming?" Karen finished. "Kelly's making some fresh bread, and Marie is making pies. I'll have some iced tea ready, assuming I have ice by then. Good enough?"

"Plenty. Thanks, babe."

"The boys are pretty well thrashed with plowing. Can I enlist them to help move some stuff in?"

"Yep. Remember that someday, we may actually get some finished paint for these rooms, so just keep the clutter down, OK?"

"Sure. Less to clean anyway."

"How are the tomatoes and peppers looking?"

"Blossoms on both. I think every seed germinated, too. We're going to be swimming in tomatoes if the weather cooperates."

"I'm OK with that. I'm sure we have a market for what we don't can or dry or whatever."

Karen and I reviewed the planting plans for our gardens as I mowed through a couple of sandwiches and some kind of tea, and the estimated man-hours to complete the work. It was, in a word, staggering. We'd have to just pace ourselves to get the initial planting done, and work on the series of follow-on plantings—some would be a week or so later than the first seeding—as time and weather allowed. Mostly, time. We were finishing up our lunch when Don Pauliano's truck came around the corner from the east, and he slowed and waved, and continued down to his parents' place. Joe and Joan appeared to be in the back of the crew-cab, which was loaded with a couple of pigs!

"Looks like Joe plans on being back in the pig farming business again," Karen said.

"I hope he doesn't over-do it. He's no kid."

"We'll send the boys down there later to check on them. I might tag along."

"Good idea. In your abundant spare time."

“What’s your plan for the rest of the day?”

“Utility player.”

“Huh?”

“Do whatever I can do around here in the house or the gardens.”

“Well, you could tidy up that pile of radio gear in the dining room. You probably want to get your computers moved out of the barn, too.”

“One of them. The rest I’ll use where they are. That’ll be my temporary office until I get the basement rebuilt. What about you and Kelly?”

“More laundry. She’s running loads on stuff that was stored. Ash got all over it, and most of the summer clothes are still in bags. Marie went over to Alan’s to bake those pies.”

“Why doesn’t she bake at home? Don’t answer. The range wiring didn’t get fixed.”

“Yep. That’s on your list, too.”

“Well, I’ll start with that. I need to go to the James’ house and salvage a hunk of cable.”

“K. Remember your gun. Your long-gun,” she said, reminding me without saying it, of the dog attack not too long ago.

“Yep. I’ll take one of the AK’s.”

“Busy day. You better get to your list, and me to mine, Especially since we’re entertaining later.”

“Sorry, not many options. This is kinda how I am.”

“I’ve noticed. After twenty years, you’d think I’d figure that out.”

“Yes, I thought you’d clue in by now,” I said as she went back inside the house, which drew a glare. “Kidding!” I said.

I finished my tea, and retrieved the AK-47 and my tool belt, and headed over to the wrecked and partially stripped house of my friend, Tim James. Tim had bugged out to the San Diego region after the quake, and after his brother-in-law warned him about a serious radiation issue at the Hanford reservation. 'Now look where that put him. Right in the middle of a radioactive cloud. God I hope he and the boys are OK,' I thought as I entered the house, with the AK ready, in case I surprised something…or someone.

The electrical panel was directly below the kitchen in a utility room, unfinished with floor joists above, several cracked, and the thick wire that fed Tim's stove was relatively easy to salvage. I didn't have to worry about the power; the entire meter panel was ripped off of the house and laying in the yard. Modern Electric had safed-up the power at least to the street.

Now with the coil of wire around my shoulder and my tool belt on the other, I awkwardly cradled the AK in my hands as I climbed the twisted basement stair. I was surprised to see a small, black border collie sitting at the top of the steps, a few feet into the front yard. I carefully looked around for other dogs, and saw none. The collie got up and moved off to the north, and sat down again, as if wanting me to follow.

"Anyone home there?" I called on the FRS.

"Yep, what's up?"

"Got a dog out here. He's looking like he wants me to follow him."

"Wait one," Karen said.

The radio was silent, and then I heard the gate, and glanced over at Carl and John trotting over, each now armed.

"Thanks," I said to Karen.

"Don't do anything stupid."

"Words to live by."

"What's up, Dad?" Carl asked.

"Him. Or her," I said, pointing to the dog. The dog had obviously been groomed, and had a collar on. "Let's see what he's up to. C'mon, dog. What's up?" I asked the thin dog as we walked toward it. He promptly got up, and headed north, looking back to make sure we were following.

"Smart dog," John said.

"Hopefully not too smart," I said.

We walked to the other end of the block, and across the street that edged our neighborhood, and up the hill towards the Interstate. The dog moved steadily, as if on an errand, checking every so often to make sure we were following. At the top of the hill, which overlooked the wrecked freeway, the dog headed towards a house that seemed to have been patched up like ours. I wasn't aware that anyone was living up this way—if they did, the census missed them.

"Weapons ready," I said. "Spread out. Carl, behind that Elm over there. John, behind that pickup. I'm calling for reinforcements."

"Yo, Emerald City, are you listening?" It was an obsolete call sign to Alan, but he was the only one that it was ever assigned to. A few moments passed.

"Six here," the proper, and obsolete reply came. "What's up?"

"Need some assistance. Some camouflaged assistance."

"Understood. Location?"

I gave him the address, and the best way to get the Army troops here, and told him to tell the Army I'd explain when they arrived. I also told them that there were three of us, armed, and under cover. The little black dog sat on the front lawn, looking at the door, then us.

Within about two minutes, three Humvees showed up, from a safe distance. Two mounted guns pointed towards the house, and a fairly weathered Lieutenant ran up towards me, in a crouch as the remaining troops, about a dozen, flared out around the house. Each had an unfamiliar radio setup on, not unlike our FRS hands-free setup. I explained the situation, and he and two soldiers went up to the front door, bold as brass, and knocked. No answer. He opened the unlocked door carefully and went in, and immediately called for medical assistance. The remaining troops entered through the back door, and then backed out to secure a perimeter. The medic team carried two good-sized satchels inside as I heard the communications officer call for a 'bus', pronto.'

"What's up, Lieutenant?"

"Civilian. Wounded in an attack. Looks like a knifing. Gotta medevac or she's a goner."

"Dad, is it anyone we know?"

"I don't know. This isn't a house I knew was inhabited. Lieutenant, do you know who it is?"

"Nope, no I.D., and this isn't my sector. I don't have a map of residents in this area."

"Well, I live down the street and I should know, and don't. Squatter?"

"Doesn't look like it to me," the Lieutenant said. "We'll leave the med team here. We're going after the guy. Lady said he headed north, over the freeway. Sent the dog for help."

"Good for her," I said.

"Mount up!" the Lieutenant yelled to his team. In a few moments, the Humvees rolled up the road, through the freeway fence, and down the steep berm to the freeway, and negotiated the broken center divider, soon disappearing up the other side, and off to the hunt.

I sent the boys back home, walking with their rifles over their shoulders, and told them to keep a wary eye. I was bothered that someone was living in the neighborhood that I wasn't aware of. I suppose I was both being territorial, and, perhaps a little fearful of what lurked beyond our 'borders.'

I looked around the property as I waited for the evac team to move the stabbing victim, as yet unseen, into an ambulance. The back yard, facing east, was recently hand-dug, with numerous raised beds—all new by the looks of them—planted and staked. 'Square foot gardening', I thought as I rounded the south side, and let myself out of the gate. The small black dog sat at the corner of the house, patiently, watching both me and the front door. The ambulance, a civilian model, showed up just then and two attendants—in military uniforms— unloaded a gurney from the back.

"Vic inside?" the first asked.

"Yeah. Medics are with her."

"Thanks," he said as they wheeled the cart up the sidewalk.

In a few minutes, they had the woman loaded up in the ambulance, and the dog promptly hopped in back and curled up next to her. The attendants gave the dog a quick look, as if deciding whether or not to kick him out, and then decided to leave him be. The ambulance then took off east, over to Valley Hospital, about five minutes away, pre-quake. The medics collected their gear and locked up the house.

"Sir, here is the key to the house."

"I have no idea who she is, or if she even lives here," I told the medic, who looked to be all of out-of-high-school.

"She said she does. Her grandparents home, they evac'd after the quake. She walked in from Montana ten days ago."

"Well, that explains why I haven't seen her before. We were in the shelter. She gonna be OK?"

"Should be. Put up a Helluva fight by the looks of the place. Guy tried to rape her she said, then he stabbed her. Looks like she got more than a piece of him though. Not all the blood was hers."

"Good. Did she say how many?"

"Just one. Mexican."

"Great."

"Don't worry, he ain't goin' far missing half of his private parts."

I just looked at the guy. "You're kidding."

"Nope. She 'Bobbit'ed' the guy."

"Serves him right."

"Yep. I just hope he bleeds out before our guys get to him."

"Can't disagree. Thanks for helping out."

"You're welcome. See ya around. C'mon Ames. Let's move it!"

The medics loaded up their gear, and headed east, I suppose to the hospital to resupply their truck. I headed back down the street, looking towards home.

A few minutes after four, in the middle of moving my last load of the day from the garage to the house, Clifton's Humvee arrived out front. Annie Ross was driving, and Clifton was nowhere in sight. I radioed to Karen in the house, that our guests were here.

"Hi, Annie. Where's your partner?" I said as she got out of the drivers' side.

"Fairchild. He said to send his regrets, and will have to reschedule."

"That's fine. C'mon in. I'll get you introduced to my wife and kids. I think you've met some of the rest of the family," I said.

"Yes, thanks."

"Karen should be right out. I think she's rounding up the kids right now. You still working on your folks' house?" I remembered from our conversations during the food-collection weeks that the home was pretty beat up.

"Yeah, as time comes. Which isn't often. And supplies are short. And money. My CO is pretty good about letting me go with a couple of the guys when we stand down."

"What do you need supply-wise?"

"Why, you know a supply sergeant?" she said with a glint in her eye.

"No, but I do have some connections, and maybe some stuff left over from our place," I said as Karen came out. "Karen, this is Annie Ross," I said.

"Nice to meet you. I think I met your parents at one of Rick's school reunions."

"Ma'am," Annie said.

"Call me Karen. Reserve 'ma'am' for my mom."

"Sorry," she said. "This is a great house," she stated, as she looked the place over.

"It was almost finished before the quake," I said. "And, was almost finished because of the quake, too," I added. "We finally got to spend the night in our old room last night."

"Where were you living?"

"The barn out back."

"Oh! That must've been rough. Since January?"

"Not bad. Good roof, wood heat, enough to eat if not much more. Better than a lot of people I suspect. Come on inside. I think Karen has a little treat prepared for you."

"That's not necessary, I was just sent to let you know…"

"I know, Clifton's not coming. C'mon anyway."

"I don't want to impose," she said quietly.

"You're not. You're a guest," Karen said. "Come have some tea."

"Thank you," she said, her eyes darting around a little. 'Her Mom's eyes,' I remembered. I'd known Tammy, her mom, since about the fourth grade. Her dad, Brian, sat next to me in Mrs. Nelson's first grade class.

Annie came inside, and then stowed her helmet and flak vest near the front door, keeping her sidearm on, and one of the (I assumed) tactical radios on her vest.

"Rick there's a pitcher of iced tea on the table. Annie, would you like apple or peach pie?"

"Peach pie! You've got to be kidding me," she exclaimed.

"Not for a minute. Home canned peaches, last summer. We found a dozen quarts of them hidden behind Rick's last stash of wine. My niece—well, she's like a niece—just made the pies fresh."

"Peach, please," she said with an eager smile.

Karen dished up a generous-sized piece of the still-warm pie, brought to the house by Marie a little while before. "Oh, my," Annie said under her breath.

I let her enjoy the pie in relative peace and quiet, with chitchat between Karen and I about the incident up the street. I thought to myself that it was odd that a stabbing and attempted rape was now almost a 'normal' thing to discuss. A few months ago, we'd have been horrified. Well, we were now too, but perhaps we were now battle-hardened. Carl and Kelly came in for a minute, and introductions made, and then they promptly disappeared again. Not my plan, but they had things they wanted to do, too—like put their rooms back together.

"That was wonderful, Mrs. Drummond," Annie said as she put her fork down on the very clean plate.

"Karen, please. Relax, Annie, I'm not your commander."

"I know it's just…"

"This isn't the Army."

"OK."

"So can you share anything with us? How things are going, really? We've heard squat on the radio. And the Air Force is continuing to cut figure-eights in the sky."

"There's not much I can tell you about that. The scuttlebutt is that the Supreme Court is here, along with the surviving House and Senate leadership. No way to know, and the higher ups won't confirm or deny anything. That's direct from my CO."

"You didn't break any rules by telling us that, did you?"

"No, sir. I heard that on open-frequency radio this morning. I asked the CO about it and he just shrugged and said, 'Could be, for all I know. Nobody's telling me anything, other than stay the Hell out of the way."

"Huh," I thought. "This Clifton guy a good man?"

"Seems like it…I mean, yes. He's only been here a few days, and is still trying to get the rest of his unit here. They detached from Mexico right before coming here."

"Is that—the Mexican Territory—settling down?"

"Not really. Think Baghdad. Well, when Baghdad was still there."

"It's not?" I asked, a little stupidly.

Annie looked at me for a moment before she answered, and glanced at Karen and I. "No, sir. Israel took it out when they took out Iran. The Iranians moved in after we pulled out, and were staging missile attacks from there."

"Obviously we haven't heard. What else from the Middle East?"

"Tel-Aviv got hammered, but not nuclear. Well, not a bomb. Radiological contamination, they figured a bomb on a small ship. We heard that it came into a marina and blew up, and then the radioactivity went off the charts. Israel took out all the Muslim holy sites after that, Mecca, Medina, Dome of the Rock, a dozen other place I've never heard of. Damascus. A bunch of sites in Iran. A bunch more in Russia and Forget-it-stan. That's what we've heard in briefings anyway."

"OK," I said, digesting what she'd said. "Back to Mexico. Are we winning?"

"We are holding territory. The urban centers are free-fire zones, pretty much run by the drug gangs. RPG's. Full-auto machine guns. Anything the Mexican Army had is now in the hands of the gangs. If there is any good news, it is that the DMZ we established is holding, because anyone caught in it is taken out. That's cut down on military casualties by about ninety percent. The flu is really bad down there among the locals, too, and our own Hispanic troops. No one knows why."

"Because it was engineered to be so," I said before I could think about it.

"Huh?" she replied.

"Maybe the Chinese designed the virus to impact certain races or genetic markers."

She let that sink in. "Why would they do that?"

"I have no idea," I said, "Unless they screwed up and were trying to take out Caucasians and instead took out either indigenous peoples or those of Hispanic descent."

"Hmm."

"Do you know what parts of Mexico we're holding? Or more correctly, planning on keeping?"

"Yeah, anything that has anything to do with oil for one. Or shipping ports. Or major industrial facilities," she said with some irritation or disappointment.

"Pretty much, anything that's worth anything," I said, looking out the dining room window at Buck, in futile pursuit of a quail. "An Empire conquers."

"Yes," she said. "But I didn't sign on to be a storm-trooper. None of us did."

34

Monday,
May First,
late afternoon

Annie took off about ten minutes to five, headed for her parent's home in Greenacres. She'd earned a two-day leave, and wanted to work on the house on her 'days off'. Just as she was leaving, Eric and Amy Moore showed up briefly, and let me know they'd be back on Wednesday to collect their things from their wrecked home, and to finalize the transaction that Alan and Ron had worked out. I told Eric that I'd like to talk to him at length about the farm, but I'd be downtown most of Wednesday on Recovery Board business. I knew that he wanted to get out of the city before dark though, and I couldn't blame him in the least. They'd cleared a good 'profit' for the afternoon, and spent some time talking with Alan and Ron about the farm. I'd get my info from them, I supposed.

The ladies had decided that it was probably easiest this week, until we were all back to something passing for normal, to share a common menu for most meals. This was partly a work-sharing idea, and partly due to no one having everything that they needed to prepare meals properly...at least in an organized manner. Everyone still had stuff in the shelters, and moving it back to kitchens hadn't happened quite yet. Tonight, we were having chicken casseroles, and fresh wheat muffins.

Ron and Alan passed through the property with Rons' Jeep, and Alan had his shotgun out and in the ready position. I closed the gate behind them as Ron shut off the Jeep.

"What's up? Why the literal riding 'shotgun'?"

"Resource protection," Alan said.

"Huh?"

"I have forty-one dollars in silver and gold in the back. As well as some other items that might be well worth their weight, if you get my drift," Alan said.

"Where in the heck did you get that kind of money?"

"All over. Lots of silver dollars, quarters, Mercury dimes, some silver Proof coins, you name it. Even got a French gold franc from one of the lieutenants. Said he picked it up in Mexico."

"Unreal. What else?"

"Five pounds of fresh butter."

"You have got to be kidding me."

"Nope," Ron said with a smile.

"What'd that cost?" They were giggling.

"Four cans of Spam that we got in a trade for a twelve-volt power adapter."

"You came out on the good side of that deal. Both of them."

"We thought so, too. But so did the guy that made the butter. He was smiling the whole time. Lives down on Thirty-Second. Hawaiian-born, got a couple of dairy cows. Makes butter, cream, whole milk, the works. Says he's working on cheese next."

"He must have more than a couple of cows to have that kind of operation. It takes something like twenty pounds of milk to make a pound of butter."

"Well, he didn't elaborate. But he does seem to have a good market for his product," Alan said.

"I'll bet. Been a long time since I had a glass of real milk. And that powdered stuff just doesn't cut it. Any chance that we can get some milk?"

"He says he's committed to his current customer base, and doesn't want to let them down."

"I can respect that. We need to find a dairyman around here though."

"Yeah. We're working on that. With the Army around twenty-four seven, it seems like people are a little less scared of going out and conducting some business," Ron said optimistically.

I thought about what Annie had told me earlier, about our foreign conquests. "Unless they should be scared. Of the Army." That drew a pair of narrowed eyes.

"Continue," Alan said. I filled him in on what Annie had told me of the U.S.'s targets in Mexico, of the rumors of similar Imperial moves in Canada. One of Annie's contacts from her ROTC program had been transferred to Alberta and Saskatchewan, as part of the Athabasca Protection Unit. This 'protection unit' was 'required', Annie said, after the collapse of the Canadian national government, and the failure of the Provincial governments to solidify control in the urban areas. Her sarcasm was thick, as only someone who was truly disgusted can deliver it.

"Seems one has nothing to do with the other. The collapse of a friendly and relatively innocuous government has little to do with us going in and scooping up their oil."

"My view, too. And possibly that of a fair proportion of the military. Rather, the Army."

"Think that's the reason the Air Force and Army aren't too happy with each other?"

"Could be. Who knows?" I said. We were all quiet for a full minute, thinking of the rabbit holes that we were now facing. Alan finally spoke.

"So who is in charge? This is not something that I would have expected the President to condone, given his history."

"Desperation makes you do funny things," Ron said.

"You think that's it? That we're that desperate for oil? For energy?" I said.

"The Middle East is a radioactive nightmare, and between the U.S. and European consumption, the fields are depleted...we saw that when the House of Saud was overthrown. Oil production in Russia won't be back for decades if then. What's left of China is throwing rocks and bullets at each other. Japan collapses without oil imports, and serious ones at that. So do we. Our civilization is unsustainable without it. India is probably relatively untouched from the war. Oil in Africa has always been a nightmare. So yes, I would say that this could be entirely plausible. We get a cheap and reliable energy source, or we're done," Alan said.

I thought about what was going on around us, here in Spokane. "So we have a government that is now choosing to ignore another sovereign nations' borders, and we invade it under the guise of 'protecting its resources," I said and paused, "And we probably have people that think that that is illegal. And those people might be here in town."

"Who's that?" Ron asked.

"Annie thought that the Supreme Court and some of the House and Senate leadership is in town," I said.

"So the billion dollar question is, if that is the case, whose side are they on?"

"Yeah. That'd be good to know. Any other news from down the road?"

"Joe and Joan send their regards. They have half-dozen pigs in his old pen. Joe's back to his cantankerous self," Alan said.

"Good for him. I wondered if we'd ever see the 'old Joe' again."

"He's stopping by the store tomorrow to work out a long-term egg and chicken supply for general sale. He says he can't do much more than that."

"At his age, he shouldn't, anyway," I said.

"He is going to start up a hatchery though, even though he said it's late for the year. Figures on selling chicks as soon as he can," Alan said. "I figured that we all ought to have a small flock for each family, too. He offered to show us what we don't know."

"Which is plenty," I replied, looking up at a Blackhawk moving quickly over the house, towards Felts Field. "Man, they're in a hurry."

"Wonder how long they'll be able to keep it up?" Ron asked.

"Why?"

"Things wear out. Rotor blades. Bearings. Engines. Either of you think that stuff is being built like it was a year ago?"

"No, probably not," I replied. "I wonder how Air Cav will operate without the 'Air'."

"Or fuel," Alan said.

We went over more details of the days' transactions, moving up to the porch and handing Karen the butter for her to split up between our homes. Alan had already given the Paulianos a share, we'd split the rest. I was interested in what people were buying, what they weren't able to get, the luxury items, and prices. Some of these were for my own curiosity; some were perhaps things I could affect through the Recovery Board.

More aircraft continued to arrive during the daylight hours, heading mostly towards Felts Field, our small private-plane airport. C-130's and helicopters seemed to be headed there, while the larger C-17's headed for Spokane International. Fairchild was closed to all but Air Force traffic, it seemed. Fairchild's approach pattern was much farther north than the International airport.   Once the sun went down, incoming air traffic all but ceased. Only 'patrol' aircraft seemed to be flying after dark, both the 'fighter cover' and the occasional helicopter.

Dinner was, we realized, the first time we'd sat down at our own dining room table since January. It was nice to have a real sit-down meal with the kids in our own home. Karen and I went over our progress for the day, and plans for the rest of the week with the kids. I found myself sounding like a taskmaster, and apologized to the kids for the 'orders' I found myself giving. After a slice of pie and getting the dinner dishes squared away, both took off for their rooms, to spend some time being 'kids'.

Karen and I continued to 'put things away' until about nine, when we were both dead on our feet. We checked on both Carl and Kelly, and they were both asleep, on top of their covers. They'd both had long days, too. Tomorrow would be not much different.

Tuesday started off well, with clear and relatively warm weather. I'd tasked myself and the available labor (both John and Carl) with conducting some test plantings of seed corn and beans, using the Ford tractor and seed drill. Alan and Ron would operate the store today, with Kelly and Marie helping them. This would be the girls' first experience in 'working retail.' Had the Army post not been present, we never would have let them work down there.

After our 'drill' tests were completed (I'd never run a seed drill before), I planned on helping Karen, Mary and her kids plant some of our many tomatoes and peppers in sunny, yet wind-sheltered parts of our gardens. Carl and John could then go back to using both the two-bottom plow and the rototiller on the three-point, and the walk-behind rototillers where needed. Plans are often folly though, as these were. Our sunny day faded to dark clouds in the southwest by eleven, and steady rain by noon. Plowing was out, planting would be miserable; so on to 'Plan B.' There was plenty to do 'inside.'

During our enforced shelter stay, I spent a fair amount of time doing garden planning, with quite a few of our seedlings already growing in the greenhouses. We had four families to feed, between the Drummonds, Bauers, Martins and Paulianos (we felt obligated to provide for them, given their contribution to us in absentia after the Domino). I also wanted to hedge our prospects, and have more food available than we would need. I planned on providing for a total of five families' needs, with more excess on top of that for sale or trade. We had fourteen acres of open ground, more or less, to work with. Around that space, on our own 'block', were two hundred and seven fruit trees, and eleven nut trees, including English walnut, hazelnut, and Black Walnut.

Potatoes, until Eric Moore came through with a Godsend, were very high on my list of food priorities. I knew that a successful crop of potatoes, figuring a couple thousand pounds planted, could return tenfold or more. My Irish heritage taught me that much.

I figured on at least an acre of corn, which should result in about two tons of corn. We'd probably need about half that for our own uses (between the families), and the rest for chickens, livestock, or sale.

If we planted wheat, which I'd just decided to do after all, I figured we'd get about 40 bushels of wheat per acre, which translated into almost twenty three-hundred pounds of flour per acre. I planned on two acres of wheat.

Tomatoes, of which we had many, could be a significant cash crop, and we could process much of the crop for our own use. We had, by Karen's count, six hundred plants, ranging from seedlings in four-inch pots to plants in two-gallon containers, some now with blossoms. Our experience showed us that yields for our plants could vary from twenty-four pounds per plant to nearly sixty. To replenish our sauce, soup, salsa stockpiles, dehydrated and fresh use, we'd need about half of our current plants for our own use, with healthy excess. Weather the previous year had decimated our 'normal' yields, bringing the per-plant yield to the low end of the production scale. We wanted to be in the happy condition of having to give the things away, rather than beg or buy them.

Peppers, including bell peppers and four varieties of 'hot' peppers, should yield a couple hundred pounds of fruit for our own use fresh, canned and dried, and potentially for sale. Karen said that we had around seventy-five plants total, with only about half of them 'healthy' looking.

Green beans, my son's least favorite food, yielded about a hundred-fifty bushels per acre, with about thirty pounds per bushel. We figured we'd need about twenty bushels of green beans alone. Dried beans for soups and more long-term storage would add on to that. We had some seeds for navy, black, and a pinto-bean cultivar for dried use.

The fruit trees, which I'd just sprayed, would yield far more than we'd use. Apples, I projected, would probably yield about ten tons. Peaches, about three. Pears, almost seven. Cherries, a little over five tons. Plums, about two. Overall, almost twenty-seven tons of fruit, just on what was already planted and growing.

All of my 'projections' of course, were based on decent weather and favorable growing conditions. A bad thunderstorm in mid-summer, and just the wrong time, could dramatically affect our yields on all of our crops. So could an early frost. So could out-and-out theft. Or worse, 'confiscation.' If that happened, especially at the point of a gun, I began to wonder if I'd be surprised.

Once the rain really began in earnest, the boys headed for the tractor shed and then the barn. I'd seen the clouds coming and figured for an early end to plowing. I tasked them with first, a clean up and organizing session for the jumble that was the tool room, and a couple hours of work on tools that we'd collected around the block. We'd 'cherry-pick' the sturdiest and best for our own use, and what we could spare, we'd ready for sale, along with other surplus items that we might have lying around. John, in an entry-level college business class, took this ball and ran with it, penciling out the essentials of a business plan for the operation. When Ron and Alan looked it over after they shut down the store in mid-afternoon (with a power outage), they had him factor in egg and chick sales, produce sales, and other goods that we might produce.

During the rainy afternoon, I got my piles of radios and computers situated, splitting the gear between the barn and the house. The house would get the older iMac and Carl's G4 workstation and my laptop would stay 'mobile.' The barn would keep my G5 workstation, the newer iMac, and the laser printer, the large-format plotter, and office supplies. I set up in the craft-area of the barn, formerly the Martins' bedroom, living room, and entertainment area. Now, my new office. I was very reluctant to move back into my old basement home-office. Somehow, the thought of being trapped under a collapsed building really didn't appeal to me, and I didn't know if the quakes were 'done' with us.

After the hardware was hooked up and tested, and just before the power went down again (we were though, getting used to having power again, however uneven its schedule turned out to be), I began to get reacquainted with my notes on the Recovery, and cobbled up a rough agenda for tomorrow's meeting. I was sure that at least a couple of my fellow Board members would have similar plans, and I was glad for it. This effort was not something that I wished to burden alone, or be solely responsible for, whether it was successful or not.

Once the power went down, I switched the laptop from 'line' power to an inverter running off a car battery, which would last me another hour at most.

Over and over again, I wondered as I looked over the rumpled pages on the legal pad, and the expanded notes on the computer, just one single thing:

'Where do we begin this?'

35

Wednesday,
May Third

Our first Recovery Board meeting was five minutes from starting, and I was at least ten minutes away. I'd left home at eight o'clock on this cloudy morning, and run into three roadblocks on the way. One, a train that was being moved for the first time since January; the second, a gaping hole with what appeared to be a large-diameter water main, bisecting Broadway Avenue, a small work crew staring at the damage; and the third, a convoy of military trucks headed north, across my path. I radioed into the dispatcher, and let them know that I was delayed. Apparently, I was not the only one, as Dispatch let me know that the meeting had been delayed until at least ten a.m.

I'd cobbled up an agenda of sorts, knowing that other members would as well. We just had so much to do.

An Army gun crew waved me through a serpentine vehicle barrier, upon seeing my 'purple' pass and checking my ID against a printed roster. The gun crew was now six blocks away from the Public Works building, far from the government campus core. I finally arrived, a little frustrated but intact. I was given a new laminated badge at the cleaned-up reception area, and I noted that the building had been cleaned and actually resembled its former self.

Walt Ackerman was in the conference room, with fellow Board members Stacey Womack, Tonya Lincoln, our chairman, and Drew Simons. Stacey looked uncomfortably pregnant, and already had her feet 'up'; Drew had traveled in from his farm outside of Cheney, about twenty miles out. Tonya was all business, and we compiled our agenda items to try to make the most use of the people scheduled to meet with us today, while Walt spoke to one of his assistants. Clete McKinnon, from Liberty Lake had not yet arrived. It was likely I assumed, that he would go through the same obstructions that I had to go through, so his delay was understandable.

"OK, for the preliminaries," Walt began, "We'll have a public meeting today at two p.m. that we estimate will run about an hour. 'Public' meaning broadcast.

The public portion of the meeting will include the reporting sections on the CERT census, utility status, et cetera, summarized from our morning meeting with additional information added as provided during the day. Questions?"

"No, surprised a little," I said. Tonya looked surprised for a moment as well. Just a moment, though.

"You talked in a previous meeting about the lack of communication between officials and the public. I figured this is the clearest we can make it. We'll meet downstairs in the Commissioners chambers for the meeting. KLXY will broadcast it live. We will have a closed session prior to that for executive issues."

"The real meat and potatoes then," Drew replied.

"I prefer to consider them sensitive issues," Walt said.

"I can't disagree with that, Walt. There are some questions that need to be asked that I would just as soon not hear answers to on public TV."

"Precisely. And speculation that fuels rumors."

At nine-fifty, Cletus McKinnon finally arrived. He was much more 'torqued' about his trip into town than I was—he had five diversions to deal with, all of them military checkpoints.

"Let's get started with our first non-published agenda item," Walt said. "Mr. McKinnon, we'll start with your commute. The reasons that you had five checkpoints is that the Army this morning began a sweep through the remainder of the east Valley, dislodging and apprehending the last elements of the Protectors in the urban area, as well as looters and non-residents who have filtered in during the last two weeks. At this hour there are over three thousand people as of this morning, who cannot produce evidence that they are residents of the homes and buildings in which they have set up house. In more cases than not, they are people that have fled rural areas for the city, upon running out of supplies or water in the outlying areas. In some cases, reports that rural homes have been attacked were listed as the reasons for fleeing to the city."

I was taken aback by this statement, and it took me a moment to respond. "Walt, most of those people probably aren't criminals. They should not be treated like they are."

"I understand. But we need to sort them out. There are a number of people that shot first at the Army patrols. Those people are no longer with us."

"Was any broadcast made regarding the searches? Was anyone warned that they needed to I.D. themselves?" Tonya asked, plainly indignant.

"Not on public stations. The operation was originated by the Army at the Federal level. Local commanders had no input on the planning of the operation," Walt said. "They believed that a warning was as good as an indication to escape, evade or shoot, and the military elected not to give that warning."

"Which, upon the first shot, could be easily interpreted as many other things. Which would to any reasonable person, cause them to shoot first, and ask questions later," Stacey said. "That is the only reasonable course of action for the citizen these days. The ONLY one."

"I know that if someone in a uniform kicked my door down, it'd be the last thing he ever did," Clete said. "Of course, if he made it there, a bunch of his friends would already be down."

"Walt, you have to stop this, and right now," Tonya said.

"Mike Amberson is attempting to do that right now." We paused as we considered what had just been told to us.

"All right. Walt, what can you tell us about what's going on at Fairchild?" Tonya asked. I hadn't prompted that; she knew something was going on through her channels. Whatever those might be.

"The Air Force has locked it down. I'm meeting with the base commanding officer at eleven. I will be getting an answer then."

"Sure you will," Clete said, rolling his eyes.

Drew Simons was next. The former professor, now farmer brought it to a fine point. "You will not get a straight answer on what or who they are protecting. You probably have that figured out. So why are you wasting your time meeting with them?"

"They asked for it, not me. I agree with you. Whoever is out there, it doesn't' really matter, unless they start getting in our way."

"And if they do?"

"Then we have a problem."

Walt's assistant, Kamela Gardner came in, with an armful of files for each of us. Instead of her 'normal' business attire, she was wearing a North Face fleece over a flannel shirt, jeans and boots. I almost didn't recognize her. "Dr. Sorenson is ready, Mr. Ackerman," she said.

"Please send her in."

Dr. Rene Sorenson, the fifty-ish County Health officer, came in. We'd heard from Walt that she was only available for about fifteen minutes, before she was scheduled elsewhere.

"Good morning, Doctor," Walt said as she came inside, and made introductions. She was known for not 'playing well with bureaucrats', which endeared her to many. Walt quickly introduced us, and I watched as she rapidly sized each of us up.

"Good morning. I've been asked to provide you a status report on the medical care and overall health situation in the county at present. The blue folder that you have been provided gives summary information as well as in-depth data on each medical facility, causes of death and diseases present in the last several months. I apologize for the dated information—this was current before the war went nuclear. I am compiling an update to this for your use, but it will not be available until next week at the earliest."

"Medical care remains far below pre-quake levels, with less than twenty percent of hospital functions in place. What does remain is general in nature, with nearly all specialty medical practices no longer in operation. Those physicians still in practice—meaning still alive and in the area, are handling many cases far out of their former skill set. These range from what we formerly considered to be childhood diseases to much more serious problems. Asthma has become a serious issue due to the ashfall, with more serious cases resulting in silicosis and pleural fibrosis in subjects that have arrived from the more heavily hit areas, or in cases where people did not take adequate precautions regarding dust masks and working in dusty conditions. This is an irreversible lung disease that normally affects sand-blasters, tunnel workers, and miners. We are hearing of more reports from the areas affected by the Rainier ash, up to and including Spokane and Lincoln counties. Other diseases include typhoid fever, acute diarrhea, at least two forms of hepatitis that are completely resistant to known treatments, continuing outbreaks of the Guangdong Flu, acute rhinovirus infections, and a significant increase in deaths due to lack of medicines that formerly maintained and managed care. These include blood pressure medicines, blood thinners, chemotherapy treatments, a dozen more. We have continuing issues with animal-bites and potential rabies cases. We continue to lose quake victims from crush injuries and infections. We had until recently, an increasing number of gunshot wounds at Sacred Heart and Valley Medical. That has stabilized in the last three weeks. Our live-birth ratio is also tipping over, with a tripling in deaths of newborn and mothers due to complications that we cannot manage without proper facilities and medicines."

Stacey Womack replied first. "Good God."

"Rene, what can we do to help this?" Clete asked.

"Can you turn back time?"

"No."

"Then not a damned thing. We are now, medical-wise, just slightly better off than your average Third World country. We don't have the pharmaceuticals, and a sizeable portion of our medical equipment and the knowledge base are gone. They're not coming back. We have no tetanus immunizations, for example. A simple nail, dirty and rusty, stepped on, has a potential to now kill you. A great potential."

I asked the next hard question. "Doctor, what percentage of our population had immunizations against common diseases, pre-quake?"

"Common diseases? Like mumps, measles, rubella, chicken pox? All of the stuff that people don't worry about?" she said with thinly veiled sarcasm.

"Yes."

"Perhaps sixty percent of adults. Maybe into the eighty-percentile range for children. There is no data on what percentage of survivors have been immunized, or have immunization records."

"What is your greatest concern, medically?" Drew Simons asked, peering over his bi-focals.

"That reports of mutations of the Guangdong Flu may in fact be real."

"Please elaborate," Tonya said.

"I have reports of a new form of influenza that is exhibiting symptoms of both the original influenza and HIV. A single infection resulting in influenza-type symptoms that can potentially be fought-off by the bodies' immune system, only later to either re-appear or kill the victim through some other seemingly minor infection. This is known to kill the subject in less than forty-eight hours after the onset of the second bout with the disease."

"Where did you hear about this?" Walt asked.

"CDC and USAMRIID. One of the Army medical triage officers gave me the packet."

"OK, so knowing only enough to be dangerous, Doctor, how do we protect ourselves?" I asked.

"Isolation from the East Coast for one. That seems to be the site of the original cases, who have been traced to people that were in the middle of a tuberculosis treatment, and then walked out before the disease was truly cured. Three 'alpha' cases. New Jersey, Quantico, and Atlanta. And, it's airborne, not vector-transmission, meaning not spread through animals, only by people."

"Isolation? How? Not like we have a helluva lot of contact with anyone outside of the state right now," Clete said, hands folded across his barreled chest.

"Then keep it that way until a cure is developed. This has a ninety-percent mortality rate."

"OK," Walt said. "Thank you, Rene. Is there anything else the Board has for Doctor Sorenson?"

"Yeah," I said. "I do. And you do too, Walt," I thought, putting things together in my uniquely paranoid way.

"What's that, Rick?"

"Do you have any idea where those planes at Fairchild came from? Originally?"

His eyes narrowed. He probably knew and couldn't tell us. "No, not really."

"Well let me play the Devil's advocate for you then," I said, playing a card that I may or may not have actually had in my hand. "If those were E-4B's--or 747's to the rest of us--they are run by the military, then there is a fairly good chance that they came from the D.C. region, and they're carrying people that wanted to get the Hell out of there. Problem is, they may have brought it with them. You may want to re-think meeting with your Air Force general. Maybe you just talk to him on a radio. Maybe you just don't talk to him at all and quarantine the base completely."

"A leper colony," Clete McKinnon said, looking at the report in front of him, and finding it as I did, irrelevant at the moment.

"Lepers have a chance of a living, or at least living for a prolonged period of time," Sorenson said. "You get this, you're done."

"Thank you, Doctor," I said. She quietly gathered her things up and left the room, obviously thinking about what I'd theorized.

"Let's take a five minute break," Walt said.

Stacey and Drew excused themselves and left the room, as did Walt. I hoped to inform the Air Force that a face-to-face meeting was not possible due to health concerns. I also hoped he spoke with the ranking Army officer to discuss the situation.

Our 'executive' session lasted through lunch, which consisted of sandwiches, apples (!!) and coffee or water. We were hoping to get an update on the 'roundup' from Mike Amberson, but he was still out in the Valley. He had, however, managed to get the word out on AM radio that the Army was 'present' in the Valley and that un-documented residents should be prepared to discuss their situations with the military, and under no circumstance should they show a weapon. People that were called 'combatants' in these situations dramatically dropped off, with only a half-dozen more incidents that involved gunfire for the rest of the day.

Over lunch, Walt Ackerman had spoken with the commanders of the Forty-First Division in person in his break from the Board business. The command elements were using the vacant fourth floor as a downtown headquarters, which had the advantage of a link into most of the County communications network and commercial broadcast abilities as well.

Walt informed them of our discussion regarding the potential new influenza, and the threat posed by it. Upon Walt's request, orders immediately went out to the Forty-First's staging area—Spokane International Airport-- to lock Fairchild down. Within ten minutes, Walt let us know that an Air Force Lieutenant Colonel using the Army radio command frequency, had 'gone off' on both the Army and the County government. The Army politely informed the Air Force officer that until the County Health Department OK'd it, no Air Force personnel, or associated civilians would be allowed to leave the base property, upon threat of immediate quarantine due to unknown pathogens that may be present at Fairchild or among its personnel. The quarantine facility would be the Geiger Corrections Facility, essentially, the County's medium security prison. The Army units fortunately, had not mingled face-to-face with the East Coast Air Force elements, but had merely arrived at approximately the same time. I could imagine that there were a number of armored Humvees with mounted weapons on both sides of the fence at Fairchild, in an uneasy showdown.

Walt spoke with the base commander over a County radio frequency. Today it was a two-star, who promptly went off on Walt and the Army, stating that travel off of the base affected National Security matters and that it was absolutely vital that Air Force personnel be given access to the urban area. Walt declined, which resulted in a tirade of expletives that a Marine would be proud of.

The 'executive session' included the straight-dope on a dozen local water distribution systems; electrical utilities; Burlington Northern railroad, which had yet to send a train into the region since January; and Rocky Mountain Petroleum, the company that shipped virtually all petroleum products into the Inland Northwest. Despite the 'brands' of gasoline that we were used to, most of them showed up in the same pipeline, and any special 'additives' were put in when they arrived at the East Spokane tank farm.

The communications segment of our meeting was both brief and depressing. I would have enjoyed having at least the hope of telephone service again, either cell phone or landline, but that was apparently not going to happen in either case. The main telephone switching station in downtown was a burned out wreck, although the ten-story building was still standing. The smaller infrastructure components were smashed up pretty well in the quake as well, but without the heart of the system, the switching center, landlines would be a long time in coming back. The cell phone system, marketed as 'different' from the land-lines when some of us dropped our land lines in favor of wireless, were inextricably tied to the landlines for functionality. Cell towers that had survived the quake in many cases had no power; those that had power had no place to send signals to with damage so great across the area. On top of all of the above, nearly all of the components for the systems were made offshore. In China. Once upon a time.

At ten 'til two, we filed downstairs into the Commissioner's chambers, where we found two television camera crews and radio crews set up. Someone had printed out name placards for each of us, and taped them to the oak paneling in front of our seats.

We sat in our chairs, trying not to look like we belonged there (hah!) as Walt introduced us to the vacant room and the two TV cameras. He turned over the public presentation portion of the 'meeting' to his assistant Kamela, who had prepared a PowerPoint presentation to be shown to the TV audience. We were reduced to looking at a ceiling-mounted monitor. Our individual screens were blank.

Kamela (who in a previous life was a communications director for a dot-com that flared briefly and burned out), presented the information clearly concisely, and in normal language. 'Almost clinical,' I thought as she explained the damage done to each water system in the County, which areas were restored to operation, and which areas would be months, if ever, to rebuild.

"Why're we here?" Drew asked me quietly as the PowerPoint slides, and Kamela's presentation, continued for the viewers at home.

"Window dressing," I said. "Makes it look like there's actually people in control and managing the situation."

"Good thing we know better."

"Indeed."

The presentation covered water systems first, then power, communications, medical care, transport and travel, food supplies, retail operations and manufacturing, and closing with a brief statement regarding funding governmental operations. This piqued my interest, realizing of course that someone other than myself had finally understood that without taxes collected, government couldn't survive. And no taxes had been collected since the previous fall. No tax payments, in money that was still used, had been made since the old Board of Commissioners had been removed. The County was broke, and needed money of some kind, to function. I supposed, it was also up to us to come up with a taxation strategy, or some other method, to fund the livelihoods of the County employees, in addition to all of our other tasks.

While the presentation continued, I mulled over the detailed CERT report that listed the deaths and damages from the quake, that Kamela was reviewing in general form. It would take me some time to take that information, and couple it with what we'd learned today regarding utilities, to come up with anything resembling a coherent 'plan.' It was a simple concept, but staggeringly difficult to comprehend on all the levels that we had to consider.

At two forty-five, Kamela wrapped up her presentation, and I noticed that the broadcast now switched over to a public service announcement on sanitation practices. I wondered where they dug that up?

"Nice presentation, Kamela," I said.

"Thanks. It's been a long time since I've had to talk in public for that length of time."

"Better you than me," Clete said. "I'd have thrown up." That got her laughing.

"Let's go back upstairs to the conference room to set our meeting schedules, if you would," Tonya asked. We headed back upstairs, stopping off at the restrooms along the way.

Back in the conference room, we recapped our day, and actually were able to set some goals on specific areas of work that we could accomplish. Each Board member was assigned, or volunteered to head up key segments of the recovery effort. Clete volunteered for the safety and security elements, which included life-safety, fire, defense and medical; Drew volunteered to address fuel and energy, which included liquid and solid fuel, bio-fuels, and hydroelectric power; Stacey volunteered to address the food production and food trading aspect; Tonya, the manufacturing, retail and service industries. Walt would (in addition to his riding herd on us and keeping the remaining County government in operation) be responsible for the communications aspect and serving as liason between the City and the County governments. I was tasked with—well, volunteered is probably more accurate—coordination of resettlement in the viable areas of the County. Which really meant keeping my finger on the pulse of everyone else's work, and determining what 'viable' really meant. We, as a committee, would have to have strategy sessions on keeping the County functioning, economically.

We scheduled our next meeting for Friday, two days away, which would give us time to review the reports given to us, in theory. I had a lot of homework to do, and a lot of work to do at home.

By a quarter to four, I was back in the Ford and on my way home. Ten blocks away from the public works building, a Humvee began to follow me, and continued east, as I turned onto our street. Ten miles plus, the Humvee was behind me.

It's a little disconcerting, being followed.

36

Wednesday,
May Third,
5:07pm

I radioed ahead on the FRS, so someone was able to open the gate for me, and told Karen that I had had company behind me the whole way home.

"Do you need us to do something?"

"If they wanted me, they'd have me by now," I replied.

"Gate's ready."

"Thanks."

I passed Pauliano's house, where a wholly decrepit early sixties Chevy pickup was parked in the driveway. I could see Joe and Joan inside, along with at least one other figure. 'Somebody's come calling,' I thought to myself.

Carl had the gate for me, and I noticed that he was still clad in his 'farmer' outfit, a pair of my coveralls, and what were once new deerskin gloves, a few days ago. They were now dirty and molded to fit his hands and the wheel of the tractor.

I parked in front of the partially opened garage door, where I noticed that the space that was recently filled with furniture, and then emptied, was full again. Of sacked potatoes!

"Perfect timing, Daddy-o," Carl said. "Eric Moore just left. You missed out on unloading the spuds and onions."

"Onions, too? Cool."

"Three hundred pounds. Six bags. And twenty-five hundred pounds of potatoes."

"More than we bargained for. Literally."

"Alan said we'd work it out. Oh. Here's the key to his house. He's not coming back to live there."

"Did you guys help him load up their furniture?"

"Yeah, most of it. Left some stuff he doesn't want. I got 'dibs' on it."

"For sales or your own house in a few years?"

"Sales. I'm not all that interested in having my own place, thanks."

"Good. You're not sixteen 'til next month."

"Yeah. We were supposed to have the Mustang done by then."

"Well, that's not happening, is it?"

"Apparently not."

"That's OK bud. There won't be gas to put in it anyway. At least not for a long, long time. I think the only motorized conveyance we'll be using will be one or two of the trucks or the van, and the tractor. Gas will be available and rationed I suspect soon, so we'll be able to travel a little bit."

"I haven't been out of the zip code for months. None of us has."

"Maybe you can tag along with me on Friday. I'll be going back downtown."

"Cool."

"Now, let's hear about the rest of your day," I said as we climbed the front steps, where Ada was laying on the concrete porch, wagging her tail. I could hear Buck inside, whining to come out.

"Is that pizza?"

"Surprise," Carl said.

"No way," I said. "We don't have any pepperoni or parmesan, among many other things."

"Joe's friend. Peretti. What his first name…Angelo. He made it. Mom traded him for tomato plants."

"That woman is a saint."

I wondered what Red wine might go with pizza….

After a dinner that not only had no leftovers, but no crumbs of leftovers, Carl filled me in on more of his conversation with Joe Pauliano and his friend Angelo Peretti. Angelo had known Joe for most of the fifty years that they'd been in Canada and the U.S., and Angelo was bringing his two grown grandsons, and a great-grandson, up to speed on the fine art of the butcher. He had worked in slaughterhouses most of his life, later as a butcher and master sausage maker. Not only did we have (well 'had') homemade pepperoni, but hard salami and three other varieties of sausage. For this, Alan paid Mr. Peretti hard cash: silver coins. I didn't ask, and didn't really care what he spent on the meat. It was well worth it.   And homemade cheese!

I filled all of the family in on the meeting at the County offices, leaving nothing out. I noticed the direct and calculated look that both Ron and Alan had when I presented the situation regarding the Flu, and the potential for yet another devastating round of losses. I also explained that what we knew was 'not much', and certainly could not be classified as 'factual.'

"No, but it's a worthy premise," Alan said. "How long does the Army hold up the Air Force on base? What's the incubation period?"

"The Doc said the mutation presents as flu, then settles down, and then comes back with a vengeance. I would expect a week, maybe two, before we know."

"Well aren't you just a bundle of happy happy," Libby said.

"Yeah. Ain't it the truth," I said. "Enough of my day. What, other than honest to God pizza for dinner, was the high point around here?"

"That Alvarez fella came in…Manny. We traded him straight up chickens and eggs for meat rabbit breeding pairs and young. Said he's very interested in more trading. Said he's making a list. I also gave him that address of the other Alvarez—that his nephew?"

"Could be. Probably a long shot, but there were an awful lot of coincidences."

"No such thing as coincidences," Mary said.

"True."

Karen had 'that look' that only shone when I was about to be surprised. "Hon, we got a packet of letters too. We waited until you got home. And a note from one of the Deputies about that girl that was attacked. She's doing OK, and her story checks out. That is her grandparents' house she was in. She should be out of the hospital over the weekend."

"Funny how fast they kick you out now that there's no such thing as medical insurance," I said, almost afraid to ask who the letters were from. "Where are the letters?"

She handed the small packet to me, a large manila envelope, still sealed. I tore it open. Five letters, unopened. "This is it?"

"Yes. Mom got a letter from my cousins in Dallas. We can talk about that later. I thought you'd want to read those first."

I quickly scanned the envelopes. Nothing from my brother Alex and his wife in Tennessee. One letter from Utah, that would be my brother Jeff and his wife Barbara, but the postage cancellation wasn't Ogden, but Provo. The envelope was edged with hand-applied black ink. Odd. Three letters from Minnesota, my oldest brother Jack and his family. One letter from Joseph, Oregon, with the name of one of my business associates printed in the corner and no return address….I thought he'd died in the quake.

I started with the letter from Utah. The beautiful handwriting belied the message within.

"March 1st

Dear Mr. Drummond and Family,

I am writing on behalf of Barbara Drummond, who has come to live with us during this difficult time. I must sadly relate to you the death of your brother Jeffery, and your niece Lynda. My name is Stephanie Larriman .I worked with Barbara on a number of community workshops on nutrition prior to the Collapse.

Three days ago, we were traveling from my parents home in Ogden back to Provo, I stopped in at Barbara's home to see how she was doing with the Troubles, and found her disconsolate and frankly, broken down, huddled in a corner near the front door. The home was unlocked, but had not been disturbed.

Her husband, your brother, had died of the Flu, as I suspect did Lynnie. Jeff was found in the bedroom; Lynnie in the bathroom. We contacted the authorities and they advised us that they would conduct proper burials per the Baptist church that Barbara and Jeff attended, and they advised us to take Barbara with us, as there are no facilities to help her at this time.

She is physically seemingly well, but I'm very sorry to say that she seems to have suffered a complete mental collapse. She continues to call out for Jeff and Lynnie, and this morning got up, showered and dressed, and began to ask for them. She seems to have no recollection of what happened, or where they are. I am writing to all of Jeff's family—we found an address book in Barb's purse. Hopefully, this will reach you all.

Barbara is welcome to remain with us as long as the Troubles last. We are trying to contact her parents or other family members in Twin Falls, but as yet of course have not heard back from them. Please write back to us when you receive our letter, and we will try to keep Barbara well.

With regrets,

Stephanie Larriman"

Karen was at my side as I finished reading the letter. It took me only a little by surprise. "I saw the black edge on the letter, and thought that this might be the case," She said. "I'm sorry, honey."

"Thanks, babe. Here. You read the rest," I said as I handed her the letters. Ron handed me a short glass of Scotch. I accepted it wordlessly.

"I'll read Jack's letters in order, first, OK?"

"Sure," I said numbly. 'So us Drummonds were not as lucky as I thought we were,' I thought to myself as Karen read the letters.

"March 20th,
Little Canada, Minnesota—

"Dear Richard, Karen, and children—

You remain in our prayers, and we hope this finds you well. We have not heard from Jeff or Alex but remain hopeful that all are well.

We are doing well, despite that which goes on around us and the events that are spinning wildly out of control in the Cities. Emily, Patrick, Jane and little Nicole are all here and doing as well, all things considered.

With sad news though, Patrick's girlfriend Deborah was found at last. She had been murdered apparently for her groceries and truck after leaving for Cloverdale. Her funeral was held two days ago. I delivered the eulogy, and spoke from James 1, on the trials that we face. Patrick, while resolute, is devastated. Dear Nicole though is persistent in getting her Uncle Pat to smile again.

The rioting seems to be held in check within Hennepin County and most of the urban areas of the Cities. Blocks on blocks of the low-income homes and neighborhood businesses are gone, and at least a half-dozen faith based colleges and universities have been sacked and burned as well. Senseless murders are all but common, and neither the military nor the police can begin to make a dent in the violence. Our two seminary students have elected to try to go back to their homes, and succeeded in getting space on an evacuation caravan yesterday morning. The caravan was organized by our lay pastor, and will head west before turning south to Nebraska and eastern Colorado, where the students' families live. The caravans' eventual destination is northwest Arkansas, where our lay pastor's family resides. Eleven vehicles formed up the caravan, with armed men in each vehicle, and a scout car within radio range ahead of the main body. I listened to some of the planning for the trip south, and for a long time, thought I had stepped into an episode of 'The Twilight Zone.' I find myself wishing that that was true, rather than the dim reality we face.

We are not long in staying here in the Cities, despite my belief that we would be undisturbed here. It is apparent to all of us that Patrick's home is better suited to what lies ahead, although vast amounts of work need to be done and quickly, to ensure us making it through the winter. Pat has a good stock of supplies on hand at the house, and his neighbors have watched over the place for the past few days since Deborah was found. I expect that we will begin to pack up our essentials in the morning, with the goal of being moved to the acreage by this Friday at the latest. I'm finding that my son has taken a much more pessimistic view of this World than I ever knew, despite his faith, and that he has certainly followed you and your precautions more than I would have. Rather, more than I did. Perhaps it is time for the father to learn from the son.

Remain safe.

All our love—

Jack and Em."

"Well that's a little more positive," I said.

"You want me to read the next two?" Karen asked.

"Sure," I said, sipping my drink. The Martins listened intently as the next letter was read—they had not received any letters or word from any of their family members since the Domino. I knew that Libby was still hoping her sister had made it through, but I held no such hope for her. The chances were just too slim.

Jack's next letter, dated March thirty-first, after the move to Patrick's farm, outlined Pat's preparations, which were not unlike my own. No root cellar, due to the high water table, but a good-sized garden, stored foods, and diesel. Pat had, on his own, figured out that diesel lasts longer than gasoline, and had aligned his vehicles and a backup generator accordingly. Jack's Subaru was parked, and any driving was now done with Pat's old Trooper, or his diesel Volkswagen Rabbit pickup. The gasoline that they had left they would use for rototillers. Pat had, unbeknownst to his parents, moved into what could only be described as a survival-based community. Twelve families on a hundred and twenty acres, of like minds regarding preparing for the worst. I could only imagine what the planning meetings for such an enterprise might be like, since the topic, whenever I brought it up, fostered nothing but overly strong opinions that ended up in alienation. I hoped that for their sakes that this community would actually function, beyond the initial weeks and months. Their power had failed repeatedly over the past week, for no apparent reason.

The third letter, dated April 7th, talked of their 'mutual aid group' meetings regarding defense of their homes from evacuees fleeing the Cities. Jack pointed out that given the location of the property, north of the Cities, it was more likely that evacuees would head south, rather than north, and generally along freeways and highways, neither of which applied to the property. The 'head of security' for the group stated that regardless, manned outposts would be established and operated twenty-four seven. Jack also expressed dismay at the reliance of the group on pre-packaged foods and the 'astounding' lack of skill and knowledge in growing food or simple farm operations.

"A little behind the curve, big brother," I said. "Hope your boy has some books on the subject, and friends with livestock."

Karen continued reading. *"There is a definite rebellion going on in the Cities, and best as I can determine, it is aligned along the split between the Blue and the Red. The Blue being those demanding public assistance, shelter, and resources, whining that the State or FEMA should take care of things. The Red being those who demand that people work for their livelihood, and who are not about to share scarce resources with those who simply will not 'do' anything. I hold both sides in contempt. They bicker while Rome burns. I have listened to reports on the radio that the Rebellion is dominant in the New England states, Cleveland and Chicago, where the Blue, I assume named after the results of the last election, seem to be in control, which means that they are seizing what they feel is 'theirs.' I actually heard a woman state on the radio, in defense of this forced thievery, that 'those who have do not share.' Incredible. The 'Reds', I assume that we are among their count, are those in the rest of the country, who 'have' things that 'they' want.*

We finally have received some of your letters. We are so glad that you have made it through the winter and are moving ahead. I was sorry to hear that Joe stopped by, although I certainly agree with your decision." (Joe, an older brother, came by the house not long after the quake, demanding that we take him in. Being a thirty-five year alcoholic, and knowing his true nature, I sent him away. But enough of him.) *"While at times, I feel that it is futile, I continue to pray for him to deal with his demons and become a productive man. I know that it pains all of us to see the waste of his life. We heard from Jeff and Barbara finally, although the letter was quite old by the time we received it, dated February 18th. Still, nothing from Alexander.*

We have tilled and prepared the land for planting in the warm week just past, but had heavy snow yet again today. Our short season, and only a single, small greenhouse, will challenge this community far beyond what they will accept. There is a continuing belief—unwarranted--that supplies on hand will suffice. I've spoken with Patrick about this a number of times, and he agrees. There are now seventy-two people on this land, up from fifty. The additional residents came to the properties from the Cities or other areas that are related in some form or other to the original members of the 'assistance group'. There are some among the owners of this land that are 'soft touches.'

While I hate to say this, nearly all of the newcomers are 'Blues.' A half-dozen of them do nothing but complain and try to direct others, while demanding largesse for their mighty wisdom. This has resulted in the alienation of at least two families from the rest of the group—and once this issue has resulted in physical violence. One of the newcomer 'Blues' was caught trying to break into a storehouse on a parcel two farms down. While he may yet survive, his right hand did not. The shotgun fired by the owner of the property saw to that. The owner apologized to the man's family for missing his head, and then went back home. Thank God that the farm that the now one-handed thief lives on is at the far end of the road. Pat did well to select this parcel, which is literally at the end of the road and the end of the group.

I fear, my brother, that our trials are just beginning.

Praying for you—
Jack and Emily"

"Indeed, they are," I said to my now-empty glass. Ron poured me another.

"At least they're out of the city. If they'd have stayed, there's no telling how they'd be now," Karen said. "Do you want me to read the next one?"

"Please," I said. I'd tried to track down my marketing manager, Greg, and our other employees right after the quake, but never found them. I assumed that Greg had been killed in the quake.

"This is pretty old. January," Karen said.

"Lucky to have made it at all," I said.

"January 28th
Joseph, Oregon

Dear Rick:

This is an odd way to start a letter, but I hope you and your family are alive to read this.

Obviously, I'm not in Spokane anymore. Right after the quake, we decided to boogie to Connie's parents' place in Joseph, after the Red Cross in Spokane shipped us south to Lewiston. Our other choice was Reno or Las Vegas, according to the FEMA idiots on the bus. They have no idea what they are doing, and actually argued about where to go while we were on our way! Connie managed to get hold of her Dad on the phone, who brought his truck in to load us up and stock up when he came to get us. We had to conveniently disappear from the shelter when she called, because they weren't letting people out to go find their own ways—I felt like we were cattle.

We've been here about a week now. I've been trying to deal with getting in touch with our insurance company, our bank, and of course our employers, but since the phones are hosed, I had to resort to the old ball-point and a legal pad. Sorry I haven't contacted you sooner.....and I hope I still have a job.

Our place was all but flattened in the quake, and I ended up with a broken wrist and a cut-up head when the ceiling landed on us. We were trapped for about three hours, until the neighbors finally dug us out. Connie and I both ended up with a mild case of hypothermia, and neither of us is over that yet. She thought I was all but dead, with all the dried blood. She wouldn't come near me until I got cleaned up. She's funny that way.

I'm not sure how long it will be before we come back home. We're hoping in a few weeks, after we heal up, that we'll be back in town and able to help you get the company back on its feet and our lives back to normal.

Write back when you can, and thank you for everything you've done for us. It's been great working with you.

Best regards,

Greg and Connie Hawkins"

"January. A lot has happened since that was written," I said. "Hope you're still OK, Greg. Enough for now. I need to go for a walk."

"I'll go with," Karen said.

37

Thursday,
May Fourth

Rain. Not just rain, but damnable rain. Hard, cold, wind blown. Utterly miserable to work in. It was apparent to me, when I finally gave up trying to sleep at five-thirty, that work outside today would be a bust. The rain pounded against the makeshift repairs on the windows; the wind threatened to tear up our new roof.

We'd had a quiet evening, both kids understandably upset with the news of the deaths of their cousin and their uncle; the plans we made last year for a summer family reunion, minus the pain-in-the-ass Joe, an impossible dream now, in this world at least.

Karen did what she could do for us of course, and I mourned with Kelly and Carl the loss in our family, realizing of course that more losses were likely, with each letter we received. Jeff had been gone since February, it was now May. No further letters arrived from Utah in that package. For all I knew at this point, Barbara may have died now. Perhaps Jack and Emily and their extended, clan too.

Quite late, the kids finally slept, and I tried to as well. I rested, but didn't really, throughout the night. Once I resigned myself to it, I got up as quietly as I could, which still woke Karen.

"You OK?" she asked.

"Yeah. Can't sleep. I'm going downstairs to get some work done."

"Wake me by seven. I want to be out in the fields today."

"Forget it. It's been pouring for an hour at least. I heard it on the roof."

"Then wake me by seven-thirty. 'K?"

"Will do," I said as I gave her a good morning kiss.

Downstairs, with Buck (Ada took my spot on the bed), I made some tea, and set up the PowerBook, with my notes from the meeting yesterday. My fingers entered the words into the computer, the responsibilities of each Board member, the impressions that I had from the CERT report.

My mind though, was far away. Jeff and Barb last summer, golfing at Indian Canyon, and that crushing drive from the first tee that Jeff had promised Jack and I would land on the green, no doubt. Well, it did, but the wrong green. Sure was pretty though, climbing high into the July early morning sky, up, up aaaaand *LEFT* like it hit some sort of force field. Jack and I laughed until our sides hurt. Lynnie tagging along, driving the golf cart like a maniac, nearly catching air on one of the bumpy cart paths. Alex and Amber met us for brunch later, where we planned 'this year's' reunion. Barb with her endless lesson planning and research, which she enjoyed more than a 'vacation.'

That was a good day. Our last good day all together.

I woke Karen at the appointed time, and let the kids sleep. There would be no fieldwork today, and the greenhouse work would keep. Karen had spoken with Alan and Ron regarding the schedule for the store for the day, and the Drummonds would have a day or two to mourn and not have to work retail, or more appropriately, 'barter.' Alan discovered his natural talent for the business; I found the negotiations unpleasant and irritating. I was never one to 'shop', but one to 'buy.' I've always hated negotiations, and when a 'new' car was needed, regularly offended the dealers by stating my best, last price on the car, cash, now. If they did not agree, I left. More than once, with a salesman chasing me. I always ended up with what I wanted for the price I wanted to pay, but usually with a headache and much frustration.

Karen was busy with building some soup mixes throughout the morning, and baking wheat and cornbread with Carl and Kelly. We'd let them sleep until almost nine, an unheard-of luxury. At thirty-nine degrees, it was a miserable day outside, with the rain continuing. My morning was spent mostly reading the CERT report through, which I laboriously translated into a graphic form, coupled with the information (and created on a typewriter of all things) of the functioning portions of the utility systems in the County.

By eleven, I was dead tired of the numbers, the analysis, the planning. I was able to prepare an analysis for a sample of the Spokane Valley near Sprague Avenue and Pines Road (one of the first 'big' intersections in the Valley when it was settled in the late eighteen hundreds). The analysis showed in numeric and graphic terms, by parcel on the Assessors maps, which homes or businesses had been destroyed, which had casualties, which had survivors in residence. When I overlaid the utility information over the same area, I was able to then determine which parts of that neighborhood had power and water as recently as the middle of April, and which parcels were not served due to infrastructure or building damage, and which parcels would not be served until extensive repairs were made, or which would never be served due to the severity of the damage and the lack of materials and labor.

The final product of the one-mile-on-a-side neighborhood was similar to the circulatory system of a human going into cardiac failure, with only the major arteries still pumping life. The periphery, those areas deep into neighborhoods or far away from major pipelines or far from substations looked like a fading patchwork, void of service. The parcels nearest major water and power lines or transformer substations, had power and water. Anything more than eight to ten blocks off of a major arterial was almost always a 'dead' zone, utility-wise.

Exceptions of course existed, and dependencies on power that could be fed to pumping stations or wells could have revitalized at least parts of the area, if power could be restored. If parts could be obtained. If trained electricians could be found.

A half-dozen paragraphs from three utilities noted that some residents, with functioning water wells, had converted them back either to backup-generator power or in one case, a combination windmill/solar power set up that used the windmill to raise the water to a surface tank, and an electric pump to pressurize the water into a home. The utility thought that the system was ingenious, but potentially dangerous due to the lack of a back-flow protection device. The concern was that contaminated water from the home could contaminate the well, or the aquifer, spreading disease. I noted that they did not mention sanitation at this particular home. I wondered where they'd put their septic system or outhouse, relative to the well.

Karen provided chili and cornbread for lunch, and I headed upstairs for a nap. I was dead tired. Ada was more than happy to join me.

I woke up after two o'clock, the rain still beating on the roof overhead. I could smell the woodstove and the baking bread from the electric oven, and hear the gentle popping of the fire. I got up and put my late Dad's black-and-red checked Pendleton shirt on, and my 'old' pair of hiking boots, thinking that I should try to do something productive around the place. Ada remained curled up on her pillow, next to the bed.

The upper floor was downright gloomy with the heavy clouds and rain. From Kelly's room, I could look out over the garage and the Woolsley's home to the south, but couldn't see as far as the end of the street for the rain. Even darker clouds were headed toward us, with winds pushing twenty or twenty-five miles per hour. Miserable. More importantly, unseasonable for May—more like March—and definitely not conducive to growing food. And, the rain had probably washed off most of my sprays on the trees.

Downstairs, Karen was snoozing on the couch under a blue-jean patch quilt, after baking a pile of wheat bread, and assembling the dry ingredients for soup, now sealed in some of the Kerr canning jars that I'd squirreled away after years of garage sales. I suspected that all too soon, the store would be inundated for requests for 'extra' canning supplies, as if there were such a thing now. We did have three canners, and one pressure-canner, but I was not about to give any of them up.

I'd been thinking about the store and I suppose, commerce in general for several days, in the back of my mind. Those of us that were 'left' here were surrounded by 'stuff', quite a bit of which was completely useless in our situation, but the remainder would be quite valuable. My internal conflict was centered around all of the empty homes around us…and that sooner or later-- sooner—we would begin to loot those houses for things to sell or things to use.

There would be no choice.

Our previous forays into these now-vacant houses were focused on food. We'd already breached the issue, but with the high ideal of using what would spoil once the weather turned warm again. I was sure that I was in a minority of people that had not already looted the neighborhood around the survivor's homes of toilet paper, money, electronics, clothes, and whatever else the 'thief' might think valuable.

'Thief', I thought to myself. Was that what we were becoming? At what point do we resign ourselves that the missing or those who evacuated will not come back, and therefore all they left goes up for grabs? Were we in a neighborhood that was one of the last to loot the remnants, or were we to be one of the first? Obviously in the days and weeks right after the quake, the criminal elements saw no such conflict and made no distinction between what they wanted and what they could take, armed or not.

I sat down quietly at a small desk in the dining room that held a number of the radios, in an untidy mass of power cables and antennas. They worked, but weren't very pretty. I'd get around to sanitizing the setup later, I told myself, and put on some headphones to listen and let Karen snooze a little longer.

Scanning the shortwave band was futile, nothing but a menu of heavy static and light static, I supposed due to the weather. I was regretting the fact that I never really learned 'radio stuff', regarding ideal atmospheric conditions, when to listen due to solar interference, etc. The AM band had our local station, which was broadcasting locations of medical facilities, shelters, and community resources and little else. A brief weather broadcast ('Continued rain through the night, with temperatures around forty'), and no national news. No reports of radiation. I punched the 'scan' button and watched the digital readout cycle through, and stop, on nine hundred, AM.

The broadcast wasn't local, but Canadian. I'd been able to pick up CBC from Vancouver or central British Columbia once in awhile when traveling before the quake, but never since the Domino. I listened as the two commentators talked about 'New Canada' and 'Free Canada.' 'New Canada' was apparently 'most' of the former country, area-wise, and seemed to include all of 'old' Canada from Manitoba 'west'. 'Free Canada' was apparently Quebec and Ontario. No mention of the Maritime Provinces. I suppose to 'Free Canada', that they didn't really matter, in a manner similar to Virginia's opinion of Maine.

The broadcast talked of the 'Free Canadians' who were now about to enact a new French-only language policy (although 'Canadian French' I knew was viewed dimly by the 'real' French), and more importantly, a wholly different form of government. They had burned their Parliament building in a revolt I gathered, and driven the coalition-type government structure from power and from, it seemed, existence. The new government was described as a 'benefit to the citizen', and 'unique to the West in its progressive nature.' A 'citizen' must of course speak French only, with native-speaking French-Canadians being the true interpreters of who was a 'citizen' and who was 'not.' The system that the commentators described, with land-based representation and requirements for military service at the behest of the Free Governor, was…feudalism reskinned and repackaged. "Good Lord," I whispered to myself. 'It didn't work in the ninth century, it won't work now,' I thought. 'At least, not for the peasantry, or 'citizens', as the commoners were now called. The new flag for Free Canada was described as a white fleur-de-lis over a wide blue field, centered between red and white vertical fields. 'Interesting they picked a symbol of the French monarchy…' I thought.

I was listening to the tone of the commentators, the clinical analysis of it, the dispassionate way it was presented, in a manner neither 'for' nor 'against.' The 'New Canadians' had established a new national government split between Calgary and Edmonton, with the judicial center in Winnipeg. 'New Canada' had retained the Parliamentary government and the Maple Leaf flag, as well as the honorary allegiance to Britain. Both governments were working to 'attenuate' the 'civil disturbances' in the urban areas. A passing comment regarding people on both sides of the Canadian/U.S. border trying to get to the other side, and believing that it was somehow much 'better' on the other side.

No mention was made of any American involvement, occupation, or presence in either 'country'. Nothing about the Tar Sands. Hmmm.

Why did this sound so…what was it I was looking for…'prepackaged?'

"What's up?" Karen said, sneaking up behind me.

"Apparently we have a new country to the north of us. Two Canadas."

"And let me guess. One speaks French and the other doesn't," she said as she loaded the woodstove.

"Yep. And the French one is now 'Free Canada'. Problem is, it sounds like a step back to the ninth century."

"Some people do not learn from history."

"Exactly. Where are the kids at?"

"I sent them up the road with Ron and Libby and Annie Ross's unit to look over the house that the girl from Montana was living in. Annie said she's going to be released tomorrow, so I thought it might be nice to get it cleaned up a little."

"Mighty neighborly of you. How did you swing that? Getting Annie to provide cover?"

"Ron's idea. He says they owed him one after he helped them set up a construction trailer down at the store for the Army post."

"Trailer? Huh. Sounds permanent-like."

"Would you want your men to stand around in the rain or snow? Or hanging around in the store to warm up?"

"No."

"Then there you go."

"You are a baking fiend today," I said, changing the subject. "How many loaves?"

"Twenty. That's it for the day."

"If I may ask, why so many?"

"A third for us, two-thirds for clients. Alan said it's a very high demand item."

"Can we afford to? I mean, do we have the supplies to keep this up without shorting ourselves?"

"Yes, because today we're baking bread made with other people's ingredients. I didn't bake the other ten loaves—the loaves that we'd be paid. I just set aside the ingredients."

I sat there with a dumb look on my face. "What did you say?"

"You heard me right. We're baking using other people's stuff. Either they don't have pans, or time, or their ovens don't work right, whatever."

"So, you bake bread using their stuff, and you keep a third?"

"Yep."

"That guy knows how to deal. I hope, so anyway. I don't want this coming back on us that we're gouging people."

"They asked for someone to do it. Besides that, they don't know who it is that's baking it, and it's apparently someone you've already traded with," Karen said.

"OK, I guess. This is just damned strange."

"No argument with that. It's not like we didn't have the time. We can't go outside today and get anything done in the garden or the fields anyway."

"True enough."

"So what's on your list for the rest of the day?"

"I ought to do some more stuff for the Board. It's not what I feel like doing, though."

"Then do that instead. After you run this bread down to the store. The customer wants it by four. And I looked over your stuff while you were sleeping. I don't know how you hope to make sense of it all."

"Yeah. It's a train wreck."

"Maybe you should quit trying to plan and let things just happen. I saw your criteria list. Shelter. Water. Power. Proximities to critical services. Step back and look at it again. Seems to me that people will figure out on their own where to live and where not to."

"Yeah, but if you had a house out of the service area, would you still want to live there?"

"Yes."

"How far out of the service area? A block? Two? Ten? How long is that do-able?" I knew I was making my point, but she'd made hers, too.

"Not very long."

"Right. You don't want to haul water if you don't have to. If there are workable solutions for shelter, water and power within a smaller area, that are close to a working transportation line of some kind, those solutions need to be identified and presented to people that have been 'making do' without since the quake."

"So what happens then?"

"I don't know what you mean."

"Do you force them to move?"

"No, but we're not going to go out of our way to accommodate them, either. We don't have the resources to," I said. "It's up to them to move or not."

"So if there were places to live with water and power, are there enough houses to fit everybody?"

"That's what we're trying to figure out. And schools. And medical care. And what do all these people do? And what do they get paid for? And what...."

She put her hand up in a 'stop' signal. "I get the point."

"Not completely. The most important question is, 'and what do they eat?'"

38

The headlights helped light up the front of the store as I pulled into the gloomy parking lot. The store was not busy, with two people with hand baskets finishing up a purchase or trade with Alan, and I noticed, looking over items that he kept behind the counter.

I parked in my customary spot, close to the door, and waved at the soldier who was under a temporary shelter (well, in normal times it would've been temporary). The triangular shelter, a glorified rain fly, was tacked on to the side of an eight by sixteen construction trailer, against the property line, and roped over to the lone light pole for support.

Inside, Alan was manning the counter alone, with Marie serving as stock-girl.

"How you doing?" Alan asked.

"Fair to middlin'," I replied. "Got a delivery for a client in the back of the Ford."

"They should be here any time now. Just leave it in the truck."

"Who's it for?"

"Fire Department. Nick Johnson. Said he knows you."

"Yeah! I've only seen him twice since the quake. I'd drop by the station once in a while with pizzas or something back before things hit the fan. Did a couple of steak dinners for them couple years back, too. His shift of parameds responded to my Mom's place when she was going downhill," I said. 'All too often those calls came,' I didn't say.

385

"He said to tell you that he's still telling the 'FEMA' story," Alan said, referring to a showdown I'd had with a pointy-haired desk jockey who fashioned himself Napoleon. "Said they're still housed over at the old mall, but whenever you have steak and cold beer, feel free to drop by. Their kitchen's pretty much non-existent, and their old station won't be repaired for another month or two. They're too short handed to handle the baking right now at their homes. Contracted with us to do it for them for the next two weeks. Twenty loaves a day for them for two weeks, and we get thirty loaves worth of materials."

"That's what Karen said. Nice contract you've got."

"Just doing my little bit to help commerce," he said with a smile.

"We got twenty-four hour security now, too?" I said, nodding my head towards the trailer.

"Yes, courtesy of your Special Forces guy."

"I suppose that's a good thing," I said. "Did he stop in?"

"Yeah for a minute. Said he'd still like to talk to you when he can."

"Good. You and I and Ron still need to figure out what to do with those M-16's, too."

"I cleaned them up yesterday. The two weeks in the shed didn't hurt them a bit. At least they don't reek like death anymore."

"How many? I never looked after we brought them out of that basement."

"Twelve in the bag, brand new or very little use. National Guard paperwork in the bag, too. Probably came from some Armory somewhere. The other two 'sixteens took me two hours to clean, each. I'd be surprised if they worked at all."

I knew that the only thing that passed as a Guard armory around was the former Readiness Center, next to the Emergency Operations Center. Both were essentially 'taken out' when a chemical-laden train derailed virtually on top of them on January fourteenth.

"Magazines?"

"Five per, full. Plus maybe five hundred rounds of ammo loose in the sports bags."

"Now the million dollar question. Do we keep them or turn them in?"

"Keep them. No doubt about it," Alan said without the slightest hesitation.

I was silent for a few moments. "OK. Say we do. We won't be able to practice with them without getting caught. If we're caught with them, it won't bode well for us."

"If we need to use them, legal issues will be the least of our problems. Besides that, I'm working on a work-around to the practice issue."

That surprised me. "And what, pray-tell, would that be?"

"I think that you ought to require that all resident-citizens in the urban area learn how to handle weapons. Including M-16's. And, I might be able to trade for a couple AR-15's."

"Who in their right mind would trade a weapon like that for anything?" I said with more than a little shock.

"Someone who no longer can use them. Aaron Watters. He's slowly going blind," Alan said quietly.

That hit me like a punch in the stomach. "No."

"Yes. He's been losing his sight for more than a year. He was selling off his gun collection before the quake, and only has his high-end rifles left, and he plans on keeping his shotguns. He figures that even blind, he can make use of them, or that Ellen McDonald can."

"What does he want for them?"

"He'd like silver. I wanted to talk to you about it before I gave him an answer, but I told him that I thought we could work something out."

"How much?" I thought, my memory going back to the silver coins that my brother Alex had shipped us, before the War.

"Pre-War he was looking for a thousand apiece. Says they're both in average condition. Good shooters, but not perfect."

"And these days?"

"If we use the standard, then they're two-hundred apiece in silver. Which I don't think is enough."

"Me either. See if two-fifty in silver will work, each. If that's not enough, we'll see what we can do. This is a stupid question, but is the store making money?"

"Yes. Of course when we run out of things, we're done. Quite a bit of stuff that's here is irreplaceable. Pre-quake, out of area, foreign, consumable. We have a high inventory compared to before the War, but a lot of that is traded or bartered. We've made about twenty bucks each day in silver or product, which is respectable, all things considered. So how long before the long arm of the tax man arrives to ruin free enterprise?"

"Any minute now, I'm thinking. I'm not sure how the County can survive without taxes."

"Well maybe not everyone that is under county employ needs to be."

"They don't have twenty percent of what they had pre-quake."

"Good. Sounds about right. Too much dead wood."

"Government still costs."

"Stupid and ineffective government costs more. Much more."

"No argument with that."

"And how are taxes to be assessed? Sales? Property?"

"No idea. Haven't gone down that road."

"Best start thinking about it. Everyone that's buying and selling here is," Alan said, looking out the window. "Here you go. Spokane Valley Fire at your service."

I turned around to greet Nick, and was instead seeing the former probationary fireman, Car Lewis getting out of a red and white Suburban. "Well, it's Probey Carson Lewis," I said as he came inside.

"None of that crap now," he said with a smile. "I'm the real deal now, Mr. Drummond."

"Depends on how many burners you've been to, according to your old lieutenant, right?"

"Too damned many in the past three months to count. And my old LT is now a captain at Station Five. Nick's our LT now."

"Good for both of you," I said. "Do you know my brother-in-law, Alan?"

"Yes, we've met. Thanks."

"Got your order in the back of Rick's Ford. How's it going, anyway?"

"Working our butts off to get the old station habitable again. No calls today so far, so that's a good thing."

"Where are you guys billeted?" I asked.

"Used to be The Dollar Store," Carson replied. It's the only place big enough for the ladder and the pumper. Thanks to the quake taking out the north side of the mall, we have a nice, big bay to park the rigs in."

"What's your ETA on getting back into your old digs?"

"July. We're scrounging some structural steel from the mall to re-rig the roof structure over the middle bay. Four of the steel web trusses split right down the middle in the quake, and the east wall veneer we lost completely."

"Lucky you got out with the gear," I said.

"Wouldn't have if the guy from the muffler shop didn't show up with his acetylene torch. We jacked up the front trusses and moved the brick out of the way, and jacked up the roof enough for the ladder truck to clear. Then had to brace it after the truck was out, or we'd have lost the whole roof. Then we had to clear all the turnout gear and tools and stuff out. What a pain in the ass."

"Yep. Know what you mean," Alan said. "Let's get you loaded. I'm about ready to close up for the day."

We went outside, leaving Marie to finish up her work. As we loaded the bread up, I asked Lewis about the other stations in the area, noticing that the Army posts' three soldiers were all outside now, two in ponchos, one under cover near a radio that wasn't there when I arrived.

"District Eight's got two stations manned, Moran and Valleyford. Their Ponderosa and Saltese stations don't have power or water, although the buildings

I guess are OK. Well, that and they've lost most of their staffing. All the old volunteer complement is either gone or converted to full-time to take up the slack. The gear from both of the closed stations was relocated to the active ones," Car said as he carefully stacked up the bags of bread in the Suburban. The Department had scrounged a bunch of food-grade plastic bags for their bread, and we were also re-using some older used bags that they provided.

"How about Nine, up north?" I asked, referring to District Nine, which handled the north end of the County.

"Four of their eight stations were lost, in addition to their Admin Nine-One-One center and their shop. So they can realistically cover about forty of their hundred and twenty square miles."

"Maybe on a good day they could do that, with phones and working radios and an Administration capability."

"They're making do," Lewis said. "We're not much better off. Five of ten stations gone, maybe thirty percent of our staff from pre-quake. We've lost eighty percent of our captains and lieutenants, and half of our admin staff in the quake, in the flu or getting shot while responding."

"I read the status reports you provided the County. You're doing pretty well all things considered."

"We need more bodies. Our guys are dead tired most of the time, and we don't have the labor or in some cases the skills, to keep the rigs maintained right. Our shop is really handling maintenance for three times the rigs it's supposed to. The mechanics are about trashed."

"Hmmm," I said, wondering if there was some way we could recruit skilled people from the local population. "Maybe we can help you there. The Recovery Board, I mean."

"Good. We need it," he said as he headed to the drivers' door. "And Nick said, anytime you wanna cut loose with a steak dinner….."

"Yeah, I hear ya," I said with a smile. "I can't tell ya the last time I had one, either."

"Oh—wait a sec," Alan said to Lewis. "Damned near forgot," he said to himself as he went back into the store through the rain, grabbed a small brown-wrapped package, and returned.

"This is from one of our locals. Remember, don't drink and drive," Alan said.

"What's this?" I asked.

"Applejack. Enjoy!" Alan said as he trotted back under the cover of the front of the store. I waved to Lewis as he backed out.

"Dang," I said. "You are just full of surprises," I said to Alan.

"Uncle Rick, Mom called on the radio for you. Said that the County was calling your number."

"K. Thanks kiddo. I better go. You home soon?" I asked Alan.

"Ten minutes. Gotta give the key to the pump to the guys manning the post."

"That working out OK?"

"So far, yeah. Had a couple guys wanting gas today, they ran 'em off."

"Great," I said sarcastically. "See you in a bit."

I headed back home through the steady rain. The southwest winds were letting up; maybe we'd have a decent day tomorrow to plant…

"One thirty-seven to Spokane," I said into the mic. Karen had responded for me, stating that I 'would respond within the next ten minutes.' I beat that by a little.

"One thirty-seven. Be advised One-oh-One will be at your location in fifteen minutes."

"Understood. One-thirty-seven out."

"One thirty seven," the automaton female voice responded.

"Who's One-oh-One?"

"I think its Mike Amberson."

"Business?"

"No idea."

"Should I set a place for him?"

"What're you making?"

"Home made chili and wheat muffins."

"Sure, I guess," I said, wondering why Mike was coming by.

I didn't have long to wait. Mike's ride-of-the-day was a freshly washed Explorer, with the gold 'Sheriff' lettering filling the entire side of the vehicle. I met him on the front porch.

"What's up?"

"Need to talk. In private."

"Let's go out to the barn. We can cut through the house."

"Sounds good."

Mike dutifully wiped his feet before coming inside, even though the remains of our living room carpet were still rolled up against the wall.

"Hi, Mike," Karen said. How're you doing?"

"Oh, OK. Need to borrow your husband for a few minutes," he said, trying to be pleasant, but being all business about it.

"We're going out to the barn for a few minutes," I said to Karen, who instantly read that as 'we're not to be disturbed.'

"K. Here. Take this thermos of tea and some muffins. Chili's not ready yet."

"Who'd you make this for?" I asked, surprised she had it ready for us.

"Sarah. The new girl up the road. I'm making her a hot dinner. Ron and Libby are still up there. Carl and Kelly came back to pick up a few things."

"K. We'll be in in a while," I said, kissing her 'hello' as I left again. Mike and I walked through the now-misty rain towards the barn.

"Nice of you guys to do that," Mike said.

"Karen's idea, but I agree," I said. We walked out to the barn in silence, and I opened the beat up outer door and unlocked the inner door, and flipped the lights on. "OK, what's up? Why the secrecy?"

"People who identified themselves as Air Force personnel rushed the barricade at the main gate at the base two hours ago. Army wiped them out."

"Holy crap," I said. "Why?"

"Guess."

"Flu."

"Yeah."

"How are you handling this?"

"I'm not. It's out of my hands. The Army is not letting us in."

"How did you hear?"

"Air Force requested permission to leave the base for supplies at noon. Medical supplies. Army countered with, 'send us a list and we'll see what we can do.' That was not acceptable to the Air Force. They wanted to go themselves, due to 'national security' issues, and informed the Army that their commanding general would be with them as they ventured off base, and the general commanded the Army to stand down. They broadcast all of this on open frequencies for anyone to hear! Well, they went for it, and they paid for it. The bad part is this: Three of the bodies in Air Force uniforms weren't Air Force. They were civilians dressed up in Air Force uniforms. They've been identified as aides to Senator Evan Milkins, Representative Victor Wyrick, and Representative Valerie Morton. Had their Capitol Building clearance badges on."

Milkins and Wyrick were two senior Democrats. Milkins from Illinois, if I remembered correctly, and Wyrick from Georgia, or someplace in the Southeast.....Morton was a Republican. Ohio? I couldn't remember.

"So it can be assumed that the two principals are at Fairchild, probably with other House and Senate leadership?"

"That's my bet. I have no idea of course who else is there. The other victims were identified as a desk two-star from the Pentagon, and two security-policemen. The second and third vehicles didn't get hit, and backed up when ordered to."

“What in the world were they thinking?”

“No idea. From what we can glean from the Forty-First command, which is not much, is that the base hospital has been secured by apparently a small group of Air Force security forces that came in on the planes. It appears that the majority of the remaining Air Force personnel are at the far end of the base, at the Alert Facility and in a row of hangars that used to handle the B-52’s. There is no communication between the two groups.”

“OK, simple enough. Dirtbags are in the hospital. Good guys are in the hangers.”

“Yeah.”

“So why all the secrecy?”

“If this is a perversion of the flu, don’t you think that everyone on that base is at risk, and might make a run for it?”

“Yeah. Which means that the Army might have a tough choice to make. Shoot anyone who makes a move to leave, or spread the disease. Which by the way, may or may not exist at the base. We do not know either way.”

“Right. Which means that innocent, and possibly healthy people will be killed.”

“Yeah. It means exactly that. But Mike, it’s not in your control. It’s not your decision to make.”

“I know. But when word gets out that significant elected leaders of the country are dying in my county, either from the flu or from our lack of giving them supplies or worse from being shot by our own troops, what do you think that will do for us?”

“Nothing good.”

“Hence my problem.”

“What has the Forty-First done so far? I mean, what have they provided the base?”

“From what I know, not a damned thing.”

"Well unless they brought it with them, there probably isn't much in the way of food or water out there. Water's probably OK, on second thought, but the base only had a skeleton crew out there after the Domino. There can't be that much food out there. It should not be that tough to rig up a staging or transfer station where the Army can supply food to the base. Army drops, backs off, Air Force picks up. They've gotta do that or this will get wildly out of control."

"Seems like it is already."

"Yeah. If it were me, I'd set up two drops. One for the hospital, one for the regular guys. Hell, air-drop it if they don't get shot at," I said.

"We'll make that suggestion to the Army. It'll be up to them."

"They've gotta do something. Right now, as far as the base goes, the base might as well be under siege. People outside don't necessarily know that though. And people tend to get a little stressed when cornered. Or irrational."

"I'm heading over to Felts Field now. Their airborne commander is over there looking over their rotary wing capabilities. They hijacked two of my deputies with flight hours, too. Really pisses me off. I don't have the manpower to spare."

"Nobody does. I was talking with one of the fire department guys earlier. They're chronically short, too. That's my nickel's worth."

"We'll see what happens. This is a no-win situation."

"Correct. Perilous times shall come," I said as we headed out the door, muffins and tea untouched.

"What's that from?" Mike asked.

"Second Timothy 3:1."

39

Friday,
May Fifth

After a not particularly restful night, I finally gave up trying to sleep and got up at five-thirty. Karen stayed in bed as I showered and dressed, and both dogs were sitting patiently for me as I headed downstairs. They were ready for their morning business, which included chasing the quail and pheasant population that both exploded this spring.

I made a quick breakfast of scrambled eggs with dried jalapenos, cornbread with honey, and strong tea. The weather looked good, with light clouds off to the east over the Idaho mountains, but clear skies to the west. Probably a good day for planting…or at least getting ready to plant. We planned on a big planting day on Saturday. With the store closed, we could field pretty much everyone, but Grace. With two-thousand pounds of potatoes, and onions on top of that, we'd need all the hands we could get.

My Board meeting was scheduled for nine, and I planned on being at the County headquarters by eight. That left me with some time to line out things in more detail for the afternoon. I planned on taking Carl, Kelly and Marie with me this morning to the County offices, so they could 'get out of the zip code' for a while. John was working the store with Ron, but took a rain check. I'd told all three that they needed to bring something to keep themselves occupied while I was in the meeting, because it wasn't safe to go wandering about. They were all excited to make the trip, even with the restrictions.

We would be losing the full-day labors performed by our indentured servants, as our wives were planning on starting up schooling again for six hours a day come Monday. Schooling would continue until early June at least, and if we could get the larger community behind it and if things worked out, we might be able to have a month or so of public schooling held at the elementary, before summer labor needs presented themselves. 'If', I thought, the pessimistic streak in me starting to rear its ugly head.

KDA, still on the air, was sounding more like a farm radio station from way-back-when, talking about crop projections, weather conditions, and the needs of individual farmers willing to trade for what they needed. I roused the rest of the family at six-thirty and radioed over to the Martins, making sure that Marie would be ready by a quarter past seven. The seven o'clock news was all-local, with only the thinnest references to the shootings at the base the day before, and repeated the lists of public facilities that would be open today, and expected road closures and utility outages as repairs were made.

Work orders for the coming days included reskinning the smallest greenhouse (ours); getting a larger herb garden established for both our use and for trading purposes; and making sure the fields were ready for large-scale planting. When those items weren't being addressed, the firewood issues and miscellaneous cleanup of pruned limbs and downed trees needed to be taken care of, and the cut and split wood racked for drying over the summer. We had a lot of wood to use locally, and would probably need more from Don Pauliano's place out near the lake. For planting the potatoes tomorrow, we'd need a half-dozen or more planter's bags, simple burlap bags to sling over a shoulder while the planter's partner manned a spade. The bags needed to be made, the shovel handles smoothed and the blades sharpened. About an acre and a quarter of ground to cover, in three different locations in the garden area. A whole lot of work, tomorrow.

"Tea's on the stove," I told my sleepy wife as she walked into the kitchen. "And nice slippers," I said, referring to her down-filled booties.

"Thanks. You gave them to me, remember. And it's not like we have a programmable thermostat anymore. And you didn't start a fire."

"It's forty-seven outside. I didn't figure we needed it."

"Its fifty-nine in here. Even when we were in the barn, we had a warming fire on days like this."

"Sorry, thinking about work."

"You think too much. Stop it," she said with a smile, "and pass me the honey for my tea."

Carl was dressed, with a mop of hair that needed serious attention. Kelly was up, dressed and ready to go. Both were working on cooking a couple of eggs for breakfast, and searching for a wheat muffin to make a sandwich. "Ten minutes, you two, and we're on the way. Make sure you're presentable, pardner. You're waaay overdue for a haircut."

"For once, I agree with you," he said. "It's a pain to keep up when it's this long."

"Been telling you that for three years," I said. We'd had running battles about his hair length since he was twelve. Just like my Dad and I had, when I was that age. I carried my 'county' radio out to the car and plugged it in. 'One-Oh-Seven' was in a conversation with 'One-Twenty-One' regarding rising water levels along the Spokane River. "It is spring guys, snow's a-meltin'. Water comes up, and goes back down again," I said to the radio.

At quarter-past, Marie and Libby were waiting for us in the driveway, ready for the field trip. "You be careful with my girl," Libby said quietly.

"Absolutely. Don't worry," I said.

"Everybody got something to do while I'm in my meeting?"

"Yes," my passengers responded.

"OK, here we go then. Karen, we're on thirty-eight," I told her as she opened the gate for us, dogs looking up wanting to go, too.

"K. Check in before you start home if you can. Someone will be listening."

I gave her a quick kiss through the window and backed out of the driveway, heading south and then west, toward town. "Sprague, Broadway or Mission?" I asked, wanting to know which road the kids wanted to take.

"We can go on any one?" Kelly asked.

"Yeah. Can't take the freeway because of the downed overpasses. We could take Trent, too."

"Sprague," Carl said, and the girls agreed.

Sprague was the Valley's major commercial arterial, once home to shopping malls, strip developments, and large anchor stores between the Downtown area and Greenacres, fifteen miles or so east, or about halfway to the Idaho state line. I knew they hadn't seen what I'd seen, the devastation from the quake, the looting, the burning. This would be enlightening, to say the least.

I drove relatively slowly, passing through two checkpoints with a wave, a third with an I.D. search. The kids were chattering about the collapsed Home Depot, the gutted Costco, the ATM machine in the middle of the street in front of a Tidyman's grocery store. Five blocks west, row upon row of recreational vehicle frames lay rusting in the burned out debris of a show lot, bracketed by burned ski-boats on twisted trailers. Apparently, fiberglass burns fairly hot.

They were increasingly quiet as we got closer to town, especially through East Central where block on block of burned homes were crumbling into their basement holes. At Sprague and Helena, I was forced to head north to Trent for the rest of the trip. A utility crew was staring at a downed transmission line, arcing in the street, and wondering what to do about it. The kids were silent as we passed more burned out businesses and piles of garbage in the streets.

We passed under the large railway bridge between Sprague and Helena, it's massive concrete posts somewhat shy of the required concrete, the reinforcing steel showing on half of the columns. Someone had cleaned up the road at least, shoving the concrete off to one side.

At Trent and Helena, where a signal used to guide traffic, a detour sign now directed those few people allowed to drive back to the west. One of the stores I used to frequent, Ames Tractor, was now a burned and collapsed brick hulk on the corner. They'd sold me many parts for my little Ford, although they now specialized in Kubota. Or did anyway, until this past January.

We continued into Downtown, and turned again onto Division, over the river. The kids grew a little more talkative, looking at the tall buildings that were the heart of the business district, now wrecked and in some cases, stripped of their skins.

Passing over the river, brown and roaring with the spring runoff, I pointed out the wrecked hotels on the north bank, the collapsed entry atriums, the cars smashed in the parking garages.

A few minutes before eight, we were parked in the Public Works lot. I shut off the Ford and sat there for a second. "You guys OK?"

"Yeah," they replied.

"We just didn't know it was this bad," Marie said. "What's that pile up north?" she asked, pointing to a red brick mound.

"Used to be REI. The camping-gear place, you remember."

"Yeah. Dad got his kayak there. And my mountain bike," she said, looking for something recognizable. "It's hard to believe."

"Seeing is believing in this case," I said. "Get your stuff and let's go inside. I should be able to square away a spot for you to hang out."

Inside, the building smelled of disinfectant and window-cleaner, and was yet again, more tidy than it had been two days before.

"Wow, this looks like nothing happened," Kelly said.

"Don't look too close, there's cracks in the concrete here and there," I said as we walked into the lobby.

"Is it safe?" she asked, Marie and Carl behind her.

"Should be fine. The building was pretty well engineered. We're over in this wing. Follow me," I said to my little herd.

Walt was in the conference room already, looking over a stack of paperwork in front of him, I made introductions, and his assistant Kamela was kind enough to allow them to either 'hang out', or work with her for the morning. Surprisingly, they chose the latter.

"Nice kids," Walt said. "Kamela's been trying to get things put back together upstairs in Engineering. No one's cleaned up up there, other than to sweep up the broken glass and replace the windows. Files are everywhere."

"Well, this bunch have their Masters degrees in cleanup. Three houses, all tumbled about. Carl helped me rebuild our place, with some help."

"And no complaints?"

"I wouldn't go that far. But maybe living in a barn for three months tempered them a little. I know I developed patience only slowly myself, and I'm still working on that one. Is everyone going to make it today?"

"Supposed to," Walt said, looking at my black armband. "You had a loss?"

"Yes. My brother and niece in Utah. Found out in one of the long-delayed letters."

"I'm very sorry. We lost our son this spring as well."

"My condolences. I pray that this will end soon," I said.

"That would be a welcome thing. I doubt however that we will see that prayer answered soon enough though." Another assistant brought a tray of coffee cups and drinking glasses into the room, with two carafes of coffee, allowing us to change the subject.

"Any guests for today's meeting?" I asked.

"Two. Mike Amberson and the Division commander for the Forty-First."

"Well! That oughta be interesting," I said without going too far.

Walt looked at me with a narrowed gaze. "Mike talk to you already?"

"A little. Stopped by the house to unload a little."

"I suppose everyone needs a sounding board," Walt said.

"Are they getting this…" I stopped my inquiry as Tonya, Clete McKinnon and Drew Simons showed up, all early for the meeting. "Well good morning all," I said as I shook hands. My armband drew their attention. "My brother and niece in Utah, back in March. We just found out," I said. All three expressed their condolences as we poured our coffee, and Walt passed out his agenda order. I noted that he planned on having us wrap up by noon again, a welcome thing.

"Let me round up Kamela, and we'll get to business," Walt said.

Each of us had a raft of notes or files we'd been hauling around. Mine was almost organized, and spread over two binders and five files. Tonya's was perfectly neat, as was Drew's 'homework,' Clete's was clipped together with a big spring clip. Within a few minutes, Walt was back with Kamela.

"Your kids are a wonder. Dug right in and started without a peep," Kamela said.

"Thanks—they've had several months to perfect the art of sorting wheat from chaff," I said.

"We've got a couple security staff up there with them, helping lift some of the big files up and keeping an eye on them for you."

"Thanks," I said.

"We ready to get going?" Walt said.

"Yes," we all replied.

We stood on Walt's request and recited the Pledge of Allegiance, and began the meeting.

For the first half-hour or so of our meeting, Walt covered his interactions with the City Recovery Board, and their almost immediate organizational collapse. Our counterpart board was apparently populated by selfish, egotistical people who believed 'service' was something that people provided to them, rather than their service to others. Recovery efforts in the heavily urbanized areas would be hampered by the infighting between competing neighborhoods. The City residents would end up fending for themselves to find effective leadership, at their peril. Walt stated flatly that the County would not be taking on the issue of the City's failure.

"Walt, what about all those folks that the Army went after the other day? What happened there?" I asked.

"Most of them are still in the homes that they had occupied. Mike and the Division commander will give us a full briefing on it. Some were rounded up as known or suspected criminals, quite a few of those were identified by other settlers as 'problems.' Some people fought back and died."

"How many?"

"Less than twenty, out of more than three thousand."

"OK, thanks."

"Speaking of which, you're up next on the agenda. Let us know what you've come up with for resettlement, if you would," Walt asked.

"OK, but remember that…"

"No apologies," Clete said. "We know the score."

"OK. Our former, and I hope, future lives depend heavily on the trappings of civilization. Running water, electricity, public utilities, and public services. The quake has damaged or destroyed the vast majority of that infrastructure system, parts of which have been repaired or salvaged by the utility and public works workers. We start there, with what we have left."

"We have defined areas," I said, rolling out a small map of the Valley, " that in this example, show what's working and what's not. Yellow for power," I pointed at the outlines, "blue for water. There is no natural gas or sewer system in this part of the valley that is operational. Everything is back on septic systems. Using this as a baseline, we can look at the population distribution at present," I said, with another transparent mylar overlay. "In this mile-on-a-side box that

I've used for this example, you can see where people are living and where they are not. They are living where the services are, except in a couple of extreme cases where people have wells and are living off the grid. Each red square represents an occupied house, based on the CERT census and some more current data. Dashed in red, means a house that could be repaired. Black 'X's' are buildings that are not salvageable."

The other board members were studying my work with interest. "The next overlay shows schools and potential public service functions within the overall Valley area, in buildings that could be repaired and adapted. Dark blue for the public service functions either existing or proposed. Green for potential agricultural areas throughout the Valley, basically the open spaces and back fields within residential areas. Brown for potential commercial centers. You can see that within the overall series of overlays, there is a significant housing inventory, within the currently served utility area, that is not populated at present."

"What are the ground rules for siting the public and commercial areas?" Tonya asked.

"I made them up, frankly. Commercial areas are within one mile of residences on the far end of the service area, at most. I consider this walking distance."

"Hope you've got good shoes, Tonya," Clete said.

"Don't worry about me. I plan on living where I work."

"And that is part of the plan, too. Encourage people to do that with shops, manufacturing, service businesses. Don't separate them like we had in the old zoning regs." I said, helping things along.

"What if people don't want to live within these service areas?" Walt asked.

"Well, I hope they like hauling water and doing without power. Restoration of services outside of these areas is completely dependent on material and labor to put things back together. From what I've read in the utility reports, we're damned lucky to have this much area served," I said, motioning to the border area.

"I would note," Walt added, "that this is happening—the resettlement— around us without our intervention. People are living where there are services. Settlers are occupying buildings in the served areas. It's obvious to me that if someone wants to live outside of the service area, they're not made of the same stuff that people inside the zone are."

"And I'm one of them," Clete McKinnon added. "My own well, my own power. Super insulated house."

"Good for you. But you're still a long way from public services, like schools and police and fire."

"I don't worry much about police at my place."

"Understood. But for the majority of people that are surviving in the Valley, it's a long way to get to a doctor, a cop, or a school. We need to fix that," I said.

Stacey replied before I could continue. "So find the right people to staff them, find the right buildings to house them, and there's a start."

"Exactly," I said. "We have three thousand people new to the area, plus our existing population. I suggest we recruit from our current and new residents, and that we establish ground rules for occupying existing homes. A homestead process."

That left them thinking for almost a full minute. "So you're saying," Drew Simons asked, "That people get a house free and clear after a period of time if they meet conditions of employment?"

"Yes, but also maintaining and repairing the place, growing food would be good, and they'll still need to be paid for their job, whatever that might be."

"Well since the County is in effect bankrupt, how do plan to effect that?" Walt said.

"There is some real money out there, just not much. Barter, trade, whatever. Get an economy going. Some jobs will be public-sector, and full-time and will not by their nature allow the worker to do anything else to support himself. Those jobs are a distinct minority, in my opinion. We've seen people in the last few weeks make things, grow things, and become business-people, just to survive. Most things that are sold in our corner store for example, aren't sold at all, but traded for something else."

We then spent an hour hammering out conditions for 'settlement' in the vacant homes and buildings. We came up with a short list of conditions, but stringent ones:

New settlers must identify themselves and all family members. Birthplace, former place of residence. County will conduct background check with military.

Must have a vocation, or be willing to be assigned a job by the center director. Public works jobs include cleanup, general labor, teachers, salvage operations, skilled trades and critical services.

Pay includes shelter and utilities and pay, in silver, depending on type of work.

Pay rates range from 0.50 per hour to 2.00 per hour in public sector.
Immediate problem is lack of physical silver.
Private sector pay varies on skills and what people will pay.
"Don't work, don't eat."

All settlers must create and maintain a vegetable garden and other food-production for their own use.

Settlers will be required to improve the plot by repairing or building a dwelling and cultivating the land. After 5 years on the land, the original filer is entitled to the property, free and clear, except for a small title transfer fee. Residency on the property is a requirement. Where adjacent homes are damaged beyond repair, that land can be used as well, and the wreckage salvaged. Businesses can also be co-located in the dwelling or accessory buildings. Businesses cannot be located solely in a former residence that could be repaired for residency unless approved by the Community Center Director.

We also established the need for two new fire stations to serve the Valley region and four new police precincts; relocate the contents of one of the public libraries far outside of the working utility area to an area that had a relatively high population; and we started to put together a list of critical skills needed for recovery—skills that were probably 'out there' in the population, but weren't being utilized. People were simply trying to survive, especially the new settlers.

One item that came up in putting 'new' people into existing houses, was the 'stuff' left behind by the former owners or residents. This was a lively discussion that finally circled back around to 'they get the house, they get what's in it. Personal possessions of the former residents are at the discretion of the new residents to preserve or dispose of. Anything else is completely unmanageable.'

The 'burden of stuff.' What was once wealth, now was burden.

Drew Simons had been busy as well. He prepared an analysis of the utility company reports, and recommended that a utility cooperative be formalized in order to facilitate better service and more far-reaching repairs and maintenance. In effect, this organization had been in place since early February, but there were still some hold-outs between rival utilities that were very hesitant to share critical spare parts, for fear that their own systems would need them. They could hardly be blamed for that.

This topic triggered the discussion of taxes and financial support for public facilities and public works. Similar to what the Federal government had proposed in doing away with the income tax (like that was a real problem for us now), we decided to propose a flat five percent tax on retail sales of new items. The barter market was un-enforceable regarding taxes, and in reality, we would be lucky if a fraction of our tax collections would actually be made.

The only 'advantage' we had to this all-but-voluntary process was that, without tax dollars, the 'public' side of the recovery effort would fail. And that was we hoped, enough for people to understand that their taxes directly benefited their security and their lives.

We took a break at ten-thirty, and I found my way upstairs to see what the kids were up to.

I found Carl on the third floor, finishing up his HALF of the floor, where he'd sorted, stacked, re-filed, and cleaned a dozen offices, all untouched since the quake and some hasty repairs. He'd filled up three garbage cans with broken items, but by and large the Engineering Department looked as if it were ready to occupy, the following day.

"You did all this?" I asked.

"Had a little help. And there she is now," he said, pointing to the much-shorter Marie. "I did the heavy stuff; Marie and Kelly tidied up and cleaned. We had a couple of staff people too, so we didn't do it all ourselves."

"Nice work. Where's Kelly?"

"She's with Ms. Gardner, over on the other side, one floor down. They're going to move the Health Department into there, I guess," Carl said.

"Good idea, since their old building is all but a pile of bricks," I said.

"How much longer, Dad?" Kelly asked, ready to go home.

"It'll be a while. Probably noon."

"OK," she said, sounding a little tired of it all.

"I better run. Don't forget Mom made you guys some snacks," I said as I headed downstairs.

"Break time!" Carl said, quickly passing me on the stairs. He nearly ran into Clete at the bottom, promptly excused himself, and headed for the parking lot.

"That young man is going to be a tall one," Clete said.

"Another inch and he's passed me. Already has bigger feet."

"Seems like a good kid. Responsible."

"He is. His Mom and I are quite proud. Probably ought to tell him that more often."

"Probably so."

We both looked at the door as Mike Amberson, Carl and a graying Army Colonel came in through the vestibule.

"Rick, nice to see you're keeping your boy busy," Mike said.

"Don't have much of a problem there. He's pretty good at self entertainment, or pitching in when called upon." I thought I saw Carl blush.

"This is Lieutenant Colonel Emory Peters of the Forty First," Mike said, introducing us.

"My son, Carl," I said as the two shook hands.

"Fifteen?" Emory said.

"Yes, sir," Carl replied.

"Same age as my youngest. His hair is about the same, too," he said. "I think he does it just to get my goat."

"Well sir, I'm about to get it cut. Too tough to maintain."

"Recommendation: High and tight. Fast, easy, and the ladies love it," Emory advised, getting a laugh from all of us.

"Thanks," Carl said as he headed back upstairs with the small bag that Karen had provided.

"Gentlemen, if you would join us," Walt beckoned.

We took our seats as Mike and our Army guest poured a cup of coffee and brought out some briefing materials for us.

"The Sheriff asked me to make a brief presentation today regarding the disposition of military and non-military personnel at Fairchild Air Force Base. Before I get into that, I would like to thank you for the opportunity to meet with you, and to let you know that the hospitality that our men have received since arriving in Spokane has been remarkable."

"Regarding the bases' current occupancy, there are two thousand two hundred and six Air Force personnel on base and one thousand two hundred nine military dependents and civilian employees. Non Air Force personnel at last count numbered six hundred one, and include Federal-level elected officials, staff, dependents and non-Air Force military officers detached to these elected officials. As you may have heard, a number of these people were killed yesterday in an attempt to leave the base, after being ordered to remain within the bases' perimeter. This quarantine is due to the unknown status of all arrivals at Fairchild over the past ten days, and the potential for a virulent influenza outbreak. At least eleven transport craft came from areas on the East Coast that were in proximity to known outbreaks of the latest flu virus. Our perimeter guard units are in full chemical and biological gear, as a precaution."

"Our orders, literally shoot to kill, came directly from the National Command Authority. The President," Peters said, looking at each of us, "is fully aware of this situation and the gravity of it."

"The base continues to be in a locked-down mode, with virtually all Air Force personnel located in and around the Alert Facility and three large hangars that formerly served the KC-135's on the eastern end of the base. The Alert Facility is locked down by the residents—the aircrews that transported the people from Virginia to the base. They are concerned that if they are infected, that they will spread it to the others. Their passengers are holed up in the Base Hospital, on the west end. The two groups have no communication between them. Our forces have been in contact with the Air Force commander, and understand the situation. Our attempts to contact the civilians at the hospital were met with directed gunfire from multiple locations. I can tell you now, that anyone in that hospital as far as I'm concerned, can rot. They've killed my men and they will receive no assistance from us. The Air Force men, women, and families are being supplied at this time, and our medical teams have set tomorrow morning as a time to begin evaluations of this group, to determine if there is any influenza among them. The incubation period should be about up by now."

"Our medical team has let me know that should the influenza virus be present at the base hospital, that there is at this point in time, no cure, and that the virus is persistent. Meaning, damned near impossible to kill. Anyone setting foot outside of that building will be shot on sight. They have been advised as much, and returned fire for the favor."

I let out a long descending whistle.

"I agree with your sentiments, Mr. Drummond. We literally cannot let this spread. The immediate problem for my medical team is that we do not know that it IS in fact present. What is present is an exhibition of extreme psychotic paranoia on the part of whoever is in charge over there."

Colonel Peters outlined the positioning of the remnants of his Division, which was by his own description, unlike anything the Army had fielded in years past, battalion by battalion, down to brigade level.

Clete asked one of the most insightful questions, or rather forwarded statements that I was completely un-equipped to ask.

"This is a Division unlike anything I've ever seen. You've got infantry and light infantry, mechanized, air support, combat support, engineering, and if you get the rest of your units here, airborne assault. Is that right?"

"Yes, sir," the colonel replied.

"In my day, a Division was ONE of those things. Not ALL. Seems like you're trying to be all to everyone, to me," McKinnon asked pointedly.

"What is now called the Forty First Division bears little resemblance to what it was six months ago. The Forty First is more properly called a Composite Division, that can provide all services, albeit limited, in task format until larger and less specialized resources are available."

"So translating, and no offense intended, you have a military force composed of surviving pieces of other units, working under a single command, to address whatever comes up until the Cavalry arrives. There were units like this after the Battle of the Bulge. Cobbled together."

"That is a perfectly fair assessment," Peters replied. "From the squad unit up through the brigades and battalions however, we are mission capable. And in our case, it was not the Battle of the Bulge," Peters told Clete.

"Ours was the Siege at Monterrey."

40

"What?" I asked.

"'Sitio de Monterrey,' the Mexicans called it, afterwards. 'Siege.' Started the first week of the War. We motored right into the city, pretty as you please. Mechanized, heavy infantry, airborne units. Damned near five full Divisions. City was quiet. We staged there for further advance to the south and along the coast, and set to consolidate the territory. We thought it was a walkover," he said, as he looked at each of us, eye to eye.

"Well," Peters continued, "It was quiet for a reason."

"If things are going well you have walked into an ambush," Clete said.

"Yeah. Well we did. Nineteen days of unremitting fire. The city was quiet because ninety percent of the civilian population was gone. They had been replaced by large chunks of Mexican military and mercenaries, backed up by front line Chinese troops and front line weapons. Nicest trap you'd ever want to set."

I felt my jaw drop. "Never heard that on the news," I said.

"No surprise there. The fact that we lost seventeen thousand men and women in and above Monterrey isn't something the Government's going to shout about either."

"Good God," I said.

"How on earth…"

"…did they do it?" Peters replied, shooting out his response like machine gun fire. "Simple. Infiltrate our units with Mexicans or Anglo-looking Mexicans or Chinese, wearing U.S. Army uniforms and speaking passable English. Use our own weapons against us. Shoot down transports on the way in with a half-dozen SAM's fired all at once at a single plane. Wreak havoc. Suicide bombs. Firebombs--building sized firebombs, pre-positioned. That was the first two days. Then they opened up with an advancing wall of mortar-fire from all points of the compass, playing hit and run. Think Mogadishu on steroids. Five thousand of their force cut off our northern ground advance when our airborne units were grounded in a sandstorm. The remains of our Mechanized units looked like the Iraqi retreat in Kuwait."

"How did you win?" Stacey asked, her face pale.

"Win?" the Colonel responded. "There is not one building standing in the urban or suburban areas of Monterrey. All roads south were blocked. We bombed the areas outside of our force-protection zone flat, went in, rescued our men, and then finished it. We escaped. It was not a win. We tried using specialized munitions to target command and control, and that had zero net effect. We ended up using the boys at Elgin to save our asses."

"MOAB's," Clete said, an acronym I'd heard before but forgotten.

"Yeah. Helluva thing," Peters replied with a tilt of his head, sizing up Mr. McKinnon.

"MOAB?" Walt asked. "What's that?"

"Massive Ordinance Air Blast Bomb. Media called them the mother of all bombs. Not far from the truth, either. We gave up estimating enemy dead at when we got to fifty-five thousand. Gathered up our dead, sent the survivors north, and kept moving south. What used to be called Mexico is now about thirty percent of the area it used to be. We now own the entire Pacific coast and eighty percent of the Gulf coast. It will stay that way."

"So what do you do with a hundred million refugees?" I asked.

"Closer to half that, now," Peters replied. "Factor the flu in, with the indigenous people getting hit much harder, and factor in the thin thread that those people lived on anyway, and the population plummets pretty quickly."

That hit me hard, for some reason. I should have expected it, hearing it already on the radio, but not in such stark terms. "OK, fifty million. Same question."

"They stay in the territory that is designated for them as legal citizens of that territory," Peters said, getting annoyed with me. "They cross the border, they die."

"What about the Chinese?" I asked.

"If there are any left alive, and I would be surprised if there are, we hand them over to the Mexicans to deal with. They're less inclined than we are to deal with them in a humanitarian manner than we are."

"You turn them over to be killed?" Stacey asked, with only a little quaver in her voice.

"They made their beds," Peters said. "What's left of the old Mexican government admitted to the fact that they'd agreed to a Chinese solicitation for assistance in defeating the U.S. militarily and economically. This opened up the door so that the Mexican people could finish invading the U.S., and that then China would become their strategic partner. The Chinese promised a sound and speedy defeat, to be treated as equals, to share in the plunder. The real deal turned out to be much different, once the shooting started."

No one spoke.

"And that, ladies and gentlemen, is enough reason for me to do what needs to be done. Period. Now if you'll excuse me, I need to get back to work. I've provided the Sheriff our deployment areas of operation, for his use, and will forward you some information on the situation at Fairchild when it is appropriate," Peters said as he stood.

Walt stood to shake Peters' hand. "Thank you, Colonel." Peters nodded to us and left the room. No one spoke.

Tonya was the first to speak. "We are luckier than we realize. By far."

"We are at that," Drew Simons replied.

"Are we ready to move on with the meeting?" Walt asked.

"Yeah," I replied. "Let's go," still distracted by the information from Colonel Peters. "Mike, you didn't look surprised by Peters' statement about the war."

"I heard it an hour ago myself," the Sheriff replied. "I reacted about the same I guess as you all did."

"Drew?" Walt said, getting us back on track, "What have you got for us?"

Our attention again was set on business and not on the War.

"Fueling issues. Fuel distribution to farm production has to set as the number one priority now and through harvest, that means getting diesel fuel to the mechanized farms within our immediate region, especially before the end of May or we completely miss the window. We're already late. Diesel fuel stocks available and projected to be available will allow farmers to plant large-scale dryland crops--wheat, peas, lentils, barley, et cetera-- by the end of May for this years' harvest. Gasoline supplies are and will continue to be extremely limited. Police, fire, emergency services and food production use only. I've formed a little sub-committee—mostly a couple of farmers and me—and we're looking at alcohol production and blending with current fuels. But we're at least a year off at getting any meaningful amount of gasohol built."

"The other thing is in regards to public transport-- Public transport along major arterials, per your idea to rebuild along established corridors. Well, there is virtually no public transport available. Nearly all buses, both Transit and school, left with the evacuees and didn't come back. Oh yeah. Propane. We're done for there. There is virtually no propane left, anywhere in the county. That affects us in a couple of ways we didn't anticipate, the first of which being moving materiel. Almost all forklifts in use in the urban area warehouses run propane. Maybe ten percent run gas. Propane is a byproduct of either oil refining or natural gas production. We don't have either locally, and what propane is being produced somewhere else, ain't coming here. And from what I can get out of the utility and energy folks, it isn't going to again, for a long, long time."

"That also affects fertilizer production," Stacey said. "The natural gas part. Without natural gas, we can't put nitrogen into a form that plants can use. Oh, I'm sorry Drew. Were you done?"

"Yes, I think so. Go ahead with your report," Drew said, obviously thinking about what she'd said, and knowing there was no work-around. I noticed a Deputy in the hallway catch Mike's eye, and saw Mike's gaze narrow at something out of my line of sight, and then he excused himself as Drew wrapped up. 'Hmmm', I thought.

"It's bleak. Thank you for putting the strong emphasis on the fuel to the farmers. That might work this year, but if we don't have diesel, and parts and fertilizers available like we've had in the past, our coming years' productions will plummet to pre-industrial age levels."

"Thanks for putting a good light on it," I said only half-sarcastically.

She smiled at my remark, until the baby kicked her and brought her right back into focus. " The Central Washington food production this year will be— well, is already—a disaster. My contacts in the Basin—these are folks I've known for years—tell me on the shortwave that up to ninety percent of the Columbia River Irrigation Project's capacity is gone. Pump stations not powered, or pumps destroyed, massive structural damage to the lined and unlined irrigation canals and trenches, no power to the crop irrigation pivots, you name it."

She went on as we listened again, to how bad things were.

"This means that the large potato, pea, squash and other irrigated crops in the Basin are gone. It also means that most, if not all, of the cherries, apples, peaches and pears grown from south of Yakima to north of Wenatchee will be dead by the end of July," she told us. "And grapes, hops and I'm sure, many other crops of lesser production."

"How are things within the counties around us?" I asked.

"Starting here, Greenbluff fruit and grain production looks good. Winter wheat throughout several counties looks like an above average yield. Lincoln County is almost all dryland, and about a quarter of that is winter wheat. Summer grains, what did get planted, make up another quarter of the farmland. They're good as far as planting and growth, but will never be able to harvest a tenth of it without fuel to run the combines. Spokane County's in about the same shape, but of course we have far less area and far less in the way of grain production here. Whitman County is similar to Lincoln as far as their planted winter wheat, but with more in the way of pea and lentil percentages typically grown there, most of those didn't get planted or are far behind what a normal year might bring. Stevens County has a lower percentage of winter wheat this year than normal, and is far behind planting schedule, and of course it's colder because of its elevation and terrain. Fuel is the number one priority, no doubt about it."

"Thank you, Stacey. About one more month, right?" Walt said as she tried to find a comfortable way to sit.

"That was the best guess, yes. And I'm ready. Believe me."

"OK, my turn," Walt said. "Rail service. We can expect commercial and passenger rail service to Montana to resume as early as June first. Burlington Northern is clearing several major rockslides and two washouts that are currently blocking the rails, and they are working them from both sides of the blockages. Rail service may or may-not be a good thing, depending on what comes our way with the flu and with refugees."

"You think more people want to come HERE?" Drew said. "I'd have thought the opposite."

"Plan for the worst," I said.

"The river will probably hit flood stage by Sunday, and will probably stay that way until after Memorial Day. Parts of Upriver Drive will go underwater. The dams are holding up OK, even with the damage and skeleton crews."

"Normal runoff?" Clete asked.

"Yeah. Rivers at about thirty-thousand cubic feet per second, should peak at a little under forty thousand."

"Now, onto the immigration issue. Mike Amberson let me know that three thousand one-hundred and six non-residents were identified in last weeks sweep, with two hundred twenty-one positively identified as wanted criminals. Fifteen individuals are in custody for firing on Federal troops after orders to stand down. Eleven were killed in direct confrontations. Most residents in the sweep area are peaceful, but frankly are barely making it on the scant food distributions that we're making from the community centers. Some are stealing from each other, and have been killed for it."

"We're sitting on a powder-keg with a lit fuse," Clete says.

"Walt, in this sweep, did anyone ask what these people used to do for jobs? What their skills or professions were?" I asked.

"Not to my knowledge. Former place of residence, social security number, name of course, and dependents. Oh, and other family members out of the area and last-knowns."

"OK. Well, that's a start at least. Maybe we can have them tell us what they did for employment, and get them back at it."

"Sure, now that the Army's scared them sh•tless," Clete said. "Pardon me, ladies. Mouth got the better of me."

"Despite your colorful language, Mr. McKinnon, I am in complete agreement," Tonya said.

"Walt," I asked. "Or anyone. Does anyone have any real news on Canada? Stacey? Anything on your shortwave network?"

"No, nothing factual. Rumors are flying though," she said. "I have a cousin up in Cranbrook. I haven't heard from her since Christmas, though."

"I know that the military's up there," Walt said. "No idea where though. Found out that from a State Patrolman who'd dropped off a vanload of prisoners and 'B.C. Bud,'" Walt said, referring to the locally grown high-quality marijuana that was British Columbia's number one cash crop. "Seems the market for 'weed' has dried up since the crash, and they were trying to bring the plants closer to the population."

We moved the meeting along, even though we were well over our designated time to adjourn. We prepared a brief list to have completed by the following Monday. Tonya, who seemed to spend most of this meeting listening and taking notes, was already working on what was being 'made' and 'grown' and determining what service and manufacturing facilities are in operation. Her task would be to finish the list of these services, and come up with what was essentially a marketing plan for letting survivors know what was available and where the jobs were. Not a task for the meek.

Clete would work up a sample document that outlined the requirements for settlers in the 'service area', ready for release by next Wednesday. He would use both my notes and Tonya's summary and our committee comments to prepare a draft.

Stacey, shifting jobs, would refine some of Tonya's work on identifying and recruiting vocations and professions for the areas to be settled and rebuilt.

At my suggestion, each board member would take some of the information from my notes (with some assistance from the County staff), and would put together information sheets for the settlers. Essentially, public-service sheets that had recommended levels of firewood for the coming winter, food requirements per family, recommendations for stocks of clothing, medical supplies, organizing neighborhood defense, and locations of critical public facilities and services. More of these little information sheets would be needed in the coming months, but that was plenty to start with. Clete volunteered to write the sheet on neighborhood defense. Stacey, the sheet on food requirements. The remainder were divvied up between Drew and Tonya.

"Prod sheets," I called them, which raised questions among my fellow board members.

"Huh?" Drew asked. "These aren't products, they're services."

"Sorry, 'prod' as in cattle-prod," I said. "As in 'to prod people into action.'"

"Then it oughta be 'sheep-prod,'" Clete said with a smile, "for the sheeple."

I would be working on preparing relatively simple maps of the initial settlement areas, starting in the Valley but eventually addressing the developed areas north and south of the City of Spokane. I had little information on the utility status in the City, and had no desire to take that on. I was glad that Walt agreed that the County should not take that on. Like our other work, my document would be printed up and distributed by the community center directors and would serve as a guideline for the settlers in finding a place to live. It would also be shown on television, for those that had working sets and were within the range of the stations.

Finally, at ten minutes to one, we adjourned for the day. Our Monday meeting was scheduled for nine. As we filed out, a new-to-me employee, with 'Communications' stenciled on his shirt, handed each of us newish hand-held radios, tuned to our own frequency. Each department, before the quake, had their own radios and frequencies to broadcast on, and now the Recovery Board had it's own. We would not have to share the radio with other County employees, and if needed, we could probably conduct some business without coming to a formal meeting. No one asked if we should return our old 'mobile' setups, which was fine with me. I kinda liked the ability to eavesdrop once in a while.

Carl, Kelly and Marie had been invited to join the County staff for lunch, vegetable-beef stew, a choice of juices, and applesauce. I was more than a little hungry myself, but wanted to get on home. The kids had shared their 'emergency snack' of miniature loaves of wheat bread with Kamela and two of her assistants, who were relishing the fresh bread, mopping up the stew with the crusts. Kamela told me as we were loading up that if the kids worked like this all the time, they were welcome back in a heartbeat.

"They beat the heck out of the civil service types that are holding up walls around here," she said as her final comment.

"Thanks. I'll let them know that," I said as I climbed into the Ford.

"You guys made quite an impression," I said.

"Beats plowing," Carl said.

"Or weeding," the girls added.

"Let's see if we have any news," I said as I backed the car out of its slot, and headed east to Division. At first we had static on KLXY, and then the station snapped to life.

"It is one o'clock p.m., Pacific Daylight Time. This is KLXY Spokane."

"Good, I wondered if we'd get something," I said as a national correspondent came on. The kids were looking out the windows at the wreckage, again I think, not quite believing what was just beyond the glass.

418

""This is ABC News Washington Bureau, reporting from Durham, North Carolina.

"The major story of the day centers around reports of an assassination attempt against the President that occurred on April 15, immediately after he had addressed the nation. The President was uninjured in the attack, although two Secret Service agents were killed and four seriously wounded. The assassin was identified as a member of the Federal security team, and was stationed at an undisclosed location where the President was in residence. Conspirators have been identified by the shooter as members and ex-members of United States intelligence agencies, four senators and two representatives, several have confessed to the attempted coup d'etat under questioning. At least two of the conspirators committed suicide prior to capture. According to sources in the FBI, all surviving conspirators are in custody at this time. The assassin is in custody and recovering from gunshot wounds inflicted during the attack. The President is currently in residence at Camp David, and Vice President McAllen remains at an undisclosed location."

"Whoa," I said, as I caught Carl's eye. He was 'watching' the radio, too.

"Unrest in several major cities continued today, with National Guard and Army troops setting up blockades on major highways serving these cities. Residents in the cities are demanding relief from both the regions surrounding the cities and the Federal Government. Senators and representatives from the region state that food and fuel supplies are at critical levels and social services have collapsed, putting many residents at risk. Areas around of Detroit and Philadelphia, where rioters overwhelmed Guard units exhibited the remains of what can only be called an orgy of looting, rape and murder late yesterday. Regular Army troops, fighting the rioters, fired automatic weapons when they came under small-arms fire and fire from captured military weapons."

"New Jersey Senator Cynthia Blackburn demanded that the Federal government cede control of all troops in the northeastern region to the states of New York, Massachusetts, Pennsylvania, and New Jersey, stating that only the leaders of those states can provide for the common good. Support for release of troops to control of the states was supported by the Acting Governor of Michigan, the Governor of Wisconsin, and several prominent mayors of larger cities. FEMA Northeast Region directors called the demand all but a declaration of secession. The President, Vice President and the Cabinet soundly condemned the requests and urged the states to facilitate recovery by calling on the individuals to take personal responsibility. Senator Blackburn could not be reached for comment, but an aide to the Senator called the Federal response 'unworthy of discussion.'"

"From Atlanta today, radiation clean up in the affected areas may take up to six years, according to FEMA, released in a report at the offices of the CDC. Areas directly affected by blast may not see repopulation for several decades, due to lingering radioactive materials with extended half-lives. The decontamination process continues in Washington D.C., parts of California and Virginia. Radioactive cleanup in the Northeast has been called off due to rioting in the area."

"The CDC confirmed this morning that a more virulent and deadly mutation of the Guangdong Flu is present in limited areas around the world, including the North American continent. Outbreaks in several East Coast cities have been reported, with extremely high mortality rates. The CDC, coupled with the U.S. Army are currently studying the disease and working on a series of potential vaccines. Sources in the CDC remain hopeful that a vaccine may be found quickly. The CDC has also stated that certain areas within affected cities have in fact been wholly quarantined, with no travel into or out of the affected areas. The CDC refuses to identify the affected areas or the cities, however. ABC's Science correspondents will be tracking this story throughout the next few days, and a special report is scheduled for tomorrow in protecting yourself against this new influenza."

'Yeah, right.' I thought to myself. 'Protect yourself my eye.'

"In news from Hawaii, the Navy has re-established a telephone line for communications purposes for very limited use by the general public and the media. All telephone communications were lost in the attack on April 15, and the Navy has since laid a new communications link on the seabed. One of the first messages received in San Francisco stated that USS Harpers Ferry had returned to Pearl Harbor after being refloated in Taiwan. The Harpers Ferry was hit while in port by a missile from a Chinese submarine on January 25th, with a loss of more than half of the crew. She will join USS Antietam at Pearl Harbor. The Antietam, a guided missile cruiser, was also heavily damaged in the Chinese attack. It is unlikely that either ship will be repaired. In other news from the islands, pleas for food shipments and water decontamination equipment have been relayed to the FEMA West Region commands. It is a known fact that the vast majority of the Hawaiian population depends heavily on imported foods and fuels from the mainland, and that no commercial shipments have been sent since mid-April."

"This is ABC News."

The local broadcast picked up a few moments later, with a flustered-sounding announcer. *"KLXY Spokane, where the current temperature is forty-seven degrees, and the barometer is currently steady at thirty point oh-one and rising with five mile per hour winds from the southwest. KLXY will now cease broadcasting, until five a.m. tomorrow morning for transmitter maintenance. For afternoon and overnight news, please turn to fifteen-ten, KDA."*

I punched the 'scan' button on the radio, and didn't find KDA broadcasting. There were no stations on the FM band either. 'Dang,' I thought.

I swung east on Trent, after slowly climbing over a raised curb in the middle of the street (no point in dividing traffic these days, with no traffic to speak of).

Again, a Humvee followed us east, from a respectful distance. I decided to check my radio out.

"Carl, hand me the walkie-talkie," I asked. He passed it to me, as he looked in the passenger side mirror at our camouflaged follower.

"One thirty-seven to Spokane," I called.

"One thirty-seven," a female voice replied.

"Anyone know why I have a Humvee following me? Happened after last meeting, too."

"Wait one," a different voice—male—replied. The Humvee slowed dramatically behind me, but was still back there.

"What do we do?" Kelly asked. I could hear her concern.

"Be advised, County has no knowledge of any protection details," the voice added, "Military or civilian."

"Well, ain't this just swell," I said, again checking the mirror. A second vehicle was now back there.

"There's another one back there, Dad. It's...I can't see it. It's not Army though," Kelly said.

"What are you going to do?" Carl asked.

"Drive," I said, looking at the upcoming intersection at Helena Street, turning south. I knew from my previous trips that I could feign a right there, sweep around either building on the south side of the intersection, and wait for the 'follower' to pass me. I could then return heading east. I hoped.

"Hang on now, this will be a little quick," I said as I hit my turn signal and turned the corner to the right, rapidly accelerating south, and then turning just as quickly left, and left again, to wait on the east side of the building on the southeast corner. "Wait here," I said as I got out of the Ford, leaving it running but locked, and un-snapped my old forty-five on my belt. I moved over to the building corner, and ducked down to take a look around the corner, my position concealed by a burned out dumpster.

The Humvee, now with a second olive-drab vehicle right behind it passed heading south at a good clip. The second follower was an early nineties Chevy Suburban, with whip antennas.

Both were marked with U.S.A.F. plates.

"Hmm." I said as I got back to the car, Carl unlocking it as I approached.

"One thirty-seven to Spokane," I said as I headed east again, this time at almost fifty miles per hour, holding the radio in my right hand as I wheeled onto Trent with my left.

"One thirty-seven, go ahead."

"Vehicles marked as United States Air Force. First is a four-door Humvee with a turtleback, second is a Suburban with tactical communications antennas, camo'd, darkened windows. Both headed south on Helena."

"Affirmative, one thirty-seven, be advised subjects are likely monitoring this frequency,"

"Duh," I responded. "One thirty-seven out."

"One thirty-seven."

"How long before they find us?"

"Doesn't really matter. I'm sure they know where we're heading."

"Do we warn Mom?"

"We do. Fire up the CB. I forgot to radio to her that we were on the way. Might be dicey getting through to her."

Carl did get through to Libby, although he had to repeat himself through the static. The little hand-held CB's antenna was far from adequate over uneven terrain and around buildings. I swept to the east as Karen came on the radio, and stopped partway up the Freya Street Bridge. The bridge spanned the Burlington

Northern tracks here, and was elevated significantly. My reception improved immediately.

"You on your way finally?" Karen asked.

"Yes. After a fashion. We seemed to have made a trip to Houston," I said, once again making reference to Apollo 13's famous quote. A very long pause on the other end.

"What can we do?"

"On our way, but we seem to have grown a tail. Two of them. Not County, not Army. Air Force plates on the vehicles. No idea why or who." At this point, if they were listening to us, I really didn't care if they knew it. I just wondered if they realized yet that they'd lost me, or if they were chasing me east on Sprague, when I was actually eastbound on Trent, running roughly parallel but well north.

"Understood," Karen said. "Advise location when appropriate."

"Location will be heard by our tail," I said. "Eastbound on a side street," I said, telling a bald-faced lie. "Not sure what the street is. Just north of Sprague. I think its part of the railroad right-of-way. Service road."

"Understood," she replied. "You watch yourself, mister. And our kids."

"All over it," I said. "Out."

"Out."

"Nice," Carl said.

"What?"

"You told them where we aren't."

"Not only that, but that service road ends at the freeway overpass, and has limited access between Helena and Fancher. And we'll be long past there by then," I said. 'Unless they've got friends,' I didn't add.

"Spokane to one thirty-seven," the radio crackled.

"One thirty-seven, over."

"Be advised, County Air One has you," the radio said, not giving away my position. "Your tail is approximately one mile west, moving rapidly."

"Now is that deception, or real?" I said to no one in particular.

"Maybe it's a lure," Marie said. "Maybe the County is fishing."

"Well, if so, let's hope they've got a little U.S. Army backup."

Ahead of me, I noticed four Humvees coming at me. "I hope these are good guys," I said. I didn't have to wait long as the lead driver waved as we passed, moving west and south, toward our tail.

"Someone's going to have a bad day," I said as the last Humvee, equipped with a rear-mounted weapon that I didn't recognize sped past. The County helicopter, a tiny two-passenger traffic unit, passed over us to the east, and seemed to be following our 'reported' position. I spotted an Army Blackhawk, with its gun crew ready, flying low over the river to the north, circling back around to the west.

"A very bad day."

41

Friday afternoon,
May Fifth

"Spokane to one thirty-seven," the radio called. We were nearly home.

"One thirty-seven," I replied.

"Please be advised, situation is resolved and investigators will be in contact later today," the voice stated pleasantly.

"Understood. One thirty-seven, out."

"One thirty-seven," the female voice repeated.

"It's over?" Kelly asked.

"Apparently so."

"Well what happened?" Carl asked.

"Might never know. That's one downfall of audio only. We, your Mom and I, used to listen to the police scanner once in awhile, and it left us constantly wondering what was really going on. Lots of times, we never knew how things ended. This might be one of them. Depends on who was following us and what the Army or the County want to share with us."

"Well that bites," Marie said. "Only the most excitement we've had in a month and we don't even know what it was!"

"I reckon I'll hear about it. Don't worry," I said as we drove by the convenience store, which I noticed, was closed. The three-man Army patrol was outside, manning their Humvee's mounted gun, and waved at us as we turned towards the house.

"Anyone listening?" I asked over the FRS.

"Affirmative," Alan's voice replied. "We're ready."

"I'm one minute out. The situation has been resolved."

"Understood. Out."

I pulled into the driveway, and Carl got the gate. The dogs came tearing up to us as usual as I parked the SUV on the side of the garage.

We got out of the car and were greeted by the rest of the family, Don Pauliano, and a half-dozen other folks we'd met through our trading network, all armed, and appearing from concealed positions up and down the street and on the property. Karen nearly cracked a rib hugging me.

"Well now. Nice welcoming party," I said, almost overwhelmed by what I saw.

"Figured it couldn't hurt," Alan said. "We heard about the same time you called that things were taken care of. Army unit on the south end of the block took care of that end, and spread the word."

"Pays to have friends in high places." I said.

"It does that," he said.

"Where's Ron?"

"Probably still walking in. He and Libby had the north end, with some help from a few more folks from the store. We didn't know which way you were coming back in."

"This didn't take long to pull off," I said.

"When you radioed in with the 'Houston' call, the store was pretty full. And everyone was armed. People these days take a dim view of stalkers or attackers."

"And I am thankful for that," I said. "Be sure to get me a list of who helped out," I added quietly. "Including the ladies and gentlemen in green."

"I can do that."

I spent a few minutes shaking the hands of those that had come to our assistance, although more than a few just waved and headed back to their daily routines, our impromptu community fading again into the background clutter.

"What's available for lunch?" I asked Karen a few minutes later as I stashed my computer in the dining room. The rest of the family was outside, even Grace, enjoying the pleasant May sunshine.

She gave me 'the look.' 'You're in for it now, bucko,' I could hear my late father say to me.

"You are followed by someone who might be trying to kill you, we call out everyone that can carry a gun, and you wonder what's for lunch?"

"Sorry, yes. I'm sorta food-centric. The kids ate downtown with the County staff. We had a long meeting."

"I figured. There's some cold fried chicken and fried potatoes in the fridge," she said. "I was scared."

"I was, too. We're OK though. I'll find out later what it was all about."

"It shouldn't have to be like this," she said with her head buried in my shoulder.

"No, it shouldn't. But it is."

When things settled back down after lunch, we gathered up the family to go over Saturday's schedule, and what we needed to do to make the potato and onion planting go smoothly.

I found myself coming down from an adrenaline high from our drive home, and trying to be 'up' to motivate the kids in particular, that this could be hard, or be harder. Planting potatoes, by hand, with two thousand pounds plus to handle, was going to be anything but easy. Grace and Mary had stitched up a half-dozen planting bags for the planting teams to use, assisted by Mark and Rachel in the cutting and stitching. A couple of old hammocks, worn and torn, supplied the heavy canvas for the bags and the shoulder slings. Marie and Kelly would be cooking with Karen and Libby for the afternoon, one of the 'batch' recipes that we'd cook up and spread among the three families. Libby had also started a batch of sourdough, that we'd keep going until we were well and truly tired of it. Ron and Alan would be busy with an afternoon on the chainsaws; John and Carl would help buck the cut wood onto Alan's big trailer, and get it ready to season at each house. I'd get to play…er, run the tractor to finish prepping the fields for tomorrow.

By three, I'd finished dressing out the three potato fields, and was about half-done with the plots that we'd set up for onions. We'd already plowed and tilled most of the fields, and to prep the potato and onion fields, I'd taken my big three-point landscape rake and pulled a number of tines off of it to allow the rake to scribe rows in the soft earth. In our old garden, we'd run stakes and string lines. With this much acreage, that wasn't practical. The three big squares we'd created for the potatoes were set far enough apart to actually be affected by the microclimate of the inner area of the block. The southern-most was lowest in elevation, one in our back field was on a slightly sloping grade to the south and west, and the northern most plot was at the high point, elevation wise, on the whole block. I was heading back to the tractor shed when I saw that Karen was flagging me down, an Army uniform at her shoulder. And this one was not in the typical BDU's. but a uniform coat and slacks. I could see the ribbons and a glint from his shoulder epaulet as I headed to the shed.

After stowing the tractor and remembering to shut off the fuel valve, I walked up to the back yard, where Libby and Karen were now talking with the Army officer, who looked to be in his early thirties. I noticed he had been provided a glass of iced tea. That meant, he must be all right with the wives.

"Mr. Drummond, I'm Mick Templemann," he said as I shook his hand and noticed the captains' bars.

"What can I do for you, Captain?"

"I'm with the Army Criminal Investigation Division—CID—and I'm charged with investigating this mornings' incident."

"Good. Maybe you can let me know what it was all about," I said.

"With some assistance from you, perhaps we can put this together."

"Let's go have a seat on the porch. Hon, is there any more tea?" I asked.

"I'll get it. You go up to the porch," Libby said, knowing that Karen wanted to hear the whole conversation.

"Thanks, Lib."

"So Captain, where are you…or were you from before the Domino?" Karen asked.

"Leesburg, Virginia. Used to work in the Pentagon. Grew up out in Odessa, though," he said, referring to a small cattle and farming town out west of town. "Nice to be back in Spokane. I played in the State 'B' basketball tournament here, a lifetime ago. Got mopped up by Republic."

"I went to Deutschesfest once out there, a long time ago. Welcome back to the real world," I said with a smile. "Things are a little different here."

"No doubt. I find that things move a lot slower outside the Beltway, and yet things get done quicker. A little paradoxical."

"There isn't much time for political bullsh•t out here. Especially not since January."

We took our seats on the front porch, now re-equipped with the old wooden chairs and tables that we'd pulled out of winter storage.

"So, tell me how things ended," I began.

"First, the deception that you put in place was key. My compliments. It did not end well for any of the six men involved. They decided to fight, which was a losing proposition from the start. The sixth, who turned out to be a deserter, survived long enough to give us a little information before he died," he said as he looked at us both, testing the waters to see if we really wanted to hear this.

"Once they realized they were boxed in, they tried to retreat to the west. There were only two ways on to that access road, which you knew and they didn't. Two of the Humvee crews engaged them from the east, and the air unit popped up and pretty much ended it before the second two ground units could engage. I was there at the end with the last Humvee. The call caught me by surprise—I was headed to Division Command when the call came in."

"So why did the Air Force want me...dead or whatever?" I asked, which gave Karen a start at my words.

"They weren't Air Force. They were using stolen Air Force vehicles, however. Before he died, the ringleader stated he was AWOL from the Air Force security police and that you were to be kidnapped and ransomed, and said that 'it worked like a charm before.' That explained the vehicles. He died before we could get anything else out of him," Templemann paused, "other than this clipboard. Your address is circled, along with three other addresses and several dates from last February, and some other numbers and letters that I can't figure out. The others have lines through them. I was hoping you could tell me why," he said as he handed me the clipboard, with a half-dozen sheets of addresses, names, numbers and dates.

"Good God," I said, knowing immediately what the sheets represented as I examined each of the entries.

"Please elaborate, if you would."

"These are FEDEX delivery addresses and dates from last February. We received a shipment from my brother. This date corresponds to that shipment. The numbers in the right column represent the weight. This symbol," I pointed to the fourth column of hand-written text, "represents the contents."

"Which was what, exactly, if you do not mind?"

"Know your periodic table?" I asked as I handed back the clipboard.

"Yes, since junior high school," the Captain responded.

"Silver and gold coins, in our case. About a hundred and ninety pounds worth. It appears that each person on that list had similar couriered shipments made during the same period. And each was probably targeted by your deserter and his gang," I said, looking down at my hands. My shaking hands. 'It was supposed to be a robbery,' I thought to myself. 'A kidnapping and robbery.'

"There must be over four thousand pounds of precious metals on this list," Templemann said as he studied the entries and added them up. "Not counting these other entries, which don't seem to correspond to your entry," he pointed out. "No idea what this one might be," he motioned to the entry below my address. The identification read 'C'. The weight, just over two pounds.

"Captain, what does 'C' stand for in the table of elements?" I asked.

"Carbon."

"What made of carbon would be worth shipping with an armed courier?" I asked, as the light came on for him.

"Jesus. Diamonds," he said as things finally clicked for him.

"Your list perhaps represents what a lot of people put up as fail-safe items of wealth. You have gold, silver, diamonds," I said as I looked over the list, "platinum and palladium, probably mixtures of these too, in looking at the entries here. And if the items that are crossed off mean that the recipients have been robbed or killed for their goods, then someone has to have a lot of metal laying around, unless they were smart enough to have the delivery made at a different address, or bugged out."

"Just like the Jews in Europe in the Thirties," Karen said as Templemann flipped through the pages. "My grandparents were some of them," he said as he continued to look at the entries.

"Earthly wealth is sometimes required to be portable," I said. "In our case, I figured we'd lost it all when the market crashed. My brother saw what was going on before a lot of people did, took some steps to make sure that we didn't lose everything."

"It looks to me that you were the last big score on this list," Captain Templemann said.

"Regardless, you better track down the other names, in case the guys you took out today have friends. That sheet is a photocopy," I pointed out.

"Thank you, Mr. Drummond," the Captain said as he stood.

"You been back to Odessa since you came back west?" I asked.

"No, sir. Haven't had time and I've no immediate family left there anymore. I still have property and the family farm out there though. My second cousin looks after it for me. His place is next door—if you can call three miles away next door."

"Well, maybe you ought to wrangle some time and go check it out. Might be more important to do so than you think," I said to the young Captain, my meaning fully grasped.

The precious metals that my brother Alex had so astutely bought with my melting retirement savings amounted to serious poundage to ship and to store. The shipment listed on the robbers' clipboard, arrived in early February, after the stock market imploded and before the vast majority of physical silver and gold virtually 'ran for the hills'.

I suppose that the pile of metal that we now had was part of that exodus. It was odd to think that I'd worked and saved for twenty-five years, only to end up with silver with a face value of forty-three hundred dollars, and fifty-five gold double eagles--eleven hundred dollars face value. Of course, I still had to remind myself, that the fifty-four hundred dollars in precious metals had cost me one hundred and seventy-five thousand dollars invested in mutual funds, as the Federal Reserve Notes evaporated. Silver at that point was just shy of thirty dollars (FRN) per ounce, and gold was a little more than sixteen hundred.   I suppose that Alex's read on the market, and converting my index funds and other mutual funds to out-of-country gold and silver funds and then selling those for physical gold and silver, put me in a distinct minority. Someone with 'money.'

Maybe it was time we started to spend some.

That night, I gave Alan the 'good to go' on buying the two AR-15's from Aaron, for two hundred to two hundred-fifty dollars in silver coins. In a separate transaction, Alan had made a long-term trade of a shortwave transceiver setup, including one of Aaron's unused antenna towers, for store credit and fresh food.

"I bet putting values on that transaction was interesting," I said to him as we watched the last of the evening sun fade to stars. We were sitting out in the back yard, under the new leaves of the big Norway maple.

"I think we both felt it was a satisfactory transaction," he replied. "You doing OK after this morning? Karen said you seem a little 'off.' She told me to buy you a drink and pry it out of you."

"And you, being the big brother, complied."

"Any chance to have a fifteen year old Scotch, well, sure," he said as he swirled the now-precious drink in the etched glass.

"Yeah, I'm OK. She knows that. Just having my doubts about how in the Hell we're going to get all this work done. It's enough to deal with with just our family. But the amount of work that is required to put a city back together? What in the heck was I thinking?"

"And your choice would be what? Bailing out? To where? You did the right thing here."

"Yeah, I know. I'm finding myself just tired. Tired of thinking about it. Tired of figuring what needs to be done. Tired of death," I thought, remembering my brother, niece and sister-in-law. "Tired of sh•t like this morning. Some bastard was picking off people who'd been smart or lucky enough to have money or whatever shipped to them. We were on that list. We were just a target. He was going to kidnap or kill us, probably all of us, for two hundred pounds of metal."

"Not the first time we've been a target," he said.

"But damn it, I want this to be the last!" I said, raising my voice when I really didn't need to. "I'm tired of being the nail that's about to get hammered.

One of these days we're not going to be so lucky. One of us is going to get killed over nothing."

"You know that the battle that we are engaged in is not visible to us," Alan said, alluding of course to the spiritual battle between Good and Evil. "And we rely on Him to see us through it."

"I know," I said, not all that encouraged by the reprimand as I looked off at the darkened earth that tomorrow would be planted. "I suppose that I've been looking for a definite end to this. There isn't one. And yeah, I know. Good and Evil and all that."

"OK, take this in the manner intended, as encouragement. I sympathize with the loss of your brother and your niece, and I know you are concerned about the rest of your family. But honestly, Rick I'm surprised at you. You're the one that's been the anchor and the organizer for this family, and for a whole lot of people beyond that. The house literally falling down around you was your wake up call. You've gotten a lot of work done. You helped a lot of people get their sh•t together while there was still time for it to matter. We are all, and you are in particular, at the point where the rubber meets the road," he said, leaning forward in his chair, the Scotch cradled in his hands. "This is your test. You need to choose how you will complete it. Are you up to what is being tossed at you or not?"

"You always put forth the easy questions," I said as I finished my drink.

"You can do this. And you know that you can do this," Alan said.

42

Wednesday,
May Seventeenth

After my talk with Alan, it took me a couple of days before I got myself back to an attitude that was more light than dark. I was finding in myself that I had to consciously make myself be positive. Without going into deep theological waters, I found in myself Faith that I didn't know that I had, and Strength that was not of me.   I also stopped worrying as much. Maybe it was resignation. Probably a more likely explanation is that I surrendered to a will that was greater than mine. (Somehow we were taught as children that surrender was a sign of weakness and was therefore bad. I was learning otherwise now.)

We finally finished planting the gardens on Friday the twelfth, with still a little snow atop Mica Peak, ten miles or so to our southeast. The departure of its' snowcap was the yearly indicator for the Drummonds that it was now safe to plant our summer garden. I was reminded several times by the kids that the term 'garden' implied something small and easily worked. The thirteen or so acres of planted ground could hardly be defined therefore, as a garden. The herb garden alone consumed more than an acre. We were all sore for days after planting the fields—those that had to be planted by hand. Even as we did so, I wondered how much more difficult next year would be, preparing fields and planting without gasoline-assuming that we were not going to get a new source by then.

The kids-ours and others now in the area-began 'school' of sorts again on May eighth, at the old Broadway Elementary. The combined school included K-12, and had forty-seven students spread fairly evenly across all grades. Karen, Libby and Mary all taught, three hours a day each, in what settled down to a six-hour school day. High points of the day for the school kids included 'recess' and 'lunch.' In a visit that I made with my fellow Board members (most of the board hadn't been out to the Valley since well before the quake), it was apparent that a fair percentage of the kids and their teachers were showing signs of malnutrition. Lunch was provided by the County from both the limited stored foods in the city and locally produced sources (grains from a local mill and bakery that had restarted, a local dairy that supplied milk, butter and eggs, and once a week, fried chicken). The new 'principal', a retired school board administrator with twenty five years of 'old school' experience as a principal, ran a good ship and would invite parents and family members to join their students for lunch each Friday. This served the dual purpose of getting the parents involved in their kid's education (which academically was far from what schooling was about, pre-War), and making sure a wider population was getting fed.

We heard precious little from the 41st Division regarding the holdouts at Fairchild's base hospital, but from all appearances, they were going to remain there until they absolutely ran out of food. The Army was not interested in ending the situation through an attack, but was perfectly willing to set up a perimeter and wait out whoever was 'in charge' at the hospital—there were people still alive in there, according to spotters.

The other groups on base, the flight crews sequestered in the Alert Facility and the other Air Force crews and their dependents camped out in hangars and accessory structures were cleared on May fourteenth of the new flu threat by County Health. The Air Force ranking officer established a no-contact zone that in effect isolated the hospital from the remainder of the base, making sure that the rest of the base personnel would be out of any line of fire from the hospital to any of the bases' new population. The Air Force crews and dependents, once released from their voluntary confinement in the small group of buildings, rapidly went about repairing and adapting Fairchild's damaged buildings for residential use and to serve whatever 'mission' the powers that be had in mind.

The Boards' work, 'organizing', 'getting information out', and getting some sort of community re-established, went relatively smoothly within the limits of what we could do, although we had our challenges. Additional newly hired County staff played a large role in helping Walt Ackerman set up a new County government, and administer new programs and rebuilt departments. Civil courts would be back in place in early June, and elections of new representatives was scheduled for early August. Our idea of putting 'flyers' out with what we thought was good information was widely accepted; my idea of establishing settlement boundaries based on available infrastructure was 'not', although the resistance to these ideas came from a different quarter than we were prepared to deal with.

Some of the five to ten thousand settlers that had come into the area since the War 'ended' had their own ideas about where they wanted to live, and began to demand that services be provided to them from the City or the County. They occupied structures that were serviceable, except for the minor issue of a lack of water and power, in what were 'prime' areas above the Valley floor or far enough out of the core of the Valley to allow some 'exclusivity': Liberty and Newman Lake neighborhoods, as an example—bedroom communities, pre-War, with no working power, water or sewage systems, and no ability to provide them, without an act of God or the resources of factories in China that no longer existed.

Things started getting interesting as we heard of minor confrontations over the issue, which seemed to build as the days went by and 'new properties' were 'discovered.' The 'have nots' were demanding their 'share'. On May twelfth, a Friday, we saw one of these situations come to a head right in front of us.

We were in a meeting (we, meaning Alan, Ron, Karen and I) with the assistant community center director regarding settlement on 'our' block, and that we wanted a say in who would settle around us. Others like us who lived here 'before' and made it this far, also wanted some input on whom our new neighbors would be, if any. (We were obviously trying to affect the ancient maxim: 'You can't choose your neighbors.')

Coming right to the heart of the matter were the facts that other areas that were being 'settled' were dealing with thieves and 'useless eaters' who would not contribute or work but demanded food, water, power, and of all things, 'entertainment.' I was not about to have this happen on our block and in our neighborhood, and was prepared to go to the mat for it. Or, in the extreme case, prepared to buy as much land around us as could be negotiated.

"You want to hand-pick people that will settle vacant homes around you?" Kevin Miller, the assistant community center director asked from behind his desk. His 'office' was actually part of a much larger room that had been carved up into makeshift cubicles. The County—well, actually the Board—had arranged for each community center to have the database showing the utility service area and the 'salvageable' properties uploaded for the center directors' use. My idea, come to life. (Now, I found myself on the receiving end of it.)

"Yeah. To be blunt."

"We've already got the so-called guidelines that the Board—you among them—created. Pretty discriminatory, don't you think?" he asked. Despite his tone, he was not opposed to the idea; it was the execution of such requests that he'd have to defend, that troubled him.

"Yes, it could be. On the other hand, more productive hands and fewer non-productive ones will benefit the larger community to a greater degree. Kevin, it's not like I'm saying that I'm discriminating based on race or religion or anything like that. I'm saying that if people are living on my block—and I call it that because I've defended it and planted it and worked it—I'd like to have a say in their selection because I know what skills we need around us. Or have a pretty good idea anyway."

"And, how do you think you can effect such a process?" Kevin worked in academia pre-Domino, and sometimes his tenure-based vocabulary reared its head.

"You work here, part time, correct?"

"Yes."

"And in exchange for that?"

"I have a house to live in…that has power and water." I knew that his former residence was two miles from a working water system.

"And?"

"Food allowances provided by the County based on my work."

"And you are allowed to grow, plant, make additional money or food or whatever on your own, at your County-designated residence, correct?" I asked, also knowing that he was also a skilled hobby-level machinist, which was a valuable source of added income for his survival….and probably more valuable as the weeks and months went by.

"Yes."

"Was your selection in this position discriminatory?" I asked. Alan was starting to smile.

"No, I was asked. I've had experience in the personnel department at the colleges and can deal with...personnel or customer-service issues."

"And if someone comes in and can do your job better, you're out?" I asked, receiving a slightly shocked look in return.

"I had not considered that, but it could be possible."

"But as long as you do a good job, you are relatively assured of your position."

"Yes, I believe so."

"This whole idea of urban settlement has the requirement of planting food crops for the settler's use. Ninety percent of the food production area on my block is already planted-by us-and that we could use labor to grow it and harvest it, for which we will share with those that will help. We also know how many houses are repairable or adaptable to wood heating for next winter, which is the defining element in resettlement. Six. We'd like to have input on who those six parties are. People that will not depend on a sole source of income—our food crops for example—for their existence. We want people that are really good at what they do because we cannot afford to evict somebody and go down that road. Generally we know when we meet somebody, instinctually, if they're going to work out or not. I'm not in the business to be a landlord. I also don't want to have to climb all over somebody to do what is expected of them. I want them to be self-motivated."

"Who do you have in mind? Or should I say, what types of skills are you trying to recruit?" He was seeing down the path.

"It'd be good to have someone in law-enforcement or the military. Medical or dental experience. Teachers. A pastor. People with primitive skills...."

"People that can perform manual labor or have multiple lines of abilities in addition to their 'other' vocation," Karen said, summing it up nicely.

"I'll see what I can do, quietly," Kevin responded. "Maybe I'll apply myself."

We got up to leave and shook hands when three men and two women barged in to Kevin's office area before we could leave. Ron and Alan already had their hands on their sidearms I noted. My old Colt was on my hip as well.

"You Miller?" the largest of them asked, ignoring Karen completely and only giving us the most dismissive of glances. He was perhaps six foot-six, well over two-fifty with close-cropped hair and perfect teeth, wearing an olive-drab utility coat, new (and ironed) blue-jeans, and some sort of snakeskin cowboy boots. The others exhibited both a sense of arrogance and subservience to the man in front of me.

"Excuse me. I think we're done here," I said as we moved to the doorway.

"Fine," the man said as he moved only slightly out of our way, looking down at me.

"I'm Mr. Miller, the Assistant Director," I heard Kevin respond as Karen followed Alan out. The two Army guards at the door were looking over our way. Ron, Alan and I hung around outside the office, listening in.

"Head for the partition over there," I told Karen softly, pointing to a masonry wall separating Miller's office from the foyer. "Stay there," I said, as she looked at me with something more than resolve.

"We need power and water, and we need it now," the spokesman for the group demanded from Kevin. Obviously, this guy was used to bossing folks about.

"What is your address?" Kevin responded, leaning forward on his desk, his flat-panel computer screen to his left.

"4314 South Bannock. West of Highway 27."

"That'd be two miles south of the utility service area then?" Kevin replied calmly.

"I don't really know. Or care for that matter."

"That area is outside of the utility service area and no water, power or sewage service is available in that part of the area. Nor, will it be," Kevin replied, firmly but politely.

"Goddammit! There's a water tank right across the highway from us! What part of what I said did you not understand?" the guy said, too loudly to avoid drawing the attention of the Army guards, now joined by two more who were apparently signaled that perhaps 'trouble' had walked in.

"I understood every word, sir," Miller said has he typed in the address and pulled up the Assessors' information on the property. "And apparently you have settled into a house belonging to a Mrs. Louanna Pickerson, aged sixty-one, widowed, who currently resides at Good Samaritan public shelter in Greenacres. That house is a wide-footprint rancher, six bedrooms and four baths, built in nineteen seventy-eight, connected to Vera Water and Power before the quake, with on-site septic system, a swimming pool and pool house, and four car garage. Sits on fifteen acres of decomposing granite and thin soils in the southern Dishman Hills. The views must be great up there."

"Listen, you little ****. We're living in a dozen houses up there and you are going to provide us services."

"Like Hell we are. That water tank you refer to has a massive rupture on the eastern side of the tank that is irreparable. Utility reconstruction to that area cost upwards of a million dollars per mile, in pre-Domino FRN's. If you have that kind of money in real silver or gold, or better yet, a mile of six or eight inch water line, and enough utility conductors and transformers to serve that area laying about, and a few thousand gallons of diesel to run the equipment, then we'll talk. If you don't, well then, I guess you can pack water and string a load of extension cord from Eighth and Pines. Which is the nearest public service to your location."

"I control that land," the man hissed, his balled fists planted on the blonde oak schoolteachers' desk. The others in his group were muttering approval. I was thinking to myself that I hadn't seen people that were both this arrogant and stupid in quite a while.

"We have a problem here?" Amy Ross in her Army BDU's asked from behind me.

"We got no ****ing problem if this **** gets us power and water."

"Mr. Drummond, your opinion on this?" Kevin asked.

"This group of people seems to have not been aware of the settlement boundaries, and have taken possession of properties that are both outside of the utility service area and, well, apparently property that does not belong to them in the eyes of the County."

"That's a damned lie," the mountain said to me, eyes narrowed to slits. "That house is mine."

"According to Mr. Millers' records, that house belongs to someone else. Regardless, it's not getting power or water. And I really don't give a rats' ass how nice the view is."

"And who the Hell are you?"

"To you I am Mister Drummond. A member of the Spokane County Recovery Board. And, I'll add, the one who drew the line beyond which settlers can fend for themselves. You and your friends here, appear to be on the other side of that line." That served to make him only angrier. "And if I might ask, you are who?"

"Michael Zantz. Also known as the guy that's gonna take you out," he said as he reached inside his oversized coat.

By then, Alan and Ron both stepped back slightly and brought their weapons to bear on his chest, as did two of the four guards. I heard the distinctive rack of a shotgun to my left. I remembered that one of the guards had an Army combat shotgun. I wondered if it had 'slugs' or 'shot' in the firing position.

"You might want to reconsider that statement, unless you are feeling particularly lucky. We live in a particularly well-armed society these days, which means that it is usually also a very polite society, as well. Of course, you can go ahead and draw, and you will all be dead before you hit the floor," I said as my eyes remained fixed on Zantz. The others froze, two of them very obviously suddenly afraid.

Zantz thought better of it and slowly removed his hand from his jacket. Alan and Ron backed up another step and lowered their weapons as the two guards moved in, and the second pair took their place.

"You four," the first Army guard said. "Back out of the room slowly with hands raised. Any bad moves and you're over," the guard said, a slight young brunette with her combat shotgun aimed and ready. "You: Loudmouth," she said to the reddening face of our opponent, "On your face, spread-eagled and hands behind your head. Simpson and Owens, take these four to detention. We will go have a little chat."

"I'm going to remember you all," Zantz said. "You better watch your back, assholes," he said to Miller and I. A machine-pistol, I thought a MAC-10, appeared in the hand of the guard searching Zantz.

"Threatening a public official is duly noted," the newly promoted Corporal Ross stated as she looked at the weapon, kicked away as the body search continued. "I might remind you Mr. Zantz," Amy said as another soldier handcuffed the prone figure, who was struggling to resist the knee in his kidney, "that under the current terms of Martial Law, that statement just got you landed in a nice, cozy detention center until your case goes to adjudication and your claim settled."

"And how long is THAT supposed to take you little b*tch?!!"

"Longer each time you open your mouth, scumbag. Get him out of here," Amy said. He was promptly moved to his feet and hauled down the hallway, none too gently.

"Thanks, Amy," I said, as Alan went over to talk with Karen.

"I'm getting really tired of these macho *****," she replied. "Fourth one this week."

"Kevin? You OK?" Karen came back to my side and wove her fingers into mine.

"Yeah, I'm great. I'm getting pretty good at pushing my little 'trouble' button under the desk," he said.

"I wondered how it was that we had assistance so quickly," Ron said.

"How big a problem is this?" I asked Kevin.

"Bigger than it ought to be. We've had good luck overall, but there are a few people like this that come in from God knows where, think they can come in and up and take over the place. Not gonna happen," He said as he straightened his desk up and started punching some information into the computer.

"So what do you do next? About the other people up there?" I said, referring to the other homes apparently occupied.

"Nothing. They'll figure it out soon enough and toe the line, go hungry or thirsty. Not worth us going after them and putting our guys at risk," Annie replied.

"And him? Or, 'them'?" I asked.

"Geiger Detention for starters to be processed. If he or his friends keep up that kind of attitude, they might find themselves working hard labor until their case number comes up for review. That might mean anything from working salvage operations to breaking up concrete with sledgehammers."

"Doesn't really matter anyway though. Not for this guy." Kevin said as he looked at his monitor. "If this is the same guy—Zantz, Michael Edward—he's wanted for suspicion of murder and robbery in Benewah County, dated one May. Long record, mostly drug related. Copy of the report is right here," he said as he read more information.

"How did you get that information?" I asked.

"It's the nasty part of my job. Background check on all new settlers in the zip code. All of North Idaho and Eastern Washington databases are linked—sort of. We're doing all the data transfers with DVD's since we haven't got the 'net. He gave me his name, and bing here he is. We'll have to get a picture of him to Benewah and see if it's the same guy."

"Well, now," Alan said. "That was fun. What're we doing for our next 'E-Ticket' ride?"

"Alan, they haven't used E-Tickets since..." Karen said, still ahold of my hand.

"I know," he said, cutting her off. "I'm showing my age."

Annie asked, "What's an E-Ticket?"

43

Wednesday afternoon,
May Seventeenth

Those that did decide to 'settle' in the utility service area went across the spectrum of the population. A fair amount of people literally walked in from points both north and south, finding that survival in a post-nuclear post-FRN America too difficult to deal with. (No kidding). I met several at our local community center and at the store who had come back to town from outlying areas when their food ran low or their gas ran out or some other technological issue came up or a medical condition brought them back. The mythic 'retreat' locations seemed to be not as well equipped as they might have been to deal with the reality dealt them. I noted that medical issues alone (a lack of insulin, for example) brought some people back, while in a few cases, people could not handle the sheer amount of labor needed to survive, coupled with a lack of human contact. In their own words, they were 'going stir-crazy.' Many it seemed, were relieved to find human contact again.

One settler who had a 'stake' in the neighborhood was Sarah Woodbridge, the slight young lady who had been attacked and successfully fought off her attacker. Sarah was adopted by her grandparents after her mother had abandoned her in favor of methamphetamine, when Sarah was ten. Her father was never in the picture. She was raised in the house up the road from ours, and attended the West Valley school district. She learned just before Christmas that her mother had died in Seattle from an overdose of some kind. (A situation, seemingly common before the War, that now is unthinkable to me.) Her grandparents, now in their early seventies, had left after the Domino for Scottsdale. Sarah had received a letter from them while she was still in school in Bozeman, back in February.

Sarah was a young twenty year old, and was in the second year of her pursuit of a Bachelor's degree at Montana State in Bozeman. Her planned degree was in Health and Human Development, with post-grad plans to work in Central America for a non-governmental organization, fostering community health programs in small indigenous villages.

Karen, Libby and Mary had all but adopted Sarah after she was released from Valley Hospital, one day later than expected, on May sixth. Sarah was at present the only person living between Interstate 90 and us for a mile in either direction. She, like many college students, had developed a 'socialist' attitude as part of living in a 'college town' (I had myself at Washington State University, a lifetime ago now). She was recognizing that in the present circumstances, that same attitude towards 'the way society ought to be' was not only dead wrong, and if pursued would end up getting her killed. Her attack was not made at random, but by a man she had befriended on the trek back from Montana. He had followed her to town, and told her that he was going to continue west, and then south, as they parted ways. Ten days later, he came back to her home and attacked her. Her injuries included mostly defensive wounds on her arms and hands, and a nasty cut on her scalp that would leave a nasty scar, under all that sandy blonde hair. She had successfully defended herself against the attempted rape, by using her grandfathers Gerber knife. She had, as one of the Army medics told me, 'lopped off his equipment'. (The Army patrol later found her attacker, a half-mile north of her home. He bled to death.)

The other kids also took to Sarah like a long-lost older sister. John, both Karen and I could tell, was smitten the first time their eyes met. Libby saw the same thing, Ron was oblivious-I wondered, when Carl fell for a girl for the first time would I be so blind? (or had he and I'd missed it at some point in the past?)

This night, Sarah would join us for Kelly's birthday party. Sarah had helped me out immensely in getting a gift for Kelly, a magnificently bound set of Rudyard Kipling's collected works that I'd been trying to find through the barter network. Sarah's grandfather was a voracious reader, with Kipling one of his favorites. Sarah found it all but unreadable. Kelly would be bowled over. In exchange for the books, I traded her shooting lessons (from Alan, the best marksman and weapons handler among us), and I told her we'd see what we could do about finding her a suitable weapon. I was really looking forward to hearing about her trip back here. I'd heard little snips, but not the whole story. Now that she was back on her feet, I'd put her in touch with the community center's health clinic medical staff, where she was quickly hired to help out.

I don't think she ever figured she'd be working with third-world medical conditions without leaving home.

May 17th, 1:50 p.m.

I was working in the northern most fields when I decided to knock off for the afternoon, with yet another ominous wall of thunderclouds coming our way off to the west. I figured that at most, I had another hour before it got here, and there were other things that needed to be done ahead of breaking a new patch of ground for a larger raspberry and strawberry propagation patch. I had (in a rare instance) my iPod plugged in, and was listening to a play list of music from last summer's big party. At the moment, The Beatles, 'I Saw Her Standing There,' which I thought was the best song they did in their early years.

I saw Karen flagging me down across the large field that was planted with corn, as I finished plowing and finishing some more land that we were going to set aside for our berries and hopefully, asparagus plants if we could find them. I paused my music, brought the Ford's throttle back to idle, and turned the FRS radio on and called her, rather than have her walk the five hundred yards or so to me.

"What's up?"

"Mike Amberson's here. It's about Joe."

I paused for a moment, and punched the call button. "Great. What's up with him now?" I said, already realizing what Mike's visit must be about.

"You better come. Now, honey."

My heart had sunk before I heard Mike tell me. I lifted up the two-bottom plow, placed the transmission in 'fourth' and drove the Ford back to the house on our new 'service road'. The old Ford's steering box, well worn before the Domino, protested at the speed that I drove, both wheels wobbling right-to-left before I steadied one of the steering arms with my boot. I shut off the ignition and rolled up to Mike and Karen.

"Rick, I'm sorry. Your brother's dead."

I looked at him for a moment and didn't speak at first. "I think I knew that. What happened?"

"He walked out of the detention center more than a month ago. There's too many to keep track of, so no one really knows what day for sure. Since then, from what we can figure, is he made his way back to his apartment. One of the patrols found him there this morning. I recognized the name on the list and came over as soon as I heard on the radio."

"Let's go."

"You sure you want to see this?"

"It'll be OK, Mike. I've been expecting this for a long time."

I gave Karen a hug as the rest of the family showed up. They knew, without knowing, that something was going on.

"I'll be back in a while, hon."

"You want me to go with you?"

"No, I'll be fine."

Mike and I got into a police Jeep, and backed out of the driveway. Within a few minutes, we were at the apartment.

Joe's unit was located on the ground floor, apparently not badly damaged from the quake. The second floor however, had collapsed on top of the first, making the complex look like a dump pile. Only by going into the pile would you see that the first floor still stood.

"You sure?" Mike asked again before we went in, a Deputy stood in the doorway ahead of us.

"Yeah. How long?"

"Day, maybe two."

"K."

We walked into the cave-like apartment, the smell of stale cigarette smoke, urine and feces thick in the air. My brother, nine years older than I, was crumpled on the floor, over an empty case of vodka bottles. The squalor of the place was unbelievable. His skin, thin and sallow, looked for the world like that belonging to a concentration-camp victim, not the holder of a Ph. D. in the United States.   In his final days, apparently he'd become both incontinent and was racked with vomiting his own blood. It was everywhere.

"Good God," I said mostly to myself. Joe's belongings-mostly covered with filth and in heaps and piles-littered the living room, dining room, and kitchen. The bedrooms were stacked with liquor boxes.

"Recovery team should be here soon. Do you have a....."

I finished it for him. "There was no will, no estate, no arrangements, no casket. My parents are buried up on the hill. I suppose we'll put him there, too."

"Let's get some air," Mike said.

"Agreed. I've seen plenty."

"If you want to have a service I can see if I can get the chaplain," Mike said.

"Thanks, Mike," I said as I looked around the apartment, that had nothing wrong with it that five gallons of gas and a flare wouldn't take care of. Empty plastic bourbon, scotch and vodka bottles littered the floor, the tables, the shelves. There were dozens of them.

We walked outside to the wreckage of the rows of carports, some cars, including Joe's rustbucket eighty-three Blazer, trapped and crushed under the metal roofs.

"Let me know where you want him buried, and I'll see to it."

"Are they done with the mass burials?" I heard someone say, then realizing that it was me that was asking the question. Mass burials were common during the early days of the first outbreak of the flu, and of course common after the Domino. The Board hadn't really asked that question, I realized.

"Almost. I can see that he's interred with your family members though."

"Thanks. I appreciate that, even though he wouldn't." The 'recovery team' had arrived in their modified Chevy Suburban. The back of the Chev was basically lined with a welded stainless-steel box that telescoped out of the back on some sort of rail, in which the dead were placed for…disposition. I walked back to the Jeep and got inside, while Mike talked to the workers, then headed back to the Jeep.

"Any idea where he was getting the booze?" I asked as we drove out of the parking lot, around the wreckage of one of the buildings.

"Liquor truck in the parking lot of the store, other side of his fence. Unmarked trailer."

"And it hadn't been looted?"

"No, it looked like a piece of crap. Tires worn out, lights broken, looked abandoned. It was half full of bootleg booze."

"Bootleg? I don't get it."

"No Washington State Liquor Control Board stamps on the bottles."

"Smuggled in before the quake?"

"Looks as if," Mike said as we headed down Sprague Avenue. No other vehicles were in sight. "Probably headed in from the Reservation on the back roads. Parked conveniently by the casino on the other side of the fence, too. No way to tell now though for sure."

"Was Joe involved in the smuggling?"

"Don't know, and probably never will." Mike replied. "Rick, I'm very sorry about this."

"Thanks, Mike. I appreciate that. You know, we've seen this coming for more than thirty years, and there was not a damned thing we could do about it. According to Joe, he 'never had a problem'."

"Yeah, I've seen more than a few…." Mike was looking for the right word.

"'Drunks', I believe is the word you're looking for. Don't worry about my sensibilities, Mike. I know him for what he was."

"Sorry."

"That's OK. When will he be buried?"

"It should be done…today."

"Will there be a casket? I mean do you have…"

"It will be supplied."

"OK," I said as I took a pad of paper off of the Jeep's dash. I sketched out the place in the cemetery where I'd buried my mother, eight years before, and my Dad, more than twenty years gone, now. "Here's where my folks are buried. If you can bury him close by, I'd appreciate it."

"I'll pass it along."

"Any idea as to when the burial will be?"

"I'd expect it to begin before four," Mike said. That was a little under two hours from now.

"We'll be there by then," I said as we pulled into the driveway.

“I’ll let the guys know. I’ll try to have the chaplain there. It’ll take some time to prepare the grave.”

“Digging it by hand?”

“Yeah.”

“We’ll help.”

“You don’t need to do that,” Mike said quietly.

“Yeah, I kinda feel like I need to, Mike.”

He paused for a moment. “I understand,” Mike said as I closed the door. The whole family met me at the door.

“Mike told me,” Karen said as I closed the front door behind me. “Are you OK?”

“Yeah, I’ll be all right. The burial will start around four. I’m going.”

“We all are, if that’s all right, Rick,” Libby said.

“Sure. That’s fine. We should have someone here to keep an eye on the place though,” I said.

“I’ll stay,” Alan said. “It’s been pretty quiet the last couple weeks."

“C’mon. Let’s get you cleaned up,” Karen said. “And you kids, you, too. Get out of those work clothes and put something nice on.”

“I’ll get cleaned up a bit, but…honey I’m helping to dig the grave,” I said.

“They don’t have a backhoe?”

“Guess not. They’re digging it by hand.”

“That’s how we used to do it, too,” Grace said. “Rick, I’m terribly sorry for all of this,” she said.

“Thanks, Mom. You know the story though,” I said.

“I suppose we all do,” Ron said.

"The thing is, I don't know how I'm supposed to feel about Joe's death. 'Sad' that he wasted his life and his talents, 'Sad' that I don't think he was saved, 'relieved' that he will no longer cause harm." That silenced everyone. "Better get moving..... Carl, would you go get a couple shovels, please?"

"Sure, Dad," he said as he gave me a hug. He was almost my height now.

"And some gloves. And there is a flat bladed spade we use to cut the sod. Grab that, too."

"Got it. Don't worry about it."

The rest of the family went off to get ready to go to the hurried funeral, and gave me some space for a while.

I heard flute music coming from Kelly's room a few minutes later. 'Amazing Grace', followed by 'Eternal Father, Strong to Save'--the Navy hymn, played perfectly, and mournfully slow. I remembered the first time that Kelly gave a recital to the family, with our cousins and elderly Aunt and Uncle there, and Joe, drunk but for a change not being offensive. He gave her high praise for her music, and this song in particular. I was surprised that she remembered his comments. She had picked it on her own and learned the music from a hymnal, after hearing it in the movie 'Titanic.'

'A fine way to spend your fourteenth birthday, dear daughter. Playing a funeral dirge,' I thought as the sky grew darker. 'A fine way.'

44

Wednesday evening,
May Seventeenth

Kelly's birthday party was a welcome chance to take a break from mourning, and celebrate life. The deaths of two of my brothers, leaving three of us (or less—since I hadn't heard from either Alex or Jack for too long) hit me harder than I showed on the outside. I think it's an Irish thing to hold such grief inside, and only let it out a bit at a time. I think that it has also colored the way I am, and perhaps not in a good way.

Dinner was well attended, and will be, even in the circumstances, a memory that I will hold dear for the long haul ahead. Our guests included of course the Martins and Bauers, Joe and Joan Pauliano, Dan Grant from over the fence for a quick bite and then he was gone again (he was now bunking at Modern Electric's offices and was on call this night), Ellen MacDonald and Aaron Watters. Aaron and Ellen told Karen and I quietly that they didn't want to upstage Kelly on her special day—they were engaged and would marry in June.

Alan and Ron were in charge of grilling up dinner—newly ground beef from one of the barter stores' clientele.

"Beat's chicken," Carl said. "There's only so many things you can do with it. And Mom and Aunt Mary and Libby have done them all," he told me as we watched Alan flip a burger, cooking over the charcoal barbeque. I think we were there as much for the aroma as for the meat.

"You obviously have not yet had chicken chili," Alan replied, focusing on his work.

"No," Carl said as he looked at me with something approaching the word 'ick'.

"Until you have, you have nothing to complain about."

The weather was very nice for a break, the dark band of clouds had blown through, leaving it a little breezy but clear. We had about an hour of daylight left, and I had some chores to attend to prior to dinner.

The menu, other than burgers on fresh wheat buns, included cows' milk (!!), fresh and ice-cold. (Again from another of our barter folk, basically what started as a hobby-level dairy was now expanding to fill the market, using scrounged equipment to pasteurize the milk, on order. The science of the dairy is almost a lost art, I've discovered.) No French fries were to be had until our new crop came in and aged, so we made do with thin hash-browns and fried onions. And for the adults, home made beer. I had a six–pack of beer from before the Domino stashed away, and that was 'it' for pre-War bottled beer. The kids had their first experience with homemade ginger root beer, which is a far cry from anything sold in a store for the past thirty years. Our kids loved it; the Martins preferred to stick with milk. (I couldn't blame either of them).

The cake, itself a work of art, was a scratch chocolate layer cake with chocolate frosting. (My mouth watered when I looked at it. How odd!)

After the singing, and the extinguishing of far more than 14 candles (Carl used trick candles that flat out would NOT go out when Kelly blew on them), Karen dished up the cake to the birthday girl and our guests. A second sheet cake appeared from the kitchen, to take care of the rest of us.

Her presents, with Sarah's help, delighted her. I explained to her that Sarah had found the collected leather-bound set of Kipling at her home, and that we'd worked out a trade for them. Her gifts included a watercolor sketch pad and watercolor pencils that I'd salvaged from my office, still in its shrink-wrap, the camel-hair brushes that I'd all but worn the handles off of in my early days as a painter (years back); some ancient sheet music that Carl had discovered in my grandparents belongings in the barn; new shoes, a blouse and jacket, and Kelly-sized deer-skin gloves that were hand-made by one of the barter folk. The shoes were most welcome, her 'work' shoes were all but held together now with duct-tape, and we hadn't found new or used ones in her size for sale or trade. Tough thing to find in a post-apocalyptic world, shoes.

The biggest box, brought out by Aaron and Ellen after the last of the birthday gifts was opened, was for both Kelly and Carl; Aaron knowing that Carl's birthday was only a few weeks ahead as well. I was wondering what they could have found the kids.

"Go ahead you two, open it up," Ellen said. "Mind the paper though, we'll want to save it."

"Thank you, ma'am," Carl said with proper respect.

He and Kelly both took out their little Leatherman tools and carefully cut the tape from the box. Under the wrapping, a plain cardboard box, that held what looked like an old Samsonite typewriter sized case.

"Careful now," Aaron said. "It's a little fragile."

Carl and Kelly both lifted the case up to the dining room table, where Kelly took the honors of opening it up. I was around the backside of the case, so I could see the look on her face, for whatever was inside the case.

"It's a radio!" Kelly said.

"Not just any radio," Carl said. "It's Army," he said as he studied the case in more detail. John and Marie were studying the radio as well, and Marie picked up the manual for the big tube machine.

"Aaron, you shouldn't have," Karen said. "This is far too valuable."

I moved around to see the front of the radio.

"I have a number of them. I know that you kids were interested in keeping in touch, and helped your folks quite a bit when the…well, when it hit the fan. This one's good to go, and I'd like to show you all how to use it."

"We'd love that," Kelly said, giving Aaron and then Ellen, a big hug.

"Where did you find this?" I asked, not yet seeing the radio in detail.

"You'll never believe me," he said.

"Try me," I said. "Let's go out on the porch." We went outside to continue our conversation.

"Fifteen years ago, they—the armed forces—quit using them. They were throwing them out by the pallet load. I got two pallets of working radios, two pallets and then some of parts. Not all were working, but I managed to get most of them up and running again. I've been restoring them and selling them off over the years. Got to the point where having fourteen of them—too good to sell I told myself-- really didn't make much sense anymore. I was planning on selling them all off, except for a couple, by the end of the year. Then we had the quake, and here we are."

"What is it? I mean, what can you tell me about it?"

"These used to be used by Army units from the sixties through the eighties. This is a Collins KWM-2A, and this setup includes a 'noise blanker', a mobile mount for using on the road, its' own power supply and the Samsonite case. There's another box of stuff I have for it at the house, including a microphone and the MM-2…sorry, that's a headphone/mic setup. I've got a TD-1 antenna— that's basically a steel tape antenna that's calibrated in meters, decimeters and centimeters in a rollout case. Let's you set up on the fly. The antenna tape has nylon loops on it so you can suspend it from trees or poles or whatever. Most of the stuff was brand new still, still in their original cases."

"These had to cost a fortune, pre-Domino," I said as Alan came out on the porch with us.

"Well, they were a bit of a collector's item, sure. The last one I sold on eBay, a little nicer than this one, sold for a little shy of fifteen hundred. But we actually need them now for real work, not just fun. Besides that, I think the younger generation ought to know how to work this stuff."

"True enough," Alan said. "We'll all need to know this stuff."

"I'm the man for it. I know these things inside and out. Good thing, since in a year or so, I'll be working on them blind."

"There isn't anything that can be done?"

"Nope," he said, staring at the beautybush, now coming into bloom, in the front yard. "Meds came from Florida. They were the only things that would keep it in check. Progressive deterioration of the retina. It's already started to get worse."

"I'm very sorry," I said.

"I'll be OK. Got Ellen to keep me out of trouble now. That woman is a prize."

"I know the type. I'm married to one."

"Yes, you are. Best remember that," he said with a wry grin.

"Thanks for selling us those AR's," I said. "We need to get trained on them. And the kids, too."

"You are most welcome. And yes, you do need to get up to a proficiency level that most civilians are not accustomed to. We're not six months into this yet, and I do not recognize my country."

"Yeah. We know what you mean," Alan said.

"So how are you planning to get up to marksman-level?" Aaron asked.

"You'll love this," Alan interjected, looking at me.

"I'm going to suggest that all adults over the age of 15 complete mandatory weapons training as part of a civilian militia."

"...being necessary to the security of a free state," Aaron said, quoting the Second Amendment.

"Precisely," I said.

"And you think our Army friends will allow that?"

"I think that they would be more receptive to it now than on January thirteenth," I replied. "They are not the same Army that they were then. The Forty-First, for example, isn't anything like it was before the war."

"Monterrey," he said, knowingly.

"How did you hear that? It's not been publicized as far as I've heard."

"The blessings and curses of shortwave radio. Sometimes you hear things that you'd rather not," he said, and then paused. "So it's true. We lost a lot of good men and women down there."

"And then we retaliated. Yes."

"With thermobaric weapons. Daisy-cutters."

"Yep."

"I saw them in 'Nam. Once. God help the poor bastards on the ground, regardless of who they were. The VC that I saw...well, you couldn't really tell they were once people."

"So I've heard," I said as Karen came out onto the porch.

"Hey you men, c'mon back inside. Sarah's about ready to tell her story. Mary and the little ones are heading home, Alan. She said not to stay up too late."

"That won't be a problem. I'm about thrashed right now," he said.

We went back inside, where the kids (as usual, pre-Domino) were piled on the couch and in the living room chairs. John sat next to Sarah with Kelly and Marie; Carl sat in one of the wing chairs. Grace had gone home with Mary and her grandchildren. We moved the oak ladder back chairs to the living room, me being careful not to get a splinter from the not-yet-repaired arm on my chair. A chunk of the dining room ceiling had neatly snapped the inch-thick oak arm, now held together with a wrap of newspaper and duct tape. In my abundant spare time, I'd have to dig out the wood glue and clamps, and do it properly.

Bozeman

"I used to live in a trailer with three roommates, a little northwest of the campus. It was cheap, and close to my jobs. I was working as a barista in the mornings, and weekends I worked cleaning houses. I made more money doing that than selling coffee."

"Anyway, when the quake hit here and Rainier went off, we got a ton of refugees right after the quake. People that were heading into Washington and Idaho that were on the road, and suddenly couldn't get there anymore. The community put them up, people camped out in every hotel and gym and school they could find. Things stayed pretty cool until the economy really started to go. I lost my jobs—all of them—inside of about three days. When the stock market dropped by half, that was the end of normal. What was that, three days after the quake?"

"Yeah. The seventeenth," I replied.

"Runs at the stores started the next day. We had enough for a week or two, basically stuff that we never really wanted to eat but had around anyway. My two roommates left the next day, heading for home. Kammie was from Cheyenne, and her dad told her to get home. Micki was from Great Falls—her Mom was in the Air Force, and her dad was a cop. They both told me to get out of town. I didn't know why, I thought things would be OK."

"By the end of the first week, I could see I was wrong. Really wrong. My car was stolen. It was a crappy Dodge Colt, but it had a full tank of gas, and gas was seven bucks a gallon by then. I had my mountain bike and my road bike inside the trailer, next to my bed. I was pretty scared, because there were people robbing people for gas money to get out of town, or whatever. The campus cops warned people that looters would be shot on sight."

"How was your power situation?" Alan asked.

"Good then, natural gas, too, so I had heat. I really was doing OK at first. I ended up with a couple of other people that I knew from my classes there, at my trailer. We were in a couple of the health-clinic classes. They lived too far away to try to make it out. Alabama and New York."

"What did you have to eat?" Kelly asked.

"We stretched out our food to last until early February. There was nothing in the stores after the first week or so, but there were some public centers where food was being distributed. By the end of February though, those were pretty much gone, too. The normal food anyway, canned stuff. After that, we had corn, wheat, mostly grains, and most people didn't know what to do with them. Lots of beets and potatoes though. We did OK…we were scared though. None of us could shoot, none of us had ever owned a gun or even held one. In early February, about the time we ran out of our own food, the University told us that for our own safety, we should move inside their perimeter, where the National Guard and ROTC could make sure we were safe. That was probably the smartest thing we could have done. Power failed the next day, and then we got a cold spell that would've killed us for sure. It was thirty-five below and we had fifty mile-per-hour winds."

"What did you do with your time?" Karen asked.

"When we were still in the trailer, we took turns keeping an eye on some of the old folks in the trailer park. They moved out though before we did, about the same time that my grandparents sent me a letter from Sun City. They have a winter place down there. They left here right after the quake, and wrote me from there when they got there. That was the last I heard from them. After the elderly had been moved out of our neighborhood, we didn't have much to do. I volunteered at one of the health clinics, the other two girls worked at the daycare center. The flu hit there about the third week of February," she said, looking down at the scarred coffee table.

I could tell by the look that she'd seen far too much for her age. She looked at Karen and I before she went on, as if to ask permission. "It's OK," Karen said. "You can go on."

"It was bad. We lost a lot of people. Both of my roommates died in three days. I never got sick. And I don't know why."

"It's OK, Sarah," John said. "It happened that way, here, too."

"They ended up doubling the size of Sunset Hills Cemetery. It was awful."

"You don't need to talk about that anymore, unless you want to," Libby said. "We're all too familiar with cemeteries."

"Mr. Drummond, I'm sorry about your brothers. Karen told me," she said softly.

"Thanks, Sarah. I appreciate your care. I'm afraid we've all lost someone in this, and may lose more before it's over."

"Yeah."

"So what made you decide to leave Bozeman?" Ron asked, leaning forward in his chair, hands clasped.

"There wasn't anything for me there anymore. Everyone I knew had died. The University was closed, the professors that taught my classes were either gone or dead. I decided to come home when the weather got better. So I did."

"How long did it take?"

"Three times longer than I thought it would," she said with a little humor, the change of subject doing her some good. "I never thought that four hundred miles would take me three weeks. I used to drive it in six hours."

"Three weeks? That seems long even to me," Alan said. "And I'm not a hiker."

"I biked part of it on top of everything else."

"And it still took you that long?"

"Yeah. The first few miles were easy. Got on the interstate and biked to Three Forks, with one flat tire on the mountain bike. That was about thirty miles, and I was thrashed. I spent the night at the state park there, with a bunch of other people—and an Army unit. I had a trailer behind the bike with most of my gear. I spent a second night at Pipestone Hot Springs, and planned on making the next day to Butte. Someone decided to start shooting at me when I was on the downhill run into town. Made it to Butte with four bullet holes in the trailer, and one scarred up frame. I hid until after dark, got my bike back out of the brush, and went into and through Butte in the dark. Things looked worse there. No power. Cars all over the place, some burned. I planned on staying there and I'm glad I didn't. I rode for hours after that, against the wind. I spent the night on the far side of Deer Lodge, and the next day, too. I left after dark, and made it almost to Drummond that night. Then the snow hit, and I was stuck. I camped in the hills above Drummond for four days to rest up. Are you any relation to whoever named that town?"

"Not that I know of," I said.

"Oh. Well back to the trip. I had fifteen inches of snow on the ground the first night, out in the clear area. I figured it'd be hopeless to try to ride in that. I camped out until it melted down some, and then decided to travel mostly at night. I heard lots of deer rifles and shotguns in the daytime. I figured guys were out hunting."

"Probably right," Ron said.

"I had a big decision to make. Try to make it through Missoula, or bypass it. The interstate was the easiest way to get through, but I was afraid of it, at least in daylight. I managed to get to the outskirts in the dark, and the Guard stopped me. I never even saw them. They had night-vision on."

"I'd'a peed my pants," Libby said.

"I nearly did," Sarah replied, laughing.

"We've had a little experience with night vision ourselves," Ron said. "Talk about an unfair advantage."

"Well these guys had some sort of infra-red thing too. They saw me coming a mile away."

"Yep," I said. "Been there!"

"I stopped when they ordered me to, I thought I was dead. They were really nice though and put me up in a shelter for as long as I wanted to stay. The weather turned to junk a couple days later, and I ended up staying three days."

"Why didn't you stay?" Karen asked.

"I didn't see the point. There wasn't anything there for me. At least here, there is something. Of course at that point, I wasn't sure that Spokane would still be here when I arrived."

"True enough," Carl added. "What did you eat on the trip back?"

"I had some dried food and some backpacking food that the shelter was giving out. They gave me a week's worth when I left. I didn't have a stove though, so one of the guys showed me how to make a cook stove out of a couple of Coke cans and alcohol. Worked great."

"So after Missoula?" Libby asked. "Sorry, you've got me on the edge of my seat."

"I made it to St. Regis the next day, that one hurt. Seventy miles on the bike, and three flat tires. I saw a few other people on bikes, too though, so it was nice to ride with them. That's where I met Guillermo. He's the one who attacked me."

"He was biking?"

"Yeah. He had a road bike and panniers. We rode from St. Regis to Cataldo. The passes—Lookout and Fourth-of-July—were a mess. Rockslides and downed overpasses. That took two days. The rail lines weren't much better. I ended up dumping the trailer at Lookout and just using the backpack from there on in. My bike broke down outside of Cataldo, and I was on foot from there. Guillermo walked with me. We walked from there all the way home. That took a couple of days. Not too much trouble, other than the wild dogs."

"And then he came after you."

"Not right away. I got home, found some of Grandpa's food out in his camper, gave it to him and sent him on his way. He said he was going down to Pasco to find his family. I did some work on the house for a few days and got the garden started. Then he came after me."

"Sounds like you did a number on him."

"He got what he had coming. I thought he was my friend. Turned out I was wrong."

"So," I asked, "You never knew about the war going nuclear? You were never in a shelter?"

"No. It was over before I got word. You guys spent that time in a shelter?"

"Yeah. Not something we want to repeat, either," I said.

"Amen." Ron added. "No offense."

"None taken," I added. "Sarah, welcome home. You've had an adventure as well. Ours was a little different as I'm sure you've heard. What are your plans now?"

"Well, I have work at the clinic from six to noon six days a week and house calls from one 'til four. Other than that, I don't really know."

"That's a good start. Maybe we can get you hooked up with some of the County Health folks, and get some more training for you. From what I hear, you're a natural."

She blushed at that. "Thanks. I never thought that I'd end up working here though. I wanted to go abroad."

"You're a victim of circumstance," Libby said. "We all are."

Our guests left around nine-thirty, and John escorted Sarah home on my old mountain bike. I heard him bring it back and park it by the back porch a few minutes later than I thought he would have. 'Good for you, John,' I thought.

Karen and I finished up the dishes and I headed upstairs as she sent the dogs out for their evening business. I was getting ready for bed and flipped on the radio as I brushed my teeth, and in my mind went over the list of things that we were running out of. The list was getting longer.

"This is KLXY News, it is ten o'clock, Pacific Daylight Time."

"Pacific Northwest Command has announced that the State of Washington will headquarter a new civilian government center in Walla Walla, at the site of the Army's new Fort Walla Walla. The civilian government, including a new civilian Governor and representatives, should be seated by the end of September."

"In other governmental news, Spokane County will be establishing a new governmental structure based on the County's townships, with elected representatives from each historic township working with the current County Administrator, Walter Ackerman, in the reconstruction efforts in the County. The Township Board will eventually replace the handpicked Recovery Board later this summer. Forty-eight Townsmen positions are available to legal citizens of the county who reside in their respective township. Candidate registration forms will be available at community centers and post offices on or after June first."

"In national news, the President speaking from Denver today, announced that representatives of the Northeastern states who are calling for open rebellion against the Federal government will be charged under the Sedition Act, passed last week by the Acting Congress. New York representatives responded by calling for the impeachment of the President and Vice President on the basis that

the Administration knew of the threat posed by illegal immigrants over the past eight years, and did nothing to stem the flow, eventually triggering the Mexican War. The Speaker of the House, upon hearing the call for impeachment, made this reply on C-SPAN: "Perhaps the congressmen and women in question should examine their voting records over their careers, because to a single individual, all of those calling for the impeachment had voted to spend Federal funds on programs that directly benefited the illegal alien population, and by such benefit, encouraged more illegals to enter the country!! I am guilty of this myself, and I'm as responsible for that decision as those administrations, both Democrat and Republican, that allowed this situation to happen over the past several decades. This is a contemptible statement made by contemptible people, who are too afraid to say these things outside of their home districts." The Democratic Party leadership declined to comment on either the calls for impeachment or the response by the Speaker. CNN news sources report that the minority leadership structure has all but collapsed. Eleven congressmen from both parties have switched their allegiance within the last three days to the Constitution party, throwing more confusion into both sides of the aisle."

"From the CDC's morning press conference, the recent outbreak of influenza, now called Guangdong H2, has a longer incubation period than originally thought, up to twenty-one days after exposure to a carrier or live virus. Symptoms of the virus include 'normal' flu symptoms lasting several days, followed by a brief recovery. The victims are then hit by high fever and life-threatening infections from any source, essentially a complete collapse of the immune system. The CDC has stated that in association with the Army, they are attempting to find a vaccine or treatment for the disease, which so far has resisted all treatment attempts in victims. The CDC has ordered that pandemic areas remain quarantined until further notice. These areas include approximately forty percent of the Eastern Seaboard, half of California, and most of the Gulf Coast and Great Lakes states."

A public service announcement for maintaining clean water came on, followed by a second for the prevention of the spread of diseases. I'd heard the first before, since February. The second was new to me.

"Weather for tomorrow, May eighteenth, the anniversary of the Mount St. Helens eruption in nineteen-eighty, is expected to be clear and warm, with overnight lows of forty-nine degrees, and highs in the mid-seventies. A cold front is expected to arrive late tomorrow afternoon from the southwest, bringing strong sustained winds of thirty to forty miles per hour with gusts of up to sixty miles per our in exposed areas. Severe dust and ash contamination is expected by three p.m., and the State Patrol has ordered all roads closed and an early curfew in place effective at two p.m. tomorrow afternoon. Winds are expected to continue through Friday. A public service announcement is expected to be made by eight a.m. Friday morning regarding the storm. Residents should make all

The national anthem played, and then static.

"What's up?" Karen asked, coming into the bedroom after cleaning up the kitchen.

"Big dust storm tomorrow afternoon and night, and maybe Friday, too. Batten down the hatches. Could be bad. State Patrol's ordered an early curfew, and they're telling us to plan for the power going out, among other things."

"Great. I just dusted, too."

"See? That's what you get."

45

Thursday,
May Eighteenth

The daylight beckoned me to get out of bed, and so far I was successfully resisting. Even the dogs were still sleeping. This day, like so many others before, I woke too early, and could not get back to sleep. It was nice and warm here, and the house was a little chilly.

At twenty-five after five, another aftershock rattled the house. Karen woke instantly, as did the dogs, growling and looking around the bedroom frantically. Within a few seconds, the shaking and the noise had stopped.

"Damn," Karen said, using a swear word that I'd rarely heard her say in all our years of marriage. "I was having a good dream, too."

"Like?"

"We were shopping in Lahaina. The kids were little. We were at that condo. And 'Baby Beach.'"

I remembered back to the vacation, the better part of fifteen years before. "Yeah. That was fun," I reminisced. "And mai-tais every afternoon."

"Mmmm."

"I'm going to get up. I've been awake for an hour."

"What's wrong?"

"Nothing, I just can't sleep like I used to."

"Three hours hoeing will take care of that problem. Or a few hours weeding carrots."

"Yeah, I'll bet."

"I'm sleeping in until six-thirty."

"You go, girl."

I dug out some clean clothes, showered and headed downstairs. Breakfast today was cold milk (I still couldn't believe it as I poured a small glass) with a homemade granola mix, complete with raisins and nuts. The English walnuts were brought home from a house down the street last fall, after the owners were forced to sell as the real estate bubble caught up with them with words to send a chill through the hearts of those buying more house than they could afford: Balloon Payment. I'd love to have that tree in my yard, as we gathered nearly a hundred and fifty pounds of nuts from that one tree.

The six o'clock news was a few moments away as I opened up the dining room curtains, re-hung for the first time since January.

"It is six o'clock a.m., Pacific Daylight Time. This is KDA Spokane, where the temperature is forty-five degrees. A severe dust storm warning is in effect for this afternoon, projected to begin in our area by one to two o'clock p.m. All public meetings and public schools are closed today, although community centers will remain open. A weather statement will follow at the bottom of the hour."

"In news gathered overnight from several sources," the announcer stated, which we had translated as 'collected through multiple shortwave broadcasts', *"we have learned that the military is establishing permanent territorial government in the Mexican territory at Ensenada. Military authorities are at this time reviewing applications for United States Territorial Citizenship for residents of the former Mexican-ruled lands. Military analysts state that more than seven hundred thousand Chinese soldiers were present in Mexico prior to the onset of the war. There is no estimate on current surviving Chinese forces in the former Mexican nation, or in the Mexico City protectorate."*

'Protectorate?' I thought. 'What the heck does that mean?'

"The United States Geological Survey reports that two major volcanic eruptions are taking place at this time, including the ongoing eruptions at the Popocatepetl volcano southeast of Mexico City and both the Kronotsky volcano and Uzon Caldera on the Kamchatka Peninsula on Russia's East Coast. The Russian eruptions began in the early morning hours of May 16th, with an ash-plume that has covered most of Alaska and western Canada, and is now beginning to dip down into the lower forty-eight states. The USGS has stated that the explosion at Kronotsky was heard more than a thousand miles away, and seismic readings were noticed across all working monitoring stations around the

world. The explosive nature of the Kronotsky Uzon eruption is expected to result in widespread effects on our climate over the next twelve to thirty-six months, with estimates of up to fifteen cubic miles of ejecta blasted into the atmosphere by midnight tonight, Pacific Daylight Time. For comparison's sake, Mt. St. Helens ejected just six tenths of a cubic mile of ash into the air in the nineteen-eighty eruption, and January's eruption at Mt. Rainier sent approximately three cubic miles of ejecta into the air. Tidal effects of the blast were noticed across the Pacific Basin, and according to the U.S. Navy, and reports of widespread devastation from the blast zone have been noted. Local news reporters are at this time attempting to contact the University of Washington climatologists in this area and at the UW Wenatchee campus and at WSU Pullman for an opinion on effects to worldwide climate conditions."

I stared at the radio for a moment. "Fifteen cubic MILES?" I said aloud to myself, wondering back into my memory. Which volcano was it? Krakatoa? Tambora? that ejected many cubic miles into the air, much into the stratosphere, and wiped out the summer for a year or three. A chill ran down my spine as I remembered the stories of the frost each month of the year, the killing frosts…of the severity of the winters. Frosts in the American Northeast that changed the face of the country at that time, when settlers gave up on the northern states and headed for the Ohio Valley. How much had they erupted compared to this one? These two—plus Rainier's…and however many Shasta had sent up. An announcement about our former Commissioner brought me back to the here-and-now.

"…Williams, charged with conspiracy and murder among a long list of charges. His trial is scheduled to begin tomorrow morning at an undisclosed location. The trial will be held under military authority, although it is commonly understood that Williams has admitted to the charges when faced with overwhelming evidence. KDA will be present in the courtroom and will report on proceedings as appropriate throughout the trial."

"That oughta be short and sweet," I said to myself in the mirror as I put in one of my contact lenses. "Followed by a long drop on a short rope."

Karen had heard the broadcast too, giving up on trying to sleep and now dressing to take the dogs out for their morning run. We talked about the implications of the report while she ate, and I waited for my tea to cool. We were both concerned with the potential—no, the reality—of a too-short growing season…this year, next year, and the year after that. Worsening weather. Harder and longer winters. Shorter, cooler summers. Probably more rain. Definitely more snow. Damn.

Once again I worked on preparing a damnable list. Stuff to do today, before the storm. I struggled to remember back a year, wondering if my—more correctly—our lives were as often disrupted by these minor emergencies then, as they were now. I supposed 'not', because now our lives depended on taking care of things like making sure we kept our crops alive, our greenhouses intact. A year ago, we were busy in living busy lives, not necessarily fulfilling, but busy. A year ago, a loss of the corn or tomatoes meant that we'd have to buy an inferior product at the store. The loss of our chicken flock to raccoons meant we'd have to buy eggs from Safeway. The barn was home to a pet rabbit only, not a bunch of 'meat' rabbits which I would one day have to kill. If the thin thread of our comforts—no, our survival—depended on one thing, it was food. This storm, and the great potential for dramatic change in the climate, threatened that thread.

For the early morning, Carl, John and I worked on securing the greenhouses as Ron and Alan worked the store, which was experiencing a typical 'run' on things, even though there was really precious little in the way of 'preps' that the store had that people didn't already have…I suppose it was a psychological thing. 'Storms a'comin. Best get ready.'

We charged up all of our batteries (some now starting to fail to hold a charge), made sure that the house was ready to close up and seal with whatever we could lay our hands on, and stored water. When the power went down, so did our water, which we'd learned the hard way, after the Domino.

In mid-morning, Carl collected refuse for his trip across the street. What little 'refuse' we had generated since the Domino consisted primarily of pre-wrapped food wrapping, and items that truly had no other re-useable functions. The quake generated enough debris in and of itself. When we were working on getting the house back in shape, we thought for about a half a minute about dumping the small mountain of plaster taken out of the house in the garden or burying it, and then discarded that idea because of the lead-based paint that was certainly in the many layers of paint applied prior to our remodel work starting in eighty-six. We finally elected to move the pile of contaminated plaster across the street to the burned-out hole of the Long's house, which would have to be excavated anyway, if a home were ever to be rebuilt there, or filled in, if not.

We all realized how much 'stuff' we'd been used to in 'normal' life. Clean clothes every day, laundry every week or so, plus or minus, meant a large pile of clothing per person, that changed seasonally and with fashion, of course. After the quake, we'd reduced our 'normal' attire to clean underclothing, and wearing coveralls, overalls, bibs or whatever over our daily wear to keep them cleaner, mostly because until the water and power were restored, washing clothing was at best difficult. This dramatically decreased our need for lots of clothing on a daily basis, and substantially prolonged the lifespan of most of our clothes. I guess I never thought much about the 'lint' in the lint screen on the dryer, it was just 'lint'. In fact, it was our clothes, bit by bit, wearing out as much as it did when kneeling in the garden or moving firewood. Our outerwear, coats, and overalls and such, paid the heavier price with dirt and grime. After a few weeks into the 'new' life we were in though, we'd pretty much got used it. It also meant that we could 'treat' ourselves to 'new' clothes once in awhile, and wear them until we couldn't stand to any longer, or until the clothes could stand on their own, whichever came first. Once we had fairly regular water and power, we managed to maintain a higher level of cleanliness, but still managed to wear coveralls or overalls to preserve our jeans and shirts. (Carl was unimpressed at first with this situation, until it was his turn to handle laundry. Amazing how fast he reformed.)

The recycling efforts within the confines of the barn, and later in our respective homes, consisted of saving anything that we couldn't find a use for. Metal cans from store-bought canned goods, paper, boxes, foil re-used until it couldn't be any longer. Extreme care in opening our home-canned quarts and pints allowed us the chance to reuse the 'flats' for the canning jars, although that was never a recommendation from the manufacturers (my late mother did this a few times when I was a kid, and money tight though. Didn't kill us then....)

By eleven, things were pretty well set for the storm. I had the kids back on garden duty, today we were trying to get as much of our acreage watered before the storm, with an hour or so of irrigation water applied to the large fields. Before the quake, it would have been simple (but a little expensive) to automate the entire operation, with fairly large control valves to operate the irrigation automatically. A commercial type controller, some low voltage wire, and the whole block could've been irrigated from one spot. I was thinking about 'salvaging' a commercial-size irrigation controller and some good-sized solenoid-operated control valves from some abandoned building somewhere, to help ease the hose dragging. In my abundant spare time, I reminded myself. Kelly and Marie were working on moving the sprinkler heads and hoses on the 'middle' acreage; Carl and John were working the 'north' and 'south' fields respectively. The two big greenhouses were automated, as long as we had power.

The seeded corn plants were now up and reaching three to four inches out of the brown soil; the wheat looking like thick-bladed grass. The thin blue-green shafts of the onions growing in their patch, as were radishes, carrots, beets, Swiss chard. Some of the potatoes were just coming up, in their blocks of the field. The burners that we used to ward off the frost a few weeks before we had scheduled to move out of the fields to summer storage. The burn barrels and their wood supplies were getting in our way as we worked the fields. Not only would we keep them there, we'd now, with the weather likely to go downhill, add more barrels and have to watch the temperature more often. Of course, if we

471

had unseasonably heavy rain, we were pretty well screwed no matter what the temperatures did.

Karen and Mary were keeping an eye on Grace, who had been having more issues with her memory. We had all noticed a marked decline in her ability to remember what she'd told us, and was argumentative when she was told we'd already heard the story. I wondered how that would play out in the coming weeks and months. 'Not well,' was all I could come up with.

We'd need more wood and soon, to season. Not just our families, but everybody. I decided to snag Carl and go look over Sarah's house, to see how it would fare the winter. I let Karen know that Carl and I were headed up to Sarah's on an errand before we left, hoping not to repeat my earlier misadventures in going places unannounced. We biked up the road on our mountain bikes, armed as usual now. Carl had my 870 Express; I had the little twelve-gauge 'blaster' as the kids called it, and my Colt.

Sarah's little black dog, "Coal", was in the fenced yard, sleeping until it heard us coming. First it barked an alert, and then realized it was 'friends' come to see him. He then decided that playing with a tennis ball was more fun than barking. He'd latched on to her when she passed through Greenacres on her way back home, and never left her side voluntarily.

"What did you want to look at? The house is all locked up."

"I couldn't remember if the place had a fireplace. If she doesn't and a woodstove or an insert, and if it isn't located about in the center of the house, she won't be able to heat it in the winter."

"There's a chimney, not very big though."

"Oil or gas furnace," I said, looking at the chimney on the north wall of the house. The chimney was a stack of pre-cast concrete blocks, cracked horizontally in a couple of locations, and missing part of it's top. "That's what I was afraid of. This isn't a fireplace. It's either a gas or oil furnace. Oil fill is over there," I said, pointing to a pair of iron pipes extending up from the basement. "No meter, so it's still oil heat."

"So she'll freeze?"

"Yeah. If she stays here. No gas, no oil, or not much oil. And she has damage to the chimney, meaning air leaks which could kill her if she does light up the furnace. Carbon monoxide," I said as I looked around the rest of the house. "And, a great big crack in the foundation."

"Now what?"

"Let's see if we can convince her to move to more suitable quarters," I said. "I need you to check on the house two doors north of Alan's place...the other side of Dan's place. It's boarded up, but I know that it has a woodstove in it, a big Schrader. Make a list of what you think it's going to need—windows, how much wall damage, foundation cracks, and look over the chimney stack. Here's a pad of paper," I said, "and here's my little flashlight," I said as I fished out my mini-maglight.

"You gonna let Mom know I'm over there?"

"I'll give you the radio. I'll head back to the house and get the car, and go over to the community center for a few minutes. I've got to meet Kevin Miller at the center, and I want to talk to Sarah about all this of course. Don't go giving a lot of detail remember, over the FRS."

"K."

"Meet me back home in an hour. We still have stuff to do before the storm hits."

"K. Be careful."

"You, too. Thanks bud."

Carl headed west, and then south, down the street toward Alan's and the Martins' houses, radioing Karen along the way. I headed south, back down our street.

Mary responded on the FRS, and I told her to pass on to Karen that I was heading over to the community center for a few minutes. Karen was in the middle of a lesson with Mark and Rachel, on the proper way to roll out dough. She was too messy to take the radio herself. I promised I wouldn't be long.

I almost took my bike, but instead drove my old Falcon van, knowing that its battery could use the charge. It had been sitting more and more lately, with few places to drive to, and the mileage not being all that great anyway. I remembered to move my 'official business' pass to the Falcon before I left.

The store was busy, with a solid dozen bikes and bike trailers at the store, and I noticed Eric Moore's farm truck. He must've had a delivery.

I waved at the three Army sentries at the gas pumps, and received a nod back. The spaces between the curbs and the asphalt I noticed were beginning to sprout weeds and tree seedlings. I wondered if, in a few years, if the road would be visible at all?

The community center was more crowded with folks than I thought it should be. There was a fairly long line waiting to get into the clinic, today staffed by two general practitioners and two dentists. I reminded myself to ask about an orthodontist. Both Carl and Kelly had braces, and obviously hadn't had any work done on their hardware since before the quake. Fortunately for them, they were near the end of their programs. They had each inherited my crooked teeth--now, like mine, they were 'straight' and as an Englishman had once told me, indicative of my nationality. 'Americans always have straight teeth.' He said that in a condescending tone. I also noticed at the time, that he didn't smile. I didn't wonder why.

I walked past the clinic entry, giving my 'hellos' to a number of our store folks, and people that I knew now as nodding acquaintances. I knocked on Kevin Millers' doorjamb, and he peered at me from the computer monitor on his desk.

"C'mon in, Rick. Got some candidates for you. Close the door, if you don't mind."

"Sure thing," I said as I came into his office.

"I've got eleven possibles. You said you had six houses?"

"Well, five now. Sarah Woodbridge is going to need to move. She doesn't know that yet, but her house is heated with fuel oil. That's obviously not going to cut it for long come winter."

"That's a fact. Any idea how much oil she's got?"

"No, the tank is in the basement. Why?"

"This building is heated with oil. We need all we can get for the winter. Heating oil is a pretty low priority right now."

"Won't be come September."

"Right. I'm trying to get somebody to notice that," Kevin said, leaning back in his chair.

"I'll pass it up the food chain."

"Here's your list. I've interviewed all of them, casually. They seem to be good eggs."

"Your name isn't on the list?" I said as I looked it over. "I thought you might be interested in the house at seventeen-oh-one."

"Tempting, yes. I looked at it with an Army sergeant. I think my equipment is about the same, and I've already moved it once. I like the place I'm at now, so I'll stay. That basement must've been impressive before they emptied it all out. I saw the collection report."

"It was. Whole lotta stuff in there."

"Belongs to the Army now. I understand they took it all, lock stock and barrel."

"Not quite true. All the canned foods were distributed. The bulk grains are still there—I don't think anybody figured out what to do with them. I'm sure the weapons lockers are empty now though. Garage still intact?"

"Yeah. The Army disabled the booby trap, collected the gasoline and diesel from the vehicles and tanks, and locked it back up."

"Nice."

"You thinking about the place yourself?" Kevin asked, one eyebrow raised.

"The tools are pretty intriguing, but I have my own shop, and I've been caretaking of two other places to the north and south of me. So far, I haven't needed anything that I didn't own before the quake. I think I'm pretty well set—for the moment at least."

"Well, one thing to keep in mind is that the machine tools at seventeen-oh-one aren't really limited to working on vehicles. The milling machine in particular. That's more of a specialty machine used for close tolerance work," 'if you get my drift,' he didn't say.

"Gunsmithing," I said for him.

"Yep," he said, a little more comfortable now that I'd broached the subject. "There is also a substantial amount of high quality alloy bar and rod stock, specialty parts and pre-built trigger sets over there that look a lot like a couple that I built for my Bushmaster. I don't think the Army grunts knew what they were looking at. The guy that lived there seemed to me a little over the top about it."

"I did the search of the house when collection was getting started. By my estimation, he had at least two years of food in the house. Never had a chance to use it though. We'll have to find the right fit for that particular house."

"Look over the list. I think you'll find one candidate that stands out."

"Who's that?" I asked.

"Randy Thompson."

I thought for a moment. "I know Randy, he's not into guns. He does all the other 'extreme' sports. He's going to set up a bike shop next door to our store."

"Sorry. Look at the file again...look at his new wife. She's the shooter. And the gunsmith."

I drew back a moment at that statement. "Really?"

"Yeah. As Darth Vader would have said, 'Impressive. Most impressive.' Her name is Anja."

"I'll take your word for it. I better get moving. Still a lot to do before the wind gets here."

"Yakima is already shut down, and it's heading into Moses Lake, according to the FEMA folks. Zero visibility with sustained winds of fifty miles per hour. Gust of ninety on Manastash Ridge."

"It's always bad on that stretch," I thought, remembering the road between Yakima and Ellensburg, and the University of Washington observatory up there. "I just hope it slows down enough to keep our corn upright and the greenhouses intact."

"Check in with me tomorrow. I can set up some face to face meetings with your choices, maybe as soon as Saturday. A couple of them are living in trailers or RV's."

"Thanks, Kevin. This means a lot to me."

"Remember me some eggs and a few laying hens and we're good."

"Will do," I said as I stood up. He had another appointment waiting, an accountant-looking fellow, carrying too many file-folders.

I made my way down the hall to the 'normal' clinic, looking for Sarah. She was over at the school though today, helping out with vaccinations provided by one of the general practitioners. The community center clinic today was transformed into a dental clinic, complete with chair, lighting, and…drills. Ugh.

At the school, the sign above the line read 'Tetanus Only.' Cuts and other miscellaneous injuries that we'd sustained in putting our houses back together could have easily resulted in a nasty, even fatal infection. The lucky happenstance that all of us were current on our immunizations saved us for the moment. I was told Sarah was on her lunch break in one of the boarded up classrooms that was unfit to use for schooling. All of the school paperwork, whiteboards, and furniture had been moved to other rooms, out of the 'clinic' wing. This was a break room for the visiting medical staff. Two cots in opposite corners allowed brief naps for the staff, when they were off duty. This particular medical center had operated more-or-less twenty-four seven for almost two months, as a way for this neighborhood to avoid bringing minor injuries or illnesses to Valley Hospital, which was dramatically overcrowded.

"Got a sec?" I asked Sarah, startling her. She was reading what looked like a medical textbook.

"Sure. Sorry Mr. Drummond. You startled me."

"Didn't mean to. A little light reading?"

"Not really. One of my supplemental textbooks from MSU. 'Where There Is No Doctor.'"

"I've got a copy. And the electronic version, too."

"Did you scan it?"

"No. Downloaded it off of the 'net. Back when we still had the internet."

"Would you get me a copy? It'd make searching for information a lot faster."

"I can do that. I think the community center's got a copy, but I can burn another." I paused for a second. "Sarah, I need to talk to you about your house. Have you thought about the winter there?"

"Not really, no. Why?"

"The house has oil heat, right?"

"Yeah. My grandfather was going to convert it to gas this year."

"And no fireplace?"

"No."

"Fuel oil's going to be, or is already, very hard to come by. I was thinking that you might want to move into a place that's more suitable to our present conditions."

"I can't afford to buy a house. All I have is my grandparents' place."

"You don't need to buy one. There are a few houses on our block that were built before the First World War. They were heated by wood or coal. Most of them—there are only six houses like this—still can be heated that way. You can basically homestead there. I think I can pull some strings there," I said with a grin. "Some of them were damaged in the quake, most of them not as bad as our house."

She had that look I suppose that I got, when faced with something that hadn't been on the radar screen.

"Think about it, but think fast. The place I have in mind is a couple houses north of my brother in law Alan's place. It's one of the best of the houses left."

"OK. How soon do I need to let you know?"

"Well, a couple of days probably. Saturday end of the day at the latest. But Sarah, you've got to realize that the house you're in will not function without a wood-based heat source. We don't have enough oil."

"OK."

"What are you doing for water? Do you have any broken pipes from the winter?"

"Just one. I capped it off. So no water to the upstairs, but everything in the basement is working. Well, the hot water heater's dead, too. I just shut it off."

"So imagine the winter in that house."

She thought for a few moments. "I'll take the house."

"Good for you."

"Will I have hot water? For a shower?"

"We'll see what we can do. If we keep our power, and the house has an electric hot water heater, you should. The houses that we've looked over don't have natural gas, or if they do, have wood heat, too. We made do with wood-stove heated water for a while. If we lose power, we lose water, too. So we need to plan accordingly."

Her eyes were beginning to show some...shock.

"It's OK, Sarah. You don't have to figure all this out on your own."

"Thank you," she said quietly. "It's just so much."

"I know it is. Stop by our place when you guys close down. Or are you staying for the duration?"

"No, I'm off at thirteen-thirty. I hope to be home before the storm gets too bad."

"We'll take a look at the place then and put some plans together."

"Thank you," she said as she stood. "I better get back to work."

"Me, too. Lots to do."

"Tell...John I said hi, okay?"

"I will. He's a good young man."

"I think so too," she said with a shy smile. "I hope his parents like me."

"They do. Don't worry about it. I've known Ron and Libby a long time. If they didn't approve of you, believe me, I'd know," I said as we walked back to the crowded hallway.

"See you later. And thank you."

"You're welcome. See you soon."

Back outside, where the immunization line was now extending just a few feet outside of the door, the western sky was turning a soft grey, and the sun was now filtered through high clouds. 'Here it comes,' I thought as I got back in the van.

"Off to the store," I said to myself as I turned on the sun-baked Sony stereo in the dash. I punched the 'scan' button on the AM frequency, and got nothing but static, until one of the lower-end stations came up. The weather service had apparently begun broadcasting on what had been ESPN Radio, a continuous forecast for the region.

I wondered why there was no 'normal' broadcast, until I pulled into the store, my little blue and white van drawing more than its share of attention. It was not often that forty year old vehicles had 'official' passes hanging from their mirrors. Alan and Ron were locking up the store, with 'shoppers' securing their purchases to their bikes and trailers, as Ron fought with the troublesome front door.

"Closing early?"

"Power's going down. They're shutting it off in sections," Alan said. "Pre-emptive strike."

"Oh. That's a new tactic."

"Beats replacing blown up parts when trees start going into lines."

"Anyone tell the girls yet?" I asked.

"No. Why?"

"I think they're baking. In the electric oven."

Ron and Alan looked at each other, and 'phoned home' the news on the FRS. Alan was promptly scolded by his sister for not letting her know sooner.

"See? Told you we should've passed it on," Ron said.

"Didn't think it was a big deal. I'll end up catching Hell for it now."

"How long 'til it goes down here?"

"One thirty. Karen said she'd need until two to get all her baking done."

"Do yourself a favor. Go out to our barn, fire up the woodstove, and THEN go home. At least she can finish baking, one way or the other."

"Probably wise. What did you find out at the center?"

"Kevin has some preliminary selections for us. He's kinda 'pre–screened' them for us."

"Good for him," Ron said. "It'll be nice to have some additional hands on the farm."

"I'm sure the kids will appreciate that. I KNOW I will," I said as we got in the van. "How's the Army sentry station working out?" I asked once in the drivers' seat.

"Good, overall. Got one Sergeant that is a pain in the ass though. Thinks we're here to serve his every need."

"Like as in supply him free stuff?"

"Yeah. I mentioned that to Annie Ross. She was going to have one of her guys have a little talk with him."

"Makes me wish Gunny McGlocklin was still around. Of course she does know a guy in Special Forces."

46

Thursday afternoon,
May Eighteenth

Sarah joined us a little after one p.m., when the community centers' patients were taken care of and had headed home themselves. The center would maintain a small staff continuously, to take care of any immediate needs that couldn't be met without a trip to the larger Valley General hospital. She arrived as I unplugged the last of the radios and other electronics from the house wiring. Despite the intentional power outage, if there was some sort of surge or lightning strike, I didn't want to fry irreplaceable hardware.

Sarah's arrival meant that just about all work ceased, as everyone but Karen--who was still hoping that she'd get her bread done--welcomed her and crowded along with us to look at the house I was suggesting she move into. Carl, per my request, had opened up the back door and inspected the place and had a five-page list of things that needed to be done, from broken pipes to windows to overall cleaning. The house was also powerless, as Modern Electric had disconnected every unoccupied house from line power as part of the restoration process. The place was pretty gloomy as the early afternoon grew dark. The sky was looking for all the world like a mid-July thunderstorm. I knew that the approaching clouds were more dirt than rain though—the color was all wrong. Thunderclouds aren't brown.

The house was sparsely furnished, but nicely so. I didn't know anything about the former occupants, other than they were married and in their early thirties. There was no forwarding address on any of the documents that the County had, and we had no idea what had happened to them after the Domino. They were just, well, gone.

The house had been remodeled at some point in the not too distant past, all the lath and plaster had been replaced, all the cloth-coated electrical wire replaced with wiring in conduit. The windows were mostly single-glazed on the second floor, double-glazed on the main. A half-dozen of them were broken, and a fair amount of cracks in the sheetrock. The place had the typical overturned furniture, broken pictures and glassware, kitchen contents turned about. The most serious damage included significant damage to the main waste stack piping and water and electrical damage from a flooded basement before the utility guys got the houses' service shut off. The water, at some point after the quake, had been two feet deep in the basement. It would take a fair amount of work to clean out the contents of the basement, fix the main drain and the supply, then attack the rest of the miscellaneous damage that Carl had noted. There were also things that we couldn't check yet, like the electrical system, although at least the panel didn't have any obvious signs of damage or shorts....other than all of the breakers tripped in the basement feed circuits. There must have been power on when the basement was flooded, which was interesting, in the big scheme of things. I'd ponder that another day.

The storm hit with more intensity than I expected, and sooner than I would have liked as well. By one-thirty, the winds were kicking up and the wall of dirt was again cresting the South Hill, headed for us. In a last-minute invitation, Libby and Ron asked Sarah to get some of her things and bring them, and her dog, back to their house for the duration of the storm. It was a nice gesture I thought, and a way for Libby and Ron to get to know the young lady that seemed to occupy so much of their son's thoughts. Ron drove Sarah and John in the Expedition to her house to get her things, just as we completely lost the view of Browne's Mountain south of us. It was coming fast, and Ron would not make it back to the house before it hit here. The rest of us headed home. Karen was taking the two loaves out of the oven as I walked in, and the power went out.

Ten minutes later, Ron radioed to me that he was at his place, and the Ford was parked behind his place. He drove right through our yard and we never saw him. The driveway was fifteen feet from where I was sitting. He must have been driving by Braille.

We lit up the two Aladdin lanterns as the place grew remarkably dark. I had both Kelly and Carl take strips of rag fabric that Karen had stashed away for braided rugs and wet them down, then place them around the window and door sills as best they could, to help keep the dust out. Most of the upstairs windows were very well sealed after our 'spring' repairs. The main floor windows still had some quake damage around their seals and trim that we had yet to touch. The rags helped a little. I ended up duct-taping the back door, on the windward side of the house. I could only imagine what it would look like tomorrow out there.

Kelly and Carl had been looking for spare time to set up the Collins radio and read the manuals, and this was an ideal opportunity. I knew that I wouldn't have to worry about them for at least a couple of hours.

Karen was cleaning up the kitchen as best she could without much in the way of light—we still had water pressure at the moment though. I wasn't sure for how long, but we had a fair amount of stored water inside the house now, in addition to barrels out in the barn. She was looking forward to taking a nap—she was pretty beat.

I told her I was headed to the basement to do a little cleaning—she knew what I was up to—I'd been trying to find some time as well for some chores, and today was the best excuse I had to take care of some maintenance. I grabbed some of the softer strips of rags and one of the battery-powered lanterns, and told the kids to come get me if they needed something. Carl grunted a response, as he was reading the operator manual for the KWM. Kelly was reading a stapled stack of papers, well used, that Aaron had provided with the set.

Downstairs, on top of my heavily damaged wet-bar, lay my fathers' blanket-wrapped Browning Automatic Rifle. I'd rescued the gun from the wrecked house in January, moved it to the barn and back to the house, and not touched it since. The weapons we'd relied on since then had included the 1903 Springfields, my Dad's Garand, shotguns, and sidearms. The BAR had not been neglected exactly, but hadn't really had a mission. I wasn't sure it would in the future either, but I wanted to make sure it would be ready, should the need arise.

I unwrapped the deadly Browning, enclosed in a wool Army blanket that my Dad had shipped it home in, although at that time it was also encased in a largish box of souvenirs from Occupied Japan. The bundle included the rifle; four box magazines of twenty rounds each, the bipod, a hand-tooled belt-sling, a three-inch wide GI belt with two soft leather ammunition pouches, and the stained and tattered Army-issue manuals for cleaning and servicing the monster. I had several other box magazines as well, although none in as good a shape as the four that I inherited.

At twenty pounds plus, I had a hard time imagining that my Dad ever slogged this thing about, but I had photographs of him with it, on top of an armored bulldozer in the Philippines. It was not in perfect shape, and had obviously seen its share of use. The finish on the walnut stock was worn through handling and use—my fathers' hands I had to remind myself. 'Peace through superior firepower' my father had once told a fourteen-year-old version of me as he cradled the gun. It was that moment that I saw that the gun was an extension of him like nothing else. It took me a long time to understand why that was.

I'd only practiced with the Browning once a year or so, for fifteen years after my father passed on. I found a spot in the hills above Priest Lake, Idaho, after the snow was gone but before the summer crowds were about, to spend an inadequate amount of time to become proficient with the rifle, but enough time to be reminded of its uses and capabilities. I'd missed a few years of practice, and never found a place in the Spokane area where I thought that I could safely use the gun and not draw too much attention. There wasn't a semi-auto option on the M1918A2, only 'fast-auto' and 'slow-auto'. The difference was about two hundred rounds per minute. I was able to hit my target, fifteen hundred feet away. I'd read that the maximum outer range was six hundred yards, but I didn't find enough real estate in the little valley to prove that fact. I did know, that of the several hundred rounds I put through it each time I'd used it, that it was quite capable of everything my Dad had told me, and all I'd read.... in capable hands, that is.

I took the better part of an hour to read, disassemble, clean, and reassemble the rifle, studying the detail of the old design, ensuring that everything would work as designed if the need arose. I retrieved eighty rounds of ammunition from one of the ammo cases, and carefully put them in the soft leather pouches. I didn't want to load the box magazines yet, especially if the old gun were to sit again, unused, for months at a time. By the time I finished with the Browning, I could hear thunder approaching from the west and south.

Next I moved on to the 1903 Springfields--the sentimental tack-driver of my grandfather's era and the other two 'shooters' that I'd had worked over by a now-deceased Army armorer who took the two 'adequate' guns, that were still well within mil-spec, and really made them over. He refused payment for the work, and asked that I make a contribution to the VA Hospital in town. I honored that request that year, and every year since then on the day that he was laid to rest. I also remember the quiet look and the thousand-yard stare, that December day when he told me of his trial by fire, in the Ardennes. The day he ran out of ammunition and fought hand-to-hand. The Battle of the Bulge.

I set the Springfields aside in their felt wraps, and systematically cleaned the rest of my Dad's war arms, his Garand and his 1911. I finished with my grandfather's 1911, which he'd had since the Great War, I found out long after he'd passed away. The same armorer who'd worked over the first of the 1903's had offered to bring the old .45 back up to snuff, as it had seen better days. For a moment, I resisted, thinking that it would lose authenticity if it were worked on. He reminded me that if my grandfather were still active duty, rather than 'gone home', he would've sent the gun to the armory for repairs and upgrades. I relented and ended up with a much-improved gun. (Although, Alan's National Match Colts still seemed night-and-day better than my grandfather's sidearm, with their adjustable sights and hand-honed internals. I was also sure that the much more modern Kimber variants would have been great too, even for the money. They were proud of those guns, you could tell by the price. They probably had reason to be.)

I cleaned the tools next, and took the can of Hoppe's and the cleaning rags upstairs. The clock read ten minutes to four, although it could have been midnight outside for all the light reaching the ground. The wind was steady, and gusting, as Buck and Ada rose from their chosen spots in front of the woodstove and greeted me. The stove rattled a bit with the low fire we had going.

Using a flashlight, I looked at the outside temperature, which had dropped to thirty-eight degrees. Had the weather been clear, we'd have a frost tonight for sure. With this storm, it was anyone's guess. No one had ever seen anything like it before, not here anyway.

The occasional crack of thunder could be heard over the wind, but we couldn't tell how far off it might be. The bay windows in the dining room, with their damp rags stuffed around them, remained uncovered by the blinds, but no rain fell. If I had ever had apprehension about the weather before, it was nothing like what I felt at that moment.

Kelly was there, huddled around the Collins KWM, ancient headphones on her head, the antenna strung from the living room wall across the room through the dining room. She'd hooked up its power supply to the inverter that I'd used for the 'County' radio, and was slowly working the dial.

"Hey, Dad. This is cool."

"You pick up anything?"

"Tons. This is way better than your radio."

"I don't doubt it. Where's Carl?"

"Sleeping I think. Mom's upstairs taking a nap, too. What were you doing downstairs?"

"Cleaning the rifles and some of the handguns."

"Oh. When do I get to learn how to shoot? I mean, shoot well."

"Soon. We're working on a training program for the settlers and kids of a certain age."

"Will I get one of the twenty-twos?"

"Probably my first one. The single shot. We'll get you up to speed on that, then move up to the Ruger, and then up caliber as you get a little older and can handle them."

"Good. I'm tired of Carl telling me that I'll never be able to do it."

"You'll do OK. You might be skinny but you've got a good eye," I said, watching her instantly improve her attitude. "That's a big part of it. You'll do fine in the safety class, too. You've already seen what a gun can do."

"Yeah. I hope I never have to use one like that."

"I hope you never do either. I hope I never do again," I said as Buck nudged me from behind, wanting attention. "What did you hear on the radio?" I asked as I scratched Buck's neck.

"The storm's all the way down into California. The Weather Service says that it's snowing in Alaska, and the snow has a lot of ash in it from Russia."

"We'll probably see some of that too. Not as bad as Rainier though. Anything from back east?"

"No, mostly south. I can't get the stations that I used to get from the east, like WWCR. NPR used to be clear too, and it's gone. There's a station out of Maine that I used to get once in awhile, and it was there yesterday on your radio. Today, it's static."

"Might be the storm."

"I don't know. Could be I guess. I haven't talked to Mr. Watters about that stuff."

"Anything on 'normal' radio?"

"Nada. TV's gone, too."

"K. I'll let you get back to listening."

"Thanks. This is the coolest thing," Kelly said as she pulled the old earphones back on.

I was headed back into the kitchen when my FRS beeped at me. "Anyone listening over there?" Ron asked.

"Yeah. How's it going?"

"OK, but we lost one of the trees out front. It's right up against the house."

"Damage?"

"Not that I can tell," he said. My radio 'low battery' light came on.

"I'm losing my battery. I'll talk to you later on the CB—preset channel. Say eight o'clock."

"Sounds good. Out."

"Out," I said as the radio died. "Dang," I said to myself, looking at the radio. The batteries were failing quickly in all of the FRS's these days. I doubted that I'd be able to find replacements for the odd little battery pack or replacement radios. These things were worth their weight in gold, early on. I wondered how we'd do without them.

"Kel, I'm going back downstairs for a bit," I said after I got her attention.

"K. I'll come get you if I hear anything important."

"Thanks, babe."

Back downstairs, I looked over our share of the stack of M-16's that we'd 'discovered,' five barely used rifles that had been looted from the National Guard, and not returned. I was sure that we'd be in trouble for possessing them, but on the other hand, I thought that having them wasn't a bad idea after all. With the fourteen M-16's, and the two AR-15's from Aaron Watters, and Alan's twin Bushmasters, we'd divided up the new guns so that each home would be equal in terms of the 'military' type weapons and ammunition. I wiped down the −16's for dust, and covered the lot with an old bedsheet. No telling how much dust or worse, ash, would filter into the house during this storm.

Alan had a substantial number of weapons other than the M-16's, including his monstrous .44 Magnum Colt Anaconda that had saved me from a couple of feral dogs; an 870 Remington Marine Magnum--a beautiful nickel-plated twelve-gauge that he'd kept on his boat when he motored around Puget Sound and the San Juan's years ago; twelve- and twenty-gauge Wingmasters; a couple of .410's; two or three 30.06 deer rifles; a .40 caliber Smith and Wesson; a goofy little Walther; a Henry Rifle in .45 Colt; some single-shot .22's and I thought a Ruger 10/22 as well; a number of old Colt single-action Army ('Peacemaker') revolvers; a stainless Colt 1991; and three 1911 model National Match models, all pre-1941. He had also for years created his own custom loads, which were kept only in his head (you'd think it was top secret or something.)

Ron had of course arrived in January without anything in the way of firearms, since he was just on an errand to pick up Marie at a basketball party. I'd loaned him my lever-action .45 'camp carbine', a 1911, a bolt-action shotgun, as well as one of the 1903's. After Gunny McGlocklin had given us weapons that belonged to a bunch of looters who'd attacked us, Ron returned most of what I'd loaned him. Ron now had in addition to the M-16's; an AK-47; two 'Firestorm' 1911's, which seemed to be good guns, and a Marlin 12 gauge pump shotgun. The other AK I gave to Alan when the M-16's came into the picture. Weird caliber that I didn't want anything to do with.

I shared what I could of my stored ammunition with Ron. Alan was all set for what he had already owned.

After the ground thawed out earlier in the spring, Alan, Ron and I had systematically unearthed buried chunks of PVC pipe that held additional ammunition and other 'valuables.' Karen of course gave me 'the look', when I told her what I was doing, but then realized that what I had done was precautionary, storing a potentially irreplaceable commodity. I'd seen six hunks of slightly damaged PVC water pipe cast aside at a construction project that I was working on, and gotten the OK from the job super to take them. I had to buy some plastic caps for them, and after filling them up with their contents (on a warm, dry day), sealed the ends with silicon caulking, wrapped them in several layers of plastic, and buried them out of the way of digging, tilling and potential wet spots on the property. Some of them had been in the ground for more than fifteen years. Let no one fool you, twelve-inch plastic pipe filled with ammunition is not a lightweight affair. Fortunately for me, Karen didn't ask me what it cost to fill them up (Enough for a decent vacation on the Oregon coast, back then, I recalled).

Alan gave me a ration of crap for being so secretive about what I'd stored and that I'd concealed it at all. I reminded him that some of—most of—the stored ammunition was put in place early in the first term of the Clintons, before the Assault Weapons ban. The canisters amounted to thousands of rounds of ammunition, some coins, and he thought oddly, laminated pages of information on capturing and filtering water, sealed seed packets, a couple Bibles, and copies of birth certificates, insurance information, family pictures, and compact discs of other stuff in the newer canister. I was pleased to see that everything had stored well, with no leaks. We test-fired some of the ammunition late one night, with no misfires. Alan thought that I would have been better off storing the raw materials for the center-fire cartridges, and of course he was probably right. I didn't however, have a reloading setup to base that decision on. He did, however, so any 'shortage' in his supply he could address. I relied on stored product only for my twelve gauges, twenty-twos, forty-five Colt, and the treasured Browning, Garand and the Springfields.

Once I was finished for the day cleaning, dusting and thinking about firearms, I set my mind on a list that Alan had given me, showing the increased demand at the store for items in short supply. We were getting low on some things too...store bought things do tend to run out. I sat in my beat-up recliner--

cut from some falling ceiling plaster back in January—and studied the many different hand-written notes on the pages in front of me.

The hand-written notes on the legal pad, noted over days and weeks of the stores' operations, listed of course the obligatory 'toilet paper' and 'feminine hygiene' items, and soaps, canned food products, and other things that were 'expected' to be in short supply once TSHTF. Later entries greatly expanded the list. I knew for example that yeast was not to be had; that iodized salt, sea salt, Kosher salt were not to be had, no matter what price was offered. Sugar had been in short supply, or expensive, for months. Honey as well. Peanut butter was a recent addition, although it had been listed early on, more requests came in for it. Vitamins, similar to 'salt', 'aspirin', 'Tylenol', 'toothpaste' and a dozen other nutrient supplements or medicinal items were simply not available. The 'home remedy' market for these was slow to take up the slack, and ineffective in most cases. Hardware items began to appear again on the list, including chicken wire, insulation and caulking.

In comparing my once-exhaustive list of our supplies to the current status of each item, we would run out of many items within two months at our current rate of consumption, just beyond the six-month mark which was my 'prep' state before the Domino. We wouldn't run out of 'food' so much as run out of 'variety.' The resupply avenue—our garden fields—would help replace much of what we'd consumed, if the weather cooperated, which it wasn't, at that moment. I was very concerned that we'd lose everything we had in the ground if the windstorm acted like a sandblaster. I'd seen it happen once, in an exposed field west of Richland, Washington. Young corn plants were worn through at the ground, as the sand from a gentle but steady wind, hit the stalks. Acres of the new field, planted by a hobby farmer, were lost over the space of a day.

I dozed off thinking about the Dustbowl, and hungry people with guns.

47

Thursday evening,
May Eighteenth

Karen roused me at ten 'til eight, asking if I wanted some supper. I checked in with Alan and Ron, their families, like ours, were lazing about and planned on going to bed soon. Kelly made us fried egg sandwiches, mine with just the right amount of mustard. Carl took two, ate them quickly, and got ready for bed. Kelly followed not long after.

"Kel, any more news?"

"Rumors mostly. The new flu has a new name. HXN dash 1."

"Where did you pick that up?"

"I heard part of a Voice of America broadcast. It went to static after about ten minutes."

"What about the flu?" Karen asked.

"The announcer said that the CDC was working on producing vaccines, but they were afraid that they were going to take too long for the outbreaks back East. I guess it's getting bad there," Kelly said as she turned the Coleman stove off.

"Anything about the storm? Local news?"

"Nope. Nothing."

"K. Thanks."

"Dad, do you think it will be like this tomorrow? We haven't seen daylight since two-thirty."

"I don't think it will be this bad. Normal storms only last a day or so. The dust should settle down soon."

"I hope so. I can't imagine being cooped up in the house for a week."

"Hon, have the dogs been out lately?" Karen asked.

"Not by me."

"You better get a mask on when you take them out then."

"You nicely volunteered him, Mom."

"Twenty years of marriage will hone that particular skill, dear daughter."

"Thanks. Both of you."

I put my small plate in the sink, and tried the tap water. The pressure had failed, with the shut down of the pumps. "We're on stored water again," I said.

"Let's hope that changes soon. I really don't want to trudge to the outhouse in this stuff."

"Yeah. We might get lost," I said, only half kidding.

I donned a light jacket and pulled on a balaclava to keep the dust out of my hair, and then my big painter's mask with the dual cartridges. I got the big maglight out, checked it, and quickly shooed both dogs out the front door, and onto the porch.

It was like stepping into a black hole.

The flashlight beam penetrated perhaps ten feet into the brown dust, which was swirling around the east side of the house. I'd heard of storms like this back in the Dirty Thirties, and in Africa when the Sahara swallows people alive. But not in Spokane. In daylight, someone could pass mere feet away and we'd never know they were there. Both dogs stopped short, at the top of the porch, as if they didn't know where they were. Buck tentatively made his way down the steps, relieved himself, and came back up. Ada followed, and they were both ready to go back inside. I patted them down, and my shoulders, before we went inside.

"So soon?" Karen asked. "And what is that smell?"

I took my mask off. I hadn't noticed it, but it was an acrid smell, almost palatable, like burning electrical insulation. "I don't know. I could only see about five feet out there. The light only went out to the tree branches. The dogs barely got off the porch."

"And they're filthy. So are you. Take off your coat and boots right there, and leave them by the door on that area rug."

She was right. My dark blue windbreaker was dirt-brown on the shoulders, sleeves, and neckband. My balaclava was no longer black, but brown. The dust filters on the inlets to the cartridges were caked with dust. Ada and Buck began to sneeze, then shake themselves free of the dust.

"Kelly, get the dustbuster. We're going to vacuum the dogs off."

"I never thought about masks for them," I said. "Hope they'll be OK."

"Smells like a vacuum cleaner bag when you empty it," Kelly said. "Only more bitter."

"Where is all this coming from?" Karen asked.

"It's probably ash from Rainier, and dirt from the Columbia Basin. All of last falls fields were probably plowed and ready for spring planting. That didn't happen, there's no irrigation out there, and voila, the Washington State version of Oklahoma in the Thirties."

"Mom was in Kansas then," Karen said. "I'll have to ask her about it tomorrow. How they…coped."

We were a week past the full moon, and I knew that we wouldn't see the moonrise tonight until well after midnight, if we could see it at all. At least for now, the wind wasn't quite so strong, and the dry lightning had stopped.

By nine p.m., both kids were asleep in their beds, and Karen was nearly asleep. I eventually drifted off, listening to the wind-up alarm clock on the nightstand tick off the time. I could still hear the occasional gust of wind swirl over the roof above us.

Friday, May 19th

I woke around four, unable to sleep any longer, and with the help of a little LED flashlight, made my way downstairs. The dogs woke and decided to stay put.

The power was still down, and I knew that there was little in the way of power for the laptop. I made my way to the kitchen and lit one of the Aladdin lanterns, this one a glass-based model, different in looks than our First-Depression era nickel plate Model 12's. Next I fired up the Coleman stove, and put on some water for a pot of tea, and then loaded up the woodstove for a small fire. Once that was going and the Coleman began heating the water in earnest, I looked outside to the west and could see nothing. In the dining room, I pushed the curtains open, again trying to see any stars. To the southeast, the waning moon was up and colored blood red. It seemed to have more detail than 'normal'. The edges of the craters seemed more distinct. Less worn. More…harsh. Funny how one's imagination runs the gamut in the early hours.

The gusty wind seemed to have slowed or stopped, although even in the house I could still sense that odd, acrid smell. I wondered how much dust and ash had been deposited by the storm, and how our crops were doing. Hopefully we'd get some rain soon, to settle the dust and wash it into the ground. I tried the radio on the 'local' stations and got nothing but static. Next, I tried the Collins, which was still set to a frequency that Kelly had been listening to earlier, as I reviewed her notes. She hadn't been able to tell where it was from exactly, but she thought 'England?' by her notes—the broadcast had faded before she had much time to identify the source. Her logbook covered three hours of listening, accounting for all frequencies she'd heard by frequency and alphanumeric title, if possible. Her level of detail surprised me. She had three neatly handwritten pages of notes, front and back, in her logbook.

"This is BBC Radio London," the broadcaster stated through even static.

"Memorial services for the Duke of Edinburgh will be televised throughout the nation beginning at ten o'clock tomorrow morning. King Edward the Ninth will deliver the eulogy for his late father, the latest in the sorrowful line of Royals taken by the influenza epidemic. Much comment has been made of late regarding King Edward's leadership, who before the present crisis was seventh in line for the Crown. The Labour Party commented that the King has shown remarkable strength in the adversity facing the Kingdom and especially his immediate family. The new Conservative Party leadership echoed the voice of the Labour Party, belatedly it appeared."

The broadcast began to waver between crystal-clear and heavy static, during which I was straining to make out the words.

"Prime Minister Stratham this day stated that radiological decontamination efforts continue in the select portions of France, Belgium and Germany that have rejected Islamist rule, with the British High Commission remaining in charge despite calls for Jihad against Britain from Islamists in leadership positions on the Continent. French Islamists in control of several cities have destroyed

notable gothic cathedrals in France, and remnants of the French military are protecting parts of Paris from the growing unrest by both religious factions and civilians demanding government relief."

'So,' I thought to myself. 'The wheels have come off the wagon over there, too.'

"The withdrawal of the United Kingdom last month from the E.U. and the resulting hostile actions against British subjects on the Continent continued this morning with attacks on British Army units delivering Islamist subjects into France. Four soldiers were killed and sixty-one injured as the last British units withdrew to within the Chunnel Zone. The joint-venture 'Chunnel' project has been secured on both ends by British Army units since fifteen March, with a twenty-five kilometer buffer zone between French units and the tunnel infrastructure."

The broadcast faded almost completely, and of course I didn't know what I'd missed. I resisted fiddling with the radio at all, waiting for the signal to come back.

".....quarantine of the British Isles projected to continue through the remainder of the year, with food produced on the Continent to be imported to the Isles subject to decontamination from radiological contamination as well as irradiation to prevent biological transmission of disease. HXN-1 influenza outbreaks in North America have spread beyond the eastern coastline cities, with outbreaks in Kansas City, St. Louis, Chicago, Dallas, and the Los Angeles region. Southern Europe, including a wide region from Lisbon to Istanbul are reporting widespread illness from both the original virus and the deadly mutation. Repeated attempts to contact the Indian Subcontinent, China, Japan and Indonesia have been unsuccessful since Friday last."

"In news from Rome, the European Union has begun using its new facilities, which replaced those in Brussels destroyed in the early hours of the War. The consolidation of European national governments is seen as a natural progression of the restructured European nation, according to their leadership. The new head of the European Union has not been publicly announced, but it is widely known that he is of Algerian birth and has lived for at least two decades in southern France......"

The broadcast faded completely and didn't come back clear enough to make out anything coherent. I shut off the Collins, and then stared out the window for long minutes.

Eventually I read, rather, my eyes moved over the words in one of my three-ring binders; this section on dealing with influenza treatment. I'd looked over my list of medical supplies earlier, focusing on re-hydration solutions, elderberry extracts which had historically served our family well in warding off the 'normal' flu virus. I found little in the way of help in keeping oneself alive in the event of a mutant virus coming after us. That, I reminded myself, was only one of the many dangers to our lives facing us right now.

By what should have been sunrise, there was a barely noticeable lightening of the gloom outside, but I could now at least make out the shape of the barn to the west, and the empty house and the damaged metal-clad pole building that used to belong to our neighbor Brad, to the north. The air was still filled with dust, which coated everything outside. I was looking out the kitchen window when I heard Buck come into the room, and nudge me with his prize of the moment, one of my now seldom-worn Reeboks. By six a.m., Buck had curled up next to my feet as I warmed up my tea and put more wood on the fire. I had moved out of the 'medical' sections of my binder, and into methods for threshing wheat. Which in our case, might be by hand.

Karen rose by six-fifteen, with the assistance of Ada, who decided that she needed to be up, too. As I poured her a cup of sweet tea and gave her a good morning kiss, the County radio came to life.

"All County units be advised of an official statement in fifteen minutes. Do not respond."

"Wonder what that's all about?" Karen asked as she sipped her tea.

"Probably the power situation."

"Any guesses on when they'll have it back up?"

"Might be awhile. Depends first of course on damage. But the dust is bad, too. It can short out the transformers and lines if it's too thick."

"So we wait for rain?"

"Maybe, yeah."

"Great. Any signs of life out back?" Karen asked, wondering about the other houses.

"No, I haven't tried the CB, and can't see that far."

"I'll give them to seven."

"You're generous. I was going to try them before the County broadcast and let them listen in over the CB."

"That's probably smarter. Is the channel set?"

"Should be. Kelly was last on last night."

"I'll try them. Why don't you go get dressed."

"What does one wear to a dust storm?"

"Plastic? Duct tape? The possibilities are endless."

"Thanks. Ever the humorist at my expense."

"When you set yourself up that way, it's pretty hard not to take advantage."

By the time I made it back down to the kitchen, Karen had roused Ron, but Alan was already up and about. The Emergency Broadcast System signal sounded on the CB and on the County radio before I could punch the 'transmit' button on the CB to have them listen into the 'County' broadcast. 'At least someone was on the ball,' I thought. I assumed that they had a way to transmit the message on all frequencies.

"This is Spokane County Emergency Operations. Power throughout Spokane County is currently shut down due to weather conditions. Weather conditions are expected to gradually improve over the next forty-eight hours with rain expected by Sunday morning. Winds are expected to decrease this morning to seasonal norms. Power will likely remain off for at least the next twenty-four hours as the power system is analyzed and repaired. Emergency service operations are extremely limited at this time, and a mandatory curfew is in effect until further notice. No civilian travel outside of shelters or residences is allowed except in cases of medical emergency. Looters will be shot on sight. This order has been put in effect by Pacific Northwest Command at Fort Walla Walla. This message will now be repeated...."

"So there you go," I said to Karen.

"Yeah. Great. What's it going to take to rig up some temporary power?"

"Moving the generator up here and coming up with a filter to keep the dust from choking it," I said, my mind working up what Alan and Ron would need to do as well.

"Better make that Job One. We'll lose the stuff in the fridge and the freezer without it. We don't have the winter weather this time."

"Well, we hope not," I said, not saying that 'this time next year, we might very well have winter.'

I went over in my head what we'd (Who? Me and the mouse in my pocket?) need to do with the generator for the house. I'd use the five thousand watt Generac and not the tractor-mounted PTO model, more to save the tractor than anything else. I could probably scrounge another Briggs and Stratton engine that'd work. I'd be hard pressed to find parts for the fifty-five year old Ford. My little generator wouldn't have the juice to run the freezer and the fridge, and was smoking more and more each time I used it. Alan and Ron had both copied my original unit and built ones of their own, Alan's a horizontal model mounted on a nearly new lawn mower; Ron's mounted on a hand-truck. Both beat my original design for portability. Ron even had a carrier for spare fuel and oil.

I radioed Alan and Ron and told them to meet me in our barn at eight for a planning meeting for power. It was a logical place to meet, because I knew that Ron would need some power cable to rig up a temporary connection to his house, and all the parts were in the barn. I also wanted to get their opinions on the list that Kevin Miller had put together for me. I hadn't had a chance to review it in detail yet. Hopefully they had, during the storm. I wondered how things were going with Sarah, over at the Martins place?

This was going to be another long day.

48

Friday morning,
May Nineteenth

A few minutes before eight, I suited up and headed outside to the barn. The sun was a clear disc in the east, above Mica Peak to the southeast. I could look at it directly, as if through a thick fog.

The dust had cleared to the point where we could see the houses behind us and even the hills around the Valley fairly clearly now. The dust seemed very high in the sky above us.

There was not a sound outside. No birds, insects, anything. It was then that I thought of the hens and rabbits, the Paulianos livestock, and the goats and cows that we'd been getting milk from. I wondered how the dust affected them…

I waved at Ron and Alan, now looking for all the world like 'Pig Pen' from the comic strip 'Peanuts', both with small clouds of dust from their knees down. Each had decent masks on, with a single 'cartridge'. Not as good as my dual-cartridge outfit, but way better than one of the silly paper masks with the rubber bands.

I unlocked the door to our former home, now beginning again to look more like a shop, and we went into the darkened room and closed the door behind us, before we spoke.

"Well, boys, looks like we're in it agin," Alan said, affecting a Southern twang.

"Everyone holding up OK?" I asked.

"Yep. Mom's been entertaining us with stories about the storms when she was a kid."

"Ron, how're things with Sarah?"

"Good. We had a long talk with her before bed last night. John crashed early. I think we were up 'til ten. She's a good kid. How 'bout you guys? Everyone OK I assume?"

"Yeah. The news was interesting this morning. I heard the BBC before dawn. They've got a new King over there. And the E.U. is now based in Rome. And they seem to have a Muslim leader."

"Huh," Ron said.

"So anything on the flu?" Alan asked.

"Got it over there too, the mutation. They reported that over here, it's on the eastern Seaboard, St. Louis, Dallas, L.A., Chicago. I made some notes. I'll get them over to you. They also said that they couldn't make contact with big chunks of real estate. Like India. China. Japan. Indonesia."

"Whoa," Alan said. "Nothing?"

"That's what I gathered."

"Before I forget, here's the list of candidates with our markups."

"Good list?"

"Pretty much, yeah. Interviews ought to be next."

"Yeah. One more thing to think about. Let's check on the hens and the rabbits. I have a little concern."

"What would that be?" Alan asked as I passed from the craft room into the woodshop.

"I'm wondering what the dust did to them. They might have suffocated."

"That'd be all we need right now."

"Yeah. My sentiments exactly."

I unlocked the door into the tool room and then opened the door to our hen-house. I was rewarded with the welcome noise of the hens milling about, looking for breakfast. Next, I headed into the 'expansion' that we'd had to add after we'd moved the Paulianos hens up to our place. Part of the addition had been reworked again, to handle the meat rabbits.

All the chickens in the addition were dead, covered with the thick dust. The rabbits in the upper hutches, were spared. The bottom-most layer though, were lost.

None of us had much to say. Half of our hens were gone. If things were this bad at the Paulianos, with a much more open—that is to say, less air-tight than our original hen-house, they might have lost all of their layers and the chicks. And their pigs. Extrapolating that out to other folks in the area….spelled disaster. Ron and Alan knew it, too.

"Dammit," Alan said for all of us.

"Come on. Let's get to it. We've got to take care of the dead ones," Ron said.

"Let's get the generators going first. These will wait an hour."

The generator work was slow. I had enough parts to build one full set of wires to connect one of the small generators to Alan's house, but not enough for Ron's. I ended up sending Ron over to the James' wrecked place to scavenge parts. It was almost ten-thirty before we were done with the wiring harnesses.

Alan quickly had his generator running, powering up his fridge and the freezer that we'd scavenged. His makeshift generator was pretty good sized, an eight horsepower Briggs running two General Motors alternators, in turn powering two large automotive batteries and two inverters. It was in effect, my little setup on steroids.

Ron's was not much different as far as output went, although he had a single large inverter and a bank of twelve-volt outlets. His inverter had come from a heavily damaged Dodge-powered RV up the street. The RV in its covered shelter, had been crushed by a fifty-foot chunk of Siberian Elm. The wood from that tree was now seasoning in Ron's back yard. Ron had planned on gutting out the RV's on-board generator, but found it had been removed already, well before the Domino. The engine powering his generator setup had come from a riding lawn mower. His design used a vertical shaft engine, as opposed to Alan's horizontal shaft.

All of the generators were now rigged with scavenged automotive air-cleaner assemblies, which were duct-taped to large-diameter shop-vac hoses. The combination of the 'regular' air filters on the stock engines, and the extra filters we'd used, caused all of the generators to run richer than they would normally. I was sure this would result in much poorer fuel economy, and probably not do the generators much good engine-wise. Would they overheat? Would the valves handle it?

Ron and John took the new harness, a beefy pigtail and a new outlet box, to wire it into their home's electrical system. Alan's had been installed long before, and he and I headed down to the Paulianos on foot with Carl, to check on their welfare. Carl carried one of the bulky hand-held CB's,

The Pauliano's house was of course dark, but the front curtains were open. I saw Joan inside and waved her to the door. I didn't want her to open the door. Perhaps some of the dust would stay outside that way. Regardless, she opened the front door, speaking to me through the tempered-glass storm door.

"Good morning," I said through the door. "You make it through OK?"

"Oh yes. We're fine. Joe's about ready to go out the back. You can meet him out there."

"Need anything?"

"No, we're fine. Everyone up at your place OK?"

"So far. We lost quite a few hens and rabbits though. The dust got them."

"Oh dear. We hadn't thought about that."

"Neither did we."

Joan moved from the door, a worried look on her face, and closed it as we headed down the steps.

The dust seemed like it was an eighth of an inch thick or so, but it was probably less. It was powdery as we walked on the grass; our footprints a clear trail where we'd walked. The color was identical to the wind-deposited soils of the Columbia Basin, formerly planted in dryland grains and a wide range of irrigated crops. Now, reverting back to its former natural state, I was sure, sagebrush and dryland grass intermixed with spotted knapweed and Russian thistle.

I found Joe, putting on a mask not unlike mine, on his back porch.

"Good morning," I said, the mask garbling and muffling my words.

"Nutin' good so far about it."

"Been to the shed?"

"Not yet. But I'm not 'specting anything but bad," Joe said. I had to process both his Italian accent and the effects of it through the mask.

We walked out to his chicken barn first. It was completely silent.

I pulled my flashlight out of my belt and played it around the darkened interior. The translucent fiberglass roof panels were half-covered with dirt and dust. Inside, the floor and roosts were littered with carcasses. None of the layers was left alive.

"Damn it to Hell!" Joe spat. No interpretation or mixed words there.

He quickly moved to the back of the barn, which held the brooder rooms. The three rooms held six brooder 'hovers,' which were all but invisible without my flashlight. He'd segregated the chicks of different ages, probably seven hundred and fifty chicks total, for the burgeoning need for eggs and meat. The rooms were ventilated differently than the rest of the barn though: Up high at the roof there were screened panels with old furnace filters in them, down low, openings to the main barn. These openings, Joe had closed up before the storm, knowing that the power would fail and the rooms would lose heat and light for the new chicks. That move had saved the younger portion of the flock. Most of the chicks were looking for breakfast. Joe scooped up one of the chicks in one swift move. The little fluff ball was almost dust free.

"Carl, let's get them fed and watered. We'll need to do something about all the dead ones."

"Can't we use them?"

"Dead meat sitting in a barn all night? No, I don't think so."

"I didn't know how long it would take for them to spoil."

"I really don't want to find out."

"True."

Joe set the small chick down on top of the brooder, and quickly walked to the last room in the barn, the semi-enclosed pig-pen. The pigs were alive, but dusty. They seemed to be no worse for the wear.

"Rick, you grab that bucket over there and wash them down. Jus' toss it on them and wet down the pen. This dust can't be good for them."

"Got it," I said, filling the five gallon bucket from the old hand-pump cistern. Three half-buckets later, the pigs were not amused by the water tossed on them, and another few gallons, and the pen was fairly wet. Joe meanwhile, had closed the loose-fitting doors to the fenced pen outside. He was visibly upset.

"You lose yours, too?"

"Quite a few. Not all. We'll help you get them taken care of and get some of the layers back down here for you."

"You think this storm is a one-time thing? You're wrong. I've seen dis before. This is jus' the first time. Rain don't come soon it'll pick up and finish off whatever's left."

"Where did you see this? Not here, surely."

"Canadian prairies. Back in the early fifties. Lost all our stock in three days. That's when I went into mining and left the farm."

"Oh."

"It changed everyt'ing for us. Never farmed again."

"I didn't know."

"Not many do."

"Do we just bury the dead? That's what I used to do with our old flock, years ago."

"That's the safe thing to do for people. Friends used to cook them up and feed them to their dogs, but I never cottoned to that."

"Then we'll bury them. How many did you have here?"

"Eighty five hens, three roosters."

"That'll be a fair sized hole."

"Better a trench. We can till up a piece deep, fold the dirt back, and backfill."

Carl found us in the main roost area. "Chicks are done."

"K. Joe, we'll be back down in a while to take care of these. You OK with power?"

"We're all right. I have a Honda generator on the side of the garage. Ron gave it to me. Got the fridge hooked up now. Freezer will be later."

"Be sure to check the air filter often. This dust...." I felt funny reminding a guy like Joe of this, but....

"I know," he said. "I cleaned it already."

"All right. We'll see you in a little while."

"K. Thanks," Joe said, shoulders slumped. I watched as he moved slowly up to the house.

"C'mon Carl. Let's head up to the house and get things in order. I want to see what we've got for news, too."

We radioed Karen and told her cryptically that we were on our way. Our radio communications protocols were definitely uneven. Almost casual when things were going well, cloaked with codewords and brief when things weren't going well. Probably not the smartest way to operate.

For two solid days, we viewed the sun and stars through the heavy blanket of dust, only going out when we absolutely had to.

We buried our dead stock, and that of Joe's, and re-worked parts of his barn and ours to help limit dust coming in and smothering the hens. His pig-pen was similarly addressed, with old blankets—tarps didn't work—hung from the roof rafters around the perimeter of the enclosure, outside of the area where the pigs could tear them down.

In off hours, which amounted to most of the time, I spent reviewing Ron and Alan's notes on the candidates for the houses on our block. I agreed with most of their thoughts, and added some concerns and questions to explore for the successful on the list. It remained to be seen when we would actually get back to this topic.

The heat during those two days also played against us, and the lack of power, and therefore, water through the Modern Electric system. The temperature on the twentieth and twenty-first rose to eighty degrees, and then eighty-five, before nightfall on Sunday the twenty-first. The fields (the corn especially) was suffering from the dry ground, and we had to watch over the greenhouses so that they wouldn't overheat. We also had to hand-water many plants due to the stress that the weather was putting on them.

On Sunday morning, after we'd spent some time in Scripture, Buck started to bark at the front door. (Both dogs wanted nothing to do with the 'outside' after the dust, which was both a blessing and a curse. Other than going out to relieve themselves, that was the extent of their outside time. Which of course meant that they wanted to play, aggressively, in the house.) A dusty Deputy Sheriff's patrol car was in the driveway. I grabbed my mask and met him at the gate.

"Paul? That you?" I asked. It'd been a while since I'd seen him. Since the Commissioners were toppled.

"Yes, sir. How are you?"

"Fair."

"Come on in," I beckoned.

"The porch is fine. I'm pretty dirty."

"As are we all. What brings you by?"

"The Sheriff wanted me to let you know something. He'd be here himself, but his wife's in early labor."

"Early," I said with some concern.

"Yes, sir, probably false labor according to our med team. They're doing OK though. The reason I stopped by is that the situation at Fairchild has been resolved."

"The hospital?"

"Yes, sir. The civilian contingent has died due to mutant influenza."

"As we feared they might. Longer incubation period than we thought...." I said out loud but not really to the Deputy.

"Doctor Sorenson agrees."

"Any other spread? Is it off base?"

"Not known. No infected victims were found outside of the hospital structure. That structure has now been burned to the ground with the assistance of several thousand gallons of av-gas and diesel."

"When did they go in? I mean, when did someone decide to find out?"

"Midnight last night. Three days since the observation post has observed any activity."

"Let's hope to God that it's contained for now."

"Yes, sir. Also, there is disturbing news about nationalization of resources from back east."

"What kind of nationalization?"

"Seizure. Food. Guns. Fuel. Medical supplies. Precious metals. You name it."

I could feel the color drain from my face as I sat down on the porch rail. "Where did Mike hear this?"

"Military channels monitored by the Forty-First Division. Federal contacts will not respond to inquiries on this. People that have asked the question have disappeared. Broadcasts that have mentioned this have been shut down."

"Possibly explaining the fall-off in news lately," I thought. "This will result in rebellion."

"Yes, sir."

"I cannot believe that this could be condoned by the President."

"Agreed. People do seem however, to be not always what they seem."

"If this is in fact the case, then we are very close to the end. Full-on collapse."

"That may well be the case."

"Then may God have mercy on all of us, because the world will not."

By Sunday afternoon, we heard over the CB that power was beginning to come back up, but there was no timeline on when it could be fully restored. Dust had coated the transformers, wires and insulators, and energizing the lines would only cause things to go 'boom.' By the end of that day, I'd contacted Aaron Watters with regards to what the deputy had told me, and we'd had long discussions about it in the family.

If someone wanted to 'nationalize' our property, they would do so, only after a fight.

We heard little on the shortwave during that time, nothing from Europe at all. National news heralded the return of the President and his cabinet to the 'Military District of Columbia.' I really had no idea what that meant. Furthermore, I was finding that I really didn't care, either. My problems were much more local than national, until national decided otherwise.

On Sunday night, the cleansing rains began.

49

Thursday morning,
May Twenty-fifth

Our weekly schedule had been shot to pieces with the storm and yet another bout of 'recovery and adaptation.' Two of my meetings of the Recovery Board, scheduled for Monday and Wednesday, were postponed until Friday the twenty-sixth. Monday the twenty-second, after two hours of 'status check requests' from the County dispatcher, my number was called. I was asked to provide a brief report on when power was turned off, turned on, and our condition. Next on the list was Clete McKinnon, 'One Thirty Eight' on the radio call roster.

No response.

This, while not unusual through the seventy-plus radio calls (not all numbers were assigned or in any regard, called that morning), I thought it damned odd for Clete. He was always listening and always responded quickly. If anyone was better prepped in Spokane County, or tougher, he'd have to be full-time military and have substantial backup. He and I talked about his depth of 'stuff' and his philosophy, which was effectively the center of his life. The dispatcher was passing his number over when I prompted her to send a patrol to 'One Thirty Eight's' location. The dispatcher made note of it, and that she would pass my request up the chain of command. Ten seconds later, she notified me that a patrol would be sent at once.

I guess the chain of command was short that day. Still, it was a long wait before Mike Amberson and another deputy showed up to give me the news. Clete's home was found ransacked, according to the Army patrol sent to check on him. Mike then checked it personally, and let me know of the signs of heavy fighting and blood in the house. Clete's body wasn't found. We presume he was killed during the fighting. The Army has dispatched a dozen soldiers to hunt down and kill those responsible. Their trails led them across the state line into Idaho, above Clete's place and over the ridge dropping towards Post Falls. It might be a while before we hear the outcome of that.

511

Clete's apparent murder was later announced on the radio, after the Board members were informed via our county radios in a make-do conference call. We listened more than talked. I'll remember Clete in my prayers for a long while to come.

The rains continued from Sunday night until deep into Tuesday, with thunderstorms skirting the city to the north and south. Power on Tuesday was back up to eight hours out of twenty-four, three in the morning, five in the afternoon and evening, with an announcement that by Wednesday, all service areas should be back up to full time service. That was a blessing, having power and water and refrigeration back up in dependable fashion.

Once the dust had settled, literally, we had a chance to get back outside and see what damage had been inflicted on our crops. Not as bad as feared, worse than we would have preferred of course. We'd lost perhaps ten percent of our crops overall. The edges of large plantings had been desiccated and wind-damaged. The greenhouses, although very dirty, survived more or less completely. Wind-caused thinning of the fruit trees had dropped perhaps twenty to thirty percent of the apples and cherries, which happens pretty much every year. There would be some hoeing and tilling to address soon, but it was far too muddy to start that yet. Once Karen and I made it back to the house with our ten-pound mud-covered boots, I broke out a hose and washed us off. I then tasked Kelly with washing down the porches and the driveway to help keep the mud and dirt from being tracked in. Futile, but it was at least something to do.

Tuesday afternoon, Alan and I reopened the store, for anyone that had the notion to come do some trading—not many were so inclined. John, Carl and Libby were helping pack up Sarah's grandparents' things from their house, in preparation for moving them. We needed more than a couple of days to make repairs properly, but she could move in her things right away, as long as we didn't have too many things in the way of our work areas. Schoolwork was completed on Monday and Tuesday morning, with Sarah helping teach Mark and Rachel in their arithmetic and spelling. Alan and I would pitch in on Sarah's place as well as time allowed and the need arose.

The store was more a gabfest than a point of sale or trade that first day. Word had gotten out about what was going on back East, with rumors flying about Federal detention camps, wholesale seizures of property and goods, executions. The two young Army soldiers talked quietly about their commanders decision not to obey an 'illegal order.' They did not talk of it openly; it was something that I'd overheard when they came in for a cup of coffee. Alan and I did our best to find out what was real and what was made up. Most of the talk was it appeared, fearful and unfounded rumor. Still, the seeds of rumor are often based in fact. We both wondered if we'd be too late in finding out the facts.

Another bone to chew on while not farming, fixing or 'jawing', was the list of 'candidates' that Kevin Miller had graciously put together. I'd reviewed the notes that Alan and Ron had made on the list and added a few of my own, along with putting together a list of questions to ask them either subtly or overtly. We needed to recruit five families to fill the remaining homes on the block that were suitable for wood heat, and a nineteen-twenties operating model. Sarah Woodbridge had taken the first house of course.

All through this sunny Thursday morning, we'd been conducting interviews of our candidates, with the goal of having all interviews done today, and settlers in the homes as soon as possible. The last interview scheduled for eleven a.m. Our venue for the interviews included an unused room at the Community Center that Kevin let us use, and then follow-ups with short listed candidates at the vacant homes. So far, we were short-listing everyone. Kevin had done an exceptional job first off, and I also thought that if people were still around after this long, they must have an inner strength that we were also looking for.

Our candidates included:

--Randy Thompson who was now running a bike and bike trailer enterprise in part of 'our' store. Randy used to work in a sporting goods store as day manager. His skills included hiking, climbing, orienteering and extensive archery skills. Randy's new girlfriend, Annika had worked with him at his store, but in hunting. She was the 'shooter', and was said to be not only a competition-grade long-distance shooter, but also a first rate gunsmith. Not qualities usually found in a woman of five foot two.

--Jake and Bonnie Callison. Jake worked as a fireman down the road at Station One, and Bonnie, originally from Bonners Ferry, Idaho, worked as an EMT. Their son Shawn had been on an AAU basketball tournament trip to Tacoma on January fourteenth. They'd heard nothing from him or any of his coaches or teammates since then. He'd attended school with Carl at University High School.

--Ray Alden and daughters Susan and Sharon. Ray lost his wife to cancer two years ago, and a college-aged son in a robbery in February, probably part of the 'Protector' gangs. They originally lived on the South Hill in the Ferris High school area, but were out of the 'service area' for utility restoration. They'd relocated to a small house on Second Avenue, east of our neighborhood, but the place was really in such poor condition that it would not serve for a winter. His girls were both grade-school age. Ray was a successful real-estate broker before the Domino, and had served in the Air Force as a navigator on a KC-135 before computers replaced most of them. His 'jobs' at present were to help Kevin Miller identify homes for resettlement and to identify parts of buildings, both commercial and residential for salvage. Kevin noted that Ray could be instrumental in creating residential/business/small industry within existing commercial zones…close to rail lines like I'd planned.

--Casey and Martha Wallace were in their late twenties. Casey's parents ran a harness shop, working in custom leather saddles and harnesses for Western and English equestrians as well as other custom leather-work required for draft-horse logging and field work. They'd been living in what was left of his shop after the attached house burned after the quake. He stated to Kevin that he has all of his equipment and gear in a mobile trailer and was ready to move 'anywhere that had running water.' They'd been hauling water from the Spokane River to their Otis Orchards home, more than a mile out of the utility service area and a half-mile from the river.

-- Bob and Margie Stoddard were forty-something newlyweds as of last June. Margie was a dental hygienist who worked over on Pines Road before the quake; Bob was a pharmacist at Safeway, now working at Valley Hospital. During college, Bob worked his way through school doing rough- and finished carpentry. They used to live in the trendy Northwood neighborhood, until their home was sacked and burned to the ground before their eyes. Both came from previous marriages, with no kids. They were living in a converted doctor's office across the street from the hospital.

--Peg Morton, single, fifty-something. Works for the state Department of Transportation as a truck and heavy equipment operator. Her ex-husband of twenty-nine years was serving in the Army, detached to Ensenada. Currently living at WSDOT shop—formerly the Central Pre-Mix Concrete plant on Sullivan Road. Her original home collapsed in the quake.

Our last candidate interview was scheduled to arrive soon, before the noon-to-eight shift began at Valley Hospital. Dr. Jim Peterson worked as a general practitioner, Lavonne "a trophy wife," according to Kevin's notes in the margin of his improvised 'settlement application.' He knew we were looking for a medical background in one of our new settlers, and Dr. Peterson was as close as he'd been able to come. Both Ron and Alan had lengthy notes about this couple. We'd interview them and make a determination at that point. Still, three pages of comments made me wonder if it was worth it. I was trying still, to give them the benefit of the doubt until a face-to-face meeting could make things crystal clear. In the final analysis on paper, if I blanked out the words that I took as a derogatory statement, 'trophy wife', and included all others on the application, they looked OK. We'd have to see.

I met Kevin in the hall, after refilling a water bottle from the kitchen's chilled (and sterilized) water supply. He had in tow, the Petersons. Jim was maybe five years into his practice, mid thirties or so I guessed. His wife Lavonne

I could see was 'high maintenance' as we used to say, wearing what seemed to me inappropriately flashy and impractical clothing given the countries current shape. Somehow, stretch pants and silk designer blouses don't do it for me. 'Good God,' I thought. 'She has sparkles in her makeup.'

"Rick, this is Jim and Lavonne Peterson," Kevin began.

"Doctor Peterson," Lavonne corrected. "Pleased to meet you Mr. Drummond is it?"

"Yes, thanks. Please come in," I motioned to the room ahead.

"Kevin tells us that you are on the Recovery Board?" Lavonne asked.

"Only until we find someone better qualified. Which will not take long," I said.

"I'm surprised that anyone would give up that kind of job," she said almost off-handedly.

"Not really a job. More an obligation. Duty."

"Still, it comes with power," she said. 'Is this her idea of pre-interview foreplay?' I thought. Alan and Ron were just taking it in at this point.

"The Recovery Board is about putting things back together so that we can survive this year and through the winter and for the coming years. It is about anything but power or political ambition."

"Oh. Sorry. My misunderstanding," she said as her husband spoke with Ron and Alan about the homes and land. She was looking at me as if I were quite naïve. I'd been looked at before by women like this one, and I didn't like it then, either.

"Please, have a seat," I said as I moved to my own folding chair.

Alan started as I considered the exchange. This woman bugged me. I was beginning to think that Kevin had her pegged. Even, understated her.

"As Kevin told you, we're interviewing applicants for settlement within the boundaries of our block."

Lavonne was silent, but I could see the wheels turning. Jim responded.

"Yes. We're currently living over on Vercler across from the hospital. My office building, actually. There's an efficiency kitchen there, and we brought in what we could from the house."

Alan and I explained our current situation, the work required on homes, and the overall goal to be mostly self-sufficient or at least set up so that we had marketable goods, food, or skills across the settlement areas in the Spokane Valley.

"Where did you live pre-Domino?" Ron asked.

"We had a home on Rockford Bay," Jim replied before Lavonne expounded on it.

"It was a wonderful home. It could be again if they'd get the power and water back up and get the windows fixed, and—" Jim cut her off.

"That's over now. We're here now. This is where we'll live."

Rockford Bay was on Lake Coeur d'Alene, thirty-odd miles from Spokane. Many people used to live in Idaho and commute to Spokane daily as the population increased, easy money flowed, and gas was cheap and plentiful. Rockford Bay had been the home of some of the largest, most expensive (and most poorly built) homes I'd ever seen. Many had been owned by Hollywood types who bought the 'bargain' real estate and were in the midst of converting the lake to Tahoe of the North, with Gulfstream jets arriving all to frequently at the Coeur d'Alene airport for a 'few days at the lake.' That was certainly over now. The couple in front of me appeared to me to be aspiring millionaires, who didn't mind the hour-long drive each way. Double that in a typical winter. Triple in a bad one, I thought. And miles from a store or a real business.

Ron had moved on to asking about the doctor's background, where he'd practiced, more of curiosity than anything else. He'd grown up in Cincinnati, moved to California, then up to the University of Washington med school where he met Lavonne. She had an uncompleted Bachelor's degree in psychology.

"Do you enjoy working outdoors? Any gardening or farming experience?" I asked. Lavonne rolled her too-blue eyes at that.

"Absolutely not. I'm from Mercer Island," she said with a tone of superiority.

"I'm sorry to hear that. You must have lost friends or family."

"Yes, I'm sure I did," she said, thinking that I missed her point. I didn't. I didn't really care where she was originally from.

"Settlement, no matter where you land," I said, already having made up my mind that I didn't want to deal with this woman on a regular basis, "will involve working outdoors. It will mean growing part or most of what you will need to eat, from root crops to fruit to small livestock. It will not be easy."

"How are we supposed to do that. I can't possibly," Lavonne said dismissively. "And where are we supposed to live? One of these little houses? With WOOD heat?" She looked at her husband with a smirk. "I suppose you want us to cut our own, too!" she laughed.

"Lavonne, I've told you this until I'm blue. This is the way it is now. Deal with it," Doctor Peterson said flatly.

"You deal with it Jim. I don't need to."

"Doctor, Lavonne, I think we're done here," Alan said for me. "Thank you for coming in. We'll see what is available. I do not think that you are a good fit for our specific needs, however."

"What is THAT supposed to mean?" Lavonne asked with too much bitter in her.

"That means, Mrs. Peterson, that I believe that you personally do not have what it takes to feed yourself and your husband and make it through what is yet to come. Your husband will be tied up with more than he can handle at the hospital and he needs to be able to rely on someone who can shoulder the load. You can't do that from what I've seen. I don't sugar coat things these days, ma'am. Good day," I said as I rose, followed by Alan and Ron.

"No one speaks to me that way!"

"Really. Well, Mrs. Peterson, best get used to it. There are no country clubs around here, and if there were, they'd be plowed up farms about now. And Starbucks went bankrupt the same time Microsoft, Google and the Big Three went down. As your husband said, this is the way it is now."

"We're leaving," she said as she spun out of the room.

"Doctor, I wish you luck," Alan said.

"As do I," Ron added.

"I apologize if I was out of line, Doctor, but we simply cannot afford to have a bad fit."

"I understand completely actually. If we had anything resembling a legal system, I'd be divorced by now," he said quietly. "She's a goddamned nightmare."

"Well, on the bright side, alimony would be pretty reasonable now," Ron said.

"Gentlemen," the doctor said as he shook my hand, then Alan's and Ron's, "it has been enlightening, if not successful. Hope to see you around."

"All things being equal Jim, I'd just as soon not see you professionally," I said.

"Agreed. Good luck."

"You, too."

After he'd left, I closed the mostly glass door behind him.

"Imagine being married to that," Ron said.

"No thanks. Don't need the nightmares," Alan said.

"So we have some choices to make. We have six seemingly good families and five houses to put them in," Ron said.

"Five on our block. On our side of the street," I said. "Seventeen Oh One on the other side of the street is repairable."

"The single-guy survivalist's place," Alan said.

"Once upon a time, yes."

"Who do you figure for that one?"

"Thompson and his girlfriend, don't you think? If she's as sharp a gunsmith as she seems," I said, recalling our earlier interview with them, which ran long because she and Alan hit it off so well with a discussion on ancient revolvers, "she's the logical choice for that machine shop. That frees up one of the other houses for the rest of the list."

"No problem with Kevin on that?" Ron asked.

"I don't think so. I'll check before we notify anyone," I said.

"So then we suggest to the candidates on the rest of the houses as far as assignments go," Alan said. "Two o'clock at your place."

"Yep," I said. "Be right back. I'm checking with Kevin right now." The five houses we'd inventoried were comparable in age, condition, and size, although some had been better cared for and updated more carefully than others. All in all, they were not all than unequal....still we were reluctant to just tell someone 'this is your house'. We'd decided to see how the candidates would select homes themselves. Another test perhaps, but illustrative of how they might work together. I was hoping myself that it didn't blow up in my face.

I found my way to Kevin's office, where he was in a discussion with Ray Alden, one of our candidates. "Ray, can I speak with Kevin for a moment?" I asked.

"Sure. We still on for two o'clock?"

"Yep. We'll meet at our place and go look over the block," I said, wondering how the afternoon would progress. Karen would have some iced tea for our guests as we toured the houses. Ray excused himself and headed down the hall to his own office.

"What's up?" Kevin asked.

"First, you made a great list. Thank you for your comments—they helped immensely."

"No prob. How was Mrs. Peterson?"

"As you described. If anything, I think you could have been more verbose and saved us the time."

"I made that assessment in thirty seconds of conversation."

"Then my apologies. You did well. The Peterson's are no longer being considered for our block. I think we're below her social status, in her opinion," I said. "I wanted to see if we could place one of our families in Seventeen Oh One."

He looked at me for a moment, realizing which house that was, and then smiled. "Sure. Who you got in mind?"

"Randy Thompson and his girlfriend Annika."

"That would be my choice as well. Go for it. I'll get the paperwork done. What about the others? Are you guys assigning them homes or what?"

"No. We'll tour them with the families and see how they work together at the selection."

"Interesting. That might work for your bunch. Doesn't work for us. We have to make the decisions and put up with the flack. 'They have a new washer!' 'They have more garden space!' 'They got a TILLER with their house!'"

"Sorry for your new bureaucratic troubles."

"They're yours too, pal, until elections anyway."

"The Board has enough to do as an oversight committee. Personally, I'm ready to move on."

"You running?"

"Running for what?" I asked probably with a dumb look on my face.

"Townsman."

"No. Never even considered it," I said dismissively.

"You ought to. You might get drafted into the position as a write in, my friend."

That stunned me a little. "That's about all I need. It's tough enough working through the foibles of what's passing for County government, lumped into the military rules of the day. We've lost two Board members in the past few days, and will have to replace them before the elections. The Board is getting along pretty well, but it is only a matter of time before we come to butting heads. Politics will rear its head sooner or later, despite the collapse around us," I said. "Maybe because of it."

"I heard about McKinnon. Who else?"

"Stacey Womack. She's leaving due to bed rest for her pregnancy. It's not yet common knowledge."

"She's the north side rep. McKinnon's the east side," Kevin pondered.

"Yep."

He snapped out of his thoughts and back to the present. "Go ahead and tell Alan and Ron that the house is fine with me. I was hoping to find someone who could use that gear."

"Your shop all set up now?"

"Yeah, but if you get a line on some milling machine oil, or stumble across some, let me know. Some bastard stole mine, and I have some custom work to do."

"I'll nose around. I'm sure there is some on our block. There were three guys heavily into machine work before the Domino, and a few others that had some hobby stuff. What are you working on?" I wondered.

"Nothing legal."

This piqued my interest as I began to smile.

"C'mon. Spill it."

"Silencers for 10/22's and other small varmint guns."

"'Varmint guns' is by definition pretty broad. I'm assuming you're talking about calibers beyond twenty-two's."

"I am, but don't spread that around."

"Not a problem. Might have need of your services myself. Know any way to quiet down a BAR?"

His head moved back a little in shock. "Browning? You have a Browning?"

"I do."

"Original. Not one of the reproduction 1918A3's," he questioned.

"Yes. Why?"

"I have one too, sort of. Only difference is, that I built mine."

"From parts?" I asked with surprise.

"No. Machined it. Dang near all of it, except the trigger assembly. I had two piles of wrecked parts to work from with those. The stock—well, I have two different stocks—was carved from a walnut tree in our back yard. The performance stock is carbon fiber composite."

"Where did you find that?"

"Friend of mine used to work at Lockheed. He made it for me there. Yours is bone stock," he asked again, more a statement than a question.

"Yeah. Why?"

"Where was it in service?"

"Philippines, Japan, North Africa."

He thought about that for a moment before he responded.

"Standard trigger, World War Two."

"Yeah. I don't know if it's seen machine work. Certainly not in the last forty years. Again, why?"

"Mine was machined from computer aided design plans and specifications for the majority of the gun. The guy who created them never sent me the trigger assembly files, and when I tried to track him down, he'd disappeared. The actual parts that I had for the standard trigger were pretty trashed. The only actual images I could find in CAD were for the winter trigger assembly, which largely hid the actual original trigger. Those dated from Korea. I'd like to find an original standard trigger to compare my homemade work to."

"It fires OK, right?" I asked of his gun.

"Yeah. But I want it to look right, too."

"So what's a 'winter trigger'?"

"Has a lever outside of the trigger guard so that you can fire the gun with gloves on. Heavy gloves wouldn't let your finger inside the trigger guard."

"So you flip a lever and it fires?"

"Yeah."

"And if the lever operating the trigger gets tripped accidentally…"

"Exactly. It goes off. My homemade standard trigger was a casting and functionally it is adequate, but I don't think it looks quite right. My standard trigger parts were more artifacts than useful: broken, twisted and rusted. I've never laid hands on a real, original one in decent shape. That's why I want to compare it to yours. Maybe create a CAD/CAM file of it so I can machine new ones that look right."

"That shouldn't be a problem," I said.

"I assume that our friends in green don't know about this."

He paused for several seconds before responding. "Actually, they do. Two of the senior sergeants were talking about their personal weapons and that they wished they had them now. Both were talking about Sixties-era Brownings. They'd like me to build them some."

"'Kevin Miller, Arms Merchant.' Should look good on a business card," I kidded him.

"Keep that quiet if you would."

"Absolutely. I'm glad we had this talk. I've been wondering how I could get some range time with that beast and not get myself arrested or have it requisitioned by a higher authority."

"This might be your chance."

"Thanks. We'll talk soon," I said as I reached the door. His secretary was waiting for him with a large stack of files.

"Damned paperwork," he said as I left.

50

Friday,
May Twenty-sixth

Friday,
May Twenty-sixth

I had planned on being present for the meeting on the 'block' to watch our new settlers hash through the process of picking their new homes. The County and the United States Army had other ideas however, and I missed the whole thing, and most of the night as well. They picked 'me' because Walt Ackerman wasn't up to the stress at his age, and with his blood pressure and no medicines to treat it.

With about twenty minutes warning, I was told to meet an Army second lieutenant at the convenience store—one thirty p.m. I was told to bring food, water, and a change of clothing, and that I would likely be back home within twenty-four hours.

"You have no idea where you're going?"

"No."

"I don't like this," Karen said as she packed some food. Muffins, dried fruit, some beef jerky (from my Christmas stocking, months ago now), and a number of water bottles and juice powder packets. "They shouldn't just shanghai you and not tell you anything."

"That might be the point," I said. "They may have really good reason not to tell me what's going on."

"What could that possibly be?"

"I don't know. Something big's going on. That's all I can figure."

"Are you taking a gun?"

"Yes. 'Colt. Don't leave home without it.'"

"Don't try to be funny now."

"Sorry. Force of habit."

My bag was an internal frame Kelty pack that I'd had since college. Whenever I went on a road trip, pre-Domino, I'd have it packed with whatever I'd need to get back home, if I had to hoof it. The pack still had some MRE's in it, and I'd re-packed it with it's spring and summer gear a few weeks before. All of the clothing was bagged up in Ziploc bags, that I'd then sucked most of the air out of with a shop vac. This resulted in less bulk, but could result in more weight if I went nuts and threw the kitchen sink in the pack. Since most of my road trips were within three to four hours drive, the pack included a small dome tent, a small stove and fuel, water filtration pack, all the comforts of home. A sleeping bag—now a summer weight model—was in a similar vacuum bag and stuff sack under the main compartment of the pack. Our 'family' road trips had similar bags for each of the family, mine more aggressive than the others. That meant, I had space for my .45 and ammunition, and an AR-10, all broken down and stowed in it's stock, packed in there, too.

Fully loaded, the pack was forty-six pounds, and I wasn't in shape to carry it far, like I'd always wanted to be. I had always been optimistic about my ability to 'pack' the thing over open ground, off road, in a SHTF scenario. I really hoped I'd never have the need of it.

"The best of the FRS's is in the pack with it's charger. And the CB and spare batteries," Karen said. "Call me when—if—you can." The concern in her eyes was obvious.

"I will. But don't count on hearing from me. K?"

"We'll be listening anyway."

"I know," I said as I hugged her. "Gotta go babe."

"I'll drive you."

I lugged the pack out to the Ford, where Carl and Kelly met us, and climbed in without a word. They knew something was up, too. Nothing like this mysterious request had happened since the quake. We drove down to the store without talking. Karen parked the Expedition in a painted stall in front of the store, where an armored Humvee and an open Humvee with a mounted gunner stood watch over things. I noted as we pulled in that the gunner looked both really pissed off and really tired. Something was definitely up.

"Carl, you take care of your Mom," I said as I got the pack out of the back and he closed the gate. "And your sister."

"Yes, sir," he said in an uncharacteristically shaky voice.

"Don't worry. It'll be OK."

"I know," he said as Karen and Kelly got out.

"I'll see you both soon," I said as I hugged them and gave them each a kiss.

"Mr. Drummond? You ready?" a female voice asked me. I spun around and saw a new officer in the form of Amy Ross.

"Amy!" Karen exclaimed. "You're in charge of this debacle?"

"Only this tiny part of it."

"And a Lieutenant no less," I said.

"Second Lieutenant, yes, sir."

"Field promotion? You were a corporal what? Ten days ago?"

"Yes, sir. My LT was killed in action. Made a mistake and it cost him and three other guys."

"Jesus! I'm sorry Annie, I thought…"

"It's OK. It happens."

"Lieutenant, we gotta roll," a sergeant beckoned from behind the wheel, in the tone of, 'unless we want our asses handed to us.'

"Annie, you watch out for my husband," Karen said after I kissed her again.

"He'll be fine. Don't worry," she said as she looked over my pack. "Probably packed a little heavy," she said with a smile.

"You never know," I said, tossing my bag in the back of the lead Humvee.

"True enough," she said as I closed the door.

"Seven to Outlook," the front-seater said into his helmet mike.

"Seven," a voice replied through a speaker. I couldn't tell with all the road noise where the speaker was.

"Can you elaborate on where I'm going?"

"No, sir. Orders."

"Understood."

Instead of heading west, towards downtown, we were headed east. 'Had I been this far east since the quake?' I asked myself. 'Only on paper,' I reminded myself as we headed east on the wreckage of the Interstate.

To my left, the twenty-screen cinema at the Valley Mall was a burned out shell, the colored steel façade still looking festive, advertising the holdovers of the Christmas blockbuster movies, and 'discounts for matinees'. How funny that sign looked.

We stayed on Interstate Ninety until we hit Barker Road. I remembered Ron telling me of their journey from Sportsworld back in January. The downed overpass he told us of then was still there, the south half still blocking the freeway, the north half pushed out of the way. We turned—at speed—through a dozed chunk of the median concrete barrier, and off the freeway onto the two-lane. The little white church that used to sit across the street from a friend's house was gone now, burned. Barker Center, one of the 'alternative' schools in the district—was mostly intact, and apparently being used for a shelter. We barreled by it without slowing down.

Eventually, we crossed the River, turned left, and headed back to the west. In another ten minutes, we were back on Sullivan Road, heading north. We ended up at the former Army National Guard building at the old Industrial Park. The Park started off life as the Velox Naval Depot in the Second World War, was surplused, and redeveloped to house one of the largest industrial areas in the County.

It now resembled its former self I suppose. Large quantities of Army vehicles, including tanks and the big transport trucks decorated the pavement. The warehouses and industrial buildings appeared to be in the process of consolidation so that the Army could use a number of the buildings.

I gave up counting troops when I got to five hundred.

"Sorry for the detour. The River bridge is down."

"Yeah, I know," I said to the driver as we headed east again, deep into the rows of warehouses. We turned right and left quickly, into the end bay of one of the buildings. The door rolled down behind us as we parked in a row of more than twenty other Humvees.

"Disembark and walk to the east, please." Annie said. "You'll be met by other personnel."

"Hokay," I said with no small discomfort as I grabbed my pack and walked through the cavernous space. The roof rafters must've been nearly forty feet up. I headed down the central aisle, in a space formerly designated for forklifts.

At the east end of the building, which was probably three hundred feet long, a staff sergeant asked for my ID, which I had to fish out, called off to my right to someone to 'stand down'. I didn't see anyone there, but it was pretty dark.

"Please advance to that door," the sergeant told me, pointing to a plastic sheet with a lighted room beyond.

"OK."

I walked the fifty feet to the sheet, passed through the slots in the panel, into a white hallway with a steel door on the other end. I walked to that door, heard a buzz, and the door opened into another darker room.

"Mr. Drummond, this way," a Marine officer directed. "You may stow your gear in the room off to the right of the conference room."

"Thanks."

"As of this moment, what you will be hearing is regarded as secret and must remain in the confines of this room. Is this understood?"

"Yes."

"Questions?"

"None. Yet."

"The other members of the meeting will be joining you in a moment. Please make yourself comfortable, sir."

"Thanks."

I sat in a none too comfortable chair on the side of the conference room table under the fluorescent lights, and waited.

Ten long minutes went by before I was joined by Mike Amberson and two of his lieutenants, Drew Simons, Warrant Officer Clifton, and a half-dozen other uniforms, including Air Force, Marine and Army. Two more civilians came in the door behind me, similarly carrying a daypack and I noted, both with sidearms. To round things out, a Navy commander joined us and sat at the head of the table, at the far end of the room. I couldn't make out his full insignia, but at least I knew rank. An orderly brought in bottled water, coffee, and tea.

"Gentlemen, this meeting is now in session. Thank you for coming on short notice, and to the civilians and local police, I want to thank you for putting up with our schedule. There are matters that we must present and discuss today that will dramatically affect the nation over the next three to thirty six months," the Navy commander opened.

'Well, this oughta be good,' I thought.

"You are in attendance at this meeting because you play a critical role in the leadership of the population, the maintenance of a system of government, and the Rasmussen maintenance of a relatively safe society."

"Good to know we're loved," Drew said. I smiled.

"Mr. Simons, Mr. Drummond, Mr. Ames, and Mr. Rasmussen are joining us today from Spokane and Kootenai County, and are civilian representatives of their respective recovery organizations. Gentlemen, I remind you that the following is classified information and is not to leave this room. Is this understood?"

We replied in unison, "Yes."

"I'm Commander Paul Hattrup. Until last Monday, I was assigned to the CDC, where we were studying the impact of the virus," he paused for several moments. "We discovered that there can be no vaccine. What appeared to initially be a complex virus is actually attacking the human genetic structure based on specific markers in human DNA," he let that sink in for a few seconds before continuing.

"We don't know who, without DNA testing of every person, will be affected by it. The genetic signature of victims does not conform to a specific race. It is, other than the single genetic marker, completely random on the surface."

"By affected, you mean 'killed,' I said, probably inappropriately.

"Highly possible, yes."

"And we're here, why?" I asked. "We don't know who's going to get this, there is therefore nothing we can do about it. Am I correct here?" I said with no small amount of irritation. I looked at my fellow civilians, and some of the uniformed men around the table. All had the same uncomfortable look. Some had fear hidden behind stony faces. 'Damn it all,' I was thinking.

"We are looking at a high probability of the complete collapse of organized government, society, and in the extreme case, civilization."

We were all shocked by that statement, and began to question Hattrup in his statement. He motioned us with his hands to calm down.

"They succeeded," Drew said, eyes focused below the solid table top.

"Who?" Mike asked.

"A few years ago, Tom Clancy wrote a book, based on the idea that extreme eco terrorists had to eliminate ninety-five percent of the human race in order to 'preserve' and 'enhance' the natural environment. In reality, that was optimistic. They wanted the human population reduced to a half-million, worldwide. Scary little scenario, except for me too real: I had a couple of them in one of my classes at WSU. They were sociopaths."

"Well I doubt that the Chinese government had this planned, but this is the hand we are dealt," Hattrup said.

"What's the mortality rate?" an Army officer asked. I noticed his Division insignia was not that of the Forty-First.

"Thirty-five percent of infected victims will die within ten days. A further fifteen to thirty percent may recover but may have critical damage to the immune system, making them susceptible to death through seemingly minor infections. Long term effects on survivors are of course unknown."

"So we're looking at a minimum of sixty to sixty-five percent of the population dying," 'Rasmussen' from Kootenai County said.

"Based on our projections and observations, yes. This genetic attack is running unchecked throughout the entire Northeast at this time, as well as in several other major metropolitan areas in the country. There are massive casualties in the Far East, which appear to have resulted in the collapse of society. Survivors within those areas do not have the skills or in many cases, the materials to fend for themselves. The media has noted that some countries are having 'communications blackouts.' In fact, these affected areas have lost much of their operating infrastructure or the skills to operate power stations, water pumps, or radio stations. That is why no communications are possible in those areas."

I thought of what that meant to our family. More than half dying. Maybe all of us if we were not among the favored, genetically. I could feel the cold sweat.

"And this is our fate," Mike said, looking at Hattrup.

"It will happen here. It will be a matter of time before it reaches the Pacific Northwest, but it will get here. Human contact with infected populations, wind-borne transmission, it doesn't really matter how it gets here, but it will. It's global, and we can't stop it."

"So we're supposed to plan for this?" the other Idaho representative, 'Ames' said. "How in the Hell do you suppose we do that?"

"You have some time due to your isolation. The reason that Pacific Northwest Command and Plains Command are in operation is to provide support for the continuation of society. Southwest Command is dealing with California and the whole Mexican situation, and they're not going to survive it. East and Southeast Commands were overwhelmed by matters political before they could do anything about it."

"This effort will fail," I said. That drew attention to me. "You'll lose sixty, or sixty five percent of our remaining population. We've already lost a significant portion to the 'flu.' You'll lose a similar percentage of your military. Critical skill sets will be lost in these deaths. The likelihood that the survivors will have all necessary skills and abilities, and be able to pass these on to others and to their descendants has got to be billions to one. We are currently unable to produce that which we consume. We are running out of pre-war supplies, critical parts, fuel. Food will run low. There are maybe two people in this room, maybe one, who know how to grow more than enough food to survive, and that's based on current technology. Not pre-industrial or Native American-level skills," I said with a pause. "And that's where we're heading," I said. "Unless I missed something of course."

I noted that Woody Clifton, the Special Forces chief, who had been leaning back in his chair, hands folded, attentive but completely silent through most of the meeting, was now looking at me. Hard.

"You probably didn't," Hattrup said.

"So why the secrecy? The charade? You expect people to misbehave once they find out that a big chunk of them might die?" Drew asked.

"Yes."

"Keeping this secret buys you hours. Maybe a few days, max." Ames said. "It'll be pretty obvious real soon now when folks start dying in the numbers you're talking about, if it happens."

"When, not if," Hattrup said.

"So what's the Federal government think that they can do about this?" One of the Army officers asked.

"This is a directive of the National Command Authority. That office is now held by the former head of USAMRIID at Fort Detrick, Maryland. His name is Colonel Peter Merrick."

I was stunned for a moment. "What?"

"The President, Vice President and the vast majority of the civilian Federal leadership are deceased due to this virus. This has happened within the past thirty-six hours after a prolonged effort to keep many of them alive at Bethesda and in several other locations."

The room erupted.

As the questions poured forth to Commander Hattrup, I tuned out a little and sat back in my chair. Six of ten dead. Unknown effects on the survivors. Would this be the last nail in the coffin?

Eventually, Hattrup regained control of the meeting.

"Gentlemen," He began again, "I realize that none of us are prepared for this. Neither is the country."

"If I heard you right, within a few weeks or months, there will be no 'country'," an Air Force Colonel said.

"That may in fact be."

"So now what?" Mike Amberson asked. I could tell that he was, like me, thinking about his wife and family, of his unborn child.

"That's what we need to figure out," Hattrup said.

"You realize that you may have brought this evil with you?" Ames said.

"No, sir. I was working on the disease, but not within the immediate area of contamination. We still have military communications that allow us to work remotely, in some parts of the country anyway."

"So where did you come from?"

"Naval Air Station Fallon, Nevada."

"I thought that was just for fighter training," the lone Marine asked.

"Not everything down there is above the ground," Hattrup replied.

"So why here? Why us?" Drew Simons asked.

"You were relatively isolated from the rest of the country due to the quake and remain so. You were infected early with the first round of the flu. This may have had benefits—plain language, you may survive where others may not. There simply isn't time to run lab trials on the effects of the mutation on people who have already been exposed to the original virus. And, I'm originally from Washington state."

"You know about Fairchild then?" CWO Clifton added.

"Yes. The victims there had not been exposed to the first virus, only the mutation. I understand it was contained within the base hospital."

"It was."

"And that the victims were cremated?"

"They were, along with the entire hospital complex, yeah," Clifton responded again.

"Then there may have been adequate containment. That there were other people around them does not help, but if it spread, it would show by now. As I understand it there have been no more losses."

"That is correct," Clifton again responded.

"Then we may pray that luck is on our side," the commander said.

"Thanks, but I'd rather have God on mine," I said.

"Amen to that," Mike added.

51

Friday afternoon,
May Twenty-sixth

"Well Commander, you've managed to drop the A-bomb on us here," Mike said, leaning forward on the table. "I'm inclined to agree with other members of this group and sh*tcan this secrecy stuff. Word is already spreading about what the government is-and is-rumored-to-be doing. If word hasn't gotten out yet that the new flu is dropping people at the rate your saying, I'll bet real money that we'll hear about it over the shortwave by the end of tonight."

"That may be. I'm not exactly working from a war plan here," Hattrup answered.

"So what exactly IS your plan?" an Army major asked.

"People in this area may have a better chance of surviving this if there is some relation between previous illnesses within the past six months and the present mutation. We were studying it in the Atlanta labs, and in Virginia when the mutation hit. A high percentage of our personnel were sickened and a sizeable portion of those, died. Ironically, four of our test subjects didn't get sick at all. They'd been exposed to the initial strain."

"So what happened after that?" I asked.

"The lab was shut down. The sh*t hit the fan. The mutation affected the entire metropolitan area. It spread like wildfire. As people got infected, or heard about others who did, they fled. The couldn't outrun it, though and in most cases, their evacuation caused the outbreak to grow exponentially."

"And we don't have any place to run to?" Ames asked.

"With all due respect, your highway systems are shot. You have no interstate traffic to speak of. You have no air travel capability. So, really, no you do not have any place to run to. We tracked people from Atlanta who evac'd to New York City. Which then caused an outbreak there. Then to Boston. Then Jersey,

Philly, Pittsburgh, and all through the Great Lakes region. A single 737 running full, with two infected patients, was responsible for that. Those that weren't infected were carriers."

"By the time they got off the plane," the Air Force officer began.

"The entire plane was exposed. Who then exposed millions from there. And there isn't a thing we can do about it."

"You said that a Colonel was in now the NCA? I have a very hard time believing that," Drew Simons said.

"That is my understanding. The civilian national leadership has dispersed to shelters or their home districts. The Acting Congress was less than seventy-five percent filled at the beginning of May, and the governors were in the process of filling the missing slots. When word got out of the mutation, people were not exactly rushing to get to D.C."

"But Hell, a Colonel?"

"He ran for state representative prior to Nine Eleven. Decided to head back to his old life at the CDC after that, gave up his private sector research, then ended up at Detrick with USAMRIID. He's a top notch guy."

"You know him personally? This Merrick fella?" Rasmussen asked.

"We've met a couple times face to face. Best microbiologist I've ever worked with, even if he was on a completely different level than me."

"So what happened to the President?" I asked.

"Mutation hit him and his family at Camp David. He was hospitalized for twenty-two days. Four of them on full life support. Still didn't matter."

"And the acting President thinks he is going to keep this quiet?"

"No. But there has been little time to deal with anything except one crisis after another."

"What about other countries? Are things as bad there, too?" Mike asked.

"Yes, from what we can tell. We have quite a few subs at sea, in complete isolation. Their crews are still healthy. For now, that is. They're monitoring things around the world. It's...grim."

"All right, back on task. Just what do you expect the people in this room to plan for?" Ames asked. "This secrecy order of yours is, pardon my directness, bullcrap."

"Sir, I believe that as a matter of course, it is best to have a plan to get out of the way of the excrement, before you throw it into the fan."

"Son, we're way beyond that around here. We've already been on the receiving end. Some, more than others," Ames said, looking around the table.

"All right then, let's play out your scenario," Hattrup said. "At three p.m. this afternoon, say word gets out that the President is dead, along with his family, and most of the national chain of command is either dead or gone for the hills. And that the reason for this is a highly lethal mutation of influenza. What happens in Spokane and Kootenai Counties?"

One of the deputies spoke up. "Not a damned thing different than any other normal day since about mid February."

"And why do you think that?" Hattrup asked.

"Commander, we've been living third-world conditions off and on for three or four months. I'd expect that everyone in this room has been shot at, or shot, someone looking to do them harm. Sometimes our own family. I'd expect that everyone in this room has already lost family, friends, neighbors in the quake, the first flu, or the war," he said as he looked at the Navy uniform with a sharp eye. "We're not like the rest of the country anymore."

Before the commander answered, I asked him, "Commander, what exactly do you expect to gain by attempting to KEEP this quiet?"

"I was hoping to avoid triggering looting, riots, and out-and-out murder."

"If I may answer for other more-qualified folks in this room, we've already seen that movie and I believe that as the Deputy said, we're not like the rest of the country anymore. I've already had to kill more people than anyone ought to, and all I was trying to do was to keep my family warm and fed. I believe that the vast majority of people left here understand that, and respect that as well. My opinion is as you already know, that you do not try to conceal this information. They need time to prepare themselves, and I'm not talking just about earthly things," I said. "Am I out of line here, gentlemen?"

The majority of them agreed with letting the information out. "Thanks. I never much cared for being the only nail sticking up."

Hattrup showed our small group a Powerpoint slide show prepared by the Department of Defense's 'Denver Task Force.' The presentation, now four days old, outlined expected losses of population, skilled and unskilled labor, industrial capability and overall production. He stated that this was the North American scenario, and that five other presentations had been prepared to address other continents and strategic relationships. DOD admitted, oddly enough, that they actually had no idea where the bottom might be, but that with already-demonstrated losses to just a few key industries and professions, modern industrial civilization was going to be 'put on hold' or 'regress' for a period of years to decades, in their worst-case scenario. Well, their 'only' scenario.

Defense was telling us that the hardest hit professional segment would be medical, and that the highest percentage of losses in the already affected areas of the country were skilled medical professionals, emergency service technicians, fire and policemen—first responders. In areas 'less affected at present', most of the emergency personnel didn't respond. This limited the spread of the disease, temporarily.

Equally hard hit, but not by disease, was food handling and manufacturing. The loss of fuel, of spare parts, manufacturing of spare parts, of fertilizer, of food-handling manpower and equipment, was predicted to devastate the nation through food shortages virtually everywhere. In food-producing regions, monocultural food production over the past several decades had eliminated most of the diversity of a 'local' diet. Areas that produced one major crop had no fields, farms, vines or trees that produced other crops needed by the human machine. While people might eat what was available and survive for a while, nutritional starvation would be real within twenty-four months. Food production nationwide was predicted to plummet far below pre-War levels, to a fraction of what it had been. The entire mechanization process had stripped away the ability to adapt equipment to non-diesel fuel in time for this year's planting and harvest. It simply wasn't possible to feed the population without tractors, combines, threshers, and 'big iron.' Neither was it possible to adapt the equipment to horse drawn operation. Among the many obstacles to that contingency was the fact that there simply weren't enough horses, not to mention people who knew how to work with them.

The fact that I found most surprising (although it shouldn't have) was this: Fifty-five percent of the nation's agricultural land that was in production last year, was not planted. This of course did not include those lands not planted, but 'held in reserve', under the CRP—Conservation Reserve Program. In pre-War days of course, the farmers were still paid not to plant. Certainly that nonsense was over now. I wondered how farmers would find enough seed to plant, given all of the disruptions in shipping and manufacturing over the spring. And what about 'Terminator' seeds that were useless for propagation after the first generation? Was there enough seed to feed us, either genetically-modified or 'heirloom?' Our personal supplies were almost all 'heirloom' varieties, but who could say how much of the nation's supply was going to be useable in a year?

The country would be 'bigger' soon too, and not geographically. DOD predicted that soon, again, it would take weeks to get across country, that communications across the nation would still be maintained to a degree, but that instant communications across the country or around the world would take at least a decade to restore for the general population. The losses of Boeing's Puget Sound facilities, of our space-launch capability, of the manufacturing base in equipment and machine tools, but mostly the loss of skilled engineers, would set us back forty or more years.

Losses of infrastructure parts and the ability to maintain them would soon be felt nationwide, as it had already affected other parts of the world. The inability to maintain power generating equipment and the losses of operators would shut down large parts of the nations electrical system. This of course would result in cascade failures of water systems, health care functions, manufacturing, and any building over three stories tall. Without power, no elevators, air conditioning, plumbing. No refrigeration.

DOD put the highest priority in their 'action plan' to securing critical power generation and switching stations, training of additional operators, and identification of spare parts and factories that could produce them. They recognized of course, that they were likely far too late in the spread of the mutation, to meaningfully affect the outcome.

They closed the presentation with the expectation that upon the loss of power for more than 24 hours, widespread civil unrest would rapidly spread and overwhelm municipal authorities and military units in urban areas.

No contingency plan was presented for that, but we all assumed I was sure, that the military units would not go down without a fight, even to their own countrymen.

The downslope of the bell curve was going to be bumpy.

We talked about the presentation throughout the afternoon, and up to what should've been 'dinner,' with one break for the restroom. We were accompanied by an MP whenever we left the room, whether we were in uniform or not.

By the time food was brought in, we hadn't really come to conclusions about how the population would react as the disease went through the area. We had ideas and expectations, but I explained that for me, I planned tomorrow happening only with God's help and direction, and that anything that I planned wouldn't be near as good as what He had planned for me in any regard.

"Con" Ames (short for Connor) said it best: "Leaving the Almighty out of it for a moment, which for me is difficult Commander, you simply need to put away your fears. What's going to happen is going to happen with this disease. You've told us that. It is up to the citizens of the respective counties to live their days in that light. I buried my wife and son, both killed from bad water they got at the hospital, last February. I didn't have to live after that, I really didn't. But God has something in mind for me in this world, and I'm of a mind to let Him have His way with me. You also ought to know that until they both took sick, I hadn't set foot in a church since my wedding day. I didn't regard myself as a Christian, I didn't regard God as relevant. Well, he showed me otherwise. My daughter and my brand new grand-daughter showed up April tenth. If I'da given up, neither of them would have lived another week. You best just give people the benefit of the doubt, cause God's steerin' the ship."

We took a break at about nine-thirty. If Hattrup's predictions were correct, then a substantial portion of our current population would become ill and die when the infection reached us through whatever means of transmission. If that happened, the survivors would need to 'contract' in the community around key resources. Water. Food. Shelter. To survive, they'd need to get along with each other. The survivors would not necessarily do that of course.

If his prediction was 'wrong' or not as severe, what passed for daily 'life' in the area might be able to continue along a path to recovery.

I passed an MP at the door as I headed out into the fenced enclosure to the south of the large warehouse, my shoes kicking up the loose gravel and volcanic ash. I looked to the southwest, to where our home was, up over the hill, beyond the Ponderosa pines that buffered the interstate. Too far to see anyway, even if the terrain allowed it. The last of daylight was fading in the northwest, and the stars were quite bright to the east.

How would I tell my family what could yet come our way?

The sentry called me back inside, and we put another hour toward that specific problem. 'Informing the Public,' that specific session was called. By eleven-thirty p.m., I took one more walk outside and looked up at the Milky Way, now clear and visible enough with little light pollution that we could now again see its true colors. I heard footsteps crunch the gravel behind me, and was joined by Con Ames, looking up as well.

"Enjoying God's creation, I see," he said.

"Never ceases to amaze," I replied.

"So what do you think our chances are?" he asked, I could see him ponder this without taking his gaze from the purple ribbon of the galaxy.

"You know, I never make a bet unless I am completely sure of the outcome. And honestly, I have a difficult time believing what I'm hearing," I said. "But on the other hand, if you told me on January thirteenth that within six months, we'd have fought the Third World War, that the United States that we'd known all our lives had nearly ceased to exist, and that Mexico, of all nations, had helped facilitate the previous two items, I'd have thought you'd escaped from the psych ward at Eastern State Hospital."

He chuckled at that. "I knew a man from South Carolina in years past. He had a bumper sticker that I'll never forget. 'South Carolina. Too small to be it's own country, too big to be a mental asylum.' Right now, I'm beginning to look at my own state in the same light."

"Balkanization?"

"That's what they're talking about," he said as he motioned toward the building, "but I think that the decision making process in that building may be critically flawed. Leaning toward the 'mental-asylum' metaphor."

"What do you mean?"

"First-responder fatigue. It's the effect of working long hours and getting restricted amounts of sleep, which messes up people's decision making ability, their judgment, their morals, their common sense. Everybody thinks that it's just being 'tired.' It's not. It's being discharged, mentally. I know people that are being hurt just doing simple things, because they've been so stressed for so long that things that should be simple kill them. A guy down the valley from me got run over by his tractor last week. Took him a day and a half to die from that. It was a stupid accident and he knew better. It got him anyway."

"I didn't know it had a name," 'First-responder fatigue,' I thought. 'Huh.'

"You sound like you have first hand experience with it then."

"I do. I think everybody does. My personal flavor tends to lean toward depression. And pessimism of course."

"Eventually, people either need to be relieved of the stress, as in removed from the situation, or they'll snap. Or screw up really badly, which is just as bad."

"I can agree with that. Problem is, there is no relief. There is no evacuation, no fall back or Plan B."

"Yeah. My point in this instance is, I think that perhaps our friends inside that building might be making really bad decisions because they've been inside the firestorm for way too long."

"You don't think that they're going to let people know about what's going on?"

"I think that part is settled. It's the follow-on actions that concern me. A lifetime ago I worked for an engineering firm down in Utah. I saw the effects of bad decision making on our companies engineering solutions. People behind desks who were working too long with too little to go on and too much pressure on them made decisions that were outside of the physical design parameters. The result was the loss of a school teacher and six astronauts."

"Morton Thiokol."

"See? You even know the name, more than twenty years later. It was a good company. It was crippled by people who were like those men in that room."

"They are, or were still around though, right? I mean before the War."

"There was a company. It bore little resemblance to the firm I once worked for."

"So what is your recommendation, Mr. Ames?" I asked.

"Word's going to get out, that's a given, whether they think it's a good idea or they make the announcements themselves or not. That endless discussion this afternoon is a prime example of what I'm talking about. Do they think that they can cut us off from the rest of the country? Were they planning on taking all our radios away? The bunker mentality that about half of that room has is completely counterproductive. Three of those guys want to lock down the REGION against outsiders. The paranoia is so thick you can taste it. Let things happen. There is nothing else to be done."

At nearly midnight, we ended our meeting. Along with most of the attendees, we were escorted to our quarters for the night, along with our personal belongings. I was pleased to see that my pack had remained undisturbed, not that I had much to hide.

We were given sleeping quarters in what had been the office portion of the warehouse. I had a half-lit cubicle with a cot, a desk, and two boxes of belongings of the former cube-farm dweller, his nameplate on his partition wall. I wondered if 'Eric Iskelson' was still alive? Certainly, he was no longer working as 'Advertising Manager.'

I fell asleep relatively quickly, thinking of course of Karen and the kids. This was my first night away since the quake. I did not sleep well that night.

52

Saturday morning,
May Twenty-Seventh

Five o'clock comes way too early when you've had maybe four hours of sleep on a board-hard cot. This was apparently not true for our military hosts, who were up and going. I did my best to imitate them, and succeeded only as a pale shadow. With some direction from a very young Corporal, I made my way to the mess hall, which had at one time been a manufacturing bay for some kind of electronics. The machines were disconnected and unceremoniously shoved into a corner. Nine rows of long mess tables were nearly fully populated.

I saw Warrant Officer Woody Clifton across the room and headed over to him after my breakfast was dished up. On the way, I noticed an Airman at an adjacent table sporting a tee-shirt that had a screen-printed image of a 747 with the text, 'E-4B--We fly the President when it really matters.' Interesting.

"Morning," I said to Clifton as I took a chair across the long table from him.

"Mr. Drummond," he responded, "Good morning." Which was said in a tone of, 'who in the Hell do you think you are telling me it's a good morning?'

"I noticed you were fairly quiet during our briefing," I said as I tried the flat-tasting reconstituted eggs. The coffee was bitter, and almost undrinkable.

"Meetings are not my strong suit."

"I understand. I like the two-ten myself."

"Pardon?"

"Two minutes of presenting a problem. Ten minutes of discussion and decision. Maybe fifteen for bigger issues. Then, get on with things."

"Yes, sir. Seems the brass missed that memo."

"You familiar with our area?" I asked, "I mean, before the War."

"Not really. Been up to Bayview a time or two with my step-father, but that's a long time ago. He had a cabin not far from Farragut. Well, I guess I have one now. I haven't been there in twenty years. Rented it out and had a local guy maintain it. Used to send me a couple of checks per year."

"Pretty country up there," I said. Bayview was a small town on the southern end of Lake Pend Oreille, about forty miles or so from Spokane.

"Fishing?" I asked. The lake was famous for it. Kokanee, brown trout, bass, mackinaw, and a dozen other species.

"No, he was trying to get me interested in the Navy. Took me to the base up there."

"Gotcha. They used to run some pretty interesting stuff up there. Last thing I saw they were testing was the a hull-model for the DDX series destroyer. Used to run all the sub models up there, too. That was last summer. Probably done with that forever," I said. "He a Navy man?"

"Yeah. He thought it would straighten me out. I thought otherwise."

"So therefore you went Army."

"Affirmative," he said with a slight grin. "That's been a number of years back obviously. He passed on before I got out of boot at Fort Sill."

"Sorry to hear that. I'm sure he'd be proud of you. Where you from originally?"

"Little town in Oregon. Joseph."

"I had a great Uncle in LaGrande. Took me down to the park down on Lake Wallowa one time. Nice little town. Maybe a little too artsy for me."

"Honestly, that's why I left it."

"Nice or artsy?"

"The latter. Bunch of useless crap."

"Well, art does have its place."

"Maybe then. They just Californized the place. I went back once, after my first tour. That was enough."

"Yeah, things change. So, getting back on topic, what do you think is next?"

"With this bunch? Honestly it's depressing. And I don't use that word lightly. The lack of brainpower in uniform in that room is astounding. You civilians and that Sheriff of yours have that figured out I think."

"I didn't want to be the one to say it, but it did seem that we had to keep feeding people the question, and then leading them to an answer."

"Seemed that way, Hell. It was exactly that way."

"OK, confidentially, why is that? I mean, some of those men have been in the service their entire career," I asked quietly.

"That doesn't mean that they deserve their rank, or even earned it."

"So let's take that ball and run with it. We decided yesterday, after hours of sitting, that telling the public what was coming, and of what had already happened ought to be done."

"And that took what, three? Four hours?"

"Yeah."

"Mr. Drummond, you and your compadres are here because you are willing to stick your neck out and decide, right or wrong. Most of the men in that room would rather bleed from their eyeballs before they'd do that."

"Then this morning's meeting will be damned short."

"That's fine by me. I've got six patrols out, and I'd like to see what they've come up with."

"Can you elaborate?"

"Nope. Not yet. They're working east and southeast. I can tell you that."

"OK," I said, finishing my last bite of powdered eggs. 'The group that probably killed McKinnon,' I thought.

"Eggs aren't bad for twenty years old, are they?"

"Not quite what I'm used to, but not bad."

"One piece of advice for you, Mr. Drummond. There are situations when the military and the Federal Government are required on a local basis. Right now and right here is not one of them. They need to let civilian authority run things and stay the Hell out of your way. What you have going on here is working. They're doing their best to make this a military action."

Our meeting was scheduled to reconvene at six thirty. After Clifton and I finished breakfast, he excused himself and headed out a door to the west, toward a guarded command center. I had a few minutes to talk to Connor Ames, Drew Simons, who joined us late, and Hank Rasmussen. Hank was a retired teacher, who before the quake was the director of one of the volunteer fire departments. I found out during the discussion that Con Ames' business, pre-Domino, was the restoration of wooden boats on Coeur d'Alene and Hayden Lakes, both sailboats and classics like Chris Craft and Hacker Craft.

I reviewed my conversation with Clifton with the group, and received raised eyebrows at my suggestion that we tell the military that we should wrap up our discussions before noon, and get back to living our lives.

"You think they'll just fold up on you like that?" Hank Rasmussen asked, skeptically.

"No. But I'm of a mind that this is a waste of time. It might be different if this were Kansas City or Fargo or someplace that already hadn't been through the wringer. Honestly—what portion of what was presented yesterday is feasible?"

"None of it," Con replied.

"My point."

"Fine with me. I have alfalfa to bale," Drew Simons answered.

"Me, too."

"You suddenly in the livestock business?" Drew asked, leaning back and looking at me a little sideways.

"Nope. Friend of ours out at Newman. He's got acreage. We're trading labor cutting and bailing for firewood."

"Wonder who got the better end of that deal?" Drew said with a smile.

"I think we're about even. It's only a good deal if both parties are happy with it at the end of the day."

He thought about that for a moment. "Agreed. Now let's start this day off right and go finish this nonsense," he said as he pushed his chair from the table.

We headed back into the meeting room, and found about half of the uniformed officers present, with briefing packets in front of them. The remaining chairs, formerly occupied by the remaining military officers, had been pushed against the wall. Apparently, others had decided that this briefing was a waste of time as well. Hattrup was present though, in a white uniform that made him stand out like a sore thumb.

"Commander, good morning," I said.

"Mr. Drummond, everyone, please take a seat if you would," he said. "In front of you is a briefing packet outlining the press releases that will begin at eight o'clock this morning. These announce to the nation that the President has passed away, and that the National Command Authority is at present in the hands of the military."

"You think this is a good idea?" One of the Air Force officers asked. "I know a lot of people who will think that this is a military coup."

"Agreed," Hattrup responded. "However, the second page details the transition process for the chain of command, to put a civilian Executive back in charge."

I was a little taken aback. "How did you come up with this overnight? Yesterday, you said that no one wanted to step up."

"That may have been the impression, yes. Military authorities across the nation have been in contact with a number of senators and representatives and presented the situation. I fully expect that an interim leadership team will be in place by one September."

"Lot can happen between now and then," Hank Rasmussen said. "And none of it good." Visions of gun confiscations suddenly popped up in my head, among other unpleasantries.

"I understand. Things take time to put together however."

"Commander, this country is quite possibly inches away from disintegration. You think we can afford to wait three months to have a new

President and Cabinet in place? I think you better try again. Three WEEKS maybe," Rasmussen continued.

"I agree," Connor Ames said. "Commander, with all due respect, we are used to making things happen quickly. The military does not move with agility, it is a plodding, awful contraption of standards, protocols, and bureaucracies. We just don't work that way." Ames looked around at us. "Frankly we do not see the need, to continue this meeting. Make the announcement. Get on with things. But mostly, and I mean this again with respect, get the heck out of the way. We've work to do."

Hattrup didn't know what to do with that. "Gentlemen, I am here to provide you the outline of events that we see coming."

"And we're telling you that by the time you get done outlining things, they're already history," Hank replied. "This meeting is a waste of time. It appears that some of your fellow uniformed officers felt the same way," he said, motioning to the empty chairs.

"Commander, nothing personal here," I said, "but there is a use for the military. There is a use for a national leadership. The military needs to protect the citizens from foreign aggressors and maintain free trade. This is an oversimplification but that's about all the mission of the military ought to be. They shouldn't be in the business of domestic *OR* international police issues, but I can understand that occasionally, that might need to happen. The national leadership similarly ought to be working to protect the national defense, our national resources, and our borders. Anything else ought to be up to the states. Or the towns."

"Amen." Con Ames added.

Hattrup paused. "I can see that I'm going to get nowhere here."

"On the contrary, young man," Drew Simons said. "The crap may hit the fan. It may not. It has here already a couple of times. You need to figure out where, exactly, do you intend to 'go' to from here? There are tipping points in the lifeline of a civilization. You are smack dab on one now. This country can tip over to a military dictatorship in a heartbeat. It can as easily, perhaps more easily, roll itself up into a fascist nation run by corporate and military interests who have thus far survived the plunge. The hard road, sir, is the one that leads back to a representative republic. Which is what this country was meant to be, before it became a mobocracy with thieves on one side of the aisle and robbers on the other. The question you have to ask yourself is, exactly what road are you on now?"

Hattrup pondered Connor Ames words for only a few seconds, then deliberately folded up his briefing papers, tied the binder cord on his file, nodded to the military officers only, and left the room. We rose, shook hands with the other service men, and as quickly we were alone. Most of them looked at us a little differently than they had before. Almost as if we were a threat.

"Well said, Drew," I said.

"Gentlemen, I believe we have work to do. I have a baler that needs repairing." Drew Simons said. We shook hands with our new friends from Idaho, collected our personal effects, and by seven a.m., we were on our way out of the building.

Drew caught a ride with a caravan of National Guardsmen heading down to Tekoa, just beyond the southern edge of the county. One of the units was ordered to drop him at his farm, after their C.O. received a radio call. I was used to seeing military vehicles only in operation. We saw five rows of American made diesel pickups though, now with new camouflage paint and a variety of weapons mounted on the beds. Some of the weapons were unrecognizeable. Our Idaho friends were driven back home in a thrashed, but current model year, Crown Victoria.

Mike Amberson hadn't been present at this mornings' meeting. I hadn't really expected him though. He did show up just as I was waving to Con and Hank as they passed the gate.

"Waste of time over?" Mike asked.

"Good morning Sheriff, and yes. That horse was put down."

"Good for you. Ready to get home?"

"Absolutely."

"I let Karen know you'd probably be back home today. Probably broke the rules in telling her that, but I really don't care all that much about their rules. This place bothers me."

"Why's that?" I said as I got into the car and closed the door. The interior panels on all of the doors had been replaced with thick welded steel, running up to just below shoulder height. The foam roof panel had likewise been replaced with a steel plate. The rear seat areas looked unfinished, waiting for more time to weld in more bulletproofing.

"It's screwed up. Not the place. The people. They don't have their chain of command figured out, and are just realizing that they aren't going back to 'normal' anymore. They're trying to get parts for those turbo-diesels and it ain't gonna happen," he said, thumbing over to a maintenance garage full of trucks, hoods up, parts laying on benches, mechanics standing around.

"What happened to them?"

"Bad fuel. Mixed with gas or something. Blew the turbos. More properly, burned up the turbos."

"Huh. Interesting modifications you've had made to your car," I said as I thumped a chunk of steel.

"Interesting times call for innovative responses."

"Well put."

We passed the front gate, where the honor guard was lowering the flag to half-staff.

"Guess words, out."

"It was on the radio ten minutes ago," Mike said as we began to re-trace the route that brought me to the meeting.

"What's on your agenda for the weekend, now that it's half-burned?"

"Taking care of the wife and Memorial Day service on Monday, out at Fairmont. You?"

"I'd like to get out there myself. My grandparents and great-grandparents graves are out there. We'll probably stay out here though. We've got a lot of work to do. Promised to help Don Pauliano get his hay in, in exchange for some more firewood."

"That's Joe's son?"

"Yeah. Lives out at Newman."

"Do me a favor. Float the trial balloon of having him replace Clete McKinnon on the Board."

"Uh, okay. I thought the Board was about 'done' though. We've got things sort of put together."

"That may be, but we still have the elections coming up for the township reps, and a smoother transition would be better. Also, I'm not sure how long Walt is going to be with us." Walt Ackerman's health had been in decline since before the Domino, and he'd gone downhill significantly as a result of the stress of dealing with our former County Commissioners. Then, to top it off, most of his prescription drugs were no longer available.

"He's failing that fast?"

"Heart. Docs don't think he'll make the end of June."

"Damn," I thought. I'd known Walt for years. One of the best of the 'old Guard,' as we called them. Professional administrators. Knew how to do a job or find the right person for it and eager to give that person the responsibility for doing it, and the credit or blame at the end. A rare quality for the past decade, I'd noticed. Most of the civil servants that I knew either micromanaged or shirked responsibility. "Who are we going to find to take his place?"

"You are my first candidate."

"Wait just a minute here, Mike," I said, with a chuckle. "Walt's assistant Kamela…"

"…was hospitalized with bacterial meningitis on Thursday. That may kill her. The rest of his staff is junior enough to be not quite useless in administration, but damned near so."

That shut me up pretty quickly. "What makes you think that *I* am any more qualified than they are?"

"You know enough about the County government, both the way it is and the way it should be. Mostly, you don't put up with much in the way of bull. That alone is a pretty good quality."

"Mike I've got my own affairs to run. How am I supposed to do THIS eighty-hour a week job, in addition to my other eighty-hour a week job?"

"You'll have help. It's not all up to you. Find the right people to put in position, and let them run the ball. They'll figure out what needs to be done. I think that you're the right man for the job."

"Given the limited population you have to to choose from."

"Well, yes, frankly," Mike said with a laugh.

"Let me talk it over with Karen."

"I already did that for you."

"And you escaped unscathed?"

"We had a good talk. I think she's OK with it. You'll need to talk to her and let me know though. I understand if you have reservations about it. It is a significant responsibility, and will be for the next few months."

"And if I decided to take the position, what sort of succession plan do we have?"

"We don't yet. Walt's job was to serve the Commissioners while they were in office. When they were deposed, he was to run the County until new elected representatives could be installed. We're starting that of course with the Townships, but there won't be, I think, any way to elect representatives from the entire County until at least mid- to late-fall. They will need a transition until after that time of course, when they may select a replacement for you."

"If I decide to take the job."

"I'm pretty confident that you will," Mike said. "When you see who I'm selecting from, you'll see why."

"Well, if I'm the deep end of the gene pool, then God help Spokane County," I said as we passed the burned shell of Macy's. Weeds were now growing thick in the parking lots, sprouting from cracks and the drifts of Mt. Rainier's ash blown up over the curbs.

Ten minutes later, I was back home in the driveway. Mike, a little too quickly I thought, dropped me off and left me to my fate.

'Thanks, Mike,' I thought as I opened the gate and was met by Ada, her tail going like mad. I could see Karen at the bay window in the dining room, rising to meet me.

"Once again unto the breach, dear friends," I said to no one.

53

Saturday,
May Twenty-seventh

"Hiya, babe," I said as I walked up onto the porch.

"Good morning. Your secret mission over?" Karen said as she came through the door and gave me a quick kiss good morning.

"Yes."

"Everyone's speculating on what's going on. At least, they were until we heard about the President. Is that what it's all about?"

"Partly. You talked to Mike, didn't he let on?"

"Not really. We had a long talk about your potential new job though."

"What do you think?"

"Mike seems pretty anxious about it. As in, if you weren't the guy for the job, he'd have a problem."

"Maybe so. I don't know. I just got hit with that on the way home. When did he talk to you?"

"Last night. Came by after curfew. We met with Alan and Ron, too."

"You've had more time to think about it than I have."

"Mike has a lot of faith in you."

"I'm not sure I do in myself though. What else did he tell you?"

"Enough, without divulging national security issues, his words."

"I'll fill you in. We'll need to tell everyone."

"Not a secret?" she asked as she squeezed my hand.

"Not for much longer." I was then mobbed by Carl and Kelly, who were both relieved to have me back it seemed. I was at least as glad to be back with them.

We gathered the family members up from throughout the fields a few minutes after I made it home and met at Alan's place so Grace wouldn't have to travel. As everyone pulled up a chair or found a place to sit on a log or the firewood pile, I asked everyone to keep things confidential for now. I told them that within the next day or so the news about the mutation, in all of its potentially ugly detail, would be broadcast locally and probably nationally as well. I told them all that they needed to be ready physically and spiritually for what might happen.

"This could take some of us, or all of us," I said with gravity. "Each of us needs to understand that clearly."

A few moments passed before anyone spoke.

"What do we tell the settlers?" Ron asked.

"Are they all moved in?" I asked.

"Yesterday was a busy one," he said.

"I'll speak with them tomorrow. I wanted to tell you all first. Like I said, this could be bad if it works here like it's doing in parts of the East, or in other parts of the world."

"You seem skeptical." Libby said, reading me like a book.

"I am. And I don't know why I am," I said as I looked over the field of corn, and the field of wheat beyond. "I'm just having a hard time believing what I was told. Maybe I just don't want to believe it. I don't know."

By ten, the wind was picking up a little, but not enough to bring up the dust. We had a cool day and if someone were sitting in the shade, they'd need a jacket.

We'd planned for several weeks to help Don out with his hay, and in exchange cutting some firewood from his land, and I was really looking forward to getting out and off of the property for a while, working on something other than my own stuff.   For some reason, working on somebody else's projects seemed more interesting than my own.

Knowing that we'd be traveling, while not exactly in unfamiliar territory, but in potentially unsafe areas, I asked the boys to round up their rifles and a couple of the shotguns, while I retrieved my own weapon from the house. Today, we'd instruct the boys on the operation of the Browning. The girls on the other hand would get lessons on the use of a shotgun. We had a .410 and a twenty-gauge for the girls, and Alan had cobbled up some 'light' loads for his Wingmaster. No sense in breaking the girls shoulders....

As an afterthought, and for humor, I grabbed one of my brother Jeff's cowboy hats, a too-tall straw hat with a band that included a bunch of ringneck pheasant feathers. Jeff had a fair number of them, but left them at our parents place after he left home. Four of us brothers decided to wear them once at Hangman Valley Golf Course, years ago, along with our jeans and western shirts—we avoided Joe during that reunion. The pro was not amused. We played a different scoring method that day, 'Disaster,' It was. I lost, having the worst game I'd had in years.

Grace stayed home with Mary and Alan and their kids. Mark and Rachel were just a little too small to help out at the Pauliano's, and I was always nervous about little kids and farm machinery. Alan was planning to work with our new neighbors on divvying up some of the more than two hundred garden tools that we'd collected over the past months, and get them started on helping out in the fields. The gardens and field work had been almost manageable so far, but soon would be beyond the ability of the Drummond/Bauer/Martin families to keep up. The additional families' labor would definitely be easier on all of us. We explained this of course to the candidates before they were selected, and none had much of an issue with working for some of their food. I wondered if they'd have said the same thing a year ago?

We loaded up our 'gear' into the rooftop bag of the Ford. I'd told the kids and the adults that they should pack for a couple of days stay, just in case something happened. That included food and water. No one argued that I was being silly, after what we'd all been through. I loaded up my bag, with two of the FRS radios and their failing batteries into the roof bag. I kept the better of the CB radios in the car and hooked up the remote antenna. As we drove east, we'd check in with the house to see what our range might be. I had no doubt that we'd lose reception completely by the time we got to Don and Lorene's.

With everyone sandwiched in and the dogs wanting to go as well, we started out with Mary and her kids minding the dogs and the gate. Joe and Joan had gone out on Thursday to work in Don's large garden--I wondered how Joe could do it at his age. We didn't have an issue driving out with my trusty purple tag identifying me as Someone Important and therefore allowed to drive my personal vehicle. Gasoline was available to folks engaged in food production purposes, still. I wondered how long we'd be able to keep that up? Behind the Ford, my little utility trailer hauled my two chain saws, oil, fuel and saw files, as well as some things that Joe wanted to move to Don's place. On the return trip, it would hold a couple cords of wood.

None of the group, myself included, had traveled this far east, to Newman Lake, since well before the Domino. This area was far outside of the 'service area' we'd established for utilities, so it was interesting to see how things had changed in just a few months since the quake and the evacuations.

We headed east along the same roads used by the Army to bring me to the Industrial Park, but would continue north on Barker to the state highway, and then toward Newman Lake. If we stayed on the highway, we'd have ended up in Idaho another mile or so east. We used to take this road to get to Silverwood Theme Park, Lake Pend Oreille, Priest Lake, and nice points north of town. I wondered as I dodged sizeable cracks and holes in the road, if I'd ever see any of those again?

The Spokane Valley is basically layers of glacial till, meaning outwash and remnants from Ice Age glaciers and the great Lake Missoula floods that began in Montana, and repeatedly washed across the region, sweeping all the way to the Columbia River and on to the Pacific. These floods swept almost all of the topsoil off of the volcanic basalt west of Spokane, creating what is called the Scablands. In the Spokane Valley, however, we were left with mixed layers of boulders, gravels, sands and some topsoil, building over the years as plants and grasses became mulch. The lower levels of this mix contain our freshwater aquifer, hundreds of feet thick below us, and ranging in depth from dozens- to hundreds of feet below the Valley floor. In recent years the agricultural side of the production in the Valley tipped to growing subdivisions instead. We were now passing through two of them, bracketing Barker, and continuing east along the state highway, just south of one of the main railroad lines.

The timing and severity of the Domino caused these neighborhoods to be abandoned in fairly short order after January 14th. Domestic water was pumped from wells in the aquifer to water towers above the Valley floor, and boosted further with electric pumps. Sewage was either piped to an incomplete—but growing—sewage collection system or treated with septic fields. The problem with this of course is that the septic systems are right above the drinking water. Without power, the water systems and sewage plants failed, regardless of damage to the supply or waste piping. The quake also inflicted massive damage to the natural gas supply system, long before the Canadian government decided that Canada needed the gas more than the U.S. did.

Incentives from the utilities over the past fifteen years made natural gas heat the only real choice for heating these new homes. Wood stoves were most often only decorative, or pellet stoves that required some form of electricity to feed the pellets into the stove and run a blower to distribute heat.

Without electricity, there was little chance that these homes would ever be livable again, certainly not in the way they had once been. It did not appear that any of the homes had been retrofitted with wood heat either before or after the quake. I slowed as we drove by, peering down the streets, looking for some sign of activity. There was none, or more correctly, no signs of human activity. I did notice a fair amount of animal tracks in the ash and dust in the streets, and of course the weed growth in the cracked pavement, the tree seedlings now a foot or more tall. Everyone was looking around, commenting on the damage at first, and what might be salvageable, as we went further along. Carl pointed out a newish Maxxum ski boat that rested uncomfortably partly off its trailer, beside a collapsed home. The trailer jack appeared to have punctured the hull as the boat had shifted forward. The white canvas covering the open bow had been cut with a knife. Obviously looted by somebody who didn't want to take the time to unsnap the cover.

I turned back toward the highway, and startled a doe and her fawn from their grazing, behind the entrance sign to the development. They took off into the rows of wrecked houses, looking for more peaceful grazing.

Within another ten minutes, we had reached the Newman Lake turnoff. The intersection had evolved over my lifetime to include a small commercial area (anchored by the liquor store/post office/bait shop), and had grown to include a small hardware store, a gas station, and an antique shop. The area used to be called 'Moab', from the Biblical town on the east side of the Dead Sea. Funny, we never had a town called 'Edom' or 'Ammon,' though. I wonder why the settlers picked that name....

"Look, they're open," Karen said, pointing to the one-time hardware store. "Let's stop quick." The store looked pretty shabby, no longer up to the standards that the Ace Hardware sign used to signify.

"In a mood to shop?"

"No, but it'd be fun to poke around."

"OK," I said.

"Might be a good idea to see what they're getting for stuff," Ron said. "Rick, did you bring any cash?"

"Silver, yes. Kids, do not get into any trouble, OK?" I said. That drew the predictable 'Daaaahhhd!'

Ours was the only 'car' in the gravel parking lot. There were however, a half-dozen bikes-two with trailers-and two horses tied up around the side of the store. They were tethered to a newly built rail.

I was met at the door by a stoutly-built older woman (to be kind), who looked at my SUV with no small degree of suspicion. Or was it something else?

"May I help you sir?" she asked as she looked at the crowd piling out of the Ford.

"Well, we were interested in seeing what you had for sale," I said. "My name is Rick. I'm on the County Recovery Board. This is my family."

"You know about McKinnon? He was a customer of mine."

"I've heard, yes. I hope they find those responsible. He was a good man. How did you know him?"

"Mica Peak Horsemen," she said, referring to one of the more serious recreational riding clubs in the area. "He taught my daughters to ride."

"I didn't know that he rode."

"Didn't the past few years. Tore up his back in a fall up on the hill. Was trying to break a stallion. Stallion won." She finished looking us over, and apparently we met with her conditional approval. "C'mon in then. Don't see many cars or trucks anymore."

"I expect that will continue. This is my wife Karen, and my son Carl and daughter Kelly," I said, making introductions. "And this is the Martin family, who live just behind us now, Ron, Liberty—Libby for short—John and Marie." Ron asked John and Carl to hang out outside, to keep an eye on the trailer, the saws…everything. Both were now wearing their sidearms, per my earlier instructions.

"I'm Rae Samuels. This is my store. My girls are at the counter there." I acknowledged them with a smile as I noticed the sign above them that stated, 'Shoplifters will be Shot.'

"Nice to meet you. We're heading up to Don Pauliano's place."

"Kit Carson Road. I know the place. His, what was it? Cousin? Lived there. That crazy Russian lives next door."

"He's the one with the draft horses, if I remember correctly."

"That's right, among other things. He's got his fingers in a lot of things right now."

"I expect that that will be a trend."

"S'long as he doesn't cross me, then that'll be fine," Mrs. Samuels said as she glanced over at Kelly and Marie, who were looking over some item two aisles over.

"Have you had problems with him?"

"Not since before the Troubles. My cousin's place is next to his. His cattle was breaking down the fences and grazing on Samuels land. He wasn't all that keen on keeping his fences."

"How about now?"

"I think since a few of his head went missing, he's minding things a bit closer."

I could tell by the glint in her eye that the missing stock probably didn't go missing on it's own, at least not permanently. "Whatcha looking at girls?" I asked.

"Canning flats. Mom said to see if there were any for sale," Marie answered, not looking up. Karen was across the store, looking at some fabric with Libby. Ron was looking at some hardware.

"Those are a fairly scarce commodity," said Mrs. Samuels.

"What size do you have?"

"Size? Wide mouth Kerr with rings. You interested?"

"More curious. How much?"

"Five dollars silver per pack of twelve."

If I'dve been chewing gum, I'd have swallowed it in shock. "Did I hear that right?"

"You think you can find some somewhere else?" Mrs. Samuels replied.

"Dad, come look for yourself," Kelly said.

"Thanks Mrs. Samuels, I'll look around," I said to her as I walked over to the girls.

"Dad," Kelly said with a hushed voice, "These things are used."

"That's OK girls, we're not buying anyway. Not these things at least. You all go back to the car. I'll see what the others have found." I feigned interest in a few things, toothbrushes and home made bar soap and poorly made candles. I did notice a gallon sized paint bucket full of used mixed brass in various calibers. That container was marked six dollars. Behind Mrs. Samuels daughters at the counter, I noticed a case with metal bars that held pre-War liquor bottles. I noticed that none of the bottles had the Washington State tax seal. Which meant that they were either bootleg, or were not what they were purported to be.

About that time, Libby, Karen and Ron were making their way towards me. John and Carl had already taken one look and headed back outside, under the wary eye of Mrs. Samuels daughters. I suspected that behind their counter, they were close to their weapons.

"See anything we can't do without?" I asked in a friendly voice.

"Nope, not this time," Ron replied in an equally jovial, and equally put-on voice.

"Well, Mrs. Samuels, we'll be heading up the road now. We'll see you again."

"Yep," was all she said as we walked out the door.

Once back in the car, I said what I felt. "That place gave me the willies."

"Yeah," Karen said. "Those girls wouldn't stop looking at us."

"Probably been shoplifted a few times, or worse," I said.

"And those prices!" Ron said. "Was she serious?"

"Looked like it to me," I said.

"Lib, your impression?"

"She's a crook. And a liar. There's more to that place than meets the eye."

"Such as?"

"Not to be indelicate here, but those girls are probably prostitutes. And there was a smell in the air that only meant one thing. Methamphetamine."

"How would you know that?" Ron asked, a little shocked by his wife.

"One of my students at the middle school had meth addicts for parents. She came to school smelling like that place. Social Services pulled her out when the City finally busted the house. Of course by then she was pregnant. Her baby died right after birth. Horrible birth defects."

"Boys, what about you?"

"We were being targeted by someone up the hill behind the store. That's why we were on the road side of the Ford," Carl said.

"How did I miss that?" I said, beginning to seriously doubt my threat radar.

"Easy. They were pretty well hidden. One got stupid though and sneezed. The other told him to shut up."

"I'm glad to be out of there," Karen said. "And let's not go back."

"Fine by me," I said as we passed along the east lake road, winding our way to the Pauliano's.

"You're intuition was right," Don said to Karen as we finished unloading the Ford.

"Mine was dead wrong," I said.

"Nobody's perfect, Rick. You have the nasty habit of giving people the benefit of the doubt."

"I do at that."

"Can't afford that anymore, my friend. The Samuels family goes way the Hell back to the eighteen nineties. They've had run-ins with the law since they arrived back then. Horse thieves. Cattle thieves. Bootlegging in the Thirties. Markham Samuels was a few years older than me in school. Quit in the ninth grade and came out here to live with his grandparents. Had a first rate dope growing operation until someone decided he was getting too greedy. What he didn't get from drugs he got from welfare and public assistance, which was a lot. He was Rae's oldest. Meanest son of a bitch I've ever known."

"What happened to him?"

"Shot, execution style up on the backside of Brevier Road, over the hill there," Don said, pointing to the northwest.

"And she was a storekeeper?"

"God no," Don said. "They just took it over after the quake from what Sergei says. That and all the acreage that they possibly can. Tried to take this place too, until he ran her off."

"She said that 'that crazy Russian' wouldn't keep his fences and that some of his head went missing," I told Don.

"That is the case from her viewpoint I'm sure. In reality, someone using a Dodge Powerwagon with a stock rack drove through the fence, loaded up a couple head, and took off with them."

"And got away with it," Ron said with disgust.

"Not completely. Sergei and his hands shot up two of them about a month after the earthquake. One got away and left a pretty big blood trail. The other, well, he didn't make it." Don said with respect to the ladies present.

"Do you think that she had anything to do with your cousin going missing?" I asked.

Don looked at me for a moment. "I hadn't thought about that." Don's cousin had disappeared not long after the quake. The story was, that he'd 'walked off' into the woods one night and not returned.

"It makes sense given the rest of the story," I said.

"Yeah. It does at that."

"What about the other stuff at the store? Is it a drug house?" I asked him as Lorene and our wives went inside. Joan had corralled Kelly and Marie for some other tasks, leaving the 'menfolk' to our work. Joe was inside the barn, cleaning out an area for more stuff, and gave us a wave as we arrived.

"Most likely, yeah. And a whorehouse. But those are in fact her daughters. And, her 'girls.'

I let out a long descending whistle. "What's the law got to say about any of this?"

"Not much law around outside the Service Area. Not much law around within the Service Area either from what I can tell."

"Not as much as we might need. Military's pretty good on keeping things in line though."

"Well, with all of your mighty pull, you might see what you can do about sending a patrol out this'a way once in a while."

"I was thinking that a garrison might not be a bad idea. And, I need to talk to you about our Recovery Board."

"News travels fast," Don said. "You want to volunteer me for something."

"I do. To take Clete McKinnon's place as the eastern Valley rep."

"You're still on the board?"

"More than ever. The Sheriff wants me to take the County Administrator position if Walt Ackerman can't continue."

"Field promotion, huh?"

"Yeah, of sorts. And definitely not something I envisioned for myself."

"Little these days is. C'mon. Let's get geared up and get to baling. Supposed to rain in a few days and we have a lot of product on the ground. Nice hat, by the way," he said.

"Belonged to one of my brothers. Resistol."

"Bet you won't find one of those for sale any time soon."

"Yeah, probably not. A little tall for my tastes, but it'll do. Thing kinda looks like a caricature of what a cowboy hat oughta be."

Don had cut all eight acres of alfalfa already, and windrowed it for the baler. He'd used a pull-behind mower, then gone back over the field with a hay rake. The cuttings had been sitting for a day or so, to get them to the right moisture content for storage.

Almost all of this was foreign to me of course. I'd baled one summer when I was about seventeen. I wore out two pairs of jeans that summer, and four pairs of gloves. I did though, have shoulders that year…I never thought to ask any questions on 'why' things were done the way they were. I was just grunt labor.

The baler was to be pulled behind Don's 8n tractor as well, and would drop the bales behind as they were packed and wrapped with twine. I'd get to drive the tractor, Don would tend to the baler, John and Carl would start off bucking bales into the bale wagon, a New Holland model that would be towed by Ron operating another tractor, this one an old John Deere. The bale wagon, a new fangled contraption to me, but ancient by the looks of it (showing my age here), basically took the bale and eliminated the need to lift the bale up and toss it onto the trailer. The man on the ground had to tip it up on end, and another man on the trailer would move the bale around on the trailer. The conveyor could be raised up so that multiple layers of bales could fill the trailer. The trailer would then be taken to Don's storage shed, and the bales placed while still stacked. One trick that the 'stacker on the trailer would have to be aware of was placing the bales correctly so that they stayed stable as they were unloaded.

"Mechanization is a good thing," I said to Don as he finished explaining the process to us 'newbies.'"

"Sure beats raking it and piling it loose," Don said.

"Yes, it does."

"One more thing. You boys have got your leather chaps on for those bales, and if you don't have a hat on for shade, you'll need one, there are some in the barn. Keep your sidearms handy."

"Why's that?" John asked.

"We've got cougar and bear up that draw to the east there. They're not all that shy."

"And you think that we'll kill one with a forty-five?"

"No, I think you'll make noise so my thirty-thirty will come into play."

"Gee. Thanks."

"Step lively boys. Day's awastin'" Ron said.

"That baler looks pretty scary," I said as the boys hopped on the hay wagon behind Ron's tractor.

"It is. Tear your arm off if you're not careful."

"Let's be all over careful then. Where'd you pick up the Deere?"

"Bought it off of Sergei. Twenty bucks in silver."

I was more than a little surprised, and Don saw my expression.

"Wasn't running. Dad and I got it going yesterday. Towed it home last weekend."

"Cool. I like deals like that."

"Got another one for ya, if you're interested. Maybe a couple."

"OK, like what?"

"My old sixty-seven Ford Pickup. I don't really need it."

"Gas for that's a little dear these days. I'm not sure we could afford the gas."

"I understand. Deal is, this one runs on ethanol. My cousin built a conversion setup. Starts on gasoline, then switches over to ethanol. He modeled it after seeing something like it in Brazil, I think it was. I left the truck with the farm when I sold it to him. Couple years ago he asked me if I'd mind the conversion. I forgot all about the truck. I haven't had it running on ethanol, but it does start up on gas."

"How much you need for it?"

"Hell, I don't know. Swap me some parts for Nellie here, and we'll call it square," he said as he patted his tractor.

"Don't you want to keep an ethanol powered truck?"

"I am. I've got Evan's Escalade. Converted that one, too."

"No kidding."

"Yeah. Nicest farm truck you've ever seen."

"Where you getting your fuel?"

"Sergei for now. He's building me a still though," he said. "Head left to the outer row. We'll start there."

"How many bales you figure we'll get?"

"Eight hundred if we're lucky, seventy pounds apiece."

"I think my back hurts already."

"Here," he said, tossing me a bottle of Tylenol. "Pre-emptive strike."

Don was figuring that the eight acres of sub-irrigated bottomland in alfalfa would net about a hundred bales per acre, amounting to twenty-eight tons. In pre-War days, the alfalfa from a single cutting, depending on quality, might sell for four to eight dollars per bale. These days, there was literally no alfalfa on the market, and only a little demand in the urban area where we lived. He was hoping to get four cuttings out of the fields this year.

In fairly short order, I found the ground speed needed by the baler to collect the cuttings and allow Don time to mind the beast. Don's tractor was equipped with a Sherman transmission, which converted the standard four-speed transmission to twelve speeds, making the tractor much more versatile (and, I was now a little envious of this option….) He had a rear-view mirror from a car mounted on the side of the hood, which allowed me to get a glimpse of him and the boys following behind us, with Ron driving the well worn and rusty John Deere. John was on the ground, Carl on the trailer, muscling the bales around as the conveyor loaded them onto the deck. The perimeter of the fields was twenty to thirty feet higher in elevation than the lower areas, and we generated quite a bit of ash dust as we passed through. Don waved Ron to slow down, to give the dust a chance to either settle out or to blow away before either man or machine started sucking it in.

"We gonna get all this baled today?" I asked when we broke for lunch, a little after noon. We were less than a third of the way done, from what I could see.

"Should. I used to do forty tons per day when I was younger. We probably have like I said, maybe twenty eight to thirty tons, total. It'll take Ron and the boys longer to get it stowed in the hay barn and over at Sergei's place than it'll take us," he said as he pulled off his now well-worn gloves. My own pair of deerskin gloves was blackened with the old rubber from the steering wheel, which now had a number of shiny spots where my hands had worked it over. "We can then get some of that firewood loaded up. I hope those lengths are OK for your trailer," he said.

"Boys? How's it going?"

"I'm glad we don't do this every day," John said, patting the dust off of his chaps.

"Be thankful you have that trailer. We used to buck them onto that big flatbed," Don pointed over toward an ancient GMC, with a now-rotted wooden bed. "That, was work."

"Thanks, I think I like this version better," Carl said.

"Farm hands," Lorene said from the porch, "Lunch is on the porch. NO ONE inside with all that dirt."

"Yes, Ma Kettle," Don grinned.

"Don't you go and start that, mister. I've been fighting a losing war with that hayfield and I'm not giving in now."

"Boys, let's wash up over at the rain barrels," Don told us. "That'll at least make us presentable."

"I've got a little favor to ask, Don." I said. "Mind if we do a little plinking after lunch?"

54

Saturday afternoon,
May Twenty-seventh

"Easy now," I told Carl as he had missed his target again. "This is not about spray and pray. This is more about precision." In a prone position, using the new-looking bipod, he'd just stitched through the target on his first try on auto, from lower right to upper left. The first target was two hundred feet away; a second was three hundred feet out, and that was Carl's target this time. "Get to know how it behaves." I looked again with the sporting binoculars downrange at Don's impromptu rifle range, at the identical targets. Don had been using them to improve his skills, teach Lorene with his Mini 14, and make some noise to keep the two-legged varmints at bay. Another set of targets was far downrange, perhaps fifteen hundred feet.

"K," he said, not taking his eye from the target, his shooting glasses and ear protection in place. The Browning was anything but quiet. His next grouping was much better, a twenty-round pattern decimating a twenty-inch circle in the thirty-inch target panel.

"Impressive," I said in my best Darth Vader voice. "Most impressive."

"Thanks."

"Next magazine, try to keep it inside of ten inches."

"Not possible," John said. "She rattles all over the place."

Before I could answer, Carl said, "So don't go full auto. Couple rounds at a time and I can do it."

"Go for it. If you can do it you get ground duty for the rest of the day. I say you can't do it," John said. Ground duty meant tipping the bales up for the trailer to self-load. Trailer duty meant muscling the bales around. Much harder work.

Carl promptly put twenty rounds into the target, seventeen of them within a ten-inch circle, three with in a twenty-inch circle.

"Welcome to the brotherhood of the spiral tube," I said.

"What's that from?" Carl asked. John couldn't believe it.

"It's not 'from' anything, I don't think. I just made it up. Alright, John, your turn."

John couldn't quite get as good as Carl's first grouping, let alone his second, despite Ron's encouragement and my coaching. I had a thought about why.

"John, do you see that black square at the lower left of the target on the first panel?" There was a one-inch square shape; in reality, it was a wood peg that the target panel slipped over. The one on the right was white, blending into the background.

"No. I can't make that out."

"Do you see the red stripe on the bale to the left of the first target?" The tape stripe was a survey-type plastic tape, about two inches wide.

"I see something. I guess that's it?" Carl could easily see both, I could see as he collected the spent brass and reloaded the empty magazines.

"When did you have your eyes checked last?"

"I've never had them checked. I mean, not since I was in middle school."

"John, I'm afraid you need glasses. You were probably lucky to do as well as you were."

"Where am I supposed to get those?" he said as he handed the heavy Browning back to me.

"We'll nose around. I'm sure we can come up with something," I said, wholly unsure that we could do that at all. "Ron, you take a couple mags and see how you do."

Ron, by the second half of the magazine, put all his rounds in the black, and the last ten inside a ten-inch circle.

"Nice work."

"Nice gun. I want one of these things."

"They may be a popular item soon," I said.

"Gents, we may want to wrap this up. Still a fair amount of hay to get in," Don said.

"Yeah, and wood after that."

"You ought to spend the night and start fresh tomorrow. You won't make it before curfew anyway," he said as we walked back to the house.

"We better send word," I said. "Don't want to worry the folks at home. How's your range on CB?"

"We have a straight shot to a repeater—meaning, a guy who passes stuff on for us. That's how we check on the folks once in awhile. He passes on messages to some guy in the neighborhood."

"I know the guy. Aaron Watters. Good man."

"Well, when I meet him face to face, I'm going to…I was going to say buy the man a beer, but we're all out of that. I owe him, anyway."

"We'll get you introduced. We go back to the early days of the end of civilization," I said with a chuckle. "What's your repeater's call sign?"

"You might get this. 'London Calling.' Know what it's from?" he asked me.

"'The Clash.' Nineteen-eighty, or eighty-one. That was a great album. Don't tell me. You're 'Casbah.'" I said, making reference to a later album with the song, 'Rock the Casbah.'

"No, nothing that musical. Fighting Irish."

"Good name for a fine Italian son."

"Dad's idea. His idea of a joke."

"Well, ya gotta admit, it is pretty funny."

"What's your call-sign?"

"Depends on who we're talking to. We have several, actually. Two for the store, one for each of the adults. I'll get you a list."

"Great. It'd be good to be able to get ahold of you in case…well, to check on my folks."

"And vice versa. I'm always amazed at how well your folks are doing at their age."

"These past couple of days has shown us that Dad's not doing as well as we thought."

"Memory?"

"Yeah, put physically he's not failing."

"That awaits us all eventually, I'm afraid."

"Yeah, but try to tell that to an eighty-five year old Italian…."

We finished picking up the bales the 'hard way', while the boys continued with Ron on the tractor. Don was driving the dirt-brown Ford truck as I bucked bales all the way to the top of the stock racks. I knew I'd be feeling it in the morning. Don needed a number of parts for his tractor that I had in abundance. The pickup ran well, based on what I was seeing from the ground, good tires, aluminum wheels, just…ugly. After we finished up our last load, and Ron was heading out for his last run with the boys, I asked Don about the truck.

"So how does this thing work?"

"I think what Evan did was create an E-Eighty-Five pickup, ten years ahead of time."

"So it's not running off of pure ethanol?"

"I don't actually know that, at least while it's running. I do know that I need to use gasoline to start it, and that once it's running at idle, I can switch it over to ethanol with a switch on the floor.

"I wonder how he did it. This can't be a stock engine."

"Numbers match," he said, referring to the serial number on the block and that of the truck. "I looked. This is the same engine that I rebuilt in nineteen eighty-six. It had a hundred and ninety-thousand miles on it then."

"I thought that ethanol fuel caused corrosion on stock engines. Either acid or water content caused problems."

"Well, I do know that the consumption rate is pretty high, but since it's a three-ninety and a four-barrel, that was always the case."

"Power seems good."

"Better than on gas. Or at least the gas I've got."

"Huh."

"The tank inside the cab has unleaded, it's eighteen gallons. The reserve tank, twenty-five gallons, is under the bed. That's the ethanol tank."

"I'll have to take a look at this in detail," I said.

"One thing, well, a couple things that I saw was that all the fuel lines have been replaced with some odd-looking tubing. There's also some sort of evaporative canister under the hood where there never was one before, and the carb's been rebuilt. Oh, there's an electric fuel pump for the ethanol, but the mechanical pump is there and hooked up to the gasoline tank. There's some sort of 'Y' fitting between them with what looks like a relay."

"Interesting. How did he convert the Escalade?" I asked.

"It's a true E-Eighty-Five conversion. Thing is, this is four years ahead of GM, from what I remember they were doing. This is either his work or something that he had done. Looks very professional. I have to blend the fuel myself though, gas and ethanol."

We showered in an outdoor spring-fed shower that was certain to either kill you through hypothermia or wake you right up. The spring, on the edge of Don's property, supplied a cistern that was used for years as the farm's sole source of water. A later well was drilled just uphill of the house, and supplied twenty-five gallons per minute, if power was available. Our work clothes were tossed into the bunkhouse clothes washer, an ancient Norge Time-Line model that dated back before I was born. They'd dry overnight on lines in the bunkhouse basement. Good thing we brought along a change of clothes....

While we were busy with the hay, Karen, Libby and the girls had been working with Joan and Lorene on cooking, cleaning and mending, after a couple hours in the vegetable garden and the small lean-to greenhouse next to the barn. I knew that Kelly and Marie hadn't had that much experience on sewing before the quake, and they had never 'mended' clothing that was worn. Soon though, I was thinking that mending would be more important than they might ever dream.

Cooking and preserving, with limited power—generator only in Don's case, and a battery bank that his cousin had installed—had changed the way that the home could be operated. Cooking was now done on the wood stove and in the wood fired oven, as natural gas was no longer an option. Lighting throughout the house had been converted before the quake to a twenty-four volt LED lamp system, which was bright enough I supposed, but limited in the areas that were lit. I was sure that was due to the design that Don's cousin had come up with. The greatest challenges were related to preservation of foods. Without a 'normal' source of power, conventional freezers and refrigerators were a thing of the past.

Joe and Don had come up with a pretty unique solution to the 'keeping things cool' requirement: They had converted two salvaged chest freezers to refrigerator units, using two temperature controllers they bought from a guy that used to make home brew. Apparently the conversion was neither all that difficult nor uncommon, if you were into making your own beer. Made sense, if you're brewing, you want a lot of cooling capacity, and a chest freezer is pretty good at that. Changing the temperature range from 'below freezing' to 'below forty degrees,' probably wasn't all that tough to do. I imagined that the equipment efficiencies between a stand-up fridge and a chest freezer were probably night and day better, in favor of the freezer.

"How often does this thing run?" I asked.

"Twice a day, so far. Could probably run less if the room were cooler. I don't really want to move it to the basement though," Don said. "Runs off the battery and inverter just fine."

"And if you do move it, you'll be running the stairs every time I cook," Lorene added from the kitchen. The horizontal refrigerator now resided in their dining room, where a sideboard used to sit.

"All the more reason," I said.

Dinner that evening was pasta with meat sauce (rabbit), fresh spinach salad, and sourdough bread, and lots of red wine. Emphasis on 'lots'. My head was spinning by the time Karen and I headed to bed at 9, in a double bed in the bunkhouse. The boys were nearest the door in their bunks, the girls in the bedroom at the far end. Libby and Ron won the guest room for the night, in the house. (We drew high cards, I lost). None of us was drawn for 'watch duty', and as a matter of course, Don and Lorene never had watch—Sergei Vlahovick saw to that.

Don told me that Sergei had on his property enough manpower to field two good-sized army squads. The available manpower included relatives and acquaintances from 'the old country' that he'd befriended since coming to the States. What he didn't have in grassland or hayfields, he more than made up for in forested range, with nearly two hundred acres of the side of Antoine Peak. He hailed from Bosnia, and made it to Washington in nineteen ninety-four. He lost most of his family in one terrible night, when a United States bomb, dropped from far too high to ensure accuracy, hit his neighborhood. He had worked as a business manager for an engineering company before their war started. He'd been raised on a farm though, and didn't have as steep a learning curve as we did—he was closer to the land. Since coming to the States, he'd rebuilt his life, and before the Domino, had no fewer than a dozen businesses running, simultaneously. Don told me he paid cash for his farm and ranchland. 'Good for him,' I thought. 'Hope it was all more or less legal.'

Sunday, May 28th

I woke up at five thirty, same as always these days, but to the sound of thunder and hammering rain pounding the uninsulated roof above us and the ground outside. The roosters signaled 'morning' as well. I'm sure that I missed their early morning call, which would've been around four a.m. I realized how sore I was before I moved a muscle. Middle age isn't for sissies.

"Good thing you got the hay in yesterday," Karen whispered as she snuggled into my shoulder.

"Yeah. Too bad we're bucking firewood in the rain though."

"Oh. I forgot that. Quit hogging the blanket."

"Here, take some," I said. I had the nasty habit of rolling over in the night, and taking most of the covers with me. She had yet to break me of that, after all these years.

"What are you doing today?" I asked quietly.

"We were going to hoe up the corn and beans, and help weed the onions. Won't be able to do that in the mud though. Probably work in the root cellar behind the house. Have you seen it?"

"Nope."

"It's nice. Carved into the hillside, thick walls insulated with sawdust. They have an icehouse too."

"Really? I've never seen one."

"Joe said they used to haul ice from the lake up to the icehouse in the winter behind horses, and then pack it in sawdust in the icehouse. They'd keep ice all the way into August."

"Good idea. I'll have to look at that. Back to sleep now, we still have time for a quick nap."

Karen hummed an affirmative, and I soon heard her sleeping. It wasn't in my nature to doze back off so quickly, it usually took me until right before the alarm went off to get back to sleep. This morning was no different.

At six, the farm bell rang, signaling that it was in fact time to get out of bed and get moving. The rain was still coming down, hard. I looked out the cracked single-pane window, and saw the steady downpour, the many puddles, and the small stream of muddy water on either side of the farm road running past the bunkhouse to the upper fields, where we'd be logging and loading wood. 'Swell,' I thought to myself. 'This'll be a whole lot of no fun.'

Karen and I dressed quietly, and roused the kids at about the same time that Ron and Libby came out of their room. None of the kids wanted to get up out of their warm beds; I couldn't say I blamed them. The thermometer said forty-three degrees.

We dashed to the house along the beat-up boardwalk, thankfully avoiding the muddy path and slippery grass. Breakfast was on, with Don and Lorene cooking up pancakes and eggs on a large cast-iron griddle, with slabs of ham in another pan. Joan was setting the table and Joe was listening to the radio in the living room. The wood stove was crackling as the tamarack burned.

"Good morning everyone," Joan said as she began to load up plates. "How did everyone sleep?"

"Like logs," I said.

"Speak for yourself, Dad. You snored up a storm," Carl said.

"Sorry. That just meant I was really tired," I said as Joan handed me a cup of hot tea, and directed me to the honey if I wanted to sweeten it.

I made my way over to see Joe, who was intently listening to the radio.

"Morning, Joe."

"Morning. You listen now to this," he said as he turned up the radio, looking at the display on the dial.

"What's going on?" I said, listening to the distant, scratchy broadcast.

"Canada. They're at war with each other," he said in his thick Italian accent.

"......erupted into violent urban battles in Quebec overnight, with Free Canadian militias struggling to maintain control of the urban centers. The warfare has centered on the proposed constitutional crisis that emerged after the death of the prime minister and his entourage from an improvised explosive device yesterday morning. Indigenous peoples of the nation, disenfranchised by the new government's recent actions regarding land ownership, sealed major highways to the cities immediately after rioting began, effectively eliminating the transportation of goods to the urban areas that are so dependent on the farms and rural industry for survival. A rioting mob was seen burning the Free Canadian flag outside of the interim prime minister's offices. This mob was then fired upon by Government armed security. An estimated two hundred civilians were killed in the exchange. Security forces then turned their weapons on the on-scene CBC television reporting team, whose cameras and microphones remained operational after they were slain."

"My God," Joe said. "How could they do this thing? How could they let it come to this?"

"Greed and ambition," I said more to myself than to Joe, as we listened some more. I noticed that Joe's hand was shaking, knuckles white with rage.

"....New Canadian government had no immediate comment, but American and New Canadian military forces were seen reinforcing border lines, described as skirmish lines, well within the Free Canadian territories. American armored units were seen as being in command of New Canadian forces, as described by witnesses."

"In news from the United States, word has come through this morning that the acting Commander in Chief, a senior military officer, has been legally replaced following a meeting of the United States Supreme Court and members of the American legislature. The Acting President, Martin David Lambert, is a former Senator from the State of Oklahoma and will remain in office until national elections can be held in November. Acting President Lambert was sworn in last evening in a private ceremony in Fort Sill, Oklahoma. The Acting President is expected to release a statement later today regarding his appointment."

"For the sixth consecutive day, correspondents and technicians from the CBC in Edmonton, Vancouver and Calgary have attempted to re-establish communications with the BBC and European broadcasters. Limited shortwave communication has been made however, but no permanent connection on a scheduled basis. It is unknown at this time what technical issues may have affected communications beyond North America."

"Calgary weather today is expected to remain wet with a low overcast and a temperature of five degrees Celsius, with winds expected to peak at twenty-five kilometers per hour. Rainfall for the year, this record-setting year that is, was this morning just over thirty centimeters. Calgary averages only forty-three centimeters per year, and we are obviously far above average. As a result of the extremely wet conditions, flooding in lowland areas of the Province remains of deep concern, along with massive outbreaks of mosquitoes and waterborne disease. Diseases in livestock not normally found in Canada have become widespread over the prairies, with little in the way of human intervention possible in the near future. Wheat and grain losses throughout the Canadian prairies are known to be widespread, if not devastating in their completeness."

The broadcast paused, seemingly a little too long. *"This is the World Report on CBC Radio One, Calgary."*

Joe reached over and pushed one of the buttons on the top of the radio, switching the station to a local station. He was silent as the religious program began, a tape from months ago. The speaker was telling the radio audience of his prophetic vision for the world, as 'told to him by God,' ten years before. I'd heard him before, always looking for a faith donation to continue his ministry...

"Joe, you OK?" I asked quietly.

"No. I'm not. This world is…it's beyond me. I dunno understand," he said slipping into a heavier than normal accent.

"None of us do."

"We lose so much, so soon," he said, just above a whisper. "This is not right. It mus' end."

I didn't have a response to that. Joan brought Joe a fresh cup of tea, as he stared out at the rain, eyes sharp but….unfocused. "It must end," he said again.

"Come on you men," Joan called to us from the doorway, obviously seeing that Joe was upset. She'd been listening in as well. "Breakfast is on and those boys will eat it all if you don't hurry," she said in her fragile, wavering voice. I had to remind myself that Joan, like Joe, was up in her eighties. Not that you'd be able to tell that, before the Domino, that is….

I recapped the news for everyone during breakfast, as Joe ate quietly (not his style) and kept looking out at the rain. When we were done, I asked Kelly and Marie to spend some time with him, and have him teach them something new. Joe used to tease Kelly mercilessly when she was younger, up to the point where the game was still funny, when he'd relent. He was as much a grandfather as she had right now. I thought that some time with him would do her good.

Don got me lined out in work that needed to be done in the barn, while we hoped that the rain would let up. We fed the livestock (chickens, pigs, and two steers; no dairy cattle or goats), moved more of the hay around in the barn, and finally in mid-morning, resigned ourselves that the rain would continue and that we'd be cutting and loading up firewood in the rain, and got started on that.

Only breaking for a quick sandwich and hot (!!) tea, we finished loading the utility trailer behind the Expedition and the back of the pickup to the top of the stock racks. The trailer, I figured, would haul two cords. Wrong. The springs were way too light for that much load, and I ended up with only a single cord there, but almost made up for it with the pickup. By three p.m., we were packed up and on the road home, with Joe and Joan as passengers in the Expedition. Ron was driving the SUV, and I was following in the pickup with Carl and Kelly. John rode up front with Ron, armed, as was Carl with me. Other than a wave to the 'storekeepers', where I noticed a motorcycle and three horses were tied up, the drive home was uneventful. The rain continued to pound at us, all the way home. The old pickup's hardened rubber wipers were wholly ineffective in keeping the windshield clear, and more than once I found myself driving by Braille.

Mike Amberson was waiting for me in front of the house, with two other police cars. I expected that tomorrow, I'd have a different title behind my name. I rolled down the driver's door window as Karen pulled into the driveway, the gate held by one of the deputies. The rain continued to wash over us.

"Hi, Rick. Walt passed away this morning," he said before I could return pleasantries.

I looked at him for a moment before I spoke. "Were you there?"

"Yes. With his wife and daughters. It was very peaceful."

"May God bless the man," I said, looking ahead without really seeing, and feeling a chill in my spine. "I'll need some time to get cleaned up and fed before I can do anything," I said, assuming that my presence was needed elsewhere.

"No rush. Tomorrow's fine. You now have a security detail watching over things here."

"You think that's necessary?"

"Yes, I do," Mike said, looking at me as if I had just asked a really stupid question. "You'll have at least one deputy watching over the house if military sentries aren't available, which they aren't at present, two at night. I wanted to talk to you about billeting them in one of the vacant houses if possible."

"Sure, I guess. What's not taken I guess would work, but will need to be worked on and furnished."

"Doesn't need to be much, but we need communications gear, sleeping quarters and a mess hall. Just someplace close by that we can put back in shape."

"All this for me?"

"All this for the office, my friend. We'll have crews from Geiger do the work," he said, referring to inmates from the medium security facility near the airport.

"If you say so," I said as I put the Ford in granny-low, and pulled into the driveway. 'Dear Jesus, please take care of my friend and your servant Walt....' I said to myself with a lump in my throat.

"Dad? You OK?" Carl asked.

"I'll be all right," I said. "I will miss Walt. He was a good man," I said as I shut off the truck. "Good men are rare these days," I said almost too softly to hear. "Too rare," I said as Kelly squeezed my hand.

"Thanks, kiddo," I said to my daughter.

55

Memorial Day,
May Twenty-ninth

"What do I wear?" Karen asked me.

"I have no idea. I've never taken an oath of office before."

"You are surely not going to wear those overalls, are you?"

"What?" I said, playing along. "I am more farmer than anything else it seems."

"Change."

"Yes'm."

"None of that Southern-pretend, please."

"I'll change. I promise."

"Well, it's almost nine. We need to be there in fifteen minutes."

"No problem. I'm a guy." That comment resulted in a washcloth tossed at my head.

I made my way upstairs and quickly washed off the garden soil and brushed some lilac and hawthorne blossoms out of my hair. We'd collected bouquets to place on the graves of my parents, brothers, and later at a different cemetery, Karen's dad's grave and my grandparents and great-grandparents final resting places. My old Key farm overalls apparently weren't up to snuff. Karen was right of course; still, I liked to pretend ignorance.

I changed into a long-unworn pair of Dockers, my lone European-made fitted dress shirt and tie, sportcoat, and dress shoes. I hadn't been this dressed up since our Christmas party, that last year fell between Christmas and New Years. I wondered if the restaurant at the resort was still there? Probably not....

I was to be sworn in as Administrator at nine-thirty, at our local community center, my choice of venue. Mike Amberson and Judge Thompson, now the senior jurist in three counties, would be the 'officials' on the other side of the Bible. My family and a few friends would attend. After the pomp and circumstance was over, we'd move on to more somber proceedings.

We collected the kids and Alan's family, and loaded up for the short trip. I'd received a new vehicle pass from Mike—this one bright yellow—and was able to keep my 'purple' pass, allowing us to have two vehicles to use, within reason. We'd made arrangements with Sarah Woodbridge to keep an eye on our places, along with our new neighbors. Once word spread that I'd been selected to succeed Walt, we'd had a busy evening. Bonnie Callison gave us a wave from her fenced front yard as we rolled by, which she and Jake were going to convert to a kitchen garden. I thought that Jake would be the one to run the Troy Bilt tiller; nope. Bonnie was all over it.

As we passed the store, closed for the holiday, I wondered if the Army's sentry post had been abandoned, until I saw the lone sentry round the side of the building. Coming west-bound though, almost a dozen Humvees were heading toward the store, slowing to fuel up.

"That's a lot of men," Carl said. Each Humvee appeared to be full.

"Yeah. I'll have to see what I can find out about that," I said.

"You can do that?" he asked.

"I think I can now, yeah."

A minute later, we parked at the front door of the community center. A half-dozen vehicles were already in the lot, and a television truck.

"Aw, damn," I said.

"Think that's for you?" Karen asked with a smirk.

"I sure hope not. If it was up to me, I'da done this in the back yard."

"Protocol, hon."

"Yeah. Great."

We made our way into the main hall, where Mike, his wife Ashley (looking uncomfortably pregnant), two of his deputies, Judge Arthur Thompson and one of his staff were waiting. The television crew was set up and ready to go, fortunately, they were not asking for an interview. I had no idea what I'd say to them, if asked....

"Good morning," I said.

"Morning, Rick, Karen," Mike said. "You remember Ashley of course," Mike said, "and this is Judge Thompson and his clerk, Harold Berk."

"Nice to meet you all," I said as I shook hands and introduced my family and friends. Karen and Libby took a seat next to Ashley, and talked of maternity issues, until the Judge beckoned Karen to join us.

"I have a role here, too?" she asked.

"You may hold the Bible if you wish," said the Judge.

"That would be an honor," she said as Alan produced our family Bible.

"I smell a setup here," I said with a smile.

"Hush now," Karen said.

"Yes'm," I said as the camera light came on behind my left shoulder.

"Mr. Richard James Drummond and guests," Judge Thompson began, "It is my honor to be here today to officiate as you take the oath of office for Administrator for Spokane County."

"It is my sad duty, as well, as I was responsible for swearing in Walt Ackerman, and the preceding County Commissioners. I pray, Mr. Drummond, that you will provide the County with the same honor, integrity and faithful service as Mr. Ackerman."

"I will do my best, your Honor." I noted he did not mention the service of the Commissioners, and rightly so.

"Please place your right hand on the Bible, and prepare to take your Oath before God and these witnesses."

I placed my hand on the worn leather-bound Bible, which was new when my great grandparents were newlyweds; our family marriages, births, and deaths recorded in the pages within.

"Richard James Drummond, please repeat after me," the Judge said, looking me square in the eye……and stated the oath in its entirety without a break for me to respond. I repeated his words, to the best of my memory.

""I, Richard James Drummond, do solemnly swear that I will support the Constitution of the United States and the Constitution and laws of the State of Washington, and that I will faithfully discharge the duties of the office of Administrator of Spokane County to the best of my ability, so help me, God."

"Mr. Drummond, may I be the first to congratulate you on the journey on which you now embark," Judge Thompson said with a grandfatherly smile as he shook my hand. It seemed that through the manner in which the oath was given…had I passed a little test?

"Thank you, your Honor."

"Congratulations," Mike said.

"Thanks. I guess this now makes me your boss," I said with a smile.

"Yes, it does. Don't let it go to your head."

"That's why I'm here," Karen chimed in.

"Ever keeping me in balance," I said, as I received hugs from my kids and more congratulations from Aaron Watters and Ellen MacDonald; Kevin Miller, and Alan and Mary.

"Mr. Drummond, may we have a few minutes?" the TV reporter asked.

"Sure, I guess. Give me just a minute."

"Sure. Thanks," the reporter said as he moved away. He didn't look familiar, and in pre-War days, I'm sure he wasn't 'attractive enough' for the image-conscious TV market.

"I guess I have an interview to do," I said.

"Your public awaits. Don't trip, Dad." Carl said.

"Thanks, son. Remind me later, to find some steaming-fresh manure somewhere for you to shovel up a hill." That drew a laugh from Karen and Ashley as they went to find a comfortable place to sit and visit.

"No problem," he said. 'Dang, he's really growing up. Sixteen in a few days,' I thought to myself.

I made my way to the entry vestibule, and out into the filtered sunshine. I heard the reporter introduce me, apparently to a live audience. 'Damn,' I thought to myself. 'Good thing I changed clothes.'

The first half of the interview was fine; I was trying not to look stupid. The second half was a little more juicy.

It began with the question that asked for my opinion on 'local law enforcement's inability to protect the public.'

"Protect them from what?"

"From criminals."

"Where?"

"All over the city. We're getting reports…"

"Show me."

"They're coming to us word of mouth."

"And what have you done with these reports?" I asked, turning the tables a bit.

"We have a list, and…"

"Get locations. Forward them to either my office or to the Sheriff or to the Army. Collectively, we have a very low tolerance for crime."

"But the police aren't doing anything," the reporter stated flatly, "except protecting specific areas. And the County is not taking care of the public."

I just about exploded. I took a deep breath. "Mr.…," I asked, fumbling for his name.

"Iverson. David Iverson."

"Thank you. Mr. Iverson, the police and the military are in fact charged with protecting specific areas. Those areas that have a population base and/or are critical to the function and operation of this City and this region. If there are criminal activities taking place outside of those areas, it is up to the individuals who are living within those areas, to defend themselves and inform the proper authorities of criminal activities in their immediate areas. Many of these critical areas are outside of the utility service areas, but still warrant police and military protection. When those reports are made, military, not police forces, will respond."

"But in the interim, there are people who are in danger from criminal elements within the city. From what I've seen it's completely beyond the County's ability to deal with."

"So, Mr. Iverson, is it your reporting style to make wildly accusatory and inflammatory statements as a matter of course, or did you learn this all on your lonesome?" My hand rested on my hip, where my Colt ought to be…

He glared at me, and I didn't give him a chance to respond before I continued.

"You want to scare the public with the shadow demon of rampant crime? I say prove it to me. If people have a criminal background, and are stupid enough to attempt a criminal activity upon people or property, it is my considered opinion that said individual may well be looking for law enforcement officers to show up, because I know a lot of people with firearms, acreage, and shovels. Citizens of this County, and of this State, have the right to defend themselves and their property. Do I make myself clear?"

"That seems quite reactionary."

"Really? Are you on the side of the criminal element now? Does the criminal need protection from the law abiding citizen?"

"That's not what I meant."

"You from around here, Mr. Iverson?"

"I was living in Fairhaven before the Domino."

"Well, this is Spokane, not a trendy little alternative-lifestyle neighborhood on the other side of the Cascades. Perhaps you ought to speak with our Sheriff about your 'concerns' or perhaps one of the line soldiers of the Forty-First. Or maybe one of our Special Forces folks."

"I really don't think that that is necessary."

"Huh," I said, thinking about that for a moment. This was a guy who liked stirring things up and didn't have the balls to back it up. "Now, with regards to the 'County's not taking care of the public?' I said, with perhaps too much calm in my voice. "That, Mr. Iverson, is a damned lie and you ought to know it by now. The remaining employees of Spokane County, the City of Spokane, and the Cities of Liberty Lake and Spokane Valley are working largely unpaid, putting pieces together to rebuild what is left of a city. Utility crews are doing the same thing. So are farmers. People are living hand to mouth, literally. This is not a nanny state. What exactly, Mr. Iverson, do you feel that the County government's responsibility is in taking care of the public?"

"People need to be protected. They need to be fed. They need medical care," he said defiantly. I wondered if he was looking like an ass on TV. He sure was making a case for that assessment in person.

"Agreed. However it is not up to the government to see that those items are provided. It is up to the government to see that those things are POSSIBLE. Do you understand the difference?"

"Frankly, no I don't," he said, almost with a pout.

"The government does not have the resources to provide those things, because that's not the function of government. With limited government, we have a framework for civilization. Without it, we have a framework for anarchy. We'd have millions of people with guns and ammunition that would prey off of each other. Eventually, the bullets run out and then you're using rocks and sticks and pointy things. There can be no safety, no protection, no peace, because someone's going to try to be king of the hill, at the expense of all others. We have a representative form of government so that everyone has a voice. Locally, we have a judicial system. We have an executive branch. We will soon have a legislative branch. Without that framework for civilization, you cannot have protection. You cannot have the ability to keep people from starving, because you're watching your back and looking out only for yourself. You cannot have medical care that is available to the public. You would have medical care available to the leaders, only. We're not going down that road. Nor are we going to create the role of 'central government' or 'central planning.' That didn't work in the communist countries, it will certainly not work here."

He didn't have a response. I continued on.

"The government's role here is to provide the ABILITY for people to grow enough food. For them to not only feel safe but BE safe through the enaction and enforcement of laws. Other aspects of what we've called civilized life, like medical care, electricity, running water, and capitalism can happen to the degree that we enjoy because we have a government."

591

"That's quite a speech. How much of it do you believe?" he said sarcastically. 'This guy is a piece of work,' I thought.

"All of it," I said. "We recently saw what happened with people posing as 'the government' ran amok around here. Two of their leaders are dead. The third will be stretching a rope one of these mornings. Their actions hastened the death of my predecessor and directly caused the deaths of dozens, if not hundreds of people. And one more thing. Police are here to enforce the law, and that does not mean the same thing as keeping you perfectly safe twenty-four seven. I fully support and encourage the individual to keep and bear arms and do both well--- your life may depend on it," I said, looking right at the camera. "I will be enacting a requirement for all citizens over the age of sixteen to be fully trained in the use of firearms, handguns included. We've seen too many accidental shootings, and too many attacks, for us to wait for either the Army or a Sheriff's deputy to arrive. We will start this training immediately."

"You think that will solve the crime problem? C'mon," Iverson said.

"An armed society is a polite society," I said, composing my parting shot. "Thank you, Mr. Iverson. I assume that you will be covering the Memorial Day services for those who have given their lives in defense of yours?" I said, words deliberately chosen. That got him off balance again.

"Why yes. That is one of our assignments today."

I doubted that that was the case. "Glad to hear it. I'll make a point of seeing you there. Good day," I said with a nod as I shook his hand. That of course was awkward for him, as he had to tuck his clipboard under his arm in order to shake my hand. To me, he looked like a goof. I expected he looked that way on camera, but I'd never see it. I noted that the cameraman had a large smile on his face.

With that, I turned and collected Karen, and shook hands again with the Judge, who was sporting a smile, his clerk, and Mike. I could tell the Judge was holding back laughter during my tirade.

"Holy crap, Dad," Carl said. "He should just take a big stick and poke a hornets nest next time," he said.

"I did get a little fired up. I really need to debate with guys like that more often. But still, I feel like I just clubbed a baby seal. It was kinda sad in the end."

"You kinda hammered on that protection of property issue a bit heavy," Mike said.

"Say it, then say it again, and close by saying it again. I wanted to get the point across."

"Someone'd have to be ambient temperature not to have heard what you said."

"Good. Then I succeeded. There are a number of people out there that needed to hear that, plain, because 'plain' is all they understand."

"Somebody in particular?" Mike asked with interest.

"The Samuels family. Newman Lake area."

"I know them. And I agree with you. We just haven't had the manpower to go after them."

"Well, I might have bought some time, but soon it'll come to a head. Best it be on your terms than theirs."

"Always. See you at the cemetery, Boss." Mike said as Ashley took his arm.

"None of that now," I said. "Your Worthiness will suffice," I said, laughing.

The Memorial Day service would start at one p.m., and Walt's burial would take place at noon. This allowed us a brief time to visit our family graves at the cemetery, across town. The graves of my own parents and two of my brothers was in the Valley, a few minutes from the community center. We'd start there, then go to town. A late lunch day today, as we probably wouldn't be home until nearly three.

At my parents' graves, we cleaned the leaves and wild grasses from the headstones, now in an unmowed field. It was odd to see the old-style headstones rise out of the dried grass, instead of the smooth Kentucky bluegrass of years before. The headstone I'd had made for Joe was a cut chunk of a granite boulder, with sandblasted name and dates. It seemed to fit the 'wild' look of the cemetery much better than the flat headstones. We placed bouquets on each, stood for a moment or so in reflection, and left for town.

The service for Walt was attended by more than forty people, including his immediate family. I wasn't aware of his military service, but he received full honors, and a missing man flyover of helicopters. Walt, I learned later from Mike, had flown HH-53 Jolly Green rescue helos over North Vietnam. I never would have guessed.

The main ceremony was held in a circle of American flags, a portion of the cemetery dedicated to veterans. A sculpted granite monument, slightly damaged from the Domino, was the centerpiece of the five hundred or so spectators seated and standing, around the site. The grass here I noted, had been mowed and seemed to have been watered as well. I knew the graves of my grandparents and great grandparents would be difficult to find in all the tall grass on the rest of the grounds.

Brief speeches were made by the Division Commander, Acting, of the Forty First, as well as vets from the Second War (as it was now being called), Korea, Vietnam, and the Gulf War. The final speech was made by a twenty-two year old survivor of Monterrey. He was a double amputee, his legs taken by a roadside bomb that shredded his Humvee, during the evacuation. It'd been a long time since I'd been brought to tears by words alone....

The service concluded in a manner that was at first predictable, and then turned ninety degrees in a way that I'd not been prepared for. 'Taps' was played by a long bugler, who had served with the Tomb Guard at Arlington. Once 'Taps' was finished, a second bugler began, and played a solemn version of what was once a protest song, Crosby, Stills and Nash's 'Find the Cost of Freedom'. I remembered the words and their perfect harmony as the notes echoed through the pines.

The service ended silently, and we filed out to the cars, and then up the hill to my grandparents' grave site. In another twenty minutes, we were headed back into the downtown area. I wanted to stop at Walt's office...'my office' I had to remind myself, and collect some papers to prepare for my new job.

The Riverside Avenue bridge over Hangman Creek was still intact, more or less, minus it's ornamental handrails. The last of the Palouse Indian wars was ended just up the creek, when Colonel George Wright hung a young brave by the name of Qualchan, who had come to talk peace per the instructions of Chief Kamiakin. In memory, the latter-day residents named a golf course after the young man. The twenty-six other Palouse who died with him were not so 'honored.' We proceeded up Riverside through Browne's Addition, past the wrecked Museum of American Cultures (more than a coincidence I thought, to see the many-million-dollar facility a shambles. 'That speaks volumes,' I thought). Kelly asked me about the second song that was played. I'd been silent I realized, since the last note of that song was played.

"It was a song by Crosby, Stills and Nash. Came out during Vietnam, and then was revised and redone by them in the early eighties. I have it on vinyl at home. We'll play it for you then."

"So it's not an instrumental?"

"No. And I don't think I could sing it and not come to tears."

"Oh."

Everyone was quiet as we drove through Browne's, past the mostly wrecked grand old eighteen-nineties houses. Karen and I had almost bought one, before we found our home. Six bedrooms, three stories, eight fireplaces, forty-four thousand dollars. Of course, that was in nineteen eighty-five….

Just west of the downtown core, we had to divert up to Second Avenue, due to collapsed brick buildings. I noticed that the Art Deco Fox Theater, where the Symphony played, was intact. 'Good old building,' I thought.

We crossed the river on Monroe, past the pile of brick that was once my office. It had either been dozed or more likely, had collapsed completely since my trip there earlier in the spring on a salvage trip. Good thing I didn't put it off…

Four Army sentries stood watch at the entry to the cul-de-sac that was the entry road to the Public Works building. I noted six or seven more at the entry to the damaged jail complex. I was waved through, apparently due to my colored tag on the mirror, and stopped at the parking lot entry.

"Mr. Drummond?" the young lady asked me.

"Yes."

"Please park in spot seven. We have some vehicles coming in that will be arriving shortly, and we'll need this full parking bay."

"No problem," I said. "Thanks."

I pulled into the parking space, in the outer row of spaces. "I'll just be a few minutes," I told everyone. "Want to come in?"

"Can we?" Kelly asked. "A bathroom break would be perfect."

"I think that can be arranged. C'mon."

Inside, I found two County workers reading what looked like a newspaper, sitting at the former receptionist's station, now a guard station.

"May we help you?" the younger of the two asked.

"Rick Drummond. I'm here to collect some files. You are?" I asked.

"Jeremy Wilson. I normally work over in the Public Safety building. Nice to meet you sir," he said respectfully. I guess word gets around…

"I'm Chris Vanderwolf. I'm the Information Systems department."

"Good. Nice to see a one-man department. Always know who's doing the work," I said, and then introduced my family. Kelly discreetly disappeared to the ladies room, followed by Karen.

"Is Walt's office locked?"

"Yes, but I can let you in," Vanderwolf replied. "I have the masters for the doors. Your administrative assistant has the desk keys though, and she's not here at present.

"Miss Gardner. We've met." He looked at me in some surprise.

"No. Sorry, Mr. Drummond. Miss Gardner passed away yesterday. Her duties were assigned to a new employee last week I understand. I haven't yet met her."

"Damn," I said out loud, remembering Kamela's sharp mind. "She will be missed."

"Yes, sir. Here you are sir," young Vanderwolf said as he unlocked the door. Walt's nametag had been removed, I noted.

"Thanks. We'll just be a few minutes."

"Nice and neat," Alan said as we entered. The office was, a little too tidy. The last time I saw it, last week was it, the desk had been buried in paper. Now, neat files were stacked and placed in racks. I noticed one had red edging. I pulled it out out of natural curiosity, flipped it open, and began reading.

'…report on cataracts appearing in several mammal species and in some humans, appears to be some form of viral onset metabolic disease similar to galactosemia. The disease does not appear to be present in bovine, canine or

feline species at this time, but continued USAMRIID monitoring is recommended.'

"What's that?" Alan asked.

"I'm not sure I can tell," I said as I looked for a signature or author, and found the signature block blacked out. "I'll need to read it through. Pass me that bag over there," I asked Alan. "I'll take some of these home for some light reading."

"You have probably six hundred pages of that."

"Probably more. Some of this is in ten-point text."

"Start with the exec summary and go from there."

"Yeah. Probably a good idea," I said, continuing my perusal of the report. "I've a lot of ground to cover before Wednesday."

"What's Wednesday?"

"My first recovery board meeting with me in charge. I have homework to do."

"Late night ahead."

"Lucky me."

56

Tuesday,
June Sixth

Some days, five-thirty is just too early; I don't care what anybody says.

The alarm (well, the radio) came on per my instructions, at just before the bottom of the hour news. The agriculture-oriented bottom of the hour news reports started off with this stunner:

"At five a.m. this morning, a low temperature of twenty-six degrees was reported in Newport, Cusick, Usk, and at Clayton, just outside of Deer Park. Temperatures in the Spokane area are hovering around forty-two degrees."

"Did I hear that right?" Karen said, now fully awake, as was I.

"Yeah," I said.

"It's June sixth, right?"

"Yep, Your boy's birthday. Sixteen."

"Do we let him sleep in?"

"After yesterday, I'm sure he'd appreciate it."

"That was a lot of wood to have him and John move."

"Had to do it though. Gotta get it stacked to season right and the seasoned stuff stored for winter," I said as I put my feet on the floor, and found Buck there underfoot. As always.

"How much do we have seasoned?"

"About five cords now. By winter, another ten seasoned. By then though we'll have probably another ten or more for next year."

599

"Does everyone have that much? I mean, everyone on the block," she asked as she dressed.

"Pretty close in total volume. Not as much seasoned and ready to go right now though. Good thing, since I've gone through two chains on the saw."

We both had half an ear to the radio as we got ready for the day. We had no warning that we'd have a cold spell, and certainly not any warning of approaching frost, a good three months early....

"...showers expected by this afternoon in the southern part of the state, according to Army forecasters at Fort Walla Walla, turning to steady rain by the end of the day, moving north."

I stood there for a second, before Karen asked me, "What's wrong?"

"We could have snow up north if this cold stays."

"This is June."

"I recognize that. But if it's in the twenties, under an overcast sky," I said as I looked out our patched-up bedroom window, "and we have rain moving up from the south, that spells snow, no matter what the calendar says."

The implications of that hit her as it did me. "What will we do?"

"I have no idea."

Our crops were doing fairly well, by our standards. The field corn was up about ten inches; potatoes were up about the same, and our tomatoes were blooming already, which seemed early. We were in the middle (we being most of the folks on the block, now that we had neighbors) of hoeing up the spuds and corn and beans, to help them stand against our prevailing winds and produce more of our vital food. The never-ending weeding, done by hand, was dimly viewed by all involved. The 'new' fields were in particular a problem where we'd turned the soil under or tilled up the sod, exposing all manner of dormant weed seeds.

The fruit trees throughout the block looked to be doing 'OK', as far as the amount of fruit on the trees. I turned over spray duties to John and Carl though, which meant that when the wind wasn't blowing and we were scheduled to spray, they needed to jump on it 'now.' We used improvised spray mixtures, some of soap, some with garlic oil, some as fungicides. Most often though, the health of the tree determined if we needed to spray it at all. This year, most all would need some spray or other; next year, I hoped we'd be able to wean some of them off the heavy schedule I had them on. Since the great majority of trees on the block were probably planted in the twenties to the fifties, and then ignored by later owners, most were in pretty tough shape. I could have spent a year doing a decent job just pruning and thinning them….

Breakfast was fresh eggs, English muffins (home made!) and honey, and tea. And, another stack of paperwork to read from my 'day job.' Outside, on what should have been a nice sunny early summer day, we had steady wind from the southwest, and a low overcast. Looked a whole lot like March ought to look.

I listened to the morning 'check in' at six a.m. on the emergency frequencies, and the coded reports sent to dispatch. Mike's operations officer would compile these into summary form for me as part of 'keeping the pulse' on public safety issues, but I liked hearing the stuff first hand. I noted that for the past three days, more looting and potential livestock theft was being reported just west of Newman Lake and spreading south into the eastern part of the Valley. I had little doubt that the Samuels clan was responsible.

'Time to act on that would be about…now,' I thought to myself.

Kelly joined me for breakfast, keeping quiet so that Carl could sleep in. She volunteered to make him a scratch layer cake (chocolate and chocolate), which was one of the best gifts she could come up with, other than the quilt she'd been making out of his old blue jeans on one side, and old t-shirts on the other. That gift would be opened tonight, when Karen and I would also give him our gifts. Mine would be one of the M-16's that we'd 'found', one of the 1903 Springfields that he'd taken a liking to, and the cleaning gear for each. Karen had hidden an acoustic guitar in my closet (hers was out of the question, and always had been. Lots of surplus clothing in there…). Carl played violin pre-Domino, and a little since then, but had always wanted to learn guitar, too. We arranged for Sarah Woodbridge to teach him, behind his back. The guitar was acquired in a trade for three bricks of twenty-two long rifle. I think Alan got the better end of the deal with that—I'd put him up to shopping for a guitar. The instrument was a little older than me, a nineteen fifty-nine model J-50. Alan said that the seller was the son of the original owner, and never learned to play. It came with a hard case and extra strings as well.

"Looks icky outside," Kelly said.

"Yeah. Supposed to rain later, and it's so cold up just north of town that they may have snow later."

"Don't look now, but it's already raining," she said. "Hope my rabbits are OK," she said, looking out at the hutch we'd cobbled together.

601

I turned to look at the large drops as they smacked into the driveway and then the windows. Within a few moments more, the rain was so heavy that Alan and Ron's places were shadowy through the veil of rain.

"Good grief," Karen said. "Kelly, get the dogs inside. They're on the front porch."

"K."

"Snow up north, huh?" Karen said.

"Yeah. Good chance by the looks of it."

I sipped my tea and was promptly distracted by an Emergency Alert signal on KDA, and a call from the County Dispatcher to me.

"One of those days, it appears," Carl said from over my shoulder.

"Happy birthday, my boy," I said as I gave him a hug. "Nice PJ's," I said, pointing to his flannel lounging pants and one of my old WSU Cougar sweatshirts.

"Thanks. They're comfy." I half-listened to the weather alert.

"Just hope you don't need snow boots."

"You're kidding, right?" he said as a second call came to me on the radio.

"Apparently not. I better get this," I said. "Grab a shower and some breakfast." Turning my attention to official business, I replied, "One thirty-seven."

"One thirty-seven, a severe storm warning has been issued for the northern half of the state, effective immediately. Significant chance of snowfall above four thousand feet, descending to twenty-five hundred feet by nightfall, projected to continue until at least midnight tonight."

"I think it's already here. Who issued the warning?"

"Army meteorology in Walla Walla, seconded by the Fairchild weather station ten minutes ago."

"Has the weather alert system been activated in addition to EBS?" I asked.

"Yes, sir, two minutes ago."

"Damn," I said to myself, before responding to the young lady running dispatch this morning. "Very well. I want local news on this now, running this as top priority obviously, with someone from the Ag Bureau on before seven for instructions on crop protection. Most people around here won't know what to do about the cold on the crops. And there may not be anything that they can do about it in the higher elevations. We need cold-weather warnings for people and animals, too. No one's ready for winter yet."

"Yes, sir, we'll run that down right now. Civilian radio frequencies are scheduled to be available within fifteen minutes."

"Anything else?"

"No, sir. Board meeting is still on for nine a.m."

"Thank you. One thirty-seven out."

"One thirty-seven."

During my first week at 'work,' I'd managed to read through about three-quarters of the stuff that Walt had cooking, meetings with staff and learning the ropes.

Today would be my first 'regular' Recovery Board meeting, at nine. At eight, I had scheduled a staff meeting with all department heads and senior managers, which amounted to fourteen people, a small fraction of the pre-Domino level. The purpose of this particular staff meeting was to lower the boom on the former goals and process of rebuilding the County government. I didn't agree with the manner that the County was reconstituting itself, and after much thought (and prayer), today was the day that I'd start refocusing the effort.

I'd received mixed reviews on my unscheduled television interview. I offended a fair number of people, probably unavoidably. There was a larger-than-I-expected percentage of the population that did not believe in gun ownership, that also believed as the reporter Iverson did, that governments responsibility was to take care of the populace. On the flip side though, it seemed that I'd made points with the military, public safety personnel, and the vast majority of the civilian population.

Still, it was I guess my nature to try to please, or accommodate everyone. I could see that in this case like most others, that just wasn't possible.

I'd gone as far as directing community center managers to schedule firearms training for the first week of July, starting with the basics of firearms safety, skill development, and maintenance. I'd called in three formerly competing gun shop owners, all avid hunters and NRA/GOA members, to craft the curriculum, set up the appropriate training facilities, and serve as liason between the County and the Army. With the Forty-First Division armorer in my office, I informed the civilian trainers that the Army would provide training on military weapons, including M-16's and M-9's. My stated goal was that I felt it the responsibility of all adults sixteen or older to be able to defend their homes, families and property through the proper use of firearms. In reality, I was trying to create a mindset in the community that police, military, and civilians were all responsible for defense…just in case someone or some force from outside the area, might have other ideas about how to run things. We'd all been scared a little by the sudden influx of the Air Force's planes, and had nothing in the way of a general mobilization of the population to attempt any meaningful form of defense.

Maybe this effort would help change that.

After breakfast, I gathered up my paperwork for the trek into town. Don Pauliano had accepted my invitation to join the Board, and he'd spent the night at his folks place. We'd carpool into town, following one of Mike's deputies all the way. I didn't really agree that that was necessary, but that was no longer my decision to make apparently.

The dash gauge of the Ford read thirty-nine degrees as we headed into town through the October-like rain. The lights turned themselves on automatically as we headed west, the sky getting darker it seemed by the mile.

"I hope to Christ that this storm is a complete fluke," Don said.

"I think you meant, 'I need to pray that this is a complete fluke.'"

"Sorry, yeah. You're right obviously," he said looking north. "If it's this cold here, it's gotta be near freezing on the hill above the farm. If the cold settles in, we'll lose everything."

"I know," I said. "And if it's colder than this up north, which it seems to be, then most every crop north of the middle of the County will be lost. And Stevens County, Pend Orielle, and everything over in the Panhandle." This would affect every survivor in the north half of the state.

We both knew what this meant. People depending on favorable weather through the growing season to grow their winter food, their survival food this year and next, could be in danger of starvation if these crops were lost.

"What do you think is going on?" Don asked.

"First, Rainier. Then Shasta. Then the eruptions over in Russia. Toss in some debris from portable sunrises courtesy of the military, and we've got a problem."

"I remember seeing a show on the History Channel a couple of years ago, 'The Little Ice Age.'"

"This might be the precursor of the modern version of that."

"Well, then we're hosed."

"Maybe so. We don't really have…at least I don't know the answer to this…any historical data for the Inland Northwest during the Little Ice Age. This was Salish land then. Not too many white folk here then. I do know that during that period from the late fifteen hundreds through the early seventeen hundreds that the native population plummeted. Part of that was due to introduced disease. Part was probably due to food shortages."

"And history repeats."

"Or at least echos."

The rest of the drive was uneventful, save the continuing broadcast on the weather. The rain seemed to come in waves, with sleet mixed in with the lighter bands. 'How much more do we have to face?' I asked myself.

After finally arriving, we took my two boxes of paperwork back into the building, showing our I.D's to a very young soldier in ill-fitting camo at the door. I'd been trying to get up to speed with as much of the recovery effort as I could, and what I'd learned over the past few days was now the focus of our early meeting. All of the regular staff was present in the conference room when Don and I appeared. Hot tea (coffee was a luxury now) was provided to us when we took our seats.

"Good morning to you all. For those that haven't yet met this gentleman to my left, this is Don Pauliano, a resident of Newman Lake. Don is joining us on the Recovery Board as representative from the eastern portion of the Valley," I said in closing my intro. "I want to get right to business this morning, and I want to express my thanks to each of you for your help so far. We've made good strides, but we obviously have a long way to go," I said. 'OK, here goes,' I thought before continuing. "My opinion, after five days on the job, is that the system is almost working. Problem is, it's the wrong system."

Dumbfounded looks from about half the staff. Not unexpected. "But we're putting things back together, as directed by Mr. Ackerman," one of the engineering managers replied.

"I understand that may be the case, and no disrespect to Walt. He was a good man and I am proud to have known him and called him a friend. But I am speaking with regards to what this government should be, and what has been recreated isn't necessarily either what is needed or what is useful in the present time. Let me expound on that," I said.

"We probably have the right number of core staff. Staff, as directed, has been trying to put the entire county back together the way it was, when the way it was is obsolete for the times ahead," I said as I looked around the hearing room. "Listen, I'm an admitted governmental outsider. I've worked with this County and other counties in my former life in private practice, which is now a lifetime ago it seems. I understand the regulatory bulls**t from both sides of the table. We are shaking things up. We have to. We have a limited amount of time before some critical issue that we're ignoring flares up and stomps us flat. I propose a significant reorganization of our efforts to date to try to pre-empt that boot to the head."

I could see that for the most part, my point was starting to get across.

"We are not a county or a metropolitan area with a half-million people and a hundred-eighty thousand residences anymore. The county, including the City of Spokane, is closer to twenty percent of our original population—and those are the ones we can find. We have more than a hundred thousand wrecked houses or apartments. We need to provide levels of service that are appropriate to that population."

"Planning Department. In our present situation we must look at the broad-brush approach. No one gives a rip if commercial enterprises are next to residential and if there is adequate space between them. Two of you folks have been working on items like that. We need to get out of that and get onto more critical decisions. You need to determine which parts of the urban area can be resettled—for commercial, residential or industrial uses—on an individual basis. Site by site, block by block. We go from there. You need to determine which areas of the undeveloped or rural county are especially suitable for agricultural use and what we can do to foster their use. If we can open up ten thousand acres of farmland for row-crop use by extending or repairing a water line, then we need to find a way to make it happen."

"This, for now, is your job. We have winter coming, sooner than we want. Right this minute, it's probably snowing in the north part of the county. It's June, and it's snowing. We need shelter for our citizens, we need commercial and industrial enterprises in operation, we need trade, we need food and clean water. We need to make sure that we're providing the people of this area the ability to survive and thrive here. Am I clear here?"

"Yes, sir," two of the planners responded. "That's a pretty tall order though for two of us."

"Then recruit from the local population. I'd lay money, real money on there being a couple of planner-types out there weeding gardens that might lend a hand," I said before moving on.

"Public Health. Doctor Sorensen has been doing a good job at keeping us informed of what's needed and what to do about it. We need you folks in Human Resources and in Community Development though to get the word out to the general population that we need more people with medical skills serving in the County. We need to make sure that our people are staying healthy. It is not uncommon now to die from what six months ago would be cured with a common prescription medicine. We've also lost as you well know, most anyone who was on any sort of prescription maintenance drug. We are now dealing with substantial numbers of borderline psychotics because there are no drugs to keep them on a more-or-less stable plane. That is taxing the medical system as well. This will be a growing problem in the coming weeks and months, as people lose whatever built-up effect of their psychiatric medicines had over time," I said. "This isn't speculation, for those of you that are wondering. We're seeing this in the borderline population. People that were working menial jobs that had been mainstreamed in the past. They're going to be a problem."

I'd seen a distant cousin once, off his medicine for 'manic depression' disorder, later called 'bipolar'. One week he was as normal as anybody else. The next week, he smashed every bit of glass in his apartment, because it was 'pretty'. We were now dealing with people like that, and worse, in every neighborhood.

"Law enforcement, fire protection, public schooling, and judicial I'll cover directly with the respective department heads, but rest assured that they'll hear about the same thing."

"Road Department," I continued, looking for and finding the once-junior civil engineer that was now the most senior in the Department. "Andy? You know better than most anyone the trouble that's on the ground and under it. Obviously we're not putting down asphalt anymore, and keeping things patched together is as good as it's going to be for awhile. I do want to talk to you in more detail about repairs to key arterials before winter. I'm thinking manual labor."

"Where do you think we can get those kinds of numbers? Even if I had diesel equipment, it'd take us months."

"Two thousand four hundred and sixty-six prisoners at Geiger. Fourteen hundred fifty-one at the interim facility at the Airport. Eighty six percent of those are male. Perhaps sixty percent of those are physically and mentally able to work under supervision."

"That's a boatload of shovels…." Andy Bach replied.

"Yep. And a lot more chain, if we're talking chain-gangs. I'm hoping not to go that route though."

"Next, I see a need for a staff person or two to coordinate urban-area salvage operations. My crystal ball tells me that we probably aren't going to get more help from the outside. The rest of the country's screwed up, too and have their own issues to deal with. I see this being a massive operation that can preserve and protect things that we will not see made in this country again."

"You're talking about building materials, or contents, or both?" one of the former Assessor's office staff asked.

"All of the above. I don't see shoes being shipped here from China anymore. Anyone here know how to make shoes?" I asked. "No. I didn't think so. How about glass? Clothing? Forged steel?" The impact of my statement caused many to ponder their future perhaps with more soberness than they had previously.

"That stuff's not coming back anytime soon," I continued. "What we have on hand, and what we do with it, either leave it in the rain to rot or preserve it and use it later, will be the difference in having or not having until we can learn to make these things ourselves."

"How do we find someone to organize that?"

"Good question. I'd start with a cattle call to the public for salvage company operators or workers. People that know how to take things apart. Then find some people who know appliances. People who work in laundries. Seamstresses, shoe-store people. In effect you are taking apart wrecked buildings with most of their contents, salvaging what you can, and storing those goods and materials in places where they can be used in the future. Think like this: You're scrounging stuff to fill up a department store."

"Where do we put it all?"

"Leave that to your planners," I said, looking at the two planners standing uncomfortably in the back of the room. "Gents, there's another task for you. Best make it high on the list."

"Alright," I said. "Telecoms. We have no decent communications system for either official or public use in the County. Or the state for that matter. I'm assigning this to the Information Systems department. Larissa? You up to another task?" I asked Larissa Monaghan.

"Sure. In for a dime, in for a dollar," she said. Larissa had been of great help to me in the past few days, tracking down all kinds of diverse information across the wreckage of the County's computer system.

"Great. I don't know how to do it, but I think you can find the right people to get something going. I don't know if it's cell phones, old fashioned copper, fiber optic, whatever, but we need to have something other than radio-based communication for general use. Official use too, but there is coming a point where we as a community just need to have faster and more reliable communications in the salvage work, in defense coordination, for emergency response."

"I'll get on it," Larissa said. "No promises."

"No problem," I said. "If it is possible though, I need to know options."

"Got it."

"Building Department," I said next.

"Yes, sir," the new Director responded.

"I think you've done a good job in keeping the public safe with regards to our infrastructure, but I think we need to have a simplified manner for the public to understand what will work in a building, with a minimum of involvement from the County. Instruct them on how to build an outbuilding or fix a house so that it is habitable throughout the year. I know that your primary focus has been on inspection of damaged buildings and condemnation so far, but that's winding down, correct?"

"Pretty much. Are you thinking structural guidelines..."

"I'm thinking structural, electrical, mechanical, and natural systems. Structural so that they build something that's not gonna fall down on them. Electrical so they don't electrocute themselves or burn the place down. Mechanical, so that water goes where it should and they don't die from carbon monoxide poisoning. Natural systems, meaning weather. What happens if we have continuous freezing weather starting on September first?"

"Bad shtuff," Brian Cavanaugh, the Director, said.

"Right. We are running out of time."

"OK. Admin," I continued. "You are about to get a lot busier. You will probably serve as support to management in all levels, in addition to probably serving a need that Justice has for administrative support. You will need some more staff for that. I will provide some more information to you later on that. OK?"

"Yes, sir," the head of administrative support replied.

"All right. In closing, I know that you have concerns about getting paid in real money. Correct?"

"Yes, sir," the response was pretty much universal.

I looked over at Don for a moment before continuing. "The biggest for the end of the meeting, as always," I said with a chuckle. "In searching the residences and the business entities of our former commissioners, we discovered a fairly large amount of undocumented silver and gold coinage. We have not been able to trace those materials back to a legal owner. Those funds have been released by the courts to Spokane County's Treasurer. I know that two bucks an hour silver isn't much, but it is all we can do right now. Back pay up to the point of your last check will of course be made."

A lot of happy faces in the room all of a sudden. "The paymaster will have your back pay in silver, by the end of business, Wednesday. Any questions or comments before we get to work?" I asked as I looked around, stacking my papers up.

"Just one, sir. We're wondering if you're considering flexible work schedules for key staff."

"Yep. Heckuva good idea. We need coverage in most positions at least five days a week though, and ideally six days, probably until the end of the year. If you have proposals to job share, work fewer days and longer hours to get the needed work done, I'm all for it. See your immediate supervisor or department head first. They have authority to OK these things. Personally, I'm going to be doing the same thing. I have a lot of gardening to tend to."

That brought a laugh as the meeting broke up. "Thank you, everyone. Have a good week."

Don and I moved towards the door. "One down, five to go," I said.

"Meetings?"

"Yeah. Monday's looking like my busy day."

"I'll see you in the conference room. Time for a pit stop," Don said.

"See you there," I said as I made my way back to Walts...no, now 'my' office. I was greeted by the sight of four Army uniforms and two Air Force uniforms, seated around my desk.

"Well, good morning," I said, triggering all in the room to rise to greet me. "Sorry I couldn't see you all earlier, but I had a staff meeting at eight."

"That's fine, Mr. Drummond," Division Commander Dennis Hughes answered. "Pardon our interruption, but we didn't have time to set up a meeting in advance," he said as one of the junior staff closed the door.

"What's up, Commander?"

"Half of the Forty-First has been ordered to Canada, effective immediately."

"I heard a little about the war, not much. Can you elaborate on the need?"

"Yeah. We're picking up a number of new territories. The directive is straight from the President. After a meeting with the Premier of New Canada, the Canadians are asking to join the United States over the next five years."

"So Free Canada is now on their own."

"Well, what's left of them. From what our intel guys tell us, it's becoming a black hole. Think 'Beirut', but in French."

"What about the Maritimes? Newfoundland, Labrador, Nova Scotia...."

"Haven't heard. I do know that everything west of Ontario is part of the deal."

"Things change quickly."

"They do indeed. With your permission, my staff has a presentation on the remaining force distribution in Eastern Washington. Obviously this affects Spokane more than other areas, mostly in force reduction."

"Not exactly what I wanted to hear, Commander."

"Understood. We are expecting a Marine detachment though, within the next two months. That should even things up around the urban areas, depending on the social situation."

"Commander, things might get real sporty here by the end of the summer. This cold snap may have killed off nearly every food crop north of the County line. Maybe not THAT far north. And you know what happens when people get hungry."

"I do. I served in Bosnia."

"Enough said."

57

Tuesday,
June Sixth
4 p.m.

I needed to wrap up my day's business and get on home. Carl's birthday dinner was planned for around six, with hand-built bratwurst and chili on the menu…some of his favorite foods.

I was worn out. In my former life, two or three meetings was a busy day. This day though, was an endless stream of demands on my time, sandwiched around one crisis after another.

'I hate days like this,' I thought as I re-read the Special Forces report on Clete McKinnon's demise. The report had been handed to me in a sealed envelope just after lunch. His remains were found seven miles from his home, about a mile from the camp of his murderers.

The report was prepared by the squad leader who tracked and ended the group of looters. The report was both thoroughly descriptive in detail, and brutally accurate with regards to specific actions taken to end the reign of this particular band. They had apparently been scouting Clete's home for quite some time, as evidenced by written notes, sketches, and plans for the attack on his house. They had planned on hitting the place when he was away. Unfortunately for both Clete and the attackers, he was there when they hit the place. Clete apparently killed five within minutes of the initial attack, and wounded several more. He pursued a small number to the place where he was ambushed, as the remaining looters swept in behind him after he'd left his house, to take everything they could carry off. They'd traveled on foot, mountain bike, and horseback away from the home to several locations, before heading back to their main camp, west of Idaho's Highway 95, in the hills above Lake Coeur d'Alene. Special Forces was credited with seventeen kills in the engagement. 'Credited?' I thought.

613

The weather had not really improved all day, but hadn't worsened, either. The endless radio broadcasts contained information on crop and livestock protection, keeping warm in the unseasonable weather, and the all-too-familiar shelter location lists was only interrupted by hourly weather reports…which were not optimistic. There was no national news worth mentioning.

Three inches of snow had fallen at the Spokane-Stevens County line before ten a.m., with seven inches of snow at the top of Mount Spokane. Snow showers fell on Deer Park, Greenbluff, and west to Nine Mile Falls, but none of that 'stuck'. The temperatures in the north county hovered in the mid-thirties. Our temperatures in the city were only a few degrees higher. North, into Boundary County, Pend Oreille County, and into north Idaho, the three-inch accumulation increased with the terrain.

Crop damage or outright loss would be massive. Lows in the mid to low twenties were predicted for the night, and daytime temperatures were not predicted to rise above forty degrees before the end of the week.

Our Recovery Board meeting this morning was to be attended by Stacey Womack's father, who had taken her place on the Board. Instead, he was trying to get his stock under cover and warm, as well as trying (probably in vain) to keep his food supplies from freezing out. Their farm property was high enough up to have received a fair amount of snow, I knew, as well as the cold expected tonight. I wondered if they had enough barn space for the lambs, foals, and calves that would need to be kept warm.

Probably not.

I had managed to plow through my day while trying to remain upbeat for staff on my 'refocusing' effort. All the while though, I knew that we were facing something that we were unprepared for….again.

In the position that I now found myself in, how was I supposed to deal with massive food shortages? What would these people eat? We were only weeks away from a major problem.

"Mr. Drummond? Got a moment?" Colonel Hughes asked as my eyes moved over words on paper, not really reading them.

"Sure, Dennis. One more lit match thrown toward a gas can?"

"Let's hope not, no," he said with a smile. Dennis Hughes, a few years my junior, was the commanding officer of the 41st Division (Composite). "Here's the revised deployment schedule. We'll have two thousand troops available, with five hundred support staff in the urban area. Reserves will total fifteen hundred, with a thousand line troops and five hundred support staff. Total complement in Spokane County will be hovering around fifteen hundred. The balance will be positioned in smaller towns within a hundred mile radius. Additional troops in transit from Puget Sound will be handling towns and cities beyond that range."

"Far cry from the ten thousand you arrived with."

"Yeah. We're still scrounging parts for the trip north. We'd planned on a warm weather transit."

"Not now."

"Nope. And cold weather gear is pretty tough to come by."

"Should be. Most of it headed south after the Domino, or is being used here. Can you enlighten me on where you're going?"

"Sure. North. That's as much info as I've got. We're assuming that we're heading to a population center, but it's anyone's guess."

"How about equipment? Are you planning on flying?"

"Nope. Ground, all the way. Fixed wing assets will stay down here, rotary wings will likely be reserved for extreme need."

"Why's that?" I asked. "I thought helos would be the first thing you'd need."

"Yeah, we do. Problem is, we're running out of blades. Nearly all of the rotor blades we've got are near or at the end of their service life. It's not pretty to lose one in flight."

"How long do they last?"

"Couple thousand hours, I think. Never used to be an issue."

"So what happens when it goes beyond service life?"

"Blades can come apart."

"Bad day for those aboard."

"Yeah. Happened a few weeks back over in the Recovery Zone," he said, referring to what used to be Seattle. "Navy lost two crews in Seahawks, which aren't all that different from our Blackhawks. Blade came off and hit the ship behind them on approach to their LZ. Took them both out."

"My God."

"Yeah. Not pretty. We grounded anything that's within a hundred hours of meeting service life, just in case."

"How many does that leave you?"

"Four. But we do have twenty-five air crews to fly them," he said sarcastically. "Those guys are now ground troops, and not all that happy about it."

"Where do they come from? The blades, I mean."

"Connecticut. I'm not even sure if Sikorsky still exists."

"Yeah."

A few minutes later, I was packing up my bag with a day's reading when the call came in on the open frequency general channel that the county used for emergencies.

"Officer down! Officer under fire!" Even through the anxiety, I knew that it was Don Paulino's voice. My heart rate immediately jumped. He'd caught a ride out to Newman Lake with the Eastern sector patrol deputy, and planned to spend the night at home, trying to keep his crops and livestock in good care. Now this.

Dispatch responded immediately. "State unit number please!"

A brief pause, before Don answered. "Seven. Unit Seven. We're a mile west of Newman Lake on Trent....Highway Two Ninety-One We came under fire...three shots...from the hills off to the northeast....damn, they're still shooting!"

"Understood. Backup is on the way."

"Good. Get medical here. He's bleeding bad."

I finished loading up my stuff and headed for the door. Mike Amberson met me on the way to his office.

“You hear that?”

“I did. Samuels clan?”

“Probably.”

“Deputy was in a marked cruiser, right?”

“Yep.”

“That’s enough for me. We’re ending this crap right now. Your tactical guy finish up his plan?”

“Yeah. Last Friday.”

“Good. Only change I want to make is this: I’m on the team too.”

“We can’t allow that Rick, and you know it.”

“I’ve known Don Pauliano for more than two decades. I’ll be God-damned if I’m going to allow people who just tried to kill them to get away with it. I’m in on this, and there is not a damned thing you can do about it.”

Mike looked at me for a moment, seeing the anger obviously. “Your wife will have my head on a plate.”

“On the contrary. I think she’d want me to be all over this. I’ve been shot at too, you know. This sh•t’s gotta stop, right damned now. I’m not losing another friend to this type of crap, and I’m not going to lose a Recovery Board member, either.”

“You think he was targeted?”

“Even chance of it, yeah. Besides that, he’s a thorn in the side of the Samuels. He’s got a backbone.”

“McMurphy’s team will be the lead unit to reach Wilson’s unit. They should be on site in ten minutes and evac Wilson and Pauliano. We’ll stage the area at dusk.”

“Fine. That’ll give me time to retrieve a certain weapon.”

“What would that be?

“My Dad’s BAR.”

Karen had heard Don's voice on my 'home' radio, and wisely did not call me on the radio about it. She did wait to hear that there was just one injury, Deputy Wilson, who was hit in the arm and shoulder. She then went to Don's folks house to tell them that he was OK. I pulled into the driveway, with a military escort, just as she was closing the gate.

"You OK?" she asked as I got out of the Ford and gave her a hug.

"Yeah. Pissed. Really, really pissed." She knew the look.

"Don't do anything stupid, Richard."

"I won't. I'll have plenty of help. Rather, I'll be a little help to them, I hope."

"What are you going to tell Carl?"

"That I'm going hunting. I think he'll understand."

"When do you leave?"

"Forty-five minutes."

"Good. Time for dinner then. Let's get inside. Rain's coming back. Brats are almost done, if Kelly remembered to put them in that homemade beer on the stove," she said. "What about them?" she said, pointing to my military escort, today a Sergeant and a Corporal, who I'd met only in passing before I left the office.

"Hadn't thought about them," I said sheepishly.

"Bring them in. There's plenty."

"Will do. You are a peach."

"I am, but don't tell. It'd ruin my reputation."

Karen headed inside, while I went to the Humvee parked across my driveway apron.

"Sir?" the Sergeant asked.

"Dinner, gentlemen. C'mon in."

"Sir, that's not necessary."

"Wife's orders. Best not disregard them." He smiled, as did the young Corporal next to him.

"Understood, sir. We appreciate that."

"My honor. C'mon inside. Bratwurst, sauerkraut, and chili on the side. My son's birthday choices."

"And good choices sir," the Corporal responded.

The rain was starting to pick up again, with wind coming from the northwest. It would not be that pleasant a night in the hills above the Samuel's place....

My Army escorts looked more than a little uncomfortable in the now crowded house. The Martins, Bauers, and Sarah Woodbridge were joining us for dinner, and helping out with the final preparations and frosting Carl's cake.

"Everyone, we have a couple more for dinner," I announced. "Sergeant, why don't you introduce yourself and the Corporal?"

"Thank you, sir. I'm Mike Green, this is Terry Reynolds. Mr. Reynolds here and I have been together since Baghdad."

"Nice to meet you," Alan said as he shook hands with both of them, and ran through the introductions of everyone, while I went to retrieve our gifts for Carl. I also changed into foul weather gear, and made sure the Browning was ready.

"No, sir, I missed Monterrey," Green replied to Ron as the Sergeant eyed another brat. "We were on mop up in Tucson."

"Sarge, go ahead and finish the brats please. I'd just pay for it later," Carl said. He'd already had two, fully loaded.

"Thanks. I believe I will."

"Ready for presents?" Karen asked.

"Absolutely!" Carl said.

We went round the room, starting with Karen. He was flabbergasted with the guitar, as was the young Corporal Reynolds.

"Mind if I try it?" he asked.

"Not at all. I don't really play yet. Just wanted to learn."

"Well, you've got a nice learner. Before the War, this was worth a couple thousand bucks."

"No way!" Carl said.

"Yeah. Pretty sure. I had a Gibson J-50, too. Mine was a sixty-one. I think this one's a little older."

"Yep," I said. "Fifty-nine."

"Nice find. Mind if I ask…."

"Tell you later," I said, receiving a nod. 'Three bricks of twenty-two long,' I thought to myself.

"Yours next, Dad," Carl said.

"John, bring those two bundles in if you would," I asked John, who seemed glued to Sarah.

"Got them."

I looked at Carl as he unwrapped the first bundle, the Springfield. He knew by the shape it was a long-gun, but didn't expect this obviously.

"Dad, are you sure?"

"Yep. I am. I pray you never have to use it as I have."

"Amen to that," Mary said.

"What's the other one?" Kelly asked.

"Something a little more modern. Hopefully our Army guests won't mind one of those in civilian hands."

Carl unwrapped the second, shorter bundle, to find one of the new M-16's.

"Whoa," he said. I glanced over at Green, and he had a grin on his face.

"Nice," he said. "Know how to use it?"

"No," Carl said.

"You will soon," I said. "Firearms training starts next Monday."

Carl finished opening up the rest of the presents, and we were then treated with cake and fresh whole milk.

"Carl, a word please," I said as he served up the last piece of cake from the kitchen.

"Thanks Dad, I really appreciate what you gave me."

"You're welcome….but listen. I'm going out tonight with those soldiers, and a few more," I spoke quietly. "Well, more than a few. We're going out toward Pauliano's and take care of some problems."

"Samuels."

"Yep."

"I heard the call on the County radio. Is Mr. Pauliano OK?"

"Yeah. But I think they targeted him and the Deputy. And if they targeted Don, that's the same as targeting me. And I won't stand for that."

"Why are you going? Why not just the Army?"

"My job to help run the County. I consider this part of my job."

"Lead from the front."

"Exactly. I need you to keep an eye out tonight though. I don't think this is something bigger than what it looks like, but I want you keep a weather eye out."

"Army patrols are still up the street?" he asked, with a little embarrassment.

"Yeah."

"What are you taking?"

"The Browning."

"Well, that oughta do it," he said with a grin.

"Yeah. I figured as much. If I'm lucky, I won't fire a shot."

"If you're lucky, THEY won't fire a shot," he said.

"Better."

58

June Seventh,
1:17 am

Endless waiting. Rain dripping off of the ocean spray shrub over my head, splashing on an old cedar log right in front of my face. Numbing cold, despite my clothing. I was uncomfortably reminded of my time on 'watch' last winter. This time though, no hot cider or coffee.   And the damned helmet didn't fit.

We'd been moving into place and then waiting for five hours. Creeping through the dark, through the trees and shrubs, finally taking our places. We hiked in individually or in pairs, from east, north, and south…into the 'back yard' of the Samuels property, which covered almost a square mile of ground. In thirteen minutes, the lead element of Kilo Company, backed up by twenty-five civilian law enforcement officers, would kick things off. 'Kilo' was a light-infantry company, undermanned at three officers and seventy-two men, from their required one hundred thirty. The infantry unit consisted of two full rifle platoons, a mortar crew, and command. Anti-armor, usually found in units like this, was gone, as was one of the rifle platoons. The combined civilian police units would serve as a single rifle platoon and would also provide communications and coordination.

Two of Mike's undercover deputies, who pre–Domino were involved almost exclusively in drug busts, would be leaving the Samuel's brothel by oh-one-twenty. They'd get on their motorcycles, same as every night this week, and head south toward Liberty Lake. They would not participate in the concluding operation, preserving their ability to serve in future missions should the need arise. Their recon, gathered over the weeks and months prior, established the movement pattern of the opponent, their size, armament, and other activities that might pose a problem.

Their reconnaissance had provided us all the probable cause that any court would ever need, although there would be no trial, not this time. The officers had observed prostitution, arms trafficking, and manufacture of drug paraphernalia and illegal drugs. Those were relatively minor offenses in the big picture these days. Murder, slavery, and torture were not. Neither was child abuse. All had been observed, and in most cases filmed, by the undercover team.

The Samuel's group never realized that one of the undercover team carried a miniature camera on his German-Army style motorcycle helmet, which was almost always placed in the corner where they sat, just up on a shelf. Tonight, he'd left that helmet behind. Sergeant Rosetti, fifty feet above me, monitored the transmission in a camouflaged hole that had been constructed right under the noses of the ineffective Samuel's patrols. The patrol path was a further twenty feet above Rosetti, just below the military crest of the hill. A half-mile further up the valley was Don Pauliano's place, which tonight was manned by a half dozen Deputies and State Troopers. Rosetti forwarded target information to the lead team, and to the support teams. We learned there were more than thirty 'viable targets' in the compound. Three of the group were on 'patrol', or were supposed to be. On typical nights we were told, they actually patrolled on fixed paths above and around the compound at regular intervals, with rifles slung over their shoulders. On nights like this, they stayed under a covered woodshed, away from the main buildings. Essentially, they were hiding from their superiors and the weather. Good for us, bad for them.

Those three would be the first to fall. Our opponents even provided us light to see each building by, one of the last outposts that was connected up to the 'grid', with mercury-vapor lights blazing on each side of the main building, small building-mounted lights near the doors, and lights in most windows. A small frame house up the hill, which served as Rae Samuels's headquarters, was brightly lit on the covered porch and main floor. She ran the entire operation from the second floor of the place, which had a commanding view of the buildings below, and views across the Spokane Valley floor. We'd heard in our briefing that at least one scoped rifle was present during normal evenings. No one was apparently on the upper floor tonight, and the balconies were empty. That meant that everyone who was of interest was in the main building.

I was relegated to covering the lesser of two exits from the main building. 'Probably rightly so,' I thought. The BAR was covered against the rain by a light oilskin canvas, that probably made more noise than it should have, even with the pine needles covering it. In a few more minutes, I would hear a single click on the military ear bud and take my final position. We would next hear a double-click, and things would begin. My job was to take out anyone exiting the back of the building—a room that had been identified as the 'cash room.' A three-man fire team below me to the left would cover the larger door, and the side of the building. They would have to exercise more discretion on targets—the larger door was the exit to the second floor brothel. 'There are kids in there,' we were told. Should anyone exit my door, there was a ninety-nine percent chance that they were viable targets. Only the upper echelon of the Samuels operation was allowed in the cash room.

I heard two Harley's start up, accelerate, and fade off into the distance. As the last note sounded, my radio clicked once. I uncovered the Browning, and trained it on the door below me.

According to recon, the concrete basement under the 'store' and the gambling area was divided up into cells, which were chain-link dog kennels bolted to the wood floors and ceiling. Within these cells, children, women, and men were physically abused and occasionally killed. We had only learned this in our briefing today. We had assumed before the briefing that the Samuels' activities were limited to theft, drugs, and illegalities of a more pedestrian nature.

I heard my radio click twice as I was wiping the rain out of my eyes. The three sentries crumpled silently in their shelter.

Several flash-bang grenades temporarily blinded me as the main building first, and later the house, lost their glass in a huge shower of light. The concussion hit me a moment later, as the guns below me opened up. I refocused my aim, wondering if anyone would come out 'my' door. Incoming rounds began to kick up mud in front of me, pass to my right, and move up toward Rosetti. I instinctively ducked behind the cedar log as three rounds hit the log to the left of me. My next question to myself was, 'where in Hell did those come from?' followed by 'Do I dare raise my head?' I hadn't yet squeezed the trigger.

No further rounds seemed to be coming at me, and I peeked above the log, my poorly fitting helmet getting in the way. The small door was cracked open, the room still lit from within, and I could see the second squad rush toward the front of the building. Firing was coming from all over the hillside around me toward the buildings, and I noticed that the second floor of the house was on fire, just as a massive explosion obliterated it completely, shaking the ground beneath me. The explosion seemed to come from below the building, under it. It disappeared, along with whoever was in it, in a huge fireball. Roof and siding rained down around the hole where the house had stood. I thought the guns were silent for just a moment, before they opened up again. I regained my composure and looked up over the top of the mossy log.

They were running now, up and into the darkness, out of the building. I took careful aim and the Browning spoke. Time after time, men and women exited the building through the cash room door, firing blindly, and I cut them down.

I went through five magazines on my own before the shooting slowed. By then, positions above me far to the right, and below and left were out of targets in their designated positions, and fired at any unfriendly that was holding a gun.

In four minutes, it was over. I promptly vomited as the smell hit me.

Mop up took a further thirty minutes, rounding up prisoners, and setting the imprisoned, free. I numbly listened to the call from Command to the waiting ambulances and transports, which were stopped on the highway, two miles away. I picked up my brass and empty magazines, wiped them down, and put them in a small, ancient canvas bag, stenciled with my fathers' serial number and Second Lieutenant rank.

"You OK, Pops?" I heard someone ask. "Yo! You hurt?" they asked again. They were asking me. I realized that my earplug was still in my right ear, and the ear bud in my left.

"I'm alright," I said flatly as I took out the earplugs and shut off the radio. Two very young soldiers stood above me, cradling their battle rifles.

"Nice ****ing shooting, old man. You really lit 'em up!" the first one said. "You can cover us any old time."

"Little old for that, thanks," I said as I crawled out from behind the log and started downhill.

"Where'd you serve?" The second asked. "And where'd you get that 'tique?" he asked of my Browning.

"Civilian. Although, I've served a bit defending my home," I said. "The gun came to me through my father. He used it in the Second War."

"Reminded me of a SAW, the way it took those guys apart," the younger-appearing of the two said. "Nice ****ing gun. Did you see that fat chick? Her head went flying!"

"How long have you two boys been in the Army?"

"I've been in two years. Petey here's a newbie. Nine months."

"Well, boys, let's go find your C.O. I have a job for you to do."

"What might that be?"

"Learning respect for the dead."

"Last I heard, we don't take orders from civvies," the older said as we reached the bottom of the hill.

That was enough for me. The butt of the twenty-pound Browning hit him right below the sternum. I brought the still-loaded Browning around and took two steps back. He crumpled as his younger companion looked on in shock, not knowing if I was a threat or not. "Listen up, sh•t for brains. We just mopped up on thirty or forty people. I just personally killed more than a half dozen. Their bodies are in pieces over there," I said angrily. "It ain't a laughing matter, whether they deserved it or not. You're job will be to collect their remains, and put them in body bags. And I mean every piece of them. Maybe next time you think killing people is fun, you'll think twice. Am I clear?" My fathers' Battalion Commander voice echoed far beyond the two soldiers in front of me. I could see out of the corner of my eye, a sergeant major coming my way.

"Yes, sir," they both responded.

"And further, boys, because right now I do not consider you worthy of the term soldier, the Commander in Chief is a civilian, so yes, sh•thead, you do take orders from civilians. Understood?"

"Yes, sir," they said as the first finally got to his feet.

"Good. Now get your asses to work. NOW!" I barked. They scurried off toward one of the newly arrived Humvees, stacking their rifles in the back.

"Problem, sir?" the sergeant major asked.

"Not anymore, sar-major."

"Nicely handled, by the way."

"Thanks. Unfortunately, I seem to have a knack for chewing ass."

"Maintains quality control."

I looked over at the sergeant, who was perhaps ten years younger than me, an 'old' sergeant if so.

"Indeed. I'm Rick Drummond."

"Cannon, David A. Nice to meet you. And they were right, those two. Nice gun. I caught the last few you took down."

"Duck shoot. Couldn't really miss from that range, especially with this."

"True enough. Pays to have disproportionate force."

"Those two belong to you?" I asked of the two men, now uncomfortably beginning to collect the scattered remains of several people that had been torn literally, to pieces.

"Thank Christ, no. They belong to the Second."

The coffee was cold, but at least I was out of the rain, sitting in a gutted school bus, converted for a mobile office. Four transports of freed prisoners were heading to two hospitals and shelters, to try to heal what would never really be healed. Four children under the age of twelve were among the freed. They all looked like death walking.

Mike and I were listening to the after-action comments coming in on the radio. We were parked just in front of the store, but I was just too tired to go see it for myself. My hands were still shaking; an hour after the last shot was fired.

"You oughta take a couple days off," Mike said.

"Yeah. I oughta. Any word on your Deputy?"

"Yeah. He's gonna lose his arm. Surgeon's can't put it back together."

"Damn," I said. "We have any wounded here?"

"Minor stuff. Cuts and bruises. Twisted ankle."

"And forty-seven enemy killed, and sixteen wounded, so far."

"Yeah."

"Recon said, what, thirty to forty?"

"Yeah, but we also didn't know about the extent of the drug lab under the house."

"That was the explosion."

"Yep. Took out fifteen or so right there. We'll spend a couple days here sorting it all out. One of the detectives did find something though that you might want to handle yourself."

"What's that?"

"Don Pauliano's cousin. His ID and credit cards were found in the wreckage. There was also a map that someone in there created, to show where the dead were buried. He's on the list. So were twenty-six others."

"So he didn't wander off after the quake. He was killed."

"All evidence says that."

"Anybody ID Rae Samuels yet?"

"Nope, but if she was in the house, that may never happen. They're still ID'ing who they can. That won't be possible in a lot of cases."

"OK, fair enough. What's next here?"

"I'll have one officer here until clean up is complete. Lieutenant Buell will be in charge of the Army clean up team. There's ordnance all over the place."

"How many more of these do we have to deal with?"

"At least one in the northern part of the County. We're still trying to locate the nest. Some smaller problem houses, nothing on this scale though."

"Good," I said. I could hear my own fatigue.

"McKesson! A moment please."

"Sir," one of the Deputies replied.

"Please deliver Mr. Drummond to his home. I think he's about overdrawn at the stress bank."

"Understood. Sir, this way if you would."

"Thanks, Mike. I'll check in with you tomorrow."

"I'll have dispatch let Admin know that you'll be off for the day."

"That'd be nice."

"Get some rest."

"I plan on it. Keep me posted on the mom-to-be."

"Will do," Mike said as I took the Browning and my gear bag, and headed for the door. I left the bus with the deputy, and headed across the debris field to the highway, where a cruiser was parked. The rain was lighter, but only just barely. It felt like November.

Twenty-five minutes of dozing-off later, I was on my own street. We passed the bunkhouse where either Army sentries or Deputies or both watched over the neighborhood, and got a wave from the lone visible sentry. The dining room light was on at my house, which surprised me. I thanked the young officer who drove me home, and he headed back to his normal duties. 'Whatever 'normal' is now,' I thought.

There really wasn't a quiet way to get from the driveway through the metal stock gate and to the house, entirely by design. By the time I made the back porch, the dogs had managed to peek out the curtains, identify me as friend, and were whining at the back door as it opened before me. Karen didn't give me a chance to get out of my wet coat before she tried to crush me in a hug and a kiss. I didn't realize how cold I was until she kissed me.

"You're an iceberg," she said.

"Yeah. Cold out there."

"I was worried."

"I know. I'm OK." Both dogs were doing their best to identify every foreign scent on me, with tails wagging like mad. I parked the Browning next to the old oak buffet in the dining room, and my mind wandered back to the endless layers of paint that I'd taken off of the Kitchen Queen. It had belonged to Karen's grandparents, well before the First War.

She knew by my look that I'd done something that I'd rather not have had to do. "Is it over?"

"Yeah."

"It was bad," she asked.

"It was bad. The only good thing is that we didn't lose any men. No injuries to speak of, either…they had slaves out there, babe."

She was speechless.

"Kids, too."

"Are they free now? Did you guys save them?"

"Most of them, yeah. Too late for some," I said numbly. "I need to get out of these clothes and take a shower. Build me a cup of chamomile tea? OK?"

"Sure."

"I'm staying home tomorrow, too. And sleeping in."

"Good. You need it."

"Yeah."

June 7th
10.30 a.m.

Buck decided it was time for me to play. "How thoughtful, you goofball. Now give me my socks," I said as he ran off with a clean pair, turning, dropping his front quarters, and growling at me.

Karen had risen a few hours ago, I wasn't really sure when. I headed in for another shower, and smelled something wonderful cooking downstairs.

By eleven, I'd made myself presentable (well, for a part-time farmer) and headed down to find the source of that aroma. Karen and Libby had just finished up preparations for brunch for the extended family and me. Brunch today was fried egg sandwiches on fresh wheat bread (with dried tomatoes thrown in), and the first batch of fresh tomato soup from our greenhouse crops.

"Good morning, all." I said to the collected relatives and friends. Kelly gave me a big hug, followed by Carl. The house was as full as it could be, with the Martins and the entire Bauer family.

"Morning. Here, I think you need this," Alan said as he handed me a cup of real coffee.

"Thanks. I won't turn it down," I said right before I kissed his little sister good morning. "Weather improve at all?"

"Well, it's warmer. That's about it. Still raining a little. Fields are a sea of mud."

"Swell."

"News of the day is that Ashley's in labor," Karen said.

"Early."

"Yeah. Three weeks early. It's twins."

I started to laugh, a little, then a whole lot. "Never been a more deserving couple," I finally said. "Is she at home?"

"No, I spoke with one of the Deputies. She's at Sacred Heart. Precautionary."

"Well, all my prayers for a safe delivery and healthy kids and mom," I thought. 'Mike's gonna be a wreck,' I thought with some level of glee.

"Store not open today?" I asked Alan.

"Not much business this morning. No one's all that interested in venturing out," Alan replied. "Can't say I blame them. What have you got planned for the day?"

"Well, cleaning the Browning for one. I'm sure it's a mess even though I got the worst of the crap off of it last night."

"We'd appreciate hearing about that when you're ready," Ron said.

"Might be a while. Still digesting it."

"Understood. Radio said sixty-seven dead. Fifty-nine of them hostiles."

"Sounds about right I suppose," I said. Carl was listening intently.

"You in the middle of it?"

"I don't know about the middle, but I went through five or six magazines. I know that I was responsible for a number."

"Well, we're glad to have you back safe and sound," Libby said. "On to other stuff. We found a roof leak. Can you help Ron with it?" She was distinctly not interested in hearing of my battle, or any battle. I couldn't blame her a bit.

"Sure. I've got some roof tar in caulking tubes out in the barn. That'll be a fun project in the rain. Other than that, I'd like to take care of miscellaneous chores that require little or no thought. I have a whole raft of things that fall into that category. I'd like to do something that doesn't involve staffing, files, the next great crisis, or anything that's related to the big picture," I said honestly. "How about you guys?"

"Ron's roof, some trades to consummate, meaning, pickups and deliveries."

"How's that going to work? You plan on driving for that kind of stuff? Gas is pretty precious for that."

"I got a lead on an old still. I'd like to use that old pickup of yours to get it," Ron said.

"Keys are on the rack. Go for it. Just remember your pass," I said, referring to the driver pass needed to use gasoline for farm uses.

"What's the policy on ethanol vehicle use?" he asked, referring to the old Ford's conversion.

"Don't have one yet. I guess we'll have staff write something up. Yet another color in the rainbow of vehicle passes."

"You might want to put some guidelines in on the stills' use too. One of those blows up, it'll leave a fair thumbprint," Alan said.

"Hadn't thought about that. You're right of course."

"Brunch, boys. Quit talking shop."

"Yes, ma'am!" Alan said. "Rick, after you."

"Oh, no. Ladies first."

"Get in line, mister," Libby said. "We'll debate etiquette later."

"As you wish." I was still bone dead tired. I wondered how long the images of last night's battle would appear before me, each time I closed my eyes.

59

Tuesday,
August Twenty-second

The rains of early June and the severe cold snap turned out to be nothing less than devastating for food crop production in the north half of Washington State and North Idaho. People who had been optimistic in the early days of that month soon realized that they were in most cases, weeks away from having very, very little to eat in the way of a normal diet.   While we worried about crime, what really scared us was hunger.

In the northern counties the June cold lasted for two and a half days, before warming to daily highs in the high forties, and lows in the thirties. The Federal weathercasters had no idea why the cold snap hit us so early and so hard, and warned us that continued unexpected weather conditions could plague us for some time. They were exactly on the mark for that though. After June eighth, it didn't rain again until deep into August. Crops that made it through the cold were seared by the heat of late June, July, and August. A record high was set on my birthday, July twelfth, for one hundred and nine degrees. That was the 'lowest' high for the following seven days.

Grains, row crops and tree fruit were hit particularly hard, with losses above ninety percent reported. Livestock losses were higher than expected too, with losses in beef, sheep, and fowl above twenty-five percent. I learned from an inexperienced farmer out west of town, that he'd just sheared his sheep a few days before the cold snap. If he had sheared them when he should have—March--I learned from an experienced shearer a few days later, his flock would have been fine. Timing was everything.

Locally we were hit, but not that hard by the cold. Almost all of our squash plants were 'nipped' by frost, and quite a bit of our apple trees thinned themselves out. Our cherry crop, less than a month away from being ready, was untouched. When the cold turned to oppressive heat and dust and smoke from unmanageable forest and grass fires, our irrigated crops were our sole hope. I wondered as the summer went by, how we'd protect our food.

I knew right away that we were in trouble. One hundred percent of the population in the County was depending on those crops to feed themselves and their families. Without a good harvest, we were either going to have people starve or become refugees in search of food, somewhere south. We'd heard from the military that the cold in British Columbia, Alberta, and Saskatchewan was far worse than what we'd seen.

With our new elected representatives in place after the June elections, we quickly made the decision to enter into trade negotiations with counties south of us for grain and other food shipments that they might be willing to sell. We had relatively abundant amounts of one scarce item, diesel fuel. Pipelines from the east filled every surviving tank at the petroleum distribution centers, and a good number of the in-ground tanks at secured gas stations. We also had a massive amount of rail equipment, including locomotives and bulk carriers, stranded here after the Domino. The rail system to the south was dependent on a single surviving line, but there was very little traffic on it, or anywhere from what we gathered.   A fair number of our townsmen were full-time farmers before the War, and they understood the situation better than a sizeable percentage of the urban dwellers. Even after all we'd gone through, some people didn't make the connection between farming and food. Between diesel fuel and food.

On this day, I was headed to Fort Walla Walla with three other men to meet our new civilian Governor, the interim State leadership, and other County representatives from around the state.

"I'm not exactly thrilled with this, Rick," Karen told me as I re-packed my backpack for the trip. She was giving me 'The Look.'

"I'm not either, Karen. But we need to have a face-to-face meeting. I need to get food supplies arranged and shipped up here or we're going to have a major-league problem. There will not be enough food to keep people alive without them fighting each other for it. We've just got the place settled down again and people are coming back out of their shells. Imagine what it'll be like around here if we have to shoot people over food." We'd had this discussion before....

"But do you have to fly?"

"Unless I want to spend two full days in a truck, and a boat ride across the Snake, yeah. I have to fly."

"I don't like it."

We'd gone over the need for my three-day trip for more than a week. My goals were to establish a steady trading relationship with trading partners to the south of us, but this would be by far the biggest trade—both in volume and need--ever. I knew that I had a few things that might be interesting to potential trading partners…but I was also going into a trading session blind to what potential partners might want. It felt like a blind date. The meeting—called the State Conference on Governance—was not exactly optional. I was specifically requested to attend, as were leaders or administrators from each county in the state. The request was hand-delivered by Army courier. We still didn't really have decent mail operations.

I was to fly to Fort Walla Walla, formerly the Army Corps of Engineers' post at the Walla Walla Airport, with two military pilots and cargo—the cargo being aircraft parts from Fairchild and Felts Field. We'd be using what had been a private plane, commandeered for military use. There really wasn't such a thing now as a private aircraft. There wasn't fuel to fly them, the government had ordered them grounded to help slow the spread of the Flu, and there really wasn't anywhere to 'go to' that was much better off than anyplace else. That was the 'official' line anyway.

The spread of the Flu had slowed, but not stopped. We were constantly expecting the death toll in Spokane County to rise dramatically when it 'got here', but found instead that we saw an increasing number of suicides and deaths attributed to other diseases or pre-existing conditions. In mid June, we saw a two–week spike in the death toll, right after the cold snap broke. Most of those deaths were attributed to exposure. From around the country we heard through the remnants of the AM and FM bands, of soaring death tolls that quickly overwhelmed some areas, and completely spared others.

It was beyond us to figure out what took some and allowed others to live. Dr. Sorenson thought that there might have been increased exposures to the genetically targeting virus carried by the wind and human transport patterns, from key infection locations. 'Sounds reasonable,' I thought. 'But what in the Hell do I know about it?' In defense, we seemed to have developed or refined our resignation to live, and the appreciation for our own fragility.

Some people just went 'barking mad' at the prospect of the Flu taking them. I thought that perhaps those folks were a fair percentage of the suicides we saw. They just got to the end of their endurance and did not see a way through. Some went the other way, and dedicated every waking minute to either serving others or living life as if there were literally no tomorrow. Some of the latter made good counselors for those in difficulty. Others turned predator, for in their own mind anything was OK, because they were going to die soon anyway.

It was unlikely to me that Sarah Woodbridge would be somewhere in the middle, but that's where I found her one day in early July, on her scheduled day off from the clinic. I'd seen her at work in the clinic, and she had a good manner and an even temperament. The girl I saw that day was unlike the girl at work, and she snapped at me when I asked her a simple question, on 'how's it going?'

"Piss off," was her reply.

"Excuse me?"

"I think I was clear enough. Piss off," this time, she was quivering.

"Miss Woodbridge, I would have expected a more polite reply to a polite question."

She turned and went back inside the back porch of her house, where I happened to be working on a rain collection system from her homes' gutters. 'Do I pursue this, or not?' I asked myself. 'In a few minutes,' I answered myself as I went back to putting the gutter screens on.

Sure enough, fifteen minutes later, she came outside. "Mr. Drummond, I apologize," she said. She'd been crying.

"Care to talk about it?"

She nodded and sat down on the steps as I descended the ladder. "I'm sorry. It was a crappy day at the clinic."

"I've had days like that before."

"I haven't," she said and then paused. "I was taking a break at work, and went over to the market," she began, referring to the clothing market at the community center, down the hall from the medical clinic. "I actually got into a fight with a lady who wanted the coat I was looking at. I was ready to kill her for it. I hit her with my fist! Why would I do that? I'm not an animal."

I thought about the right thing to say. "Sarah, I could blame it on stress, and I'd probably be right. But I think you need to look inside yourself for that answer."

"I've never done anything like that before in my life. It would have never occurred to me to do that."

"Was she hurt?"

"No, I think she was more surprised than me. I scared her for sure. I apologized, but I don't think it mattered. Doc told me to take a couple days off."

"Good idea," I said. "Sarah, we've never really talked much about your background, but what sort of value system did you grow up with? Did you attend church with your grandparents?"

"Well, not really. I mean, at Christmas and Easter. That was about it. My grandfather was raised Catholic and didn't like the priest. My grandmother, well, that was another story. She hated the church. She never told me why."

"OK, without getting all preachy here, has anyone ever asked you if you believe in God? In Jesus Christ?"

"No, not really," she said. "Not before the War anyway."

"Well, maybe it's time you figured out if you do. A lot of people wonder how I deal with what we're going through. Why I act the way I do. The reason is because I know that I'm only here for awhile. I'm going elsewhere after my time on Earth is done."

She looked at me, not knowing what to say. "It's OK if you don't have an answer. My faith is what works for me. Some people can't figure that out."

"I've just never thought about it," she said. "I don't know enough to know what questions to ask."

"I can help you out with that if you like, but I'm not exactly a pastor. Closest thing that I did in that fashion was serve in a youth group."

"So what do I do, just pick up a Bible and start reading?"

"Well you could, but I can help you with some guidance along the way. You will have questions. You also ought to have the right Bible for you. Not all of them are the same. Some are pretty tough to read. Others, well, aren't translated all that well."

"You've done this before," she said. I could tell she was feeling better.

"I've done this before."

"So how do people just start believing?"

"Most adults only with difficulty. It is far easier to ask a child and have them come to believe in Jesus Christ than it is an adult. Most adults, if they have not found Christ by the time they're eighteen or so, never will, no matter what. At least, that was what we learned before the War. Now? Anybody's guess."

"And that's how you cope? By just believing?"

"No, not just believing. By praying, by dedicating my life to Christ, by using Him as an example for my life. By extension, using my life for others. I can show you where to start with only a half-dozen Bible verses."

She was thinking about it, and that was a good start. "Thank you. I'm sorry I snapped at you."

"It's OK. We all have our moments."

"You don't seem to."

"Oh, don't be so sure of that. I bury a lot of stuff that I shouldn't. Then, I blow off at seemingly unexpected moments."

"I haven't seen that."

"Few have. Just as well," I said. "Sarah, it's a good thing you feel badly about what happened today. It means you have a conscience. There are a whole lot of other people in this world that see absolutely nothing wrong with stealing, killing, whatever, just to get what they want. You're not one of those."

"Thank you," she said softly as our conversation paused. "On a different topic, do you think things will ever get back to...you know, normal?"

"Normal being the world before January eighteenth? No. We're too far down that road for things to be 'the same' as they were before. We're now in post World War Three America. We're now living with a genetic killer that we don't know if we're immune to. The economy is a wreck, and will be a long, long time in repairing. But mostly, we've all changed. We aren't really interested in 'American Idol' anymore. Stuff like that doesn't matter."

She laughed a little at my reference, I was glad to see that she was getting out of her funk. "I used to watch that show. Remembering it now it was like I was watching myself watch that show."

"I know what you mean."

"You said that the economy would take a long time to get back to normal. I don't understand. We still use money, we still buy things."

"Yes we do. But we also trade. And we don't use paper money anymore, right?"

"Right, I just don't see the difference."

"The difference is that silver and gold are real. Paper money is just that. It can be worth whatever you want it to be by printing a number on it and calling it legal. Well, it wasn't legal, it wasn't money, and it wasn't worth what people were led to believe."

"OK, I guess I understand," she said. I could see she didn't yet though.

"Sarah, our economy used what was called a fiat currency. Fiat means, literally, fake money—a monetary system that is not backed by a metal value. Once upon a time, our dollar was backed by silver and gold. We were on the 'Gold Standard', where one ounce of gold equaled twenty dollars. That went away in the First Depression. We've been on a downhill slide since then. We hit the ground, then started digging. There isn't one person in a thousand now who would take what little real money they have and risk it in the stock market, or in a bank, or in any sort of institution that plays games with money. The word 'dollar' meant a unit of weight of gold—measured against the Spanish piece of eight. Didn't know that, did you?"

"No."

"We're so far removed from what was 'money' in historic times that we have to learn it all over again. That's part of the problem. The economic engines of nations run in cycles. There's booms and busts, and probably always have been. By allowing our government to be run by the bankers and corporations, and that's what's happened to us, we allowed the government to blind us to what our dollars were worth. We finally got to the point where 'digidollars' were all that mattered. Not many people used cash—meaning paper—before the crash. They all used credit cards. Debt went rampant. People were financially destroyed. The economic winter I'm afraid, will be a long one. The real winter might not be any picnic either."

"How are John and I…I mean…"

I smiled. "It's OK. It's a poorly kept secret, you and John."

"Thanks," she said as she blushed. "How are we supposed to make a start?"

"Same way your great, great grandparents did I suppose. The hard way."

"It's like we're back in the nineteen twenties."

"Not really. More like eighteen sixty-six, and this is the South. Reconstruction era."

"I wish I knew my history better."

"Not too late to learn. Read."

She gave me a big hug, a quiet 'thank you,' and quickly went back inside the house. I went back to finishing up the water collection system, and then headed home.

That was a better day than I thought it would have been. Good kid, that Sarah. I could imagine the stories she'll tell her grandchildren, and hoped that our history would not fall on deaf ears.

My too-heavy travel pack in hand, we headed to the Ford for the short trip over to Felts Field. At least the weather was relatively nice, with a mostly-blue sky today. For weeks we'd had the dust and haze of what was called the Dirty Summer.

"So what happens in Walla Walla?" Kelly asked as I looked over the elm seedlings growing in the cracked street.

"I get to meet with my fellow county leaders and beg for food."

"Seriously, Dad," she said.

"I am serious. That's my primary reason for going."

"But we're OK with our gardens, aren't we?"

"We're OK, and our immediate neighbors will be OK. I cannot say that for the rest of the county. We were counting on a decent year for growing, and we didn't get it."

"What are you going to trade them?"

"Good question. I need to find out what their needs are, and work the problem from their side of the table. With God's help, it'll work out for both parties."

"Sounds like fun. Not." Carl said from behind the wheel. Karen and I were letting him drive today. He had his 'provisional' license, but there really wasn't a 'permanent' license to get these days.

"How do you plan on getting the food north?" Karen asked wisely.

"Yet another, in a long line of questions to resolve. I'm not completely sure of the condition of the rail system down there, or outside of our county for that matter. Or the roads. If we can send stuff by train, then we're good. I'm not sure of the highways down there either, but Tim James made it here from the Tri Cities, so Three Ninety-Five was still OK at that point."

"How much food are you trying to get?" Karen asked.

"Kinda depends on what's available. I'm going for grains mostly, but if there are other crops available, we'll see what we can do. We're talking many tons of stuff."

"Well, what kind of stuff?" Kelly asked.

"Wheat, barley, oats, corn. Grain crops mostly because that's what I think they've been able to grow down south. The Basin's irrigated crops—peas, beans, potatoes, and corn—were devastated by the loss of irrigation. Corn is a priority, but I'm not hopeful on that. Wheat is a big one, oats and barley, and I forgot lentils, important or critical as well."

"So, just for fun, how many pounds are you trying to get?" Karen asked.

"I said tons, not pounds. Something on the high side of six thousand tons, closer to seven."

"Seven thousand tons?!" Carl asked.

"Yeah."

"How did you figure that out?"

"Of grains, if we can get maybe two hundred fifty to three hundred pounds per person, that will go a long way toward keeping people fed. Doesn't provide everything of course for a balanced diet, but a good chunk. Fresh vegetables will be a premium...." I said. "Everything will. Meat will be scarce. Fruit **is** scarce. Nuts are hard to find. I'm trying to avert a major disaster. I know we'll have a minor disaster even if I'm successful."

We turned from Park Road onto Trent Avenue, and headed west toward Felts Field. As we approached Freya, an Army sentry unit, who requested—despite my colored tag—that we leave the vehicle for a search, stopped us.

"Lieutenant, care to enlighten me?"

"Are you Mr. Drummond, sir?"

"I am."

"Sorry sir, we are searching all vehicles, orders of the Duty Officer. Four vehicles were found last night with partially completed IED's. All were Ford Expeditions, similar to yours, right down to the color, license plate and your mirror tag."

I was stunned. "What the Hell?"

"You heard me correctly, sir."

"Time for a new ride."

"Yep."

"Who was putting them together?"

"Don't know that sir, no one was apprehended. The work was incomplete though, but recent. They seemed to have been waiting for some parts to complete them."

"I would like to see your duty officer immediately."

"Yes, sir, he asked that he be informed when you arrived."

"Lieutenant, exactly how long have you known about these car bombs masquerading as my vehicle?"

He looked at his watch. "Nineteen minutes, sir."

"Good enough. Who's the duty officer today?"

"Colonel McCalister, sir."

"Thanks." 'Colonel', I thought. 'Got promoted.' McCalister had been largely responsible for overturning the tyrant local government of Spokane

County, which then was run by my predecessor, Walt Ackerman. I hadn't seen him since the early days of Walt's tenure. I'd heard he'd been ordered elsewhere.

"Hon," I said to Karen, "You get this Ford home, put it in the garage, and do not drive it again. If you need a car, have Carl put your Crown Vic back in service," I said. "Carl, you got that?"

"Yeah. Just swap out the battery and gas, right?"

"Well, might help if you take the Vic off the blocks."

"Duh, Dad."

"Turn left up ahead, through the gate, and park where they tell you to. Do not stray from where they point you."

"What'll happen if I do?"

"Don't go there," I said sternly. "Security Police have absolutely no sense of humor."

"Gotcha."

We parked in the designated space, far away from the old terminal, and three infantrymen, M-16's at the ready, immediately surrounded the car eyes scanning a 'perimeter.'

"Sir, if you would, instruct your family to proceed directly to Hanger One, on foot, and double time," a soldier said without really looking at me.

"Done. Karen, kids, move it, now. And double time. Leave what you don't need."

"Mom?" Kelly asked.

"Just do it honey. Go!"

They headed to Hanger One, about fifty feet away, and through a side door. I was mystified. Things were settling into a routine, weren't they?

"Sir, with us please?" The lead soldier asked, without really asking.

"Will I get to say my goodbyes to my family?"

"I believe so sir, but that's at the Colonel's discretion at the moment. Ready?"

"Yep."

"Leave your bag," he said as he saw me reach for the pack. "We'll take care of that. Go."

I half-sprinted to the old terminal, where two more soldiers were scanning the opposite fence line. I noted the barrel of a bolt-action sniper rifle peeking over the parapet of the terminal, pointing to the hillside on the north bank of the Spokane River. Felts was Spokane's first airport, built in the twenties on the south bank, and named after a local Army pilot who died in his plane. Before the War, it was primarily a light-aircraft terminal.

I made my way inside and was quickly escorted away from windows and into an interior space. Colonel James McCalister rose to meet me.

"Mr. Drummond. Sorry for the inconvenience."

"What in Pete's name is going on?" I asked.

"You are being targeted for assassination, it appears."

"OK, I know I've pissed off more than a few people, but who…"

"By our intel, several well-connected members of the Samuels family."

"I thought we were done with that."

"Not remotely. That particular family appears to have connections far and wide. Think of an organized crime family with deep-seated commitments and interests that stretch beyond a normal lifespan."

"What?"

"You appear to be interfering with their plans to accumulate property, businesses and placement of people of their choosing in positions of power that would best suit their interests."

"How did I do that?"

"You encouraged and demanded that the new government be representative of legal land owners within the county. You placed those elected representatives in positions of power."

"As opposed to…"

"Representation bought and paid for."

"We thought we were…we thought we had ended the Samuels problem at Newman Lake."

"Out there, sure. There are other…cells you might think of them. I think that they see you as a continuing threat."

"So let me guess what they were planning."

"No need to. They left us a written plan. Simultaneously decoy a number of vehicles identical to yours in places that you have visited or plan to visit. Park them in places of key and critical importance, remote detonate them. Then when your vehicle is actually spotted, leave it up to the Army or law enforcement to wipe you out with friendly forces."

I sat there not saying anything.

"Two hundred men are now on, and around your home property, up to a half-mile radius. There is no perceived threat at this time within those boundaries."

"Exactly who is responsible for this?"

"That's what we're trying to figure out."

"What about my family? My friends?"

"Unknown if they are being targeted as well. Doubtful, but a possibility."

"Colonel, we cannot live inside a protective cordon. It's impossible."

"Understood. Mr. Drummond, force protection is in place until actions currently underway are terminated. Your family will be escorted home by our security forces. Security will be maintained until we find those responsible for this planned attack—which I believe will be fairly soon—or until you return to Spokane, when other arrangements may be required for your safety."

"Dammit," I said more to myself than anyone else. "Is my flight still on?"

"Yes, sir. Less than fifteen minutes."

“I’d like to say my goodbyes to my family.”

“I’ll see to it. There’s a set of BDU’s in the room behind you. Please change into them before you leave the building. And wear your helmet. Your civilian clothing will be bagged and sent home with your family.”

“Is this your idea of camouflage?”

“Yep.”

“Swell.”

“I’ll be waiting for you in reception.”

“Thanks.”

McCalister rose and left the room, leaving me to change. My heart was pounding as I changed out of ‘civilian’ clothes. At least the uniform was worn somewhat. No nametag. No rank.

I stuffed my Colt inside the uniform blouse, grabbed ‘my’ helmet, and left the room.

“Hon, I’ll be OK. Listen to the Colonel’s men, OK? I think he’s not telling me everything, and I also think he’s closer to finding who’s responsible than he’s letting on.”

“Rick, this scares me.”

“Me, too. Be strong for me OK?”

“I’ll pray. A lot.”

“Me too.”

Kelly was holding back tears as we met in the corner of the hangar, doors closed. Carl was obviously holding his emotions in check as well. I’d already had a private word with him that he may have to hold more responsibility than he’d been used to until I got back. In other words, he was the man of the house until then. He didn’t like the sound of that anymore than I did. Both kids gave Karen and I a few minutes of privacy before I heard the engines warm up.

“I love you most.”

"Nope, but a close second," I said.

"Stinker," she said through her tears, blowing her nose. "You come back to me."

"I intend to. Twenty years isn't anywhere near enough of you sweetheart."

"Stop or I'll start bawling again."

"Can't stop. You know that."

"When will you be back?"

"Coupla days, probably late in the day. Flights are VFR only."

"Meaning?"

"Visual flight rules. Daylight. We're supposed to be wheels down by twenty minutes after sundown."

"And if you're late?"

"I will be coming home…nothing will keep me from you and our children."

"Mr. Drummond?" A thirty-something Captain asked. "It's time."

"Thanks."

"C'mon you two. Big hug," I said to the kids as they did their best to squish me. "And no fighting over my iPod. It's in your Mom's custody until I get back."

"Least of our worries, Dad." Kelly said.

"Good. I love you both. You take care of your Mom until I get back."

"We will," they said in unison.

I gave them both a squeeze, then kissed and 'dipped' Karen in the fashion of World War Two's returning soldiers, which made her laugh.

"I'm coming home," I said as I headed out to the plane.

"You better," Karen said.

I was no sooner in one rear seat of the big Beech King-Air, than the co-pilot piled in and the pilot stuffed the throttles forward. I had no chance to look back as we headed towards the east end of the runway on the taxiway, quickly turned around to the southwest, and accelerated up and away. Karen and the kids were nowhere to be seen as we passed the hangar and terminal.

We were gone.

60

Tuesday,
August Twenty-second

We climbed out at about five thousand feet, headed south-southwest across the Palouse, towards Walla Walla. The late morning sun was warm in the cabin of the plane, despite the air conditioning. I didn't have headphones or a mic, and was pretty much isolated from conversation with my pilot and co-pilot, unless I wanted to yell. I tried that once, and the front-seaters were not particularly interested in communicating with me, but were fairly well focused on their own tasks. I'd flown on small aircraft before, but never saw this level of intensity on the part of the pilot before. I put in a pair of earplugs that normally resided next to my ancient table saw, which dulled the engines enough to be tolerable. I later learned that air traffic control was literally non-existent, and that the navigation information for the plane, formerly integrated into the global positioning system, was as stone dead as the GPS satellites circling the earth. Put a whole new spin on getting from 'A' to 'B', which increased in complexity as the wind below us kicked up dirt and ash, obscuring most of the ground references along the way.

Our flight south took us along State Highway One Ninety-Five for a portion of the trip, as far as Rosalia, just south of the Spokane County line. Why we veered west after that was anybody's guess, we went cross-country from there towards our destination. I recognized a few things on the way, the most prominent being the Snake River. I couldn't tell if we were 'upstream' or 'downstream' of the Central Ferry Bridge, which was the main highway crossing of the river in these parts.

By two p.m., we were on 'short final', which normally meant as I recalled other flights, that we were in plain sight of the airport and that our airspeed should have slowed markedly. The dust below was almost like a ground fog, and I was very nervous as we descended, too quickly I thought. We did slow, but nowhere near what I'd experienced in single-engine aircraft. We were within fifty-feet of the runway when I finally saw the concrete. As soon as we were down, the pilot killed the engines and we coasted out to a stop. A tow vehicle then dragged us to a hangar.

"Nice flight, guys, but what was up with that descent? Seemed fast and steep."

"Lower we fly, more ash we ingest. Kills the power plants pretty fast. You did pretty well—you don't look green at all," the co-pilot said.

"Not the first time I've done that."

"Most guys puke, regardless. Back seat does it."

"Try riding in the back of an ex-Russian helicopter some time on the other side of the world. That'll pretty much give you a cast iron gut."

"What was that?" the pilot said, looking over his shoulder towards me.

"Nothing. Something I did in a previous life," I said as the plane was unhitched from the tow tractor. The pilot looked at me a little funny as I awkwardly climbed out, reassessing me perhaps. The hangar door closed behind us. I then noticed the dust masks, bandannas, and goggles that the ground crew wore. Reminded me of the Air Force guys serving in Iraq…not long ago.

"Mr. Drummond?" asked a young lady from the other side of the hangar.

"Yep, present and accounted for."

"Good afternoon. I'm here to direct you to your quarters. I'm Barbara Cole, on the Governor's staff." Miss (?) Cole seemed about thirty, all business, with the air of a bureaucrat about her. 'Damn, there I go judging people in the first three seconds, again.' I said to myself.

"Nice to meet you," I said as I shouldered my pack. I thought I could feel the butt of the disassembled M16 in my pack nudge me.

"You…aren't military, are you? I was under the impression…" she said as she looked at my uniform.

"No. I'm not. Long story."

"That's fine. This way, please," she said as we headed out through a glass door into a plywood-enclosed walkway, lit by a string of incandescent lamps. "The official reception begins at sixteen hundred hours, followed by a buffet dinner. The business session will begin at nineteen hundred. We're not sure when it will wrap up. Business sessions tomorrow will begin at oh-nine hundred. There will be a complete packet for you in your room."

"Who else will be in attendance?"

"That will be in your packet. It's changing almost hourly depending on circumstance," she said, not looking back at me as we entered a glass vestibule for the Walla Walla Airport terminal building. "Your shuttle bus should be right out the main door, and will take you to your quarters."

"Thank you," I said, and she was gone. "Huh," I said a little under my breath.

My 'quarters' were at a former 'Super 8' motel, about a mile away. At least it was a non-smoking room. I shared the trip over to the motel with two other conference attendees--mayors from Wenatchee, another from Clarkston, just across the river from Lewiston, Idaho. We agreed to get our gear unpacked (I noticed that Jim Evans, from Wenatchee, had a pack similar to mine, although his rifle was in a scabbard. It appeared to be a lever-action Western-type rifle) and meet in the lobby or other suitable space to discuss things prior to the reception.

By three p.m., I'd reviewed the briefing packet, and made my way back to the lobby. There were fifteen of us in the lobby area, and the 'manager' seemed a little nervous about us hanging around and talking in low tones. He discreetly made his way into a small office behind the check-in desk, made a phone call (phones!) and within a few minutes, a shuttle bus appeared, and we were ushered back to the Airport for the reception.

I had changed back into my civilian clothes, not taking the bait to dress up any more than I did on the 'job' in Spokane. Today, that meant some worn Carhartt's, a button-down shirt, cowboy boots (shiny, for a change), and my Colt. Most other attendees I noted also had sidearms. One guy, from Republic I later learned, had a matched pair of Colt Peacemakers, well used. I mentioned that my brother-in-law had saved my life with one of those, he replied. "Yep. These've both done that for me, more 'n once't." I noted he looked at my nametag hanging from a lanyard, and for the briefest moment, his eyebrows twitched. 'What was up with that?' I thought.

Over the months since the quake (and even well before), I'd been practicing my 'listening' and not my 'talking.' I was hearing a lot of the same issues that I was dealing with, in spades. Thank God that I didn't have lynchings going on, as some of my peers did…sex offenders were being dealt with quickly and quite publicly. So were murderers. So were horse-thieves. I tried to keep a relatively low profile, to get a sense of how smaller towns were dealing with things. Being the administrator for Spokane, however, made me the big fish in the pond. I neither wanted the attention, nor the impression that our needs were any more crucial than anyone else's. We did have by far though, the highest population and population density I guessed, than anyone else in the region.

Our 'reception' included 'beer' that was apparently a micro-brew, cloudy and quite strong; local, pre-Domino wine; and soft drinks the like of which I'd never had before. Ginger beer, being one of them. 'Grub', as the Yakima delegate called it, included fresh-cut potato chips, deep-fried, a stir-fry of vegetables in a vinegar sauce, apples, plums and grapes. I wondered what 'dinner' would involve.

The meeting attendees, not all in positions of leadership it appeared, included representatives from a large area of eastern Washington; the surviving populated areas south of Seattle and the Bellingham region; eastern and central Oregon (but no one from west of the Cascades; and a dozen or so representatives from Idaho. A 'sphere of influence' meeting, it appeared. By four p.m., when the reception was officially to begin, we already had a fairly full hangar, and I was working on my second Wheat Beer. I tried, and could not remember, the last time I'd had a cold beer.

"Ladies and gentlemen, we're about to get started. If you would please take a seat," a middle-aged man asked from a podium, which appeared to have been assembled from a stack of pallets, and covered with plywood. "Governor Hall will be arriving momentarily."

I took a seat at a round banquet table, which was set with 'hotel type' silverware, tablecloths, and dried flower centerpieces. (It was odd).

"So, Mr. Drummond is it?"

"Rick, please," I responded to Clair Chaffee, from Potlatch, Idaho.

"OK, Rick then. Know anything about this Governor?"

"Not even a first name."

"Odd, isn't it?"

"In a long string of odd. Yep."

"Ladies and gentlemen, Governor David Hall," the Suit announced. We rose as the fifty-ish Governor took the stage. 'Executive hair', I noted, remembering an ancient Dilbert cartoon strip, where only guys with Executive Hair were promoted to the sacred halls of Management. Applause, a polite amount, sounded before we took our seats.

"Thank you everyone for coming. I know there are a number of invited guests that were not able to attend this meeting, and I'm hoping that they will be able to arrive soon."

"This meeting is not being broadcast across the state, or in the region, because I want this to be a working meeting between leaders in the region. There are critical issues facing Washington, Idaho, Oregon, and indeed many states in the nation. There are issues that we can help to find solutions to. There is little that government can do to fix things."

"Good God. A politician who knows how things work on the outside," someone said loudly from the back. The Governor immediately started laughing.

"Please, do me a favor. Don't call me a politician." The room immediately erupted into applause. This guy was good.

"In a former civilian life, I ran an insurance agency. I've never held elective office. This is an interim role for me, and I do not intend to run for office at the end of my two-year appointment. For those that may not know how I come to you today, I serve under an appointment put forth by the two surviving Senators from Washington and Oregon, one Representative from Washington, and the United States Army Reserve, where I served from age eighteen until six weeks ago. The President reviewed this request for my service to the State of Washington, and approved it as submitted, with the conditions that I do not run for a succeeding term. I am here to do what I can to help the State get its feet back under it, and put in place conditions where normal governmental functions can take place. That is not to say a restoration of the former state administration, but an agile government that provides for the safety, security, health, and welfare of our residents."

"Governor Hall, may I ask a question?" one of the men at the table in front of us asked.

"Certainly."

"What was your role in the Reserves? Your rank?"

"Brigadier General. I was the commanding officer of the Seventy-First Regional Readiness Command. The command was located at Fort Lawton, in Seattle. I happened to be at a meeting in Los Alamitos, California when the Schumer hit the fan. The vast majority of survivors from the RRC were put on active duty and headed south, serving in other units, myself included. I was wounded in action in El Paso on the third day of the War and spent two months in recovery."

Two men at different tables toward the middle got up, and began a slow round of applause, that spread until all of us were thanking the Governor for his service. A minute or so of that was enough for the man, and he motioned for us to be seated.

"Thank you. It has been an interesting journey to this point. Let us make the rest of our journey less so."

The Governor outlined the work session for us, based on what he understood of each of our specific immediate needs. This was a trading session really, and we were getting set to see what we could do for each other. 'How enlightened', I thought.

The meat and potatoes of the session was a listing of specific needs, spelled out by each community, through information that in my case, I had provided to the Forty-First Divisions logistics branch. Food shortage projected, being the particular need that would cause us a crisis over the next few months. In the 'Plus' column, a massive amount of salvaged material available for trade. Sixty-one diesel train engines, including tugs, long-distance heavy-transport engines. Four hundred rail cars, various types, available for use in trading purposes and transport upon repair of trackage to destination points. Heavy manufacturing of metals, including forging, casting, machining and custom fabrication. Medical community that continues to provide a higher standard of care than other areas within two hundred miles, including areas outside of the Domino impact area….Diesel fuel, undetermined quantity of recent refinement…

I wasn't prepared to see 'our' diesel on the trading block. We'd filled most if not all of the surviving 'tank farm' tanks with diesel and gasoline from refineries in Montana and Wyoming. I had hoped that that fuel would get us through the winter. The fuel distribution network, I understood from the military, was on a rotation to fuel specific parts of the nation based on projected weather. Well, since the weather was anything but stable, that seemed to me to be a stupid way to prioritize….at least our tanks were relatively full…until now anyway.

I could feel that there were several sets of eyes looking at me, folks that I'd met in the pre-meeting reception, now sizing me up for some horse-trading. This would be an interesting experience. I wished Alan were here. He was way better at this than I was. Pre-War, I was the kind of guy who knew what he wanted to pay, and pay it. No more, no haggling with dealers. This is my price and that's it. Meet it or don't….it's not like I need to buy this here or now…Well, that way of life was gone. I needed food, lots of it, and needed to find a way to meet our needs and not give away the store.

"Yeah, seven thousand tons, maybe more, primarily grains, here's the list of what we're looking for," I said to the small crowd gathered around a table labeled 'Region Two.'

"That's not a lot to ask for," said an overall-clad man from Lexington, Oregon. I couldn't tell if he was being facetious or not.

"Depends on if you have it or if you don't. We have a lot of mouths to feed," I said as the crowd moved on to the next table. Each of us took turns talking about what we 'needed' and what we 'had'. This would give us time to study, and to plan some trading.

"Let me tell you this, you look like a guy who doesn't quite know where to start here, Mr. Drummond, not to be insulting or anything," the man said. 'Arnie Tremmel' was his name.

"Mr. Tremmel, a perfectly fair assessment. No offense taken."

"Advice, if yer interested."

"Sure."

"You have more rail equipment sitting unused than anyplace in three hundred miles. The lokies that was in the Tri-Cities were all moved out right after the quake. The yard at Pasco is empty, except for them that wasn't fit to move."

"Lokies?"

"Engines. Locomotives."

"Got it." I felt like I was back in school, and hadn't done my homework. And, it was 'finals week.'

"Mr. Drummond, Spokane County has the market effectively cornered on the railroad system in the Inland Northwest. There are only a handful of operational locomotives between here and Boise, between here and California. That's your bargaining chip. Most of those here cannot ship what they have. Your list there is their salvation."

"So I need to start a railroad," I said.

"That'd make the most sense, if you have the manpower, the skilled manpower, that is."

"I'll have to look at my census."

"Your request for food in the quantities you're talking about is easily doable," Arnie continued. "Your county gets a cut...a percentage...of what you ship. There's lots of stuff out there and damned little way to move it. These guys know that. That's why they're looking at you like you're either going to screw them or save them. Most, the former though."

"Thanks for the advice, Mister.."

"Call me Arnie. You know how much that grain is, in volume?"

"No, I've never tried to figure it out."

"One train, a hundred-ten cars long, common load, will be about twelve-thousand tons, in one trip."

"So this is doable."

"Yep. As long as the trackage is intact. And so long as there's a way to transport the grain to the elevators...."

"That's being worked on. We lost the south leg of High Bridge in the quake, and there isn't a work around at that point. Lines head west and south, and we'd have to reconstruct lines to connect to the Basin somewhere west of town. Problem is, the further we head west, the more damage we encounter. South of town is better, but the lines aren't exactly robust. Most of them were pulled up in the past twenty years."

"Rail's the way of the future, but you probably knew that."

"Well, I did for human transit, but apparently I've been thinking inside the box of Spokane County and not looking at the region. Thanks for the kick in the head."

"No problem. Now, let's talk business."

"Sure. What do the folks of Blackhorse Canyon and Willow Creek need?"

That shocked him. I'd not only been to Lexington, but knew it fairly well. My firm had a project there ten years back.

"You know where Lexington is?" he asked with some surprise.

"Yeah. Did a project for Morrow County, way back when. Nice little town. Chemical spill restoration along the creek after a semi rolled into it."

"I remember that. It is a nice town, despite the present difficulties. I'm the Mayor."

"Nice to meet you. Like I said, what're you in the market for?"

"Here's my list," he said as he handed it to me. 'Building materials. Medical supplies. Pharmaceuticals. Wood fired stoves, Water purification equipment, Sewage treatment supplies, High-grade steel stock…'

"Your water and sewer plant go down?"

"Yeah, in April. We ran out of chemicals for the water treatment system, and we're needing parts for our pumping systems for both water and sewer. Lost one of the water supply pumps in the quake, the second is on its last legs. It was supposed to be replaced this fall."

"Got the specs on it? And the chemical types and quantities?"

"Yeah. You think you can get this stuff?"

"Our sewage treatment plants are off line pretty much forever. Most of the mains were destroyed in the quake, and we're back on septic systems almost everywhere. Given that fact, and the number of plumbing and equipment warehouses in town, I'm pretty sure we can have somebody come up with a work around. I've got an engineer on staff who used to run the main wastewater plant. He'd know."

"I would really appreciate this," Arnie said.

"Glad to do it," I said. "Let's go find out what kinda trouble we can get ourselves in. And another beer."

I didn't get far in my wandering around the room. I was headed to 'Region 1', which comprised the Walla Walla/Pendleton/Tri-Cities area, and was sidetracked by a representative of the Governor's office.

"Mr. Drummond, a moment if you would?" the shapely young lady asked. 'Navy uniform. Interesting,' I thought.

"Sure."

"The Governor would like to have a word with you."

"No problem." 'Sure, no problem at all,' I thought as I was directed to the Governor's temporary office, in one of the conference rooms off of the main meeting area.

"Mr. Drummond, nice to meet you. Dave Hall."

"Governor, my pleasure."

"Please. 'Dave' is fine," he said. "Something to drink?" he asked. I noted he had a fresh glass of beer himself.

"One of those would be just fine."

"Pretty good stuff. I just wanted to thank you for your kindness on behalf of my nephew on my wife's side. I believe that you met right after the Domino."

"I'm sorry sir, but what was his name?"

"Marine by the name of Scott McGlocklin. Lieutenant Colonel these days."

That brought back a flood of memories, both good and bad. "Yes, sir. I knew him as a Gunny. McGlocklin is quite a man. First Marines, if I remember right. How is he?"

"Doing pretty well. He and his family have relocated to Bend from Camp Pendleton. He'll be heading up the Marine detachment in the Oregon Zone."

"Good for him. Last I'd heard he was headed to Mexico."

"That was a while back. He made it through that cluster with only two purple hearts and minus a finger. He was strongly encouraged to consider standing down to a position that would allow him to remain on this side of the grass."

"I didn't know orders like that were given."

"Not by the military, by his wife and parents. And his daughter. His son Manuel was damned near killed by vigilantes, who accused him of being Mexican."

"Good God."

"Yeah. Doesn't matter where you go, idiots are still present."

"I've seen that too."

"Anyway, Scott asked me to pass on his thanks. Mentioned something about his wife wanting to get a recipe for scrambled eggs, hot salsa and cheese hot enough to make him sweat."

I laughed at that. "Sure. I'll dig it up. We made him breakfast one morning after he saved our asses in a little skirmish."

"He mentioned that there was a little 'dust up.'"

"Sure, little by his standards. Plenty big by ours."

"Perspectives change," Hall said as he finished his beer.

"Indeed."

"You getting what you need?"

"Apparently so, yes. It would seem that I have more valuable items than I possibly realized."

"Arnie tell you that?" Hall said.

I paused for a moment. "I smell a conspiracy," I said with a grin.

"You've got rail power. A lot of it. It's quite valuable and scarce. Stands to reason. Part of my former life was figuring out how to get stuff from A to B. You have the means to do so, nobody else does around here right now, outside of what the military has running, which isn't much, either."

"We'll have to see what we can do to put the resources to the best use then."

"I'm glad to hear that. There are too many cases around the country where hoarding and selfishness and governmental seizures are the rule of the day."

"Can't eat trains."

"Can't move grain without them."

"Yep," I said. "My thanks, Governor," I said as I finished my beer. "Still some things to attend to. Give my regards to Gunny McGlocklin."

"Will do. And send those recipes up the chain of command some time. I'll see that he gets them."

"Will do," I said as I shook his hand. 'Good man in charge,' I thought to myself. 'What if we were not so lucky?'

Following our dinner buffet of barbequed beef, fresh vegetables, ice water and...yes, more beer, Hall's Secretary of State provided a briefing on the conditions outside of the Pacific Northwest with regards to trade. The presentation rapidly went off course, when an off-handed comment was made regarding governmental seizures of private property. The volume of conversation in the room rapidly overwhelmed the speaker.

"Ladies and gentlemen! Please!" The speaker said as he hushed us down. "I can provide only limited information on this. We do have FEMA Region Ten's assistant director here. Jack? Can you help me out here?"

A roundish man climbed up on the riser, and to the microphone. "I'm Jack Kessler, with FEMA," he started. There was a low growl in the room.

"Now before I get started, let me say that FEMA is not really a player in this region right now. Most of our resources are going to other areas. During the first ninety days of the crisis—starting with the Domino—we were very active. Things as you know changed dramatically after that and Region Ten was largely stripped of useable assets that weren't at that time being used. Meaning, staff."

He continued on. "My background here is not one of government. I was a branch manager for a credit union until it hit the fan. Two other directors have served in this region since January. I've been on the job since May. So, in that light, please do not view me as a bad guy. I'm a kid who grew up in Union Gap, after all."

That seemed to settle things down a little.

"OK. Now on to what some of the rest of the country is seeing. This is from the horse's mouth, so to speak. I was at a Western and Central region meeting six days ago, so I have this on pretty good authority. Things aren't great out there, and a lot of what you've been hearing is most certainly true. Let me outline what I know."

"There are activities by State governments that are in direct violation of the Constitution. Properties...private properties...are being seized. This is not happening, and will not happen, in FEMA regions west of the Mississippi. These are not Federal actions."

"And how are you going to guarantee that?" A voice from behind me asked.

"Governors in Regions Six through Ten have discussed this and have decided to uphold the Constitution's intent. The same cannot be said for most of the leadership in Regions One through Five, comprising most of the Eastern Seaboard, the Ohio Valley, et cetera. There are areas of rebellion—and that is the correct word—in each of Regions One through Five, fighting the seizures of private property. Predominantly urban areas in Regions One, Two and Three— the northeastern states—have had virtually all private properties confiscated. About half of Region Four, centered around Atlanta and progressing throughout Florida, but excluding most of Kentucky, Tennessee, Alabama, and portions of Mississippi, the same. Region Five—centered in Chicago and the Great Lakes— has active rebellion against seizures taking place throughout rural Minnesota, Wisconsin, Michigan, and western Illinois."

"This is, ladies and gentlemen, a concerted and coordinated effort on the part of the leadership in these regions to redistribute wealth in these cities and states. It started with the banking industry through repossession. It went downhill from there when the political powers in those areas saw the potential."

I asked the next question. "And what of the role of the Federal Government in this fight? You're telling me that the entire Eastern Seaboard--the home of the Federal Government—is in the heart of an area that has had all private property seized?"

"Correct. The President and the Acting Congress are adamantly against these operations. It is the State governments, encouraged and sponsored by what we can only call extremist elements, that are directly responsible for these measures."

I continued. "So, you mentioned 'redistribution of assets.' What I interpret from that comment is that the assets are being taken by those in power. And kept. Not a redistribution at all?"

"It is being marketed—and that is the correct term—as a 'sacrifice by all on behalf of the common man.' That is a direct quote from a television commercial that I saw in Kansas City."

"First, I resent being called 'common.' It belittles me, you, and everyone else in this room. There is no such thing as a common man."

"Franklin Delano Roosevelt would disagree with you, I do not," Mr. Kessler replied. "You are correct in your summation, sir, in my opinion. The Federal Government is powerless to stop this process, short of an open civil war, and frankly, those in the affected areas flat out do not have it in them to resist. They do not see this as a particularly large problem. Some, even many, view this as a good thing."

"Until the boot heel of their masters begin to cut off the flow of air to their lungs."

"Well put."

"So, what are we talking about here? Secession?"

"On the part of the rebellious areas, I don't actually know. We're not about to secede; we have, and continue to operate, under the rule of law and the Constitution. There is a whole lot of military support heading to the areas that are fighting seizure. I can tell you that factually."

"What a freaking mess," a tough sounding female voice said to my left.

"Amen to that."

Wednesday afternoon
August 23rd
1.45 pm

Most of the day, until our work session wrapped up at noon, was spent brokering deals. I did not have a knack for it, but managed nonetheless. Or, perhaps, put up a good show. Either way, I was mentally worn out. A little hung-over, too.

Spokane County would get her grain, in the form of wheat, corn, rice from California (the biggest surprise of the day, through a third-party trade), and tons of fruit from various locations, some dried, some ready to eat. To say I was stunned by our good fortune would be a severe understatement. The northern counties, from Okanogan all the way over to Idaho's Boundary County, also negotiated successfully for food. In trade, they'd be sending lumber. A whole lot of lumber.

To pay for our grain and food supplies, pending the successful acquisitions of short-stocked items, we would supply diesel fuel (some, thank God not much); water pumping and sewage equipment; salvaged building materials (mostly glass, used insulation, and sheet metal); and, manage and oversee the creation of a regional railroad system, centered in Spokane, but linked to the Northern Tier states through recently repaired lines in north Idaho. That task would not be a job for me. I'd need to recruit somebody from what was left of

Burlington Northern Santa Fe or Union Pacific. What I knew about railroads, well…was precious little.

I was one of the first of the attendees to be heading back home. Most would head home with military traffic from Fort Walla Walla to points within their 'A.O.' although, some others would fly or go by rail.

"Mr. Drummond, you good to go?" my pilot, a young looking first lieutenant asked.

"Yep, I think so," I said, shouldering my pack. "I'm Rick."

"Bob Henson," he said as I shook his hand.

'Good looking kid,' I thought. 'Young.'

"I'm thinking that you didn't sign up to fly prop planes," I asked as we headed out to the apron.

"No, actually, F-16's or 22's."

"Not too much traffic in those these days."

"Nope, but we can always hope."

"We taking that Beech back to Spokane?" I asked, pointing at the plane that brought me.

"Nope, we've got a nice, new Cessna today. One Seventy Two R-GA model. G-One Thousand glass cockpit. Very sweet little plane."

"Glass cockpit meaning flat panel display for the instruments."

"Yep."

"I've never seen one of those in a small plane."

"Not many around. Spendy upgrade, but worth it. Of course, hard to say when they'll build another one of these," Henson said as he checked the starboard wing tank for water in the fuel.

I put my pack in the rear seat, laying down across both seats. Henson's flight bag, about half the size of mine, was already in the seat.

"Go ahead and buckle up. I'm only waiting on the tower to send down the weather report. We're supposed to get wind later this afternoon, and that'll be something to avoid."

"Why's that?"

"Storm coming in from the south, according to the Army meteorologists. If we get caught in the air in that, we lose all visibility. ILS and GPS are gone, so we'd pretty much be up a creek without a paddle. We need to be wheels down by seventeen hundred, latest."

"We gonna make it before then?"

"Absolutely. We're only about a hundred fifty miles away, cruise speed at one three five knots, no problem."

I looked at him, still looking for an answer.

"A hundred fifty-five miles per hour, more or less," he said. "Sorry. I keep forgetting I need to translate that for civilians."

"Or, non-pilots," I replied.

"Yep," he said. "Here she comes. Tiffany, what've we got today?" he said, looking toward the tail of the plane.

"Only the weather for you, contrary to your desires," the slight, and very pretty blonde said. She'd obviously seen him coming a mile away.

"One can hope, sweetheart. And one can dream."

"Front is moving faster than they said. And coming from the south-southeast. You better move or you're on the ground until tomorrow."

"Rog. See you tomorrow for dinner. My place, about seven."

"In your dreams, pal," she said, spinning on her heel and moving back to the air-traffic control building. Yet, she did look back, and there was more than a necessary amount of motion in her hips.

Lieutenant Henson climbed into his seat, buckled in and closed the door, quickly moving through his pre-flight checklist as I stayed out of his way. At least this time in the air, I'd have headphones, so I'd at least be able to carry on a conversation.

Five minutes later we were airborne, and moving north-northeast towards home. I spent some time looking down and around at the rolling hills, trying to pick out landmarks.

"I take it you are in pursuit of that young lady," I said to the young Lieutenant.

"Until she catches me, yep. I knew her back home in Bakersfield. Went to school with her older sister. Never dreamed I'd run into her up here."

"How'd she end up here?"

"Family died when the Mexicans downed a C Seventeen in her neighborhood. Took out six hundred people on the ground and on the plane, and the only reason she didn't go with them was a trip to Costco for supplies. Her dad worked for the weather service down there, and she was going to follow in his footsteps. She's really just getting back on her feet."

"And your story?" I asked as I admired the colorful displays on the instrument panel…noting the 'dead' GPS unit.

"I was with the Four Ninety Seventh Combat Training Squadron in Singapore before the balloon went up. When we pulled out of there, I ended up at March over in Riverside. Reassigned the whole squad all over the place. I was assigned to the One Twentieth Fighter Wing. Used to be the state of Montana's Air Guard unit. Damned good pilots there."

"I assume that you saw more than your share of action over Mexico."

"Yep, I did. Right until that God-damned Chinese SAM took my plane apart."

"You're a lucky man."

"No, that bastard Chink was the lucky one. He was lucky that one of our A-10's shredded his ass before I could do it personally," he said, bitterly. "Oh, ****," he said looking across me, out the window.

"What?" I looked out to the south. The storm was obviously going to overtake us. "Oh."

"This might turn out to be a really interesting day, Mr. Drummond."

"How long?"

"I've been doing this shuttle service a lot but only in Oregon. I've never seen one move that fast. Ten minutes, max, and if we're not down, we've screwed the pooch."

"OK," I said. We were a long ways away from a highway, or a flat piece of ground for that matter. The Palouse is nothing if not a definition of rolling hills.

"How well you know this area?"

"Pretty well," I said. "Used to travel a whole lot down this way."

"Any landing strips down here?"

"Lots of ag strips down here for crop dusters. Nearest one I know of is at Dusty. That's a ways yet, other side of the Snake, maybe fifteen miles from the bridge."

"Not going that far," he said, looking out at the wall of dirt coming toward us. It seemed like it was only a mile or three away. "We got about three minutes to be on final, or we're done."

'New York Gulch,' I said to myself. 'That's New York Gulch below us.' "The Snake is just over that next ridge. The highway we just crossed will head east, then north. It'll cross the river at Central Ferry. Big bridge, one of the County port docks is on the south side of the river. Fertilizer plant on the north side, east of the bridge. Big State Park on the west side of the bridge. If I remember right, there should be a decent flat field there."

"Running out of options. I can't land this thing on the spaghetti string highway down there."

"Nope."

"Obstacles. Can I approach from the west clear?"

"Trees, not too thick but maybe fifty feet high if I remember right. There is an opening…a clearing… on the beach area and another north, right in the park. Remember, I'm doing this by memory."

"Better than plowing into a hillside blind."

"Or going for a swim."

"That, too."

The dust and wind was hitting us already, but we could still see…for now.

"There! The bridge is to the east of the field."

"This could be rough. We're landing in one ungodly crosswind," Henson said to himself. "We're going in pretty hot. You might want to tighten up your five-point."

I did as instructed, tugging the safety harness tighter as we swung northwest, and Henson swept us in a steep right hand bank to approach the clearing. I hoped it was as smooth as it looked from a few hundred feet. I glanced to the south bank of the river, and saw not the shore but just airborne dirt.

"Brace," the Lieutenant commanded as he tried to settle the bucking plane into a glide path, the wind shoving us into a wild yaw. I placed my hands on the dash, in a knowingly futile motion to keep me from smacking the dash should things go badly.

We touched down on the port landing gear and bounced up, the Cessna threatening to flip over. A second bounce and he jammed the throttle back and applied the brakes, trying to tip the starboard wing down into the wind. In vain, however.

"Oh, sh•t," were the last words I heard from Lieutenant Robert Henson. The port wingtip grazed the ground as the wind from starboard picked up the plane and tossed us out of control. The plane then rocked to the left and tore into a grove of Black Locust trees on the north edge of the clearing. The trees came at us far too quickly and I heard the prop hit the branches.

I don't really remember much after that. I do remember thinking of Karen on our wedding day, and all the buttons on that gown.

I was dreaming that my mouth was full of blood, and woke coughing. It wasn't a dream, and I was nearly choking on the blood from a tear inside my cheek. My tongue was swollen, and when I coughed, a searing pain tore through my left side. I had to have cracked a whole bunch of ribs. My head hurt too, and when I touched the sore spot, my hand came away with caked and clotting blood.

I noticed that some of my teeth were loose. Oddly, my glasses were still on my head. I'd foregone putting my contact lenses in for the trip back.

The dirt was blowing into the wrecked cockpit of the Cessna, which was still sort of upright, but buried in the grove of trees. I could barely see...but I saw enough of my friend the young Lieutenant to know that he had died instantly...brutally. I strained further to look around, but couldn't really make much out. I did know that I was covered with blood. My blood. The wind was howling outside.

I don't know how long I sat there, buckled into the wrecked plane, my Velcro-strapped Ironman watch was gone, and I couldn't reach my pack in the back without feeling the stabbing pain from the bottom of my ribcage to nearly my shoulder. Finally, I fished out a tiny LED flashlight that was on the zipper pull of my travel vest, which gave an eerie green light. The starboard door was still latched; half the windscreen was gone where the tree had come in, killing Henson. I had no idea why my ribs on the left side—toward the middle of the plane—were hurt. Nothing on the left side of the dash was recognizable as coming from an airplane. The technological wonder of the flat-panel instrument screens were cracked and...covered with blood. It appeared that I had coughed while unconscious, spewing a mouthful of blood on the dash and myself.

I found one of my water bottles on the floor, and spent a number of minutes picking it up. I drained the bottle completely. I was immensely thirsty. I finally hit the release on my seat harness, instantly creating a searing pain in my chest, and then relieving it almost completely...and then it was back. I took a mouthful of water and spat it out, trying to wash the blood out, a futile move. I then took a large drink, and tried not to vomit. One of my bandannas was put to use as a dust mask. Thank God it was already tied. I could never have managed to tie it. I closed my eyes, leaned my head against the right side of the plane, began to pray, and passed out.

I woke again, this time it was completely dark. The wind was still blowing, harder than I remembered from whenever I was awake earlier.... I had no sense of time. I wondered how I would get home. My ribs still hurt, every time I moved, breathed, or just sat still. I needed to get out of the plane to relieve myself, and to figure out my 'next move.' The young man whose body sat next to me, was responsible for shuttling me back to Spokane. There was a small bundle of packages that went with us, but nothing in my opinion worth dying for. I did not regard myself as worth that sacrifice, either.

Awkwardly, I moved to open the passenger door, and ended up shoving it hard to get it to open. Once that was done, I pivoted in my seat, and eased my way out of the plane. That must have taken me a good five minutes.

I was standing in water or mud, or both, just over the tops of my hiking boots. 'How could that be?' I thought. 'We landed on grass and weeds, didn't we?' Working with the little LED, I moved the seatback forward, and pulled out my heavy pack. It hurt a lot to do that, but there were things in there I needed. First aid kit for one...

I had a choice. Drag the pack through the water I was standing in, or attempt to make my way to higher ground, that, if the plane hadn't spun around, would be on the left side of the plane, through the trees. I first fished out a two D-cell maglight that had been converted to LED. I had changed the batteries...a year ago. I checked them a few days ago and they were still good. The diffuse light was good for lighting up stuff around me, but not a penetrating beam over distance. Even so, I saw more of the Lieutenant's body than I wanted to. I found my extra space blanket, unwrapped it with great difficulty, and covered his body.

Next, my compass. North was in front of the plane, not to the left of it. I'd have ended up walking into deeper water, had I followed my first hunch. I put the bag on my 'good' side, which only hurt like Hell times five. Henson's bag, I carried with my 'bad' left hand.

I remembered through my pounding head and the pain in my side, that there were buildings to the north of where we'd landed. One was the entry trailer, a single-wide office type building that the state parks workers used to collect camping fees. There were caretaker buildings to the west, probably in the water that was around my ankles—I knew they were at a lower elevation. There were buildings to the south too—probably in deep water. Restroom, picnic shelter. Nothing useful to me.

Dodging the thick thorns from the black locust trees, I made my way through the brush, struggling to see through both the trees and branches, and the dust. It was as thick as fog. I was constantly having to stop and adjust the bandanna. It was a poor substitute for a real mask.

I was sweating profusely by the time I saw that I had missed the trailer. The entrance road, asphalt with curbs, was completely silted over with windblown dust, which then had grown grass over the past growing season. I doubled back, and sat under the carport on the north side of the building. The pack fell off of my shoulder under the canopy, and I left it there. Gingerly, I lay down on the small deck, and used Henson's bag as a pillow. The last thing I did before falling asleep, was tighten the bandanna.

"Daylight." I said to myself. I still had no idea what time of day, minus my watch. And no spare in my pack. At least I could see without the flashlight. My ribs were definitely cracked or broken. I thought to myself long and hard as I lay there on the deck of the best way to move from horizontal to vertical. What worked 'best' was rolling to my right, and easing up, very, very slowly. My head throbbed, and I noted that the deck had a pool of dried blood. At least my mouth had quit bleeding. I was cold. My feet were wet still, of course, I hadn't changed into dry socks before sleeping. It was only maybe, fifty degrees out. It had to be late morning, the sun was visible as a circle above me in the dust, easily viewed with the naked eye. This was August, I reminded myself. It should be quite warm at this time of day, at this time of year.

I had almost a quart of fresh water in the external canteen, and triple that in a flexible bladder in the pack, and two smaller pint sized bottles. I had a four day supply of MRE's, fresh from my friends in the Forty-First, and a total of a week's worth of other food, at moderate consumption.

"Well, Rick, you are well and truly screwed this time," I said to myself. "Does anyone even know where you are?" I asked no one. "Not bloody likely," was the answer. "And your wife and family are mourning you. Ponder that for awhile."

'Did the plane have an emergency locater? Do those things still work without satellites?' I asked myself as I climbed to my feet, and made my way around the trailer. The door next to the deck that I'd slept on was locked and barred from the inside, I guessed. The door on the far end of the trailer though, was unlocked. I proceeded inside, without my Colt in hand. I doubt I could have fired it even if I wanted to. I was beginning to see double.

The place had been gone through, but a long time ago, by the amount of dust on the papers and maps scattered around. After checking the place out, I went back out, collected my things and Henson's bag, and went back inside to change and get cleaned up. I couldn't see the plane from the building, through the dust in the air and the thick trees. It wasn't more than fifty yards away though.

The trailer had a lunch room with a couch and table, two small offices, a ticket counter, and a full restroom in the back. I doubted it worked, but I thought I'd try it just in case. My flashlight played around the darkened trailer, and I found that by some miracle, there was water pressure in the lines, and there was a flush toilet that still worked.

"There are yet miracles in this land," I said aloud with slurred diction.

I then saw my reflection in the mirror for the first time and took two steps backward.

My face was stained and covered with dried blood, and my tan shirt and travel vest were similarly stained. My outer shell hid most of my clothes during my original assessment. My hair was matted with dried blood. I had a cut on my cheek that had scabbed over. Whatever had hit me, or that I had hit, cut me there and loosened some molars. I didn't know that I was that big of a mess. I stood and looked at myself for only a moment more, set the flashlight down on the back of the toilet, and got myself cleaned up.

A half-hour later, I was more presentable, but still a wreck. My feet had been wet enough to leave my soles shriveled and painful to walk on, and my boots were soaked. The cut in my scalp was a straight line, as if a knife had sliced me, and aside from the clotted blood and the hair mixed in with it, there wasn't much I could do about it. The left side of my ribcage was bruised from just under my shoulder to just above the lowest rib on that side. Through the skin, they didn't feel right. Cracked or broken. And it hurt to move, breathe or sit still. It was nice to get into clean, dry clothes, before I ate a 'breakfast' MRE. I still had no idea what time it was, but the sun was showing that it was well past 'noon' and on the decline.

I needed to figure out what my next step was. My body presented my next step, telling me that it was time to rest. I made my way to the couch and tried to get comfortable.

When I awoke, it was utterly black. I fumbled to find my flashlight, and then remembered, for whatever reason, that there was a watch, minus its band, in one of the pockets of the backpack. I hadn't checked to see if it worked, but the batteries usually lasted for years.

"Four-twenty a.m." I said aloud, and then noticed the date. "Sunday. August twenty-seventh." Four days since we'd left Walla Walla. "Four days."

'How long was I in the plane before I woke up?' I wondered. Karen and the kids had to be dealing with the fact that I wasn't coming back by now..... 'How do I get home?'

I was hungry again, and ate two of the home-made granola bars that Karen had made me, and dug out a map of the state. I was sixteen or seventeen miles from Highway Twenty-Six, thirty or forty miles from Colfax, the Whitman County seat. A good hundred miles from home.

I lay back down on the couch and thought about that trip, on foot: 'Impossible.' When I woke up again, it was daylight, with relatively strong sunlight beaming in, but it was cold in the trailer. The watch said eight-thirty. It was still Sunday, thank God.

'Breakfast' didn't appeal to me yet, but I carefully brushed my teeth and tried not to mess up my mouth anymore than I had too. My mouth was still bleeding.

My pack held a small multi-band Grundig radio, and a hand-held CB radio. My first step would be to listen for a signal on the CB radio. The Grundig was a receiver. Good for news, not for bailing my sorry butt out of this situation.

The valley I was in would certainly limit the signals coming in or being broadcast. I would need to climb the hill to the north of me at least I thought, to get a signal out. That was a good country mile, relatively steep terrain, more suited to sheep than humans. With my ribs being the problem they were, it would be a long, hard climb. If I fell, I realized, I could do more damage than might be survivable, assuming that I didn't already have life-threatening injuries....

I packed my fanny pack with two MRE's, the two smaller water bottles (after filtering the tap water from the sink), gloves and a hat (which I later realized was a waste of time. It hurt to put on my banged up head). The radios were put inside the deep pockets of my travel vest, still crusted with my blood. By ten a.m., I started my hike. My boots were still damp. My .45 was on my side, but I really hoped that I wouldn't need it.

There had been a small farm to the northwest of the state park, on the west side of the highway. I remembered that the residents had sheep, cattle, pigs, and horses, all crammed into the narrow canyon leading up from the river. The farmhouse, or what was left of it, came into view as I reached the base of the hill that was my target. The home and at least one of the barns were burned to the foundation. No sign of human activity was visible. No animals for that matter, either.

The climb wasn't just hard on me, it was excruciating. I switched back from east to west along a zigzag path, which was easier on the pain in my side and my throbbing head, but took far longer than I had anticipated. By noon, I was a little more than halfway up the hill. Thankfully I was only having to deal with going through grassland, rather than sagebrush, which is also present on some hills. The climb went easier as I got higher, and the hillside flattened out a little.

At one o'clock, I was at the top of the hill, which afforded a decent view of the park below. The plane was invisible in the heavy trees on the side of the clearing, but I knew about where it must have been. I could see the damage to the bridge more clearly now. The bridge superstructure was intact, but half of the approach was gone on the south end, leaving a good quarter mile of 'nothing' where the road should have been. To the east of the bridge, I knew there had been a fertilizer plant, which was supplied by barges coming up river, and then distributing the chemical fertilizers by truck to the farms in the region. I couldn't see that for the side hill in the way.

I sat down, carefully, and took a long drink from my water bottle, draining the last of it from the first bottle. I shucked off my shell, and enjoyed a few minutes of the sunshine before I tried the CB.

The radio was set to 'scan' any active frequency, and briefly lock on to any broadcast on any of the channels. I watched as the digital display cycled through a half-dozen times, before locking on a garbled broadcast, then moving on. Channel twenty-seven, I noted.

Was anyone looking for us? Maybe, given the weather and dust, it would have been foolish to fly a search for us. I punched up channel nine, and broadcast 'Mayday,' repeating it for five minutes. The risk of course being, that someone would come looking for us that wasn't about to rescue us. I really didn't see much choice in the matter. I knew when I started up the hill, there was no way that I'd be walking home.

Nothing. I waited another five minutes, and tried again, this time on twenty-seven. I heard some garbled traffic but mostly static, but couldn't tell if they were responding to me or not. I decided to go ahead and give our approximate location, and let the cards fall where they would. When I released the 'push to talk' button, there was no response, no garbled traffic, nothing. I repeated my broadcast on channel nine. Nothing.

After fifteen minutes of this, I put the radio back on scan, and it locked on twenty-seven. Maybe they'd heard me. Maybe, they were 'good guys'. I continued to repeat my 'mayday' and location every five minutes until I thought it prudent to head down the hill, at three p.m. It would be a slow walk, and if I was lucky, I would make it down safely. Two hours down? Three?

"No wind. Good for me," I said to myself as I headed back down the hill, being overly careful of my footing. 'One slip and that could do me in,' I said to myself.

By five minutes to four, I was back on the 'flats' again. The descent went much better than I thought it would, but I still hurt like Hell. I was nearly out of water too, I noted when I thought I heard a voice. I headed for cover, which must have looked funny to the casual observer, since I was moving so awkwardly. 'Friend or foe?' I wondered, not for long.   I moved to open ground as the mounted patrol came into sight. I thought for an instant, 'when was the last time an active U.S. Army patrol rode horses?'

"You Mr. Drummond?" the lead soldier asked, obviously riding with experience in the saddle.

"I am. And damned glad to see you."

"How about the Lieutenant?"

"He didn't make it."

"Understood. Can you direct me to the aircraft?"

"Yeah. Maybe a hundred yards through there," I pointed. "Lieutenant Henson is still in the wreckage."

"We'll take care of him. Morgan, see to Mr. Drummond's injuries."

"Sir," a young medic replied.

"Let's head to the trailer," I said. "That's where I spent the night."

"Helo will be here any time, sir. You'll evac to Spokane pretty quick."

"Let's hope to God my next flight goes better than my last one."

"Yes, sir. You weren't the only flight downed in that storm. So far though, you're the only survivor that's been found."

"Anyone tell my wife yet?"

"I believe so, sir. Your mayday call was heard by a farmer, who relayed it to Colfax, and then up to Spokane. We weren't that far away. I take it you did not hear the reply?" he asked as he looked over my head wound, pulling on medical gloves.

"Nope. Radio crackled, but nothing I could understand. I had to get to the top of that hill to get any sort of signal at all."

"You took quite a shot to the head here," he said. "You'll end up with some surgery on this to fix it right."

"Yeah. You oughta see my ribcage."

"Let's then."

I took off my shell and shirts. "Holy ****," the medic said. "You hiked that hill with this?" he said as he examined me, making me wince.

"Yep," I said. He looked at me pretty hard.

"You've got six broken ribs. Probably a couple more that are cracked."

"That's what I figured."

"Need something for the pain?"

"Nice shot of scotch would be good."

"I was thinking more on the lines of morphine."

"Can't. I'm allergic to it."

"Porter! You got any of that whiskey left?"

"Yeah. Need some for medicinal purposes, right?" I could hear the smirking tone of voice, but couldn't see the speaker.

"My patient does, yeah. Now if you please," the medic said.

"You got it boss," the voice said, now more serious. "Sheeeit!" the soldier said as he saw my injuries. "You can have it all, sir."

"Nope, just a shot or two. Thanks," I said as I took the small metal and glass flask. I noted the 'Airborne' logo etched into the glass. The bourbon was quite good, I thought as the medic put some sort of antibiotic on my head, and looked over my cheek. "I'm thinking this isn't an Airborne unit," I said as I handed the flask back to the young owner.

"My great-grandfathers. Hundred and First. He was a Pathfinder on D-Day."

"Thanks. That was good," I said. "My father and grandfather served in the Second War. Too bad it wasn't the last of the wars," I said, beginning to feel the liquor, too soon.

"Let's get that shirt back on you," the medic said.

"Works for me. Coldest August in memory."

"You oughta see Canada. Snow all the way from Edmonton to the border."

The patrol commander, 'Parkinson', came back over to the deck of the trailer where I was dressing with the assistance of the medic. "How's he doing?" he asked the medic.

"Fair for a soldier. Effing spectacular for a civilian," the medic said, then listing my injuries.

"Mr. Drummond, did you happen to find a small bag in the aircraft after the crash?"

"Yeah. Belonged to the Lieutenant. It's inside the trailer. Why?"

"Sorry, that's above my pay grade," Parkinson replied.

"So was it me or the bag you guys were sent to retrieve?" I asked.

"Both."

"Good to know one's rank in the world," I said as I heard a helicopter approaching. "Would you mind grabbing my pack?" I asked as the Blackhawk came into view. "Doesn't pay to travel without it."

The big helo flared and settled into a pasture north of our would-be landing strip, and a half-dozen men quickly left the ship and headed over to us and to the wrecked Cessna. I was directed onto a folding stretcher and strapped to it, and was efficiently transported to the idling helicopter as my pack, accompanied by a pile of my stuff that hadn't been re-packed, was put in beside me. A Captain held the bag that I thought had been Henson's flight bag, and within a few more minutes, I was hooked up to two IV's. A twisted black body bag, containing Bob Henson's remains, was placed behind me, with two of the men that had traveled on the Blackhawk. Without waiting, we were off the ground moments later. The rest of the men remained on the ground.

I dozed as we traveled 'home', and didn't really rouse until I felt the ship wheel to the left slightly on approach, and begin to settle in to land.

I could feel the cool air as my stretcher was lifted, and then settled on a gurney. I looked around and saw the familiar sight of downtown Spokane, from the roof of Deaconess Hospital. I was quickly whisked inside and into the trauma center, as the Blackhawk spooled up and took off again.

"You're a sight for sore eyes," I said as I saw Karen for the first time.

"So are you," she said as we kissed. "You're a mess."

"Been a tough day or two."

"It's been four. Almost five," she said in a quivering voice. She'd been crying. A lot.

"Sure. But I missed most of them. Slept or out cold. Kids here?"

"Outside," she said, almost in tears.

"Bring them in."

"No, not 'til you're cleaned up a bit."

"Oh….OK. Go ahead and tell them. I'll be OK. I love you," I said as I squeezed her hand.

"You most," she said as she headed out of the curtained area. Someone was working on cleaning my head.

I relaxed as I lay there, someone cutting off my hair and scrubbing my head, and prayed to my Savior my thankfulness.

'Home,' I said to myself.

END